WHEN BLOOD BURNS

BOOK ONE
IN THE
CYCLE OF AWAKENING

ANDREW STEVENS

astevenswrites.com

VALDRYR
DURIBOR
DURALIAN MOUNTAINS
FAER'ELAS
KALINOR
LIOTHA'S FALL
MOUNT DICENDIA
THOUSAND PEAKS
DOR'DRAGOS
DRAGONS KEEP
E.
TER'ALAS

AL'ISA
SAH'NARA
NORTHREACH
LONELY PINES
THE VALE
JEB'S POST
VALEHOLD
SOLANTRIA
SOLHARBOR
ONG ISLE

Copyright © 2025 by Andrew Stevens
Cover design by Rachel St. Clair
Cover illustration by Sutthiwat Dechakampu
Map by Andrew Stevens, design elements by Rachel St. Clair
Author photograph by Douglas Brauner

Self-published by Andrew Stevens
P.O. Box 25402
Colorado Springs, CO 80936
https://join-the-awakening.com

First edition: July 2025

ISBNs:
979-8-9929519-0-5 (ebook)
979-8-9929519-1-2 (trade paperback)

To my wife...

We have weathered many storms. You have put up with my passion, and on occasion, pulled me down when my head soared a little too far above the clouds. You are the line that grounds me, the light that guides me through, and the love that makes it all worthwhile. I couldn't be who I truly am without you. Never stop believing how much you mean to me.

To my past self...

We always knew we had these gifts, but it took some time to learn how to dedicate them to a project and see it through. We struggled to believe, and we wasted our time doing so many things that didn't really matter. But we did it, we finally did it, and this is just the beginning.

To the believers...

Mom, Dad, Alane, John, and all the others. You know who you are. You believed in me, you believed in my gifts. You'll never truly know how much of a difference that made. Thank you!

To the dreamers and creatives...

You have a gift. Don't settle for anything less than using it to the fullest. Don't let your future self regret the years wasted. Reach for the stars, take the leap. There's no better time than right now.

CONTENTS

PROLOGUE

SHADOWS

The last of the candles dwindled, nearing the end of its life. Smells of dust and old tomes clung heavy in the air as the darkness of the archives closed in around a lone figure sitting in a chair, a heaping pile of books scattered before her.

Nalaen pushed aside her long, flowing sea of red hair as her eyes, shimmering with a fiery glow, focused intently on the pages before her, hanging on every word.

She felt it now–felt the weight of apprehension closing in upon her. Her whole life had led to this moment. She'd grown up without a mother, stolen from her within moments of first opening her eyes to the world. She'd sought answers to explain why for so long. She'd sought the truth. She'd sought purpose.

It was all laid out before her, the lines of interconnected events all leading to the climactic moment that had defined her sole intent since her very first breath. And yet, it was all wrong.

Thousands of years prior, Dro'Kal, the last of the Wyrmlords, was slain, his thirst for power a corruption that could not stand. It was Liotha, the first queen of the dragons, who ended his reign of terror. It was she who ignited the long-standing war with the humans, with the ones called the Dragonbloods–those vile abominations who had somehow risen from the one race that had never claimed mastery over the arcane. And yet, she vanished soon after, her fate never fully explained. A new Queenmother was chosen from amongst the Scions and for nearly two thousand years, these wars raged until the day Nalaen was born. And then, mere days after her mother was slain, a deal was struck, vying for an end to the bloodshed. But why then? And why had her mother's death come at such an untimely moment?

Nalaen needed to know the truth. She'd been scouring the archives for weeks, trying to piece together what had actually happened between Liotha and Dro'Kal, and how the conflict with the humans first began. The books suggest Dro'Kal overstepped his bounds–that his greed came at a detriment to the kingdom. But before becoming queen, Liotha was basically a nobody. How could someone like her rise against *him*? And why? Dro'Kal was one of the most powerful wyrms in the dragons' history. And while history has muddled the rumors, it was no mere coincidence Dro'Kal's fall was at the same time magic began to diminish and the ancient races started to collapse. Even in the dragons' domain, where magic still flowed, it felt... weaker, less prominent. Most of the official records indicate there was no direct correlation between these events, but Nalaen didn't buy it. History is always written by those in power, and the truth is often skewed in their favor.

Nalaen had been noticing slight variations between pages within tomes; subtle differences in penmanship and ink, indicative of alterations, but she needed more proof. It all came down to the mystery surrounding her mother's death. If she could solve that riddle, then perhaps she could follow it back to the beginning. To solve that mystery, she'd need to do the unthinkable.

Standing up from her chair, she snatched several tomes off the table and headed for the front of the archives. She followed the line of lonely torches down the columns of tall bookshelves, passing thousands of historical texts, wondering how many of them contained their own lies. Fortunately, near the front of the archives, sat the one who might have answers, the only other individual in the archives at so late an hour.

He was an old dragon, having lived several of Nalaen's lifetimes over. His frail, hunched over figure in human form showed his age. As Keeper, he was head archivist, ensuring the histories of their kind were preserved for generations to come. And, if Nalaen's suspicions were correct, he was likely privy to whatever edits had been made.

"Explain this," Nalaen said, taking the top book off the pile she was carrying and placing it down before the Keeper. She flipped to the last page she'd been reading, staring up at him intently.

The Keeper glanced at her, his eyebrow raised. He picked up a pair of nearby spectacles and leaned forward to glance at the tome.

"I'm not quite sure what you mean, Princess. This is the recount of Queen Liotha's ascension."

"I know what the tome is. I've read it many times over. I mean this," she said, pointing between the two pages. "These were not written at the same time. This tome has been altered."

The Keeper cleared his throat and reached for the book, a look of further questioning. He glanced between the two pages, then sat back and shook his head.

"I'm not sure why you suspect so, Princess. There appears to be no difference to me."

"Oh, it's close, I'll give you that, but there are subtle differences in the strokes and lettering. The ink is much newer, too. Do not take me for a fool, old drake. Someone's altered these. A Keeper's job is to study and preserve the history of our kind. One does not ascend to such a prestigious position without merit. Or should I assume you rose to this position by some other means? Should I assume you neglect your duties in maintaining the integrity of this archive?"

The Keeper cleared his throat, fidgeting ever so slightly in his seat before straightening his glasses and sitting upright.

"Princess, I take my job quite seriously, I assure you. If anyone had tampered with these, I would most certainly know."

"Is that so?" Nalaen questioned. "This is not the only tome." Nalaen slammed down the other books she'd been holding in her arm, opening each to the pages where the changes had been made. When she finished, she looked back up at him with a glare. "All of these have been edited. So, tell me, Keeper. Either you are incompetent, or you are a liar. Or perhaps, it's a bit of both."

She watched the Keeper's eyes shift nervously between her and the tomes. A small bead of sweat trickled across his temple.

"Princess, sometimes edits are necessary to clarify details," he fumbled. "I don't quite recall, but I believe some such edits were required before my time as Keeper. It's a common practice, and one that is carefully curated by the Keepers, I can assure you."

"Clarity," Nalaen scoffed, remaining calm despite the growing rage within her. "Or covering up the truth?"

"Princess, this is madness. What you're suggesting is—"

"Treason? Yes, it is, Keeper. I expect the histories would not be kind to the one who allowed them to be altered under his very nose."

"This is preposterous. When Kyrian hears of—"

"Kyrian!" Nalaen roared, her eyes flaring, the dull glow from before bursting to life in a brilliant, fiery red. "Kyrian is Herald, *I* am the rightful heir to the throne, and soon, I will be crowned Queen. You best choose wisely who to place your loyalties with. That pretender has sunk his teeth deep. Even into you, it would seem."

The Keeper shook, his fear readily apparent now that his feeble attempts to stand up to her had worn out.

"I... I don't know what you want from me, Princess. I didn't mean to—"

"I want the truth. Who altered these? Was it Kyrian?"

"I can't— I can't say for sure," the Keeper quivered.

"More lies. Your usefulness is running out, Keeper," Nalaen said, her claws slowly extending from her human hands, her face shifting, revealing a hint of the dragon within. She dragged her claws across the Keeper's desk as she walked around it toward him.

"They'll kill me," he said, almost begging.

"They'll kill you?" Nalaen laughed. "I've already studied some of the forbidden magics. By the time I'm through with you, you'll be begging for death."

The Keeper quivered again, more beads of sweat dripping down his bald head. His eyes darted about the room, looking toward the exit, perhaps hoping someone would come to save him.

"It wasn't Kyrian. At least, I— I don't know, for sure, that it was."

"Go on," Nalaen said with a smirk, continuing to walk toward him.

"It was a wyrm. I don't know his name. I've never seen him before, nor seen him since. He just showed up with orders containing the royal seal allowing him private access to the archives. I don't know what he changed, nor why. But they threatened to–"

"I don't care what they threatened you with. You are the Keeper," Nalaen said, drawing close. "A letter shows up bearing the royal seal and you just let its carrier in without questioning the validity or purpose of such a visit? I wonder how the other Keepers would feel about such a betrayal. Or perhaps, they took part in such behaviors, too? Either way, this cannot be tolerated."

"What– what are you going to do, Princess?" the Keeper asked, his eyes wide in terror.

"I'm going to find the truth," Nalaen said, calming herself. Her claws retracted, her human hands returning, though her eyes remained bright. "But first, I'll need access to the Vault of Shadows."

"The Vault of– Princess, how do you know of such things?"

"I have my ways," she replied.

"Well, then you must know only an order from the High Council can permit its opening."

"You know as well as I do such a request would be futile. Given what I've discovered here, I cannot raise suspicions. You will open the vault," Nalaen fumed, a hint of the dragon reemerging.

"It is forbidden without the highest approval. It's the one oath all Keepers are sworn to uphold above all else. I do not know exactly what will happen when I open it. The knowledge there is–"

"Necessary," Nalaen said, finishing his sentence for him. "Whatever lay hidden in that room, I believe I can trust it above what these archives have to offer. If I am going to uncover potentially thousands of years of lies, the knowledge and magics documented within will be necessary. I will not ask you again. Open the room."

As she spoke the final words, Nalaen's eyes flared brighter again. Normally, mind magic wouldn't work on most dragons. But she'd seen how spineless the old, frail Keeper was. His mind was already weak, and in this state of terror, he'd likely be susceptible to her persuasions. The Keeper sat still, staring into her eyes, his face twitching intermittently for a few seconds. Nalaen watched the willpower slowly drain from behind them. After a few more seconds, he nodded, rising to his feet.

Nalaen followed him as he approached the back wall behind his desk. The Keeper pulled out a key from around his neck and placed it in a small opening, barely noticeable against the wall's smooth surface. The sounds of a locking mechanism clinked, followed by the grinding of gears. Gradually, the outline of a door appeared. *So, that's where it was hidden. Clever.*

As the door swung open, Nalaen tried to keep her focus on the Keeper, maintaining her connection to his mind, but her eyes were drawn to the dark room on the other side of the door.

Stepping inside, the Keeper waved his hand in front of him. A row of torches lining the walls of the room flared to life, illuminating the giant metal door before them. Nalaen stared in awe at it.

It was a massive circle, adorned with depictions of the creation of the world. It showed the dragons, the first and most powerful of the magical races, descending from the skies, four enormous beings of an almost formless shape casting them down from the heavens. The Architects, they were called—the creators of Velasia. Two of light, two of darkness. Balance. They had given the dragons the power to be the world's stewards. And though it was the greatest gift given to any of the races, the Architects also bestowed with it a limitation—the dragons' magic would not go unchecked. If they did not rest and recover in their human forms, they risked tapping their power to its limit and succumbing to the primal beasts within. Apparently, even the gods feared what dragons might become. But where are the gods now?

Feeling her connection slipping, Nalaen focused back on the Keeper.

"Open it," she ordered.

"Please don't make me do this, Princess," he begged. "I was told there was a cost."

"Open it," she ordered again, prodding him forward.

The Keeper hesitated momentarily before he moved forward to the base of the door. Nalaen followed, watching closely his every move. Slowly, he lifted his hand, placing it on a small mold near the door's base.

"En tenebrem de lucia, nos vocatia a foras. Ecese vitalia man, et mai en umbral incedio no maius," the Keeper spoke in the ancient draconic tongue. Nalaen tried to remember her teaching.

From darkness to light, we call you forth. Behold my life, and may you walk in shadow no more.

For a few seconds, nothing happened. Nalaen thought perhaps the old drake had said something wrong, but just as she was about to tell him to try again, the Keeper started to convulse. A few seconds later, his whole body jerked, and what sounded like a whimper emanated from his mouth.

Nalaen watched in wonder as distorted lines appeared in the Keeper's arm, slowly beginning to pulsate. She could see bulbs moving through his veins in the direction of the door.

Blood, not life. Vitalia could be translated both ways. Behold my blood...

The Keeper screamed, trying desperately to pull his hand away from the door. His sheer terror washed over Nalaen, severing her connection to him. It didn't matter. He needed no compulsion now. He was trapped. The door, it seemed, needed a blood offering to open.

An ingenious magic. Quite the surprise for anyone who tried to open it themselves.

Nalaen covered her ears at the Keeper's howls of agony. Though the scene of his body slowly shriveling and folding in on itself was quite grotesque, she couldn't look away. After what seemed like an eternity, the Keeper's cries were silenced, ending with the sound of flesh and bones collapsing into a pile on the floor. As it settled, Nalaen swallowing down some bile that had crept up into her throat, she heard a loud sound, much like the first door opening, but amplified tenfold. She watched as the door shifted and changed, the images moving about its surface in circular patterns until, eventually, all were settled in a new scene.

The Architects were now gone, the door seeming somewhat dimmer than it had before. Near the base of the door loomed a giant, formless shadow, seeming to reach up toward the dragons soaring above. And between them, lines spanning the surface of the world. It was a chilling scene–one Nalaen's mind was struggling to comprehend. Her thoughts were cut short when, with a hiss, the door creaked open ever so gently.

Nalaen felt a dark magic seeping from within the vault beyond. She'd heard stories of what tomes and artifacts lay beyond the mysterious door. She didn't know how much of what she'd heard was true, but one thing that was certain was the forbidden knowledge within. And if the rumors about those magics were true, there was likely at least one capable of helping her uncover the secrets surrounding her mother's death. If she could do that, then perhaps she could uncover the truth about it all. What had happened to the world's magic? Why had the ancient races disappeared? What role had the humans played? And, most importantly, was there any possibility of fixing it?

Now, all would be revealed. Now, she would finally find the answers she'd sought her entire life. Nalaen would uncover the lies. She would find the truth. With the dark secrets waiting just beyond the door, nothing, nor no one, would stop her.

With a sinister smile, Nalaen stepped into the shadows of the vault beyond.

Chapter One

RESTLESS

It was early afternoon, a gentle breeze causing the fading gold and red flowers in the field below to sway back and forth, their rhythmic dance symbolic of the teetering feelings swirling through Mara's head. It reminded her of fire. It reminded her of the greatest pain she's ever felt.

It had been fifteen years since the day that had changed her and her brother's lives forever but Mara remembered it like it was yesterday...

The dragon had come out of nowhere.

They were celebrating their tenth birthday, going with their parents to meet Uncle Yoren for lunch. Everything had gone well enough. The twins ate their meals while enjoying their gifts from Uncle, though their father, Harran, hadn't approved. Their Uncle served the Order of Scales—the knights who protected the realm from dragons, within whose veins flowed a fragment of the dragons' power. He was technically their great uncle, for Dragonbloods lived roughly twice as long as normal humans did, but they just called him 'Uncle'. His gifts that day had been related to such things. For Kai, a cloak, fashioned like the one the knights wore, albeit much smaller. And for Mara, a book about the Order's history. Mara loved to read and remembered diving right into its pages.

In life, their father had always been vocal about wanting something else for the twins—something safer, something better, according to his point of view. He didn't want them to follow in Yoren's footsteps. Their mother, Calista, never seemed quite as concerned, usually more focused on keeping the peace between Harran and Uncle Yoren. He had always meant well, and he tried to uphold their father's wishes, even though he knew how the twins, and Kai especially, loved hearing his stories and the tales of fighting dragons in wars long past.

After lunch, having eaten their fill, they parted ways, the twins heading home with their parents at the promise of more presents.

That's when the dragon appeared.

As they rounded the corner of the street, coming into view of the edge of town, they started to hear what sounded like shouting. A few seconds later, the nearby wall exploded in a cloud of dust and debris. The four of them were knocked aside, Kai and Mara sent sprawling in one direction, their parents in another.

Mara sat up, blinking, trying to force the darkness out of the corners of her eyes. At first, she only heard the beating of her own heart. It sounded like thunder in her ears. Gradually, it faded, and she began to hear other sounds. Screaming, more buildings breaking, the distinct crackle of flames. She tried to focus, tried to understand what had happened, saw some of the nearby buildings were already consumed in fire.

She turned and saw Kai lying still next to her. Her heart skipped a beat. She prodded him but he did not move. She looked up and around, desperately searching for her parents. She couldn't see much through the dust and smoke.

Hearing a scream off to her left, she turned. Something large moved within the smoke, causing it to swirl about, the sound of more buildings being torn apart. There were other sounds, too, more... grotesque. At the time, she did not know what they were.

She heard her own heartbeat growing louder. No, not her heartbeat; there were vibrations in the ground, a beating sound like drums growing steadily louder. The smoke swirled more furiously, moving in Mara's direction.

Terrified, Mara prodded Kai again, fiercely trying to wake him. After a few seconds, he began to stir. When he sat up, Mara pointed at the approaching clouds as something darker moved within them.

Mara held her breath as the face of a massive dragon emerged from the smoke, its gaze immediately landing on the helpless twins lying all alone in the street. Its eyes twitched when it saw Kai's cloak–the distinct black and red colors, the emblem of the Order etched upon it. It opened its maw wide and roared, red slime dripping from fangs the size of Mara's forearm.

It was the loudest sound Mara had ever heard. It pierced her ears, sending pulses of electricity down the back of her neck. Mara began to whimper, her heart beating at a blazing speed. She could see Kai felt the same.

From somewhere behind them, their father appeared, waving his hands to grab the beast's attention. It turned its head, focusing on him. He moved down the debris-ridden street, trying to lead the dragon away. That's when it charged.

Mara felt strong arms grab her and her brother from behind, lifting them up and pulling them down a nearby alleyway, away from their father and the dragon. The last thing Mara saw through tear-filled eyes was their father, through smoke and ash, arms waving, walking bravely toward the charging beast.

And then, he was gone.

A familiar voice, much like her father's, brought Mara back to reality.

"What are you thinking about?" asked Kai.

Wrenching her thoughts away from the nightmare, Mara stared at the field for a few more seconds. Wiping her tears away, she bent down and plucked several of the nearby flowers on the edge of the field before joining her brother, who was kneeling beside their parents' grave. Mara sat down, placing the flowers at the foot of the gravestone.

"Just trying to comprehend how it's been fifteen years since their passing," Mara said, trying to keep Kai from seeing her face. "It feels like forever, but also, not. Does that even make sense?"

"Hm," Kai pondered. "I know what you mean. I can't believe it's been that long, either."

They sat in silence for a minute, both staring at the words inscribed on the gravestone. *In life, so in death – together, always. Harran and Calista Grayscale.*

"Do you ever wonder, Mara," Kai said, his voice solemn. "That this is not the way things were supposed to be?"

"You mean that Mom and Dad died?" Mara asked.

"No. I mean, I guess. Of course, I wish they hadn't, but that's not really what I mean."

"What *do* you mean?"

"I mean everything after their death. Joining the Order, becoming... whatever it is we should call ourselves."

"Dragonbloods..." Mara said, confused. Kai glanced over at her with a hint of frustration in his eyes.

"Mara... we're not Dragonbloods–not *real* Dragonbloods. Sometimes I struggle to even grasp the point."

"The point is to protect the lands from the dragons. You know that. What's gotten into you?" Mara had heard Kai talk like this before, but never in quite such melancholy.

"Not *real* dragons. You know as well as I do the capital, its people hiding safely behind the protection of the Wall, care little for the Order anymore. The threat of dragons is as far off to them as we are to becoming actual Dragonbloods. Plus, there's still the peace accord. Maybe the elder dragons are really done fighting finally."

"The capital may not care about us, but out here, we do matter. Out here, beyond the Wall's protection, we can still help save lives. The elder dragons might not be a threat, and the wild dragons have grown scarce, yes, but they're never truly gone. We must keep believing we'll always have a purpose here."

"Purpose..." Kai said, sounding even more dejected. "They look down on us, Mara. All of them. They barely even let us help in the fights against the small dragons. If the elder dragons ever returned, we're useless."

"We can still help..." Mara said, trailing off, even though she knew his words weren't entirely untrue. It's a thought many of those without the dragon's blood had discussed often. What *if* the elder dragons returned? Perhaps, then there would be dragon's blood again, at least. But the thought of it brought a hint of fear to Mara's heart.

"I know you don't believe that, Mara," Kai said. "You're just trying to make me feel better. I don't think it's going to work." Kai bent his head forward, staring at the ground.

"I'm sorry, Kai. I don't think we're useless, but I understand how you feel. It's not the same. *We* are not the same. I just... I don't know what to do about it."

Kai lifted his head and glanced at Mara. There was a pleading look in his eyes. She could see the wheels spinning, even as he tore his gaze away and stared at the gravestone again.

"Have you ever wondered," Kai started, pausing momentarily. "Have you ever thought maybe Father was right?"

"Father? About what?" Mara asked.

"About us not joining the Order. He wanted a different life for us. I think that's what I meant earlier. What if we were supposed to do something else?"

"Something... else?" Mara asked, a bit taken aback to hear Kai say it. "What else would we do? This is what you always wanted."

"It *was*," Kai said. "But I'm not so sure it is anymore. I'm tired, Mara. Tired of waiting for something that might never happen. I wanted so much to avenge their deaths–to kill that damned dragon that took them from us. To kill every dragon everywhere. I wanted it more than anything. I still do, but also, I don't. I don't know what I want anymore," Kai finished, his shoulders sagging. He turned away from Mara, trying to hide his despair, but she saw it clearly.

Mara inched closer, putting her arm around his shoulders.

"It's okay, Kai. It's okay to question how life turned out. I've thought about it, too–how things might have been different if they hadn't died. What we might have done instead."

Kai lifted his head and stole a quick glance at her, letting out a partial smile.

"What would you have wanted to do?" he asked her.

"Hmm," Mara thought. Of course, she knew the answer right away, but wanted to make it seem as though she had to give it some thought. "I probably would have opened a library, or a bookstore."

"Why did I even ask?" Kai said with a smirk.

"What about you?" she asked. "If you could do anything in the world, what would *you* do?"

Kai's brow scrunched for a moment, his eyes wandering somewhere off in the distance.

"I don't–" Kai started. "I don't know. It's not that I haven't thought about it, I just never found the answer. I know there's something missing, I just don't know what it is."

Mara smiled sympathetically toward her brother. If she was being honest, she felt it, too. Yes, she loved books, and loved the idea of being around them the rest of her life, but that wasn't everything she wanted out of life. She, too, felt like something was missing.

"Well, keep thinking about it," Mara said, focusing back on Kai. "I'd like to know when you figure it out. And who knows, maybe somehow, it will find us." Mara tried to make her final statement sound confident, but she heard the doubt in her own voice.

At her words, Kai let out a half-hearted smile. She knew he doubted it, too. If he couldn't believe it, Mara would just have to have enough hope for the both of them. She just needed to try harder, for Kai's sake.

"Well, we should probably–" Kai started, cut short by a familiar sound.

A distant bell rang, its sound drifting through the valley. Kai sat up straight, then looked at Mara with excitement.

"A dragon has been spotted!" they both said at once.

***

By the time they got back, the castle was a blur of activity as knights scurried down hallways, most of them headed toward the armory. If a dragon had been spotted, it meant everyone needed to be ready to be called upon. And as was the case for most of the lesser dragons that roamed too close to human lands, only so many knights would be chosen.

On their approach, they saw the knights were already forming up in the courtyard.

"Go ahead," Mara said, knowing exactly what Kai was thinking. "I'll catch up."

Kai nodded, his face aglow with a large smile. He turned and raced after the others.

It warmed Mara's heart to see him excited every time this happened. Her smile faded quickly, however. She knew it was only temporary, but at least this would satiate his restlessness–for a little while. That is, so long as he was chosen. She prayed he would be chosen.

In truth, a dragon sighting was a glorious event for the whole Order, as it did not happen very often, and seemed to be growing longer and longer between occurrences. If Mara remembered correctly, the last sighting was nearly half a dozen moons ago.

Instead of catching up, as Mara had told Kai, she headed for where she knew their uncle would be getting ready. She hurried down the hall, hoping to catch him before he met up with the other leaders to choose the hunting party.

Down a few short hallways, Mara came into view of Yoren's office. Her uncle was still inside, briefing a few officers. As Spear of the Scalewarden, Yoren was second-in-command of the Order. It was a position in which he served honorably, though she knew he had never wanted to lead. Some of the best leaders never did.

She waited patiently by the door, and once the others left, she slipped inside.

"Where is it this time?" Mara asked.

Yoren glanced over at her from behind his desk, then turned his attention down to a large map on the desk's surface. He stuck his finger out, tracing a line between several points of interest.

"It was last spotted headed southeast, about an hour ago, near the north-central tower. It seems it's injured and can't fly, but it's big, and it's still moving at great speed. We need to ride out right away to try and intercept it before it reaches one of the towns."

"A big one? Will it be dangerous?" Mara asked.

"Nothing we can't handle, Mara," Yoren answered, standing up and giving her a reassuring smile. "I'm sure your brother has already joined the others in the arena?"

"Yes, of course. Kai always wants to go on the hunts. He's so restless these days."

Yoren chuckled, a broad smile forming. With his grey hair and beard to match, he was a kind-hearted man, soft-spoken and good to all the knights of the Order. But despite his aging appearance, Mara knew her uncle was strong, and a good fighter. He'd rightfully earned his station as Spear, through both the strength of his arm and of his character.

"Go fetch your armor and meet us in the arena," Yoren said, standing up from his desk. "We've got a dragon to slay."

Mara hurried off to the armory, finding it mostly empty by now. It didn't take long to don her armor, which she'd done hundreds of times before. After it was fastened securely, she rushed through the hallways, entering the arena in the outer portion of Dragonscale Keep. It was basked in the light of the waning sun, unlike the larger section she'd just left, which had been built into the side of the nearby mountain. The only surefire defense against a dragon's fire was dozens of feet of rock and dirt.

Dragonscale Keep was the heart of the Order of Scales, named for the scale-like armor they wore into battle. It was forged from a special steel found in only two known locations in the world. It kept the knights cool and was able to dissipate a great deal of heat, as was oft the case when facing dragons. When Mara stepped out into the light of the sun and saw the whole of the keep gathered there, the glint of daylight reflecting off the knights' armor, she paused momentarily. It was always a mesmerizing sight to see.

In the arena stood roughly a hundred Dragonblood knights, quietly awaiting the Scalewarden's choosing. Mara scanned the line of knights, spotting Kai a few rows from the front, his armor polished and glistening with the rest. He was easy to spot, not only because they were twins, but Kai had an air about him that drew one's attention.

He was tall and handsome, his jet-black hair long enough so that it covered some of his face, though it was brushed to the side in its usual manner. He was very particular about it sitting on the left. His eyes were dark, same as his hair, and there was an intensity behind them that sparked a certain sense of energy in those who met their gaze.

Knowing there was no way she could get to him now, Mara skirted her way around to line up in the back with the few who were still forming up.

"Our scouts report a wyrm of exceptional size has crossed the northern boundary and is heading southeast. Its behavior is erratic, abnormal, and for whatever reason, it does not fly. Our brothers and sisters were able to herd it away from the villages, but the beast still moves at an alarming pace. We must ride out quickly to avoid any bloodshed," Karg called out, his voice echoing throughout the arena.

Karg was the oldest living Dragonblood. By the way he carried himself, you wouldn't know, the white-as-snow hair on his face and head the only signs of his true age. Karg had been one of the Order's fiercest warriors, boasting the highest known dragon kill count to date. The Great Dragon Wars had been a long and hard-fought struggle, and more dragons were slain during the roughly ten-year span of the wars than what had been recorded in the previous two thousand years before that, though accounting was less reliable the further you went back in the Order's history. Karg's lofty kill count was in large part due to the scale of the wars. However, striking the killing blow to so many dragons was no small feat, and the man had earned his station as head of the Order, to which the title of Scalewarden belonged.

"We will bring thirty warriors with us. As soon as I call out your name, head to the stables and prepare your mounts to ride," Karg continued.

"Cyrus Bladesong, Thorlan Brighteye, Caliena Steelheart..." Karg began, naming the knights one by one, each falling out of line and moving quickly down the rows, headed toward the stables.

Several of the others nearby Mara heard their names called and fell out of line. She focused on Karg's shouting, a small bead of sweat running down her face in anticipation of hearing her or her brother's name.

But no such call came for Kai or Mara, and when the last had been chosen, Mara let out a deep breath. Those who remained slowly began to shuffle back into the keep to return their armor and get back to their daily duties. Grunts of disappointment filled the air around Mara as she pushed her way through the crowd, heading toward where she'd seen her brother.

After a dozen paces, she finally saw Kai through the commotion. He was walking after Karg and Yoren, trying to catch up with them. Mara rushed to catch up herself.

"Uncle," she heard Kai call out.

Yoren stopped and turned around, Karg slowing to look back. Yoren waved him on and the Scalewarden continued with the others.

"Uncle, please," Kai said as he approached.

"I'm sorry, Kai. The Scalewarden has chosen."

"Can't you ask him to let me come?" Kai begged.

"Not this time, Kai. I will put in a good word for the next one, I promise."

"He said it's a big one. What if it's—"

"I don't know, Kai. I suppose it's possible, but—"

"Yoren," one of the knights called out, waving to him. Yoren turned and nodded to the man.

"I'm sorry, Kai. I must go. Next time..." Yoren reached his hand out to put it on Kai's shoulder, shaking it firmly before nodding. As he turned, he saw Mara approach, giving her a short bow before hurrying to join the others.

Kai stood there and watched the riders mount their steeds, heading for the gate. Within a minute, there was nothing but dust as Mara stood next to her brother in silence. She turned to Kai and tried to touch his arm, but he stepped away, looking at her in frustration.

"You see? What's the point," he said, then spun and stormed off inside.

Mara stood there in silence a bit longer, her feelings mixed. She knew he wasn't mad at her, but his tone still hurt. She didn't blame Kai, though. In truth, things *were* much different than they'd expected, and even she was beginning to doubt her earlier words.

Perhaps this is just the life we've chosen. Perhaps this is all we were meant for...

CHAPTER TWO

QUEENS

"What exactly are we looking for here, Sister," Talesa asked, kicking a loose stone from a nearby pile of rubble. "There's barely anything left of these ruins."

"I'll know the spot when I find it. It's been a long time, and I was very young."

"You'll just... know?" Talesa asked in the tone she always used when she wanted to annoy her sister rather than get an actual answer.

Nalaen rolled her eyes and ignored her.

"Keep looking, Sister," said Sorn. "You will find it. Nalaen's connection to Mother was the strongest and I'm sure she will be able to sense her when she draws near the spot."

Why does he always have to acknowledge her...

Nalaen, or Sha'Nalaen, per the ancient ways of dragonkin naming, was the oldest of the three siblings who were presently scouring the ruins of the old dragon fortress. As she looked at her brother, Sorn, and her sister, Talesa, standing in these ruins in their human forms, a flood of thoughts swept through her mind. The flight had been long and arduous. Fortunately, they were far enough from human settlements that there was no danger, so assuming their human bodies was a good chance to conserve what remaining energy she had for what she was about to do.

The night her mother died was something she'd relived a thousand times over. Nalaen hatched first, then Talesa, then Sorn. The other eggs were stirring, but they never got the chance. A giant, metallic orb crashed into the middle of the clutch, Nalaen and her brother and sister just barely out of range when the thing exploded, sending the three of them hurtling, slamming them against the far wall. Nalaen was the only one not knocked unconscious by it, and the blurred images she saw in those moments had served as the source of her nightmares for many years.

She watched her mother dive toward the eggs, a look of pure horror etched across her face. After realizing all were lost, her mother turned to Nalaen, both love and sorrow in her eyes. Nalaen would never forget the look of desperation and despair and how much it pained her to see her mother in such anguish, even though Nalaen hadn't fully understood it at the time.

But then, a different look came upon her mother's face. This look was of pain, but not a pain of the mind—it was a physical pain. Her mother's face writhed and twisted momentarily, her eyes wide in shock, before slowly rolling back into her head. After several moments, which in Nalaen's mind now felt like an eternity, her mother's eyes closed, and her lifeless form slumped to the ground.

From the far side of the courtyard, Nalaen could hear shouting, but she did not have time to even try to comprehend it. One of the Queensguard emerged from the other part of the fortress, running forward to defend the Queen as the other one grabbed the three hatchlings and retreated with them in the opposite direction. As they were carried through the archway, Nalaen—the other two still unconscious—looked back to see the Queensguard who had stayed suffer the same fate as her mother. As they rushed toward the end of the hallway, a horde of dragons sprinting out into the courtyard, the last image Nalaen had of her mother was of her corpse lying in the middle of the courtyard, surrounded by her dead children, the Queensguard dropping beside them.

"Sister, are you alright?" Talesa asked, waving her hand in front of Nalaen's face.

Nalaen snapped out of her hellish thoughts. A stroke of memory hit her, and she stepped forward, ignoring her sister again. The images of that night whirling in her mind, nearly as vivid as the night she was there, she began to see the keep as it had been so very long ago.

"Over here," Nalaen gestured, her brother and sister following as she walked between two lines of stones, presumably a long corridor at one point. Nalaen walked slowly, the images of the great halls of the dragons coming to life around her.

The keep had been called '*Dra'lith Fa'Liotha*', meaning 'Liotha's Fall' in the tongue of dragons. Though it was not the largest or most impressive structure the dragons had built, it was one of the most meaningful, especially for those who held Liotha in high regard. Liotha was revered by many as the greatest of the Queenmothers and the one who led the initial onslaught against the humans in rebellion for their attempts to harness the power of the arcane. She was the queen who united many of the clans against a common foe. No one could have foreseen that Liotha's brief crusade against the humans would bring about the rise of the Dragonbloods—a faction of men devoted to protecting humanity with their newfound powers from drinking the blood of the elder dragons that were slain in the battles brought to their doorstep. Little did the dragons know the very act of seeking to save themselves was what led to their undoing.

And so it was for many years after Liotha fell to these abominations. Her followers would strike out in revenge and the humans would repel them time and time again. Since the heart of the dragon's empire, Dae'calum Dor'Dragos, was so far to the east from where the humans dwelt, the dragons needed a base of operations closer to human lands. And what better place than to bolster the shrine of their Greatmother Liotha and use it as a pivoting point with which to strike out at the humans.

For thousands of years, the wars raged between dragons and men, ebbing and flowing throughout the centuries, with no side an apparent winner. That was, until the end of the Great War. Since Liotha's fall, no other Queenmother had been slain; at least not until Sha'Mora, Nalaen's mother.

Liotha died because she was too bold, but Sha'Mora's downfall was something else entirely. The dragons had been safe inside their fortress and repelled all attacks before. Because of their location, it had been easy for the dragons to see any attacks coming and to control the battle from the skies due to the higher altitude and cold temperatures that the mountain provided. Somehow, the Dragonbloods had been able to sneak in unnoticed and lay siege to the keep in a manner of minutes, slaying Sha'Mora and many of her Queensguard before the dragons even had a chance to respond. The few dragons who returned to the capital were questioned, but none could explain how the events of that night unfolded. At least, that's what the accounts told. Nalaen knew there was more to it.

And that was exactly what Nalaen was here to do now. As the three of them continued down the row of stones, Talesa was the first to speak.

"Sister, I know that you've told us the story a thousand times, but what exactly do we expect to find in what is left of these old ruins, even if we *do* find where Mother died?"

"Don't worry, Sister. I have a plan." Nalaen was not normally one known for patience, nor courtesy. She loved her brother and sister, but years of thirsting for vengeance made little room for such trivial emotions.

"Nalaen," Sorn said. "We know that's what we're looking for, but we were hoping you'd shed some light on your plans once we get there."

Nalaen cast her eyes sideways at Sorn. She'd always had a slightly softer spot for him. Maybe it was because he was different, less angry, and more in awe of the world than her and her sister. Or perhaps, it was just that he was her little brother and not seen as a threat, since only female dragons could rule. Or maybe it was something else entirely. Whatever it was, it just... was. It both infuriated and softened Nalaen at the same time.

"When we get there, I think I might have a way to figure out what happened that night; to figure out how mother was killed."

"What!? And you're just now telling us!" Talesa was more than a little upset. Nalaen had always been close to her sister, but never *too* close. Nalaen was the firstborn and was therefore destined to rule once she came of age. But naturally, should anything happen to Nalaen, her sister was next in line. It wasn't common, but there had been instances in the dragons' history where elder sisters met an untimely demise at the hands of their youngers. Nalaen didn't want to take any chances. That being said, she did appreciate Talesa's keen ruthlessness and hunger for blood, a trait they both shared, but her sister delighted in it more than was probably healthy. Pointed in the right direction, it could be a powerful tool; one

Nalaen intended to use extensively in the days to come. But right now, it had no place. Nalaen had work to do and she didn't want her sister getting in the way.

"Quiet, Sister. I am the Queen heir, and I do not answer to nor have to tell anyone anything, not even my own blood. Now, if you'll let me focus, I am trying to conserve my energy while navigating based on crumbled ruins and near hundred-year-old memories."

Talesa sneered and turned off to the left, stepping over the crumbled row of stones and off in her own direction. Sorn watched quietly. As Talesa moved out of hearing distance, Sorn picked up his pace and came up beside Nalaen.

"You think you can find the spot? It was so long ago and there really is almost nothing left of the old fortress."

"Yes, Brother," Nalaen scoffed. "I can find it." Though he could be annoying, she was glad he was there, and she softened her tone. "I was digging deep into my memories to remember what the keep looked like all those years ago. You and Talesa were both knocked out, but I remember it quite vividly. I believe we have several more halls and then we will come into the courtyard where it happened."

"How will you be able to find out what happened?" Sorn asked.

"It's... complicated. Just trust me."

In truth, Nalaen did not want to offer anything else. Partly because she did not want anyone to know what secrets she'd dug up in recent days, but in part it was more of a sense of pride that vengeance should be hers and hers alone. Of course, she would use others to her own ends to get there, but the knowledge and the plans would all stay in her head. She did care for Sorn, but he was too naïve. And Talesa, she was too unpredictable.

When Nalaen was first brought back to the capital, she was a newborn with no mother. Though she was heir, Queenmothers are not allowed to rule until their 100th cycle from hatching. To the dragons, a cycle is a little less than what humans consider a year. While Nalaen waited for her time to come, she had spent a lot of time planning and studying. Though the dragons did not know what happened at the keep on the night her mother was slain, Nalaen, through her study of the forbidden magics, had uncovered a way to divine it.

When Liotha came to power, she was the first Queenmother. Before her, the Wyrmlords had ruled. The situation surrounding her rise to power, and of Dro'Kal's fall, is a murky tale, full of dark secrets, and undoubtedly, lies. However, rumors spread amongst some of the dissenters, accusing Liotha of delving into magics that were considered unnatural. When Nalaen started her studies as heir to the throne, she'd been required to study what was written of the Queenmothers before her. When Nalaen came to read about some of the rumors surrounding Liotha, she became infatuated with seeking them out. As such, she came to discover knowledge of these dark magics and why they were forbidden. And of the Vault, where the majority of them were kept secret.

Nalaen knew her brother had his suspicions. Sorn had always been an inquisitive sort, and he often spent time in the library with Nalaen—when she would allow him. He'd watched her over the years as she'd wrapped herself in a blanket of secrecy. When they were younger, Nalaen talked to Sorn more than anyone else because he understood her more than anyone else. But over time, things began to change.

She knew it hurt him, but she couldn't let him know what she was up to–not fully, at least. At times, he would drop hints or make comments to her about the things that concerned him, but it was never direct. Nalaen knew he would never confront her directly.

"I trust you, Sister. Lead on," Sorn said, though Nalaen could clearly see the tide of questions he was holding back.

Nalaen hesitated slightly, knowing her brother was more observant than he let on. What her sister Talesa lacked, Sorn did not. And that was one of the reasons why she was glad to have him by her side. Sorn was clever, but he knew his place. Talesa constantly questioned hers.

As Nalaen turned, the images of the great keep flooded her vision again. They rounded a corner of the long hallway, coming upon a larger area where the stones were spread out. A flood of emotions filled her as the memory of the last sight of her mother came rushing back. This was the room the Queensguard had retreated to with Nalaen and her brother and sister; the room where they fled shortly before taking flight back home.

Nalaen crossed the open space toward the center of the room, Sorn close behind her. As she turned, she saw the remains of several archways leading out to various points in the keep. This had been the central room and it led to multiple key points within the keep. Her eyes fell upon a particular archway. She knew it was the path to where her mother fell.

"It's just down here," she muttered.

They picked up the pace and made it to the remains of the courtyard where she and her brother had been born. The area didn't look much different than anywhere else they'd been in the ruins, but as Nalaen approached, she felt it. It was a slight tingling in the back of her neck, and in her fingertips. It was more than the range of emotions running through her. There was a latent power here–the presence of her mother's blood.

"Stay here," Nalaen told Sorn. He obeyed.

Nalaen walked to the center of the area and bent down, reaching her hands out, palms facing the ground. Yes, despite the huge gap in time, she could still feel her mother's presence.

Dragons are creatures deeply rooted in the oldest of magic. As dragons age, they become more in tune with the magical essences of all things; earth, air, fire, water, light, darkness, and all that lay between. Though most of the other races have some magical affinity, dragons have the strongest connection. With the other races wiped out, dragons are now the only ones who wield magic naturally. During the course of her studies, Nalaen was taught about such things. She was also taught there are some of the old magics that should not be trifled with, even for a dragon. These magics included shadow, blood, decay, and death, amongst others. It was said that, because a dragon's entire essence is so intertwined with magic, delving too deep into these dark arts could twist them into an abomination. There were stories of dragons who'd gone astray. And, in fact, the root of why the dragons are now ruled by females is directly related to a time when the great Wyrmlord Dro'Kal was seduced by the power of these magics. The stories tell he nearly destroyed the kingdoms, twisting into a horror the likes of which had never been seen. When Nalaen was younger, she'd thought the tale was only a myth meant to persuade young queens, and to explain why it must always be a Queen who rules. As she grew older, Nalaen learned there were truths to the tales, though she presumed those, too, contained exaggerations and misleading information.

Over the course of thirty cycles, Nalaen pieced together loose findings until she'd finally stumbled across the details about the Vault of Shadows. Once her knowledge became complete, she'd learned a great many things and developed skills that many, especially her brother, would not approve of. One such skill was that of being able to relive the moments of another's life by communing with the magical essences in their blood–a skill she was planning to use now to find out what had happened to her mother.

As Nalaen stared at the ground, she focused all her energy on what was left of her mother's essence below the surface. The blood had run deep, and it was difficult, but Nalaen could still feel it. In truth, this was not the first time she'd performed this ritual, though it was the most extreme. She'd previously practiced it on several corpses of dragons that had died, most of natural causes. Through it, she'd been able to see their last moments as she worked to hone the skill. But their deaths were fresh; her mother had been dead a long time. She presumed she'd have to expose herself to the magic longer, which could potentially be dangerous.

She focused on her task. Her mother's essence was clearly there, but it was elusive. Additionally, she detected the essences of many other dragons in the direct vicinity. It would be difficult to pinpoint her mother through it all. She pressed further, searching intently for it.

While Nalaen tried to focus, Sorn watched her curiously. There was a commotion off to the side and he saw Talesa approaching. Her gaze was fixed on Nalaen, one eyebrow raised. She glanced briefly at Sorn before edging closer to her sister. She circled Nalaen as her gaze turned more inquisitive, studying her sister's mannerisms. Dragons are able to communicate with each other through their magical connections, speaking directly to each other telepathically. Sorn was proficient in it, but he would not dare attempt it on his sister at the present. Talesa was much bolder, and Sorn knew what she was thinking.

He came up and touched Talesa's shoulder, just as she was about to try and commune with her sister.

"She needs to focus. You should not interrupt her," he said carefully.

"I'm just going to take a peek," Talesa said, brushing his hand away.

"I don't know what she's doing, but it is not any magic known to me. You don't know what the side effects of interrupting her might be."

"I don't care. I want to know."

"I meant the side effects for you, Sister. It is unwise. You should leave her be."

Talesa stopped, eyeing her sister more cautiously now. For a few moments, it seemed as if she would continue, but eventually she rolled her eyes, glared at Sorn, folded her arms, and went to lean against a nearby wall.

Suddenly, the wind picked up and swirled about them. Talesa and Sorn watched Nalaen, noticing her skin was now a pale greyish color. Her eyes were closed, but he could see them darting back and forth underneath her eyelids. Her hands were still in their outstretched positions, hovering over the ground, palms down. The winds swirled more around Nalaen's location, emanating from her.

Sorn and Talesa approached her, shielding their eyes from the snow that was now forming a vortex around them.

"Nalaen, are you alright?" Sorn called out, raising his voice as much as he could over the wind.

Nalaen did not move. Sorn echoed his previous question, but still nothing. He reached out to put his hand on Nalaen's shoulder, but Talesa snatched his wrist and pulled him back.

"Like you said, Brother. Just let her finish. I want to see what's going to happen." Sorn looked at her, an eerie calmness in her eyes now as she watched her sister. He nodded, hesitantly.

Nalaen, completely unaware of what was happening in the real world, was lost in the memories of a place and time long forgotten. She could sense them all, the dragons that had died on that night so very long ago. She could feel their thoughts and hear their shouts as they rushed in to defend their dead queen against an unknown foe. Then, she listened to their cries of pain, all meeting the same end her mother had. But through it all, she could not locate her mother's memories. She strained harder, trying to drown out the noise of the others.

As she pushed herself further, she began to hear whispers, faint echoes of something beyond the night of her birth. The whispers sounded like words, but Nalaen could not comprehend them. They seemed to be the voices of dragons, but no dragon that Nalaen had ever known. Then, she remembered her teachings. She remembered this keep had been erected on the site where Liotha had fallen, hundreds of years ago. It must have been dragons before even her mother's time. Nalaen knew she had dug too deep, and yet she was curious. Could she read their memories, too?

As she pursued them, she started to see images. The mountains were covered in a blanket of snow, the waning light of the day casting an orange glow against the soft, white background. The world was still. Nalaen found herself walking along the crest of a hill, her footsteps falling eerily quiet on the soft powder below. As she came upon the top of it, she looked down over the valley. A thousand snow-covered trees spread out before her as a slight breeze trickled through them, scattering the powder in small tufts down to the valley floor. The sun still shone its waning light on a few of the treetops, but it was fading quickly. Below the thick tree cover, it was getting darker by the minute.

Nalaen looked around for any sign of life, but there was nothing save her and the air in between the vastness of the peaks and the valley. There was no sound but the slight whistle of the wind as it whimsically flittered to and fro amongst this expanse at the top of the world. Nalaen felt herself getting lost in the soothing peacefulness of the vision, when suddenly her ears perked at a faint sound on the wind. It was a sound Nalaen knew well. Wings.

She looked up, her eyes searching for signs of approaching dragons. She realized the sound was coming from behind her and turned, shielding her eyes from the light of the sun beyond the rolling hills to the west. As she squinted, a shape came slowly into view. A lone dragon, flying up from the human lands. As it moved closer to where Nalaen stood, she could see it was dressed for war. As it drew even closer, she could see the dragon was battered and bruised, struggling to stay aloft.

Soon, she realized it was a female—one of the most majestic dragons Nalaen had ever seen, adorned in purple scales. She knew instantly that it must be Liotha. But despite her air and magnificent form, she looked tired from whatever battle it was she'd just left behind. And it almost looked as if she was holding something in her arms.

Just as Liotha was about to pass over where Nalaen was standing, another sound caught Nalaen's ear. This sound was different. It sounded like voices, but not dragons. There was a far-off shout, and then a quick mechanical sound. Nalaen turned around and looked down into the valley, which was now even darker than before. As she scanned the tree line, her eye caught a small, flickering flame amongst the shadows. The flame lifted up and held momentarily, then suddenly moved down toward the ground. As it did, Nalaen heard another mechanical sound and then a whirl, as if something were flying quickly through the air. Then she saw it-a small, dark line lifting quickly into the sky, a slight glint at its end as it caught the disappearing rays of the sun. A dozen more lines followed shortly behind it.

Nalaen watched in horror, trying to cry out, though no sound came from her mouth, as a flurry of massive bolts went sailing straight at Liotha above. The first round all missed, but just barely. Liotha dodged haphazardly, as if she were trying to understand what had just happened. She dove down, trying to force them to adjust their aim. As she dove, Nalaen heard the same sound as before, and then another hiss as a second round of bolts flew into the air. The bolts missed again. Nalaen saw Liotha slow, as if hesitating, and then quickly veer off in the direction she had originally been headed. Once more, Nalaen heard mechanical cranking and shouts, then a third volley of bolts sailed up after the fleeing target. This time, Liotha was hit, plummeting down and crashing into the snow on the hillside just beyond her.

Nalaen cast her eyes down and surveyed the bloody scene along the slope of the hill several hundred yards from where she stood. She could see the blood stains smeared across the snow and rocks where Liotha had crashed into the earth. With her keen eyes, Nalaen could see her well enough, and so far, she had yet to move.

As she watched, hoping for signs of life, she heard the shouts of men and the sound of hooves, the ambushers riding out of the forest and up the hill. Nalaen looked back and forth, hoping that Liotha would get up and fly away. As she began to lose hope, she thought she caught a slight stirring from Liotha herself. The Queenmother appeared to move her head slightly and open her eyes, though she did not move any more than that.

The mounted men reached the crest of the hill several moments later, halting their mounts and dropping to the ground. Nalaen counted a dozen or so of them. They grabbed their spears and cautiously approached the motionless form on the hill. They spread out, though five or six of them headed directly toward Liotha from the front. Nalaen held her breath. The Queen showed no sign of movement now. Perhaps Nalaen had just imagined that she'd seen her open her eyes before.

All of a sudden, Liotha sprang, snatching up the closest man to her right, and with her tail, she swatted another one to her back left and sent him reeling down the hill. The other men raised their spears in defense and started forming a circle around her as the rest of the men joined the fight. The Queen slowly inched her way backwards, head up and ready to strike at the first man who dared to engage her. She was limping, and it was apparent in the way she moved she was in a great deal of pain. She also kept one of her legs tucked in tightly, still looking as if she was holding something. Nalaen could see blood spurting out from the wound where the massive bolt had pierced her hide.

Even injured, she was not to be taken lightly. They were clearly Dragonbloods. No other men could have taken down a Queenmother so easily, though Nalaen had to wonder why she was alone. They formed a tight ring and closed in on her. Liotha moved her head from side to side, eyeing the ranks of men, as if she were searching for a weak link to attack first. After a minute of neither side taking the first move, one man stepped forward. From what Nalaen could tell, he looked taller and larger than the rest. Liotha focused in on him and poised, ready to strike. The man slowly inched closer and Liotha opened her maw and showed the man her glowing throat, a low crackling sound emerging as she readied her attack. The man stopped, but kept his raised spear pointed at her midsection. The two stood there for a few moments, locked onto each other's gaze.

Then, Nalaen saw it. She tried to call out, but again, no sound came from her mouth. It had been a diversion. One of the men on the opposite side of the ring from the man who'd moved forward had inched his way behind Liotha. He'd placed his spear on his back and was holding his hands up. But he made no motion, just stood there at the ready. Nalaen's brow scrunched, confused at what was happening.

Then, suddenly, the larger man leapt forward with his spear. Liotha was ready, and she let loose a roar as the flames began to spew forth. But they never even touched the man who was rushing in for his strike. And then Nalaen understood. The man in the back was what the Dragonbloods called a "Fireblood"–a rarity in their Order, who could manipulate fire itself. The large man leapt, pulling his spear arm back as far as he could, then releasing it with all his might straight into

Liotha's throat. The fire from her belly stopped immediately, her eyes rolling back into her head.

Nalaen watched the great Queenmother draw her last breath, and the world slowly faded to black.

Nalaen listened in the darkness. She could hear voices again, the souls of many others slain throughout the years. Then, she heard it. It was faint but distinguished from the rest. It was a soothing voice. One that sounded familiar. She was talking to someone in low, soft tones. Images slowly faded into existence around Nalaen as she realized who it was.

"There, there my children. It is time to wake up. The world is ready for your flight to begin."

It was Nalaen's mother. She could see her clearly now, in the room where Nalaen had been born. She was lying next to her clutch of eggs, none of which had hatched yet, close as to keep them warm and sheltered from the cold of the night. Nalaen saw her egg amidst all the others.

"My Queen," came a voice. It was one of the Royal Guards. "Preparations have been made. We leave for Dor'Dragos first thing in the morning, as you requested. The High Council has been made aware and are eagerly awaiting your arrival."

"Excellent. Did they send a reply to my message about the accord?"

"Yes, Queenmother. They have already sent the offer of a truce, and are expecting a reply anytime from the humans. They will be ready to discuss it in more detail upon your arrival."

"Very good. Make sure all are ready, then. My hatchlings should awaken any minute, and I would like to leave before first light."

"As you wish," the guard replied. He bowed, turned, and left.

Mother was planning to go home in the morning? One more day and she would have survived, along with all my brothers and sisters...

Nalaen's thoughts were interrupted by a distinct sound–a gentle cracking. She watched as her younger self crawled its way out of one of the eggs. It was weird to see it this way, but the sight brought warm feelings. She saw her brother and sister do the same shortly after, struggling to break free from their own temporary prisons. For just a moment, Nalaen was pulled back there, reminded of her first few moments of life and the instant affection she'd felt for her mother.

But it was not meant to last.

There was a loud crack, and everything happened as it did before. The explosion sent the newborns reeling. Nalaen watched from her mother's eyes as she saw the devastation of her clutch. She saw her mother look at her and her brother and sister, she felt the sheer terror and despair as her mother realized that most of her offspring were lost. She saw her mother look her way, checking to see that Nalaen and her brother and sister were okay. Heat began to fill her lungs and Nalaen felt the burning embers of rage swelling up in her mother's throat.

Then, Nalaen felt pain–immense pain, as if something had pierced through her scales, deep into her body, nearly reaching her heart. The darkness around grew even darker as she fell to the ground. All Nalaen could hear was the slow beating of her mother's heart between shallow, bated breaths. Amongst the slow, rhythmic sounds of her mother dying, Nalaen started to hear something different. It was muffled at first but became clearer after a few moments. She could hear two distinct voices, though the first sounded a bit more youthful than the second.

"Is she dead?"

"Not yet, I can still sense the beating of her heart, but it's fading fast. It won't be long."

"To kill a queen in one blow. The intelligence we received proved to be correct. Without it, we could have missed the Queen and her kin. How did you come by it again?"

"It was a message delivered by a courier from the dragons themselves, though it would not tell me its master's name, only that someone on their side wanted to see the war ended swiftly."

"A gift, indeed. It seems both sides want the war to be over."

The voices continued, but Nalaen could feel herself losing consciousness. She'd stayed in these memories too long. Darkness was closing in around her.

She strained to hold on just a few seconds longer. Someone had betrayed her Mother. One of her own. What monster would do such a thing? She needed to know more.

As Nalaen lost her hold on the magic, slipping back to reality, she heard footsteps. She heard grunting as a man grabbed the spear and wrenched it from its fleshy hold. Nalaen felt another tinge of pain and a slight spike in her mother's heartbeat, though it quickly faded again and slowed even further than before as more and more blood rushed from the now open wound.

The humans spoke further, one of them shouting, but Nalaen was being lifted out of the visions, pulled back into the real world, where her brother and sister were waiting.

Just before she opened her eyes, she caught one final word that stood out from the others, the murderer's voices barely clear enough to understand: "Grayscale."

CHAPTER THREE

NO-BLOODS

Mara traced her fingertips along the crenellations of the top of the wall outside the keep, her eyes wandering the surrounding hills, watching for signs of her uncle's return. It had been three days, and she was worried. She was always worried about her family. Aside from reading, it's probably what she spent most of her time doing.

With a sigh, she turned away and cast her gaze down to the middle of the arena where Kai was sparring with one of their friends. Brol was nearly Kai's size, just a few inches shorter, but he was nowhere near her brother's aptitude in combat. Brol could hold his own for a little while, but Kai's fury nearly always got the best of him.

Mara could tell Brol was quickly approaching his limits.

The two boys dodged and weaved, Kai pressing his attacks with the wooden training spear, Brol dodging and deflecting as best he could. Mara saw Kai score two hits—one in Brol's shoulder, another across his leg. The boy managed to dodged several more attacks before Kai pushed in again, bringing his spear in a wide arc and sweeping Brol off his feet.

Kai reached out his hand to Brol, lifting his friend out of the dirt and taking his spear so Brol could dust himself off.

"Well done, Kai," Brol said, clapping him on the shoulder. "Maybe one of these days I'll stand a chance against you."

"Well done for a No-blood," a nearby knight called out, walking in the direction of the two boys with his own wooden spear. "How about a real fight?"

Mara sighed heavily. Bran Lightfoot, aptly named for his speed and agility, was a complete ass. "No-bloods" was the term used for Kai and Mara and the others who did not have dragon's blood in their veins. Though most of the Dragonbloods weren't mean or overtly condescending, a few were, and Bran was one of them, seeming to especially delight in taking any chance he could to get under Kai's skin.

"Sure thing, Bran," Kai shot back. "Let's see if you fight half as well as you run your mouth."

"Oh, I assure you, my spear will touch your chest before I even break a sweat."

Even from her perch atop the wall, Mara could see Kai's jaw clenching. Her brother was exceptionally skilled for his age and experience, but against a full blown Dragonblood with nearly ten years more training, she wasn't sure he stood much of a chance. That wouldn't stop Kai, though. He rarely backed down from a fight.

The two boys circled each other, both keeping the dull points of their practice spears trained on the other, though Bran held his loosely, an obvious taunt. Kai held his spear properly, as they were trained to do—both hands, adequately spaced apart, his stance wide and his feet firmly planted with each step. *Good, Kai. Don't let him get to you.*

Bran made the first move, moving in quickly, trying to catch Kai off guard. There was a reason he'd earned his surname of Lightfoot. Mara watched as he ran, bobbing and weaving in with a shocking speed. Kai reacted, bringing his spear up, barely managing to deflect the quick blow. As Bran bounced past Kai, he swung his spear backward, clipping Kai in his heel. Kai winced, but recovered quickly, spinning and bringing his defensive stance back to the ready.

It was a hit, but not a lethal one, though Mara knew a blow like that with a real spear would likely cause some damage. However, in the rules of sparring, it was only considered a minor blow. In order to score a winning hit, you needed to hit torso or head, though head was off-limits in unarmored fights.

Bran dodged back in again, this time feigning a direct attack to sweep hard right, coming around Kai to get behind him. Kai kept his defense strong, following Bran almost as quickly as he leapt around. Bran continued, throwing several jabs, each one missing until, finally, he landed a quick thrust against Kai's shoulder. Kai reeled again, this time taking his own jab back at Bran, who moved easily out of the way, Kai's strike hitting nothing but air.

Mara could see Kai was getting frustrated now. His grip was a little off, and he wasn't minding his feet as much. Though Mara much preferred reading over fighting, she'd never forget the instructions that had been drilled into their minds. She decided it was best she headed down to the arena and see if she could catch Kai's eye to remind him to keep a cool head. It wasn't one of his strongsuits, but she had to try.

As she descended the stairs, the boys exchanged more blows. Bran continued to dance around Kai, never staying within striking distance for more than a couple seconds. Kai jabbed several more times, more misses. Bran struck two more blows, one on Kai's thigh, another on his hand, though Kai still managed to keep him from scoring a critical hit.

By now, Kai was furious, and he was getting sloppier by the second. Bran, seeming to notice, pressed in, this time coming for a direct attack. Just as Mara came around the corner from the stairs, she saw Kai leap toward Bran in a counterattack. The two boys collided, Kai's spear hitting Bran firmly in his shoulder, Bran's spear narrowly missing Kai's chest. In a grunt of anger, Bran lashed, bringing the butt of his spear up and cracking it into the side of Kai's head.

Momentarily stunned, Kai reeled backward, trying to keep his footing. He shook his head and reached his hand up to his ear, withdrawing it, a few drops of blood on his fingers. His gaze met with Bran's, who wore a cocky smirk.

"You're gonna pay for that," Kai yelled, beginning to rush forward.

Just then, the horn blew from one of the guards atop the gatehouse. The knights were returning.

After a short while, the doors to the keep grated open, and a few seconds later, Karg rode through on his horse, proceeded by their uncle, the rest of the host behind them.

Kai stopped, staring at the procession as Karg and Yoren eyed them curiously. Backing away, Kai bowed, offering the standard salute of the Order. He eyed Bran on the other side of the horses, his gaze intense and cold. His stare was pulled away from Bran when a large cart passed between them.

Most of the dragons the knights had slain over their years of service were small—no larger than maybe two or three horses at the most. But this beast—this was something else. The knights had laid its body across two carts, with a decent gap between them, part of its belly sagging, nearly scraping the ground. From snout to tail, it must have been at least sixty feet. Its scales were shades of darker gray, not shiny, though polished enough to still reflect the rays of the early morning sun. There were large spines along its back, from the tip of its tail to the nape of the neck. On all four of its legs were massive, razor-sharp claws, extending at least half a foot. The dragon's wings were folded in and laid on top of the cart, but Kai imagined what they must have looked like fully stretched. The beast could have easily blotted out the sun the entire length of the column of knights, and then some. It must have been quite the sight to see before the life was taken from it.

Amidst the bustle of the arriving party, many others had emerged from the inner keep, marveling at the kill. A dragon always caused a commotion, but as word of the beast's size spread, nearly the whole of the keep was soon inspecting it. Forgetting about his prior angst, Kai moved in closer to join them and get a better look at the dragon.

Haunting images floated across Kai's vision—images he'd tried so hard to shove deep down inside. He saw the massive beast emerging from the smoke as Mara woke him. He saw it drooling, staring down at them with fire and rage. He heard Mara's scream as it barreled toward them. He saw his father walking bravely toward it, waving his arms. He saw the whole scene fading away as their uncle pulled them to safety.

"Now *that's* a dragon," came a voice off to Kai's side, pulling Kai from the hellish nightmare he'd relived a thousand times over.

The voice belonged to Daxon Lockewood, though everyone just called him Dax. He was a head shorter than Kai, lanky, and nearly always wore a smile that stretched across his face. He'd joined the Order the same time as the twins. "Those teeth look like they're longer than my forearm, and maybe even wider, too."

"That's 'cause you're a twig, little Dax," said Brol. Brol walked up and placed his hand on Dax's head, messing his hair, to which Dax stepped aside and swatted him away. "But you might be right. This thing is huge. Must have taken all thirty to take it down," Brol finished, turning to Yoren.

Kai gave a half-cocked smile, looking back at the beast, traces of his nightmare still lingering. Though his friends jested, there was truth to their words. It wasn't the beast that had killed his parents, but it was roughly the same size. This close, Kai could now see the size of the beast's head, its mouth wide-open. The dragon's jaw was easily as long as Kai's arm, and it was full of rows of fangs that looked like they could bite a man in half as effortlessly as a spear sliced through parchment.

The beast's tongue was sticking out of its mouth, lying on the surface of the cart. It was long, a deep red color, and still glistening with saliva–or blood, Kai wasn't sure which. Either way, Kai's thoughts ran with images of those massive jaws coming after him, the slithering tongue begging to pull him in and devour him whole as a young boy.

"Don't worry, Kai," Dax said, placing his hand on Kai's shoulder. "It's very much dead."

Kai smiled at Dax, pretending to laugh, but unable to shake the images in his mind.

"A beauty, isn't she?" came another voice from behind them all. Yoren stepped up beside the three boys, admiring the beast with them.

"Yes, Spear," Dax said, using Yoren's official title. "She?"

"Yes, female. She put up a good fight, but as you can see, was no match for our warriors."

"Were there any casualties?" asked Brol.

"No, fortunately. Our knights from the tower pressed her south, away from the villages as best they could. With her wing injured," he said, pointing, everyone's eyes following to see a large tear in the left wing, "she seemed unable to fly, and was heading for the farms below the south-central tower, but we cut her off just in time, pushing her back toward the mountains where we eventually cornered her. She still put up a good fight, nearly got Cyrus there, along with a few of the others, but luckily no one was seriously injured. Though, it did give some of the farmers quite a scare to see a huge dragon barreling toward them as our knights rode up in force from behind!" Yoren laughed out loud, many of the other knights around joining him. Kai gave half a smile but remained quiet.

Kai saw Yoren glance his way, but his uncle was immediately waylaid by several knights who were eagerly inquiring about more specifics of the hunt. With his prior irritation returning, Kai decided to get some air and headed up onto the outer wall.

After taking one last look down below, seeing everyone still talking happily amongst each other, he turned back and leaned over the side of the wall facing outward. Dragonscale Keep stood tall on a hill overlooking the valley, with the village of Eastend sitting comfortably far below, under its watchful gaze.

Kai glanced over at one of the nearby ballistae–"Dragonkillers" they called them. He'd marveled at them in his early years, fascinated with how efficiently they earned their nickname. They could release a volley of ten arrows in a manner of seconds before needing to be reloaded. Still, even with the keeps weapons watching over the valley, Kai always wondered why anyone would have wanted to live so close to the border, especially in earlier times when the threat of dragons was much higher.

Fortunately, since he'd been alive, it had been relatively peaceful, and Kai had many fond memories growing up there. Normally, they brought warm feelings, but today, they were more like hollow echoes of a past life when he was full of hopes and dreams. He'd always dreamt of the day he would walk these walls, carrying a spear, bearing the emblem of the Order on his back. Today, it felt like a sham. It felt meaningless.

"Beautiful day, isn't it?" Yoren spoke, coming to stand beside Kai.

Kai glanced sideways, but kept his gaze forward, his cheeks turning red, his jaw clenching. A nod was all he could offer in reply. Yoren stood there for a moment in silence, casting his gaze down into the valley, as Kai was. Kai waited, uncomfortable, knowing his uncle was looking for the right words.

"I know you're restless, Kai," Yoren said at last, after taking a deep breath. "I know this isn't how you wanted things to be. Trust me, this isn't what I had in mind, either. Nor Karg, nor the others. In truth, everyone is a bit restless."

Kai looked at his Uncle for the first time, acknowledging his words as he examined his somber nature. Kai looked back over his shoulder, still hearing talking and laughing as tales were still being spun down in the arena.

"Seems like *they're* happy," he said, tilting his head to the side.

"For the moment," Yoren replied, acknowledging the commotion. "But it won't last. It is peculiar, though..."

"What is?" Kai asked, his ears perking up.

"The beast. Usually, only the young ones that don't know any better wander down into human lands. This one is old. It's full-grown, probably several hundred years old by my guess. What reason could it possibly have had to expose itself? It's a feral dragon–nothing like the ones we fought in the wars, but they're still clever enough. It should know better."

Kai scrunched his brow, contemplating his uncle's words. A hint of excitement filled his mind.

"What do you think it could mean?" Kai asked.

"I don't know–not yet, at least. But I plan to think on it a great deal." Yoren paused, meeting Kai's gaze, seeming as though he had more he wanted to say. After a moment, he cleared his throat, turning his attention away awkwardly. "We will hold the Fire at dusk, and afterwards, a feast to celebrate. Will I see you there, Kai?"

Kai followed his uncle's gaze back to the arena where the knights were already beginning to hack away at the dragon's corpse, the smell of fresh blood just now beginning to fill the air.

"Where else would I be?" Kai replied quietly.

"That's my boy," Yoren said, smiling. He placed his hand on Kai's shoulder. "We'll get you out there yet, Kai. You have my word." Yoren moved to leave but stopped just before entering the doorway leading to the stairway down. "Oh, and Kai... let's keep these concerns between us, eh? I don't want anyone to start getting any crazy ideas until I get this sorted out."

Kai nodded, his mouth edging on a frown. Yoren nodded back with a smile and left, leaving Kai alone. Kai went back to leaning on the edge of the wall, his expression returning to its earlier state. *Where else, indeed...*

***

The evening festivities started at dusk when the horns blew, signaling the start of the Dragon Fire. As was customary, the dragon's corpse was burned, though not entirely. The claws and fangs were saved, along with the head, which was to serve as the Order's trophy. Since this was the biggest dragon in decades, its skull would be preserved and mounted on the wall along with the others, most of which were from the Great Dragon Wars. As such, there was quite the excitement within the keep.

Kai and Mara and several of their friends, all of whom joined the Order at the same time, gathered around the huge bonfire in the middle of the arena. They watched excitedly as Karg handed out the teeth and claws, trophies for those who'd participated in the hunt. Everyone thought it was exciting–everyone but Kai.

Kai had several of his own trophies from past hunts, but nothing like what they were receiving now. He watched in quiet contempt as they claimed their prizes, one by one. It wasn't until Haran, another of their friends, elbowed him that he realized he'd been staring into the fire well past that portion of the ceremony, thinking on what his uncle had said earlier. When he came to, he saw Karg was giving his closing speech.

"And so, we honor our brothers and sisters who placed their lives in danger to defend the realm. It is for this very reason that we celebrate this evening, for the slaying of a beast this large is no small feat. It renews our faith in the Order's calling; that we will defend the realm at all costs, ensuring the dragons of old don't get any ideas, and that they stay where they belong far across the Thousand Peaks."

"As one last reward, the knights who rode today shall be seated first at the head tables. You have earned the honor to fill your bellies with ale and food ahead of the rest. Now, let's go christen this night with good food and drink."

Karg stood, a nearby knight handing him his spear. When he received it, he raised it high and shouted.

"One bond!"

"ONE BLOOD!" came a glorious shout in return, echoing throughout the open space.

Karg bowed, then waved his free hand, signaling for the honorees to leave first for the dining hall. Kai watched, his mood not improving, though he tried to cast it aside. He was, after all, used to being seated last.

Kai's friends stood around talking, waiting for the others to filter out. Mara was chatting with several of the girls, Haran and Dax also with them. They were laughing and, Kai thought he heard, talking about joining future hunts. He saw Mara glance his way several times, in addition to Vi.

Vi was what they called her, because no one knew her full name. For whatever reason, that's the way she wanted it. Even Kai's uncle and the other knights just called her Vi. Kai had to assume his uncle knew her full name, but if it wasn't important enough to share, then Kai supposed it wasn't worth it to press the matter. Still though, he'd always been curious.

Vi was tall, like Kai, with black hair to boot. In many ways, she looked a lot like the twins. Kai assumed she was from a noble family, perhaps in the capital, just like his mother, Calista, had been. But where Kai and Mara had dark eyes, Vi's were an emerald green. She was beautiful, though Kai tried to pretend he didn't notice. She was also a peculiar girl. It was quite normal for most girls to give Kai their attention, but she hardly ever did. And when she did, it wasn't like the other interactions. Not that he cared, really, but it made her much more... intriguing.

At the moment, however, Kai's mind was elsewhere, and he avoided everyone's gaze. He stared back into the fire, half wishing that everyone would go on without him.

Brol walked over and kicked Kai gently. Kai looked up at him, his expression unchanging.

"What's eatin' you?" Brol asked.

Kai sucked in a deep breath, then let it out slowly.

"Just tired of being left behind, I guess," he replied, hiding his true feelings.

"I know what you mean. I wish we could have joined the hunt. I'm dying to get out there and do something."

"You and me both."

Brol stood in silence for a moment, looking at the fire. The last remnants of the dragon's flesh sizzled, the large fire finally starting to grow smaller.

"Well, looks like everyone's about left. Let's go drown our misery in some ale, eh?"

Kai glanced at the dwindling crowd, then up at Brol, his mouth forming a half frown.

"I guess some ale would be nice, take my mind off things."

"Now that's the Kai we all know and love," Brol said with a grin.

Dax came over and slung his arm over the taller boy's shoulder, a silly expression on his face as he looked at Kai.

"Well, what the hell are we waitin' for? I don't know about ya'll, but we
don't get to drink every day around here. Let's go get some ale before the fearless
champions drink it all!"

Kai rolled his eyes at the remark, but Dax's ridiculous grin was just too much.
Slowly, he cracked a smile. He looked at Brol, his own mouth twisted in a grin.

"Careful Dax," Kai said with a smirk. "Don't get too excited. Remember
what happened last time you drank."

"Uh, I have no idea what you're talkin' about, Kai," Dax said, trying to keep
a straight face. "That goat just came out of nowhere and I fell on top of it."

"Riiight..." Kai said, grinning.

All three boys broke out into laughter, remembering when Dax tried to ride
the goat. He lasted longer than they'd expected, but it was absolutely hilarious
when it ran under a low-hanging branch and knocked Dax flat on his back.

It felt good to laugh. That was exactly what Kai needed right now. He still
had much on his mind, but at least he had his friends. And tonight, ale. That
would help, too. But Dax was right, and they needed to get moving before even
that was gone.

"Alright, let's go you three," Mara said, approaching the group, giving each
of them a sly smile. "I'm hungry."

"You heard the lady," Dax said, tilting his head to the side.

"Lady?" Kai remarked, finally coming to join the others. "Suck up," he
added as he gave Dax a light punch on his arm.

Everyone chuckled and followed Mara and the other girls into the keep,
joining the rear of the line entering the dining hall.

Inside, the tables were littered with all sorts of foods–roasted boars, cheeses
of various types, and at least three different kinds of bread. Kai spotted the one
called Honeybread. It was his favorite, and seeing it brought another smile to
his face.

He cast a look over the area, seeing the final tables with enough open seats for
their group of eight–Brol, Dax, Haran, Mara, Vi, Riesara, Catlyn, and himself.
He glanced toward the head tables, seeing most of the knights seated there
already, eating and drinking, conversing heartily between bites and sips. The
sight brought a hint of his prior mood back, along with the yearning to be sitting
amongst them, but a call from his sister brought his attention back to his friends.

Almost everyone had already taken their seat. Mara was sitting, Vi on her
right, and the seat to Vi's right was open. Brol saw Kai eyeing the seat and must
have seen the hint of nervousness on his face, as he quickly smiled and slid
into the open seat across the table from there. Kai gave Brol an annoyed look,
swallowed, then took a deep breath and moved to sit down next to Vi.

Vi gave Kai a quick glance but said nothing. Kai tried to hide the fact he
was blushing, hoping desperately that it worked. Looking over at Brol, who was
hiding his laughter behind his hand, made him think it didn't. Kai kicked at
Brol under the table.

"Finally," Mara said, bending forward to look at her brother.

"Yeah, yeah," Kai replied, turning to her, trying not to make eye contact with Vi as he did. "I'm here. Everyone can eat now."

"Oh, thank the makers," Dax jeered. "The illustrious Kai has arrived. Let the feast begin."

Everyone laughed, even Kai. He winked at Dax, then reached over to fill his cup with the ale that had been set before them. It was Fire Ale, Kai was pretty sure. It wasn't his favorite but, as its name implied, it packed quite a kick. He lifted the drink, everyone else doing the same.

"To friends," Kai said, smiling at everyone.

"Friends," everyone replied.

They all lifted their drinks to their lips. Kai gulped his, felt the burning in his throat, but continued to take heavy sips until his glass was emptied. When he set it down, everyone was staring at him with wide eyes.

"What?" Kai offered in reply. "Like Dax said, how often do we get to celebrate? So... let's celebrate."

With a grin, Dax and several of the others followed suit, finishing their own glasses. Vi smiled at Kai, then also downed hers.

"Impressive," Kai offered.

"Well, you do have a way with words, leader boy," Vi coaxed, her tone flat, using the nickname she'd given to him a while back. Kai knew her sarcasm all too well, as it was the staple that defined almost every conversation with the girl.

"I told you not to call me that," he jabbed back.

"And that's why I call you that," she replied quite matter-of-factly, scrunching her nose in a vexatious manner.

Kai gave her a flat stare in reply, his lips curling upward slightly on one side.

"Words aren't exactly my strong suit. That's more Mara's area of expertise," he said, raising his voice.

"Hmm?" Mara inquired, looking away from her conversation with Catlyn.

"Vi said I had a way with words," Kai said. "And I told her that's more your thing–when you speak, that is."

"Hey, I speak," Mara said, scolding Kai with her face. "Just when it's important."

"And that's why you're better with words," Kai added. "Because you think before you say things." He tapped his forehead and smirked.

"Now, that's the smartest thing you've said all week," Vi jabbed, smiling her snarky smile.

"Vi's got a point," Mara added, joining in. "You probably should work on that," she finished with a wink.

"Rude," Kai replied, frowning. "But fair, I suppose. Anyway, that's enough words for now. I'm hungry. Shall we?"

"Yes, but first..." Vi replied, reaching out and filling her cup with ale again. "Another round? But this time, think you can beat me, leader boy?"

Kai looked at her, at the filled drink, then around the table at everyone, all of whom were watching the interaction, waiting to see what he would do. Finally, Kai dipped his head, reaching out to refill his own cup.

"If the lady thinks she can outdrink me," he said, lifting it, a bit more boldly now as the first glass was already starting to make his head feel lighter. "Let's have another. After all, we probably won't be killing any more dragons for a long while. Might as well make the best of tonight."

Chapter Four

EMBERS

S omewhere up in the Thousand Peaks of the Vale...

The night was dark, the woods quiet and still. Several hunters sat around a freshly stoked campfire as the smell of smoke filled the crisp air. The world was silent, like a breath drawn, masked only by the sound of a gentle easterly wind as it exhaled. The crackling of wood echoed into the night, slowly shedding the last hour of its life, giving way to a bed of burning embers below.

Though the fire glowed hot, the men sitting around it still showing their breath in the cold mountain air. Up this high, it was nearly always blistering cold. The hunters didn't typically come up this far, but they'd been sent deeper into the mountains to hunt.

The steady decline of the woodland creatures had happened steadily over the years. And now, spotting an elk or bear or any of the other creatures the hunters normally killed, was rare indeed. They had no idea why it was happening, but it was a strange phenomenon—one that had the Lodge worried. If their fortune didn't improve, they would be in for a rough winter.

They sat around the fire, laughing and telling stories in between bites of warm meat, freshly cooked over the coals. They'd been fortunate to catch a few rabbits, at least, which would keep them satiated long enough to continue the hunt. They talked of the preceding day and how odd it was that they hadn't come across anything larger, noting even the typical mountain wolves were silent on this eerie night.

"Maybe the dragons are about and have eaten all the animals!" said one of the hunters—a middle-aged man named Kanir, who sat up and looked at his comrades with a smirk.

"Hah, wouldn't that be our luck! Maybe we will find this dragon and kill it. Then we can feed the villages for a whole year," jested Yoghar, a large man with a deep voice and a dark brown beard who's size almost made the other two hunters look like youth sitting next to him. He was muscled from head to toe, intricate tattoos adorning his exposed arms, and a large beard hanging low from his face, tied in two loose braids.

"You shouldn't joke about such things. Dragons are often spotted in these hills, and if they were to return in greater numbers, we'd have much worse things to worry about than starving." The third man, Jarren, was an older man in years to the other two, though his gray hair was just barely starting to show. He was thin and unkempt, an ever-present look of paranoia about his face that did not belie his true nature. "Besides, you can't eat dragons. Meat's tainted."

"Oh, lighten up you old spook. There are rarely dragons in these hills. And when they do show up, the Order makes short work of them," jeered Yoghar as he reached over and clapped the man on the back.

Given Yoghar's size, and the small, gangly stature of Jarren, the jokingly pat on the back almost knocked the smaller man off the log he was sitting on. He coughed, choking on his meat. Kanir laughed, followed by Yoghar, which echoed through the shadowed trees around them, traveling up the side of the mountain, hitting some far-off surface before echoing back.

"It's not just a myth, you know—the elder dragons. During the wars, they were all over these mountains. Rumor has it one of their main fortresses was just a short trek further into the mountains. They say some of the dragons that still roam these parts may be a few of the beasts from the wars that lost their minds to the animal within. There's no knowing how many truly remain, hidden away in caves and the dark corners of the forest."

"Jarren, all the elder dragons were finally defeated in the Dragon Wars. There haven't been any sighted since before we were even born. Don't worry, old man. I think we're safe here." Kanir was younger than Jarren, but the clasp on his grey cloak indicated he was a respected member of the Lodge and the leader of the group currently present.

"Retreated, but not dead, my father told me. Some still live, far across the Thousand Peaks, pushed back by the Dragonbloods. They could still come back one day." Jarren's tone was sharp, but there was an apparent manner of respect he showed the higher-ranking man.

"Oh, your father told you that, eh?" Yoghar scoffed. "I bet he told you stories of witches and trolls as well, huh? I heard they lived in caves around these hills and came out to eat overly paranoid hunters who strayed too far up the mountain!"

With that, both Yoghar and Kanir laughed again, the sounds of their voices echoing through the mountains once more. Jarren, annoyed and slightly embarrassed, turned away from them and set about finishing his helping of meat. The other two laughed again as they watched their comrade's discontent, though this time, not quite so loud.

"Sorry mate, I'm only joking," Yoghar said, his voice softening a little. "I'm sure we're perfectly safe out here. Based on the quiet, I'd say it's just the three of us here for miles." He paused as he looked around at the shadows, then up at the night sky. "Anyways, I've got to piss." Yoghar took the last bite of his meat, tossed the bone in the fire, and started walking off into the darkness.

As Yoghar stepped just past the edge of the fire's light, he stopped and pulled down his trousers to relieve himself. The woods were silent as he stared into the shadowy abyss, save for the sound of his fluids hitting the forest floor. Finishing, he grunted in satisfaction, yanking up his trousers. He started to turn to head back but heard a slight rustling sound coming from somewhere in the night. He paused and listened. From the dark came a sound, like the cracking of a stick. Yoghar quickly fastened his belt as he peered, straining his eyes for any sign of movement.

"Yoghar, you all good out there?" Kanir called out.

"I'm fine, just heard something out in the woods. Might be our luck has picked up. Bring my spear."

Jarren turned and looked at Kanir, a curious look on his face. He grabbed his bow as he stood, while Kanir grabbed his own, also grabbing Yoghar's spear. They headed over to the edge of the light to gaze into the darkness with their companion.

"What did you hear?" Jarren asked, his spine tingling, the talk of dragons still fresh in his mind.

"I don't know, just some rustling somewhere out there. Sounded like it was maybe fifty feet or so out that way," Yoghar explained as he pointed up the mountainside. "Must be something larger, too, because I heard a twig snap."

All three peered into the night, but the dark was so thick up here in the mountains and the light of their fire drowned out so quickly, they saw nothing but black staring back at them.

Yoghar nudged Jarren as he joked, "Maybe it's a dragon, eh?" Jarren merely responded with a glare.

After a few more moments of silence, convinced whatever it was had gone, the three turned back toward the fire.

You should put more weight in the words of your friend, a voice called from the darkness.

The three men spun, weapons at the ready. Yoghar was the first to speak, "Who's there! Show yourself!"

No need to be alarmed. I just want to talk, the voice calmly replied. It was a woman's voice, but unlike any the three men had ever heard. It was deep, yet still feminine in nature, seeming to come from the very night itself. And even though the circumstances of this encounter should have been disturbing, the voice had an almost soothing nature to it.

"I said show yourself," Yoghar called out, shaking the invasive thoughts out of his head. "This is your last chance. Otherwise, I'm coming out there swinging. And I can promise you, I rarely miss."

Alright, no need to get violent. I will come into the light.

The three men peered into the darkness, weapons at the ready, not knowing who or what was about to come out of the shadows. They backed slowly toward the fire, away from the edge of the darkness, straining their eyes to look for any signs of movement amongst the void in front of them. There was a large rustle in the dark. After a few seconds, which seemed like ages, the men spotted a hint of movement. At first it was formless, seemingly taking on a shape of its own, a lighter shadow amongst a backdrop of shadows. But gradually, the form came into better focus as it neared the edge of the light.

Jarren, tightening his grip on his bow to the point of near pain, whispered to the others, "It's a ghost, descended from the ruins. I knew we weren't alone out here."

The others shot quick glances at him, this time much more serious in nature, before turning their eyes back toward the approaching stranger. After another moment, all three men watched as the form of a woman stepped fully into the circle of light.

The woman was tall—much taller than any woman they had ever seen. Yoghar was a big man by all accounts, but this woman must have been at least several inches taller than him. She wore a long, red tunic with a large hood that covered most of her features. Her head was bent forward, the cloak leaving shadows across her face, but strands of her bright red hair flowed through the opening in her hood, the color intensified by the flickering flames casting light from their fire.

The men had never seen anything quite like her before. Though they felt entranced by her uniqueness, they also felt a cold chill run down their spines as they struggled to understand what exactly was going on. Who was this woman, and where had she come from? Was there any possibility that she was merely a ghost of someone fallen in a long-ago battle? Confusion hung in the air about them. There were always rumors about ghostly apparitions spotted in these hills, especially after the Great War, when so many died and not given proper burials. But they were just tales to keep the children out of the hills. It couldn't possibly be true, could it?

"I am no ghost, I can assure you of that," the woman said calmly.

Again, Yoghar, being the bravest of the bunch, was the first to speak.

"Who are you and what are you doing out here? Where did you come from? Remove your hood so we might have a better look at you."

"My, my, so many demands. Quite bold of you," the woman replied. There was something different in her voice now. It sounded somewhat more human than it had before, when it had echoed out of the darkness. "You wish to know who I am and where I come from? Very well..."

The woman reached up toward her hood, pausing momentarily, slowing her ascent as the men tightened their hold on their weapons. She pulled her hood upwards higher on her head so they could see her face fully, revealing more of her long, wavy red hair. As she did, she slowly raised her eyes.

As her gaze met theirs, they felt another chill as her piercing red eyes seemed to see into their very souls. And not just red, but glowing, too.

Jarren thought he saw a flash of light in her eyes; not from the fire, but almost as if it had come from within. He looked to the other two to see if they had seen it, but their gazes were still fixed firmly on her, entranced by her appearance. He swallowed and looked back at her, her eyes meeting his directly. Her gaze felt strange, as if she was searching his mind for something. He felt confused, and fearful, but could not look away. After what seemed like an eternity, the strange sensation passed, and something else took hold. He stumbled backwards, nearly falling over, before regaining his composure. Though Jarren did not know why, he knew what he had to do. He dropped his bow, turned on his heels, and began to run down the mountain.

Yoghar and Kanir snapped out of their own trances when Jarren's bow hit the ground, just in time to see his form disappear into the darkness behind them. They kept their raised weapons pointed toward the stranger while calling to Jarren, but soon the sound of his footsteps vanished with him.

"What have you done to him?" Yoghar yelled, taking a step closer. "Are you some kind of sorceress? I have never seen anyone with eyes like yours."

The woman's ominous manner of arrival aside, her demeanor up to this point had been relatively non-hostile. But now, there was no denying her intentions. The men could see the malice burning behind her eyes. She was no normal woman. There was something more to her, though they still could not say exactly what it was.

"First a ghost, and now a sorceress? You humans truly are simple creatures," she scoffed, her voice returning to the otherworldly sound they'd heard before. "I am not some cheap dabbler in tricks, nor am I a figment of your imagination. No. I am afraid, for your sake, I am something much... more." The woman laughed, a deep, throaty laugh. Her eyes flickered, just as Jarren had seen before, but this time, Yoghar and Kanir saw it clearly.

No longer having any reason to hold back, Kanir loosed the arrow he had notched and Yoghar lunged at her with his spear. Both weapons missed their target as the woman stepped aside easily, receding into the darkness from which she'd come, a strange gust of wind ensuing. Yoghar barreled into the night after her as Kanir readied another arrow. Kanir could hear Yoghar's enraged grunts as he swung his spear, though it sounded like he was hitting nothing but air. There was a rustling, followed by more sounds from his companion, a large thud, and then, silence. Kanir kept his bow aimed, frantically scanning for any signs of movement. No more sounds came from the darkness, and only the crackling of the fire continued, though at this point it wasn't much more than glowing coal.

Kanir wanted to chase after Yoghar, to make sure he was alright, but fear kept his feet firmly planted in the assumed safety of the fire's dwindling light. He flicked his bow back and forth, looking for any signs of friend or foe, but still, nothing.

Now do you believe the words of your friend—Jarren, was it? The voice from the darkness had returned.

Kanir felt as if his soul leave his body. Though terrified, he mustered up a response. "What did you do to him? Where's Yoghar?"

Yoghar is here, with me. You don't need to worry for him anymore. As for your other friend, I merely sent him on an errand.

"Yoghar, can you hear me? Are you alright?" Kanir called out.

There was more rustling, then something landed across the fire from Kanir. For a moment, he couldn't tell what it was, but as he strained his eyes in the now dim firelight, it came into focus. It was Yoghar's arm! He could see the tattoos clearly.

Kanir felt a deep dread wash over him, understanding now the futility of the situation. This was it. This was his end. He eyed the fire, the dying flames symbolic of his own approaching fate. He mustered up the courage for one final question.

"Who *are* you... really?" Kanir asked as he stared into the dark, all hope gone from his body. From within the blackness of the night, a much larger shadow slowly loomed over him, it's stark outline an eerie contrast against the stars above.

I... am vengeance.

And with a flash, the night was cold and dark yet again, the last embers of the hunters' fire fading to the sound of wind and wings.

CHAPTER FIVE

TREMORS

Aerin watched as Haromir raised his hand, signaling for the others to be quiet. The room sputtered to a hushed silence, all eyes focusing on the Huntsmaster as he cleared his throat.

"I know that you all are worried due to the game shortages. Trust me when I say that we are all concerned. But it is the job of this group to ensure the people are not left hungry, and it is the members here in this room who will see it done. However, we cannot do that if we are bickering like a pack of wild dogs over the last few scraps of food."

Aerin watched Haromir, waiting for him to continue. As the Huntsmaster's apprentice, Aerin attended all Lodge meetings to observe, and, if necessary, advise. Normally, these meetings were a cheerful occasion. But today, Aerin felt like there was a sickness hanging in the air. Even Haromir himself seemed stricken with it, his eyes dark, his face weary. The council members—representatives of the Lodge from the nearby villages—looked much the same, though there was more fear in their eyes. It was their job to provide for all the people beyond the Wall that bordered the central Vale. Here, outside its protection, the people needed to work together to survive.

Though things had always been more of a struggle beyond the Wall, the potential food shortage they were confronted with was not something any of them had ever faced before. There were always ebbs and flows in the local game population; some years were very prosperous, others not as much. But the last few years had seen the latter, and it was showing no sign of getting better, each worse than the last. No one knew why. No matter, it was the Lodge's responsibility to figure it out. But instead of answers, the group gathered here today had zero evidence of what was going on and were now fighting amongst themselves about what to do.

"Brothers and sisters," Haromir continued. "I know we have faced many trials together over the years. The situation may seem more grim than we are accustomed to, but this time will be no different. As long as we work together, we will meet this challenge head on and survive it."

"What news from the hunters who haven't returned? We just got word a dragon was seen east of the towers," asked one of the members.

"We have already sent a raven to the Order, requesting they investigate the missing hunters. We can only hope they will return soon, and unharmed," Haromir answered, eyeing Aerin quickly before offering a smile to the council. "As far as the dragon, we're told it has been slain."

"We–"

Haromir stopped abruptly. There was a commotion happening outside the room. Everyone else must have heard it too, for they turned their heads toward the doors on the far side of the room. The commotion got louder until, suddenly, the doors burst wide open. Jarren, one of the Lodge's hunters who'd been sent up the mountain to look for food, was making his way straight for the meeting table with a trove of hunters and curious townspeople close behind him, trying to keep up as they bumped into each other to squeeze through the doorway.

"Ah, Jarren, I was just talking about you to the council. I hope you have something good to report."

Jarren stopped in front of the table, an odd look in his eyes as they darted back and forth across the council members. He stood there, staring at them, but made no move to speak. Aerin eyed Jarren closely. There was something in his eyes that brought a funny feeling to the back of his neck.

"Well? What news have you? And where are Kanir and Yoghar?" Haromir repeated.

Jarren shifted nervously where he stood, still not saying a word. He looked as if he wanted to speak, but for some reason was unable to. Haromir cast a glance at Aerin, nodding toward Jarren, then moved around the table to where Jarren was. Aerin followed. Haromir put his hand on the man's back; he was quivering, his skin pale, and sweating profusely. Now that he was closer, Aerin could see the sweat dripping down his brow, and he could hear his erratic breathing. Something was definitely wrong.

"Is everything alright? Did something happen?" Haromir asked.

Jarren turned slowly, looking directly into Haromir's eyes. There was something oddly blank about them, though Aerin could not place it. Haromir put both his hands on the man's shoulders and spoke gently.

"It's alright, Jarren. Tell us what happened."

At those words, Aerin thought he could see some life come back into the man's eyes, and the quivering seemed to lessen. After a few moments, Jarren slowly began to speak.

"S-something h-h-happened in the- the m-mountains. We s-saw a w-woman there. Kanir and Yo-Yoghar, they..." Jarren trailed off, a pained look in his eyes. "The v-voices... I can't-"

"Yes? Kanir and Yoghar? What happened? Where are they? And what is this about a woman?"

Jarren began shaking again, more violent than before. He grabbed his head and knelt over, bending down toward the ground. Haromir put his hand on

Jarren's back to comfort the man, but he immediately pulled away, wincing as if in pain. Haromir gave Aerin a concerned look, turning to the rest of the crowd gathered in the room. All the faces staring back at them looked just as confused as he felt.

"Aerin, will you please have someone send for the healer?" Haromir whispered.

Aerin nodded and scanned the crowd, spotting one of his fellow hunters who was reliable. Pushing his way through the others, he leaned close to the man and relayed the Huntsmaster's request. The man spun and ran off, Aerin returning to Haromir, who was now kneeling next to Jarren.

"Jarren, sorry, that was a lot of questions. Let's try this again, more slowly. Would that be alright?" Haromir asked.

Jarren looked at Haromir, the same hazy look in his eyes, but he seemed to understand and nodded slightly.

"Alright," Haromir began. "Let's start with where you were in the mountains. Can you tell us that?"

Jarren stood up slightly, though he was still hunched over, his eyes lowered toward the ground. He stood for a moment, saying nothing, but finally started to speak.

"We- we were in th-the mountains, be-between the n-northern and cen-central w-watch t-owers. Maybe a... a day's w-walk up th-the mountains. Made camp b-below the snow."

"Alright, I think I know where you mean. Thanks for that." Haromir smiled at Jarren. Jarren seemed to relax slightly. "Okay, so you were in the mountains. And Kanir and Yoghar- they were there with you?"

Jarren nodded, several times, his eyes darting quickly between Haromir and Aerin.

"Okay. And where are they now?"

Jarren turned his head away from Haromir, keeping his eyes low. He made no reply.

"Where are they, Jarren? Are they alright?"

A few more moments of silence passed before Jarren finally spoke.

"I- I d-don't know..."

Haromir looked again around at the crowd, frustration and exhaustion in his eyes. Aerin put his hand on Haromir's shoulder, dipping his head to his superior. Understanding, Haromir nodded back.

"Alright, so they were there with you," Aerin started, taking over. "And you said a woman was there? Tell us about this woman?"

Jarren's eyes met Aerin's, sending shivers down Aerin's spine.

"I- I d-don't kn-know. She c-came f-fr-from the night. R-red hair, b-b-burning eyes." As he spoke, he began to tremble more, and he grabbed his head again, covering his ears. "Th-the voice. H-her v-v-voice."

Hearing a murmur run through the crowd, Aerin looked up. Everyone was whispering to each other, though most eyes were still glued to the strange scene unfolding in front of them. Aerin wasn't sure what to make of it, but he was certain the crowd wasn't helping, and Haromir looked like he needed as much air as Jarren did. Aerin stood up and turned to face them.

"Alright, that will be enough. Please clear the room. We need some time with Jarren to make sense of all this."

The crowd looked at Aerin, then to Haromir. Blank stares filled most of their faces. Haromir, seeing their gazes, sat up straighter and cleared his throat.

"You heard him. Do as he says." As the words left his mouth, several groans and scoffs could be heard from the gaggle of onlookers, but they reluctantly started turning and slowly pushed and shoved each other out of the council room.

As the last of the gaggle shuffled through the doorway, Haromir turned to the council members. He looked at them sternly. "You too," he ordered. "Jarren is obviously in no state to give an actionable report at this time. After the healer tends to him, and we figure out what ails him I will try to get more answers. Once I have something of value, I will call for a conclusion to this meeting. Perhaps by midday tomorrow, we will adjourn."

Aerin watched the soured faces of the council members, which seemed more indignant than the looks they'd gotten from the crowd. He sensed someone was about to object.

"Haromir, we are supposed to be the eyes and ears of the people in all manner of affairs which affect our ability to provide for the masses. Surely, we should be here to help find answers," argued one of the council. There was a slight murmur of agreement among the others present.

"That is true," Aerin cut in. "And once we have some time to attend to Jarren's mental state, you will be. You will find your usual quarters are available. Please see Valen up front for the keys. If we are not able to adjourn by tomorrow, and if there is no sign of when we will be able to do so, then you may return home, and we will send ravens once we have something of use."

The council members rose, rather indignantly, and slowly meandered out of the hall, giving sideways looks to both Haromir and Aerin before skirting around the quivering mess that was Jarren still on the floor. Aerin followed the last of them to the door and closed it, catching the last few looks of discontent from them before he closed the door, finally leaving them alone in the room with Jarren. He returned to Haromir's side, waiting for the Huntsmaster to speak.

"Thank you, Aerin. You are doing well to handle yourself in such a manner."

They both turned to look at Jarren, who had hardly moved from where he knelt. Aerin had always felt sympathetic toward the man. In truth, there were few who really liked Jarren, but he was one of the best trackers they had. He was a loner and had no family. He'd lived with his father until his passing several years back. It was his father that had taught him how to track, though his father had not been a member of the Lodge. The old man had been seen as somewhat of a town spook. He was always telling wild stories about magic and the old ways of the world, especially dragons. In kind, it seemed Jarren had taken to some of his father's eccentric ways.

When his father died, Jarren seemed lost in the world. It was sad, but they finally convinced Jarren to join the Lodge because of it. Fortunately, Jarren had been amenable as it gave him the opportunity to continue to have someone looking after him. And though he was a bit childish in the way he needed looking after, his tracking skills had become of great value to the Lodge.

Just then, there was a loud knock on the door that startled Aerin from his thoughts. Aerin moved to answer it.

"Yes, what do you want Valen? Were the council members giving you trouble?"

"Ah, no sir. They all just left a moment ago, but the healer is here now. Would you like her to come in?"

"Oh, yes, of course. Please send her in right away."

"Very well," Valen said with a short nod of his head.

Aerin watched as Valen retreated to the entry hall, returning a moment later with Miria, the town healer. Miria was a good friend of the Lodge, as they had regular need of her skills. She'd saved many a man who been attacked by wolves or mauled by a bear. Once, long ago, she'd even treated Haromir when his leg had been sliced pretty good by a giant boar. And her skill with medicinal concoctions was without peer beyond the Wall, perhaps even the Vale itself, save for the capital.

"Ah, hello my friends," Miria said smiling as she came through the doorway, greeting Haromir and Aerin with a slight bow. "I was told you had quite the predicament—something about Jarren acting like a madman. More so than usual, I assume," she finished with a slight chuckle. Aerin grinned, though it was short-lived.

"Well, come see for yourself. He's gotten himself into quite the stir." Aerin turned as he spoke, leading Miria over to the sad slump of a man in the middle of the hall. Jarren barely moved as they approached.

Miria bent down beside Jarren, examining the man's posture, noticing the small puddle of sweat that was forming on the ground directly below his head. She put her hand on his forehead. Jarren flinched slightly, but mostly seemed to not mind.

"Good heavens, he's warm," Miria exclaimed. She lifted Jarren's head up, looking directly into his eyes. Aerin watched her intently.

"I– I've never seen anything like this. What happened to him?" Miria had an estranged look as she asked the question.

"We sent Jarren, Kanir, and Yoghar on a hunt. Since we've had an unusually low number of sightings, we thought that maybe the creatures had moved into the mountains for some reason. The three of them were to venture up the mountains until they either found something to hunt and bring back, or at least positive signs of wildlife in the area. They were to return within a fortnight either way. Today marks day twenty-three since they left. According to the few ramblings I got out of Jarren, he said that he left Kanir and Yoghar in the mountains and indicated something might have happened to them. He also said something about a woman with burning eyes and hearing voices. So, I don't really know what to make of it at this point."

Miria gave Haromir a curious glance as her eyes moved downward, resting back on Jarren.

"Did he say anything else?" Miria asked.

"Not really. He began stuttering pretty badly as he told us all this, and then shortly after he came to the state you see him now. He was quivering something awful on several occasions. It seemed to increase as I pressed him for further information, and we didn't want to make matters worse, so we tried to ease up."

"Strange indeed," Miria acknowledged. "We need to get him over to my place right away. Do you have something to lay him on and a couple men to help carry him over?"

"Yes, we have some carrying racks in the lodge. Aerin, can you get a couple others to help?" Haromir asked.

Aerin nodded and rose to get help.

He returned promptly, four men behind him and set the rack down. Miria and Haromir helped Jarren lay on it, Jarren eyeing everyone warily, though he stayed silent. Aerin watched him in return, studying the man, looking into his eyes as they bounced across the people in the room.

While they carried Jarren out, Aerin's thoughts grew conflicted. On one hand, he could tell that Jarren had obviously been through something to put him in the state he was currently. But on the other hand, the man was known for the occasional hysteric, though it had never been this bad.

Aerin couldn't shake the fact that something strange was going on. They were in the middle of the worst hunting shortage they had ever faced with no sign of what had happened to the animals. And now, two of his brothers were missing, the third claiming something unnatural might be afoot. It couldn't be a mere coincidence, could it? Haromir had put Kanir in charge of the scouting mission and he was one of their best. It's unlikely that Jarren would have left without him knowing. Although, Kanir wasn't happy that Jarren was going with them. Maybe they had been unkind to Jarren? Tricked him, even?

Whatever it was, Aerin felt like he was on the edge of a cliff, an invisible force slowly pushing him toward the edge. He hoped the feeling was just fear of the unknown. He hoped the feeling would pass. Though he tried to push it aside, Aerin couldn't shake the image of the intense emptiness behind Jarren's eyes, almost as if the man he knew was fading, and something else was taking over.

CHAPTER SIX

NIGHTMARES

J arren woke to the sound of his own heavy breathing. He sat up and looked around, confused.

Where am I?

The room was quite dark, and there was very little he could make out. He was lying on a bed, that much he could tell. Straining his eyes, he noticed a low, flickering light coming from underneath what appeared to be a doorway on the other side of the room.

Someone must have a fire going.

He rose and stumbled through the darkness, heading for the light while trying not to trip. His hands found the wall and he followed it.

Just a few more steps.

He reached the corner of the wall. The doorway was just to his left. He slid his hands from the wall to the door, feeling the change from smooth wall to wooden molding in some sort of pattern. Though the light was coming under the door, it didn't provide much light with which to see. He ran his hand down, feeling for a handle or anything to grab to open the door.

Ah, there it is.

He pressed down on the latch holding the door shut until he heard an audible click, followed by a slight movement as the door inched inward. Pulling the handle gently, the light from the room beyond flooded in. Though it was not very bright, it still hurt his eyes momentarily. He turned away, looking around the room behind him. It wasn't very big, the only occupants the bed and a lone nightstand, as best he could tell. After a few seconds, his vision cleared, and his eyes adjusted to the new light. He turned back to the doorway and peered through. He glanced quickly down the hallway, noting there wasn't much to see, his eyes drawn to the next room. It was a bit larger than the one he was leaving, but it, too, held very few objects. There was the fireplace on the wall opposite where he was now. In front of it was a chair, facing the fire. It appeared as though someone was sitting in the chair, but he could only make out rough shapes amongst the flickering shadows as the flames of the fire danced their slow rhythms. Jarren peered from side to side, eyeing the other two walls. They were blank, other than a mural on either side. He tried to make out what images they bore, but the light was still a bit dim. He cautiously took a step forward.

"Hello?" he called out softly. There was no reply, and no movement from the chair. A slight shiver ran down his spine. He took several more steps forward, his eyes focused intently on the seat and whatever mystery it held.

"Hello? Can you hear me?"

Again, there was no reply, and no indication that his presence had been acknowledged. He took several more steps, this time edging to the left of the chair to get a better view before getting too close. Something about the whole situation felt off to him.

As he moved closer, a hint of movement caught his eye off to the left. He spun quickly, but there was nothing there except the mural on the wall. At first, it just seemed to be painting of a man standing in a forest. But as Jarren was about to turn away, a bright flicker from the fire further illuminated the man's body, triggering a strange feeling. Jarren inched closer, studying it. The man held a bow and appeared to be a hunter. Something was oddly familiar about him.

Jarren, confused, began to turn again, but another flicker of movement kept his attention firmly fixed on the painting. The image started to move. Were his eyes playing tricks on him in the dim light of the fire? He shook his head and refocused his eyes. No, he was sure the picture was, in fact, moving. He could see the slight sway of the trees as the man bent over, studying something on the ground. He looked up and moved his head from side to side, as if looking for something. Suddenly, he stopped and stood up straight.

Jarren watched, awestruck, as the figure of a small boy came into the bottom right-hand corner of the painting. The man turned and Jarren saw his face.

No... it can't be. Jarren felt slightly weak. The man, though he had to have been in his thirties, had the undeniable features of his father. Jarren squinted, inching closer. He was certain it was him. And that meant the small boy was- *How can this be? Am I–*

"What do you see, Jarren?"

Jarren spun, a jolt of energy flowing through him. From where he stood now, he could see the chair from a better angle. He saw an arm rested on the armrest, though he still was not able to see their face.

That voice...

There was something both terrifying and calming about it; and its tone felt oddly familiar.

"Who are you?" he asked. "And where am I? Why do you have a painting of my father, and how did it-?"

"Come closer," the mysterious figure beckoned.

Jarren wanted to resist, but something about the voice compelled him to act. He took several more steps around and to the side of the chair until he was only a few feet away. He could see now that upon the chair sat a hooded figure, though he still could not see any of their features. Finally, the figure moved. Its head lifted slowly as Jarren watched, the world feeling like it was coming to a halt as time slowed to but a trickle.

And then, from the void of darkness behind the hood, Jarren saw a familiar sight–an image that sent a thousand pins into his skin and a dull throbbing pulsating through his head. Eyes, as bright and as fiery as the setting sun, burned beneath the hood, staring straight into his soul.

Jarren stumbled backwards, his head reeling from the sudden surge of energy swirling about his skull. He felt weakness begin to overcome him and he struggled to keep himself from falling over. Then, he heard it, recognizing it at last.

Jarren, it is time...

The voice from the woods–it was her!

Jarren felt himself sick as the tingling in his entire body grew worse. He struggled to keep his eyes open, watching the dark figure rise from her chair and step toward him, her red eyes fixed on his, boring into what little consciousness he had left.

Jarren...

Everything began to fade to black.

"Jarren!"

Jarren twitched as he awoke, beads of sweat sliding down his face. Everything was still dark. He writhed and lashed out, sending his arms out to push away the demon from beyond. His hands felt flesh, but his vision was still clouded in darkness.

"No. Get away!" he cried out. He felt a pair of hands grab him, the voice called out again.

"Jarren, wake up!"

Jarren opened his eyes at last. The light from the sun shone down through a window above where he was laying, its brightness blinding him temporarily. He blinked a dozen or so times before his eyes finally adjusted. He saw the face of a woman standing over him, her hands trying desperately to hold him in place. He eased his resistance but eyed her cautiously. She seemed familiar, though he could not remember from where.

"There, there now. That's it. Can you understand me, Jarren?" The woman smiled at him. She was an older woman, wearing a simple, green shawl draped over the top of her dress. Her silver-streaked, wavy brown hair was tied in a bun in the back by a small, green piece of cloth. That, and the number of wrinkles forming on her face, indicated she was later on in years than he. Jarren was still wary of his situation, but the woman did not seem a threat, and her warm smile helped put him at further ease.

"Y-yes, I can... understand you," he said finally.

"Ah, there you are," she replied. Jarren thought it an odd reply. Her voice was calm, but with his head still throbbing, it sounded as though it was echoing through a stone corridor.

"Y-yes, here I- I am..." he shot back. "And wh-where is *here* exactly?"

"Oh, very sorry. It's just that this is the first time you've spoken since you returned. I am Miria, and you are at my home in Northreach. This is where I bring all my patients."

Patient, Jarren thought to himself. *What happened?* He tried to remember, but his head was foggy. Miria seemed to sense his confusion and continued.

"You came sprinting into the middle of town the day before yesterday in quite the troubled state, and you were ranting about some woman in the woods. You weren't making much sense..."

Woman in the woods...

Miria continued to talk while thoughts came rushing back to him like a bolt of lightning. His head began to hurt more. He placed his fingers on his temples, attempting to ease the throbbing, trying to remember everything that had transpired. It wasn't all real, was it?

"Are the headaches still bothering you? Let me get you another dose of the Alderberry tonic."

Jarren sat up and watched as she walked out into the other room. He heard the creak of a hinge, followed by the light clanging of glass. The sound, though to a normal ear would have been hardly a thing, seemed to reverberate through the room and into Jarren's head. He felt dizzy, so he steadied himself on the bedpost.

Miria returned a moment later holding a small glass vial, along with a cup of water. She handed Jarren the vial and told him to drink it all down. He willingly placed it to his lips and let the sticky fluid run down his throat.

Rather sour, he thought to himself, swallowing the last of it. He let out a grunt, handing the vial back to Miria, who handed him the cup in return. He took it and began to drink. Jarren hadn't realized how thirsty he'd been. The cool water felt like heaven to his dry throat as it washed away the tart tonic taste. He drank the entire cup in one sitting, taking a deep breath when finished. His head started to clear, and he felt his focus coming more in line.

He looked at Miria, who was standing there, a gentle smile on her face as she studied him. When he finished, she reached for the cup.

"More?" she asked. Jarren nodded, wiping the remnants of water from his face and handing it to her. "I should say, you must be thirsty. You've barely been conscious since they brought you here, and you were sweating like a shipwright in broad daylight when you first arrived."

She chucked, then turned and walked out of the room, though she continued to talk to him.

"You worked up quite a sweat on your way back to the city, and I could tell when I saw you at the Lodge that you were very low on fluids. We got you to drink some water before you fell asleep, but it wasn't much. So yes, drink all you need," she said as she rounded the corner and came through the doorway, carrying another glass.

Jarren took it as she handed it to him and downed it as well, not stopping to catch his breath until he drank every last drop. Again, he took a deep breath and wiped away the drops of water left on his face.

"More?" she asked again.

"No, th-that will be... be e-enough f-for now," he said forcefully, his breath still catching up. "I'm– I feel a bit better."

"Good. I should hope so. And how's your head feeling?"

"It still hurts, but– but a bit less f-foggy now."

"Yes, lack of water will do that. I'm sure it will get better, and the tonic should help your headache subside shortly. Is there anything else you need?"

"No... no, I– I think I'm good. M-might rest a bit more."

"Okay, well feel free to rest as much as you need. I will leave the cup here on the table. The water well is outside and to the left. Drink as much as you want. There is also some food in the cupboard next to where the water is. Should you get hungry, help yourself. I will be out front in case any customers come in. If you walk past the water well, it's right down the hall and around to the right. I will come check on you in a while."

Jarren nodded sleepily. Though he'd apparently just slept for some time, he still felt exhausted. He was pretty sure the tonic she'd given him was starting to take effect as well, or perhaps it was the water. Food did sound good, and he heard his stomach grumble, but sleep first; he'd get something to eat after another nap. Jarren laid his head down on the pillow, dozing off almost immediately.

A large sound, something akin to thunder, woke Jarren with a start. He sat up instantly in his bed. The room was pitch black again. He felt an uneasy sense of déjà vu.

Either I slept the rest of the day, or I'm back in that nightmare.

After rubbing his eyes, he looked in the direction he remembered the door ought to be. He could make out a very faint line of light at the bottom.

Just like before...

He turned in bed and let his feet hang off, carefully lowering himself onto the invisible ground beneath. His feet hit the wood floor, and he stood up straight. He felt the bed beside him and used it as a guide as he took several steps toward the door. He remembered the room had been rather empty, so he wasn't too concerned with tripping over anything. He was more concerned with what was awaiting him on the other side of the door.

After half a dozen steps, he was at the door, reaching his hand out to feel for the handle. He found it easily and pulled, the same creaking sound as it glided open. The light from the next room was dim, but this time, it was only emanating from a small oil lamp on a stand across from where he was.

It's not the nightmare, he sighed, a huge sigh of relief.

He looked to the left down the hallway, seeing a doorway about two thirds of the way down, more light coming from within. The hallway continued past that, but it was dark. He took several steps down the hallway toward the open room, noticing there were some paintings on the wall.

Where those there before? I can't remember.

He stopped to look at the nearest one. It was a picture of the mountains, somewhere along the Spine in the Thousand Peaks. He studied it to see if the painting was moving. Fortunately, it was not. He checked another, just to be sure. It was a clearing in the woods somewhere, and there was no snow. The picture was at night, and it looked familiar. It reminded him of where Kanir, Yoghar, and he had made camp. It seemed odd, but then there were many such places in the mountains, and he'd camped in more than one clearing in all his hunts. Shrugging, he turned his attention to the third and final painting.

Jarren stopped cold, staring dumbfounded at it in horror. There it was, as clear as the memories in his mind, as if the painting had been extracted from his consciousness. Except, in this version, he could clearly see two bloody corpses around a fire–the very same fire he'd been sitting at with Kanir and Yoghar. One corpse was torn in several pieces, one of the arms close to the fire.

Tattoos. Yoghar?

The other corpse was surely Kanir, and his was closer to the fire, a bloody trail of his innards leading away into the darkness.

Jarren blinked several times and shook his head. He felt sick to his stomach. There was no doubt he was dreaming now. When he'd left, his friends had still been very much alive. They were just joking and having a bit of fun with Jarren when– and then he remembered her, the woman with the red hair. There *had* been a woman there, he thought. Jarren's head began to pound, the confusion settling back in, only making it worse. He tried to force himself to wake up.

Jarren...

Jarren spun, startled, looking both ways down the hallway. He saw nothing. He felt like he was losing his mind. He tried to tell himself he was in a dream, but his consciousness would seemingly not let him escape it.

Jarren.

It was *her* again.

The voice came from down the hallway where the lit room was. He didn't want to follow the voice. He tried to turn around but couldn't.

Come, Jarren!

His feet began to move on their own, pulling him toward her. He shook his head, trying to stop himself. It only made his headache throb more fiercely. All he could do was stare into the void before him, awaiting what lay beyond.

It is time, Jarren.

The voice echoed from the shadows beyond the door, louder than before. He turned away from the darkness, not wanting to see whatever was there. He didn't want to look, but every bit of his being seemed to be forcing him to. As his gaze turned, he could see now the shadows were swirling in some sort of a dark vortex. Then, from the center of this vortex, a pair of bright, red eyes flashed open. Jarren could feel those eyes burning into him, taking over his mind. He tried to resist, but it was useless. He felt himself slowly slipping away, being drawn into whatever evil that had its grasp on him.

Just as it was about to devour him, there was a jolt of energy, and he was awake again. At least he thought he was. He sat up in bed and looked around. There was a candle burning on the nightstand next to the cup Miria had brought him earlier. It was dark outside, but at least the room wasn't pitch black. He hoped that was a good sign. He felt his forehead. It felt warm, and there was sweat dripping down his face, just like the last time. He turned and leaned over to grab the cup of water. It was full, so he drank it vigorously. It wasn't very cold, but it tasted fresh—and real. He was pretty sure he was out of the nightmare.

Jarren stood up and walked over to the door leading out of his room. It was cracked slightly, so he just pulled the handle. The next room had a few candles lit. He looked left down the hallway. It looked just the way it had in his nightmare. The room down on the right was lit, the corridor beyond was dark. Though it didn't seem as dark as it had in the dream, the sight of it still made him cringe and second guess his consciousness.

Please let the nightmare be over.

He took slow, cautious steps down the hallway until he was within a few feet of the doorway. He eyed the dark corridor beyond, expecting to see the horrific void at any moment.

"Creeping around, I see." Jarren leapt backwards and nearly toppled over himself as Miria's shadow appeared in the doorway of the lit room.

"Jumpy, are we?" Miria loomed in the open doorway with her hands on her hips. Jarren looked at her, cringing slightly at the light, while he tried to slow his breath, and in conjunction, his pounding heartbeat.

"S-sorry, you—you just st-startled me, th-that's all," Jarren replied as he stood upright.

"Startled you? You look like you just saw a ghost!"

"A gh-ghost w-would be welcome." Jarren tried to read Miria's face, but her features were hard to make out amidst the backdrop of light. He realized she was joking with him, but felt embarrassed, nonetheless.

"Alright, well let's get you something to eat, yeah? I'm sure you're starved." Jarren only nodded in reply as he put his hand on his stomach. It was still settling from the fright, but he could feel it now beginning to churn in want for sustenance.

Miria turned around and headed into the room, Jarren a few steps behind her. "You can sit at the table, there," she pointed. There was a medium-sized table in the center of the room with three chairs around it. The table was overall simple in design, but it's red-brown wood was offset by an immaculate shine. The chairs followed design in a similar fashion. Jarren sat down and ran his hand across the table's top, feeling its smooth caress against his fingertips. He'd never seen anything quite like it. Of course, he'd seen plenty of redwood furniture, but he'd never seen one quite so red or so polished and smooth.

"Here you go," Miria said, startling Jarren, lost in his thoughts.

"Jumpy indeed. Careful not to spill it. It's still a bit hot. I'll get you some bread to go with it." She turned and walked back into the kitchen area, grabbing a loaf of bread from a cupboard. She broke off a generous piece and brought it over to the table, setting it down by Jarren and then taking a seat across from him.

She sat there and smiled. Jarren looked back at her, forced an awkward smile, and nodded. "Th-thank you," he muttered. He looked down at his food, his mouth watering. He looked back up at Miria, who continued to smile. He felt weird and wasn't sure what to do.

"Please, eat. I'm sure you're starving. It has been two days at least since you ate, and who knows how long before that."

Jarren still felt awkward with her sitting there just watching him, but his compulsion to satiate his stomach overcame his desire to be polite. He ripped off a piece of bread and dipped it in the stew, brought it up to his mouth, and took a small bite. It tasted like the stew his mother used to make when he was a boy. It tasted like heaven.

No longer able to contain his hunger, he began to rip off pieces of bread and drown it in the stew before placing the hot, soggy chunk in his mouth. He felt some pain from the heat of the stew as it singed his tongue and the sides of his mouth, but he didn't care. He was so terribly hungry, and the food was so terribly delicious.

"I can tell you like it," Miria said, sounding rather pleased.

"Mhmm," Jarren let out between bites.

Miria got up and walked over to the counter, grabbing the rest of the bread, and brought it back to the table. She set it down beside Jarren's bowl.

"Feel free to eat the rest of this, and there is more stew in the pot. Help yourself to it. I'm going to retire for the evening. It's been a long day. You are free to stay another night, should you wish, or you may leave. I believe you are feeling much more yourself and I'm sure you're ready to get home. Plus, I know that Haromir is very eager to speak with you. He keeps coming by to check on you. If you do leave, I will send him over to your house. And I took the liberty of washing the clothes you came in with. They aren't dry yet, but you can come pick them up tomorrow. They should be ready by then."

Jarren looked at her empathetically, though the thought of her undressing him while he'd slept made him blush. He sincerely appreciated what she'd done for him, but wasn't quite sure the words to say at the moment. Miria, sensing his hesitation, added, "Oh, and don't worry about the tab. The Lodge has already taken care of it."

Jarren continued to remain quiet but nodded his head in understanding. In truth, he'd totally forgotten about the necessity to pay. He wondered what Haromir would have to say about all this. He was sure that no one would really believe that some woman in the woods had bewitched him. But it had to be true. It was all so vivid. Plus, there were the dreams.

"Alright, well, have a good night," Miria offered.

Pulled from his thoughts, Jarren looked up at Miria. Though his mind was a bit jumbled with everything, he managed to get out a quiet "Th-thank you," just before Miria exited through the doorway.

He felt awkward, sitting there alone now eating her food. But she had offered it to him, and he *was* still hungry. Plus, the Lodge had paid for it. He did want to get out of there as soon as possible. He needed to sort things out and he thought that perhaps being in his own space would help him get his head straight.

Jarren gobbled down the rest of the bowl and grabbed the remaining chunk of bread, then headed for the hall. He took one last look down the dim hallway before turning and heading out to the shop and into the streets of Northreach.

Outside, the streets were dark, but there was enough light to see his reflection when he closed the door to Miria's shop. He looked at himself for a moment, as if he were studying the man looking back. He felt like he didn't recognize himself.

Lost in thought, a slight movement in the reflection of the window caught his attention. There was a shadowy figure lurking on one of the side streets. Jarren spun quickly, searching the dark corridor, but he saw no one. He turned back to look in the window where he had seen it, but there was nothing there now.

Realizing how late it was and how dark the city seemed, Jarren took rushed steps east along the alley toward the center of town. He wasn't as familiar with this side of town as he'd rarely had any reason to come down here. There were many taverns and brothels scattered about this side of Northreach, both of which Jarren had never had the urge to partake in. Plus, the Lodge paid well and provided much of what was needed, and that was on the western side of the city. Jarren mainly only went from there to his home and back.

He walked cautiously, his head down low. There weren't many people out at this hour. By his account, it must have been somewhere around eleven or midnight, maybe later. There were a few drunks stumbling about while the shadows of street cats skulked along the side alleys, rummaging through trash, searching for tossed-out food scraps. Several people eyed Jarren as he skirted past them, trying to give a wide berth. One even called out to him asking for some spare change. But the manner of his behavior felt almost sinister, his voice more of a hiss than that of a drunk or beggar. Jarren quickly shied away and crossed to the other side of the street, though it wasn't much better.

The brothels and houses of less tasteful business were open, and though most were quiet, a few of the streetwalkers were outside. Since the streets were mostly devoid of potential customers, they were more aggressive, and as Jarren walked past one such place of business, a woman emerged from the shadows and touched his arm.

Startled, Jarren jumped slightly to the side. He looked at her. It was dark, and hard to see her face, but as she stepped out into the street after him, one of the streetlights gave him a brief glimpse of it. Already on edge, he nearly toppled over himself as he saw the face of the woman from the woods!

Come with me, he heard in that same dreadful tone he'd heard in his dreams.

Tripping several more times and nearly losing his balance trying to get away, Jarren finally caught his feet under him, taking off in a near sprint. He ran as fast as he could, hearing the woman calling out to him, laughing. He ignored it, not stopping until he rounded the corner and made it to one of the main streets. He paused there to catch his breath, trying to tell himself that it was just a side effect of his condition and that he was still seeing things. Plenty of women had red hair.

But not like hers...

Though it was late, there were a few more people here on this street and the lights were a bit brighter. It was also a more prominent part of the city, so he was hopeful there would be no more strange encounters. He started walking again, though he kept his pace brisk.

He moved along this street for several minutes with no more encounters or strange sightings. Thinking he was out of it, he relaxed his pace some. His house was just two or three streets up and then a right on Wickers. He would be safe at home soon. There was a side street just up ahead. He wasn't usually out at night, but he was pretty sure this one was Carlon street. He looked to his right as he crossed it, looking for the sign he expected to see. There it was. "Carlon", in bold lettering. Jarren was about to turn his attention back ahead when he noticed a shadowy figure moving his direction some thirty feet or so down Carlon. He couldn't make out if it was a man or a woman due to the large hood over their head, but something about them made his stomach feel queasy. Jarren picked up his pace again and crossed Carlon in haste.

After some seconds, Jarren looked back over his shoulder. The hooded figure was still there, seemingly now following him down the street, still about thirty feet behind him. Jarren quickened his pace again as much as he could without running. His stomach took a quick lurch as he made eye contact with whomever was hiding in the shadows of the hood. He began to feel a slight tingling at the back of his skull, as if some force was slowly pressing on it. He reached up his hand to rub where it hurt, but the sensation continued.

He came to the next street and crossed immediately, this time heading diagonally to get to the opposite side. His street was the next one, and when he saw the signpost for it, he moved into a full-on run. Though he could barely breathe and was feeling nauseous, he kept going, being so close to home. As he rounded the corner of Wickers, he slowed just a hair, managing a quick glance backwards. The mysterious stranger was still there, seemingly keeping up with him. This spurred Jarren into full panic mode as he pushed himself as fast as his legs would carry him.

He could see his house down at the end of Wickers. It was a dead-end road, which didn't help his cause at the present. But if he could just get inside, he would surely be safe. He fumbled in his pocket, trying to find his key. It wasn't in its usual place, further terror ensuing. Did he have his key? In his panic, he nearly forgot that Miria had washed his clothes. He frantically searched the other pockets. After several moments, he felt a lump in his breast pocket. He reached inside the pocket there, feeling the cool metal of a key. He pulled it out, just as he reached the steps of his house. He ascended them and pushed the key toward the lock, looking behind him. He didn't see anyone on the street, though he wasn't sure that made him feel any better. It was fairly dark, and his pursuer could be hiding anywhere.

He tried to slow his breath and calm his trembling hand, but it was no use. It took him several tries before he finally got the key in the lock. He turned it and heard the lock release. Never had a sound sounded so good to his ears. He pressed open the door, rushed inside, and slammed it closed behind him, locking it immediately. He glanced out the small window in the door, but he couldn't see much through the cloudy glass.

Jarren put his back against the door, his legs feeling weak, and fell into a sitting position against it. At last, he was safe in his house. Perhaps the stranger had just passed by his street. Perhaps he was just being overly paranoid. Breathing a huge sigh of relief, he stood up and headed toward the kitchen to light a candle and get some water.

Rounding the corner, he froze. There, in the center of the dark room, stood a figure shrouded in shadows. Jarren tried to move—to turn away, but he couldn't. Something was holding him in place. He could feel his muscles twitch as every fiber of his body ached to run, but there was nothing he could do as he watched the figure draw closer. Jarren tried to cry out, but no sound came from his mouth. It was as if the very shadows were sucking the breath from his lungs. He could feel his consciousness slipping as a deeper darkness closed in around him.

The last thing Jarren remembered was the flicker of red eyes amidst the shadow, and an all-too-familiar voice echoing through his thoughts.

It is time, Jarren. I have something I need you to do.

CHAPTER SEVEN

QUESTIONS

Mara was deep in thought, the words spinning in her head as she rushed to write down some notes; so deep, in fact, she didn't notice Kai leaning on the table as he peered over her shoulder to see what she was writing.

"Mara," he whispered in her ear. Mara jumped, her quill scratching a thick line of ink across the paper.

"Oh, Kai... hey. I didn't notice you come up."

"Uh huh," he replied, grabbing a nearby chair and pulling it over to the table to sit down next to her. "Seems you're pretty engrossed over here. What are you reading now?"

"Oh, I was just reading about Paren Blackhammer. He was the original builder of Dragonscale Keep. Did you know that he designed it after the architecture of his homeland? He was from a place known to us as the Sah'naran Desert, of which the capital is Sah'nara. Of course, in the tongue of his people, it's Sah'hanar Ah'ran– I think, but of course that's too complicated for most of us in the Vale to pronounce, so they just went with Sah'nara."

Kai looked at his sister while she talked, his eyes a tad wider than normal, bobbing his head up and down, a superficial smile adorning his face. Mara smiled as she talked, barely taking a breath in between thoughts, oblivious to her brother's masquerade.

"He earned his name Blackhammer because of the mighty black hammer that he wielded in battle. He was a large man by all accounts, even for the Order. But of course, that's what most of the people from Sah'nara are like– they're just large people. And I don't mean large, like, you know, fat. I mean large like their average height was somewhere around twenty-one hands high. But Paren was even taller than that! The books differ in their accounts, but he was somewhere between twenty-four to twenty-six hands tall! That's at least two heads taller than you or Uncle! Can you believe that?"

"No, no, I really can't..." Kai responded, a hint of sarcasm in his voice.

"Well, like I said before, he designed Dragonscale Keep based on the architecture of his homeland. He did have to make some adjustments, of course, because they only have Torrium and Khastite rocks in this region, so he had to make some adjustments. Did I say that already? Anyway, he knew that the Order mainly had people from the nearby areas, so he wanted it to be somewhat of a mixture of the two styles. He–"

"Mara," Kai said, giving her a look she'd seen many times before.

"I'm doing it again, aren't I?" she asked, blushing. Kai nodded, a sincere smile now showing as he looked into her eyes.

"Sorry Kai, I just– I just love learning more about the Order's history. The books Uncle gave us as kids didn't even come close to what this place holds. There are *so* many stories, and I feel like we don't have nearly enough time to read them all. I want to know everything!"

"Mara, you've been reading these books almost non-stop for years. By my count, I'd swear you've read all of them."

"All of them? No. But I have read half... maybe?"

"Good gods, Mara. That's impressive," Kai said, his eyes wide. He smiled for a moment, but it slowly diminished, his eyes cast downward.

"Guess I can't blame you, really. The Order in those books is not the same Order we're living in. I wish I was more of a reader so I could get lost in the tales of the old days."

"Still on about this, I see," Mara sighed. "But of course you are."

"I'm sorry. I just don't know what to do with myself anymore. I wish..." Kai said, pausing. "I wish what Uncle said was true."

"What Uncle said? What do you mean?" asked Mara.

Kai looked around at the two other people in the library, then back at Mara, his behavior causing Mara to raise an eyebrow.

"Uncle told me not to talk about it, but when they came back from the hunt, he said something about the dragon," Kai whispered. "He said it's the biggest dragon we've seen in a very long time, and it's old–old enough to know better than to wander into human lands. But even more curious, it had been wounded by something."

"Wounded? What would wound a dragon of that size?" she inquired, suddenly growing quite interested.

"What indeed," Kai replied. "Another dragon, perhaps, though it's hard to imagine another one even bigger, unless..."

"Unless it was an elder dragon," Mara said, catching on.

"Unlikely, right? I mean, it's strange, but maybe it was just another big one. If there's one, there must be more."

"Yeah..." Mara's eyes glazed over for a moment. "Was Uncle concerned?" she asked, looking back at Kai.

"Maybe? It's hard to tell with him, you know. The fact he told me not to say anything makes me think maybe there's something to it."

"Hmm," Mara let out, sitting back in her chair. She hadn't given it much thought, but it made complete sense. Dragon disputes did happen, and the

Thousand Peaks were massive. There could easily be more than one of the older beasts roaming its near endless valleys and peaks.

"Any thoughts in that head of yours?" Kai smirked. "Anything in those books that might give an answer?"

"Um, no... well, I don't know. Maybe?" Mara answered, her expression changing as quickly as her thoughts. She saw Kai's face, a hint of hope behind his eyes. "I can look," she added, hoping to fuel the spark. "I'm sure there's some explanation."

Kai's eyes lit up even more at her words.

"Well, I need to get to my post soon, but let me know what you find out," he said, standing.

"Of course," Mara replied, giving him a hint of a smile.

She watched him leave, a happy expression across his face. It brightened Mara's mood to be able to help, giving Kai a sense of purpose, even if it ended up being nothing in the end. But still, what he'd said was odd. Besides, Mara would get to read more books, so it was a win for both of them.

Mara set her current books aside and went back into the aisles. *History section for sure. Maybe something about a time when there was no war, or at the start of the war?*

She perused the books for a while, reading the titles, none of them seeming to be what she was looking for. Running her fingertips across the spines, she continued until one caught her eye. It was one she hadn't seen before, but the title, *A Study of Dragon Blood*, piqued her interest. She'd perused the sections on science and magical studies several times already and hadn't seen anything else that talked specifically about dragon blood.

This one must have been misplaced.

Mara examined the book's cover for a moment. Most of the books she'd been reading had been well-worn, but this book seemed to be in quite good condition. The cover itself was a dark, almost a burgundy red color. There were no markings on any side of the cover other than the front.

Perhaps it's newer...

She opened it, her fingers slipping across the surface of the inside cover. It was smooth, with few flaws, though the papers were a different texture than all the other books she'd read. On the first page there was a short introductory paragraph, hand-written in thick, black ink:

An accounting of Mordan Oathsworn's research on dragon blood.
Transcribed by Fenris Oathsworn, Mindwarden of the Order, 212th year in the Age of Reckoning.

Mara gasped. *The 212ᵗʰ year in the Age of Reckoning!? That means this book is... over 2,000 years old! How is it in such good condition?*

Mara sat there, her eyes wide with excitement and confusion. She turned the page and saw that the next one was full of smaller words that filled the whole of it. She flipped through further pages, skimming through the book for anything that stood out to her. As she flipped through, something caught her eye and she stopped. Manually flipping backwards through the pages, she stopped when she found the image she'd glimpsed moments prior. It was a picture of a dragon, which filled nearly the entire page up and down. She turned the book sideways to look at it from the proper angle. The creature walked on two legs, with razor talons and two large wings attached to its other limbs, folded into its body. Scales covered it from head to toe, and four main horns protruded from its skull. The creature itself looked rather majestic, the artist showing no lack in skill in its recreation. There was a word beneath the creature, along the edge of the page. It read, "Sha'Liotha."

The queen!

Mara quickly flipped through more pages, which held images of other dragons, followed by a hefty section on dragon parts. Fully intrigued, she returned to the second page of the book and began to read the first few lines of text:

> *This is an accounting of the study of Queen Liotha and her kin's blood after their defeat. It has been preserved, under the assumption that royal blood is the key to unlocking the full potential of our Dragos'viren.*

Dragos'viren... I've seen that before. Mara set the book down and picked up her notes, sifting through them momentarily. "Ah hah!" she exclaimed. Realizing she'd said it out loud, she lifted her head to see if anyone was looking. There were a few sideways glances, and she immediately put her head back down, returning to the book.

"Dragos'viren was the original name of the Dragonbloods back in the first few centuries of the Order. I knew I'd seen it before," she whispered to herself.

Mara continued to skim the page, hastily reading over the text in eager anticipation. There was a letter on the next page, apparently written by Fenris himself.

> *My dear brothers and sisters. I thank you for seeing me on my recent visit. I have gone to great lengths to procure my uncle's research, and it has proved most beneficial. Though his notes were in somewhat of a disarray, I believe I have been able to organize them into some semblance of order. My uncle's research on dragon blood was nothing short of astounding, and it is my strongest desire to see it furthered in the coming years. The following pages and illustrations should help*

us all do exactly that. Though I encourage you to read this book in its entirety, I would like to summarize some of my conclusions up front.

In later pages you will find illustrations portraying the physical appearances of many different types of dragons. As you well know, the purer the blood, the more potent its effects on those who've been somehow predetermined to stomach it. Though we still need to do more research in that regard, we do have a much better understanding of how to identify the purest of dragon bloods. Based on the colors of the skin and eyes, the size of the dragons, and several other notable physical features, we have discovered how to ascertain, with relative confidence, the purity of their blood. Brighter colors in both skin and eyes are a good sign, along with the overall size of the beasts. However, we have noted that their coloring fades rather quickly after death, especially the eyes.

I have consulted with my dear friend and trusted colleague in the arts of magic, Lyrielle Vesarian, on the matter, and we have come to some profound conclusions. We fully believe that dragons, being creatures of immense magical capacity, possess blood that is directly infused with the essence of that magic. This is, of course, what gives us our powers as dragos'viren. The stronger the magical connection dragons have, the brighter the colors of both skin and, most especially, the eyes. This further proves our theory, though it means that observing dragons' eyes before their death is of the utmost importance. Capturing a dragon alive would be even better, if the possibility were to exist.

I sincerely hope that you will read all my notes on the matter, and hopefully my words here have confirmed the importance of it. And, though I need not remind you of it, this information must only be shared between the most trusted of allies. In the wrong hands, it could prove disastrous.

I am humbled to be able to share them with you so that they might prove fruitful in your continued work.

Your Brother in Blood,
Fenris Oathsworn

In the wrong hands, Mara recited to herself. *What have I found? How has this book been left here in the library all this time?*

"Hey, Mara."

Mara jumped, startled by the voice looming over her. She turned to see Vi standing to her right, looking over her shoulder at the table. Mara quickly closed the book, blushing.

"Oh, hey Vi."

"Hey, don't mean to pry, but you were glued to that book. Something good I take it?"

"Sorry, Vi. You know how I am with books," Mara squeaked, followed by an awkward laugh.

"Yeah, I know you love these things. Anyway... the others are heading to dinner soon. You joining us?"

"Um, yeah, just one second. I'll be right there. Need to put these back."

"Alright. Me and the girls will be out in the hall. Don't take too long."

Mara nodded, still blushing as she picked the books up off the table. She walked back into the aisles, putting each book back in their place. When she got to the herbalism section, she stopped in front of the empty spot where she'd gotten the strange book. She stared at it, unmoving.

The Mindwarden usually lets me borrow books when I ask, but this book is... special.

She stood there for several more moments. She heard a shout from the door across the room. It sounded like Vi. She tucked the book into her bag, covering it with her notes, then walked out to greet Vi and the other girls.

"Hey, you good?" Vi questioned.

"Yeah- yeah, I'm fine. Just tired is all."

"Okay. Well, we're going to go catch some fresh air first, then head to the dining hall."

"Actually, I'm going to head back to my room. I think I need to lay down for a few. I'll meet you guys in a bit, if you're still there." Mara felt her cheeks turn warm. She hoped they didn't notice.

"Alright, Mara. See you in a bit then. Let's go girls." Vi gave Mara a peculiar look, but turned and walked off, Catlyn and Riesara close behind her. Mara watched them briefly before turning to head in the opposite direction toward her room.

I can't wait to read more of this.

CHAPTER EIGHT

DESTINY

"What is she doing?" Talesa questioned, irritation in her voice.

Sorn looked over at Nalaen, who was sitting cross-legged on the ground in their camp on the edge of the ruins. Her eyes were closed, but Sorn could see the flicker of her pupils as they darted back and forth. Sorn had spent many years studying the ancient arts alongside Nalaen. Talesa, on the other hand, had never cared for things that she didn't view as useful.

"She's communing with her *delisae*, I believe," he retorted.

"Her what?"

"Oh, dear sister. If only you'd spent more time studying *all* the ancient magics and not just the ones used to kill and destroy, then perhaps you'd know what that means."

"But killing is so much more fun. You should try it some time, Brother," she sneered as she ran her tongue across the blade of the dagger she'd been fidgeting with. There was a sly smirk on her face, as if she were joking, but Sorn knew better.

"Yes, well, a *delisae* is what you call one who has been swayed to come under another's control. She's communing with the human she found in that camp."

"Wait, you can do that?" Talesa quit playing with her dagger, her demeanor shifting to a more serious nature. She narrowed her eyes and looked at Nalaen.

"Relax, Talesa. She can't do it to us. It only works on weak-willed creatures. Many humans can be controlled, but not all. That's why she chose the one called Jarren. The other two were, unfortunately, stronger of mind." There was an odd inflection in Sorn's tone as he finished his sentence.

"I wish I had been there to rip them all limb from limb, even this Jarren. What good is a human to us anyway?"

"He will help us find Mother's killer, Sister," Nalaen said sternly as she approached, a slight hiss in her voice.

"Ah, Sister, there you are. Done playing with your pet?"

"He is a means to an end. We cannot safely search the human villages without arousing suspicions. Plus, we have more important matters to attend to."

"Yes, well, I didn't come all this way to watch some human run around doing our dirty work. You promised me blood, but so far you seem to be keeping it all to yourself," Talesa spat, eyeing a bloody sack sitting off to the side. There was a deadly look in Talesa's eyes. Sorn had seen this scenario play out a hundred times before. Talesa knew her place under Nalaen, but she couldn't ever let it be easy. She loved to challenge her sister's authority. Sorn was worried that one day it would escalate to something beyond just a challenge.

"I did what I had to do. I knew we would need a scout. And now, we have one. We also have the proof we need to bring before the Council."

"Proof?" Sorn questioned.

"Yes, proof. The Council will need proof the humans are pressing further toward our home. I intend to deliver it to them."

Sorn eyed the sack, realization setting in. *So, she means to lie to them...*

"You should dispose of this human and let me scout. I'm sure I could find this Grayscale faster," Talesa butted in, still seemingly stuck on the prior argument with her sister.

"Ah, aren't you the sly one Sister," Nalaen replied with a sarcastic smile. "I know what you're after. No, I will not ruin our element of surprise. The humans believe we're upholding the accord. For now, I want it to stay that way."

Tsch. Talesa let out a slight hiss as she gritted her teeth. "Mother would have never used a human to do a dragon's job."

Sorn winced as Nalaen's eyes lit up. The red of her pupil filled her whole eye as the pupil itself returned to its distinct dragon form. Her voice grew deeper, echoing across the desolate ruins around them.

"How dare you speak of Mother as if you knew her. I was the only one of us who ever even saw her face. I was the one who watched as the light slowly left her eyes. No, Talesa, do not speak of which you know so little." Nalaen's eyes began to return to their more humanoid form as the red dimmed, her anger subsiding. "Mother was killed because she underestimated the humans. I will not make that same mistake."

Talesa kept her eyes glued to Nalaen. Sorn noted her fists clenched tightly around her daggers, the glint of their black, polished surfaces reflecting the sun across the glistening snow. Though Talesa had backed a step away during Nalaen's outburst, she stood defiant in the face of it. He looked to Nalaen, who held a similar stance. Sorn could feel the tension in the air, as if a frayed rope were resisting its inevitable fate amidst the onslaught of a storm's fury. And to his own stomach, he felt it turn. He worked up the courage to do what he'd done more than a dozen times before, though it never seemed to get any easier.

"For now?" he choked out, then coughed and cleared his throat. They both eased slightly as they turned his direction.

"What?" Nalaen questioned. Sorn cleared his throat again.

"You said 'for now', Sister. What is your plan?" he asked, a little louder this time. Nalaen relaxed some more, but Talesa's stance remained.

"Yes, for now. We're going to need help. As much as Talesa might think she can kill them all single-handedly, we need to return to the High Council for aid." Nalaen looked sideways toward Talesa as she spoke, an air of superiority gently lifting her chin.

Talesa let out another *tsch* sound, though she leaned back and her muscles relaxed. There was still tension in the air, but Sorn felt the worst of it had passed.

"The High Council?" Sorn questioned. "I doubt they will support our cause. You remember, they did not give us permission to come to the human lands, right? Kyrian will not be pleased. What makes you think he will even listen?"

"Kyrian is Herald. *I* am Queen."

"Not yet, dear Sister," Talesa jabbed, still scowling. Her sly smile returned, now that she'd found a new thorn to press into her sister's side.

"Quiet, Talesa. I will be queen soon enough, and they *will* listen."

Sorn cleared his throat, shifting uneasily. Nalaen, hearing him, rolled her eyes and looked in his direction.

"What is it, Sorn. Speak up."

"Not to take sides, but Talesa has a point. You are not queen yet. And while you remain so, Kyrian has supreme authority as Herald–a position he's held for quite some time now."

"Speak plainly, Brother. What is your point?"

"Yes, what I mean to say is that he is likely to use any fault of yours as an excuse to keep his station and power. If he can prove you are unfit to rule, he may yet convince the Council to delay your ascension. We must be tactful in our approach. He is dangerous, as you well know."

Nalaen let out a sigh, shifting her stance. Familiar wrinkles formed on her brow, and she began to pace back and forth. Sorn could see her lips moving, though he could not hear if she was speaking from this distance. It was a scene he'd seen her portray countless times before. She was smart and methodical; he admired her for that. But she could be arrogant and hot-headed too, which often came at the cost of the prior. Sorn tried to be tactful in his reminders of that.

He knew it was best to let her think. He turned his attention to Talesa, who was still brooding, but it seemed her heightened state had calmed. She, too, knew what her sister was doing, and had reoccupied herself with her daggers further away from the group.

Though they were siblings, all three of them were so very different. Sorn knew this better than any of them. As a male in dragon society, especially in the royal family, it was his duty to merely advise and support his sisters. As such, he had developed a keen awareness of his surroundings. It turns out, there is much one can learn when sticking to the shadows.

Studying his sisters now, he thought about how even they were so very different, almost so much so that one would be hard pressed to call them sisters without already knowing.

They were both about the same height in human form, and had similarly wavy hair, but where Talesa's was a dark brown, bordering on black, Nalaen's was a fiery red, matching her eyes. Talesa was always dark and brooding, and she liked to wear clothing and adorn herself in such a way that accentuated that persona. Nalaen, on the other hand, though she could get just as mean and snarky, she didn't embody it like her sister. Nalaen appreciated the finer things afforded to a princess such as herself, and she wore a variety of colors, though red was always her favorite.

While they were both dangerous in their own rights, Talesa was so much more unpredictable. Nalaen was no less dangerous, but she was typically much more calculated in her approach. She was honestly more like Sorn than she was Talesa. But, as he'd noted before, she had her impulsive moments. Because she was heir to the throne, Nalaen had a certain air of superiority about her. When they were younger, it wasn't as apparent, but as she'd gotten closer to her ascension, it reared its head more frequently—and more aggressively.

It started about twenty cycles ago. Sorn had observed his sister disappearing on many occasions. She would frequent the archives, scouring ancient texts and manuscripts documenting the history of dragonkind. As heir, she was allowed near unconditional access to such things, though there were things even a queen-to-be was not allowed to read. Normally, it was expected for a future queen to gain knowledge of the ancient ways, but what Sorn had observed in her behavior these more recent cycles was something beyond mere academia.

Nalaen had always craved knowledge, as was her nature. But as she gained more, so came the hunger for that which was forbidden. One time, Sorn had gotten a quick peek of one of the texts she'd taken and had in her study. It had strange symbols on it, something he was not familiar with.

When she caught him peeping at the strange book, she was furious. Sorn had never seen her react in such a way when it came to knowledge. Before, it was quite the contrary; she'd often enjoyed showing Sorn what she was studying. They'd spent many nights discussing various aspects of their history, or odd texts about the old magics of the world. This was how Sorn knew about the mind-control magic. Those days seemed but a distant memory to him now.

He continued to watch his sister in silence for several more minutes, waiting to see what she would say. Tired of waiting, he decided to take a seat on one of the broken walls of the ruins and cast his gaze out over the vast, snowy mountain peaks. One could see for miles from where they were now. There seemed to be no end to the mountains as they stretched westward toward home.

He sat there for a moment, soaking in the beauty of it all, trying to let his mind wander from the stress of their tasks at hand. He knew there were hard days ahead, and all he wanted was to be of some use. But part of him also wanted to just spread his wings and soar away over the mountains to somewhere far beyond where there was no backstabbing, vengeance, or talk of war. Sorn loved his sisters, Nalaen especially, but he couldn't shake this nagging feeling that her quest for vengeance was going to bring ruin to them all.

He'd studied the dragons' history. He knew what war had done to their nation. And while the dragons were considered the strongest species in the world, even they had their limits.

"Where do your thoughts roam, Brother? To home, perhaps?"

Sorn turned to face Nalaen, who was standing behind him, sharing his gaze out over the mountains.

"Beyond home," Sorn said with a slight smile, keeping his gaze outward. "Do you remember when we were younglings, Nalaen? Do you remember how simple life was, studying in the library or practicing our magic? And to our trips to the western coast? I always loved it there."

"Of course, I remember. You always got so much sand in your hair, and I had to help you clean it off so it wouldn't get stuck in your scales."

"Ha, yes," Sorn chuckled. "So much sand..."

"Why do you ask?"

"I was just thinking about the pressure of it all, you know. Don't you tire of it? Don't you ever wish to be free of the burden of living up to others' expectations?"

"Sometimes, yes." Nalaen shot Sorn a quick smile before continuing to look out over the horizon.

"Do you want to talk about what you saw in the memory of Mother's death?" Sorn asked, finally mustering up the courage with Nalaen's temper subdued. "Anything besides the name?"

"No, I don't wish to speak on it. Just trust me, Brother. If there is something urgent, you will be the first to know."

Nalaen quieted then and said nothing for a minute. Sorn could see there was more she wasn't saying, but he didn't want to press it. He imagined the sight had been painful. He could see it wore on her. Nalaen's eyes were dim, her power diminished. She looked tired. *She's been tapping a little too deep, I fear.*

"Do you remember the history of the queens?" Nalaen asked, finally breaking the silence.

"Of course, Sister."

"Then you remember how Sha'Liotha came to be the first?"

"Yes," Sorn replied, nodding. "At least, what little there is to know."

"Dro'Kal nearly destroyed the world in his thirst for power, but she put a stop to it. She started a legacy of queens who stood to defend the world from those who would destroy it, restoring the ancient decree and bringing balance."

Sorn listened quietly, knowing full well the stories of Liotha and her rebellion.

"The legacy that she started is the same legacy I now carry. We do not share the same blood, but her legacy is still mine to uphold. It was a legacy that Mother carried, though she did not live to see it through. The humans have grown too strong, dabbling in magic they do not understand. They seek to undermine the order of all things. It's only a matter of time before they look west to our lands. This cannot be tolerated any longer. I will finish what Mother started. I will finish what Liotha started. My destiny is to walk that path, and I cannot deny it," she said, pausing momentarily. "It is my privilege–and my burden–to carry this weight. I should think you above all others would understand."

Sorn studied his sister's eyes as she stared at him. Though their glow was faint, there was a fire of determination still burning within. Sorn had known that fire his whole life. Though he never knew their mother, he knew it was surely the same fire that had guided her path all those years ago. He wasn't sure he liked where this fire was leading them, but he couldn't help but admire and respect her for it. He would not be one to stand in her way.

"I understand," Sorn sighed, casting his gaze to the west. "Do you really think they'll buy it?" Sorn added, looking at the bloody sack off to the side.

"I don't know," she said, her eyes following. "I'm sure many will question it. We'll just have to make it convincing."

"I'll help as best I can," Sorn said with a smile. "To Dor'Dragos then?"

"To home," she corrected with a tired smile. "But first," she yawned, "I need to recover my energy. We'll leave first thing in the morning and discuss our plans on the way."

"Think I might survey the nearby caves for a bit then. After all, I'm rested well enough, and I've been intrigued to finally see them for myself."

"Very well, Brother," she replied. "Just make sure you're ready to leave by first light."

"I'll be ready, Sister. Rest well," he nodded, standing and stretching. "Rest well."

CHAPTER NINE

MESSAGE

Aerin approached the raven's nest. Haromir had given him a message to send, informing the Order of the update surrounding Jarren's return and his unbelievable, yet worrisome, accounting of the night in the woods.

As Aerin ascended the ladder leading up into the loft of the lodge, all was quiet. *Strange.*

Normally, the birds heard them coming and started talking, as only crows do. But today, there was nothing. After a few more rungs, Aerin reached the top and poked his head through the floor. There, on the bottom of the roost right in front of his face, was one of the ravens. It lay deathly still. He scanned the rest of the small roost, spotting the still bodies of six other birds.

Aerin looked back at the nearest bird, puzzled, trying to understand what possibly could have happened. It did not appear to be the doing of a hawk, or any other wild animal. The birds were without a scratch, though their feathers were quite ruffled. Aerin grabbed the raven with his bare hands and held it up, the bird's head rolling to the side. *Broken neck?*

He picked up another. It was the same.

Rushing down the ladder, still holding the bird, Aerin burst through the door into Haromir's office.

"The ravens are all dead."

"What?" Haromir questioned, looking up from his desk. He held a plate of cooked potatoes, setting it down along with his fork. "How?"

"I don't know, but it seems like their necks are broken. Here, look," Aerin said, approaching Haromir's desk and setting the bird on it.

Haromir prodded the bird with his finger, noting how loose its neck was.

"How could this have happened?" Haromir asked. "Were there any other signs of a struggle?"

"No blood, nothing," Aerin replied, just as confused as Haromir seemed to be. "They're all like this. It's almost as if–"

"A human did this," Haromir said, finishing Aerin's thought. "One of ours? But who would do such a thing?"

"Who indeed," Aerin asked, puzzled. "Has there been any word from Jarren yet?"

"No, nothing yet. I sent Logan to go check on him at Miria's. You don't think–"

"I don't know what I think. Jarren, the food shortage, the dragon sighting. All of it is happening at the same time, and now this. It can't all be a coincidence, can it?"

"I don't know. It is strange. Begs one to question, at least. I'll look into the matter further, but for now, I have an important task for you. Well, make that two, now."

"Whatever you need, Huntsmaster," Aerin said, bowing.

"I trust you above all others on this," Haromir emphasized, a serious tone in his voice. Aerin nodded, his interest piqued by the compliment, but he made no response. "We need to ask Valehold for more time. We just don't have the stocks we need for the yearly trade. And because this is a bit sensitive, I don't want word of this getting out and causing the wrong reaction. Can you promise me to keep this matter private, Aerin?"

"Yes, sir. Of course," Aerin replied.

"Good. I have a letter here for Valehold."

Haromir folded up a piece of paper and placed it in an envelope that had been sitting on his desk. He flipped it over and placed it down, reaching over to grab a small ceramic pot of wax he'd preheated. He carefully poured a small blob of brown wax onto the line where the envelope closed. He set the pot back in its place and blew on the wax a few times before reaching up to the front of his desk to grab a metal stamp with an oak handle, the seal of the Lodge on its underside. He placed it down in the middle of the wax and pressed, then withdrew it. Satisfied with the seal, he placed the stamp back in its holder and picked the letter up, blowing on it several more times to ensure the wax had cooled. After several more breaths, he looked back up at Aerin and reached out his hand holding the letter.

"Here you go, Aerin. This is for Lord Valeheart's eyes only. It is my formal request for an extension. We need that food for Winter, and if the Vale doesn't help, people may starve. Please keep this safe until it has been delivered. Can I trust you with this task?"

"Can one of the others not deliver it? I want to help you find out what's going on, and to go look for Yoghar and Kanir. They may still yet be alive."

"I know you want to help, but this is urgent. The Order will look into the matter of Yoghar and Kanir. Which brings me to the second request. After you have delivered this message, head straight away to Eastend and inform the Order of what happened here with Jarren. I don't know what it might mean, but perhaps they will understand. They are much better suited for such things, and if our brothers are still alive, the Order will find them. I will work on getting some new ravens, but that may take some time. For this task, you are the only one Essie trusts, and she's the fastest horse we have. If we don't get word to Valehold soon, I fear they may send our goods elsewhere. I just hope our justification for why will be understood. Lord Valeheart is not a particularly kind man."

Aerin sighed. The yearly trade with the inner Vale was a critical source of food for the surrounding villages. Crops grew much better there, whereas out here, there was much more wildlife for hunting. At least, there used to be. Aerin understood the urgency of the task, even though he didn't approve of merely being a messenger.

"I understand, sir. You have my word. I'll get it to Lord Valeheart."

"Very good. Thank you, Aerin. Hopefully, by the time you get back, we will have this all sorted out."

Aerin stared at the plate on Haromir's desk.

"Everything alright, Aerin?" Haromir questioned.

"Oh, sorry... yes. Was just thinking about potatoes."

Haromir's eyes landed on the dish, then came back to Aerin, followed by a puzzled expression.

"Jarren's favorite," Aerin noted, saying his thoughts out loud. "Do you think he'll be alright?"

"Hah," Haromir chuckled. "Yes, his favorite. Don't worry, Aerin. I'm sure we'll get him sorted out, too. Just worry about your task. Won't be many potatoes if we don't get this message to Valehold."

Breaking his odd trance, Aerin looked back up at the Huntsmaster. He nodded, his lips drawn in a thin line. Now was not the time to reminisce about trivial things. After all, he was right. If Valehold didn't hold their supplies, there'd be a whole lot more than potatoes that were in short supply come winter.

"Safe travels, friend," Haromir called out as Aerin bowed and left the office, heading out toward the supply room, grabbing one of the sacks and shoving half a dozen essentials—rations, water pouch, wrappings, a change of clothes, and a few other miscellaneous items—into the pack. Satisfied, he left and headed for the back door leading to the stables. On his way out, he opened the small coat closet and retrieved his winter coat. It was getting colder outside, especially at night, and he didn't want to get caught in a pinch without it. The journey should only take a few days, perhaps a week in total to Eastend. He'd be fine without much else.

Outside, he turned the corner of the lodge and came into view of the horse stalls, which currently housed three mares. Essie's stall was the furthest to the left. They kept her separated from the other horses, partly because she liked the last stall the most, as it had the most sunlight, but mostly because she was a pain and a bad influence on the younger horses. Essie had let him ride her on several occasions, but she wasn't always amenable to such things. He hoped today was one of her good days.

Before walking over to her stall, he stopped around the side of the stable and grabbed another sack, this time filling it with a dozen apples and a handful of carrots. The barrels were looking awfully low, but he knew if he was going to coax the old shrew to carry him to Valehold, he'd need to come bearing gifts.

Once the bag was full of his offerings, he hurried around the stable and down to the last stall where Essie lay, silently soaking up the sun. Upon his approach, she neighed slightly and shook her head. She looked at him momentarily as he came into view over the top of the stall door, but quickly turned her head away, pretending to ignore him.

"Oh, come on, old girl. Don't be moody today, I need you. Haromir's got a special task for us. See... I come bearing gifts." He reached into the bag and grabbed one of the carrots, holding it out over the top of the stall door, smiling at her. Essie turned her head slightly to look at Aerin, but when she saw the carrot, she shook her head and neighed loudly at him.

"Okay, okay, you got me. Don't worry," he said, placing the carrot back in the bag, grabbing an apple instead. He held the apple up, waving it so she could see it. "I know you like apples best. Don't worry, I grabbed a whole bag of 'em."

Essie turned her head and looked at Aerin, ears back, staring at him as though she were reading his mind and deciding whether or not she liked what she saw. Aerin swallowed; he wasn't the best rider and he'd only ridden Essie a few times. He motioned with his hand, beckoning for Essie to come take the apple, a pleading look in his eye that he tried to make seem sincere. Essie stared at him several more moments before finally coming to a decision. She slowly stood and meandered over to Aerin, snatching the apple from his hand. Aerin recoiled slightly, still unsure of the mare's opinion of him at the given moment. Essie, too, retreated several steps backwards and eyed Aerin cautiously as she chewed.

"That a girl. Let's get going and I'll give you some carrots, too," Aerin said as he pet her. With her seemingly calm, he stepped over, retrieved the saddle, and within a minute had it fashioned tightly about her. He grabbed his things and mounted, settling himself in the saddle.

Essie shifted a bit under his weight, pawing at the ground a few times, but it otherwise seemed she would allow him to ride.

"Alright. Here we go," Aerin said, reaching into his sack for a carrot. "As promised. One more for the road." After she quickly munched it down, Aerin gave her a slight kick and they were off.

Chapter Ten

MAISIE

Jarren trudged along at a meandering pace, his conscious still weighing on him. He hadn't wanted to kill the birds. It had been *her* idea, though he didn't quite understand why.

Hearing voices up ahead, he slowed his pace even further and crept cautiously forward. As he came around the bend in the road, he leaned up against a large tree, peering around it to see the outskirts of a town in the distance as several people walked down the road ahead of him. Lonely Pines, as it was called, wasn't a large town by any means, but it was the largest between Northreach and Eastend, which was his eventual goal. It was a quaint town, and one Jarren had visited quite frequently on his many hunting trips throughout the area. It was a good place to catch a rest and restock supplies, as was his normal routine.

Though he was still a bit far off, he could see the town was abustle with the comings and goings of its inhabitants as they no doubt made their preparations for winter. Jarren stood there, peering around the tree suspiciously, conflicted. Because of his frequent stops here, there were several in the town who knew him quite well, including Gaston the Innkeeper and Maisie—the girl who ran the front counter at the town trader.

I like Maisie, she's nice to me, Jarren thought to himself as fond memories of his last stop ran through his head.

No, we mustn't attract unwanted attention. She won't like it, the other voice in his head countered. He didn't like this new voice.

But why, she's kind. She won't bother us.

No. No distractions, no attention. We have a mission from her and that is all that matters.

"Hey there, sir. Is everything alright?" A man sat upon a halted horse-drawn carriage in the middle of the road, looking down at Jarren with a peculiar expression. Jarren jumped, turning toward the man, quickly averting his eyes to the ground as he pulled the hood of his cloak up over his head. He hadn't even realized he'd wandered into the road.

"No, I mean... yes. Everything is fine."

"Okay... well if you want to catch a ride the rest of the way into town, you can hop on back."

Jarren raised his head slightly, looking past the man to the back of the wagon. It was full of what looked like an assortment of vegetables, most of which Jarren couldn't recall the names of.

"I wouldn't- no!"

"Eh?" the man questioned, growing more confused.

"Sorry, I- I mean, no. I'm fine."

"Alright, suit yourself then. Have a good day." The man slapped the reins and whistled, the chestnut horse started trotting, the cart lurching forward. As they rode past Jarren, he saw the man looking back at him curiously. He pulled his hood down and moved back behind the tree, out of the man's view.

Stupid, Jarren heard in his mind, grabbing his head with his hands as he leaned against the tree.

"Sorry," he offered out loud, his voice growing softer.

Sorry? What did we say? Jarren's face contorted as the voice in his head scolded him.

"No attention, I know. I... didn't hear him."

You're an idiot. Perhaps she should have chosen better.

"Well, maybe I could– could've heard him if... if you weren't so loud!"

Fine, I'll be quiet, but don't screw this up. Wait until dark, go to the tavern. No one knows you there, and it will be a good place to ask about Grayscale.

"Right, good— good idea. Dark, tavern, ask about Grayscale."

Nothing else.

"Nothing else," he repeated.

Jarren hated this new version of his conscious. Not that it had ever been nice to him, but since *she* came into his life, it was even worse. He retreated into the woods, away from the road, and found a comfy place to sit down and wait for dusk. As he sat there, resting his back against a tree, his eyes darted back and forth as fast as his thoughts were racing back and forth in his head. The areas directly beneath his eyes were dark, his eyelids heavy. He only now realized how tired he was, trying to remember when he left Northreach and how exactly he'd ended up here. But try as he might, it was all a blur of darkness and shadows.

Though he wanted answers, he couldn't help but yield to the growing weariness in his head. He looked up, calculating the time of day based on the bits of sun he glimpsed through the green canopy above.

It's two, maybe three hours until dusk, he thought. The idea of sleep made sense. Jarren dropped his head and rested it on his knees, letting himself get swept away by the overflowing darkness within as he closed his eyes and succumbed to sleep.

Jarren awoke in a state of confusion. Lifting his head, he looked around. It was nearly pitch black, and all he could see were shapes in the darkness all around him; shapes that seemed to twist and turn, mocking him as he stood and began stumbling through the dark woods. He realized he was walking, but how, he knew not. Visions raced through his mind. Voices echoed, calling to him–taunting him.

He saw the faces of Haromir, Aerin, and others. They told him how worthless he was, how insignificant. They told him they hated him. The visions disappeared, the faces of Kanir and Yoghar coming to him, twisted and contorted in agony, the smell of death heavy in the air.

"No," he pleaded out loud, "it wasn't my fault."

Yes, it was. You abandoned them!

"Yes, but she made me."

Yes, because they were not important. They were not chosen, like you. She needs you. She will protect you.

"She needs me..."

Jarren felt a hard bump on his head as he fell backwards into the earth, pulled out of the nightmare. He groaned in pain, placing his hand on his forehead. A slight bit of blood formed from a small gash. Jarren wiped at it several times before placing his sleeve over the area to curb the bleeding. After several minutes, the pain subsided and the bleeding stopped. Still on his back on the ground, he sat up, holding his hands out in front of him to avoid any more collisions. He looked around. It was still very dark, but up ahead he could see a faint light coming from some unknown source, its beckoning glow distorted by the forest's undergrowth. He reached out to one of the shadows in front of him, feeling the familiar sensation of wood and bark. He used it to pull himself up, one hand still held out in front of his face to avoid whatever hit him just a moment ago.

Once up, he breathed heavily, placing his hand again on his head, the pain, though less now, was still there, a throbbing reminder to be more careful. He stumbled forward through the darkness, moving toward the light up ahead. It gradually became brighter, and he found it easier to navigate through the woods amidst the fractured rays of light on the forest floor.

At last, he reached the edge of the forest and peered out into the town from behind a large shrub. He could see now the light was emanating from several buildings, lamps hanging outside to guide weary travelers, or the occasional inhabitant who was out late working. From where Jarren crouched, he could see the tavern. Though he was not a normal customer of such places, he knew its appearance well enough from his countless trips here. Besides, taverns were usually hard to miss, especially at night, as they tended to be the busiest places in town after dark.

Things seemed relatively quiet about town. There were a few lone people walking through the streets, going about their business, and one group of three, laughing as they went along, pulling their overcoats tightly around themselves. There were a couple men hanging out in the front of the tavern, trails of smoke swirling about them as they momentarily braved the brisk night air to satiate their unsavory habits.

Confident it was quiet enough, Jarren decided to make his move for the tavern. He emerged from the forest, pulling his hood back over his head, walking hurriedly toward the welcoming warmth the tavern would offer. Walking through the town, his eyes darted back and forth, peering from underneath his low hood at the few people still out and about. He could not see their faces, but felt a tingle in his forehead, not sure whether it was the wound pulsating, or the sensation of their stares as they bore into him. He swore he overheard some low conversation off to the side, aimed at him.

Jarren picked up his pace, exchanging quick, awkward glances with several of the men outside the tavern. He skirted past them, waving the smoke away from his face, wanting to get inside and ask his questions so he could be on his way as quickly as possible.

Passing through the doorway, the smell of smoke and booze assaulting his senses, he immediately began to regret his decision. But the warmth of a large hearth on the right side of the large open area beckoned him to stay. The tavern was not as full as he'd expected, but there were about a dozen patrons sitting at various tables throughout, a dull hum accompanying their scattered conversations. As Jarren entered, several of them turned to look at him, their stares causing his head to pulsate yet again. He scanned the room quickly, looking for the most secluded table that wasn't too far from the hearth. He spotted a quiet corner near the back of the room, on the same side as the fireplace. Still feeling stares from some of the patrons, he made for the table. To get there, he had to pass between several inhabited tables, each containing several men, empty drinks strewn about before them as they sat there, laughing about something. When Jarren passed between them, trying to avoid eye contact, he accidentally kicked one of the chairs, a terrible sound ensuing as he nearly lost his footing.

"Hey, watch where you're going there, buddy," one of the men called out, though Jarren couldn't discern which. He saw all eyes were now on him, the pulsing in his head like the steady beat of a drum, and he felt the darkness creeping into his vision.

"S-sorry," he managed to spit out before continuing to the table he'd marked as his destination.

Idiot.

When at last he reached the table, he sat down, pulling his hood down even lower, trying to ignore the several lingering stares throughout the tavern as most went back to their business. He sat there in silence for some time, not knowing exactly how long, his head down and his eyes scanning the surface of the table in front of him. He found himself lost in the swirls of the wood's rings as they flowed across the polished surface like a thousand tiny rivers all circling each other, headed to some unseen vortex pulling them into the abyss below. Jarren found himself being drawn into the same abyss, some intangible force pulling at his soul. The sounds of the tavern faded into the background.

Through it all, one voice became louder and clearer. He tried to focus on it, tried to understand what it was saying, but it was elusive, like a shadow in the darkness. He recognized the voice, but it felt different–foreign, yet becoming increasingly more familiar. He knew there were words being spoken, but he did not understand them.

As Jarren sat there, lost in his thoughts, he began to hear another voice, louder than the rest. He tried to push it aside, but it repeated itself, louder this time.

"Can I get you a drink, sir?"

Jarren snapped out of his trance, rushing back to reality to see a large man standing over his table, a soft, but puzzled look on his face. Jarren shifted uncomfortably and looked up at him, blinking.

"Hey, are you alright?" the man asked, resting his hands on the table. Jarren looked up at him again. He was a large man, by most accounts, and by Jarren's guess maybe in his sixtieth winter. He had a hard face, the lines of age beginning to take a hold, and his beard had a hint of brown, with shimmers of gray throughout.

"I'm fine..." Jarren replied, trailing off, unsure of what else to say.

"Alright, well, name's Garis. I own this here establishment. Can I get you a drink?"

"A drink?"

"Yes, this is a tavern, y'know. We serve drinks here."

"Oh, right. I, um, no– no thanks."

"Okay, well if you're not going to have a drink, I'm going to have to ask you to leave. These tables are for paying customers."

Jarren looked around, several stray gazes from the closest tables directed his way. He shifted again, uncomfortable with the attention.

"I'm not... not here for a drink, just pass– passing through and..." he paused, "I'm looking for someone. Can you... help me?"

"I see a lot of people come through here, so maybe, but that depends on you buying a drink or not."

"I see. Got any food?"

"Nope, sorry. Kitchen staff all left a short while ago."

"Fine, I guess I'll have a drink..."

"Great," Garis said sarcastically. "What'll it be?"

"Oh, um... I don't really know. Do– do you have any honey mead? Something light?" It was the only thing Jarren had ever really had that contained alcohol.

"Something light... okay, sure thing buddy. I'll be right back," Garis chuckled as he headed back to the counter on the other side of the room. He stopped at several of the occupied tables on the way, chatting and laughing with the patrons there and taking empty cups before heading behind the counter. Jarren watched him as he moved back and forth, grabbing various things for whatever concoctions he was brewing up.

After several minutes, he left the bar area with a tray full of drinks. He stopped at the same tables as before, placing cups down for their respective consumers. He nodded and smiled at the other tables, getting the same in reply. One of the men looked at the last drink on the barkeep's tray and laughed, and Jarren thought he heard some comment about a woman's drink. The barkeep grinned and nodded, then shook his head, looking in Jarren's direction. The rest of the table followed his gaze and Jarren sunk low in his seat, trying to ignore the laughter.

Moments later, from under his hood, Jarren saw Garis's legs standing beside his table.

"Right, here you are. One light mead, from the last barrel of the summer batch from Briargate Farms. It's all we have that's light. Anyways, that'll be three silvers. Would you like to pay now, or do you think you'll want more later?"

"Um, this... will be all," Jarren affirmed while fidgeting through his pockets, looking for the bag of coins he'd brought. As he searched for it, he returned to his previous question. "So, you said you can help me with the person I'm looking for?"

"Aye, I might be. I know most of the folks who come through these parts, though I don't reckon I've seen you before. But then, you don't strike me as the usual tavern-goer, eh?" Jarren shook his head. "Right, well, who is it you're lookin' for? Friend of yours?"

"No- I mean, yes, sort of- friend of a friend, you might say."

"Right... okay then. This friend of a friend got a name?"

"It's Grayscale. Know any by- by that name?"

"Grayscale, eh? The name does sound vaguely familiar. Maybe one of those lads from the Order, if I were to guess. Tell you what, my night girl is currently in the back washing dishes, and she might know your, um, *friend*. My mind's not as sharp as it used to be, but she's got a mind like a steel trap, that one. I'll go ask her."

"Alright. Thanks for your help."

"Sure thing, buddy. Appreciate your patronage. I'll send my girl over if she knows anything. Oh, and when you find your coin, you can leave it on the table."

Jarren nodded and waited for the man to leave, still trying to find his bag of coins.

I'm sure I grabbed it.

He continued to search, growing more desperate. He checked his pack, which he'd hung around the back of his chair. Rifling through the clothes and other items he'd packed, he found no sign of it. He looked up, confused. Suddenly, he remembered his coat pocket. He moved his hand up, feeling for the bag. His hand found the familiar lump in his right breast pocket, and he reached inside to pull it out.

Relieved, he opened it and pulled out several silver coins, placing them on the table, along with the sack.

"Jarren?"

Startled, Jarren looked up to see the face of Maisie, the girl from the town store, staring back at him. Jarren, unsure how to react, sat there staring at her. She wore a brown bodice that covered a long, green dress underneath, her low neckline exposing more of her cleavage than made him feel comfortable. She was smiling warmly at him. Jarren's eyes flitted between her face and her breasts several times before he blushed and bowed his head low, embarrassed.

"Jarren, it is you. I thought that looked like you from across the room. How are you?"

"I- I'm f-fine. Surprised to see you here, is all."

"Oh, yes, I know," she said, grabbing a chair and sitting down across from him. "Times are tough, and my hours at the store don't pay for everything we need, so I work nights here on occasion. It's not the best job, but the tips are good. But anyways, enough about me. How are you? I'm kind of surprised to see you in here."

"Oh, yes. I was just– just looking for a place to... warm up."

"Ah, well we do keep the fire lit late into the night. Oh, but Garis said you were looking for someone? Someone by the name of Grayscale, was it?"

Jarren smiled slightly and nodded, anxiously looking at Maisie, trying to keep his eyes locked with hers. He squirmed in his seat, the sounds of the tavern growing louder in his ears as he tried to focus.

"I don't know him too well, but he's passed through on several occasions on his way to and from the northern mountain towers. He's usually with a couple other knights and he always buys their drinks. Yoren, I think his name is. Not sure if that's helpful, but I don't know any more than that."

The barkeep called out from behind the bar, waving in Jarren and Maisie's direction. Maisie turned to him and he tilted his head toward a group that had just come in and seated themselves on the other side of the room.

"Sorry, I need to go help Garis with some customers. I'll be back after. Do you need anything?" she asked, standing up. Jarren just shook his head, his face pointed down toward the table again.

"Alright, well I'll be back in a minute. I'd love to catch up!"

Jarren watched her walk away, mixed feelings flowing through his head. On the one hand, he was glad to see her, but the other voice in his head didn't like it.

No distractions, he heard it say. *Besides, she probably doesn't even like you. She's just being nice. No one likes you.*

Jarren began bouncing his leg up and down rapidly, his anxiousness growing.

Maisie met with the new group and took all their orders, returning to the bar to get started on their drinks. She returned a few minutes later, but Jarren was already gone, a handful of silvers left in the middle of the table. She reached down and picked them up with great curiosity. She looked around again, then headed to the nearest occupied table, asking the men if they'd seen Jarren leave. They shook their heads, looking toward the table where he'd been sitting. Maisie returned to the counter with a frown. She dropped the coins on the counter for Garis.

"Ah, good lad," he said, nodding, placing the last of the ales on the tray for Maisie. He looked at Maisie's perplexed face, then down at her hand, as she stared off at the wall behind him.

"Looks like he left you quite a nice tip too, eh?"

"Yeah..." Maisie exhaled, trailing off. Garis waved his hand in front of her face.

"The drinks, lass. Table's waitin'."

Maisie came to, looking down at the tray. She shot a forced smile at Garis, then picked it up after placing the extra coins in her pocket. She walked over to the table, placing the round of drinks in front of the men there. They thanked her for them, but her mind was elsewhere as she stood up straight and headed for the tavern's main door.

Outside, Jarren watched from around the corner of a nearby building, the shadows concealing his figure, as Maisie emerged from the tavern and looked out into the streets. He wanted to cry out; he wanted to go back to her and tell her everything. But something deep within his mind kept him silent, his thoughts of asking for help quickly fading into nothingness.

As Maisie retreated back inside, Jarren turned and headed for the woods, disappearing once more into the cold, dark undergrowth of the forest. No longer apprehensive, there was only one thought on his mind now: *Eastend*.

CHAPTER ELEVEN

DOR'DRAGOS

There was nothing Nalaen liked more than to feel the power of the wind beneath her wings. Their time spent in human form, walking on two legs–it sometimes made her temporarily forget just how good it felt to stretch her wings and soar, as dragons were meant to. But all magic has its limits, even dragons. Even Nalaen.

Nalaen pushed her thoughts aside. There was no point dwelling on what was out of her control. It was time to focus on what lay ahead. There was only one thing left now standing between her and the vengeance she'd waited so long for. Kyrian and the High Council.

Kyrian Orae'tor, Herald of the Dragon High Council, was no friend to the royal family. Nalaen knew as much, as she had watched his pervasion of the High Council and its members blossom during the years after her mother's death. Nalaen and Sorn had studied all the members of the High Council, deciphering which ones would remain loyal to her once she took her rightful place as Queen. In truth, it had been a difficult task, as Nalaen had been excluded from many of their secretive meetings. Though she participated in matters of state for the dragon kingdoms, it was only in an obligatory manner. Nalaen came to understand it was all for show, and that she was being excluded from the *real* Council meetings. But there was hope.

Not all of the High Council felt as Kyrian did; or, at least there *were* a few loyal to the royal family for many years after Queen Sha'Mora's demise. High Councilor Lyriae Corignas, specifically, helped keep Nalaen abreast for many years, and was the one who initially told Nalaen of these secret meetings. Nalaen hoped that Councilor Corignas would take her side in the coming days. If ever Nalaen needed allies, it was now. She knew now that her mother's killer was a member of the Order, thanks to her pet, the human Jarren. The Order was a strong and fearless enemy, wielding the power of the dragons against them.

Abominations. We shall rid the world of them, once and for all. Then, nothing will stop us from eliminating the rest of the vile humans and stopping their heinous acts of subjugation.

But still, the thoughts of someone on her side betraying her mother still haunted her. Could it have been Kyrian? Or perhaps one of the councilors?

Nalaen looked to her left where Talesa flew. Talesa and she had rarely ever seen eye to eye, but at least against their mother's murderers, they were of one mind. Nalaen was the stronger of the two, but she still had a healthy fear of her sister–the same fear that has kept many Queens of the past out of harm's way when those closest to them wrought betrayal. Studying Talesa now, Nalaen *was* glad she was on her side.

In her true form, Talesa was an impressive sight. She was darker than Nalaen, almost black, with green scales that flecked up her back, culminating at the top of her spine, before ascending to a green crown of spikes set upon her head. She and Nalaen shared many of the same features, though where Talesa was green, Nalaen wore red, and Talesa was just a tad smaller than her sister. Talesa's powerful legs rippled with energy, the ability to shred enemies within seconds–a feat Nalaen had seen in practice–due to her razor-sharp talons, which were longer than Nalaen's own. Where Nalaen preferred fire, as many other dragons did, Talesa had a certain taste for getting up close and personal with her kills, watching the life slowly drain from their eyes as she poked and prodded them. It was unnaturally cruel, even for a dragon, but again, Nalaen couldn't dispute the results her sister achieved. And it was why Nalaen had a healthy respect for the killer she knew her sister to be.

Turning to her right, Nalaen watched her brother glide through the air, a much more peaceful mannerism to his flight than Talesa. Nalaen did have to admire Sorn, for what it was worth, even though he was a male. He was larger than her and Talesa, which was oft the case for males, but Sorn hadn't trained in combat like she and Talesa had. He preferred to use his mind to solve problems. Be that as it may, Nalaen couldn't help but see the warrior he could be.

In Sorn's true form, he was a lighter gray color that shifted almost indistinctly into a pale blue. Similar to Talesa, it was spottier toward his tail, the blue growing more prominent up his spine and onto his head. His crown wasn't as spiky as his sisters', but his head was larger, his fangs several inches longer than both her and Nalaen's. If Sorn ever had the mind to, he could probably bite one of their necks clean in two, but Nalaen knew he never would. In fact, Nalaen had rarely even seen him angry. She hoped the day would never come when she saw his true rage emerge, unless of course it was directed at their enemies. She, however, had little hope of it; it was not his way. She wondered how he could have come from the same mother that she and Talesa had.

Nalaen turned her attention forward, straining her eyes against the rising sun as the first glimpse of Dor'Dragos, or Dragonhold, as the other races called it, came into view. Though Nalaen had always felt it a prison, being trapped there all those years, barred from breaching the city's walls unless escorted by the Royal Guard, the sight now instilled a pride in her. After Nalaen had come into her own, growing bolder and more indignant of the palace rules, she'd ventured out on her own on more than one occasion. She toured the kingdoms of Ter'alas, the lands surrounding Dor'Dragos, in her later years, and even some of the lands beyond, but had never found anything more grand or awe-inspiring than home. It was a magnificent city, which only now did she truly appreciate and understand.

The city itself was enormous, scaling anything she'd seen in her wanderings. Though she'd barely scratched the surface of the world, and had not yet explored the human lands, she doubted there were any cities that could rival Dor'Dragos. From one end of the city, you could barely see the other side of it. The city was a near perfect circle, divided into several separate sections, each housing various levels of dragons. The northern sections were reserved for the nobility and families of higher status, the southern sections more for the working class and lower-income inhabitants.

The architecture itself was marvelous, the work of thousands of craftsmen over a multitude of millennia. Though there was a common theme amongst the various architectural styles, there were dozens of sections of the city crafted in varieties that made them unique. One could easily mistake their craftsmanship as that of mimicking those of the Kalinari, Duril, and other ancient races of the world, but in truth, it was quite the opposite. The dragons, being the oldest creation, had been the original inventors of many styles found throughout Velasia.

Though Nalaen was somewhat relieved to be approaching home, gazing once more upon the great city of Dor'Dragos, she knew it would be short-lived. They had a task to accomplish, and they could not truly return until she had seen it done.

Now that they were closer, she could see the images of her *dragonai*–her people. At first, they were just specs, but because of their hasty approach, she could now make out their forms–large, small, and everything in between. The humans believed the size of a dragon equated to its strength, which wasn't wholly untrue, but Nalaen knew better. It was the magical essence, innate to all *dragonai*, that only the strongest among them could truly assess, though there were physical features that often gave it away. Seeing them now, Nalaen felt a renewed sense of purpose in her mission. Though she was not Queenmother yet, she owed it to them all to avenge her mother's death. She owed it to uncover her kil and ascertain the true history of her kind. And more importantly, she owed it to herself, to prove to them she was worthy of their loyalty. Today was the first big step in making that a reality.

Nearing the outermost edge of the eastern part of Dor'Dragos, Nalaen spotted the unforgettable pinnacle of *Cor'Sha Mataer*-the Seat of the Queenmother, Nalaen's home. It was a grand palace that had been built in the very heart of Dor'Dragos, recognizable for the massive spire rising several hundred feet above the rest of the city. On the sides of this spire, were two great wings, extending outwards and over, casting great shadows upon the nearby areas. It was a vantage point for the Queenmother to watch over her people, and a symbol of the unwavering protection she provided all *dragonai*.

The infrastructure itself was expertly crafted with the rarest and strongest of minerals, a substance called *inga'lapelli*–or Dragonstone, as most of the world knew it. The sight of it now, in all its glory, further renewed Nalaen's resolve. As her and her brother and sister drew near, they flew around to approach from the northern side, where a large landing platform had been crafted. Nalaen saw the Dragonguard were waiting for her, several of them rising in the air to greet and escort them in. By the looks on their faces, Nalaen already knew she was in for an earful.

As they rounded the corner, the platform coming into full view, her suspicions were confirmed. There, down on the precipice of the rise, stood Velicos, the royal family's caretaker. He was an ancient dragon, who had started his service to the royal family nearly 1,200 cycles ago, under the care of Nalaen's grandmother, Sha'Valiara. He was a good servant, and extremely loyal, but Nalaen knew he'd have a mawful of words for her, and she wasn't in the mood. She needed to save her patience for Kyrian and the High Council.

As Nalaen descended, landing gracefully on the platform, she shifted back into her human form, a swirling mist of red appearing, then vanishing in an instant as she emerged from it. Talesa and Sorn did the same, just behind her, as Velicos came up and gave a quick bow out of respect, two female maids dressed in elegant, but plain grey and red robes–the standard dress of the family's servants–behind him. Nalaen shot him a quick sideways glance but continued walking toward the gateway to their home in a hurried manner. Velicos rose quickly, coming up beside her to match her pace.

"Your highness, forgive my forthrightness, but where the hell have you been? We've had the royal guards out looking for you for over a week!" Velicos paused, looking down at the bloody sack Nalaen was carrying. "What is that?" he asked.

Nalaen's eyes looked sideways in Velicos's direction, then down at the sack in her hand, but she made no motion indicating she intended to respond to his questions.

"*Filia*–" Velicos pleaded, a term of endearment he had used for as long as Nalaen could remember, "Please. The crowning is less than a cycle away. We cannot take unnecessary risks. Your life is more important than you know."

"My *life*!" Nalaen exclaimed, raising her voice as she stopped and turned to face him. "My life is nothing if I do not respect my mother's legacy. She is not here to rule because she was slain by men–men who still walk this world, though I shall remedy that soon enough." Nalen turned and continued walking.

"Your Highness, what is this you speak of? What do you mean?" Velicos asked, the numerous lines of his age showing. He trailed behind her, slowing his pace. "Where... have you been?" he asked in an accusatory tone.

"Mother's killer. I found him."

Velicos let out a noise that sounded like the cross between a sigh and a gasp. He picked up his pace, the increased effort along with his age apparent in his de-meanor. He looked at Sorn and Talesa, exchanging worried, questioning glances with them. Sorn made no reply but offered the old dragon a look of surrender. Talesa shot him her usual, evil grin. He let out another sound amidst hurried breaths, then strode to get back in step with Nalaen.

"How can this be? And what exactly are you planning? You know crossing into human lands is strictly forbidden!" Velicos lowered his voice and continued. "You could be punished for this. Kyrian will not like it."

"Kyrian be damned. *I* am set to be Queenmother, and he should do well to recognize that," Nalaen stated, a cold tone in her voice. "He has grown arrogant in his position as Herald."

"Princess, you cannot say such things out loud," Velicos whispered, looking around to see if any of the guards had overheard. Fortunately, the guards were walking a good distance behind the party, their eyes facing forward, unmoving. "As it stands, he is in the highest position of authority in the dragon kingdoms. The title of Princess does not carry as much weight as you might think."

"Maybe not, but Queen does. And when I am so, he shall know his place once again." Nalaen stopped, turning to the old dragon. She could see the weariness of his age. He was tall, but his years saw him hunched forward, his shoulders not as set as they once were. He wore a long white beard upon his face, as white as the snow-covered peaks of the nearby mountains. His beard trailed down to about his mid chest, tied neatly with several silver clasps. His eyes glowed a deep blue, though Nalaen thought they seemed dimmer now than they once had, yet there was the same kindness in them, the same look of ever-present concern for her and her family's well-being. She bore no ill will toward him, and in fact, it was quite the opposite. But at the present moment, he was an obstacle in her path, and she simply couldn't afford any distractions.

"I know you are no friend to Kyrian, Velicos," Nalaen spoke softly, trying to smile. "I know you are loyal to me and my family, and for that, I thank you. But right now, I need allies more than scolding. I must meet with the High Council—to ask for aid. I do not know what allies our family still has, but I'm hoping you can help us with that."

Velicos looked at Nalaen, his eyes squinting as he deciphered her words. A smile slowly grew on his face—the same one Nalaen had grown fond of all these years. She couldn't help but smile, ever so slightly, in return.

"You have the same fire in you, *filia*, my princess. I guess I've known it for some time now, but you are just like your mother. And I cannot deter you any more than I could her, once that fire has been stoked." Velicos grabbed Nalaen's hands in his own, pulling her off toward a side balcony, his eyes darting sideways, and he gave a slight nod toward the guards and other servants. He turned and waved for them to stay as they moved to the ledge, overlooking the city below. He stood there momentarily, gazing down at it, a heavy sigh slowly leaving his lungs.

"Somehow, I knew this day would come. I just didn't want to lose you like I lost her," he said, looking at Nalaen with a smile. "You must be careful, *filia*. There are just as many dangers within, as there are without." Velicos looked up toward the mountains to the east.

"I know, Velicos," Nalaen replied. "And you won't. I will be careful, but I cannot stand idly by any longer. Are there any still loyal to the royal family?"

"There are some, yes. The sway of Kyrian and his allies is strong. Even here," he warned, looking at the guards. "But blood runs deep, and there are many who would see a Queen on the throne yet again. I will do what I can to find them."

Nalaen nodded. She should have never doubted the old drake. Though he was always keeping up formal appearances, time and time again he'd proven his loyalty. And now, yet again, he was by her side. She wasn't sure what kind of connections he had, but if anyone could do this, it was him. Nalaen gave Velicos a hug, then gave him a short bow, to which he replied with his own short bow. She returned to her brother and sister at the other end of the balcony, Sorn waiting patiently, while Talesa fondled her knives. As Nalaen approached, Sorn came up beside her.

"Will he help us?" Sorn questioned.

"Yes," Nalaen replied, keeping her voice low. "He will seek what allies remain." Sorn nodded his approval.

"So, what now?" came Talesa's voice from behind them, a look of irritation as she sauntered over.

"Now," Nalaen answered with a sly smile, lifting up the sack, "we bring our *proof* before Kyrian and the Council."

CHAPTER TWELVE

LIES

The High Council presided in a grand building, not far from the palace. It was known as the Tempus of Fire. If the palace was the heart of the dragon empire, the Tempus was the lungs, breathing life into it, ensuring it stayed ever beating. The empire could not function without both. The High Council itself was comprised of twelve members and the Herald–the speaker and leader in all matters of state. Members sitting on the council were chosen from the thirteen Scions of dragon society. Each Scion was representative of the different highborn broods–vast factions with considerable power and influence. Any who wanted to hold claim to a position on the High Council must have the full backing of their Scion, though it was almost always the Scion leaders who held such positions.

Though not all dragons in the world come from one of these Scions, most of the city's inhabitants were either connected through blood, or through their declared allegiance, gaining access to the many benefits such affiliations brought. To sit on the High Council was one of the greatest honors each Scion could bestow. And in the most extreme circumstances, when the royal family should be unfit or unable to provide a queen, one would be chosen from amongst them. However, it had only happened several times throughout the reign of the Queenmothers. Nalaen knew, though, that before, during the time of the Wyrmlords, it had been commonplace for rule to change between Scions. She also knew there were still those who wanted to see it return to such.

As they approached the building from the ground level, Nalaen couldn't help but marvel at its splendor. Though it still paled in comparison to the palace, it was the only other building in the whole city that even came close. In similar fashion to the palace, it was crafted using a good portion of Dragonstone. But unlike the palace, which was almost entirely red, the colors and sigils of the thirteen Scions adorned each segment of the building's circular construction. Additionally, the inner segment, representative of the Herald, sat slightly higher than the rest, its pinnacle seen even from Nalaen's position on the ground.

Thinking of it now made her scoff, realizing the arrogance of the dragon it currently represented. She wanted to fly up there and shred the banner to pieces, but she knew better. In the world of dragon politics, one must be careful. Strength is not measured in teeth and claws, but in blood and allegiances. And that was one thing Nalaen did not believe was in her favor at the present. She didn't know how many allies Kyrian had, but she assumed it was many. He could have won over the entire Council by now.

Walking up the steps, Nalaen could see the place was a hive of activity, as was quite normal for the Tempus. All matters of state were handled there, from economics, to alliances, to war. If there was any serious change happening within the dragon empire, you could be sure that it had been discussed there. Today, the busyness outside suggested a High Council meeting was likely in session.

Good. Let's go interrupt it.

Up the many steps leading to the main entrance of the Tempus, which alternated in color for each Scion, the names of the greatest among them were engraved along their surfaces. It was said this was done so that any who entered this great house would remember all who had come before, in service to the dragon empire.

Nalaen never had any love for politics, and as such, was little impressed by the spectacle. However, she understood the nature of it, as well as its necessity in supporting her rule. Reading some of the names as she ascended the last of the steps, she wondered whose names she'd allow to be carved next.

Realizing she was attracting a growing audience of onlookers from the Tempus's main foyer, she focused her attention ahead. It was always a spectacle when she came to the Tempus. As future Queen, all there knew who she was, but Nalaen was unsure of the nature behind their stares. Whether it was in reverence, or detest, she could not say.

As they entered the main foyer, Nalaen ignored the crowd and headed straight for the doorway leading into the central chamber of the Tempus where the High Council convened. Approaching the closed doors, the Chamberlain looked up from his desk off to the side, gasping from behind rounded spectacles. He quickly scampered down to block their way, standing no higher than Nalaen's chest as he looked up at her.

"Uhm, I'm sorry Your Highness," he bumbled, straightening his glasses, "but the Council is currently in session. I must ask you to wait outside. If you have a matter of importance, I can see that it reaches the Council's agenda for the next meeting."

"Yes, I'm sure that you can," Nalaen replied, unamused, continuing to head for the doors. The Chamberlain placed his hand on her arm, trying to slow her, when Talesa appeared, her dagger at his throat before Nalaen could even react. Talesa hissed at him, lifting him slightly off the ground with her other hand. From the corner of her vision, Nalaen saw the two guards standing in front of the doors grip their weapons and head toward them.

"Sorry, sir," Sorn's voice came from behind them as he cleared his throat. "You will have to forgive my sister, but we've just traveled a very long way, from across the mountains, and our message is urgent." Sorn bowed as he spoke, looking up to see Talesa ease up slightly. She gave him an expression of distaste until she saw the guards, wherein she reluctantly let loose her grip on the Chamberlain, rolled her eyes, and placed him back on the ground.

"F-f-from across the mountains? Oh my..." the Chamberlain stuttered, his look of terror toward Talesa shifting to one of scorn. "The Council must hear of this immediately! Guards, escort them in!"

Nalaen looked back at Sorn, who shot her a quick wink, the realization of what he'd just done sinking in. She smiled and nodded at him before turning to follow the Chamberlain in, the guards on either side. He opened the doors and proceeded inside, his head held high.

As the doors opened, Nalaen could hear the recognizable echo of Kyrian's voice. It came to a halt as the group entered the audience chamber. It was a large hall, room enough for several hundred dragons in their human forms. Each Scion had its own section along the outer rim of the room, directly in line with where each Councilmember sat. The vaulted ceilings high above caused voices to carry beyond their normal volume. Protruding from the ceiling were thirteen dragon sculptures, the original leaders of each Scion. They were intricately carved, no details left out, the perfect depiction of their models.

The Council itself was seated around a large, circular ring-like table in the very center of the room, its core empty, a map of the Old World painted on the floor, the dragon kingdoms of old at its center. Kyrian sat at the far end of the room on a raised platform, just beyond the table. There was a gap in front of him in the table itself, so that he could walk into its center whenever he felt the need.

Fitting, Nalaen noted to herself. *He always loved being the center of attention.*

Currently, Kyrian sat on his dais. Nalaen tried to hide her pleasure at the sour look he was giving her.

"Chamberlain, what is the meaning of this? I told you, no interruptions, not even for our errant Princess." Kyrian barked, a demeaning tone as he cast his eyes from the small dragon to Nalaen. "But welcome back, Princess. Enjoy your little... excursion?"

"Sorry, your Majesty, but the Princess just informed me that they returned from across the mountains. I thought you'd want to know right away!" The Chamberlain bowed as he spoke, then stood up, raising his head, a smug smile adorning his tiny face as he cocked his head toward Nalaen. A gasp went around the room, followed by hushed whispers between the members of the Council.

Your Majesty? This really has gone too far...

Nalaen walked forward, entering the gap in the table opposite Kyrian, and several of the nearby Councilors immediately grew silent.

"Oh?" Kyrian remarked, appearing to be apathetic, though Nalaen knew he was probably delighted to hear the news. "I hope it wasn't too far, Princess. The border rules are strict, and no place for a future queen. I should hope you have a good explanation for this."

"I do."

"Well, then please enlighten us," Kyrian waved his hand forward, a devious smile forming.

Nalaen collected herself before she began her reply.

"While we sit comfortably in our halls, forgetful of the atrocities wrought against us in our own lifetimes, the memories of loved ones lost a fleeting reminder we've so carelessly cast aside, our enemy grows bolder. While scouting the reaches of our eastern border in the mountains, I came across this..." Nalaen sneered, playing the part as best she could, though she meant most of the words. She tossed the sack with the head in it at the feet of Kyrian's chair.

Kyrian bent forward, eyeing the sack warily. Seeing the blood-red stains in the sack, he looked up and eyed Nalaen, raising one of his eyebrows.

"What is this?" he asked.

"See for yourself," Nalaen challenged, smirking.

"I don't think I will. Why don't you stop playing games and just say what you mean to say," Kyrian replied, meeting her challenge.

Nalaen stepped forward toward Kyrian, keeping her eyes locked with his. When she reached the sack, she bent down, grabbed one of the corners, and lifted. After a few seconds, the head rolled out in the direction of Kyrian's seat. Several of the closest councilors stood up and gasped at the sight of it.

Kyrian reeled back himself, lifting his feet as the head rolled his direction. It stopped short, almost perfectly, the eyes facing him. His face turned to disgust, and for a few seconds, Nalaen reveled in his reaction. But finally, Kyrian recovered and turned his gaze back to Nalaen, gaining control of his composure.

"This is a serious accusation you bring, Princess," Sorn said, back to his prior demeaning tone. "*If* this is true, the implications of it could have dire consequences for the realm. Are you sure you found this... human, on our side of the mountains?"

"I am," Nalaen replied, her eyes cold. "And I can offer proof that he was no mere wanderer. Because from his thoughts, I came to know our late Queen's murderer." Another gasp went around the room, this time louder, as remarks rose up from around the table. Kyrian's face changed, his smile fading into a look of confusion.

"From his thoughts? That is not a magic taught in our schools these days. So, the errant Princess has learned some of the ancient magics on her own. I should have known you'd be so curious. Begs the question what else you've studied in private. If only our late Keeper were here to weigh in on that."

"If only..." Nalaen replied, her heart racing slightly.

"And what exactly were you doing on the border, anyways?" Kyrian continued, Nalaen releasing the air she'd been holding in her lungs. She regained her composure and continued her charade.

"Our borders have long sat unguarded, the assumed safety due to the peace accord made all those years ago with the humans. As Queen, I plan to make sure we do not fall prey to their treachery. And it seems my mistrust was correct. We cannot expect the humans to uphold their end of the bargain."

"The humans' treachery is unquestionable, but it's been a long time, Princess. They've given us no reason to doubt the integrity of the accord. You're sure this human isn't just some wanderer who lost its way?"

"As I said, I learned who my mother's killer was. A *sangure*," Nalaen spat, the word vile on her tongue. "A random wanderer would not know such things."

"You're not building a good image for yourself so close to Ascension Princess. But seeing as it is just a lesser magic, and that you only used it against a human, we may be willing to let it slide." Kyrian paused, a cruel smile beginning to form. "If... you can provide real proof your claims are as you say. It's well-known the Dragonbloods are the ones who killed your mother."

"I have a name." Nalaen looked around the room, taking care to look at every Councilor there. More whispers were exchanged. Nalaen tried to not show her disgust.

"A name?"

"Grayscale. With one act, I learned what countless others could not. And now that we know who to truly blame for the Queen's death," Nalaen continued, her eyes unmoving from Kyrian's, studying his face for any hint of change, "and for the deaths of my brothers and sisters, no matter my... *sins*, this new information must be decided on. Punish me as you see fit, but only after I have found and brought justice to her murderer. I request leave to repay the blood debt that is owed."

Nalaen's eyes never left Kyrian's. Her words were meant specifically for him—to see if he would show any sign of his guilt in the affair. If anyone would have betrayed her mother, who more likely than the one to inherit rule of the realm. She also knew he might be persuaded if she placed the blame on someone else, which wasn't untrue, but also not the whole of it.

Kyrian kept his gaze locked with hers, but did not seem to reveal any sign of his possible guilt. Even still, Nalaen was not convinced. *I will find out sooner or later, snake.*

"Herald, if I may," came a voice from the table. Nalaen quickly looked over, her eyes resting on Councilor Corignas, who was now standing.

"Yes, Councilor Corignas. What is it?" Kyrian responded with an irritated inflection.

"Herald," she said with a nod and slight bow. "Though the Princess's actions might be questionable, and must ultimately be answered for, aren't you forgetting something?"

Kyrian sat up, looking at the councilor with a questioning look.

"As you well know, this Council was founded on the laws of our ancestors, sworn to uphold them in all matters. As it now stands, I believe the Princess has just made a request." Councilor Corignas looked at Nalaen as she finished her thought, then back toward Kyrian, as whispers reverberated once again amongst the councilors.

"Yes, and?" Kyrian questioned, unsure of where the councilor was going.

"According to our old laws, should a Princess, who is waiting for her time to be crowned Queen when no Queen currently sits on the throne—when that Princess makes a formal request to the High Council, there must be a majority vote against it to prevent her request from being granted."

Nalaen was taken aback by this fortunate turn. She looked around the room at the councilors. Several of them nodded their heads, while others asked questions amongst each other. They all looked back and forth between Councilor Corignas and Kyrian, whose face was becoming redder by the second. Nalaen could see a drop of sweat inching past his temple. He nervously wiped it away, standing up and looking around the room.

"Thank you, Councilor, for your gracious reminder." His voice hinted at disdain, though he tried to hide it. "Very well. We shall put it to a vote then. Just remember when casting your vote, if this goes wrong, the end result could be war, and we all here remember how that went last time." Kyrian eyed each of the members of the council, giving them all a stern look.

"All those in favor of the Princess's request, please stand." Nalaen watched him carefully, following his eyes to see the others' reactions. She could see some of them fidgeting in their seats, eyes averting as he looked at them. Others, she could not read.

Initially, no one stood. Nalaen held her breath, looking at Councilor Corignas. Slowly, the councilor stood back up, looking at Kyrian, then around the room. Nalaen watched as the others exchanged glances with Corignas. Nalaen waited, looking for any other sign of movement but no one else stood.

Kyrian smiled, first looking at Corignas, then at Nalaen.

"It seems you are out of luck, Princess." Kyrian said, his mouth forming a foul grin.

A slight shuffling sound came from the left side of the room. Everyone turned to look, seeing another councilor, Councilor Yseran of Scion Aurius, standing, smiling and nodding at Councilor Corignas, who returned her gesture with a nod. Kyrian's eyes lit up, his expression turning sour. After several more moments, more shuffling came from the other side of the table, just off to Nalaen's right. It was Councilor Siraena of Scion Viridian. She too exchanged nods with Councilor Corignas before looking defiantly toward Kyrian.

Following suit, three more councilors stood, then another. Kyrian looked at each of them, his expression growing more and more infuriated. Nalaen watched in amazement, finding it hard to believe that so many had stood up. She started to count them.

One, two, three... four, five, six. Six!

Currently, six councilors were standing, all of them female. The rest of the remaining councilors, who were still sitting, were male.

Shit, Nalaen thought. She was glad for the six, but she needed seven to make it a majority. Would any of the males stand up? She had little hope, but still held her breath in anticipation, watching them as they looked at each other, then to

Kyrian. He was staring them all down, a more obvious pressure being applied through his gaze now.

Several of the male councilors were resolute in their intent to remain seated, but Nalaen's eyes zeroed in on one of them, a councilor named Hiraeo Sidentis of Scion Te'nebrum. He was looking between the others and Councilor Corignas, mostly avoiding eye contact with Kyrian. Nalaen watched him, hoping he was leaning her way. She looked back to her brother and sister. She could see that Sorn had made the same observation. Talesa, looking bored with the proceeding, was playing with her knives.

Typical.

She turned back to see what Councilor Sidentis would do. She saw him nod in Councilor Corignas's direction. Nalaen could feel her heartbeat intensify, its sound echoing in her ears, as time slowed to a crawl.

Finally, she saw Councilor Sidentis start to move, staring at Kyrian as he did so, the questioning look gone from his face. Once he was at a full stand, he looked to Nalaen and smiled. Unbelieving, Nalaen barely managed to return the gesture. She looked at Councilor Corginas, mouthing a silent "thank you". The councilor nodded with a smile.

"You would side with our rebellious Princess?" Kyrian shouted, no longer containing his anger. "And I thought this a reasonable body, but I can see now that madness has taken hold."

"Councilor Corignas," he said, turning to her. "You started this. Would you please see the Princess out so we can further discuss this in privacy?" He waved her off as he walked back to his seat, sitting down and placing his head in his hands, his fingers massaging his temples. "There must be some... limitations set forth if we are to allow this dangerous game to ensue."

Councilor Corginas nodded, turning toward Nalaen and skirting around the edge of the table to come up beside her. She bowed gracefully, before drawing in close.

"Best do as he says for now. We don't want to anger him further by your presence. Let me deal with him, and then I will report to you on our final decision." Nalaen gave her a look of concern in reply. "Don't worry, I have a plan."

Nalaen nodded, still worried, but also grateful for the councilor's support. They turned and headed for the door, Sorn, Talesa, and the guards in tow, followed by the now mopey Chamberlain. As they neared the exit, Nalaen turned her head to look back, seeing Kyrian glaring at her from atop his pedestal. She wasn't sure how this would all turn out in the end, but no matter what, she felt an immense sense of victory.

That's one win at least, she thought, smiling.

Once outside, the councilor bowed again, then turned to head back inside the audience chamber. Before passing through the doors, she turned to Nalaen. "You have won today, but the fight is not over. We will discuss the details of your request... and your punishment. Please do try not to get into any more trouble. And let's try to avoid dabbling in the old magics, okay?"

"You have my word, Councilor. *We'll* do our best–" she paused, looking at her sister. Talesa uncrossed her folded arms, throwing her hands up in the air, followed by an immature gesture as she turned away, rolling her eyes. "We'll do our best to behave," Nalaen finished with a smirk.

Councilor Corignas bowed one last time, then reached for the doors and began closing them. "See that you do," she said with a smile a mother would use when she was berating her child. "I will come visit you when we're convened."

And with that, the doors closed. Nalaen stood there for a minute, soaking it all in. She had come here today looking for a fight. Though it hadn't gone exactly as planned, she'd at least made it through that fight still standing. Now, all she had to do was wait and see how much that victory would cost her.

They turned to leave, Nalaen noticing the original crowd from before had grown. As they started to walk out, the crowd parted, the same dead stares they'd seen walking in still on their faces. Nalaen looked to the side, seeing the Chamberlain had returned to his chair. He was glaring at her from it, his spectacles scrunched up to the side, his nose raised slightly.

Make that two wins...

Chapter Thirteen

DEVIATION

Aerin looked up at the gates of the Vale's massive wall, Essie shifting nervously below him as they approached the armored guards checking everyone who wished to go through. Aerin reached down and patted her neck.

"It's alright, girl. I know it's a strange sensation. I remember the first time I came near it. They're just going to check our papers and make sure we're allowed to pass." Essie bobbed her head up and down, whinnying, as if she understood, but didn't like it.

The Wall was no small feat, and it was one of the most intriguing things Aerin had ever encountered in his life. Encased with some sort of magical apparatuses, it hummed with a slight energy. To Aerin, and most humans, it had little effect, as its intended goal was to identify and root out anyone of magical origins. To them it *was* harmful. But even though the sensation was nothing more than a dull hum in Aerin's ears, it still set him off the hairs on the back of his neck.

Construction had begun near the end of the Great Dragon Wars, many years before Aerin was born, because of the increased threat the dragons posed. Since the threat of the elder dragons has since been nonexistent, all it did now was serve as a border, giving the rich—and those lucky enough to live in their shadows—their own separate space to thrive. The lands within the Wall, surrounding the capital of Solantria, are rich farmlands, and all manner of trade with the outside world flows through the largest human port of Solharbor, sitting just to the south of the capital.

It was for this reason that the lands beyond the Wall traded yearly with Valehold, the bastion that stood as the gateway to the inner Vale.

Aerin turned his attention ahead, trying to ignore the slight vibration building in his skull. He watched those ahead of him slowly filing through with nods from the guards. As they got closer, he overheard an argument between the guards and a younger-looking couple. He realized they were being turned away, the woman pregnant and crying. Aerin saw the man looking at him as they walked back the way he'd just come, a look of desperation as he tried to console her.

"What's your business in the Vale?" asked one of the guards, Aerin turning quickly to see he was now next in line.

"Aerin Peratos, Emissary to Huntmaster Haromir of the Lodge. I come with a very important message for Lord Valeheart. Here are my papers." Aerin pulled the letter out of his vest, coupled with the papers authorizing him passage, and showed it to the man. The guard took it and eyed it carefully, then did the same to Aerin and Essie and all of Aerin's packed items. Eventually, he handed the items back and nodded.

"Alright, seems legit, but, eh, good luck with the Lord. He's been in an exceptionally foul mood as of late," the guard said with a smirk.

"Of late?" said another guard nearby. "He's always in a foul mood."

They chuckled between themselves, a third joining in. Aerin smiled and nodded, trying to ignore them. He wanted to get through the Wall as quickly as possible.

As he passed between the gates, the hum grew stronger momentarily before, gradually diminishing, and as they moved away from the Wall, it disappeared entirely. Aerin sighed in relief, patting Essie to help calm her down.

They quickly came to the fork in the road just beyond the gate, one direction leading into the heart of the Vale, the other heading up the side of the large hill wherein Valehold sat overlooking the Wall and the lands beyond. He gazed up, seeing he had several hundred feet of winding road to climb to get up the city's gates, which loomed large and foreboding above. There was a line of people steadily climbing toward it–traders and merchants, farmers, and more. Though traffic between the Central and Western Vale wasn't heavy, Valehold served as the only gateway to the western lands, attracting a good bit of trade, though it was rare for most merchants to travel west. Aerin himself had never been sent to Valehold, but he knew others who had. As he looked at all the people and the sheer size of the walls up above him, their stories didn't quite do it justice.

"Alright, girl. Let's get this over with, eh?" Essie cocked her head to the side, eyeing Aerin in her peripheral. She let out another whiney, then started trotting up the incline.

The climb was slow, but after a short while, they reached the top. There were hundreds of people on the landing leading through the large gates. There were various merchant stalls parked outside, a few with customers. Through the gates, Aerin could see hundreds more. Overhead, he saw the recognizable banners of the Vale, blue with a large sun and star symbol, a sword at its center – the seal of Solantria, the capital. Aerin recognized that one, but below those banners waved grey flags, a symbol of a shield with an iron gate in the middle of it. He presumed it to be the symbol of Valehold's lord.

A handful of guards watched these gates too, but unlike at the Wall, they weren't checking anyone here. Instead, they stood, silently watching the crowds as they came and went, their mere presence a deterrence for anyone thinking about acting on the wrong side of the law.

Once through the gates, Aerin came into a wide roadway leading into the heart of the city. The street was lined with houses and shops, dozens more merchants selling directly out of their carts. There were hundreds of people moving about the streets, some haggling with vendors about their various goods, others hauling the items they'd acquired one way or another, and others still just casually strolling along. Aerin even noticed a few shady characters eyeing unaware passersby. Aerin turned around to check that all the sacks attached to his saddle were well secured.

Essie, too, seemed a bit distraught by the sheer number of people, especially in such a tight space. The road was wide enough, but there were so many people it still felt claustrophobic. Aerin calmed her as best as he could, but there was no doubting that they both felt out of place.

When they reached the end of the street, they came into a large, open space. People were busy about their errands here too, but it didn't feel nearly as packed. Before them loomed a large keep, which Aerin presumed could only be the house of Lord Valeheart. It was the highest part of the city, towering well above the castle's walls, the only other building coming close, a tall steeple off and to the left, which looked to be some sort of religious center. There was another gatehouse guarding the entrance to the main keep, smaller walls extending off the sides to separate it from the rest of the city.

Aerin headed straight for the gate, not wanting to waste any time. As he approached, one of the guards came out to greet him.

"Hail, traveler. What business do you have at the keep?" The young man, probably somewhere around thirty winters, wore an extravagant set of polished platemail, which glistened in the afternoon sun. He wore no helmet, his long, black hair well-kept and tied in a small bun behind his head. His dark beard was trimmed, unlike most of the guards Aerin had passed coming in. There was a look about him and Aerin could tell the man commanded some manner of respect, most likely a captain of some sorts.

"Good day, sir. I am Aerin of the Lodge. I come bearing an urgent message for the Lord, from the Huntsmaster himself." Aerin pulled out the letter again, handing it to the knight. The man examined the letter, his eyes resting on the seal.

"I see. I can't guarantee you an audience with the Lord himself, but you can deliver the letter to Steward Albright in the main lobby. I'll have one of the knights escort you in."

Aerin nodded, then started to ride forward, but the knight stepped in his way.

"Sorry, no horses inside the keep. You'll need to stable him–" Essie snorted and kicked her feet. The knight cocked his head to the side, quickly examining Essie, then smiled. "Erm, her... in the guest stalls," he finished, pointing to the stables down the right alleyway against the wall.

"Ah, of course. Thank you..."

"Captain Garlan, at your service," he said with a short bow. Aerin dipped his head in reply, then turned Essie and headed for the stable.

"Nice man," Aerin said out loud.

Essie let out a loud snort, followed by a blow with her lips.

"Hey, he changed what he said."

The stable was mostly empty, with only two other horses occupying the ten stalls. Aerin felt it best to put Essie down on the far end by herself. As they approached it, she let out a throaty neigh, the other horses poking their heads out to look.

"It's alright, girl. It's not the stable back home. No sunlight here, but this should hopefully be quick. I'll let you have the last of the carrots. And if you're good, I saw some fruit and vegetable vendors on the way in. I'll get you something for the next ride."

Essie whinnied, reluctantly walking into the stall. Aerin grabbed the last two carrots from his sack and handed them to her. He patted her as she chewed, then walked out, closing the door and heading back to the gate. When he got there, the Captain was waiting for him with another guard.

"Very good," Captain Garlan said. "This is Barret. He'll escort you to the Steward's office and see that you at least get your message delivered. Good luck, my friend." He bowed again, extending his arm toward the gate as the other knight led the way. Aerin nodded his thanks to the Captain before following the knight through the gate.

Once inside, Aerin looked around. The gatehouse led into a large courtyard, two rows of statues leading to the front door of the keep. The statues were carved from some type of white stone, exquisite and regal. Behind them, on either side, were four square pools of water. There were paths that diverged in the middle, going right and left toward well-maintained gardens with various trees and shrubs. Aerin had never seen anything so grand.

"Sir," the knight Barret called out, bringing Aerin back to reality. "This way, please."

"Uh, yes... sorry. Coming."

The keep itself was much bigger than it had looked from a distance. As Aerin approached the doorway, he strained his neck to look up at it, estimating it was at least four or five hundred feet to the top. More of the grey flags clung to its sides, constant reminders, just in case one forgot.

As they entered, they came into a well-lit foyer. There was seating around the edges of the room, some of them occupied by people that Aerin could only guess were of some nobility, as their mannerisms and attire were of a much loftier quality than the masses outside, and for that matter, Aerin himself. They passed looks of judgement as he entered.

Aerin followed Barret into a room on the right where a man sat behind a desk stacked high with various papers. As they approached, the man looked up at them with a flustered expression, rolling his eyes.

"What is it now, Barret? I don't have time for any more interruptions." The man, who could only be the Steward, peered around the bulky knight to look Aerin up and down, an immediate frown forming. By Aerin's judgement, the Steward was well into his later years, but the large wig on his head made it difficult to tell exactly. Aerin had heard stories of men from the Vale who wore wigs of white. Apparently, it was some sort of fashion statement for the rich and wealthy. He'd only ever seen one once before when a rich merchant harbored his ship in Northreach. It had seemed silly then, and it still seemed silly now. Aerin tried not to chuckle.

"Oh, is something funny?" the Steward inquired.

"No, no sir...," Aerin said, assuming a straight face as best he could.

"And who is this, exactly, that the Captain thinks he can cut the line in front of the both the Duke of Charsborough and the Magistrate's cousins?" The Steward asked, looking to Sir Barret.

"Steward, this man is an emissary from the Lodge, sent here on behalf of the Huntsmaster with an important letter for his Lordship." The Steward leaned sideways and looked Aerin over again.

"I see... I've never seen you before, Emissary. You must be new."

"Yes, sir. Well, I mean, no sir. I've just never been here before," Aerin fumbled, frowning.

"So, you're new... anyways, let's see this *important* letter."

Aerin walked around Sir Barret and up to the edge, leaning over to hand the letter to the Steward across the abnormally large desk. The Steward sat back in his chair, his hand outstretched, waiting just out of reach. Aerin leaned over further, bumping against the desk to place the letter in the man's hand. The Steward eyed him uncomfortably as he waited, finally snatching the letter with a sigh as it reached his hand. Unsure how to react, Aerin straightened back up and stood there waiting, trying not to let his mixed emotions show on his face.

The Steward reached over to a fancy-looking knife sitting on his desk, bringing it to unseal the letter.

"Ah, excuse me, Steward," Aerin said quietly, clearing his thought. The Steward just looked up at him with dazed eyes. "That letter is for the Lord, if you don't mind." The Steward just kept staring at Aerin with an unblinking stare, before finally folding his hands, a smug smirk ensuing.

"Listen, Emissary. I'll explain this because you're new. That is not how this works. You bring your requests to me, and if I don't deem it a waste of the Lord's time, then *I* will bring it to *him*. Understood?"

Aerin, now frustrated, was seriously considering punching the man squarely in his pompous face, but with Sir Barret standing right next to him, he figured it wasn't worth the risk. Aerin just offered a flat smile and nodded as the Steward returned to his task with another sigh. Aerin watched him open the letter and start reading.

When he finished, the Steward looked up at Aerin for several seconds from behind the letter before folding it and standing up.

"I will go see if the Lord is available," he said with a sigh. "I believe he may want to see this himself. Please wait here. You may take a seat, but please don't make a mess," he said with a taste of disdain, looking Aerin up and down another time. Aerin clenched his jaw and turned to go find a seat.

While he waited, Aerin got more annoyed looks from the others waiting in the lobby. He tried to ignore them, looking at the paintings on the walls. There were several of the keep itself, some of various exotic-looking fruits that Aerin didn't recognize, and one very large painting of a man in showy armor with a similar wig to that of the Steward. Aerin figured it must be Lord Valeheart himself. The man looked to be even more pretentious than his Steward, though Aerin found that hard to believe.

After an uncomfortably long time, the Steward finally returned, his face and mannerism in a perturbed state. When he saw Aerin, he frowned, but waved him over.

"Lord Valeheart is greatly distressed to hear this news..."

Aerin let out a small sigh of relief.

"The only reason he looks forward to Winter is the annual fattened boar or elk from the hunters beyond the Wall."

Aerin's relief instantly turned to a frown.

"However, if the Lodge cannot provide its share of bounty as a trade on time, the Lord regrets he cannot exchange goods from the farms in return. And he trusts the Order can handle this nonsense about your missing hunters. His Lordship is heavily preoccupied with the Winter preparations and cannot provide any additional assistance unless your trade arrives–on time and in the agreed upon quantities." The Steward held out the letter, an underwhelming expression on his face.

Aerin wanted sorely to object, but he was so mad that he snatched the letter and turned and stormed out without a word, Sir Barret at his heels. He took one last look back at the Steward before rounding the corner to the doorway, seeing the haughty man's insufferable face one last time. *I'm never coming back here, or I* will *punch that man in the face.*

Once outside, he headed straight for the gate. Captain Garlan was waiting for him.

"Ah, so you've met with the Steward then, I see," the Captain said with a knowing grin.

"Met and wasted my time. I hope I never have to see that man ever again."

"Yes, that's the usual reaction we get from most visitors with any sense about them. The Steward is... an acquired taste, if you will."

"An acquired taste? I've eaten raw meat I could stomach better than him. No, that man is impossible. The Lord too, it would seem."

"Alright, easy now. That is my Lord you're talking about."

Aerin suddenly felt uncomfortable, realizing he'd probably spoken out of turn.

"Sorry. I'm just frustrated. The Huntsmaster entrusted me with this task, and I've failed him."

"What exactly is this task that you were sent here for, if you don't mind my asking?" Captain Garlan inquired.

"We're facing a serious shortage of game, and it may have something to do with the strange happenings going on in the mountains," Aerin noted, his voice sullen.

"Strange happenings?"

"Yes, ah... here's the letter. I suppose there's no harm if you read this, given your status. At least one person with a level head here should be aware of it." Aerin handed the Captain the letter, staring off into the distant sky as he thought about how he was going to deliver the news to Haromir.

"Hmm, I see," Captain Garlan mumbled, finishing the letter. "This is very odd. And the Lord refused to offer aid?"

"Yes, of course. He can't be bothered with all of his no doubt *important* duties. They said we should just wait for the Order of Scales to respond to our plea, and our trade agreement will not be able to be upheld."

"I see... I *am* sorry, my friend. If that is what the Lord said, then I cannot provide you any aid." Captain Garlan paused a moment, stroking his beard. "However, I can still provide you assistance in another way–as a gesture of good faith for the information you've shared. While the Lord may not give much weight to your mysterious claim, I am Captain of the Royal Guard, the safety of the Vale and its people is my sole purpose and duty. I cannot act contrary to the Lord's wishes, but I can see to it that you are properly supplied for your trip." Captain Garlan walked over and whispered something in Sir Barret's ear, who promptly turned and retreated into the hallway built on the side of the gatehouse.

He returned several minutes later, a large sack slung over his back, which he handed to the Captain. Captain Garlan inspected the sack's contents briefly before handing it to Aerin.

"There, this should get you back to Northreach–or, is it to Eastend, then?"

"Yes, I have a message to deliver to Eastend. Hopefully, it is more well-received."

"I'm sure it will be. I have never met anyone from the Order, but I have heard the tales. If what they say is true, those old warriors have saved this kingdom more than once from the fiercest foe we have ever known. If they are still serving that oath after all these years, then I'm sure they can help you with your plight."

Aerin thought heavily on the man's words. He gazed admirably at the Captain, a swell of respect rising in his chest. Though the man was younger than most of the guards, not to mention the fools in charge, he was better than all of them. It's too bad *he* wasn't the one in charge around here.

Aerin smiled at the Captain, thanking him for the supplies before heading back to Essie, who was waiting impatiently for his return.

"Sorry, girl. That took a bit longer than I'd hoped, and unfortunately, their reply was not good. On the bright side, the Captain provided us with some snacks for the next ride," Aerin lifted the sack as he finished, showing it to Essie. She sniffed it cautiously, followed by a low whinny. Aerin placed it inside the now almost empty pack he'd originally prepared for their trip, then grabbed hold of the saddle and pulled himself up.

As they passed the gate on the way out, Aerin saw the Captain coming out to wave goodbye.

"Safe travels, friend. Oh, and to the misses," he said, bowing low as he looked at Essie. "I do apologize."

"Captain," Aerin started, remembering something. "You are an honorable man, and for that, I am glad we have met. There was a couple outside the Wall on my way in. The woman was with child, and the guards there turned them away. Might there be anything the Captain of the Royal Guard can do about that, at least?"

"Hmm. My area of influence rests primarily within these walls, but there may be something I can do about the treatment of people at the Wall," he said, his face scrunched in thought. "Thank you for bringing it to my attention. I'll see what I can do. I hope we meet again, Emissary," he finished with a bow.

"Likewise, Captain," Aerin replied, nodding.

Aerin kicked Essie's side and she turned, heading back the way they'd come through the main road leading out of the city. It was no less crowded, despite the sun setting lower in the sky. Several men were now walking up and down the street lighting the streetlamps in preparation for the approaching evening.

They made much better time heading down than they had coming up, and it wasn't long before they were at the bottom and heading back to the Wall. The trickle of people was smaller now, with only several men pulling carts on the road ahead of them. Aerin saw the guards up ahead, who spotted him as he approached.

"And how'd it go with the Lord, eh? I'm guessin' he wasn't much help by the look on yer face," he blurted out, laughing with the others. Aerin ignored him and rode on, passing through the large archway, wanting only to get some distance from the Wall and the hum, which had returned. He saw the couple was still outside, the husband pacing back and forth as the wife sat resting on nearby rock.

Aerin heard the guards still laughing amongst each other as he reached the fork in the road. He stopped there and paused, the words of the Captain coming back to him.

Aerin reached inside his sack and grabbed a few items, holding them out toward the distraught husband.

"I think you need these more than me," he said.

The man was taken aback by the generosity, hesitated a moment before he came and took the items with a bow.

"Thank you, kind sir," he offered.

Aerin bowed his head and turned Essie, who snorted when she realized he'd given away some of her treats. Aerin smiled, pulling out an apple from his pocket and handing it to her.

"Saved some for you. Alright, let's get to Eastend. We've got a message to deliver."

Essie shifted under him, shaking her head with a series of snorts.

"I know," he said, patting her neck, "but we've got another message to deliver. We need to do this for Yoghar and Kanir—for the people beyond the Wall. We need help, otherwise those apples of yours are going to get scarce come winter. Perhaps the Order can help with all of our problems."

Essie stomped her feet lightly, giving Aerin the sense she didn't like what he was saying, but after a moment, she turned and pointed down the western road.

Aerin heard a commotion behind him and turned around to see what was going on. He saw a knight with black hair and much fancier armor talking with the Wall guards and pointing toward the couple outside. Two of the guards came out to the couple, one of them the one who'd turned them away in the first place. Aerin watched as they escorted the couple to the gate, passing to the other side. The fancy knight waved in Aerin's direction, to which he returned the gesture with a wide smile before kicking Essie and starting off on a gallop along the western road.

"To Eastend we go. Let's hope they are more amenable than the Lord of Valehold," he said out loud. Essie neighed in reply.

If only the world was filled with more men like Captain Garlan.

CHAPTER FOURTEEN

CRIES

Mara sat up in her bed, some strange sound stirring her from her sleep. The room was dark, and she could not see the other side of it. Waiting, she sat there silently, listening.

There it is again. But... what is it?

It sounded strange, like nothing she'd ever heard before. It sounded faint and distant, echoing through the corridors of the keep from some unknown source. She placed her feet on the floor. It was cold. She reached her hand over, feeling for her boots in the darkness and slipping them on. She knew her coat was on the wall, above where she kept her boots. The room felt abnormally chilly, so she grabbed that as well and pulled it tight around her. Standing up, Mara crept quietly out of the room, using the wall to guide her to the door.

Once outside, Mara could see several lone candles going down the hallway toward the exit of her dormitory section. The candles weren't bright enough for her to see much, but they at least helped guide her way out.

She heard it again and could tell the sound was coming from somewhere beyond the end of the hall. Quietly she crept forward, being careful not to wake anyone else. It was deathly quiet, which seemed odd, but it was the middle of the night.

Once she reached the end of the hallway, she peered out, looking both ways down the corridor that led through the central part of the keep. There were a few torches lit, which emanated more light, but it was still quite dark. There was no movement in either direction. She stopped there for a minute, waiting for the sound to repeat itself. After a short time, it came again, sounding as though it had come from the right. A chill wind blew from the direction of it, causing the hallway torches to flicker.

Strange.

She continued after the sound, heading down the corridor, watching for any signs of movement. She heard it once more before reaching the end, a bit louder this time. Another flicker.

Once she reached the end of the hall, she stopped and waited. She knew the right hall would take her to the arena, whereas the left went into the center of the keep. There were still no signs of movement. She thought she would have seen someone by now, but it seemed the entire keep was asleep, though there were always guards on the walls outside. Maybe they couldn't hear it from out there.

It came again. Mara looked left, its call guiding her deeper into the keep, so she continued on. The corridor coming up on the left went into the heart of the keep, a place she had not been often. As she came closer to it, she heard the sound again, and it was coming from that direction. She stopped as she rounded the corner, unsure whether she should proceed.

Hesitating, the sound repeated itself, louder and, somehow, more desperate. Still seeing no one, Mara decided to go, creeping along the long hallway. She could see a large room up ahead, this one a little bit brighter than the rest of the keep. As she neared the room, she slowed her pace, listening for signs of anyone who might be inside. But all she heard was the faint sound of the wind, which seemed to be coming from in front of her. The air got a little colder and she wrapped her arms around her tighter to keep her body heat from escaping.

Stepping into the light of the room, she could see it was empty, with only torches lining the wall. What stood out to her was the enormous door at the far side of the room, its surface depicting an epic battle between man and dragon. *Garn fighting with the dragon queen Liotha.*

Behind the doors was the room known as The Heart. It was meant for important matters, and typically only the Scalewarden's closest advisors met there. Mara had never been permitted entrance. Mara approached them cautiously, pressing her ear against its surface. It, too, was cold to the touch. A chill ran down her spine as she stood there, waiting for the sound.

In response, it cried out again, and Mara pulled away, looking at the doors. It was much louder now, and was definitely coming from behind them. The room was normally off-limits. She questioned whether or not to proceed. Turning back, there was still no one coming. She inspected the doors further, eyeing the two large handles in the middle. She walked over to one of them, tugging slightly. The door was heavy, but not as heavy as she'd expected. As she pulled, it slowly creaked open, the sound of metal grinding against metal causing an echo to reverberate down the hall behind her. She looked back, but other than the fading echo, the keep was still silent.

She poked her head around the edge of the door, peering inside. Nothing but darkness stared back at her. She felt a chill wind blow from inside the dark room beyond. The sound came again, much louder this time. Mara knew she was close. It was somewhere in this room, or somewhere just beyond it. Mara turned to her left, looking at the torch on the wall in the outside room. She walked over and grabbed it, pulling it out of the sconce. It came freely. She turned back to the cracked door, holding the torch up in front of her to see if she could see anything, but the light's reach was limited. She could see the short set of stairs leading downward. Turning one more time to look for anyone, she squeezed inside.

The room felt even colder in here, the fire from the torch casting little heat, though she held it close. She could hear her footsteps echoing through the darkness as she descended the wide stairs. There were only ten or so steps until she reached the bottom floor, though she had been too distracted to count. Once there, she nearly bumped into a large table in front of her. The table was circular in nature, but it had straight outer edges that extended several feet before hitting a point, then moving onto a new edge. In front of these edges were large, ornate chairs. Mara placed her hand on the nearest one, feeling its smooth surface. She held up her light to try to see the entire table, but the darkness prevented it from reaching that far. *Why does the darkness seem so... dark here?*

She reached her hand down to the table, feeling its surface. It was smooth, with some sort of filigree carved into it. As she held the light up, it formed some design, which also looked oddly familiar to her.

The mysterious sound came again, causing her to jump. It echoed loudly in the room, as if it was coming from just on the other side of the table.

She moved slowly toward where it had come from, edging around the table, holding her light up to guide her steps. Reaching what she thought was the other end of the table, she turned, looking for the wall. She could not see it, so she slowly stepped forward, toward where she thought the sound originated. As she looked around, something above her caught her attention. There was an archway built into the stone above her, seeing a large pair of feet. At first glance, they looked almost lifelike, causing her heart to leap in her chest. But holding her torch up higher, she could see it was only an ornately carved statue. The light of the torch did not reach the upper half of the man's body, so she couldn't tell who it was.

Mara then realized she could hear the faint sound of wind coming from in front of her. And then, the sound cried out once more, Mara quickly turning her attention back toward its source, which was through the archway just ahead of her in the back of the room. After several more steps she saw a door, much smaller than the one she'd come through previously. It was engraved with the same design she saw on the table, the door itself made entirely of metal. She touched its surface, and it was even colder still, so much so that Mara recoiled in pain.

Why is it so cold?

Mara inspected the door further, bringing her light in close. She could see the hints of frost near the cracks along its edges, and a cold wind blew from underneath.

Strange...

Mara thought she heard a sound, but this one was different, much softer than the one she'd been following. She brought her face closer to the door, getting her ear as close to it as she dared without touching it. She paused and listened carefully, trying to calm her breathing. She could hear the wind coming from behind the door, but there was something else, too; something almost human.

There it is, but what is it?

It sounded like the cry of a child, though it was ever so faint, barely audible over the wind. Mara quickly pulled back, now worried that some child was stuck out in the cold beyond the door, though she had no idea how this passage could possibly lead outside. She searched and found the door handle. She tried to pull, but this door was heavy—much heavier than the first. The chill of it burned her hand, and she recoiled in pain again. She tried to think quickly of what to do.

An idea came to her. She brought the torch up, placing its fire on the handle. She left it there for 10 seconds or so, then pulled it back, checking it with her free hand. It was still just as cold. She put the torch back and waited a bit longer, then checked again. No difference. *Strange. Maybe if I pull quickly with both hands...*

Mara looked around for somewhere to place the torch. By a stroke of luck, there was a holder on the side wall, next to the door. She quickly placed the torch there, then grabbed the door's handle with both hands, straining to pull it free. There was a slight crackling sound, as if ice was breaking, but the door still did not move. She braced her feet against the wall, trying to pull more vigorously, her hands burning from the cold. More sounds of ice cracking, but the door still resisted.

With a renewed sense of urgency, Mara tried once more, pulling with every ounce of strength she could muster. The sound of ice cracking intensified, and she thought she could feel the door budging ever so slightly. With one last surge of strength, pain shooting through her fingertips, Mara heaved on the door. A loud sound of ice cracking echoed through the hall, and then, at last, the door swung free, a massive gust of cold wind bearing down on her from beyond.

The torch on the wall instantly went out, leaving Mara alone in the darkness, staring into the icy void beyond the door. Mara felt cold—so cold. She heard the cries of the child coming from the icy dark in front of her. She stumbled forward, feeling for some grip, her body starting to grow numb.

She held her hand up in front of her face and peered into the darkness. Just as she was about to take a step forward, there was a loud cry, and a black shadow flew past her. She jumped to the side, turning around to watch the shadow of what looked like a bird fly through the room, traces of light from the keep's hall beyond reflecting along its feathers. Mara strained her eyes to see it, when suddenly the wind stopped and the door behind her slammed shut. In the same instance, her torch sparked back to life, its glow illuminating the room again, and she saw what had flown past her. It was a black raven, sitting on the table in the center of the room, staring at her, its head cocked to the side.

Mara felt herself drawn to the raven's gaze. She felt the world around her begin to spin, like a vortex, drawing her closer to it. She began to panic, her mind struggling to understand what was happening.

With a flash of light and a jolt, Mara awoke, finding herself back in her own room, the dim light of a nearby lamp flickering gently on her nightstand.

It was just a dream? But it felt so—

Mara looked down at her hands. They still felt numb. She touched her face. *Freezing! But... how?*

There was a loud knock on Mara's door. She shook her head, still in a daze, and stood up slowly to answer it. Before she could get to it, the knocking intensified, followed by Kai's muffled voice from the other side.

Mara cracked the door, the light from the hallway almost painful on her still tired eyes.

"What is it, Kai?" she said, blinking.

"A message just arrived from the Lodge. Uncle wants to see us right away."

"A message?" Mara asked.

"Yes. From the hunters. A raven just delivered it, and it sounds urgent."

"Did you say a raven?" Mara asked, stunned.

"Yes..." he said, giving her a strange look. "That's how messages normally get delivered. Rough night?"

"No, sorry... I just–" Mara paused, trying to calm her mind. "Just give me a minute."

"Alright. Just hurry. I don't know why Uncle wants to see us, but I think it might have something to do with the message."

Kai was clearly excited, and before Mara could respond, he zipped off down the hall, leaving her alone with her thoughts, staring out into the empty hallway.

It's just a coincidence... right?

There was only one way to find out.

CHAPTER FIFTEEN

OPPORTUNITY

Kai sat outside Yoren's office, bouncing his knee up and down. *Where is Mara?*

He could see inside his uncle's office from where he sat and was watching him talk to a couple of the older Dragonbloods, Thorlan and Cyrus. It seemed the two of them were arguing with each other, Yoren attempting to moderate as best he could. From where Kai sat, he couldn't quite make out the details of the conversation. He was pretty sure he heard his and Mara's names, though.

Kai leaned forward as far as he could, trying to discern what they were saying when Mara rounded the corner of the hallway and stopped to stare at him, a confused smile forming.

"Ah, just stretching," Kai said, awkwardly shifting into an actual stretch before sitting back in his seat.

"Stretching. Right," Mara said with a giggle, her arms crossed.

"Fine, you caught me. I was trying to listen in on their conversation," Kai said, tipping his head toward the doorway to their uncle's office. He stood up and came closer to Mara. "I think I heard our names."

"Our names? What are they talking about?" Mara asked, her tone indicating her curiosity was piqued.

"Well, if I knew that, I wouldn't have been leaning forward, now would I?"

"Right... Do you think it has to do with what Uncle wanted to see us about?"

"Maybe," Kai shrugged.

They both turned their attention to the heated conversation. After a moment, Yoren looked their way, nodding to the two of them. Kai saw him mouth a few more words, Thorlan and Cyrus turning to look out at the two of them, Thorlan glaring and Cyrus the opposite. They both then turned back to Yoren, bowed, and took their leave.

As they left, Yoren waved to Kai and Mara, beckoning them to enter. Kai heard Thorlan mumble something under his breath as they passed by. Cyrus, on the other hand, greeted them with his usual smile—broad and genuine. He was always kind, and Kai had enjoyed the time spent with them over their years learning how to be Dragonbloods.

Kai smiled back to Cyrus and proceeded into his uncle's office, Cyrus bowing and taking his leave.

"Kai, Mara," Yoren began, nodding at the chairs in front of his desk. "Please, have a seat."

Kai and Mara did as they were told, each taking a chair. While he was their uncle, he was still the Spear, and the position demanded their respect. It was something they'd had to get used to over the years.

"Now, I'm sure you're both wondering why you're here," Yoren continued.

Kai nodded earnestly, looking at Mara, her nod more apprehensive.

"Alright," Yoren chuckled. "I can see Kai, at least, is eager to know. Well, I promised you I'd put in a good word with the Scalewarden, Kai. He agreed, so we'd like to ask you and your sister to join the party that's going to investigate the missing hunters."

"Missing hunters?" Kai said, his excitement fading.

"Yes. We just received a raven from the Lodge. Three of their own have gone missing. It's been about three weeks, which means they would have been out when the dragon came through. And according to them, it's possible the hunters wandered up near its path. Considering the danger, they asked us to send a team out to try and locate them."

"Why don't they just send some of their own people?" Kai asked, not fully understanding the nature of the request. It sounded more like an errand to him than the duty of a Dragonblood.

"The hunters aren't trained in fighting dragons, and with the sighting of one so recently, they're a bit spooked. Plus, they're busy dealing with their own issues, compounded even more with several of theirs missing. Besides, I thought you wanted an opportunity to get out there, Kai?"

"I do. I just didn't think it would be tracking down a couple of lost hunters in the woods."

"Well, that's the thing, Kai. I'm pretty doubtful that you'll find them."

"Huh?" Kai asked, even more confused.

"I think what Uncle–I mean, the Spear–means is it's probable the dragon got them..." Mara chimed in, finally breaking her silence.

"I don't want to rule out they might still be alive, but if I'm being honest, that does seem the most likely outcome given the circumstances. And if that is the case, we'll need people who are experienced in tracking dragons to confirm it."

"Okay," Kai said with a sigh. "And what about what you said earlier, Uncle? About the dragon?"

"Kai, I told you we needed–"

"I already told Mara what you said–about its size and injuries."

"I see," Yoren said, giving Kai a stern look, which quickly faded into a condemning smile. "Well, then I suppose Mara's already given it some thought. Find anything?"

"Nothing definite," Mara replied, her cheeks turning red, followed by a smile. "The lesser dragons were driven out of their homes in droves during the wars, for obvious reasons. That was the last time a dragon of that size was spotted—well, other than... but that was an isolated incident. But that doesn't really explain why it would be happening now."

"Yes," Yoren said, a distant look in his eyes. "I do remember. But you're right. It doesn't make sense for it to be happening now. The Huntsmaster's letter did make mention of a wildlife shortage, and now that I think about it, our own hunters have been coming up a bit short these days. Perhaps the two are somehow related."

"A wildlife shortage? Strange. That could make sense why it would wander out further, but if true, that just presents more questions..." Mara said, trailing off.

"Strange indeed," Yoren admitted.

All this talk was beginning to get Kai excited again, though he cared less about the wildlife and more about the appearance of large dragons. If whatever was causing it to occur was starting up, perhaps more would be sighted. Perhaps, even while they were out.

"When do we leave?" Kai butted in, causing both Yoren and Mara to emerge from their thoughts.

"Hah," Yoren chuckled. "Back to your eager self then, I see. You will leave first thing in the morning. Cyrus is already informing the others. Caliena will lead your expedition, and you'll have one other experienced knight. Bran Lightfoot."

"Caliena," Kai groaned. "*And* Bran?"

"Yes. Is that a problem?" Yoren asked, his eyebrow raising.

"It's just..." Kai started, but saw his uncle's stern expression. "No, sir. It's fine."

Yoren nodded, though he continued to study Kai for a few more seconds.

"I was also given permission for you to bring several of your friends along. This is a good opportunity to get some field experience and stretch your legs."

Kai's eyes lit up, and when he looked at Mara, he could see that even she was a bit perkier at the mention of their friends.

"How many?" Mara asked.

"Considering there's not much going on at the moment, I don't see why you can't bring six."

Kai and Mara exchanged broad smiles.

"Mara, you may leave. I need to have a brief word with your brother."

Mara glanced at Kai, giving him the usual look that said she knew he was about to get a scolding. Kai tried not to smile, exchanging an awkward stare as she walked out the door.

"I trust that whatever is going on between you and the other knights," Yoren started once Mara was gone, "will be over by the time you come back. If we are to function as a unified body, we can't be bickering amongst ourselves."

"I... understand," Kai said, holding back his true thoughts.

"I know it's difficult, serving without dragon's blood in your veins, but you must do your best with what you've been given. We all have our purpose to play. It might be taking longer for you to find yours, Kai, but keep your head up and your mind focused on what matters most. If you do that, I believe it will find you."

Kai nodded. He wasn't sure how much he believed his uncle's words, but he at least appreciated the effort.

"Safe journey," Yoren said as Kai stood, making for the door. "Look after your sister."

"Yes, sir," Kai replied.

***

The next morning, Kai woke up well before dawn. He yawned. Sleep hadn't come easy, his excitement getting the better of him. The candle beside his bed still had about a quarter left, so he knew it was still a bit early, but he couldn't stay in bed a minute longer.

Outside, the stars still shone brightly in the sky, the hint of the first rays of sunlight somewhere beyond the horizon. With all his things ready, Kai decided to go up on the outer wall and watch the sun rise.

As he stood there, gazing up at the stars, his thoughts drifting through recent events, he quickly came to dwell on the thoughts of the recent dragon attack and what it might mean. If the dwindling animal populations and the appearance of an older dragon were linked, it could mean more was going on than just another random sighting. And though Kai didn't know what explanation might be hidden behind these events, the thought of it excited him, nonetheless.

"Couldn't sleep either, I see?" came Mara's voice from behind him.

"No. Of course not," Kai replied, smiling at Mara. "Am I so predictable?"

"When I saw your door open, I wasn't surprised. And yes, you are predictable. It wasn't hard to find you."

Kai grinned, letting out half of a laugh, turning back to gaze at the stars.

"I'm trying not to get too worked up about this. It's probably nothing, but part of me–"

"Wants it to be more?" Mara finished Kai's thought as she came up to stand beside him.

"I really am predictable."

"To me, at least," Mara said, smiling as she bumped her hip against him. "Part of me hopes it's more, too. I just hope it isn't something bad."

"Yes, I expected you'd think that. Is it bad that I do hope that?" Kai asked, a hint of embarrassment showing in his expression. "Not that anything bad happens, just–"

"No, I understand. I know what you mean. If I'm being truthful, I've thought about that a lot lately. Part of me hopes that things change for us. I know you're hopeful about this, and I'm hopeful that it can somehow lead you to something better."

"My little sister, always looking out for me," Kai jested, bouncing his hip against her this time.

"Big sister," Mara corrected, giving him a sly look.

"You were only born minutes before me, and by my count..." Kai replied, lifting his hand up to measure the distance between the top of her head and his.

Mara pushed Kai gently, smiling.

Kai pretended like her push had sent him off-balance, grinning at her. It had been a running joke ever since they'd turned about thirteen and he'd shot up nearly a head taller than her. It was around then he'd filled out into his body, looking more like a man than a child.

Kai glanced back up at the sky, noticing a light blue hue faintly along the ridgeline of the distant mountain peaks.

"Looks like dawn is almost here. We should probably go see if the others are getting ready," Kai said, growing more serious.

Mara followed his gaze, then nodded solemnly.

"Time to find out for ourselves what's going on. You ready?" Kai asked, feeling a pulse of apprehension and excitement at the same time.

"Ready as I'll ever be, I suppose," Mara said.

Chapter Sixteen

STIPULATIONS

Nalaen stood quietly, her eyes scanning the room she grew up in. It brought back a flood of memories, not all of them good.

The room had changed greatly over the years as she grew from a young hatchling into a full-grown adult. Though the room had changed, she could still see it now as it was all those years ago. She'd grown up without a mother, and she'd never known her father. She presumed he might still be alive, but there was no telling. The fathers of young dragon princesses were of little concern, and they were rarely ever known. The Queens shared their bed with whichever suitors they thought would yield the strongest offspring. Once they performed this deed, they were almost never included, nor formally recognized, as part of the family. Such was the way of the Queenmothers; or so, at least that's what Velicos had told her all those years ago. Soon enough, she would know for herself.

As she walked about the room, there were remnants of her days as a hatchling. The room itself was large, because hatchlings did not learn to assume their human forms until after a few cycles. Nalaen learned when she was five. Velicos had told her then that it had been early, that she had a gift. She didn't see it as a gift. Rather, it felt more like a curse, never fully understanding why the gods would limit them so, only to disappear and never be heard from again.

But because she'd started out her life with scales, there were scorch marks and gashes that remained on some of her furniture, as well as along the walls. She ran her fingers now across the headboard of her bed. Though it had been painted over at least a dozen times, she still felt the groove marks of where she'd scratched it repeatedly with her hatchling claws. She'd had many nightmares as a youngling, mostly involving her mother's death, but there were others about the creatures who'd killed her mother. As a child, she saw them as demonic beings of immense power. Now, she knew better.

"I remember the first time you had a nightmare," came Velicos's voice from behind her. "You were only a few days old. It was right after they brought you back from the front." Velicos came up to stand beside Nalaen, who was still staring at the bed. "It was the most heart-breaking sound I had ever heard. And you had them so frequently, we didn't know what to do. I tried to have the painters cover it up, hoping that maybe, over time, you'd forget. But how could I have been so naïve..."

Nalaen looked over at Velicos, a warmth in her heart swelling that she tried to suppress. Apart from Sorn, Velicos was one of the few who'd actually been there for her and supported her as she grew. She'd grown bitter at a young age, often causing trouble and being reprimanded for it. That was not how a princess was supposed to behave, they said. The whole kingdom judged her for it. But Velicos, he never did. He had been a faithful and loyal follower. She'd never fully recognized or appreciated it growing up. In fact, she was mean to him more often than she cared to admit. Part of her wanted to hug him now, to tell him how much she truly appreciated him, but the thoughts of her plans came sweeping in and she buried those feelings deep down within her vengeful heart.

"Did you have any luck finding allies?" Nalaen asked, her tone cold and flat.

"I did put out a call that the Princess needed aid, but I had to be careful. If word of this were to get to Kyrian, he'd most certainly put a stop to it. We shall wait to see who responds. But as I hear, you had some support from within the Council itself?"

"Yes. Councilor Corignas was a somewhat unexpected turn of events, though I had hoped her loyalties would remain with us. She was bolder than I anticipated, and she saved us when failure was imminent. It would seem Kyrian has not been able to sway the Mothers as much as he has the Wyrms."

"Yes, I expected as much. He has many allies, of that, I am sure. There are whispers in the streets that many would see a Wyrmlord on the throne again. These whispers started to surface some years after your mother was slain. Many felt the Queens had grown too arrogant, and that the wars in the human lands would eventually come to our gates. That did not come to pass, but it was enough to sway many to Kyrian's side in the early cycles, and he has nurtured that sentiment since. I never suspected he would be so bold as to assume the throne for his own, but you must be careful, Princess. I know he will try to use your situation to his own ends, and I fear it may lead us into a conflict far greater than your plight with the human who killed your mother."

"I will be careful. Once Mother's murderer has been brought to justice..." Nalaen paused slightly, contemplating her words. "When they see I am fit to lead this kingdom, then I will return and deal with Kyrian and his conspirators. With him out of the way, we can lead the dragons into a new dawn. We have sat idly by for far too long, the world too long forgotten who its true masters are. We used to be a great civilization–the keepers of this world. Mother knew it, and she tried her best, but she underestimated the humans. I will not make that same mistake."

"Sister." Sorn appeared in the doorway, bowing respectfully as Nalaen looked his way. "The Councilor is here with news from the High Council. She's waiting for you in the Reception Hall."

Nalaen's eyes lit up, a smile forming as she nodded to Sorn. He bowed again, then turned and left. As Nalaen left the room, she stopped close to Velicos, leaning toward him and placing her hand on his shoulder.

"We will see our family's position restored. I promise you. And it will be in part because of your help. The royal family thanks you for your loyalty."

Velicos stood there quietly for some time after Nalaen's departure, contemplating all that she had said, a troubled expression etched in the lines of his weary face.

He walked over to her bed, looking down at it, his eyes focusing on the paint-covered claw marks of her youth. He wished they could go back in time. Things were much simpler then. Though Nalaen had been through a lot, and he did not want to see her relive her nightmares, it had been a time when she relied on him wholly as her caretaker. It was a gift—the greatest gift he'd received over his long years of service to the royal family. Though there were many proud moments over his long lifetime, none touched him quite so much as those years that Nalaen looked to him like a father. And nothing pained him more than when she treated him more like a servant.

She was not his daughter. She never had been, and she never would be. But he had hoped that one day she would at least understand how much he truly cared for her. He was proud of who she had become, but he also harbored a great deal of fear for her future. He ran his fingers over the marks on her bed, his heart heavy.

"The nightmares never truly left you, did they, my sweet *filia*."

***

Downstairs, Nalaen descended the long staircase leading down into the main foyer of the palace. The Reception Hall, which was off to her left, was the main area where the royal family entertained its many guests when they came to call. It had seen little use in recent years.

When Nalaen was a younger, she remembered spending a great deal of time in this room, as hundreds had come to pay their respects to the family after her mother's death. But over time, visits came less and less often. Eventually, they stopped altogether.

Entering through the doorway, past the two guards at its entrance, she saw that Councilor Corignas was there talking with Sorn and Talesa. There were several trays on the small table near where they were seated—an assortment of refreshments at the ready. Several servants were waiting on the far edge of the room, standing by in case their assistance should be required. Nalaen waved them away as she came up to sit on the couch across from the Councilor. Seeing her arrival, the Councilor moved to stand, but Nalaen motioned for her to remain seated.

"Good morning, Councilor," Nalaen offered.

"Good morning, Princess."

"I presume by your presence here that the Council has made its decision?"

"Yes, the Council has…" the Councilor started, eyeing Nalaen closely. "It took some deliberation to talk Kyrian down from his fit, but I believe we've come to an agreement that will satiate both your thirsts."

"Go on," Nalaen said, her eyes narrowing.

"The High Council has agreed to grant your request–" Nalaen smiled, looking over at Sorn, "–on several conditions." Nalaen's brow furled as her eyes focused intently back on the Councilor. "You may exact your revenge against your mother's killer, if you are indeed sure you have the correct person."

"I am."

"Very well, then once this human has been found, and you must do so with the utmost tact, being careful that there is no… collateral damage. We don't want to incite another war. Once found, you are to bring them back to Dor'Dragos to stand trial before the High Council. We will decide his fate and you will *quietly* wait out the remainder of your time until coronation."

"What?" Nalaen raged, barely able to contain the beast within.

Sorn sat up, apprehension apparent in his features. He waved his hand, trying to calm her.

"These ridiculous conditions are no doubt Kyrian's doing?" Nalaen asked, ignoring Sorn, though she tried to calm herself.

"These conditions are from the Council. As a whole, we felt it best to prevent another war from breaking out. Many of us understand and support your motives, Princess, trust me; but we must ensure that your results are… precise, and appropriate, if you understand what I mean. We have an accord to maintain. Due process must be adhered to."

"The Council thinks so little of me, then?" Nalaen stood and began pacing back and forth.

"We have faith in our Princess. These are merely precautions, should any–" she stopped, her eyes darting in Talesa's direction, "–complications arise."

Nalaen saw the Councilor's eyes land on Talesa. Her sister also saw, understanding the gist of what the Councilor was saying. Talesa moved to object, but Nalaen silenced her with a wave.

"My sister understands the objectives and will not overstep her bounds. As for the Council, I don't appreciate being confined to these… limitations. Is there anything else I should know?" Nalaen questioned, more sarcastic than anything.

"There is… one more thing, your Grace."

Nalaen turned and stared hard at the Councilor, who bore a serious look of her own. Nalaen had to give the Councilor credit. She had a certain commanding air about her. Not many could hold their composure so calmly in Nalaen's presence.

"More? What more could there possibly be?" Nalaen asked, her anger flaring once again.

"In order to ensure these conditions are adhered to, you will be taking a small contingent of the Royal Guard with you–both for your own safety, and for the success of the mission. And apart from your brother and sister, you may take no others."

Nalaen's eyes lit up as she was no longer unable to contain herself.

"So, the Council wants to babysit me *and* take my vengeance away! The guards are no doubt in the employ of Kyrian. Do you think me such a fool?"

The Councilor stood, walking over to Nalaen, pulling her away from the main doorway into the Reception Hall, her eyes darting toward the guards outside. She spoke loudly enough for only Nalaen to hear.

"Princess. You are not wrong. I have no doubt that these guards are in Kyrian's employ. And I do not know what his play is, but there is good news. One of them, Drae'tar Kavriel, is a friend. He is the second highest-ranking member of the guard that will be escorting you. I have been working to gain allies in the guard for some time, but Kyrian has a tight grasp on them. His lead drake, Drae'vir Cathan, will be in charge. He is too close to Kyrian, and I could not get to him, so we must rely on Kavriel for information about their objectives. But you must do so carefully, so as not to alert the others of an insider. Do you understand?"

Nalaen's anger lessened as the Councilor spoke. She was still furious with this final requirement from the Council, but she nodded to the Councilor slowly. She would find a way to get around these hindrances. No host of Kyrian's would keep her from the blood she was owed.

"I understand," she said out loud, calming herself enough to lie.

Talesa had been waiting for her chance to speak, and she approached the two of them.

"You understand? They think that we need to be watched like hatchlings. They want to take away *our* vengeance, and you *understand*? You've grown soft, Sister." There was a cold look in her eyes, defiance emanating through the hiss between gritted teeth.

"Quiet, Sister," Nalaen said in a soft, but menacing tone, walking closer to Talesa. "I will explain everything once the Councilor has left." Talesa looked to the Councilor, then back at Nalaen. She grunted and retreated to her seat on the couch. Nalaen watched her sister sit, then moved back over to the Councilor.

"Thank you, Councilor Corignas. Though I do not like it, I accept the High Council's decision," she offered, loud enough for the whole room to hear. "When can we expect to leave, then?"

"Your escort should be ready by this evening. If you wish to leave tonight, which I'm sure you do, that would be best. If you leave under the cover of darkness, that should draw less attention." The Councilor bowed to Nalaen. "Oh, and Princess..." she said, looking squarely into Nalaen's eyes. "Do try to be careful and return to us in one piece. The kingdom needs its Queen. Plus, I sincerely want to see Kyrian disappointed at your successful return." The Councilor let out a sly smile, then turned on her heels and left.

After the Councilor was gone, Nalaen went over and sat on the couch across from where Talesa was sitting. She motioned for Sorn to come closer. Once they were all close, she leaned in and started talking softly.

"Kyrian is granting our request, but of course, he wants me on a leash. The Councilor said that the escort is *mostly* loyal to Kyrian, but there is one—the second-in-command, Drae'tar Kavriel—who can help us. We have no idea what Kyrian is planning exactly, but we can assume that it is no good and we cannot trust any of the others. We must rely on this Drae'tar to aid us."

"Why don't we just kill the others and be done with it? I'm just itching to spill some blood," Talesa said, a strikingly nonchalant mannerism as she sat there.

"No, that won't do," Sorn interjected. "The Princess can't just go around killing guards she suspects of disloyalty without reason. Sister," he said, turning to Nalaen, "who is the guard in charge?" Talesa rolled her eyes and scoffed, but Sorn and Nalaen ignored her.

"Drae'vir Cathan. I believe that's what she said. Sound familiar?"

"I might know who that is. If he's in charge, it must be one of Kyrian's closest guards. I've seen several skulking about in the shadows, never more than an earshot away from the Herald. But, if he's a Drae'vir, then he only outranks our wyrm by one—Drae'tar is just below Drae'vir. If we can somehow dispose of him on accident, or show he's acting out of line with our orders, then our wyrm can take charge and keep the others in line."

"Hmm... that could work. Good thinking, Brother," Nalaen said, nodding. Talesa scoffed again, then stood up and headed for the door.

"And what of this requirement for us to bring Grayscale back alive?" Talesa objected, a bit too loudly.

"Quiet," Nalaen shushed her sister, looking at the doorway. "I will come up with a plan, but there's no way I'm letting them steal my vengeance."

"Our vengeance," Talesa interjected, garnering a sharp look from Nalaen.

"Yes, *our* vengeance..." she added with a scoff. "We will have his blood before this is over."

"We better," Talesa butted in. "You promised me blood."

"And you'll have it. Just make sure you're ready before dark, sister," Nalaen responded as Talesa headed for the door.

"Oh, I will be. I will have blood, one way or another." Talesa stormed out of the room without looking back, hissing at the guards as she passed by them. Nalaen and Sorn watched her leave, both smirking.

"She's the one that needs a leash..." Sorn said, breaking the awkward silence that had befallen the hall.

"Indeed," Nalaen chuckled. "We better find a way to soothe her thirst soon, or there's going to be a literal bloodbath."

Sorn smiled at the comment, but they both knew well how true Nalaen's words were.

"Come on, Brother. Let's go get ready."

Chapter Seventeen

SIGNS

"What do you think killed it?" Brol asked as he bent down to inspect one of the gashes where dried blood now sat. One of the nearby horses snorted nervously.

"I don't know," Dax replied, "but I sure as hell know I don't wanna stick around to find out. Anything that can kill a bear this big, well, I don't want to know what it could do to me."

Mara watched Kai and Caliena and several others squat next to the massive bear carcass, examining it from afar as she listened to Brol and Dax's exchange. They'd come down cautiously early in the morning after making camp for the first night on a ridgeline above. They'd heard the howl of wolves the previous evening, though they hadn't seen any, but out of an abundance of caution, decided to camp above where the wolves would normally roam. But now, it seemed wolves were the least of their worries.

When they first spotted it from afar, its light brown fur stood out against the rocky slope it was strewn against. But it wasn't until they got a bit closer did it become clear this was no ordinary bear. Mara had heard tales of wolves and bears of exceptional size that lived in the mountains, but that's all they had ever been–tales. She'd never actually seen one, or known anyone who did, and there had never been any attacks as long as she was alive. Like the recent dragon, animals of this size rarely wandered this close to the settled lands beyond the mountains. And even though they were much further into the mountains than Mara ever cared to go, they were still leagues from the heart of Thousand Peaks where such creatures normally dwelt.

But it was more than just the mere presence of the bear that unsettled Mara.

The bear's light brown fur was long and thick, dried blood soaked into it near at least a dozen puncture marks along its back. As she looked at the massive wounds inflicted on the enormous predator in front of her, the concern at the forefront of her thoughts was not a pleasant one. *It must have been a dragon. But the one that was slain... or another?*

Mara scanned the terrain around them. The bear was facing southwest, as if it had been running away from the two large mountains, which she knew were part of the so-called "Spine"–a massive chain of mountains that split the Thousand Peaks in half. It was called the "Spine" due to its resemblance of a massive dragon's spine. Mara didn't know what they'd find north of the Spine, but from the reports in the Huntsmaster's letter, that's where they'd pick up the trail of their missing hunters. *Great.*

"We should follow where it came from and see what we can find out," Kai said. Everyone just looked at him with blank stares, Mara most of all.

"Kai, are you mad?" Dax exclaimed.

"Well, that's where they said to look for the hunters–north of the Spine, right? It's a bit out of the way, but we're also out here to find out what's going on, aren't we?"

"Will you two shut up so I can think," Caliena barked, looking up at Kai through narrow eyes. Caliena Steelheart was tall for a woman. Almost as tall as Kai, she wore her long, golden hair in a braid that ran down her back, a red metal clasp at its end. She had bright green eyes and dainty features, though she was anything but. She was almost as hardheaded as Kai. He had been butting heads with her ever since the start of the mission. Caliena had been informed of their secondary agenda, as she was the leader of the group and Yoren said she needed to know everything. It didn't seem, however, that she put much stock in there being any other explanation other than the obvious.

"Uncle–er, the Spear," Kai corrected, "did say for us to keep an eye out–"

Caliena stood quickly and drew close to Kai, getting in his face.

"That will be enough, Kai," she said, loud enough for Mara to hear, but not the others. "This isn't our priority, and you're supposed to keep this quiet."

"Everyone already knows," Kai replied, standing his ground and keeping his face close to Caliena's. "I told them."

"You told them?" Caliena said, this time much louder. "But of course you did."

"We're all out here on the same mission, aren't we? They should know what our mission is–all of it."

"You're an arrogant shit, Kai. Just because your Uncle is the Spear, doesn't mean you can do as you please. I am in charge of this *mission*," she said with a hint of disdain, "and you will do as *I* say. Is that understood?"

Mara watched Kai's face grow red, her heart beating a little faster in apprehension. She'd seen Kai lose his temper for less. Kai glanced her way, blinked, then slowly unclenched his jaw and backed out of Caliena's face.

"What's done is done. Are we going to follow the path or not?" he prodded.

"What do you think, Bran?" Caliena asked, turning to her peer.

"I think we're wasting our time with this *secret* mission," Bran said matter-of-factly. "It's quite obvious the hunters were killed by the dragon we slew, and that's most likely what killed this bear, too. Animals get hungry enough and they go lookin' for food. Dragon's no different. Either way, we got to find what's left of these hunters so we can be done with this damned excursion. But that pass *is* the easiest way through the mountains."

Caliena looked at the mountain pass, then back at Kai and Bran.

"That's going to take us a little out of the way," Caliena said calmly, examining a map she'd brought from the Order. Mara caught a hint of annoyance under her breath. "This map is dated, but it appears Bran is right. The gap ahead of us is the clearest way to the northern side of the Spine. If we follow the mountains northeast, it might take us longer to find a safe passage through."

A cocky smirk formed on Kai's face–the first since they'd left Dragonscale Keep. He looked around at the others, who were all staring at each other, each seeming as if they were thinking the same thing as Mara. *This can't be our best option.* Dax's overly expressive face was the only one Mara could read clearly, as was usually the case.

"I don't like it, but if that's what the boss lady says," Dax said, garnering a slight sneer from Caliena.

"It is. Now move out. We've wasted enough time here bickering," Caliena called, circling her hand in the air, and shooting Kai a pointed look.

Everyone mounted their horses and skirted around the bear as they fell in line behind Caliena. Mara came up beside Kai, who was staring down at it with a hollow expression.

"Are you thinking what I'm thinking" Mara asked quietly enough so no one else could hear.

"I'm rarely thinking what you're thinking, Mara."

"Why didn't the dragon eat the bear?" Mara asked.

"For the first time, I guess we are thinking the same thing. Strange, isn't it? If the dragon had come east looking for food, why wouldn't it have eaten it? Unless something scared the dragon, too."

"Scared a dragon that big? Seems unlikely. Doesn't make much sense. First the dragon, now a bear this large. They don't usually come down here this far, as best I know," Mara admitted.

"Maybe the dragon chased it this way? Maybe they fought and that's why the dragon was injured?" Kai stated, more of a question.

"Maybe, but that still doesn't explain why it didn't eat it."

"Wasn't hungry? I don't know what to think. We're headed through the pass, so maybe we'll find more clues along the way." Kai shrugged, moving to his own horse.

"Maybe..." Mara was sure there was more of an explanation, but it still eluded her. The obvious answers seemed unthinkable. This mystery was becoming even more puzzling, and with this new discovery, Mara only had more questions than when they'd started. There was only one way to get answers, and Mara really didn't like where it was taking them.

CHAPTER EIGHTEEN

ESCORT

Nalaen watched the tip of the sun as it dipped below the skyline of the mountains west of Dor'Dragos. Standing on the precipice of the landing, she gazed out over the vast city that was destined to be hers. This was a place she'd spent a lot of time, especially as a youngling. She loved coming up here to watch the sunsets, feeling the wind against her face as the last rays of the setting sun faded into the city's fires below. At night, the city glowed near bright enough to almost make one think the sun was still just barely in the sky. The light did not reach everywhere, though. Shadowy figures prowled hidden alleys and the quiet corners of the city. Some districts were worse than others. But up here, above it all, Nalaen only felt peace. Or, at least, she presumed that was what peace felt like. Perhaps she would know true peace soon enough.

Nalaen's dreamlike trance was broken by the sound of approaching wings. She looked up to spot a group of wyrms approaching.

"Seven, peh!" Nalaen spat. "Does Kyrian really think so little of me? It will take more than that to control the future Queenmother of Dor'Dragos."

Nalaen strode toward the center of the platform as the wyrms landed with a torrent of wind, strong enough to knock even Nalaen over if she didn't steady herself against it. Despite it, she stood defiantly in front of them. She seemed so small compared to them in her human form, but she stood there like an immovable object, staring at the one she presumed was in charge. The wyrms shifted one after the other into their own human forms, coming up to stand before her.

One of them bowed low, an air of ego about him as he reached for her hand. Nalaen's skin crawled as she offered it to him, but it was a gesture she'd grown accustomed to tolerating. The wyrm pressed his forehead to her hand, then stood back up, looking her in the eyes. He was handsome in his human form—and tall. He had long black hair, and his eyes glowed a bright yellow. His muscles were well-defined in his fitted armor. It was a dark black metal etched with scale-like engravings over its entirety. And about their backs hung red cloaks, the symbol of the royal family in the middle. It was the common outfit of the elite Royal Guard.

They should be loyal to the me, not that snake. They forget who's crest that is...
Nalaen forced a smile.

"Good evening, Princess. I am Drae'vir Cathan, and we are pleased to be at
your disposal for this mission of great importance. We've been briefed on all the
logistics, though I'm sure you'll have more to discuss on the way." The Drae'vir
stopped, noticing Sorn and Talesa approaching from the archway of the landing's
main entrance.

"I see everyone is here now," he continued, nodding to the new arrivals. "We all
know who you are, but you may not know us. Allow me to introduce everyone."
The Drae'vir waved his hand and the others gathered around.

"I am Galen Cathan, Drae'vir in his majesty's—erm, your Majesty's Royal Guard." The Dare'Vir shot Nalaen a sideways glance, realizing his mistake.
Nalaen raised her eyebrow in disapproval. "Sorry, Princess. I'm just used to re-
porting to the Herald for the moment. Forgive my stupidity."

Nalaen read the hollowness in his words.

"But, continuing on... this is Drae'tar Mykael Kavriel. He is my second,"
Galen waved his hand toward the wyrm right behind him. Mykael came forward
and bowed his head to Nalaen. He did not reach for her hand, instead pulling his
sword from its sheath and bowing low before her, holding it outstretched with
both hands.

"My claws and blade are yours, Princess," he said, keeping his head bowed
before finally looking up at her, smiling as he stood. Nalaen merely nodded, trying
not to portray her inner approval at his approach over Galen's. She could sense
the slight tension between the two of them as Mykael fell back in line.

"And this is Drae'ko Lirael, Drae'ko Fareen, Drae'ko Masila, Drae'ko Vecana,
and Drae'ko Zateros," Galen offered, one by one. Each guard bowed, holding
their fists to their chests, offering similar pledges as Mykael had done, although
none seemed quite as sincere.

"These are the finest warriors the High Council could offer for your mission.
Can I presume they are to your liking?"

Nalaen looked to Galen, then back over the others. Holding her head high,
she walked up to them and inspected each from head to toe. It was a customary
gesture, as was fit for such an occasion. She needed to know she would receive
only the best from her soldiers, and they needed to know they had her approval.
Such had been the way for thousands of years. The choosing of a mate happened
in similar fashion, and more often than not, mates were chosen from the same
crowd—the strongest and fiercest of the warriors in service to the throne.

However, this time it was different. Though Nalaen was going through the
customary motions, she was inwardly piercing into the souls of the guards she
knew Kyrian had personally chosen. She wanted to look each of them in the eye,
hoping to instill some manner of doubt in their choice of allegiance. She wanted
them to fear moving against her.

Despite their motives, Nalaen had to admit they were an impressive bunch.
Should she ever be in the position of choosing a mate one day, she couldn't do

much better than the wyrms standing before her at this very moment. It was unlikely that any of them, save perhaps Mykael, would ever be one of her suitors.

Traitorous eyes the lot of them. We will see where your loyalties lie before this is through.

"Well enough, Drae'vir," Nalaen offered, nodding to the wyrm. "These will be sufficient."

"Excellent, Princess. If there is nothing else, shall we depart?" Galen looked first to Nalaen, then Sorn and Talesa.

"Yes, let's get moving. We have a long flight back to Dra'lith Fa'Liotha, and personally, I'd like to get started with our plans as soon as possible once we've had a decent rest."

"Ah, the old fortress. That is where your mother was slain, was it not?"

Nalaen shot the Drae'vir a deadly stare.

"Bold question, Drae'vir," she replied, letting out a slight hiss. "But yes, it is."

"Sorry, your Highness. I merely meant that it is a poetic place from which to strike out at her killer. We were informed you discovered who it was?"

"Yes, I did. I will brief you on the way. And take care how you speak of our late Queenmother. Understood?"

"Of course, Princess," Galen said, bowing once more. "We will follow your lead."

Nalaen turned and walked over to Sorn and Talesa. She leaned in close, ensuring the others could not hear them.

"Keep your eyes on them, both of you. If you can spot any weaknesses in any of them, we may be able to use that to our advantage. Also, do not say anything to them of our plans or what we've gone through to get here. I don't want anything useful to reach Kyrian's ears in their reports. I will give him nothing to use against me upon my return." Sorn nodded, Talesa shrugged.

"And sister," Nalaen added, "keep your blades sharp. You will have blood soon enough. We all will. Are you both ready?"

Sorn and Talesa nodded in unison. Sorn looked mildly concerned, though he tried to mask it, while Talesa was openly displaying her approval at Nalaen's final words to her.

"Alright," Nalaen called out, addressing all those on the landing. "Let's be on our way. And do try to keep up, Drae'vir."

Nalaen's eyes flashed red at her escorts before being enshrouded in a swirling mist, the sound of wings bursting forth from their fleshly prison as she took to the night sky. It was a long flight back to the border of the human lands, but at last she was on the way to fulfill the promise that had been put off for far too long.

Vengeance was coming for the lands of men.

CHAPTER NINETEEN

REVELATION

As he rounded the corner, Aerin could see the road ran straight, the rolling green hills that surrounded Eastend rising and falling like waves. Farms and homesteads speckled the crests and valleys, and looming beyond them, the white peaks of the mountains stretching as far as the eye could see. It was quite the sight to behold, and now, so near his destination, Aerin felt a renewed sense of purpose.

He'd stayed the night at Jeb's Post, and though Jeb had been nice enough, his words of warning about traveling east with the recent dragon sighting had Aerin questioning what he was getting himself into. Still, he hoped he could do more than just deliver a message.

My friends need me. I am more than just a messenger. I can help... somehow.

Essie, almost as if in response, let out a loud whinny and quickened her pace. Turning his attention to the scenery ahead, Aerin saw that she, too, had noticed the farms.

"Atta girl, Essie. We're almost there. I'm sure the Order will feed us quite well. And worst case, we can see how the market in Eastend fairs. Perhaps their harvest has been good down here in the south."

Aerin patted Essie on the side of her neck and gave her a gentle kick, picking up the pace further. The thought of warm food and a break from riding sounded superb. He imagined Essie felt quite the same.

They made it to the edge of town in short work, and though Aerin wished to stop, his eyes were focused on the keep set against the mountains beyond. From here, it looked small—nothing notable nor innately special about it. But Aerin had heard stories of the keep built into the mountains, with halls magnificent and grand, large enough to house a thousand men. Aerin, of course, had no idea if the stories were true, but he was eager to find out.

The town of Eastend was quaint, and though it wasn't as large as Northreach, it still felt very much alive. The troubles they had in Northreach did not seem to extend this far south, which made Aerin wonder if, perhaps, the wildlife around these parts was in better supply.

After skirting the center of Eastend, the road continued straight toward the mountains. As the hills began to rise at a much steeper pace, it wound to the left, following the side of one hill until it wrapped back to the right and up, disappearing from view.

The road was rockier here, loose stones skittering away from Essie's feet. At this proximity to the mountains, he could hear her footfalls more clearly as they echoed against the cliffs closing in on them.

After rounding the first corner and turning right, Aerin could begin to see the tops of the walls of Dragonscale Keep. And after another hundred paces, the gate came into view. It looked less grand than he'd been told, though he presumed the outer portion of the keep was nothing compared to its inner halls. And even from here, the part protruding from the mountainside seemed quite small.

Less gaudy than Valehold. Let's hope its inhabitants are more grounded as well.

Approaching the gates, he heard a call from somewhere up above. Craning his neck, he saw the hint of an outline inside one of the tower windows.

"What business do you have with the Order of Scales, rider?" the silhouette called out.

"I am Aerin of the Lodge. I come bearing news from our master—and to offer my aid, if the Lord will have it."

Aerin shifted in his saddle, waiting for a reply. There was silence for a long moment before he began to hear the clanking of chains from behind the door. A few seconds later, the doors slowly opened.

Aerin waited patiently, spotting several men on the other side. Once the gates were just wide enough, the group emerged, the gates, coming to a halt. One of the men, a grey-haired man with a neatly trimmed beard strode up to stand in front of Aerin and Essie.

"You're from the Lodge?" the man asked in a suspecting tone as he eyed Aerin and his equipment. "We weren't expecting anyone."

"Aye, sir," Aerin said, trying not to sound nervous. "I was sent to deliver an update on the missing hunters situation. Our ravens... become indisposed, so the Huntsmaster sent me. I also thought, perhaps, I might offer my aid, in whatever way I can be of use."

"I see," the man replied, scratching his beard. "My name is Cyrus Bladesong. I can take you to see the Spear. He will hear what you have to say and decide if he wants to present you to the Scalewarden or not. We would welcome any additional news you might have pertaining to your lost brethren, at the very least. You may follow me..." Cyrus paused, giving Aerin a questioning look.

"Aerin, sir," he replied.

"Pleased to meet you, Aerin. Right this way then."

Aerin nodded with a smile, gently tapping Essie with his heels to follow Cyrus through the gates. The other men eyed him warily, Aerin smiling to them with more nods.

Inside, he saw the courtyard of the keep was filled with knights coming and going, some of them practicing at various stations around the edge. He heard the clang of weapons as some of them sparred, and heard the grating of metal as others sharpened spears and other weapons.

"You may stable your mare over there," Cyrus said, pulling Aerin's eyes away from the scene at hand. Aerin's gaze followed, seeing the stables off to the left. He nodded and turned Essie to the side.

After quickly bustling Essie into one of the empty stalls, he locked the door and returned to Cyrus, who was waiting patiently for him.

"I don't suppose you have any feed for her?" Aerin questioned. "It's been a long ride."

Cyrus nodded, then waved to one of the nearby knights.

"See to it that Aerin's mount is fed and given some water," Cyrus ordered. The knight he was addressing nodded, then turned and ran off toward the stables.

"Alright then. Let's go see Yoren," Cyrus said, beckoning Aerin to follow.

Cyrus led Aerin through the main gates set against the side of the mountain. Once inside, Aerin saw the interior of the keep was quite plain. It seemed the stories had exaggerated a few of the details. It was not nearly as open as they'd made it out to be, though the hallways were big enough for perhaps half a dozen men from side to side, and high enough for two standing on top of each other. *They probably didn't want any dragons squeezing through here easily*, Aerin thought to himself. *Makes sense.*

What did catch Aerin's attention was the shafts of light coming from above. He was pretty sure it was daylight, reflecting through some sort of cut stones inlaid into the ceiling in steady increments along the hallway. It was nearly as bright inside as it had been out in the courtyard. He marveled at the simple, yet highly effective ingenuity.

After leading Aerin through a series of hallways, which caused him great confusion, they at last came to what looked like a central area that branched off in various paths through the underground fortress. They turned down another hallway with a bunch of doorways, stopping in front of one of them, Cyrus motioning for Aerin to wait with the two other knights who'd come with them.

"Sir, there's an emissary here from the Lodge. He says he has news, and wishes to offer his aid," Aerin heard Cyrus say to whomever was inside the room.

Several moments later, Aerin saw the one they referred to as the Spear emerge from his office. Aerin eyed the man, immediately sensing an air of respect about him, as was apparent in the way Cyrus and the other knights bowed to him and stood up a bit straighter in his presence.

"Emissary Aerin," Cyrus offered, waving his hand in Aerin's direction. The Spear's eyes focused on Aerin, and Aerin felt his heartbeat intensify. It seemed as if the Spear was measuring him. "And Aerin, this is the Spear, Yoren Grayscale."

"We weren't expecting any emissary. Has there been news?" the Spear questioned.

Aerin hesitated, not sure if he was meant to speak yet or not. A quick nod from Cyrus cleared up his confusion.

"Yes, sir... Spear," Aerin bowed, doing his best to show respect.

"Please, Aerin. Yoren will do," Yoren offered.

"Of course, Yoren. I was sent with a message from the Huntsmaster to inform you that one of the missing hunters returned to us."

Both Yoren and Cyrus's eyes lit up at that.

"One of them returned? Well, that is good news. But only the one?" Yoren asked.

"The hunter who returned is named Jarren. He's always been an odd sort, but he's one of the best trackers we have. When he came back, he was raving like a madman and talking some nonsense about what happened in the mountains. We tried to get something sensible out of him, but we couldn't get much of anything, so we sent him off to be treated by the local healer, in hopes she could get him to a better state. I don't know his status now, as I was sent to Valehold. I assume they haven't sent any more ravens to inform you of all this?"

Questioning looks of growing apprehension went around the group, and Yoren eyed Cyrus with a serious expression. Cyrus returned his look and shook his head.

"No. No more ravens have come," Cyrus said, shaking his head in reply to the questioning look from Yoren.

"You said he was rambling on about what happened?" Yoren asked, turning back to Aerin.

"Yes. Most of it didn't make any sense. He said there was a woman with red eyes, and she–"

"A woman with red eyes? Are you sure that's what he said?" Yoren cut Aerin off, his eyes growing wider.

"Yes. It was all we really got out of him. Is that supposed to mean something?" Aerin asked, confused.

Yoren turned to Cyrus and whispered in his ear. After several seconds, Cyrus nodded, whispered something back, motioned to the two knights, then turned and hastened back down the hallway with them. Aerin watched them, not quite sure what was happening.

"Come with me, Aerin. We better bring this before the Scalewarden. He needs to hear this right away."

Aerin followed Yoren down the short hallway, passing several doors on the way back. There, a larger and more ornate door stood. Yoren nodded to a gentleman in a cubby beside the door, then opened it and motioned for Aerin to follow him inside. As Aerin entered, he heard the ringing of a bell echoing through the halls behind him.

CHAPTER TWENTY

RUINS

As they walked in between the massive mountains, Kai couldn't help but look up at them in awe. Most of the present party had only ever seen the mountains from a distance, though they'd had a few short excursions during their training years. But being this close now, he fully realized just how large and majestic they truly were. There was an eerie beauty to them as the winds howled throughout the rocky crags, sending gusts of snow this way and that across their frozen surfaces. The rocks here lining the sides of the mountains and cliffs were a slate grey, peeking out from beneath the blanket of snow, casting large, jagged shadows beneath Kai's feet.

Kai didn't like how many potential hiding spots there were up above. The scattered rocks and boulders provided plenty of cover, should an enemy wish to hide amongst them. Fortunately, though, whatever enemy had slain the bear would probably have been too large to hide easily. The thought still ate at Kai's mind, and he felt a slight anxiety set in as his eyes dodged between the cliffsides and rocky slopes above.

Wrenching his eyes away, he noticed most of the others were in a similar state of paranoia. He didn't want to dissuade them from being cautious, but he also didn't want everyone so on edge they'd miss something more obvious. He brought his mount over next to Mara's and spoke quietly.

"Everyone's kinda freaking out a bit, me included. Any ideas how we can distract ourselves with something else?"

"Oh, my *big* brother is freaking out, huh?" Mara jested, her nose scrunching into a familiar smirk.

"Yes, he is. And you are too."

"Well, you're not wrong, but I didn't think you'd be the one to admit it first. Just thought I'd take advantage of that."

"Hah, you're funny. You got your jest out. So?"

"I don't know. Maybe a song or something?"

"Not a bad idea, but not sure I want to make too much noise if this thing is actually still out here. Maybe when we get further away from here?"

"Yeah, that makes sense. So, hmm... what else? Oh, I have an idea!" Mara guided her horse away from Kai and over to Catlyn, who had been trotting alongside Mara just moments before.

"Hey, Catlyn. First thing you're going to do when we get back to the keep?" Mara looked at Kai and winked. Kai, taking the hint, sped up to come alongside Dax.

"Oh," Catlyn said, pausing momentarily. "Well, I would love a hot bath. I think I can feel this cold in my bones." Several of the other girls smiled at her answer and moved closer to ride together.

"Oh my god, yes!" said Riesara. "A hot bath would feel so amazing!" The girls started talking amongst themselves.

Kai glanced up ahead at where Caliena and Bran rode together in front of the group. Bran glanced backward, hearing their words, snickering. Caliena continued on, seemingly ignoring it altogether.

"What about you, Dax?" Kai asked, ignoring Bran.

"Well," Dax said, looking toward the girls. "A hot bath does sound great. It's cold as hell out here, and my rear is hurtin' somethin' fierce." A murmur of laughter went around the group at his words.

"Alright," Kai said out loud so everyone could hear. "It's think it's fair enough to say that we *all* would like a hot bath when we get back. But, besides that, what else? I, for one, want to eat a whole loaf of that sour bread they feed us. What's it called again?"

"You mean the goat bread? Syrbread?" Dax asked.

"Syrbread! That's it! I kinda thought it was gross when we first ate it, but it grew on me, and it sure does sound good right about now." More laughter went around the group, followed by a handful of nods. All except Bran and Caliena.

"With all the yapping you're doing, it'd be a wonder if the whole of Thousand Peaks didn't know we were comin'," Bran said, sneering at the group.

Kai's face flushed with anger. *Who does he think he is...*

"Sorry we're all friends here except you two," Kai retorted.

"I have friends. I had to leave them to babysit you all on this stupid errand."

"No one's making you stay," Kai shot back. "You're free to go. I think we can handle ourselves just fine."

"Huh," Bran scoffed. "You wouldn't last a day out here without us."

Kai thought he heard Bran mutter "no-bloods" under his breath.

"What did you just say?" Kai yelled, his anger flaring.

"That's enough you two!" Caliena shouted, finally turning around. "I can't think with you two cock fighting. You're not impressing anyone here. Both of you shut up. In fact, I want everyone to be quiet for the next hour. We're heading into the northern mountains, and nearing where the hunters might have gone. We need to focus and pay attention for any signs of their passing."

Even from where Kai stood, he could see Caliena's nostrils flaring. As much as he wanted to object, he knew she had her limits. Kai nodded, then cast his gaze toward Mara and the others. They all nodded, but exchanged expressions of annoyance when Caliena turned back around.

Kai saw Bran mutter something to her, holding up his hands in a gesture of innocence. Kai heard Caliena scoff, then watched as she pushed him away. After that, Bran kept his distance and went further up ahead, but not before shooting one more smug look Kai's way.

Kai felt a nudge on his arm and looked over at Mara, who'd drawn close.

"Good job," she whispered.

"Hey, not my fault. He's being an ass. And I'm pretty sure he called us 'no-bloods'."

"So what? It's just a dumb expression they made up. It doesn't matter. You need to learn to let things go, Kai."

"It's disrespectful–and degrading. I won't let him treat us like children."

"We know we're not. I appreciate you standing up for us, but you really gotta learn when to quit."

"Yeah, yeah," Kai said, shirking back into a foul mood. He knew she was right. *She's always right.*

"Sorry. I don't mean it that way. You're always thinking about others, and you're stubborn," Mara said, winking at Kai. "It's why you'll be a good leader someday."

"I prefer determined, but sure, I'll let you call it what you want."

Kai looked up and saw they had rounded the edge of the mountains, finally coming into view of a larger swathe of the Spine as it trickled slowly eastward, disappearing from sight the further south it ran. Everyone noticed the same and stopped to take in the scenery ahead of them. To the north, it was a lot more open, the massive, rocky mountains of the Spine giving way to smaller, smoother hills speckled throughout the landscape before them, broken every once in a while by higher peaks. It was a serene and peaceful view, setting Kai's nerves at ease now they were through the rocky pass.

"Alright, everyone. Let's follow the mountains southeast now," Caliena called out. "We'll stay up on the hillside, as long as it's not too steep, so we have a better vantage point. Keep an eye out for any signs of passing–men or beast. We're going to need to see if we can kill something before making camp, just to ensure we can eat again before too long. But we should be able to make it a couple more hours before we need to find a place to rest for the night."

Everyone nodded again, but didn't dare raise any objections. Kai saw Caliena signal to Bran before he nodded and started riding further ahead of the group, most likely to scout ahead.

The party moved along at a steady pace for another hour or two, talking quietly amongst each other in small groups, their temperaments more relaxed as time went on. They discussed what each of them wanted to do when they returned, and about what life might be like as real Dragonbloods. Kai didn't care much for it, knowing it was a dream they would likely never achieve, so he instead turned his attention out to the landscape to the north, watching for signs of anything that stood out against the blanket of snow-covered treetops and rolling hills. The going was steady, and they made good time, but gradually the slope of the mountain started getting steeper, slowing them a bit.

Caliena called the group to stop and take a short break. Kai dismounted and found a nearby rock to sit down for a rest. As his eyes scanned the horizon, he caught a hint of something that seemed out of place against the backdrop of the scene before him. It was on a hilltop, roughly a few miles north.

"What's that?" he asked, pointing. Everyone's eyes followed.

Caliena stood up, placing her hand over her eyes as a shield against the sunlight. Kai saw her brow furl, then she pulled out the old map she'd brought, studying it.

"I think those are the ruins of the old dragon fortress," she said, shrugging.

"Dragon fortress?" Kai asked, suddenly very intrigued.

"That's what I said," Caliena replied with pursed lips, seeming uninterested.

"What–" Kai started before feeling Mara's hand on his arm.

"Liotha's Fall," she said quietly, answering the question he'd been about to ask. "Where they defeated the first queen of the dragons."

"I remember…" Kai said, looking back toward it. "They taught us about that in our first year, right? I didn't realize it was this close."

The others gathered around, each casting their eyes north to see the ruins for themselves.

"Two- or three-day's ride at most, maybe more in bad weather. It was where they gathered to strike out against us in the Dragon Wars. The last bastion, far from their homeland."

"A bit too close for comfort."

"Yes. Uncle was there that night when they slew the last queen and ended the war."

"Two queens died there. Guess they finally learned their lesson. So, that is the last remnants of the life before peace. Pretty crazy it's right there." Kai paused, deep in thought. "We should go check it out," he said, getting a bit excited.

Everyone around seemed interested, but Caliena was still sitting quietly a ways away from the group.

"We should go check it out," Kai said a bit louder, ensuring she heard him.

Caliena turned his way with a slight frown.

"Our objective is to find the hunters. We need to keep moving east along the mountains."

"The mountain is getting steep, anyways," Kai pressed. "The horses can't take much more of this. Plus, we need to make camp in an hour or two anyways, right? Why not do it there? Wouldn't the ruins provide some natural shelter?"

Caliena glared at Kai but made no reply. Kai couldn't tell if she was considering his words. Her expressionless face was too hard to read.

"I'm guessing we can make it there in a short time. It's got a good vantage point to survey the surrounding area, too–to look for the hunters, of course…"

Caliena looked back at the ruins but said nothing. Kai waited in apprehension, hoping she'd see the reasoning in it.

At that moment, Bran reappeared from down the hill. He climbed the mountain and came up to speak in a low tone with Caliena. Kai watched, noticing Bran cast his gaze out toward the ruins. They seemed to be arguing, but he couldn't make out their words. Finally, Bran looked up at Kai, grunted, then turned and headed back down the mountain in the direction of the ruins.

Caliena turned and came closer, stopping a dozen paces short and staring at Kai with a flat expression.

"Fine. We go to the ruins," she said. Everyone started getting excited. "But–" she added, cutting off their murmurs. "Just for the night. We make camp, get some sleep, and survey the land at first light to decide our path from there."

Kai gave Caliena a smirk. It was the first time he'd smiled at her, probably ever. It felt weird, but he was too excited to contain it. They were going to see a real piece of the Order's history–a real piece from when the Order was as he wished it to still be, even though he knew in his heart all they would find were more relics of a past all but forgotten.

CHAPTER TWENTY-ONE

CONVERGENCE

The last rays of daylight cast a glowing red hue on the tops of the stone structures still standing amidst the scattered rubble of Liotha's Fall. Shadows crept beneath this fiery canopy, creating dark pockets of black, and Kai was almost certain he saw them writhing at the group's approach. *Just my mind playing tricks...*

For a place where dragons once dwelt, it seemed an appropriate cemetery.

Kai shivered and wrapped his cloak tighter, puffs of icy mist hanging in the air before him. It was naturally colder with the waning of the day, and with the heights they'd climbed to get atop the smaller mountain, but this was something more. A storm was coming.

They'd felt the sinister bite of the easterly wind before they even saw the dark grey clouds on the horizon, menacingly approaching over the treetops as they'd made their way up the base of the mountain. Once in view of the ruins, they saw the clouds were indeed heralding a storm their way. And if there was any truth to the tales of those who'd dared brave the Thousand Peaks during Winter, they were in for a rough night.

Kai felt a sense of dread creep over him as he gazed into the approaching abyss. He wanted to explore the ruins, but imminence dictated other priorities.

"We need to hurry and make some manner of shelter before that reaches us," Caliena barked, sizing up what seemed to be a reasonable section of the ruins that would provide some protection from the cold and wind. "Use our tents to cover this section here. We'll need logs and the such to make something big enough for all of us. The horses will need shelter, too." She called out names and assigned duties. Kai was to go with the boys to gather wood for the horses' shelter, Mara and the girls had been ordered to start clearing the snow and preparing the tents. Caliena and Bran were going out to hunt, noting the storm might delay their return and their supplies would be stretched thin.

"They don't trust us to catch anything," Kai said, tying his horse up to a wall that would serve as the animals' shelter.

"Shoot, I wouldn't trust me neither. I mean, I can wrastle a sheep or hogtie a steer in less than a minute, but I ain't no good with a bow," Dax said in his matter-of-fact tone, tying his horse up next to Kai's.

"Now that's something I'd like to see," Brol chimed in with a grin. "Dax wrestling a goat."

"Oh no, not a goat. I said sheep. You don't wrestle goats. Their horns'll getcha. I once saw a man lose an eye tryin' to do that. But sheep, shoot... that's easy."

Brol and Kai exchanged questioning looks before Kai pat Dax on the shoulder.

"You are somethin', Dax," Kai said with a grin. "But I was being serious. Maybe we're not the best choice to hunt. I mean, I'm okay with a bow, but that's beside the point. The point is they don't trust us to do anything important."

"Well, I reckon building a shelter is pretty important with that there storm comin'," Dax said, turning to gawk at the approaching clouds. "Looks nasty."

"Yeah, sure... I guess. I just meant—"

"We know what you meant," Brol interjected. "Sucks, I know. But Dax is also right. Someone's gotta build the cover. So, let's build the best damn cover they've ever seen. Except, maybe we leave a corner kind of weak and make that Bran's spot..." he finished with a sly grin.

Kai's serious expression turned upward.

"Hah! Wouldn't that be somethin'. Bran waking up all cold and wet," Kai said, grinning "Thanks, Brol—and Dax. Always know how to make me feel better. And I suppose you're right," he sighed. "That storm's getting closer every minute, and I sure as hell don't want to get caught out here in it."

The boys got back to gathering, finding as much wood as they could carry before heading back to where the horses had been stabled. Fortunately, there were plenty of logs and broken branches protruding from the snow just down the hill from the ruins, and it wasn't long before they had a good pile going.

Kai sized up the pile, satisfied they had enough to at least get started. He saw Mara and the girls had fully cleared the area in between the ruin's walls and were already working on draping the tents over the top. The boys got started patching gaps in the wall next to the horses, in addition to some measure of roof that would protect them from the snow. By the time they were done, he saw the girls had nearly finished their own tasks.

The boys still had some wood left over, so they brought what they could and helped the girls finish getting the tents draped over the top and sides until they had a nice-looking box with a small entrance in the front. They placed some larger pieces on the top and sides in hopes nothing would blow away.

"Think she'll hold under the wind?" Brol asked.

"I think so," Kai said, stepping up and giving one of the sides a good tug. "As long as it doesn't get too crazy."

Worried glances were cast about the group before all eyes gazed up at the storm clouds. The wind was already starting to pick up, and Kai noticed the low howl echoing through the canyons.

"Wonder how our hunters are faring?" Kai said, his eyes following the slope downward into the valley. There was still no sign of Caliena or Bran.

"I hope they're back soon," Mara said. Kai shot a sharp look at her, but kept his mouth shut. Even though he didn't care if they were back, his stomach had been reminding him for some time now that it'd been too long since he last ate.

"We still have some food left, but if we get stuck out in this storm too long, we should probably be sparing," Vi chimed in as she dug through their sacks.

"We can ration those out, but Mara, I think it's time to get that fire started," Kai said. "Looks like we don't have much light left."

The sky had grown darker, Kai just now realizing the sun had dipped below the horizon. He surveyed the surrounding hills, searching for any last signs of Caliena and Bran. *Good luck*, Kai thought, nodded, then joined the others inside.

Shortly after the fire was in full swing, Kai sat back and basked in its warmth. The fire's glow momentarily got his mind off his stomach, but several moments later, a large gust of wind wrapped around the enclosure, its icy fingers slipping through the makeshift shelter and causing the fire to flutter.

Everyone eyed the walls and roof, listening as the storm finally set in upon them. A few flakes of snow fluttered underneath several sides of the tent covering, those nearby moving sticks and their supplies around to seal up the gaps. Once the holes were better secured, everyone scooted closer to the fire.

Mara stood up and peeked out the front door flap. She stood there for a moment, Kai waiting to see what she would say.

"How's it look out there, Mara?" Brol asked.

"Miserable. I can barely see anything. It's snowing pretty good. That came on so quick."

Kai frowned. It seemed the rumors about the storms out here were true.

"Bet Caliena and Bran are regretting their choice now," Dax said, elbowing Kai.

"Yeah, guess they got the short end of the–"

"Shh," Mara said, waving her hand up in the air.

Kai raised an eyebrow, everyone in the tent growing quiet.

"What is it, Mara?" Kai asked.

"I think someone's out there."

"Caliena and Bran are finally back?" Kai said.

"No... I don't think so. It sounds deeper. Much deeper than Bran, but I can't quite tell. Maybe the wind is just playing tricks on me, but it sounds like voices."

Kai stood and came over to the opening. Mara stepped aside and let him poke his head out. Snow instantly started covering it and he shivered, trying to focus his ears to see if he could hear what Mara had heard. For a few seconds, all he heard was the wind. But then, a few seconds later, something caught his ear. It was faint, but clearly different. It *did* sound like voices.

He peered through the snow but couldn't see much. He could barely see the horses nearby in their covering, huddled closely together for warmth. They were shuffling a bit but otherwise seemed calm. Beyond that, it was a wall of white.

Kai listened again, waiting for the voices to return.

"Blast this storm," one of the voices–a male–called out.

"Barely made it here in one piece," came another, sounding quite similar to the first.

"She said find shelter. Some portions of the ruins still stand. We just need to find the best spot, and find it quickly."

Kai turned inside and stared at the others. Who else could possibly be out here in this weather? They'd seen no one else in the ruins as they'd crafted their own shelter.

"Did you hear it?" Mara asked, breaking Kai's inward monologue.

"Yes. Someone's definitely out there. But who could it possibly be?" he said.

"Maybe it's the hunters?" Catlyn offered, looking hopeful.

"One of them said 'she'. There was no woman with the hunters, was there?" Kai asked.

"*She*?" Mara said, clearly confused. "Do you think they mean Caliena? Maybe some of the others came out to help us?"

Kai simply shook his head. Something felt wrong, and somehow none of the logical answers seemed to make sense to him. The tone of the strangers' voices set him off.

"I'll go take a look," Kai said, turning back to the doorway. "Stay here." His gut told him it was a bad idea, but someone had to do it.

"Kai," Mara said, reaching for his arm. "It's fine, right?" Her eyes were boring into him and he could sense her apprehension.

"It's fine. I'm sure there's a perfectly logical explanation. Perhaps we can even help each other." He forced a smile, hoping his words were convincing. Then, without hesitation, he stepped out into the cold abyss.

He scanned the surrounding area, but could only see the horses. They were stirring more now. *These newcomers might be spooking them.*

"Do you smell smoke?" came one of the voices from behind the wall of white, beyond where the horses were clustered.

"Someone's here? I thought she said these ruins were empty," came the other.

Silence ensued and Kai grew uneasy. He stepped forward, getting closer to the horses' shelter, holding his hand up to shield his eyes from the flakes hurtling toward them. When he made it to the wall, he patted the nearest horse, trying to reassure it quietly while still listening and scanning for the strangers. He glanced back at the tent, saw several faces poking out from behind the doorway, though he couldn't tell who they belonged to. He waved his hand, telling them to stay.

Kai peered around the edge of the wall. There were some sections of the ruins in front of him, but he couldn't see anything beyond them. His mind raced, trying to decide what to do. Reluctantly, working up the courage, he readied himself and rounded the corner, making for a low wall within his view. He stopped there, hesitated for another second, and looked back. He could no longer see their tent. *Damn this storm.*

Kai stood up and peered over the wall, scanning the next area. Still, he saw nothing but white and a few scattered stones from the ruins. The area was more open, and he wasn't sure now where his next move would be.

He felt a hand graze his arm and spun, coming face to face with Brol, who quickly held his hand up to cover Kai's mouth. Dax was right behind him, and Mara behind him. Kai tried to talk, but Brol's hand kept his voice muffled.

"What the hell, guys. You nearly gave me a heart attack," Kai said after Brol removed his hand.

"Sorry buddy," Dax said, crawling up next to him. "Didn't want to leave you out here on your own. Could easily get lost in this mess."

Kai gave them all a hard stare, but slowly pursed his lips, happy for the company.

"What do we have here," said a voice to their side.

All four of them spun to the right, seeing a large figure emerge from the snow, an exquisite sword in his hand pointed right at them. The storm raged all around them, the man's black armor standing out in stark contrast, a red cape flailing furiously behind him. And the man was tall—much taller than Kai.

"Some poor lost souls trapped in the storm it seems," said another, dressed in the same manner, his own sword held high.

"Who are you? And what are you doing out here in the middle of nowhere?" asked the first.

Kai raised his hands, unsure of how to respond. He was stunned by their appearance. Who were they, exactly? Kai had never been to the Wall, but he'd heard stories, and these men were dressed much too extravagantly to be simple Vale soldiers.

"We're just resting for the night. Looking for some lost hunters. Are you from the Vale?" Kai asked, still wary but more intrigued now than anything.

"Lirael," the first called, scanning Kai and the others. "Bring her. She'll want to see for herself."

Almost as silently as he'd appeared, the second left, vanishing into the storm.

"No, we are not from the Vale," the first sneered. There was something about the man's eyes that were off-putting, but with the storm, Kai couldn't explain what exactly it was. It almost seemed as if they had a slight glow to them.

"Then where?" Kai asked, growing more suspicious.

"You'll know soon enough. How many of there are you?"

"Just the four of us," Kai lied, swallowing.

"There are more than four horses over there" the man said, flicking his head toward the wall. "By my guess, seven or eight. Where are the others?"

Kai glanced toward the wall. From where he stood, he couldn't see any of the horses, though he heard them now, their nervous snorting clear as he focused on it. *How could he know how many?* Kai returned his gaze to the man.

Kai's desire to take some sort of action was increasing by the second. Internally, he was sizing up the man, wondering if the four of them could take him. His hand instinctively moved to the spear's handle at his back.

"I wouldn't do that," the man said.

"Why not?" Kai asked, suddenly emboldened. He saw the looks his friends were giving him out of the corner of his eye, but every second they waited, his apprehension grew.

"I would kill you before you even drew the weapon from its hold."

Somewhere, deep down inside, Kai believed him. But reason wasn't one of Kai's strengths. Just as Kai was about to take hold of the handle, he felt Brol's hand on his arm.

Kai looked at his friend, seeing him mouth the word "don't". Kai returned the gesture with widened eyes, pleading for his friend to back him. Brol's eyes cut downward, toward his right hand. He had ahold of his own spear, the hand hidden from the stranger's view. Kai instantly understood.

Kai nodded to Brol, then turned back toward the man, holding his hands out in a surrendering gesture. With one quick movement, he dove to the side, gripped his spear, and came up facing the stranger. At the same time, Brol whipped his own spear out and brought it up toward the man. The stranger reacted faster than Kai could track, bringing his sword up and deflecting Brol's awkward strike. The spear went flying, the stranger bringing his sword up and within inches of Brol's throat, all while keeping his eyes trained on Kai. When Kai saw this, he tightened his grip on his spear, gritted his teeth, and took a step forward.

"Ah, ah," the stranger said, shaking his head, pressing his sword against Brol's throat. Kai saw a thin line of blood drip down his friend's neck.

"Coward," Kai said. He continued to grip the spear tightly, though he knew he should stop. "Why don't you point that at me."

"Kai, please," Mara begged. More than her words, or tone, there was true fear behind her eyes. Kai glanced at Brol, his own eyes pleading for Kai to stop. Kai clenched his jaw but softened his grip on his weapon.

"That will be enough," came a voice from somewhere beyond the veil of the storm. It was a woman's voice.

The man sneered at Kai, his lip curling upwards in a grin. After a few seconds, he lowered his sword and placed it back in its sheath. He turned and bowed to the shadowy figure emerging from the wall of white.

"Forgive me, Princess. These two were having..." he paused, eyeing Kai with a sideways glance, "...reckless thoughts."

Princess?

Kai peered into the storm, watching the new figure emerge. She was tall, like the other two. Her face was veiled by a dark hood, draped over the top half of her face. Though the lighting was poor, and the snow made it hard to garner precise details, he thought he could see strands of red hair blowing in the wind. She had an air about her, too. Whatever kind of princess she was, he could sense the power she commanded. But it wasn't just her station that Kai felt. It was something... more.

The woman walked toward the group, finally stopping a dozen paces in front of Kai. She reached up and slowly removed her hood. As her features came into

Kai's view, he felt a tingling in the back of his skull. With every inch of her face revealed, the sensation grew stronger.

And then he saw her eyes. Though it was faint, he clearly saw a glow there. And at the moment her eyes met with his, he felt the sensation pulse even stronger.

"Kai, they're..." Mara started, stuttering.

"Dragons, yes," replied the woman coldly.

You should plan your next move more carefully, came words from all around Kai, almost as if they were in his head. He looked around at the others, their faces still fixed on her.

They can't hear me. Only you.

Kai shook his head, looking back at her. Her red eyes were staring straight at him. The pulsing in the back of his mind felt dizzying.

What is your name?

Kai placed his hand on the back of his neck but there was nothing there.

What is happening? Kai thought to himself. He felt confused, like a fog had settled over his mind.

We're just having a chat. Now, your name?

My name is... Kai started, then stopped. *No.* "No," Kai said aloud.

"What's wrong, Kai?" Mara asked.

So, came her voice in his head again, *it's Kai then. And why are you here, Kai...?*

The confusion returned, a thrum of energy feeling like it was vibrating the back of his skull. She still wanted his name—his full name.

Kai... he thought. *Kai Gr–* a hand on his arm stopped him.

"Are you okay?" Mara asked, drawing close behind him. "What's going on?"

"I..." Kai started, still feeling confused. "My head. I– I can't... she's in my head. Somehow." Kai gripped his head, covering his ears.

"Stop it!" Mara called out, her voice muffled. "What are you doing to him?"

"Just trying to get to know each other, my dear. Nothing to worry about. But if he won't tell me, then perhaps we'll introduce ourselves first."

The Princess waved her hands, more shadows emerging from the storm all around them. Most of them were dressed in similar armor to the first two they'd met. There was another woman, looking much like the Princess, her hair black, her eyes glowing green, an even colder expression cast their way. There was also another figure behind the Princess, barely a shape, a pair of blue eyes the only feature he could see through the storm. As Kai raised his head, he saw the others' eyes were now glowing faintly as well. As he stared in awe of them, his heart racing, her words drifted across the raging wind, coming into clarity.

"Princess Nalaen, Heir to the Dragon Throne, Daughter of the Slain Queen, and I have come for vengeance."

There, amidst the ruins of a forgotten past, ten sets of dimly glowing eyes stared back at Kai. The storm had brought with it the answers to their mystery. For the past, it seemed, had not forgotten them.

Chapter Twenty-Two

SACRIFICE

Mara's heart pounded as she stared at the group before her.

Heir to the Dragon Throne? How could this be?

"What do we do, Kai?" she asked.

"I– I don't know..." he mumbled, seeming to still be a bit confused.

Kai's mannerism only drove home what Mara already knew. These were elder dragons, somehow, here in the flesh. They'd heard all the stories, knew all there was to know, and yet, they had just been stories. Now, it was real–too real.

"What do you want?" Mara spoke up, hoping her nerves would not show through her words.

Nalaen grinned, some of the others around her laughing. The woman next to her with black hair licked her lips, her smile more unnerving than the rest.

"Well, you must know," Nalaen said. "You don't think I would tell you all that and then just let you walk away, now do you? My sister has been itching for a fight, though you don't look like you have much fight in you. Perhaps one of you can prove me wrong? Maybe Kai, perhaps?"

Kai lifted his head, his eyes focused on the Princess. Mara saw the anger in his features.

"I've trained my whole life for this," Kai said, cold and hollow.

"You can't," Mara said, holding tight to Kai's arm. "How can we–"

"She's right, *Dragonblood*," Nalaen said, almost spitting the word. "That's right, I know what you are. I recognize the attire. But what I don't understand is why I sense no magic in your blood–no trace of my kin flows through your veins. Has the Order fallen so far they recruit helpless children now?"

"We're not children," Kai said through gritted teeth, taking a step forward and pulling his arm away from Mara to grip his spear with both hands.

"Sister, I tire of this. Will you end him quickly?" Nalaen said. The woman with black hair stepped forward.

"With pleasure," she said, two daggers flashing into her hands, too fast for Mara to even see where they'd come from.

"Kai..." Mara said. Her throat felt dry. "Don't lose your–"

Kai was already off, leaping at the black-haired woman. She merely stood there and smiled, waiting for him to draw close. Kai's movement felt slow in Mara's mind, every step an eternity, every breath bringing him closer to the inevitable fate Mara was sure to come. They'd trained their whole lives for this, but they weren't ready–not fully. Mara turned her head to Brol and Dax. She felt a scream in her throat but heard no sound. The world began to spin.

Brol and Dax gripped their own spears, stepping forward to help Kai. Before they could draw any closer, two of the dragon warriors intercepted them, moving so quickly they barely had time to react. Brol was knocked to the ground, disarmed. Dax took a heavy blow to the chest, knocking the wind out of him, also disarmed. The warriors kept their swords leveled at the group, preventing anyone from interfering in the fight. All Mara could do was watch it unfold, praying for some miracle to stop it before Kai met his end.

Kai finished his approach, swinging furiously. The woman was already gone, sidestepped, tapping Kai on the back of his head with the butt of one of her knives. Kai stumbled forward, recovered, and spun back toward her. She kept moving, keeping to his left. Mara saw her move faster than anyone she'd ever seen, save some of the senior Dragonbloods. Her knives came up, Kai swung again, missed. As Kai spun to track her movement, Mara saw the line of blood along the side of his cheek. The woman licked the edge of her knife, her eyes glowing stronger now. Mara feared the worst.

"How long will you play with him, Sister," Nalaen said, smiling. Her eyes were steadily growing brighter, too.

Kai grunted, charging again as the black-haired woman coaxed cheers from the others. Slightly caught off guard, the woman reeled, deflecting Kai's sudden attack. Kai pressed her, swinging his spear around in a spinning arc, then stabbing straight for her face. Each attack was parried, each with more ease. Kai stepped back, swinging again as he leapt past her. From what Mara could tell, it was another miss.

The woman turned to face Mara's direction, a smile on her face. Mara held her breath. Kai had drawn blood of his own across her cheek. The woman's expression shifted as she seemed to notice the same thing. She reached up and wiped her fingers through the blood, scoffing as she flicked it away. Kai smiled.

"That's enough, boy," she said, her eyes flaring brighter. Her features started to shift, Mara catching a hint of the dragon beneath. Her teeth grew slightly longer, her face elongated. Then, even faster than before, the woman bolted straight for Kai. It was so fast, Mara barely kept track of her. Mara closed her eyes, starting to cry out.

A clash of metal, a grunt, and a nearby dragon fell to the ground grasping his chest. Mara looked around, confused. Where was Kai? And who was that now sparring with the black-haired woman?

Mara strained her eyes, trying to comprehend what she was seeing. It was Caliena.

The black-haired woman grunted, let out a deafening screech, then pressed at Caliena, who continued to parry her onslaught while everyone around scattered, confused.

The Princess looked at the bleeding dragon, her face portraying her own confusion. The others bolted to her side, trying to protect her from whatever hidden attack had injured their comrade.

Mara felt a touch on her arm, looked back to see Bran crouched behind her.

"Time to go," he said, then pulled her away from the group. Mara looked past him, seeing Kai propped up by Dax and Brol, a smirk directed at her.

"Kai, what happened? How did you–"

"Bran," he said, lifting his head. "Thank you," he added, directed at the man.

"Yes, yes. We'll have time for thanks later. Meanwhile, dragons..."

Bran nodded, then disappeared into the darkness of the storm back toward Caliena, who was still going toe-to-toe with the black-haired woman.

"Right," Kai said. "He told me they already moved the others. We need to get the horses and get out of here."

"Are you alright?" Mara asked, looking Kai up and down.

"Yes, I'm fine. Just twisted my ankle something fierce in the struggle. And I lost my spear. But go ahead. We'll follow."

Mara nodded, glad they were away from the danger, but knowing it was still very close. She didn't know how long Bran and Caliena could hold up against a whole group of dragons. Even as actual Dragonbloods, she doubted they could fight that many.

They started off through the snow, quickly finding the horses, the remaining four in quite a fit of nervousness. Mara helped Brol and Dax get Kai in his saddle, then she climbed on her own horse, trying to calm it as best she could. It took a minute, but finally she and the others were racing off down the hill, away from the fighting. Mara gazed back over her shoulder, hoping Caliena and Bran were alright, but she could see nothing through the haze of snow and darkness.

The sound of the fighting began to fade as they made their way further down the hill. Mara felt better, but they still didn't know where they were going. She supposed anywhere was better than where they'd just come from.

"Where–" Mara started, cut short by a sudden rush behind her. She turned around just in time to see a full-sized dragon barreling down on them through the canopy of white. "Kai!" she called out, the last thing she remembered before darkness overcame her.

***

Kai rolled on his side, a terrible pain throbbing through his whole body. His head was cloudy, thoughts of the fight with the black-haired woman coming back to him. He remembered them getting on the horses, then... darkness. *What happened?*

He sat up, looking around. He remembered Mara's scream.

Mara.

He searched frantically for her. He saw the horses, strewn about nearby, some of their guts draped across the snow, followed by splashes of deep red.

One. Two. Three. Where's the fourth? Where's Mara?

He stood up, the pain in his side forcing him to take it slow, the determination to find his sister causing him to ignore it. He limped forward. He saw Dax lying still next to one of the dead horses.

He heard a groan to his left, saw Brol reaching for his head, trying to sit up.

"Brol," Kai called.

"Eh," Brol mumbled.

"Brol... Dax." Kai pointed, Brol suddenly opening his eyes, following Kai's arm to spot Dax. "I'm going to find Mara. Help him."

Brol nodded, and Kai turned. He saw trails of blood etched in the snow. His stomach lurched into his throat, a terrible feeling setting in. He staggered forward, following the trail, praying he'd find his sister still alive at the other end of it.

The storm was thick, and darkness had almost fully set in. Kai could scarcely see more than a handful of feet in front of him. He continued to follow the trail, which quickly became more than just blood. More entrails, seemingly from the last horse.

Too much to be Mara. Come on, Kai. He groped his side, moving faster.

And then he saw the body.

The last horse, but no Mara. Kai sighed heavily and kept moving, searching everywhere his eyes could see. He saw the snow was piled in odd ways, as if something incredibly large had crashed down there.

He followed the piles, and after a few more steps, noticed a strange light up ahead. He took several more steps toward it, then froze.

It was her–the Princess. Her eyes were glowing a bright red, and she was staring right at Kai. In her arms she held the limp body of Mara.

"Thought you'd just ride away, Kai?" she said, her tone deathly calm. Her haughty air of superiority from before was no more.

"Let her go," Kai said, trying to match her demeanor with his own. "If you're looking for a fight, I'm right here." Even as the words left his mouth, Kai remembered he no longer had his spear.

"Says the boy who barely escaped my sister's clutches, and she was merely toying with you. I will not afford you that same gesture. Besides, it looks like you have no weapon. How exactly do you intend to fight?"

Kai gritted his teeth and clenched his fists, but in truth, he had no idea. His mind raced, searching for something. Perhaps, if he could somehow stall her. Maybe someone would come to help.

"You never answered her question..." Kai said, dipping his head toward Mara.

"What question?" Nalaen asked, narrowing her eyes.

"What *do* you want? Why are you here after all these years?"

"I *did* tell you. Vengeance. My mother was slain by your kind in these very ruins."

Kai remembered the stories. His mind continued to race, his eyes searching for something he could use, some way to get Mara away from her grasp. But how?

"We weren't even alive then. She has nothing to do with your mother's death. Let her go. And if it's vengeance you seek, then take me."

"You?" Nalaen scoffed. "You're nothing. You're no one. My vengeance will not be satisfied solely by killing random *sangures*... random *Dragonbloods*, especially one with no actual blood in his veins. No, my vengeance will only be quenched by the blood of one man."

"Who?" Kai asked, curious, but he still needed to buy time.

Kai saw the Princess pause, eyeing him through narrow eyelids, as if she were pondering whether or not she wanted to answer. Kai eyed Mara, she began to stir slightly. Nalaen looked down and smiled.

"Looks like dear Sister is coming to. Won't she be delighted to discover her current predicament."

Kai's eyes grew wide. *Sister? How did she–?*

"Yes, I know," came her reply. "I can clearly see the bond between you two. Now, tell me, Kai. Tell me of the one I seek, and maybe I will let her live. The man I seek... this Grayscale. Tell me where I can find him and no more of you need to die."

Grayscale. Kai's expression shifted, the world beginning to feel as though it was spinning. She was back for Yoren! The stories were true. His uncle had been there that night.

Mara's eyelids began to flutter, opening a few seconds later. Her gaze met with Kai's, and for a moment, he saw confusion flood her features.

"I can see you know him. A mentor, perhaps? Tell me, or you will hear her screams even in death."

"Kai?" Mara said, growing terrified. She struggled in Nalaen's grasp, but the dragon held her firm. "Kai? What's going on? What does she mean?"

Kai's shoulders slumped, a weakness taking over him he could not fight. What was he supposed to do?

"I–" he started, barely able to speak. "Please, let her go and I will tell you."

"Where?" Nalaen roared, her eyes flaring brighter. A gasp from Mara and Kai saw the Princess's fingertips elongating, resembling her dragon claws, the tip of one of them drawing a drop of blood from Mara's throat.

"Stop. I'll tell you. Just let her go."

The features on Nalaen's face grew more deadly, her face and jaw swirling in a transformative pattern, her claws growing even longer as she held up her hand, as if to show him.

"Where?" she shouted even louder, her voice growing deep and ethereal.

"He's–" Kai started, but a whistling sound cut him short. He felt a gush of wind as something passed closely by his head.

There was a roar, the Princess reeled to the side, her claws passing across Mara's face as she let go. Blood splattered across the snow. A second later, as Kai began to sprint toward her, he felt the presence of someone close behind him. He turned, seeing the faces of Cyrus and Yoren on either side. He wanted to smile, but Mara needed help. Yoren nodded to Kai, then charged forward toward the Princess, who was starting to recover from the attack.

"Dragonbloods," Kai heard Yoren call out. "To me!"

Kai ran up to Mara, who was still hunched over in the snow, blood all around her, the two men rushing past toward the princess. He grabbed her and turned her over, staring into her bloody face. Her eyes were closed, several gashes crossing her eyes. She was shaking, though from the fear of what just happened, the pain, or the cold, he could not know.

Yoren came over and knelt beside them. Kai looked up at him as he held his sister tight.

"Is she okay?" Yoren asked, reaching out to touch Mara's arm.

"I– I don't know. She's hurt badly," Kai replied, his own voice shaky.

"Let's get her out of here. The others can take care of the dragons."

Kai continued to hold Mara, still weak, but an anger was welling up inside him.

"It's your fault," Kai said.

"What?" Yoren asked.

"It's your fault," Kai repeated, looking at his uncle with angry, tear-filled eyes. "She came for *you*."

"What do you mean, Kai? Who came for me?"

"That dragon. She's the daughter of the Queen you killed all those years ago. She said your name–*our* name. She specifically said she's back for the man who killed her mother. For Grayscale."

A distant look filled Yoren's eyes, the realization of Kai's words seeming to hit him like a boulder. He turned his gaze up the hill toward the ring of Dragonbloods who now surrounded the princess, now in her dragon form, roaring and lashing out at the group surrounding her. There were flashes of light beyond them, more fighting further up the hill.

"I'm sorry, Kai," Yoren said, his demeanor somber. "I will fix this. Get your sister to safety."

Kai looked at him, his anger still strong, but he knew his words were true. Mara needed help, fast. Kai stood, Mara still in his arms, turning his back to Yoren.

"Take care of her, Kai. And... take care of yourself. You are more than you know–both of you. I– I know your father would be proud."

Kai continued to walk away, making no acknowledgement of Yoren's words. He heard his uncle turn and sprint up the hill to join the others.

Kai picked up his pace, continuing down the hill. He remembered there was a small stream just up ahead, and perhaps he could clean Mara up before they figured out how to get out of there. After several dozen slow, steady steps, he heard it bubbling in the darkness.

Kai knelt beside the stream, placing Mara down gently. She was quiet, Kai fearing the worst, though he pushed the thoughts aside and ripped off a piece of his sleeve. He dipped it in the water, wrung it out, then began to pat it gently on Mara's face. He continued for a minute until her face was clean, two long scars now exposed that ran across her face. Her eyelids were scratched, but he couldn't tell if her eyes were damaged. He lifted his head up to the sky.

Kai had never been one to put much stock in the gods—the creators of the world known as the Architects. Some say they disappeared long ago, others still worshipped them as if they listened to the cries of those who still held faith. Either way, Kai needed a miracle, and for the first time since he could remember, he cried out to them.

A commotion to the side, Kai peered through the snow and darkness to see the battle had moved down the hill, just up the stream from them. Fire was burning through the trees above, illuminating the hillside. He prepared to get up and move Mara again, but a sound caught his ear—a voice he recognized.

It was Yoren. He could see them now, Yoren and a dragon fighting alone. It seemed neither was winning, both bearing red splotches that caught the light of the fires above. Both breathing heavily.

Kai watched as the dragon roared before shrinking back into the human form of the princess. She was panting, her eyes barely glowing now, several cuts along her arms and legs. She spat blood on the nearby snow, stood up straight, and squared off against Yoren.

Yoren raised his spear toward her, spitting a spat of blood himself. Kai saw him faltering slightly, noticing a steady line of blood down one leg.

Both of them began to circle each other, only a short distance apart.

"You fought well, Grayscale. But it is not so easy to kill a queen when she's ready for your attack," Nalaen said. It was clear she was tired. She might have even been bluffing, but Yoren looked bad, too. Where were the others?

"I did what I had to do to protect my people," Yoren replied. "But I am sorry for your loss... for what it's worth."

"Sorry? You don't get to be sorry. Not here, not now," Nalaen spat. "And really? Protect your people? You mean the ones who slaughter and enslave anyone with magical blood in their veins? No. Humans are a blight upon this world. A stain that must be removed."

Kai watched in silence, holding Mara close, part of him wanting to get up and move Mara away, no matter his uncle's fate. But something held him there. A voice inside, telling him his uncle did not deserve this. He *was* just protecting their people. He couldn't have known the repercussions all these years later.

As Kai wrestled with his thoughts, he caught a hint of movement in the shadows of the trees behind Yoren. Kai strained his eyes, focusing on it. It moved again, a hint of light catching it, the form of the woman with black hair flashing briefly into clarity.

Kai hesitated for a moment. The woman crept closer, then leapt from the shadows.

"Uncle!" Kai called out instinctively.

Yoren spun just in time to parry her attack as she leapt at him, both her knives aimed at his chest.

Nalaen's eyes widened and flashed toward Kai and Mara, then back to Yoren, the realization of what Kai had just said setting in. She screamed in rage, then began walking toward them as Yoren struggled against the sister's onslaught. Apparently, she was not as tired as her sister.

Yoren stole a glance in Kai and Mara's direction, noticing Nalaen walking toward them.

In a burst of strength, Yoren bellowed, his own eyes flaring to a bright yellow glow. Kai had only ever seen it once before–the true strength of a Dragonblood unleashed. He parried another attack from the black-haired woman, spinning his spear around to smack her upside the head with the butt of it. As she bounced backward, he swung the spear around, swiping it across her face, a spurt of blood scattering about the snow around them, slicing open her cheek. She fell backward, Yoren instantly turning to chase after Nalaen, who was drawing closer to Kai and Mara with every second.

So fast was Yoren's speed, Nalaen could not react in her weakened state. He tackled her, his spear driving into her shoulder, and they crashed into the stream, only a short distance up from where Kai knelt clutching Mara.

She lay, unmoving, pinned down by Yoren as her blood turned the stream red. Kai watched it flow slowly down, past him and into the darkness beyond. *Was she dead?*

A gurgle and Kai quickly turned back, seeing the black-haired woman standing behind Yoren, a look of satisfaction etched across her bloody face, her knives buried deep in Yoren's back. She met Kai's gaze with a maniacal expression.

Kai's eyes widened in horror. His eyes met with Yoren's. Yoren's eyes cast down to the stream of blood flowing down the water, to Mara, then back to Kai. He pointed, lifting his hand up to his mouth. With the light in his eyes flickering, Yoren slammed his head backward, hitting the woman square in the face, blood bursting from her nose. He let go of his spear, turned, and tackled her down into the snow behind him. Kai saw the two daggers still protruding from his back, gushing streaks of blood flowing from them.

Kai looked down at the blood-red water, his mind racing to understand. *Drink.*

Kai glanced at Mara, then back at the water. He quickly dipped the strip of cloth in it, soaked up a bunch, bringing it above Mara's mouth. He used his other hand to pull open her jaw, then squeezed the bloody water out and into her mouth. He did this several more times, not knowing how much blood was needed, nor how quickly it would start working. But if there was a chance it would heal her, he would take it.

After several squeezes, Mara started coughing, a bit of blood spurting from her mouth. Relieved, Kai set her gently aside, leaning down to cup his hands in the stream. He lifted it up, took a drink, then did it again.

At first, he felt nothing. Slowly, he could feel his heart begin to pound faster, his head starting to spin. He heard Mara speaking, her words jumbled.

"Kai. What's happening. I can't see. Why do I feel–"

Darkness closed in around Kai, fragmented images of Mara fainting, of the princess's limp form stirring, of the black-haired woman limping away from Yoren's still body toward her fallen sister, of shouting as knights rushed down the hill, of a dragon flying away, of Cyrus's face over him.

And then, nothing.

CHAPTER TWENTY-THREE

BLOOD

"You should probably get some rest and let that heal," Sorn said as he approached Nalaen, eyeing her bloody shoulder. She was standing still, staring down at the splattered bloody snow where the man named Grayscale had fallen. Sorn bent down, touching his fingers to the frozen blood. Even though it had been their objective all along, it didn't feel right.

"I'm fine," Nalaen said, turning away from him.

Sorn knew she was lying, but the wound hadn't been mortal, and though it still looked nasty, it was simply a matter of rest for her to fully recover.

"Are we sure he's dead?" Sorn asked.

"Yes, Brother," Talesa said. "I saw the light fade from his eyes before I got Sister out of there. And you see how much blood colors the snow. He's dead."

"He apologized at the end. Why?" Sorn asked, looking up at Nalaen.

"Because he was about to die, of course," Talesa remarked casually as she attended to her scars, most of which were already healing quite well. "He put up quite the fight, but in the end, he died like the vermin he was."

"He was protecting his family," Sorn stated, directed again at Nalaen as she stared off into the distance, the next morning's sun just beginning its ascent for the day. "And it seems you've already forgotten about the scar on your face, Talesa. You're lucky to be alive."

"Well, here I am, still breathing, and he isn't," Talesa scoffed, giving Sorn a sarcastic look.

The storm had passed, and the fighting was over. All in all, it had gone in the dragons' favor. They'd only lost one of their own, Drae'ko Masila, while the humans had lost at least three before retreating. For Sorn, it didn't feel like a victory.

"His family, yes. It's unfortunate they got away," Nalaen said, breaking her silence.

"They were not our target, Sister," Sorn exclaimed, taken aback by his sister's words. "We got what we came for."

Nalaen turned and shot Sorn a glare—one that made him feel uncomfortable. He'd seen that look before, and it never meant anything good. It also meant he'd overstepped his bounds.

"They *were* not our targets, but I cannot let them live. The name of Grayscale shall be wiped from the surface of this world, never to be uttered again by those who still live. I will hunt until the end of time if I must, but they *will* die, just as he died." Nalaen looked back at the blood-soaked snow, the light in her eyes flaring, as if an unyielding oath that could not be broken had just been made.

Sorn watched Nalaen, though he dared not speak another word. Rarely had his sister been in such a mood, but from the handful of times he'd seen it before, he knew there was nothing he could do but stand aside as her fury took flight.

"Good," Talesa said. "I got a taste of that boy's blood, and now I want more."

"And you will have it, Sister," Nalaen said. "Your actions last night saved my life. I will not forget it."

Talesa gave Sorn a sly smile.

"But we must come up with a new plan," Nalaen continued. "We were fortunate last night. They were outmatched. But they will not be as easy of a target now that they know we are here—now that they know our strength. They will hide in their fortress, no doubt. We must assess their full strength and devise a plan to strip it away."

"Princess," came a call from the side. Galen walked up to them, eyeing the bloody area in the snow

"So, he's dead then?" he asked.

"Yes," Nalaen answered.

"Then it is done."

"No, it is not."

Galen's eyes narrowed, his expression shifting. Nalaen turned to meet his gaze.

"My mission was to find and kill Grayscale. One is dead, but there are at least two more. I will not return home until all those who carry the Grayscale name have bled dry."

"Princess, I must respectfully disagree—"

"You can disagree all you like, Drae'vir, but that does not change the fact that I will not be leaving. Your mission was to escort and protect me, no?"

"It was..."

"Then fulfill your duty, as I fulfill mine. Our Queen's memory deserves as much."

"Very well, Princess. But I must warn you, Kyrian and the Council will likely not approve."

"Better to ask forgiveness, as they say," Nalaen said, trailing off. Her expression was resolute. Galen looked at Sorn and Talesa, hoping for something more. Sorn gave a slight shrug, his gesture telling the dragon there was no fighting with his sister.

Galen let out a sigh, then nodded to Nalaen.

"I trust you have a plan?" Galen asked.

"I do."

"Care to enlighten us?"

"Soon, but there is something I must do, first."

"Very well. I will go to the others in the ruins, and we will await your word. Everyone could do with more rest to recover. I will be there, waiting."

With that, Galen gave a half bow, then turned and stormed off, whispering something under his breath.

"So, what *is* our next move, Sister?" Talesa asked.

"I must commune with my *delisae*. He may be of use in getting close to the humans and finding more about these young Grayscales."

"Ack," Talesa spit. "The human again?"

"He has his uses. We will give him some time to get close to the humans. We can learn about our enemy from the inside–how they work, their strengths, and... their weaknesses. Then, we will plan our attack."

"Ugh. Call me when you have blood that needs spilling, Sister," Talesa yawned. "Until then, I will get some more rest as well." She immediately stood and stretched, walking off without waiting for any reply.

"Talesa..." Sorn chuckled, "always eager to kill, never eager to plan. But that is a good plan, Sister. However, it's more than that, isn't it?"

"More than what?"

"This is more than just the boy and his sister. You and I both know your aspirations are grander. If Kyrian finds out–"

"He will not find out."

"How can you be sure Galen has not already sent word?"

"Mykael has kept me informed of their conversations."

"I see. But can he keep Galen from sending messages in private? I do not know Galen's control of magic, but I can imagine he's learned at least a few tricks rising to his station as Kyrian's eyes and ears in the Queensguard."

"I'm devising a plan with Mykael to remedy that. But worst case, we will adjust as needed. I do not fear Kyrian. In time, he will pay for his crimes," Nalaen hissed, her eyes betraying her hatred. Sorn thought he detected something deeper there lurking in the back of her mind.

"He is dangerous, and devious, but crimes? That might be a difficult stretch. Is there something you're not telling me, Sister?"

"No," Nalaen retorted quickly. "Just his pervasion of the Council, and his efforts to undermine my claim to the throne. He will pay for his attempts to cast aside our family."

"Indeed..." Sorn acknowledged. He knew there was something else, but Nalaen was getting agitated. "Either way, I'll keep a closer eye on Galen. I may be able to monitor his magical output without him taking notice. Just in case."

"Thank you, Brother. Your mastery of magic is quite impressive–for a male. You, too, continue to prove yourself useful. Speaking of which, do you remember how to perform *acroturas*?"

"The projection magic? Yes, why?"

"We no longer have the element of surprise. The Order knows we are here. Let's send them a message—one that can be seen for a hundred miles," Nalaen said, a treacherous glint in her eye.

Sorn let out a sigh. Nalaen was clever, but never shied away from a display of power.

"Tonight?" Sorn asked.

"Tonight."

CHAPTER TWENTY-FOUR

REVERENCE

A horn blew, echoing through the halls of Dragonscale Keep. It was time for the ceremony to honor the fallen.

Aerin had heard whispers of what happened throughout the keep ever since they'd returned the day prior. He tried to piece it all together based on what he heard, but it had been broken and inconsistent. However, one thing echoed clearly between them all.

Yoren Grayscale, the Spear of the Scalewarden, was dead.

Aerin had only shared a few words with the man, but it had not taken him long to understand how important he was to the Order. Karg was in charge, but Yoren, it seemed, held the largest sway over the hearts and minds of all. Based on the somber atmosphere around the keep, it was a wound they would not soon recover from.

Yoren's niece and nephew, the twins Kai and Mara, also seemed to be in trouble—Mara especially. What ailed them, Aerin was not quite sure, but he heard mention of various controversies surrounding it, though none of it made much sense to him.

Everyone in the dining hall around Aerin rose when they heard the horn. They had been expecting it. Quietly, they left the tables, leaving their messes behind, and set off toward the arena. Aerin filed out behind them, drifting down the halls as more of the keep joined the procession.

Over the past few days, Aerin had felt quite welcome. But after the tragedies of the past day, he'd felt more and more excluded. He'd come to the Order hoping to help, but it only felt like this was all somehow his fault. He was the one who'd come bearing bad news. He was the reason Yoren and the others rode out. And even though he knew it wasn't directly his fault, he still felt like Yoren's death was, in part, because of him.

As the procession rounded the corner and came into full view of the arena, he noted three pyres had been erected of stone and wood. They were situated in the middle of the arena, a small crowd already gathered there as the rest of the keep filed in. Torches were lit around the arena, and there was one lone torch in the middle of the pyres made of metal, intricate lacework adorning its bronze handle. The ceremonial torch.

As Aerin took his place, he gazed solemnly at the three bodies. Two of the knights he did not recognize, but the third, Yoren, lay on the middle pyre. Even in death, he appeared grander than any of the knights he'd met in Valehold or otherwise. Aerin felt humbled to be in the presence of such a protector of the realm.

A tear etched its way into the corner of his eye. Though he did not know the man, the overwhelming sense of grief surrounding him seemed to draw it from his eyes. The somber nature of all eyes cast Yoren's way permeated Aerin's mind, forcing him to choke back the beckoning grief.

A change in the air stirred Aerin from his struggle. Looking up, he saw all eyes had been cast to his left. The Scalewarden, Karg Wyrmsbane, approached.

Aerin had never seen a more magnificent sight. The Scalewarden was adorned from head to toe in the grandest armor he'd ever laid eyes on, its glistening silver plates starkly contrasted by the red filigree laced across the breastplate and greaves. The symbol of the Order–a spear emblazoned in flames–stood out clearly from the polished metal. At his back, Karg wore a flowing, blood-red cape.

In his hand, he carried a spear of exceptional craftsmanship. Even from where Aerin stood, he could see the intricate designs carved into its bronze shaft, flowing upwards to the silver tip at its head. It looked like flames.

Everyone stared at the Scalewarden, apprehension in the air. Aerin could see he was mustering himself to speak, the grief clear in his features. His shoulders, even in the spectacular armor, seemed to slump forward. His balance appeared to waver slightly, and it looked as though he was using his spear to lean on. He kept his eyes fixed firmly on the pyre where Yoren's body lay.

"Today," he started, moving his eyes across the crowd, "we gather to mourn three of our own under the light of a moon we never thought we would see again. They were brothers, sons, friends... and family." Karg choked on his words. "No matter who they were in their past lives, the bond of blood shared between us made them so much more than just fellow knights of the Order. We all feel the pain of their absence."

"As Dragonbloods, they swore an oath to protect this land and its people from the fiery wrath of the dragons. Yesterday, they died defending that oath, though none of us could have anticipated it to happen so suddenly. We will never forget their sacrifice, both to defend this land, and to protect the next generation–the blood of our blood. Though not all here can fully understand the blood-bond we share at this time, you may soon know. For if the dragons have returned, our stores of blood may soon be filled again. But that is a problem for the coming days. Tonight, we mourn."

Karg turned to one of the knights next to him–the one called Cyrus. Cyrus handed him what looked like a pendant, and Karg walked forward toward the leftmost pyre, Cyrus close behind.

"Bran Lightfoot, son of Halron Davenport," Karg said, lifting the pendant above his head. "He protected our own, sacrificing his life to help them when they were outmatched and unable to fight. His quick thinking and courageous acts saved the Order from mourning any others this day. We honor you, Blood of our blood."

"*Blood of our blood*," came a somber reply from all around Aerin.

"May your memory live on in the halls of our forefathers," Karg said, laying the necklace across Bran's chest. He backed up and bowed, everyone around the arena doing the same. Aerin followed suit.

Karg turned and passed Yoren's pyre, moving to the other knight. There, he paused again, taking a new necklace and holding it high.

"Kalin Hightower, son of Ganis Hightower, the father who still stands beside us," Karg said, turning as an older man approached. Karg handed the stalwart man the pendant, who then stood up beside the pyre, bent forward and kissed his son on the head, placing the pendant across his chest as Karg had done.

"Blood of my blood," Ganis spoke, the pain of grief filling every word.

"*Blood of our blood*," everyone replied again.

With teary eyes, Karg and Ganis exchanged a firm shake and a brief hug, Karg leaning in to whisper words to the father. After a moment, Ganis rejoined the crowd and Karg moved to stand before the final pyre.

Here, he paused, staring at Yoren for several seconds.

"Tonight, we honor the loss of one of our best—of one who could have easily served in my stead as Scalewarden. Yoren Grayscale was the best of us, and in many ways, he was just as much the leader of this Order as I was. Without his gentle hand and careful guidance all these years, I fear I would have been lost. There were... choices I made, many years ago. Choices I regret. Yoren was the one who showed me things could be different—that things could be... better. He was integral in helping me build a brighter future for the Order, even if that future was one where we were no longer needed."

"But that future is no more," he continued, his eyes scanning the crowd. "We expected the dragons would return one day, though we did not think it would be in our lifetimes. They caught us unprepared. But they will regret the day they returned to our borders, breaking the peace accord that's stood for nearly a hundred years. They will pay for taking the lives of our brothers."

Karg turned his eyes back to Yoren's body, his anger softening.

"You have passed into the great beyond, Brother. Your days of service have come to an end. Though it will not be the same without your guidance, we will carry on in your memory. Enjoy your rest, and worry not, for it may be soon that I will come to join you in those sacred halls. And when that day comes, we will eat and drink and share tales of battle into eternity."

Karg reached over and exchanged his spear with another from Cyrus. This one was not so grand as his own, though it, too, was adorned with elaborate patterns. Aerin recognized it as the spear Yoren had carried when they'd first met.

Karg approached Yoren's pyre, his eyes wet with grief. Aerin did not know how he could keep them from gushing forth, Aerin's own tears now flowing freely after Karg's brief speech.

"Blood of our blood," Karg shouted, lifting the spear high.

"*Blood of our blood,*" came an echo from the knights.

"May this spear go with you into the afterlife, Brother," Karg spoke as he placed the spear across Yoren's chest. "Until another proves their worth to take up your mantle, may it guide you and keep you safe in the lands beyond."

A lone tear ran down Karg's cheek. He laid his forehead on Yoren's hand, all the knights watching quietly.

Aerin was not sure how long this lasted, but it felt like an eternity. He had to avert his eyes for some time, the scene of the old man, looking as if he might now be weeping, was too much for him to bear. When at last he felt a stirring in the crowd, he looked up to see Karg standing solemnly in the center of the pyres, the bronze torch in his hand.

"From fire you came, and to fire you shall return. Let the flames of this world burn, sending you on to a peaceful forever slumber, knowing full well that you have served the Order faithfully to the end."

Karg turned and walked to Bran's pyre. He brought the torch over and lit the kindling, setting it ablaze. He did the same for Kalin, then approached Yoren's.

"Goodbye, old friend," Karg said quietly, lighting the pyre.

Karg handed the torch off, then took a knee before the ignited pyres. All around Aerin, the knights began doing the same. Aerin joined them.

There was another long silence as everyone watched the flames, the flickering light of the fires casting their yellow glow around the arena. Though sad, Aerin felt humbled to be in the presence of such a company as the knights who surrounded him. He did not belong amongst them, but he would do what he could to help them recover from this.

Karg stood, looking around at the host surrounding him. His sadness was gone, and the fires of anger burned clearly in his eyes again, the flickering light of the flames making it even more apparent.

"Continue your mourning tonight in whatever way you see fit. Tomorrow, we begin preparations for war. We will not let this attack go unpunished. The dragons have forgotten their defeat. We shall remind them."

Karg nodded his head and moved to leave, the edge of the circle creating a gap for him. Suddenly, there was a flash of light, followed by a gasp from the arena.

There, atop the highest peak of one of the distant mountains, the glowing shape of a dragon's head took form. It was shining a bright orange, a swirling torrent of flame and magic. The dragon's head rose from behind the snowy peak, its neck appearing, gradually looming higher above the top of the mountain. Then its wings appeared, cresting the sides of the peak, spreading out wide around it, their glow casting an amber embrace of the snow-covered mountaintop.

Finally, the image of the dragon seemed to settle. Everyone in the keep stared in awe of it, some seeming apprehensive at what it might mean. Aerin, himself, felt a cold chill run down his spine.

The spectacle of the dragon reared its head, then let out a roar, echoing down the mountains and through the valleys. Eyes grew wider and Aerin's heart beat loudly.

Just as suddenly as it had appeared, the image of the dragon faded into darkness, the red hue in the snow fading back into a pale reflection of the moon's light.

Everyone around the pyres stood there for another minute, silence in the air aside from the crackling of the pyre flames.

"So, it begins…" Karg said, breaking the silence. All eyes rested on him, the weight of his words fully settling in. A low hum of voices began to fill the air as those in the arena started speaking amongst each other.

Aerin stood alone amongst them, his eyes still cast upward to the now dark peak. He did not know how he could be of use against such a foe, but one way or another, he was going to atone for sending Yoren and the others to their deaths. Somehow, he was going to take revenge against the ones who murdered Yoghar and Kanir, against this so-called princess.

Somehow.

CHAPTER TWENTY-FIVE

SUBTERFUGE

It was early morning when Jarren knocked timidly on the massive iron gates, the hairs on the back of his neck pricking with every thump of the large, iron lever.

This is it, Jarren. This is what she commanded. Don't fail her.

The voice in his head had only grown louder in the past two days. It seemed more eager, more desperate than it had before. And now it urged him to infiltrate the very heart of the ones known as Dragonbloods.

When no reply came from beyond the gates, Jarren tried to force himself to walk away. No matter how hard he tried, compulsion kept his feet planted firmly in the dirt. Uncontrollably, his hand reached for the iron ring and knocked once more.

"Who goes there?" shouted a voice from atop the gate. Jarren shivered.

"I-it's Jarren," he replied.

"Jarren? Jarren who?" the voice asked.

Idiot. He doesn't know your name.

"Jarren... from the Lodge."

"The Lodge? One moment."

Jarren waited, shivering once more. He stared at the large gates before him. They didn't seem to be the gates of an evil order. They just seemed like normal gates.

She never told us why...

After an awkwardly long wait, the gate creaked open, the metallic clang of its iron hinges sending a strange sensation down Jarren's spine. He took several steps back from the gate, the feeling of apprehension growing.

"Jarren?" said a knight in steel armor, the infamous crest of the Order of Scales on his chest, a red cloak at his back.

"Yes?"

"That is your name, correct?" the knight asked, his forehead scrunched in a questioning manner.

"Oh... yes, Jarren."

"Very well, Jarren. Follow me."

Jarren followed the knight, who turned on his heel and headed for a large doorway at the other end of the wide, open area just beyond the gate. Jarren looked around, instantly noticing three stone piles in the center of the arena. They appeared charred, as if a fire had been lit atop them.

To honor their dead, said the voice in his head. *They will need more before this is over.*

"You say you're from the Lodge?" the knight questioned, looking back at Jarren.

Jarren quickly averted his eyes, feeling a sudden pulse of guilt wash over him. Jarren glanced up at him quickly, nodded, then cast his eyes back down toward the dirt.

"Interesting. We've already received one hunter. We did not expect any others to come."

Jarren's shame was quickly replaced by fear. Who could possibly be here? Was someone looking for him?

"Wh–" Jarren stuttered, then swallowed.

"Eh?" the knight asked, eyeing Jarren with a confused look.

Relax. Everything will be fine.

Jarren wanted to relax–felt compelled, even, but his hands were still shaking. Jarren shook his head, the knight eyeing him strangely once more before continuing forward to the gate. He pressed it open enough for them to fit through, then waved his hand for Jarren to proceed.

Inside, the hallway was lined with torches, a long passage leading straight into the mountain. Jarren marveled at it, forgetting about his anxiety for the time being.

The knight closed the gate behind them, then took off down the hall, motioning for Jarren to follow. He tried to keep in step with the knight, continuing to investigate the area. They passed down several hallways that went off to the left or the right, each time Jarren paused for a moment to look down it, each time the knight clearing his throat in an effort to hurry Jarren along.

Finally, they entered a section of the keep that seemed to be some sort of central area, with several larger hallways branching off in different directions. Jarren gazed curiously down all of them.

"This way," the knight said, ushering him down one to the left.

They walked a short way before coming into view of another two hallways and an open doorway, which appeared to be an office of sorts. He saw a large man inside, a gray beard formed around an exhausted face. He was rifling through papers at the desk inside.

"Wait here," the knight ordered, then moved to stand in the doorway.

"Excuse me, sir," the knight said, clearing his throat. The man inside the office looked up, Jarren eyeing him with curiosity.

"Yes?" the man inside asked. He sounded as flustered as he looked.

"We've got another visitor, Cyrus. He says he's from the Lodge."

Cyrus scrunched his brow, leaning to the side to eye Jarren curiously.

"Another? Odd," Cyrus said. He stood and came around the desk, the knight moving aside so he could come out to greet Jarren.

"His name is Jarren, sir," the knight said as Cyrus exited the room.

"Jarren? Jarren... that name sounds familiar." Cyrus paused, eyeing Jarren with renewed interest. "Giraud, would you go fetch Aerin, please? We'll see if he can verify this man."

Aerin? Jarren's eyes widened. *Aerin.*

Who is this Aerin, the voice questioned.

He's a friend... sort of. Nice, and not a threat. Probably.

Let's hope so...

Jarren snapped out of his thoughts to see Cyrus standing closer, eyeing him with a curious expression.

"Do you know Aerin?" Cyrus asked.

Jarren nodded, blushing. His hands started to tremble more.

"Why have you come?" Cyrus asked, seeming to notice Jarren's shaking.

Relax, Jarren. Calm your mind. Everything will be fine.

"O-okay," Jarren said aloud.

"Okay?" Cyrus said. "Are you alright? You seem nervous."

"I– I... I'm–"

"Jarren! What are you doing here?" Aerin asked, appearing from down one of the hallways.

"Oh... hello, A-Aerin," Jarren stuttered, his brow furling as he spoke the words. He felt his face grow red again.

Aerin gave him a strange look, confusion littering his face.

"What? How? Jarren, when I left, you were still at the healers. Why are you here now?"

Jarren shrugged, giving an awkward smile in reply. His mind fumbled at the words to say, but then, as if by force, the words came to his mind.

"I came to help. The dragons, they killed Kanir and Yoghar. I want to help the Order get revenge any way I can."

"Dead?" Aerin said. "It's true, then."

"This is the one you told us about?" Cyrus said, turning to him.

"Yes," Aerin said, his eyes staring off at the ground.

"Well, that is fortunate," Cyrus said. "Perhaps you can tell us anything else that might be of use, Jarren."

Jarren nodded, smiling. He liked being helpful. *What should I tell them?*

I will guide you, replied the voice in his head. Jarren nodded again.

Both Cyrus and Aerin turned to look at each other, exchanging puzzled expressions.

"Excellent," Cyrus continued. "But right now, I have more important matters to attend to. Aerin, you're well acquainted with Jarren. You can vouch for him?"

"I do know him," Aerin replied. "And normally I would, but everything that's happened..." Aerin trailed off, eyeing Jarren, seemingly staring past Jarren's eyes and into his soul. Jarren tore his eyes away awkwardly.

He suspects us.

Don't worry about him... for now. We will deal with him if he becomes a problem. Right now, I need you to assess the true strength of the Order and its leaders. Find out what preparations they are making, how many there are, and anything else that might be of use to me.

Yes, m'lady, Jarren replied in his head. He looked back up to the small group present—Aerin, Cyrus, and the knight who'd escorted him in. He tried to think of a way to get alone and figure out how to do as she asked.

"I'm s-sorry," Jarren said. "It's been a long w-walk. I need some rest."

"Yes, of course," Cyrus said, turning to the other knight. "Giraud, can you find Jarren a guest room? Perhaps right next to Aerin's quarters? We'll let him get some rest and see if that clears his head a bit."

"Yes, sir," Giraud said. "Right this way, Mr. Jarren."

Giraud headed down the same hallway that Aerin had come from, and Jarren quickly moved to follow. He cast wary glances at Aerin and Cyrus, tipping his head forward briefly before scuttling off after his escort.

As they moved down the hall, he could faintly hear the exchange of words behind him.

"Odd fellow, isn't he. Is he trustworthy?" Cyrus asked.

"Normally, yes. He is odd, but there's something different about him now. I'll keep an eye on him, Cyrus," Aerin replied.

We may have to deal with him after all. I'll think of a way to get rid of Aerin shortly. I must leave you now, but I'll speak with you tomorrow. Just remember what I said. Get to know them and what they are up to without drawing suspicion.

We're not going to hurt him, are we, Jarren asked.

Not hurt him, no. Just get rid of him.

Okay. I won't fail you, m'lady.

Please, call me Mother...

Yes, Mother.

Chapter Twenty-Six

DRAGONBLOOD

Kai twisted in shadows, muttering unintelligible words, a terrible pain beyond anything he'd ever known pulsing through his very core. And he felt hot–so hot.

Drenched in his own sweat, Kai opened his eyes to stare up at the ceiling of a strange room. It swirled in his vision, the stones seeming to swap places. He tried to focus, felt dizzy, tried again, turned over and hurled onto the floor beside his bed.

His head still spinning, the taste of vomit in his mouth, he looked up and surveyed his surroundings. The walls seemed familiar, but he did not know them.

A flood of thoughts suddenly overcame him, visions of his Uncle fighting the woman with the red hair, another woman, her sister, sneaking up behind him. He saw the princess, her glowing red eyes boring into Kai as she inched closer. And then he saw the images of his uncle's final moments.

Another wave of nausea washed over him. He rolled over and hurled again.

Maybe I am dead, too, and this is my eternal punishment.

Then Kai remembered drinking the blood–the dragon's blood! Was this...?

"Kai? Oh, thank the gods, Kai. You're awake!"

Kai glanced up to see Cyrus entering through the doorway, someone behind him, a woman. He sat up, wiping his mouth clean, though the foul taste remained on his lips. The woman rushed past Cyrus and placed a cool, wet rag on Kai's forehead. It was the best feeling he'd ever felt in the world.

"Can you understand me, Kai?" Cyrus asked, moving to the head of the bed.

Kai nodded slowly, his head pounding.

"I can see you're feeling about as expected," he said, eyeing the pile of vomit on the floor. "Good. It means you're coming around, though you might try aiming for the bucket next time."

Kai turned to the side and noticed a large bucket sitting just off to the side where he'd relieved himself. He glanced back up with an embarrassed expression.

"It's quite alright. It hits some harder than others. You tried to regain consciousness a few times the past day, but all you were doing was rambling, mostly incoherent nonsense. It's good to see you alert now, though I'm sure you must still be feeling quite terrible."

As if I needed the reminder...

Kai looked up to see the typical Cyrus smile, warm and sincere. After a few seconds, it faded, a look of great sorrow ensuing.

"Kai, I– I don't know how to say this, but..."

"I know," Kai barely managed to say. "I saw it before I..."

"I'm so sorry, my boy. He was–" Cyrus paused, his eyes glazing over. "He was a good man. He–" Cutting short, Cyrus just moved closer and placed his hand on Kai's shoulder.

It was my fault, Kai thought. *I'm alive, somehow, and he's...* Kai felt grief take over him, felt like crying, but he couldn't at that moment, realizing how incredibly thirsty he was.

"Water?" Kai asked, his voice horse and quiet, his throat burning.

"Ah, yes. Marie, keep tending to him. I'll fetch some water."

Kai closed his eyes and lay there, waiting for Cyrus to return. He tried to focus on the cool rag sitting on his forehead, tried to ignore the voices creeping around his skull, reminding him over and over it was his fault his uncle was dead.

He felt a hand on his shoulder and jumped slightly, his eyes cracking open to see Cyrus had returned with a glass of water. Momentarily forgetting his demons, he tried to sit up. Everything hurt, but he managed to scoot up in the bed enough to take the drink and tilt his head backward, sipping it down. As soon as the water hit his throat, he began to drink furiously.

He finished the cup in a few seconds, handing it back to Cyrus and looking up at him.

"More?" Cyrus asked. Kai nodded greedily.

Why am I so thirsty? The glass of water barely sated his thirst.

After downing three more cups in similar fashion, Kai felt his thirst finally beginning to subside, his body calming down a bit. He was still warm, but it didn't feel like he was burning up anymore.

"That's enough," Kai said, handing the cup back to Cyrus for the last time. As Cyrus took it, a sudden fear shot through Kai. *Mara!*

"Where's Mara?" Kai asked.

Cyrus's smile faded again.

"She's still asleep in the other room. She's hardly moved a muscle, but she seems to be doing okay. Not like you, that is. I mean, she's a little warm, but not burning up like you were. But we are a little worried since she's been so still. It's not what we'd normally expect from someone who'd just–"

"Take me to her," Kai said, sitting up. His muscles felt a little weak, but he pushed through it. A wave of nausea forced him to take it slow.

"Kai, maybe you should–"

"I'm fine. Just take me to her." Kai swung his feet over the edge of the bed and placed them on the floor. The cold stones felt good against his bare toes.

It took him a few seconds to steady himself into a standing position. When he felt ready, he nodded to Cyrus, forcing the rising vomit in his throat back down with a quick swallow.

"She's just next door," Cyrus said, heading out of the room and turning left into the hallway and entering the next door down.

As Kai entered the room, he immediately felt a strange sensation, the hairs on the back of his neck pricking up as if a bolt of lightning had struck nearby. It was an odd feeling, and Kai couldn't fully explain it. As his eyes landed on his sister's still form, he snapped back to reality.

He hurried over to her side and knelt down, looking her body up and down as she lay there under the covers. A good portion of her face was wrapped in cloth, covering the scars. She appeared peaceful on the surface, her sleep seemingly much more contented than his own had been. But it was what was going on beneath the surface that put Kai off. He felt his sister's physical presence, naturally, but she also felt... distant somehow. It was hard to describe, but either way, Kai didn't like it.

He reached out his hand to touch her.

"I don't know how she's going to take the news, Kai," Cyrus said, his words somber.

Kai paused and thought. *He's right...*

He pulled his hand back and stood, his mood shifting back to embarrassment. How could he tell her? It was all his fault, after all. All of it. *No, I– I don't want her to wake just yet. I need to think this through.*

Kai stood and headed for the door, moving past Cyrus with his head cast down toward the floor.

"Where are you going?" Cyrus asked.

Kai paused in the doorway. He looked at Mara again, then glanced back up at Cyrus.

"I need to think," Kai said, giving Cyrus a flat stare. "And get some fresh air."

He turned and hurried down the corridor, finding his way out of the infirmary. He'd been in this part of the keep a few times, but he still had to orient himself for a few seconds to remember which way led out toward the front gate. He still felt a bit nauseous, and his head was foggy.

"You're awake?" came a familiar voice from off to his left.

Kai turned to see Vi walking his direction. Immediately, his face flushed. He looked down, trying to hide it.

"Oh, hey Vi. Still lurking around corners, I see," he said awkwardly. Though it was meant as a joke, he could not smile at the present. He glanced up, seeing a slight smirk on Vi's face.

"Oh, you know, gotta remain dark and mysterious..." Vi said, her own reply sounding awkward.

Both of them stood in silence for a few seconds, Kai assuming she was just as unsure as he was about what to say.

"So, I-" Vi started.

"I need to-" Kai said, cutting her off.

Both of them stopped, looking awkwardly around for another second.

"Sorry, I–" Vi started again.

"Sorry–" Kai said, then stopped again. "Sorry, you go..."

"How is she?" Vi asked, casting her eyes toward the hallway Kai had just emerged from.

He followed her gaze, trying to decide the words that made the most sense.

"She's okay. At least, I think she's okay. She hasn't woken up yet, but she sleeps peacefully. Not like–" Kai stopped short, not wanting to change the subject. "I'm sure she'll wake up soon."

"That's good to hear... I guess," Vi said. "Did they try to wake her?"

"No, I– I guess it's better if she wakes on her own. Makes sense, I suppose."

"Sure..." Vi said.

There was another long pause, the silence making Kai feel hot again.

"Are... *you*, okay?" Vi asked after another moment, tilting her head forward.

No.

"Yes," Kai replied, feeling his face blush again. "I'm fine, I just need some air, and some time to think."

"Okay," Vi said. Her eyes and tone made it seem though she wanted to say more, but she simply smiled at him.

Kai dipped his head, tried to smile, then turned and headed down the hall away from Vi.

"I'm sure Dax and Brol would like to see you up and about," he heard Vi say after a few steps.

"Thanks, Vi," he offered, turning back to give her another nod. "I'll find them later." *No, I won't.*

In truth, he sincerely hoped he didn't see any more of his friends. He didn't want to talk to anyone right now. He wanted to be alone. He got a few curious stares as he wandered down the halls, but none of them dared talk to him. He didn't blame them. He probably looked about as bad as he felt. Plus, after what had happened...

He thought he heard a few quiet comments between people as they passed by, the thought causing him to heat up again, but he pressed on and soon made his way up the staircase leading atop the wall outside.

The chill breeze felt good as he emerged atop the wall. He saw the hour was late, the sky nearly full dark. In the waning light, he saw only the usual guards at their posts. Breathing a sigh of relief, he leaned against the wall and looked down to the rocky ledge below.

I'm a Dragonblood now, he thought. *Why does it feel so... empty? So bad.*

His mind raced with thoughts, the demons returning to haunt him. He saw Yoren's last moments again. Kai remembered the harsh words he'd said to him. He saw the agony in Yoren's eyes. He saw the knives go through his back. He heard the thud as his body fell into the bloody snow. He saw the light leaving his eyes as he looked directly at Kai for the last time. His Uncle had sacrificed his life to keep him and his sister safe.

A wave of grief overtook Kai, tears welling up inside. They'd been held at bay until now, but he could not hold them back any longer. And so, Kai wept.

He didn't know how long he'd been standing there crying, but when his tears finally stopped, he saw the side of the wall was covered in his sorrow. Embarrassed, he glanced around to see if anyone had noticed, then ran his hand along the surface and flicked the tears off over the edge. He watched them scatter, falling out of sight toward the ground below.

Thoughts filled Kai's head—dark thoughts. He stared at the rocks below, contemplating things he could scarcely believe. Were things really so bad? He finally had what he'd always wanted, but what had it cost him? This was not how Kai had wanted it to happen.

Kai leaned further forward, feeling his arms weak, his head heavy. He held his breath, his heart beating faster.

Kai...

Kai pulled back, looking around in confusion. He was certain he'd heard a voice, like a whisper, but there was no one there. He shook his head. The voice had almost sounded like Mara's.

With his mind now on his sister, he looked back over the edge. He shook his head again, fully realizing where his thoughts had been just moments before. How could he be so foolish? How could he leave her? Mara needed him. In fact, right *now*, she needed him.

Shaking away the last remnants of his dark thoughts, Kai headed for the stairs, descending quickly and heading for the infirmary.

He made it there in short time and went straight to Mara's room. No one was there at the moment and Kai sighed in relief. His sister was still lying there motionless, just as he'd left her a short while before. He moved to the side of the bed and sat down next to her. He took her hand in his, noticing her body felt oddly cold. Or perhaps, it was just him who felt so warm.

He squeezed her hand, staring at her face.

"Mara," he said aloud. "Mara, I need you. Please wake up."

He continued to stare at her intently. There was no sign of stirring. The hope in Kai's heart shrank, the dark thoughts edging their way back in. He squeezed her hand once more. *Mara...*

"Kai?" Mara squeaked, her voice weak. "Is that you?"

"Mara," he said, his heart leaping in his chest.

"Where am I? What happened?" she said, her head turning. "Why can't I see?"

"You're safe," Kai said, holding her hand tightly. "We're in the infirmary. They bandaged your face."

"Infirmary? My face? What hap–" she paused. He could feel her heartbeat intensifying. "We were... I remember... She–Oh Kai, how did we escape?"

"We escaped because of Uncle," Kai said, his voice heavy.

Mara turned toward the sound of his voice. It seemed she sensed the weight behind his words.

"Uncle? What happened, Kai? Where is he?"

"He's..." Kai started, trying to finish, the words caught in his throat.

"Kai?" Mara asked, her voice higher. "Kai, where's Uncle?"

"I'm sorry, Mara," Kai said. He felt like crying again, but he had no more tears to shed. He laid his head down on her stomach and wrapped his arms around his sister. He heard Mara sniffle. He felt the pain flowing through her body as she began to quiver.

Kai wanted to say more, wanted to explain everything. He wanted to tell her that their uncle had saved them, that everything was going to be okay, but he wasn't sure he believed it. It wasn't going to be okay, at least, not while the princess and her sister still drew breath. It wasn't going to be okay until he set things right.

Kai lay there and held Mara as she sobbed. He stared at the wall, his thoughts slowly changing from sorrow to anger. They nearly took everything from him. They nearly took his sister. And now he was going to use the new power flowing through his veins to end them all.

All he had to do was figure out how to use it.

CHAPTER TWENTY-SEVEN

SORROW

It was late on a brisk morning, the chill winds of Winter slithering down the hills, twisting about the gravestones of warriors past. Some of them, Mara knew, others remained lost to her memory. No matter, there was only one she was here to visit.

After the ceremony, which the twins had still been unconscious for, Yoren's ashes were set aside for a proper burial. Once the twins were awake and feeling up to it, the funeral had gone ahead, his ashes brought here to be joined alongside his brothers and sisters who'd gone before him. The twins would have preferred he be buried next to their father and mother, but such were the traditions of the Order. Now, Kai and Mara had two graves to visit each year.

Mara reached up to her face, feeling the scars from the dragon princess. The wounds, though they still pained her, had healed quite well. Kai's choice to have her drink the blood might have very well saved her life. But at what cost? Kai had said it was Yoren's idea. That he motioned for Kai to give it to her. But the pain of how it all happened made her feel like crying all over again. She'd already cried so much.

Trying to distract herself from the thought of it, she glanced up from the fresh grave. The funeral had recently concluded and the last of the knights were fading out of earshot. Mara saw Kai standing alone off in the far corner of the cemetery. He was gazing up at the mountains, still as stone, only his hair moving as the breeze brushed it across his face.

Mara frowned. Kai had not been the same since the other night. It was to be expected, of course, but this felt different—like something deeper was troubling him. Kai and Uncle had never quite gotten along, but Mara knew he still cared for Yoren, and that his death had cut deep. Still, Mara couldn't help but feel there was more to Kai's grief. He'd told her everything that happened after she'd been injured by the dragon princess. At least, she presumed he'd told her everything.

Mara's eyes glazed over as she looked back at her uncle's gravestone, the words written there going blurry for a few seconds. She brought her hand up and rubbed her eyes, assuming it was just remnants of her tears causing her vision to go foggy. After a few seconds, everything went back to normal.

> *Here lies Yoren Grayscale, Blood of Our Blood,*
> *Spear of the Order of Scales.*
> *May his blood always burn with the fires of justice*
> *May his spear always pierce the darkest of nights*
> *May his soul forever rest in the halls of the brave*

Bending down, Mara placed a book against the headstone. It was the same one he'd given to her all those years ago, on the day their parents had died. She smiled sorrowfully and stood, heading toward her brother.

"How are you doing?" she asked, coming up beside him.

Kai's eyes shifted her way, but he kept his gaze upward toward the mountains. Mara knew he may need a few to formulate his thoughts, so she waited quietly.

"I think... maybe I was wrong earlier," he said slowly.

"Wrong? About what?"

"What I said before, about things not being as they were supposed to. Maybe this is how it was supposed to be. But maybe..." he said, pausing. "Maybe I just wasn't who *I* needed to be."

"What do you mean, Kai?" Mara asked, inching closer and taking his hand. He looked down at it as she took it, then up at her. That's when Mara saw there was something different in his eyes. They were distant, as if a part of him was no longer inside. They were Dragonbloods now, and one of the gifts of that was what the knights called "dragonsight" – the ability to see further than normal humans, and the ability to see better at night. There were changes that would happen to them, but this wasn't that.

"Maybe what was wrong this whole time was me. Maybe *I* was not who *I* needed to be. And maybe I am now, or maybe I'm on the path to becoming that person finally, but either way, I can't help but feel everything was wrong before because– because *I* was wrong."

"Kai, you can't say that. We can't change who we are. We can try to be different, yes. We can learn from our mistakes and try to be better, but our mistakes are not who we are. No matter what happened, Kai," she said, placing her other hand on his arm, "that isn't who you are."

Kai tried to force a smile, his face twitching. He turned back to look at the mountains. Mara knew there was a great deal of pain he was hiding from her.

"I want them dead, Mara. All of them. For what they did to you. For what I– for what they did to Uncle. I know I shouldn't feel this way. I know Father wouldn't approve. But they took everything from us. They almost took you, too. I almost– I don't know what I would have done if you..."

Mara saw Kai's face twist in emotion, though she could tell he was doing his best to hold it in. She wrapped her arms around him, trying to keep her own tears from coming back. Despite her attempt, a few seeped out and onto Kai's sleeve.

"It's okay, Kai. I'm still here. Thanks to Uncle, I'm here. And thanks to you."

Kai glanced her way, his eyes moving from her to the gravestone. As they stood there, Mara still hugging him, she felt his skin grow warm. At first it was barely noticeable, but soon it was undeniably warm. Letting go, she looked up at Kai's face. His eyes were glued to Yoren's gravestone, his jaw clenched and his face turning red.

"What is it, Kai? Are you okay?" she asked, her eyes following his.

He looked down at her, the strangeness in his eyes seeming even more apparent.

"I'm going to fix this, Mara. I'm sorry they took him from you. Maybe this is who I was supposed to be all along, maybe it isn't, but either way, I'm going to fix this."

Kai's words struck Mara hard. Her brother had changed—was changing—and she wasn't sure it was for the better.

Chapter Twenty-Eight

ATTACK

The night was cold and still, chill winds sweeping down from the shadows of the mountains above as several guards on the Order's south-central watchtower paced along its ramparts. It had been two days since the dragon's warning atop the peak. As such, the towers were on high alert.

One of them, a knight named Lania, wrapped her cloak about her as she stared up at the mountains. The cold had a firm grip on her, but it wasn't as firm as the looming fear in the back of her mind. She'd never faced an elder dragon before, and hoped she wouldn't have to tonight. There were four guards stationed at each tower. Two of them were sleeping, while she and the other knight kept the night watch. Word had been sent that more knights would arrive soon to bolster their defenses along the border. Lania had hoped they would have arrived already.

It was dark, but the sky was clear and the moon mostly full, casting a luminous glow over the nearby snow-covered slopes. Her eyes darted back and forth between the shadows of the mountains, watching for any sign of movement. But as of yet, there had been no sign of the dragons.

Lania sighed, the heat of her breath creating a puff of steam that disappeared quickly. She sniffled, taking one last look as she turned to head back south along the rampart. A flicker of light caught her eye to the north. Her eyes grew wide.

"The beacon's been lit!" she shouted. She turned and saw the other guard looking in her direction. She pointed, yelling again, this time louder. "The beacon on the north central tower! It's lit!"

The other knight, who was manning the ballista, stood and faced the tower. "That's not the beacon, Lania. That's the entire tower! It's been set ablaze."

Lania strained her eyes, realizing he was right. It was too big to be the beacon. The watchtower *was* on fire.

Just then, a gust of wind blew past the two of them. Lania spotted a quick movement to her left. It swooped low, around the tower, disappearing into the shadows below.

"Attack! We're under attack! Light the beacon," her partner yelled, sitting back down and trying to track their attacker with the ballista.

"Yes, call for help little one."

Lania and the other knight spun, looking over toward the edge of the tower where the voice had come from. There, between the roof and the tower wall, a shadowed dragon craned its neck, staring at them. Its eyes were aglow, a mouthful of fangs curled into a wicked grin.

"Light the fire," it commanded, sounding somewhat feminine in nature.

"What?" Lania asked, taken aback. She glanced up at the knight above her. His face looked the same as hers.

"You heard me. Light the fire."

Lania paused, confusion written all over her face as she contemplated the dragon's words. Her spear was strapped to her back. She glanced sideways toward it, then at the torch on a pillar in front of her.

"Decisions, decisions," the dragon said, bouncing its head back and forth. "Do as I say and warn your friends. Or, take your spear and try to save your own skin. It's a tough choice but let me make this a bit simpler for you. Grab your spear and you die before it even leaves your hand. Light the fire, and you still die, but at least you will be allowed to fulfill your duty first." The dragon paused, looking deep into Lania's eyes. "So, which will it be?"

"Why would you want us to warn the Order of your presence?" Lania asked as her eyes narrowed.

"Because I want them to leave the safety of the keep. Your signal will tell them we have come. The signal fire will call for aid. And I'm desperately hoping they are as *honorable* as the stories say."

Lania and the other knight glanced at each other, both seeming to weigh their options of what to do next. The knight could possibly angle the ballista down enough to shoot the dragon, but he'd have to turn quickly. Lania saw it in his eyes. She blinked, time slowing as he began to spin, bringing the weapon around in a blur of movement. He aimed it where the dragon was and let loose a bolt before Lania could even decide what to do. It soared through the air, disappearing into the darkness below, the dragon already gone. A second later, a shadow loomed behind him. Lania screamed a warning as an arm came from within the shadow, the flash of something metallic with it. Before the knight could even let loose his spear, blood was spilling from his neck. His head dropped forward, his body slumping deeper into the seat. Below where he sat, a pool of blood began to form on the tower floor.

Lania looked up from his bleeding corpse to see a large woman with black hair, eyes glowing a fierce green, a similarly wicked smile staring coldly back at her.

Lania felt her nerves faltering, understanding fully the gravity of the situation. She heard muffled shouting as the shock set in, blurring her vision and dulling her senses. The other two guards burst from the tower below, up the stairs with spears in hand. They saw the scene and their dead comrade, raising their weapons to come to Lania's aid, looking for any signs of the attacker, who was now nowhere to be seen.

Lania couldn't move; couldn't rush to stop them. She saw another flash of movement behind her comrades, the woman popping out of the shadows as her daggers sunk deep into the back of one of them, through a gap in his armor. As he let out a grunt, the other spun to face the threat. But the woman was fast—much faster than anyone Lania had ever seen. She dodged the swing of his spear and came in close, bringing her dagger up and straight into his throat. He slumped over, grasping at it for a second before he, too, was dead. She walked over to the first knight, who was bleeding out from his wound, trying to crawl away, though he hadn't gotten very far. She reached down and put her arm around his neck, lifting him up as she brought her face down, placing her cheek against his, licking a splatter of blood off it. Then, she brought her dagger up and ended his misery, slicing his throat as she'd done the first guard.

The blood-crazed woman stood up and laughed, walking back over to where Lania stood stunned, sliding behind her and bringing the edge of her blade up to Lania's throat. She grinned, looking in Lania's eyes from the side, then up at the dragon, who was nor perched on a new spot along the wall.

"You are the last. Consider it a gift that we are giving you the chance to fulfill your duty. The others chose poorly. So, what will it be? Either you light it, or you join them and we light it anyways. I will not ask again."

Lania looked again at her dead friends. She'd served with them all at the tower for nearly two months, though she'd known them even longer. They'd spent a lot of time together at the tower. She was scared her life would be over soon, but there was an anger welling inside her, replacing the fear she'd known earlier. She glanced north, saw the flames still engulfing the other tower. She knew what needed to be done.

She turned her eyes to the dragon, her nerves still trembling, but with a renewed resolve.

"I will light the fire," she said firmly.

"Good," the dragon replied, grinning again. "Sister," she added, nodding. The sister nodded back, easing up and removing the dagger from Lania's throat, though Lania felt her remain close, feeling the tip of the dagger pressing ever so gently into the back of her neck.

Lania began to walk slowly toward the beacon. She grabbed the torch off the wall and moved to stand over the unlit pyre. There was wood and oil in it, so it would ignite instantly once she dropped the torch in. She would only have a short second or two as it flared up to do what needed to be done.

The woman followed her, standing close by. Lania eyed her as she raised her arm out over the fire, holding the torch firmly for several seconds. The woman held the knife up toward her, nodding her head downward.

Lania sucked in a deep breath, concentrating as she prepared for what she was about to do next. She loosed her grip on the torch, letting it fall. As the sound of metal hitting metal rang out, followed immediately by the roar of rising flame, Lania moved as swiftly as she could.

She dove away from the woman, gripping her spear as she rolled. When she came up to her feet, her spear in hand. In one swift move, she put the tip of her spear at an angle under the supports holding up the basin of the pyre bowl. She pushed upward with all her might, the leverage of it enough to tip the fiery bowl over in the opposite direction.

Flames and burning oil poured onto the floor of the tower, the fire moving instantly along the stone. The oil continued to spread, the fire following it, reaching one of the support beams of the roof as flames rose up it, climbing to the top. Lania continued to move, trying to keep the fire between her and the woman, who was circling toward her rapidly.

As Lania stared at her through the flames, she could see now the draconic features of the true creature within. Lania heard the sound of wings as the other dragon took flight, ascending away from the now burning roof. The black-haired one glared at Lania, then stopped and laughed as Lania kept her spear trained on her. She stepped through the fire, growing and changing as she did. The flames did nothing to her skin. It was then that Lania fully realized the fire would not keep her safe.

Seconds later, the top of the tower exploded as the woman took on her full dragon form. Lania was thrown from the top of the tower and sent plummeting toward the ground. As she fell, she saw the face of a dragon looking down at her. Accepting her fate, Lania closed her eyes, knowing she'd done the best she could to warn the Order of the dragons' presence. She did not want to die, but she embraced it, knowing in the end, she'd faced her demons as any true Dragonblood should. As she impacted the rocky crag below, she knew only peace.

Nalaen landed on the top of the burning tower, coming up next to her sister, who was staring down at the dead knight.

"Defiant, just like the others," Nalaen scoffed. "I should have just let you kill her."

"They will know something's wrong now," Talesa replied. "And yes, you should have."

"It's no matter. I had hoped to set a trap, but this will do. They will still come, if even more urgently. We'll just have to make sure with some... convincing." Nalaen's gaze turned down from the tower toward several lights in the distance. There was a small town below, past the foot of the mountains. Lights were igniting in the houses, and a bell started ringing.

"You want more blood, Sister?"

Talesa's eyes followed her sister's to the village. A sinister smile grew, Talesa's throat rumbling with an insatiable heat.

"Let's pay the local towns a visit, shall we?"

The two sisters grinned as they leapt into the air, a gust of wind fanning the flames of the burning watchtower as they descended toward the helpless village below.

Chapter Twenty-Nine

WAR

"If the watchtowers are burning, we can only assume one thing—they are trying to draw us out of the keep!" Thorlan exclaimed, addressing the crowd gathered in the Heart.

Kai watched as the heated debate continued. On one side, Thorlan, one of the Order's oldest veterans, was arguing caution, while some of the younger knights, led by Caliena, were arguing haste. Though he hated to admit it, Kai wanted to side with Caliena.

"You would have us hide in here like scared sheep while the dragons prey on our brothers and sisters?" Caliena objected, standing up as she raised her fist. "This is what we've trained for. This is what we live for."

"No, Sister Steelheart. I merely mean we need to be careful and devise a plan so we don't leave ourselves exposed. These dragons have proven their strength. This so-called Princess is a threat we should not underestimate."

"So, we will just let the surrounding countryside burn as we devise the perfect strategy? We can't keep sitting here doing nothing. We've already wasted too much time. If the dragons want a fight, then I say we give them one!"

Many of the younger knights started cheering, Caliena shouting out, riling them on as she aimed a challenging expression at Thorlan. Karg sat in his chair, his fingers on his forehead, just sitting and listening to the bickering between the young and the old. So far, Cyrus had simply sat quietly next to him, glancing over to watch the Scalewarden's reactions. Based on what Kai had observed, the Scalewarden seemed indecisive.

"Quiet, everyone!" Cyrus shouted, finally taking a stand. "We must calm down if we are to decide what to do. Bickering amongst ourselves will do no good to our comrades out there—if they are even still alive." The uncharacteristic volume and intensity of Cyrus's voice brought the room to a hasty quiet. Even Kai was stunned by its intensity.

Cyrus stood and walked a few steps over to where Karg was seated. He rested his hand on the man's shoulder, bending down to lean close to him. Kai tried to read his lips as the rest of the room watched in silence.

When Cyrus finished, Karg looked up at him, his face blank, his eyes searching Cyrus just as much as Cyrus's were searching him. As before, Kai observed doubt, an uncharacteristic hesitation within their normally strong and fierce leader. And if he was honest, the old man seemed to look frailer than he had just weeks ago. Perhaps Yoren's death had affected the old man more than he'd let on.

At last, Karg turned, looking over the silent crowd. He smiled weakly.

"My brothers and sisters," Karg began. "Old and new, alike. Given recent events, we are all of us feeling the loss of our Spear." His eyes continued to scan the group, resting on Kai and Mara as he finished his thought. He frowned at them and nodded.

"But as we always have, the Order must endure. Not for ourselves, but for the sake of the realm. If we fall, there will be no gate to hold back the tide of the dragon horde from ravaging the people west of the Wall. I know many of you have little experience fighting elder dragons," he said, looking at some of the younger members, then to Caliena. "That is a tragedy, but nonetheless, not an experience you should seek to meet head on without a solid strategy." Caliena's face turned red at Karg's remark.

"Normally, I would have consulted the Spear on such an occasion as this. Ever wise was his advice. But since I am without counsel, I must ask for another's. Kai, Mara. Please stand."

Kai glanced at his sister, confused. Why would the Scalewarden call upon them? His eyes darted around the room before moving back to Karg, giving him a questioning look.

Karg nodded, his expression serious.

Kai and Mara stood slowly.

"We have in our midst the first new Dragonbloods in over fifty years—the niece and nephew of one of the finest warriors I've ever served with." A hushed murmur went around the room. Karg eyed them and it grew quiet. "Kai, Mara—you two have become Dragonbloods in the most peculiar way, yet it was clearly for a purpose. Yoren is no longer with us, but I believe he gave us a gift—both of you. Though you have much to learn, I believe you have a destiny before you that none of us could have predicted. Yoren's blood, the blood of the Grayscale line, flows through you, as does the blood of the dragon Princess. I do not believe that is merely a coincidence."

It was the first time that fact had been told to a wider audience, and it was apparent in the reaction amongst the knights it was not well received. Kai glanced around the room, feeling himself growing upset by the looks and whispers of many eyeing them. He turned to Mara and leaned closer.

"You see, even now that we are one of them, they still look down upon us."

Mara glanced at him, concern in her eyes. The red hue in her cheeks intensified and she shifted nervously in her seat.

"So, knowing that, I'd like to ask your advice," Karg continued.

A gasp went through the room. All eyes focused on the twins, many of their gazes unpleasant. Ignoring them, Kai turned to Karg.

"Our advice?" Kai asked, trying to sound confident, though he was sure that's not how it came across.

"Aye," replied Karg.

"What should we say?" Kai asked, turning to Mara. She'd always been the smarter one, more strategic. Kai was hoping she would have an idea, but the discomfort she was feeling at the present was apparent. Clenching his jaw, Kai looked around the room, glaring at everyone. He did not like how the attention was affecting Mara. He felt his body grow warm as he stood to face Karg and the assembly.

Kai eyed Cyrus for a moment, the man's expression different than expected. Kai had always admired Cyrus and had enjoyed training with him in his younger years, but his features were hard to read at the present. Kai felt their only ally in the room was Karg.

"Scalewarden," Kai began. "I'm not sure what you expect from us," he continued, waving his hand toward his sister. "But if you want the truth, I think we need to act. The Princess took our uncle from us. And before her, our parents were slain by another of the monsters. I've waited fifteen years for the opportunity to bring its kind to justice. Perhaps, now is that time."

Kai paused, his thoughts racing to find the right words.

"The dragons are on our doorstep. They've made their intentions clear. We've beaten them before, when their numbers were greater, so why should we hold back now? I say we march out and meet them head on before anyone else loses a father or a mother... or someone else they love."

There were grumbles amongst some, while others turned their attention to Karg, hopeful expressions that Kai's words would sway his mind in their favor. Caliena was one of them, and she nodded to Kai, the hint of a smile on her lips.

Karg eyed Kai for a moment before turning to gaze across the group, his eyes eventually landing on Cyrus. The older knight stood there, seeming to be deep in thought.

"And what do you say, Cyrus?" Karg asked, drawing his attention.

Cyrus eyed Kai for a moment before he spoke.

"I think we've all had a long day, and that we could all do with a rest to freshen our minds for what we must decide. While I do not think any individual's words should be heeded over the others," he said, glancing back at Kai, followed by Caliena and Thorlan, "there is one truth that has been said here today. Whatever we decide, we must do so quickly, lest more pay the price for our indecisiveness. I say we rest tonight and reconvene in the morning to make our final decision."

"A sound judgement, Cyrus," Karg said, nodding to the man. "We will reconvene in the morning, just after first light. Have you anything else to say before they are dismissed?"

Cyrus glanced up at the room, lines forming in his aged features.

"Ready yourselves for what is to come, Brothers and Sisters. For whatever we decide, there is no question that war is upon us."

CHAPTER THIRTY

FAVOR

"What the hell were you thinking, Princess?" Galen shouted. "Your orders were clear. Kill the human responsible for your mother's death and return home. We did that. But then you said that there was more of his family, and I allowed you to stay to finish this. Yet, now you're attacking towns and villages and killing humans needlessly to fuel your vendetta of rage. This has gotten out of hand, and I cannot stand by any longer. We need to return home immediately."

Nalaen stood by, patiently waiting for Galen's rant to end, her face unyielding of any emotion. She had no intention of leaving, and it was time, it seemed, that her tolerance of Galen's presence came to an end.

"Are you quite finished?" Nalaen asked, her face remaining expressionless.

"I am not finished until you are safely back home where you belong..." Galen replied, his own resolve unwavering.

"Where I belong? Why is it that you were sent here, Galen?" Nalaen asked.

Galen scoffed. "To escort you on your mission and keep you safe, of course, Princess."

"No, Galen. That is not your true task. Please, tell us why you were really assigned to escort me."

"Princess, I'm not quite sure what you're implying, but you seem to be mistaken."

"Oh, I'm not implying anything. Do you really take your Princess for such a fool? I know the schemes that Kyrian is ever whispering in the shadows. Do you expect me to believe that his most trusted guard would not be intimately involved in them?"

Galen's eyes widened, his face turning red, a sour expression forming. He opened his mouth to object, but Nalaen cut him off.

"Very soon, I will be Queen. Kyrian is only Herald until that day comes. When I rise as Queenmother, do you expect me to just let these schemes of Kyrian's, and those who partook in them, go ignored? I can assure you, there will be grave consequences for any such cohorts."

"We have the chance here, now," Nalaen continued, "to do something that has eluded our kin for thousands of years. We have the chance to end the humans that rose up all those years ago—the humans who have stood between us and our true purpose as the stewards of this world. Have you forgotten, Galen, or has Kyrian uttered promises of some new vision that seems better than that? Promises to see a new era where a Queen no longer sits on throne?"

With that, several of the guards shouted out, voices echoing their distaste for Nalaen's words.

"You must be very careful, Princess," Galen spat. "You are not Queen yet, and those are very serious accusations to throw out toward the one who's led this kingdom in your mother's absence since you could barely fly."

"You mean the Queen *he* let die?" Nalaen raged. "It's easy to rule a kingdom from the safety of its walls. My mother was out trying to usher in a world where dragons did not cower like rats trapped in a cage. And yet you remain loyal to the very one who wants to ensure the cage remains." Nalaen's body began to transform as her rage grew. Talesa stood by off to the side, smiling as she eyed the wary guards loyal to Kyrian and Galen. Only Mykael stood amongst them, calm and reserved.

"So, tell me then, Drae'vir. What has your lord commanded of you?" Nalaen's transformation reverted as she collected herself.

"I do not answer to you, Princess. Until the day you are Queen, you are merely a pup to be watched over. I am in command here, and I order us to head back to Dor'Dragos at first light." Galen's nostrils flared as he stood facing Nalaen.

"Well, then we shall have to remedy that," Nalaen said, smiling. Galen's eyes grew thin as he eyed her with a questioning look. "Tell me, Drae'vir. How does one rise to a position such as yours?"

"Through proven merit and years of service," Galen replied, his face showing uncertainty at what Nalaen's goals were.

"Or?" Nalaen asked.

"Or? What do you mean? What are you playing at, Princess?"

"Have we strayed so far from the old ways that you have forgotten? Have you ever heard of *cona'ceratus*?"

Galen's expression shifted at the mention of the word from ancient draconic tradition. It meant trial by combat.

"Yes, I have heard, but—" Galen started, stopping short when he saw Mykael striding out toward Nalaen. "Mykael, what are you—" The sudden realization set in. His anger began to swell as he looked at the others, similar expressions accompanying their guttural growls in reply.

"Mykael, you have sided with the Princess? I should have known you would betray us."

"Silence," Mykael said. "*You* are the traitor. I am loyal to the *throne*. You seem to have forgotten our oaths. Though the Princess does not hold the title of Queenmother yet, I live to see that she does. I will not hide in the shadows and plot against the rightful ruler of our kingdom. You'd be wise to correct your ways before I correct them for you."

Mykael came to stand beside Nalaen, his chest up and his head held high. He flexed his muscles as he gripped his sword's hilt, staring confidently at Galen.

Galen stood there for a moment, locking eyes with Mykael, his anger fuming. But then he shrugged his shoulders back and shifted his demeanor, relaxing with a grin.

"Lofty words for one such as yourself. I always knew you envied my position. Just didn't think you fool enough to try and earn it this way. But very well, if it's a fight you want, then I will gladly give you one." Galen turned his gaze from Mykael to Nalaen. "Princess, once I dispose of this wretch, I expect you to leave with us tomorrow willingly."

Nalaen chuckled, grinning at Galen before turning around. She leaned in closer to Mykael before walking away.

"Make it look like a good fight at least, will you?" she said slyly, smiling at him.

"Of course, my Queen," Mykael replied, bowing his head to her.

Nalaen walked back and joined Talesa, who was leaned against one of the nearby walls. Talesa, who had so far seemed to be minding her own business, glanced up at her momentarily as Nalaen joined her.

"You really think Mykael can beat him?" she asked.

"Oh, I know he can. Galen is strong, but his pride will be his downfall. Mykael has been training for this day. This fight has been a long time coming."

"Had some intimate conversations with the wyrm, have you now?" Talesa asked.

"Not like that," Nalaen replied, eyeing her sister with a menacing look. "But... I must admit there is a certain appeal in the thought of it. He is a fine specimen." Nalaen watched Mykael as he drew his sword, Galen doing the same, beginning to circle each other.

"So, is this the form you prefer then, Galen?" Mykael called out. "Of course, it makes no difference to me. I can best you with either sword or claw."

"Hah! Such arrogance. You don't want to fight me in my true form, Drae'tar. Let's see your skill with the blade."

"Very well," Mykael replied with a smirk.

The two warriors began to circle closer, each taking swings and exchanging parrying blows.

"Well, you are soon to be Queen," Talesa said, continuing their conversation as if there wasn't even a fight going on. "You'll need plenty of specimens to sire our family's future."

"That is true," Nalaen said, more to herself than to Talesa. She watched Mykael and Galen continue to exchange blows. "In truth, I hadn't really given it much thought. But once we've had our revenge, things will change. Once I am Queen, we can finally take some time to enjoy the... *finer* things in life." Nalaen smiled as she watched Mykael move, the way his muscles tensed as he parried Galen's blows and returned with his own.

Talesa looked up finally, a smile forming as she watched the battle intensify. A little blood was already dripping from the two wyrms' bodies. They were only minor scratches so far, but its aroma seemed to draw her attention.

"Ah, how I love the smell of blood," Talesa said, smiling a devious grin as she continued to watch the two wyrms fight.

Both were sweaty, breathing heavily as they circled each other again, each waiting for the other to make the next move. It was clear they were both tired, but it seemed Mykael had the upper hand. He pressed in, pushing Galen back toward another part of the ruins. The other guards were cheering for Galen and hurling insults at Mykael, but the two of them stayed focused on each other.

"What's wrong, Galen? Had enough?" Mykael taunted.

"Not even close," Galen quipped.

Galen leapt forward, lunging straight for Mykael's midsection. Mykael, surprised by the sudden aggression, barely had time to react. He deflected the blow, keeping it from piercing straight through his body, but Galen's sword still clipped the side of his stomach, opening a small gash in Mykael's flesh.

Mykael winced in pain and spun sideways, away from Galen as he pressed his attack. Galen, emboldened by his strike, continued to move on Mykael, who was barely keeping his attacks at bay for the moment.

More shouts and cheers rang out from the guards as the tide of the battle seemed to change. But as Galen continued to push in, he was getting more tired. Mykael was worn, but his defensive stance had helped him conserve some energy. Galen's attacks became more and more erratic, and Mykael kept his footwork and stance steady.

"If Galen wins, I think I'll bed him tonight," Talesa remarked rather nonchalantly. Nalaen looked at her sister in a momentary shock before chuckling.

"He won't, but sure. If he wins, he's all yours," Nalaen scoffed, Talesa smiling in reply.

"Don't be so sure, he's getting beaten back. I can almost taste the blood from his wound."

"Don't be gross, Sister. Just wait and see."

As the words left her mouth, there was a grunt from Galen as he lunged forward again. He missed, and Mykael saw his opening.

As Galen tried to recover from his failed blow, Mykael spun his blade around and underneath Galen's sword, lifting it up in the air, Galen's arms with it. Mykael launched his shoulder into Galen's chin, sending the wyrm stumbling backwards, drops of blood splattering from his lips. Not waiting for Galen to recover, Mykael brought his sword in low, aiming for the leg. Galen swung his sword wildly, trying to parry while not losing his balance completely. His parry only slowed Mykael's blow.

Mykael's blade bit into Galen's leg, causing a spurt of blood as a large wound opened. The gash caused Galen to continue stumbling backwards, this time losing his balance entirely. As he fell, he spun around and then, in a cloud of smoke, his wings appeared, and he took to the sky. Assuming his full dragon form, he rose higher. His leg was still bleeding, but he ignored it and swooped up before spinning and diving back toward Mykael, who was still on the ground, sword in hand.

Galen dove quickly, but Mykael was ready, dodging out of the way at the last second as Galen swooped back up in the other direction, trying to avoid the nearby ruins. He flew higher, turned, searching for Mykael, who was now nowhere to be seen. His head swerved from side to side.

"Come out and fight me, coward," Galen bellowed.

"I am not the one who flew away when I was losing," came a voice from somewhere in the ruins. "But if you want to fight in the sky, then I shall litter this ground with your blood!"

There was a flash from within the rubble as the true form of Mykael shot straight up from directly underneath Galen, claws extended in an attack that sent Galen reeling out of the way. Galen tried to dodge, striking back with his own swipe.

From below, Nalaen and Talesa saw several fresh wounds on Galen's left side, in addition to a claw mark on Mykael's wing. The two of them watched the wyrms square off in the sky, facing each other and circling as they had done before. Both were injured, and it was hard to tell who would triumph. Both were impressive in their dragon forms.

Galen was large, even for a wyrm. He had been known to be a fierce drake, and he was respected for his brute strength and skill in combat. Mykael was a bit smaller, more the size of the average wyrm, but what he lacked in size, he made up for in agility. As he swooped around the sky, Nalaen couldn't help but admire the ease with which he danced circles around the larger drake.

Nearby, Talesa was watching with a similar interest.

"Your wyrm is fast, I'll give him that," she acknowledged. "But one blow from Galen's claws and he's finished. I thought I preferred his human skin but now that I've seen him fight, I think we'll celebrate his victory in our scales tonight."

Nalaen scoffed. She wanted to banter with her sister, but she was enthralled with the fight. It was going better than expected. She was rooting for Mykael, and would certainly satisfy these sudden urges she was having with him later should he be the victor, but the real reason she wanted him to win was to get rid of Galen. The wyrm had been a thorn in her side for far too long. He had shown he was vehemently loyal to Kyrian, and that was one thing she could not stand. If there was anything Nalaen wanted besides her revenge, it was to see Kyrian, and any of his lackeys, lying in pools of their own blood. Nalaen hoped today would be the first.

As she focused back on the fight, Nalaen saw it was at a standstill. Mykael was still flying circles around Galen, but so far, he'd only come in to inflict minor damage, being careful not to get caught by the larger wyrm's slashes.

Mykael swooped in for another attack, feigning at the last second and rolling away. The feign left him a few seconds at Galen's back, which he used to close in, aiming an attack at Galen's wings. But just as he came in, mere feet away from a successful attack, Galen spun backwards and twisted, coming down on top of Mykael, who was caught off guard by his sudden movement.

The two plummeted toward the ground as Galen grabbed hold of Mykael, seemingly planning to smash into the ground and crush Mykael beneath him. Mykael struggled to get free under the force of the larger drake's dive.

As the ground drew close, Mykael was able to get a claw free, swinging it upward, raking Galen across the face. This caused Galen to reel, slowing their descent, which allowed Mykael to dive away and out of harm's reach, just moments from impact.

Barely able to divert his dive, and with one eye bloody, Galen lost sight of Mykael momentarily as he circled up, trying to catch a glimpse of the speedy drake. He caught a hint of movement below him, but when he realized it was only Mykael's shadow, his eyes grew wide.

The downward force of Mykael's dive was enough to send the two of them hurtling back toward the ground. Caught off guard, Galen scrambled, trying to slow their descent and shake off Mykael, who was now on his back clawing his wings. Galen let out a roar as Mykael's teeth dug into the back of his neck, claws continuing to slash at his wings.

The ground was fast approaching and it seemed Galen could do nothing to stop the imminent collision. At the last second, Galen rolled, Mykael still clinging to his back. By the time Mykael realized what was happening, it was too late. He tried to let go and fly away, but there was no time.

The two wyrms slammed into the ground, Galen landing on top of Mykael. For a minute, neither of them moved. Nalaen, Talesa, and the others stared, breaths held as they waited to see what happened.

Slowly, Galen's body started to move. He rolled over onto his feet, away from the sight of the crash. As he moved, they could see Mykael's lifeless body still lying in the dirt. Galen stood over him, looking down with a blood-soaked smile. He prodded at Mykael's body, but he lay deathly still.

Satisfied, he turned and stared down Nalaen, letting out a roar of victory as he reared up on his hind legs, wings spread out. He came down with a crash, a cloud of snow puffing up, partially clouding Nalaen's view.

As the snow settled, everyone gasped. Mykael's body was gone. Noticing their faces, Galen spun and saw for himself. He flung his head in every direction, snarling as he kicked up more snow. He let out a roar, fire rising in his throat, preparing to unleash it when Mykael showed himself.

Catching a hint of movement nearby, Galen fixed his attention on the nearby ruins. He brought the fire up into his throat, unleashing the full might of his breath on the ruins. Flames beat against the stone for a dozen seconds as Galen expelled every ounce of fire he could muster. Part of the wall crumbled under the intense heat and sheer power of the assault.

As he finished, Galen tried to catch his breath, watching the ruins for any more signs of movement. Everyone else watched from afar, wondering if Mykael was finally finished.

Still trying to regain his breath, Galen panted, eyes twitching back and forth as he held his ground. Unwilling to move closer, Galen drew a deep breath in again, wanting to make sure there was no chance Mykael was still alive. He reared his head back, preparing to unleash another torrent of flame.

He never got the chance.

As Galen opened his mouth, sucking in the last bit of air he could muster for a second attack, a sword flew out from behind the scorched wall, straight into Galen's open mouth, embedding deep within the soft flesh at the back of his throat.

The blade's strike was true. Galen's eyes rolled into the back of his head, his body slumping over onto the ground with a large thud, sending another cloud of snow into the air. Everyone watching was stunned.

As the snow settled, Mykael strode up to Galen's corpse in his human form. Reaching his arm inside the dragon's maw, he ripped the sword from within the soft tissue in the back of his throat, blood and other fluids spewing forth. Mykael wiped the sword clean on the dead dragon's corpse, then lifted it high in celebration of his victory.

Nalaen smiled, glancing over toward Talesa to see the disappointment on her face.

"Such a shame," Talesa said, pouting. "He was a fine specimen. But such is the way of things. Now I shall have to find another to sate my craving tonight."

"Mykael is mine," Nalaen sneered, watching her sister's eyes gaze in his direction.

"Yes, yes, I know, Sister. Enjoy the spoils of your victory. Just try not to get attached, okay."

"He is merely a means to an end. But he will do, for now," Nalaen assured her. "Hopefully, the others will fall in line so we can do as we please."

With that, both smiled deviously.

Nalaen walked toward Mykael, who was walking slowly, but confidently her direction, a slight limp in his step. There was a cocky smirk on his face as he came up to her, putting his sword back in its sheath.

"I told you to make it look like a good fight, but for a moment there, I thought you were going to lose," Nalaen scolded him playfully.

"Hah," Mykael laughed, wiping sweat and blood from his forehead. "Galen didn't go down easily, but in the end, the result was the same. Is the Princess pleased?"

"I am," Nalaen replied. "I trust that you can get the others in line now, Drae'vir?"

"Of course, my Princess." Mykael bowed, glancing toward the others. They were all watching the spectacle, sour expressions directed at their new captain. "They will do as they are told."

"See that they do. Starting tomorrow, we have preparations to attend to."

"You think the humans will come?" he asked.

"Oh, they will come. We razed their towers and burned their villages. If they are not cowards, they will come. And we will be ready for them."

"I'll go prepare the others then," Mykael stated, starting to bow.

"No, not yet."

"Is there something else the Princess requires?"

"Yes, there is," Nalaen replied, a coy undertone on her lips as she gave Mykael a playful smile. "Come with me."

Nalaen turned and walked toward the shelter in the ruins that had been built for her. Mykael smiled, watching her walk away. He glanced toward the other drakes with a look of satisfaction. They scowled at him as he turned and trotted after her.

CHAPTER THIRTY-ONE

BURNING

Mara tried to focus her eyes, the words on the page blurring. It was happening more often now. Her eyes felt incredibly dry. She gazed up from the book in front of her and stared at the wall for a few seconds, trying to let her eyes readjust. *Maybe it's just the lighting? How long have I been reading?*

Mara stepped out into the hallway, noticing the light crystals above had gone dark. *Night already?* Shrugging, went back into her room to retrieve another candle from within her cabinet and brought it back to her reading desk. She lit it on the already burning candle and set it on the other side of her book.

The words weren't blurry now, though her eyes still felt a bit dry. They felt a little warm, too. *Perhaps it's time to turn in for the night. I need to be up early for the meeting.*

Mara had left the meeting earlier, parting ways with Kai and heading straight for the library. Not that she expected anyone to listen, but Karg had asked for their opinion. She'd been too flustered with all the attention to think properly at the moment but still intended to try and find some answers to at least offer something–if the Scalewarden were to ask again.

She'd been reading about past battles, trying to find anything that might help. So far, nothing from the past had happened quite like how it was now. Sure, several dragon queens had waged war on the humans in the past, but it had always been at a greater scale, seemingly more about indifferences and large-scale change. But this–this was personal. The princess had come specifically for Mara and Kai's uncle. Her fight was with him, and now, it seemed with her and her brother. So far, it didn't seem that a full-scale war was afoot. Mara had counted only a small handful of escorts with the princess. If that was all, then perhaps the dragons didn't mean to incite war. Perhaps, they didn't even know, or approve, or her actions.

Perhaps we're looking at this all the wrong way...

A loud knock pushed Mara from her thoughts, the frantic sound of a familiar voice drawing her to the door. When she opened it, she was face to face with a very red and flustered Brol.

"Brol? What is it?"

"Its..." Brol said, taking a deep breath. "It's Kai. Something's wrong."

Kai? Mara's mind raced with a hundred different scenarios.

"What happened?" Mara asked, closing the door behind her and heading down the hallway with Brol.

"I'm not sure. We were training. He was trying to figure out his new abilities. He was pushing himself. I've never seen him so upset. It's like he–"

"Brol," Mara said, grabbing his arm. "What happened?"

"Sorry. He passed out. He was turning red, his skin hot to the touch. I've felt someone with a high fever before, but this was different."

"Where is he now?"

"Infirmary. He's there now, getting water. They're trying to cool him off with wet rags. I came to get you as soon as they took him back." Brol's expression was grim. Mara could tell he was obviously shaken up by what had happened. Her heart raced at the thought of it. She had known something was off with Kai, but she hadn't pressed him about it.

"Thanks, Brol. I'm glad you were there." Mara smiled quickly and picked up her pace.

They hurried through the keep, saying nothing more as they made their way to the infirmary. On approach, Mara noticed Dax and Haran standing outside the doorway leading inside.

Mara simply glanced at them as she moved past, the expressions on their faces similar to how Brol's had been, causing further haste in her step. There were only a dozen rooms in the infirmary, and at the moment, only one of them was occupied.

Inside, Mara found Kai lying on his back on the bed, his shirt removed, two nurses leaning over him on either side. One of them held a rag to his head, a bucket of water nearby. The other held a cup, trying to force small sips of water between Kai's lips.

"What's wrong with him?" Mara asked, directed at the one holding the rag, her head turning when she heard Mara's words.

"We can't say for sure. We've sent for the Bloodmender. He should be here any minute. Hopefully, he will have a better answer."

Mara knew the Bloodmender well. He was the best healer in the Order, having a special gift for sensing the illness in one's blood. She was certain he'd have an answer.

Mara moved closer to the bed, the nurse giving Kai water stepping aside to let her by. Kai's eyes were closed, his skin a pinkish hue. Sitting on the bed next to him, she gently touched his hand. It felt incredibly hot. His face twitched at her touch, his eyes fluttering beneath the eyelids, but they did not open.

A shuffling in the hall brought Mara's attention to the doorway. After a few seconds, the familiar face of the Bloodmender appeared.

"Hello, Mara," he greeted warmly. "I've been told there's something going on with Kai. Let's have a look, shall we?"

Mara nodded, a small smile forming, reassured by his presence. She stood and moved aside, letting the man take her place beside Kai. She watched as he checked Kai's heartbeat in his wrists and felt various areas of Kai's skin. He whispered under his breath on several occasions, Mara straining to comprehend his muttering, though she didn't get much. She found herself clenching her fists as she watched him, white-knuckled under the strain of her anxiety, when finally the Bloodmender turned to her with a frown.

"This is strange, I must admit. It's not a fever, as far as I can tell. The source of his heat seems to be intrinsic, from somewhere deep within. It's like his blood is... burning, but there is no infection or obvious source I can trace. His heartbeat is strong—quite strong, perhaps *too* strong, especially for someone who's unconscious. But I can't say why. I'm going to need some more time with your brother, Mara, to fully assess and refer to some of the Order's older notes."

Mara nerves trembled at what she was hearing. Her legs began to feel weak. Her eyes focused on Kai, the room around her growing strangely darker on the edges of her vision.

"I'm sorry, Mara," the Bloodmender continued. "I don't mean to worry you. I'm sure we'll get to the bottom of this. I just haven't seen anything like this before."

The darkness grew, crowding in on Mara's vision. She squinted, feeling tears forming. She turned to look at the Bloodmender in confusion, the black in her vision following as she did. She closed her eyes again for several seconds, hoping it would go away.

"Are you feeling alright, Mara?" he asked, standing.

Mara opened her eyes, the darkness slowly rescinding.

"Y—yes, I'm fine," she lied. "I'm just worried about Kai."

"Understandable," he replied.

"How long will it take?" she asked, looking back at her brother.

"I can't say. I will do some more tests and see what I can sense from his blood. If that fails, the Order has a whole archive on rare historical cases. I will consult my predecessors' notes to see if there's something like this that I've maybe forgotten."

Archive, Mara thought. *Perhaps I can help, too.*

"Very well. Let me know if there's anything I can do to help, or if you learn anything. I'll go... get some rest and check back on him shortly."

"An excellent idea, Mara," the Bloodmender said. "If anything changes with him, you'll be the first to know. You have my word." He placed his hand on his chest and dipped his head forward.

It made Mara feel a little better, but the possibility of her being able to help gave her the most hope. If there *were* any documented cases of this happening before, Mara would find it. Whatever ailed Kai, there had to be a clue somewhere in the Order's library.

Despite feeling tired, and the concern of her changing vision in the back of her mind, Mara found a new surge of energy. It carried her step as she left the room, taking one more glance back at Kai before heading down the hallway.

Outside, all her friends were standing around chatting quietly. Dax and Brol had been joined by several others, including Vi, Riesara, and Harran.

"Hey, Mara. Any news?" asked Brol when he noticed her approach.

"Nothing yet," Mara sighed. "But the Bloodmender is looking into it. He says he's never seen anything quite like this before, but he's going to do some more tests and look into the medical archives to see if anything's ever been documented."

"I'm sure he'll figure it out," Vi said, coming up to place her hand on Mara's arm. "How are you doing?"

"I'm... okay," Mara said, trying to hold back her tears as best she could. "I'm just worried."

"Of course. Kai is strong, like you. Whatever this is, he'll pull through. Maybe this has something to do with–?"

"It's possible," Mara said, knowing where Vi was going with her question. It had only been a few days since they'd recovered from the initial effects of the dragon's blood. "Actually, I'm going to the library to look into that. Want to join me?"

"Sure. I've some free time," Vi said with a smile. "Riesara?"

"Sure, I'll come too," the other girl said, smiling as well.

"Boys?" Vi asked.

"Dax and I have watch duty here soon, and Harran just finished his, so he's going to get some rest, but let us know if you find anything, Mara," Brol said.

"Sure," Mara said, sniffling. "Good luck with watch."

"Thanks," said Brol, nodding before the three boys wandered off.

"Well, shall we?" asked Vi.

"Yes, let's go," replied Mara. "I'm sure I can find something on the topic."

CHAPTER THIRTY-TWO

ACCUSATIONS

Aerin paced about his room, his thoughts focused on Jarren's odd behaviors. He kept replaying it all in his mind, trying to decide whether it was just Jarren's usual odd self, or if there was, in fact, something else going on. Aerin was worried he'd grown overly paranoid with all that had happened of late, but he couldn't shake the thoughts of the strange story Jarren had told upon returning from the mountains.

A strange woman in the mountains. Burning eyes. Voices.

Initially, Aerin hadn't given much weight to it. But now that elder dragons were confirmed to be back, perhaps Jarren had had an encounter with one. Perhaps, the Princess even.

"I wonder..." Aerin said aloud to himself. He had a wild idea, but would need to speak to someone to confirm. He knew nothing of magic, or what powers the dragons were capable of, but perhaps it was possible his friend had been affected by it in some way.

Aerin stood just as there came a loud pounding on his door. Cautiously, Aerin stepped toward it. As he came within a few feet of the door, it swung open, two armored knights bursting through the other side.

Surprised, Aerin stepped backward.

"Can I help—"

"Aerin of the Lodge?"

"Yes..."

"You need to come with us."

"Okay..." Aerin said, still wildly confused. "May I ask what for?"

"The new Spear will inform you."

"New Spear?"

"Yes, Cyrus Bladesong has just been appointed the new Spear of the Scalewarden."

"Ah," Aerin acknowledged as he followed the men out into the hallway. He was still confused as to the nature of the intrusion but was less worried since he was being taken to precisely the man he'd intended to go see.

The knights hurried Aerin down the hallways through the keep on their way to Cyrus's new quarters–the very same room Cyrus had brought him to meet Yoren. Aerin felt sad at the change, but also happy to see Cyrus, a man whom he respected greatly, assume such an esteemed position.

As they approached the room, Aerin noted Cyrus was busy at work, several knights coming and going, each of them seeming to increase the lines of stress showing in the older man's features. With the dragons back, it seemed the title of Spear brought with it many new requirements of the man.

One of the knights escorting Aerin approached the door and knocked, waiting for permission to enter. As he did, Aerin heard muffled words, including his name, but nothing else comprehensible. Instead, he studied Cyrus's face, trying to decipher from his shifting expression what the nature of this meeting might be. What Aerin saw there did not fill him with hope.

Eventually, Cyrus looked toward Aerin and waved for him to approach. Swallowing, he stepped forward and entered the room, followed closely by the other knight.

"I've just been told some distressing news, Brother Aerin," Cyrus began after a long sigh. "They said our meat stores have been ruined. And based on an initial glance of all the evidence, it seems it may have been you who did it."

Aerin's face contorted in confusion. *Me? How–*

"While I find that hard to believe, I must ask, Aerin–can you offer any possible explanation of this? Did you know about the meat being spoiled?"

"No," Aerin denied, his heart racing. He tried to think if anything had happened–if he'd made a mistake in some way. "I had no idea. How did it get spoiled?"

"Brother Tarson says the cellar door was left wide open for several days. All of the ice was melted, and it seems like nearly all the meat is spoiled."

"I always make sure I close the door, I swear," Aerin replied, getting more worried by the second. He got nasty looks from the two knights. "Someone else must have gone in there."

"Lies!" one of the knights scoffed, presumably Tarson himself. "You were the only one who's been in the storerooms in the past few days. The kitchen staff only restocks once a week, and they were the ones who found it. It had to be you. Besides, the meat that was somehow allowed for you to take back with you is still preserved with extra salting."

"Is this true?" Cyrus asked.

"Yes, it is true," Aerin sighed. "I resalted it two days ago, just to make sure it would be safe for the trip home. But I resalted *all* the meat that I could get to! And I'm sure I closed the door."

Cyrus looked at Aerin with a curious glance, then at the others, his eyes seeming to be weighing all that had been said. Finally, he sighed.

"We will have to take this matter before the Scalewarden. He will decide what is to be done." Cyrus paused. "All our meat is ruined?"

"We're still going through it, but everything that's at least on the surface seems to be. That, and the supply the hunter saved for his trip home," answered Tarson.

"Very well," Cyrus said, sighing again. "Throw out the spoiled meat so it doesn't ruin the rest. And I'm sorry Aerin, but we'll need to requisition all the meat I promised you. Winter has nearly started and we're going to need it."

Aerin's face turned grim. He felt defeated, not knowing what else to say. He was so worried he'd somehow actually made a mistake, he completely forgot about the previous matter he intended to bring up with Cyrus.

"Alright, let's go see the Scalewarden," Cyrus acknowledged, standing.

Aerin nodded sorrowfully.

***

"My new Spear," Karg said as Cyrus and Aerin entered the room, the two knights right behind them. "And our helpful hunter. What can I help you with?"

"Scalewarden," Cyrus replied, ignoring the initial remark with a half-hearted smile as he jumped straight to the issue at hand. "There's been an accusation by these knights that the hunter here has ruined our food supplies. They say they found the food storeroom open and the Order's share of the meats unsalted, which caused them to lose their preservation and become rotten. It seems the meats we promised Aerin he could take back to the guild with him are still intact, however."

The Scalewarden raised an eyebrow, watching Aerin as he narrowed his eyes. Aerin's face turned red as he looked toward the ground.

"And what does the hunter have to say for himself, Spear?" Karg asked.

"He claims that he properly prepared all the meat and closed the door."

"And do you believe him?"

"I... I'd like to, sir. I've had a handful of conversations with the man. He seems honest and hard-working, and he's never given us any reason to doubt that. I find it hard to believe he would deliberately do anything to hinder us." Cyrus paused, looking at Aerin, who glanced up at him with sorrowful appreciation. "And if it were a mistake, it would seem out of character," Cyrus added.

"I see," Karg said, pausing as he scratched his beard. "Who discovered the spoiled meat?"

"The kitchen staff. They say it seems to have been left open for several days."

"And there was no one else who's had access to the storerooms?" Karg questioned.

"Not that we're aware of. With Aerin's skill with a bow and his offer to help, he'd been put in charge of hunting and preparing the meat while we focused on other matters. So, other than the kitchen staff, who only gets supplies from the room once a week, it should be only him."

Karg's expression shifted from confusion to something Aerin could only describe as surety. His heart sank, his mind certain his fate was sealed.

"Scalewarden, if I may…" Cyrus said, drawing Aerin's gaze.

"Yes, Cyrus?"

"Allow me a day to look into the matter myself. I will personally check with the staff and inspect the storeroom to make sure there isn't some other explanation. If it isn't Aerin's fault, he can aid us in restocking our stores before Winter fully sets in. We're already pressed as it is, and we need every person we can get to be ready to fight."

Karg sat silently for a moment, pondering Cyrus's words. Aerin's heart beat faster again, hoping the Scalewarden would allow Cyrus to prove his innocence.

"As Spear, this is beneath you. I know I've asked much of you in filling this new role, and I would not have asked if you weren't up to the task. But even you have your limits, and we need you working on preparations for what is to come."

Aerin's heart sank again.

"Besides, the evidence seems clear."

Aerin heard Cyrus sigh, his shoulders dropping as he did. He turned slowly to Aerin, a look of apology in his features. Aerin felt tears welling up, but he suppressed them, trying not to look too pathetic in the eyes of those present.

"Aerin of the Lodge," Karg said. "Your services are no longer required, and you are no longer welcome in these halls. Please pack your things and leave before the sun sets." Karg turned his attention to Cyrus. "Cyrus, please assign a knight to keep an eye on the hunter until he departs the gates."

"I will escort him myself. It's the least he deserves," Cyrus said with a bow, an annoyed expression forming as he turned and nodded to Aerin.

Aerin nodded back and solemnly turned to leave with Cyrus, the two knights stepping aside, both staring at him with looks of condemnation.

Outside in the hall, the two of them walked in silence for a minute. Aerin was still trying to figure out what might have gone wrong when Cyrus finally spoke.

"I'm sorry it came to this, Aerin."

"It's not your fault, Cyrus," Aerin replied. "You tried. I appreciate you trying."

"I just have a hard time believing it was you."

"It's possible. I'm sure I took care of everything, but my mind has been preoccupied lately with Jarren." At the mention, Aerin suddenly remembered his thoughts from earlier. "Oh, that reminds me, actually. I wanted to speak to you about him. I guess you'll have to keep an eye on him now."

"He's an odd one, for sure, but seems mostly harmless. But you're still skeptical, I see."

"Normally, I wouldn't be. Normally, he *is* harmless. But there's something off about him right now that I just can't place. And I was thinking about what he said about seeing the woman with the burning eyes. Do you think he encountered one of the elder dragons out there?"

"I suppose that's plausible. You think the encounter had some effect on him?"

"Something like that. I won't pretend to know much about dragons, nor the powers they wield, but it does seem odd that only he survived. His companions–Kanir and Yoghar–they were both exceptional hunters, some of our best, even. Seems odd that Jarren, the weakest of the three, was the only one to survive, doesn't it?"

"Yes, that is odd. Hadn't really thought about it too much," Cyrus admitted. "Maybe he fled. Maybe she let him go? But if she killed the others, why not him?"

"The thought crossed my mind. But yes, why indeed? Jarren is a great tracker, but hardly much use outside of that."

"Maybe she just wanted us to get spooked–spread rumors of her arrival to sew fear in the surrounding areas," Cyrus suggested.

"That would make sense. And it did have that effect–at least on the Lodge. But the lord of Valehold dismissed it without so much as a wink. Not very effective of a fear tactic if you ask me."

"Hmm," Cyrus said, scratching his beard. "I'll have to think on it some more. Either way, I'll try to keep an eye on the fellow."

They rounded the corner, coming into sight of Aerin's room.

"Well, it's not like I have much to pack up. It shouldn't take but a few minutes."

"Take all the time you need," Cyrus said, his face solemn.

Aerin nodded and headed inside, packing what little he had. It was mostly just the supplies he'd brought with him. He was low on rations, but fortunately had some coin, so he'd have to make a stop in Eastend to restock.

With everything in his sack, he left the room, glancing back sorrowfully one last time. It wasn't much, but he'd grown fond of the temporary home. *Oh well*, he sighed. *Time to get back to my real home.*

Outside, Cyrus greeted him with a thin smile.

"All set then?" he asked.

"All set."

From where his room was, it was only a short distance out to the open-aired courtyard where the stables were housed. As they exited the main gates leading inside the mountain, Aerin headed toward the stable, back to the corner where they'd been keeping Essie away from the other horses. As Aerin rounded the corner, she greeted him with the stomping of her feet, bobbing her head up and down.

"Hey girl," Aerin called out as he came up to the stall door. "Well, I have some bad news. Looks like it's time to head back home. And I'm sorry, but I don't have any treats for you at the moment."

Essie snorted as she turned away from him.

"Hey, don't be like that. It's not my choice. We'll stop in town, so I'll see what I can find."

Essie snorted again, turning to the corner to munch on some hay. Aerin opened the door and came inside, grabbing her tack and saddle from the nearby wall. As he approached her with them, she sidestepped away. He stepped forward and she moved again.

"Oh, come on Ess. We need to get home. We'll pass through Jeb's Post on the way back, and you know he always gives you a few apples."

Essie looked at him with a look that seemed to say she didn't believe him.

"Something happened," Aerin admitted, his shoulders drooping. "It wasn't my fault, but they told me to go. So, you see, we *have* to leave." Aerin looked at her with a pleading look.

Essie shook her head, snorting again, but she shifted a little back in his direction.

"Thanks, girl." Aerin stepped forward and slid the saddle on her back. Essie shuffled her feet a bit but ultimately stayed put.

Aerin finished fastening all the straps and made sure everything was situated before leading her out of the stall. He hopped up on her back and together they headed for the gate.

Just short of the gate, Aerin called Essie to a halt, glancing back over his shoulder up at the towers of the keep. Cyrus was still standing near the awning on the other side of the open arena. He waved and Aerin nodded back in reply.

Aerin turned back toward the gate at the sound of the doors creaking to life. As they swung open, he gazed out into the barren fields beyond, and the forests beyond that, past the town of Eastend. He sighed one last time, then kicked Essie gently.

"Let's go home, girl."

***

As Aerin left and the gates closed behind him, Jarren watched intently from the shadows of the ramparts.

It is done. He's leaving.

Very good, praised the voice in his head. *Now, the twins. We must know more about them.*

Yes, Princess. I will try to get close to them.

See what you can learn. Anything that will help me understand their personalities and traits.

Very well...

Jarren wrapped his cloak a bit tighter around himself as he turned with a sorrowful expression. He didn't like hurting his friends, but Mother demanded his obedience. He was not strong enough to resist her compulsions, and he hated himself for it.

CHAPTER THIRTY-THREE

PUZZLES

Mara read most of the night, only getting a few hours of sleep before she was up again, heading straight for the library. She'd skimmed through several dozen tomes, but so far none of them had clued her in to any possible explanations for what was happening to Kai.

Her vision blurred as she read the words on the page in front of her, several black spots forming where words should be. She squinted, closing her eyes tightly and rubbing them. She was sure it was just the lack of sleep and how stressed she was, but it was happening more frequently now, which did have her a little worried. *Need to focus. Need to help Kai.*

Her vision improved after another minute, and she continued. The book before her at the present was titled 'The Bloodrite', written by one Garet Mindsmith. Mara knew the man well enough as he'd authored several dozen books in the library, most of them pertaining to many of the things the Dragonbloods had gone through over the years. It was the most promising book she'd delved into so far, and though the book covered a great many side-effects of drinking dragon's blood, none of them matched what was happening to Kai.

She lazily skimmed another page, waiting for something to catch her eye. She mumbled to herself as she skimmed, not realizing she was even doing it.

"Adverse reactions... Hives. Weakness in the limbs. Red eyes, sometimes blurry vision..."

Oh, well that might explain what's happening to me.

"Gradually improves over time, three to five days in most cases."

I'm almost there.

She continued to scan, looking for any heat-related illnesses. Best she could find was that fevers were common, but usually mild, and never debilitating. Plus, the Bloodmender had been quite sure it wasn't a fever.

Seems to be the only thing he's sure of...

She flipped the page and continued skimming, her vision getting blurry again. She blinked hard and reopened her eyes, the words coming back into focus. One of them caught her attention–a name. Fenris Oathsworn. *Where have I...*

"Oh!" Mara said aloud, suddenly remembering the mysterious book she'd found earlier about the study of dragon's blood. She'd read the book from cover to cover since removing it from the library and was appalled she hadn't thought of it sooner.

There had been several passages that hadn't made much sense at the time, but now that she thought about it, with everything going on, there was something in particular that stuck out to her.

The book had spoken about the effects of not just the elder dragon's blood, but specifically the powerful effect that Liotha's blood had had on the Dragonbloods who consumed it. It had been clear that some dragons' blood was much more potent than others, and based on Fenris's research, Liotha's had been the strongest they'd ever encountered. And, in fact, the very first Fireblood came from consuming it.

Fireblood. Overheating? I suppose it's possible, but there is no direct mention of it...

Mara rifled through her stack of books, looking for one she'd skimmed earlier on exactly that topic. Mara had read the book about the Firebloods–the rarest of rare abilities that only four Dragonbloods had ever possessed, of which Garn, the first ever Dragonblood, was also the first Fireblood. The only problem was, based on what had been documented, none of them had issues with overheating like Kai. There were only four, and Garn's case was never formally documented, but the other three never struggled with issues other than the normal side-effects.

"I wonder..." Mara said aloud.

"You wonder what?" came a familiar voice off to the side, startling Mara.

"Oh, hey Vi," Mara said, looking up at her, blinking several times as her friend's face came into focus.

"Goodness, Mara. Did you even sleep last night?"

"I got a couple hours," Mara said, yawning.

"A couple hours? Mara, you can't do that to yourself. I know you want to help Kai, but-"

"I'm fine," Mara said, her tone a bit on edge, which surprised even herself. "Sorry," she added, her face turning red.

Vi smiled and sat down in the chair next to her.

"It's okay, Mara. We're all worried, but you won't be much good to Kai if you don't get enough rest."

"I know..." Mara said. "I just– I think I'm close to finding an answer, and then it just turns out to be nothing. There's got to be something in these books."

"I figured I might find you here when you weren't at the meeting this morning."

"Oh, right... I forgot," Mara said, feeling a bit worried about not showing.

"It's fine. No one really expected you to be there."

"Did they make a decision?" Mara asked.

"Yes. They're sending two dozen knights to scout the towers and check for survivors, and to report on whatever else might have happened. Based on what they discover, we'll decide the next steps. Everyone else is preparing for war, and they're gearing up knights to send out to protect the local towns."

"Sounds about right," Mara replied, her mind wandering.

"But enough about that. What are you looking at now?" Vi asked, looking down at the pile of books in front of Mara.

"Oh, right. So, this is interesting... I remembered something from the book on– a book I read before. It reminded me of this *other* book, the one about Firebloods."

"Firebloods. The super rare ability where Dragonbloods can control fire, right?"

"Yes, that's it," Mara replied.

"Pretty wicked if you ask me. But what's it got to do with– wait, do you think that's what's going on with Kai?" Vi asked, suddenly seeming much more intrigued.

"I don't know. Like you said, it's very rare. There've only been a handful of them, and as far as it's documented, none of them have had anything like this. So, you see, just when I think I found something, it's–"

"Ms. Grayscale," said someone toward the front of the library. Mara and Vi both looked up to see a knight walking toward them.

"Yes?" Mara asked.

"Ms. Grayscale, the Bloodmender sent me. He said to tell you Kai is awake."

Mara turned to Vi, her eyes lighting up as she did.

"Thank you," Mara replied, dipping her head to the man. He returned with a bow and promptly left.

"I guess I should clean up," Mara said, looking down at the pile of scattered books.

"I'll take care of it," Vi said as she began to start picking them up. "Go see your brother."

"Are you sure?" Mara asked, blushing.

"Yes. Go!" Vi said, waving her hands.

"Thank you, Vi," Mara said, heading for the exit.

"Oh, and Mara," Vi called out. "Get some rest."

Mara smiled back at her friend as she rounded the corner.

***

When Mara entered the doorway of Kai's room, seeing him sitting up and talking with the Bloodmender, she felt a surge of joy flow through her. It had been less than a day, but the toll it had taken on her was more than she'd realized. The lack of sleep probably didn't help.

Kai spotted her a second later and turned away from his conversation with the Bloodmender to cast a weak smile her way.

Without hesitation, Mara came up and wrapped her arounds around him, squeezing him tightly. After a few seconds, she felt his arms wrap around her, too. It wasn't firm; a bit shaky, even.

"Hey, Mara," Kai said through quivered lips.

She squeezed him again for a few more seconds before pulling back and looking into his eyes. She saw it, then–the weariness. His skin was paler than normal, several dark rings under his eyes. His lips looked chapped, even though they'd been giving him water since the start of everything. His hair was matted from sweat, which she could smell. But all that aside, he was awake, and at least for the moment, he seemed okay.

"Don't you ever do that to me again," Mara said, putting her hands on his cheeks. "Did you find out anything?" she asked, turning to the Bloodmender.

"Unfortunately, no," he replied with a slight frown. "I was just telling him it was clear this is a heat-related illness, which caused his body to go into a state of shock. But I still can't determine the root cause. Somehow his body is generating an abnormal amount of heat."

Mara looked back to Kai with a look of concern. He returned the look and shrugged with a half-smile.

"Could this be related to the dragon's blood?" Mara asked.

"Yes, it's possible. Normally, we perform the Bloodrite in a controlled environment. The manner in which you two came to possess the blood in your veins was... unconventional, to say the least. Still, even in the early days when much less was known and the Bloodrite wasn't as curated as we've done in recent years, there has never been a documented case of a reaction like this. That's not to say it's completely out of the question, but it is a mystery."

"So, what do we do now?" Mara asked.

"Well, we may not know exactly what's causing it, but we do know what it's doing to you, Kai. Until this passes, and hopefully it does, you're going to need to take extra precautions when you feel your body heating up. And water–drink lots of water."

Mara glanced up at Kai to see him rolling his eyes. She elbowed him gently and he turned to her with a smirk.

"I will," he said. "Anything else?"

"I recommend you rest quite a bit for the next few days, and no strenuous activity."

Kai rolled his eyes again.

"I missed the meeting," Kai said, looking back and forth between Mara and the Bloodmender.

"So did I," Mara answered, to which Kai raised his eyebrow. "I was... busy, but Vi filled me in. They are sending knights out to scout, and to protect the villages. I know what you're thinking, and you heard him. That's out of the question."

Kai pursed his lips and looked away. Mara could tell he was trying not to roll his eyes again. After a second, he looked at the Bloodmender.

"So, when can I?" he asked.

The Bloodmender glanced at Mara briefly before replying. "I can't say for sure. If all goes well, perhaps a couple weeks."

"A couple weeks!" Kai exclaimed. Mara could see his face turning red.

"Until we know exactly what's going on and what's triggering it, it's better if you avoid excessive physical activity. I know you want to help, Kai, but if you pass out again, you're not going to do anyone any good. We'll get there, I promise. Just need to give it some time."

Kai glanced at Mara before turning his head away from them both.

"I'm sorry, Kai," Mara said, reaching her hand toward his. He pulled his hand back at her touch, keeping his focus toward the wall.

"Perhaps we should let him get some more rest," the Bloodmender said, standing and heading for the door.

Mara looked back at Kai, wanting desperately to say something to make him feel better, but she did not have the right words. She needed rest herself. Perhaps, once they'd both rested, they could talk more productively about it.

"I'll come by later," Mara said, standing. She saw Kai's eyes turn her direction, but he continued to face the wall. After a second, he nodded, then lay down and closed his eyes.

Outside in the hallway, Mara approached the Bloodmender.

"I was in the library doing my own research," she said. "Trying to see if I could find anything about his illness myself."

"I see. And did you?" he asked.

"Nothing specific, no. But there was one thing. It doesn't quite make sense, but just a hunch. How much has been documented in your medical notes about Firebloods?"

"Firebloods?" he asked, raising an eyebrow. He glanced Kai's direction. "Based on what I know of the Firebloods, while it might explain some of Kai's symptoms, we don't have any notes about these specific symptoms happening with any of them, though they are quite a rarity."

"It was just a hunch," Mara said. "I came to the same conclusions as you. There are no notes, that I can find, with this happening to any of them."

"I see. Well, I'll keep it in the back of my mind as I continue to try and understand what's ailing your brother. But in the meantime, it looks like you could use some rest yourself."

"Yes, I know. You're not the first person to tell me that. I plan to go do that right now, in fact."

"Good to hear, Mara. If you need anything, you know where to find me. I'll continue to keep an eye on him."

"Thank you," Mara said, trying to smile.

She felt her body growing weak, as if it was beginning to go to sleep on its own. Even her facial muscles seemed to be dysfunctional. Sleepily, she found her way out of the infirmary and headed for her room. Her mind was still racing with everything that had happened, but she found it harder and harder to focus. The black spots were back, and seemed even worse than before.

When she finally reached her room, she collapsed onto her bed, letting the darkness overtake her before she even realized.

Chapter Thirty-Four

OBSTRUCTION

After Mara and the Bloodmender departed, Kai was left alone in the room to stew on his thoughts. He'd heard them whispering about him out in the hallway, though he hadn't discerned much of what they'd said.

"Left behind again," he said aloud, uncaring if anyone heard him, though it had been quiet in the hallway for a few minutes. "Even as a Dragonblood, I'm still useless."

He looked up toward the ceiling, his face a mixture of pain and frustration. "When will it ever end?" he asked of the gods above, though he doubted they heard him, or even cared, if they existed. "When will my life actually matter?"

He realized his temperature was rising again, and his thirst had returned, which made him even more angry. He turned to the side and saw the wooden cup sitting on the nightstand. He reached over and snatched it, spilling a bit of water on the floor. Apparently, someone had filled it up for him. He cursed under his breath, lifting the cup to his lips, downing the glass in a matter of seconds, spilling a few more drops, this time on his bedsheets.

He still felt thirsty. He looked at the cup in his hand, then to the large bucket of water they'd set beside his bed. He began to grip the cup tightly for several seconds, fighting the growing urge within him. Losing to it, he hurled it against the wall with a grunt. It clanged around on the floor for a few seconds before it began to roll. Turning away, Kai laid back down and closed his eyes.

Kai gasped as he woke, visions of fire filling his head. A short flare of light clouded his vision, forcing him to squint.

He had no idea when he'd fallen asleep or for how long. His heartbeat was strong, somehow audible in his ears. He heard the fading crackling of fire, though he knew it had only been in his dreams. Looking around, trying to orient himself, he assumed he'd been asleep for some time. He also assumed the strange moment of brightness when he awoke was merely an aftereffect of waking so abruptly.

"I must have passed out hard."

He sat up further, blinking the sleep from his eyes. He glanced at the lamp beside his bed, noting someone must have turned it down while he was asleep. Seeing the bucket of water next to it, he realized he was parched. Remembering his fit of rage before passing out, his eyes scanned for the cup amidst the dull glow of the flickering lamp. He spotted it on the floor near the corner of the room, blushing in the dim light. *Guess I overreacted a bit. Hope I didn't break it.*

He slid his feet off the bed and walked over to it, picking it up with one hand. He looked it over, checking for cracks. There was a small chip along the rim, and the cup had some strange black lines along the side, but it seemed to be mostly intact, and he didn't think much more of it.

He returned to his bedside, dipping the cup in the half-full bucket of water. Holding it up, he watched for any leaks. *All good.*

He downed the glass, then another, then another.

Feeling a bit better, he set the glass down next to the bucket and let out a deep sigh. He was still frustrated about his restrictions, but now that his body had had plenty of rest, his mind was trying to figure out something more productive to do than just sleeping and tossing cups at walls.

"I've got to get a grip on this. Whatever is going on, I can figure it out. If I don't, I'll never get the chance to prove myself. This is it. This is your moment, Kai. Time to step up and get your shit together."

Kai glanced at the doorway. He'd been told to take it easy. If he passed out again, he'd never hear the end of it, especially from Mara. *As long as I'm careful, no one will know.*

He had no idea how long he'd stared at the door, deciding whether or not he should go. He was pretty sure it was night, so it'd be unlikely anyone spotted him. Thoughts of all the knights leaving without him kept coming, finally tipping the scales in favor of him getting out of bed. He couldn't miss it. He could prove he was fine. He could prove he had control over whatever this was.

With a renewed sense of determination, Kai headed for the door. Stopping a few feet short of it, he glanced down, realizing he had no shirt and was only wearing his lower undergarments. Blushing again, his eyes circling in confusion, he turned and looked around the room for something to wear. Off in the corner, on top of the lone dresser, he saw what looked like clothes folded in a neat pile. Walking over, he saw that they were, in fact, his clothes. It seemed someone had washed them for him. *Well, that's lucky.*

He took a minute to properly dress himself, still feeling a bit embarrassed that he'd almost walked out in his underwear. Once complete, he ran his hand through his hair, realizing it was also a bit of a mess. He combed it to the side as best he could without a mirror.

Satisfied he was more presentable, he headed out into the hallway, glancing both directions. All was quiet, only the small flicker of the torches lining the walls making any sound, further confirming it was probably sometime in the middle of the night. He nodded and left the room, hanging a left and heading for the main exit.

Out in the main passageway of the keep, it was much the same. All was quiet and Kai only passed two knights in the hallway, probably on the way to their shift on the wall. With an awkward nod, Kai passed them and turned down the hallway leading to the inner training ward. While most of their training happened in the outdoor courtyard, the inner training area had several unique things—namely, the Grinder.

Named the Grinder for a reason, the platform that extended from nearly one end of the hall to the other contained a series of contraptions meant to test the true speed, agility, and strength of those who survived the Bloodrite and became Dragonbloods. And though many thought its name was because of putting one's skills to the grinder, what was more appropriate was the toll it took on many young Dragonbloods. Kai had seen it for himself many times, though he had never been allowed to use it as a 'No-blood'.

It was what he'd been attempting to finally do the other day when he first passed out.

"Alright, this time is going to be different," he said, taking a torch off the wall and heading around the room to light the others. "Don't push yourself too hard. Take it easy, take it slow, think through each step. Keep your head on straight and you can do this."

Kai felt awkward speaking aloud to himself, but there was no one around at this hour and he felt like if he didn't say the words aloud, he might forget and lose his cool again. He couldn't let that happen. He couldn't be bed-ridden while everyone else was out there fighting a battle that should be his.

His mood soured as his thoughts drifted to his uncle. He was the reason the princess was here. Kai still blamed Yoren for everything. But Yoren had also paid the price for his sins, and Kai still felt shame that it was partly his fault.

"No time to be sad. I'm still mad at you, Uncle, but that doesn't mean I won't fight in honor of your memory. You failed me—you failed us. But I failed you, too. I won't fail Mara. I'll become what I was always meant to become."

Kai set his torch back on the wall and stared at the Grinder for a few seconds, assessing it in a new light. He had many challenges ahead, but this was the first. It wasn't going to be easy, but failure was not an option.

"Alright, let's get to it," he said, rolling up his sleeves and pulling himself up onto the starting platform. "Time to prove to the world what you're made of, Kai."

CHAPTER THIRTY-FIVE

TWILIGHT

Mara stirred from a restless sleep full of dark dreams. She felt strange, like she was still trapped in one of them, though it seemed she'd hardly slept at all. She tried to open her eyes, but she couldn't.

Am I still asleep?

It felt like she was awake. She tried to open her eyes again. She felt her eyelids moving, but everything was just... blank. She forced them shut, blinking hard, then opened them again. Still, nothing.

Odd. I must be dreaming. But it feels so... real.

Mara moved her hands, feeling the sheets on her bed as if she were there, awake. She forced herself to sit up, moving her hands around to steady herself. It all felt so real. She could even hear the ruffling of her movements in a gentle echo throughout her room. At least, that's where she assumed she was.

Sitting up, she tried to focus. She tried to force herself awake. Perhaps her vision was just taking longer to recover than the rest of her body. Mara didn't know, but whatever it was, it felt strange, and she didn't like it.

She furled her brow, concentrating as hard as she could, drawing on every ounce of strength she had to bring her vision back to life. She could feel the beads of sweat forming along her hairline. She reached up and attempted to touch her eyes. She jerked backward when her fingertips brushed her bare eye.

Panic began to slowly creep in. Mara tried to calm her breathing, every breath sounding like a gust of wind. She heard a drop of sweat as it slid down her nose, dropping off the edge and landing on her hand. She could hear every sound as if they were amplified. Her heart was beating faster in her chest, sounding like drums reverberating through the walls. Her panic grew.

What is happening? What is wrong?

Her thoughts went to Kai.

"Kai," she called out, the echo of her voice crashing through her room. She placed her hands over her ears and around her head, pulling it down as she brought her knees up in a fetal position, tears beginning to run down her face.

"Kai!" she called out again, this time louder.

Mara heard the distinct clang of a metal door handle, the lever being pressed downward as the latch unhinged. There was a shuffle and the sound of a voice in the hallway. It was Kai's.

"Mara?" she heard clearly, though it was still muffled. She could hear a hint of desperation in his voice.

"Kai," she said once more.

A second later, the sound of her own door started, the same metal against metal sound of the latch shifting. Kai burst into the room, his entry sending waves of sound throughout Mara's room that bounced off the walls and escaped into the hallway, echoing down the corridor until it finally faded.

Every sound felt like a hammer against Mara's head. She could hear Kai talking to her, but she couldn't focus on what he was saying with the pounding in her skull, even though she still had her hands over her ears and her head tucked between her knees. Mara tried to block it out, but it only grew worse.

And then she felt Kai's hands on her shoulders.

The sounds began to fade as his voice came into focus.

"Mara? Mara, what's wrong?"

Mara slowly lifted her head, desperately needing to see her brother's face. There was nothing. No Kai, no darkness. Just... nothing.

She heard Kai gasp.

"What? What is it, Kai? Kai, I– I can't see you. Is something wrong with my eyes? Am– am I still dreaming?"

"Mara... your face. Your scars are basically gone, but your eyes, they're... different."

"Different? What do you mean, different? Kai, what's going on?" Mara started to tear up again, the fear of something terribly wrong setting in.

She felt Kai's firm grip on her shoulders as he brought her closer and hugged her, a gentle shushing sound as he put his hand behind her head.

"It's alright, Mara. Let's go find Cyrus, or the Bloodmender, or someone–anyone. I'm sure someone can help. I'm sure it'll be alright."

Mara sobbed in Kai's embrace, but a spark of hope ignited with his words. After a minute, she felt calmer, forcing herself to her feet with Kai's assistance. He led her to the door, out into the hallway. It felt so much like a dream still. Her inability to distinguish where they were, what direction they were headed, and what was around her made her feel like she was trapped in some sort of nightmare. Mara had never given vision much thought before this, but now that it was taken away from her, she realized just how much she'd always depended on it–taken it for granted.

Now, she relied on Kai. Walking down the halls of the keep with him as her guide was more reliance than she'd ever given him before. It was a simple thing, really–to hold someone's arm and let them guide you. But being forced into this sort of reliance on someone else was a strange feeling.

Mara wasn't sure where in the keep they were now, but she knew it had to be somewhere near the center when she started to hear voices echoing through the hallways. It began to get louder in her ears, like before. As her panic grew, so too did the thundering of every little sound. Mara heard familiar voices, but the sounds were becoming so deafening that she had to cover her ears to try and block them out. It was as if a swirling torrent of darkness and fear was slowly drowning her, the immensity of it booming in her head.

And then, a voice rang out from the loudness that started to bring Mara back. It was Cyrus.

"Mara? What's wrong, Kai? Is everything alright?" he asked gently, his voice soothing, helping calm the storm that was raging in Mara's mind. It took her a minute to calm down again, and she started to hear Kai's voice in reply.

"Something's wrong with her eyesight. Mara, it's alright. Cyrus is here. He's going to help get you to the infirmary so we can get you some help. Hold on to me." Kai squeezed her arm with his free hand, leading her a new direction. Mara could feel Cyrus's hand on her other shoulder. The presence of both of them was comforting, and it helped keep the panic at bay all the way to the infirmary.

When they arrived, Mara heard Cyrus speaking with one of the women who worked there. She thought she recognized the voice from before.

"Yes, there's something wrong with her eyesight. Can you get Baelin to take a look at her?" Mara heard Cyrus inquire with the nurse.

"Yes, of course. Bring her in here and we can find a bed for her to relax on."

Kai and Cyrus led Mara into the infirmary, bringing her to a bed like the one she'd stayed in when they returned from the mountains with her injuries. They'd seemed serious at the time. Now, they seemed to pale in comparison.

"I'll go fetch Baelin right away. Please make yourselves comfortable," the woman said.

Mara heard wood grating against stone, which unnerved her. It hurt her ears, and she winced slightly, but it didn't last long, and she relaxed when Kai reached out and grabbed her hand, squeezing it gently.

"Are you in pain, Mara?' Kai asked.

"The sounds. It hurts my ears," she said.

"Oh, sorry. It was just the chair. I'll try to be more quiet."

They waited in silence for some time, the only sounds in the room the soft breathing of Kai and Cyrus. As Mara lay there, she began to listen to their individual breaths. After a minute of focusing on them, Mara could distinguish subtle differences between the two.

Cyrus's breath was steady and drawn out. She knew it was him because Kai was holding her hand and was closer. He'd always been a calm man, and his breathing was no different. Kai, on the other hand, was quick and irregular. His breathing was shallow, and Mara thought she could even hear his heart thumping rapidly in his chest. She could sense he was in pain, too. She didn't know exactly how, but she could feel it. It was on his breath, and in the pulse of his hand, which was steadily growing warmer.

The sound of distant footsteps pulled Mara from her strange trance. She listened carefully and thought it was more than one person. The footsteps grew louder, and Kai and Cyrus stirred, rising to their feet as several people approached.

"Greetings, Baelin," Cyrus said, shaking the man's hand.

"Hail, Brother," came the familiar sound of his voice. "She's having trouble seeing, I've been told."

"Aye, seems that way," replied Cyrus. "Ever seen anything like it?"

"A sudden onset of blindness? No." Mara's heart sank. "But let's have a look. I've seen dozens of different reactions to the dragon's blood. Everyone reacts a bit differently, so this could just be something new."

Mara heard the shuffling of feet as the two men moved her direction, one coming close to her bedside.

"Good evening, Mara," came Baelin's voice. It, too, was calm and soothing, setting Mara at ease. "Can I ask you a few questions?"

"Yes..." Mara said, a slight quiver in her voice. She felt Baelin set something on the bed by her side.

"When did you first experience trouble seeing?"

"This morning–" Mara paused. *No.* "No, that's not true. It's been a few days now. Since... since Uncle's burial."

"A couple days? Mara, why didn't you say something?" Kai asked, sounding shocked.

"Sorry, I–" Mara started.

"It's okay, Mara," Baelin interjected. "Kai, if you don't mind."

Mara heard Kai breath a heavy breath through his nose.

"Can you see anything at all? Or is it total darkness," Baelin asked.

"I can't see anything. It's like darkness, but also... not. There's nothing there at all. I don't know how else to describe it."

"I see."

Baelin asked the nurse to fetch a candle. Mara listened as she walked off, returning after a minute.

"Thank you," Baelin said. "Now, Mara. I'm going to wave this candle in front of your face. Let me know if you sense any of the light."

"Okay."

Mara heard the flicker of the flame as the candle moved closer to her, but no light reached her vision. Mara could hear Kai's breathing slow, then come to halt. He was holding his breath.

"Anything?" Baelin asked.

"No, nothing," Mara replied. Kai let out his breath and the flame on the candle flickered ever so slightly, a puff of heat swelling into Mara's face, making her flinch.

"Nothing?" Baelin said, letting out a short sigh. Mara felt Baelin pick up what he'd set down on the bed earlier, followed by rifling sounds as metal clanked into metal. After a few seconds, the rummaging stopped, and Baelin leaned back in toward her.

"Mara, I have here a magnifier. It will help me take a closer look at your eyes to see what's going on. Is it alright if lean in close to examine your eyes?"

"Yes, go ahead."

"Thank you, Mara. I'm just going to take a look to see if I notice anything out of the ordinary." Mara nodded.

She could feel Baelin move closer, his own breathing steady and light as his exhales gently kissed her face. It felt strange to have him so close to her, but she knew she could trust him. She could tell by the rhythm of his heart. Now that he was so close, she was almost positive she could hear it. It was steady, like Cyrus's breathing. It had a rhythmic pulse to it—one that set Mara further at ease.

Baelin made several soft grunting sounds as he examined her eyes, but said nothing as he carried on, carefully examining each one thoroughly. At last, he sat up, muttering to himself.

"I'm not quite sure what to think, to be honest," he said. "There's a clear change in your eyes. We've never had someone go blind from the Bloodrite, so I've never seen eyes change like this before. For someone's eyes to lose all their color—to go gray—well, it could just be a side effect of the blood, or it could be..." Baelin stopped, and Mara felt his hesitation. "I'm going to need some time with Mara to assess her blood. But for that, I need to focus, and I need the room free of distractions."

As Baelin finished his sentence, the torches throughout the room flickered momentarily, everyone looking up and around at them as Kai let out another heavy breath.

"Kai, are you feeling alright? I was a bit surprised to find you out of bed already this morning," he asked. Kai let go of Mara's hand and stood quickly.

"I'm fine," he replied. "I was feeling much better after some rest and wanted to sleep in my own bed. It was a good thing, otherwise I wouldn't have heard her."

Mara felt guilty. She could tell Kai wasn't fully telling the truth. He was still recovering from his mysterious ailment and now all the attention was being paid to her. She felt her panic creeping back in. *If I'm blind forever, how will I help Kai?*

"Okay, Kai. Let me spend some time with your sister and I'll come find you as soon as I know anything. Just take care of yourself, okay. If you need water, there's still some in your room."

Kai let out a heavy breath again.

Mara reached her hand out in Kai's direction, waving it around as she searched for him. She waited until she felt his fingertips touch her own. She wrapped her fingers around his hand and squeezed him, as he'd done for her earlier. His demeanor softened a little.

"It's okay, Kai. I'm sure Baelin will take good care of me, just as he did you."

"Mmm hmm," Kai mumbled. "I'll be outside if you need me."

Mara smiled as Kai's fingers slipped away. She listened to his footfalls as he left the room and disappeared down the hallway.

"I'll go with Kai," Cyrus said. "Keep me updated as well, Baelin."

"Of course, Spear. Soon as I know anything."

"Be at peace, Mara," Cyrus said. "I know this is scary, but we're all here for you. I'll let the Scalewarden know what's going on. And I'll keep an eye on your brother until you're on the mend."

Mara felt the sincerity behind his words but also sensed the doubt as he finished. She wanted to believe she would get better, that this wasn't permanent, but she was struggling to believe it herself.

Baelin scooted closer as Cyrus left.

"Alright, Mara. Like I did with Kai, I want to see if I can sense anything from your blood. To do that, I'll need to take hold of your wrists. May I?"

Mara nodded.

"Thank you. I'm just going to place my fingers here," he said, taking hold of her wrists and placing a thumb on the inner side of each wrist. "I'm going to need to concentrate, to see if I can sense anything with your blood. If you can, try to relax and breathe normally. The quieter the better so I can try to discern the source of what's going on with your body."

Mara nodded again, trying to focus on her breathing and calm herself. It took a little bit, but gradually she felt her heartbeat fall steady, her breathing matching it. As she quieted, that's when she began to feel it. It was a strange sensation, like an exterior presence moving through her body. She felt it in her arms first, and it slowly moved up toward her chest. Her heart beat a little faster as the feeling surrounded it. She tried to calm it, but it was difficult. It was like something unfamiliar was there and her body was adversely reacting to it.

"It's okay," he said, trying to reassure her. It didn't help. "I know this is weird, but I need you to try and remain calm."

Mara tried, but her heart and the rest of her body didn't want to cooperate. After a few more seconds, Baelin let go with a quick gasp.

"What?" Mara asked.

"It's– it's nothing," he replied, a hint of concern in his tone. "This is a lot, I know. Maybe you should get some rest first, and we'll try again later."

Baelin stood abruptly, Mara sensing his own breathing faster than it had been before. It unnerved her. She didn't know what to think of it.

"Would you like me to put the lamp out?" Baelin asked, the reversal in his tone bringing Mara back to reality. "Oh, sorry, I guess it doesn't–"

"It's okay. Leave it on. I like feeling its warmth."

"Understood. Is there anything else I can get for you for the moment?" he asked.

"No, I don't think so. I'll just rest now."

"Very well. I'll check on you in a bit but just call out if you need anything."

Mara nodded and laid her head down. She lay there quietly, listening to the sound of his footsteps as he disappeared down the hall. Her mind returned to his strange reaction. What had he seen in her blood?

Despite the fears weighing on her, she felt tired–not physically, but emotionally. With tears rolling down her face, Mara lay for some time before finally succumbing to the exhaustion.

Sleep did not bring the peace or rest she needed. Nightmarish visions danced in her head, images of living in a world of total darkness at the forefront. But there were other visions, too–things that made her uneasy. Things that made her think the worst was still yet to come.

Chapter Thirty-Six

SPARK

When Kai left Mara in the room with Cyrus and Baelin, he headed straight toward the training hall. His previous attempts with the Grinder the night before had all ended in frustration. But feeling himself overheating just thinking about the possibility of Mara being blind, he needed a distraction. It was time for round two.

When Kai arrived at the training hall, it was still empty. With most of the knights preparing for battle, there was little cause for them to be training. Because of the morning light coming through the shafts in the ceiling, the arena was well lit. He headed straight for the starting platform.

Last night, he'd tried to take it easy and be mindful of his condition. He almost let his nerves get the best of him several times, but fortunately he'd been aware of it enough to hold back. Now, with Mara at the forefront of his thoughts, things were different. He needed to get this figured out so he could be there for her. He needed to control it so he could help put a stop to the ones who'd did this to her. It was time to take things up a notch.

Kai stepped in front of the entrance to the course, staring at it for a few seconds. Off to the right there was a lever attached to a large wheel. Kai grabbed ahold of the lever and began to turn it. As he did, parts of the large platform began to move. The entirety of the Grinder stretched nearly the length of the arena, so it was about 200 feet from start to finish, but it was designed in such a way that one could not simply go straight through. There were vertical jumps up to platforms and platforms that swung back and forth. There were two circular sections that spun around with counter-spinning bars, and there were several parts where one had to swing between ropes or hold onto bars above the head. All in all, it looked daunting. It was dangerous, too. There was a reason they only let Dragonbloods use it. Kai had seen several of the less-experienced Dragonbloods take some blows that would have gravely injured, or possibly even killed, someone without that strength flowing through them. Kai stood there watching all the parts move, reaching his hand down to touch the sore spots on his arm where he'd taken a pretty good blow last night. It was sure to turn into a bruise soon.

Clenching his jaw, Kai's hesitation turned into a look of determination. His eyes narrowed as he studied the movements of the various obstacles near the front of the course. He tried to remember which ones hit him before. He began to shift his weight, mimicking the movements on the platform as he planned his path. Kai took a deep breath, trying to focus himself.

And then he was off, jumping onto the first platform, a narrow walkway with horizontal bars that came from the sides every foot or so. Kai managed to dodge the first two bars that came toward his midsection, but the third one hit him in the right leg, causing him to lose balance. He landed on the hard stone floor on his side with a groan. He immediately got back up and walked around to the front.

Focus. You can do this.

He watched the bars move in and out, trying to commit their pattern to memory. There were about twenty bars he had to get past for the first section of the walkway. Kai bobbed again, waiting for his moment to go. After a few seconds, he started another attempt. Kai made it past the first two again, barely moving his leg in time to dodge the third, which grazed his calf. He took another step forward when one up high and to the left slammed against his head, knocking him sideways as another hit his arm on the way down. He landed on the ground again, same as before, though he managed to get his hands out to soften the blow. Kai slammed his fist on the ground in anger.

He sighed heavily and got back up, moving to face the course a third time. Like before, he studied the patterns of movements, hoping to learn them as best as he could. And for a third time, Kai moved. He made it another step further this time before getting knocked off.

For how long this continued, Kai didn't know. He must have tried two dozen times, getting knocked off every single time. His body ached from all the blows. He reached around and felt new bruises already forming on his head and arms, and he felt blood from a blow above his right eye. And he was hot—ungodly hot. Kai took his shirt off and threw it to the side. The cool breeze from the windows across the room touched the drips of sweat running down his back, sending brief chills along his spine. It felt good against his aching muscles.

Kai clenched his jaw, ready to make another attempt. He faced the course yet again.

Come on, Kai.

Kai clenched his jaw, determination filling his eyes. He slowed his breathing and honed his focus as he was taught during his earlier training days. It was something he'd always struggled with. And it was hard now, his mind in a disarray, but he tried with all his might. His breathing slowed. His vision focused. He could feel the energy building in his tired muscles. Three breaths. *Focus*. Two breaths, in and out. *Control*. Last breath. *Relax*.

Kai was off, moving gracefully across the first platform, dodging every bar as they came hurtling toward him one after another. One, two, three, four bars were behind. Five, six, seven, eight more passed. Nine, ten, eleven, twelve. Kai was doing his best yet. Not a single bar had even grazed him. He kept moving, dodging, ducking, and inching his way forward one step at a time. Everything felt like it was in slow motion, Kai watching the bars whiz past his body as he moved between them.

Three more to go. That one moves out, and then... Kai had miscalculated one near the very end. As he moved within several steps of the next platform, the bar he hadn't anticipated came right behind the one before it, only six inches between them. Kai dodged the first one, but he wasn't moving fast enough to avoid the second.

He found himself on the ground again. Kai rolled onto his back, defeated, laying there on the cool, stone floor.

"I thought I might find you in here," came a voice from the side. Kai sat up and searched for its origin. It was Karg. "Though I believe Baelin told you to take it easy?"

Kai blushed, offering half a smile with a shrug.

"No matter. I see the Grinder is thoroughly kicking your arse, anyways." Karg let out a chuckle, followed by a gentle smile. Kai didn't usually interact with Karg except on formal occasions, so the nonchalant nature of the Scalewarden's approach set him off. Especially considering the fact he'd disobeyed the Blood-mender.

"Yes, well, I needed to clear my head, sir. Apparently, a good ass kicking was what I needed," replied Kai. Karg let out another short chuckle, then walked over and reached his hand out to help Kai up off the floor. Kai frowned, continuing to sit on the ground.

"You know, your uncle was sitting in about the exact same spot once, but he took my hand when I offered it."

Kai looked up at Karg, slightly embarrassed. This was the Scalewarden, after all. Kai's previous frustration melted a bit when he saw Karg's sincere smile, and he lifted his arm up, grasping Karg's hand with an awkward smile of his own.

"Uncle had trouble with the Grinder too, huh?" Kai asked nervously.

"Oh yes," Karg replied, a slightly louder laughter ensuing. "I saw your uncle fall often, especially on this first part, which he attempted many times over in the days after he completed the Bloodrite. The wars were raging, and he was eager to prove himself. He wasted no time and spent many late nights training, trying to hone his skills for the coming battles." Karg paused a moment, the lines of thought etched across his face. Kai leaned against a nearby part of the course, waiting for him to continue.

"It was late one night, and I found him trying to do the course. He kept getting knocked off the first platform. His problem was that he tried to memorize the pattern of the bars." Kai blushed at the mention of the very same thing he'd been attempting to do, averting his eyes toward the course for a few seconds. "But the trick isn't to memorize it, because it changes ever so slightly each time. It was designed to fool those who would try to do just that. Anyone can memorize a pattern, after long enough. The course was designed to change every rotation of the cogs. It is meant to test reflexes, balance, and most importantly–focus. You must possess all three to complete it. Your uncle was one of the best warriors I'd seen in a long time. He possessed superb reflexes, and his balanced stance with the spear was unparalleled. What he was missing was focus. And what he lacked in focus, he tried to make up for in smarts. And he was smart, mind you. Trouble was, he couldn't outsmart the course. It is just a machine, after all, and it only does what it was created to do. And so, he repeatedly failed."

"You see, the course was meant to prepare young Dragonbloods for facing the real threat. One cannot memorize a precise pattern of movements or attacks to take down a dragon. One must focus and be observant, reacting to the dragon's attacks as you plan your own, looking for openings in which you may strike. As a trainee, you're primarily only taught to defend, because that is all that should be expected of you. But to master the art of attack, especially against a foe such as a dragon, one must hone their skills beyond the physical limits of what humans are normally capable of. That is why we don't let those without the blood do the course. Do you understand, Kai?"

Kai nodded slowly as he thought over Karg's words. He looked back at the course, eyeing every part of it for a minute. He could feel the bruises on his body throbbing, remembering each blow he'd taken. He turned and looked back at Karg with a questioning expression.

"So, how does one learn focus, exactly?" Kai asked.

"That, my boy," Karg said, his lips turning upright into a smile, "is what every new Dragonblood must learn for themselves. When I told your uncle he needed to focus more, he told me off. He said that he *was* focused and that he could figure the course out—that he was almost there. He just needed more time. As expected, it didn't work. He continued failing for many days after that. Eventually, one day he came running to me, waking me up before the sun had even risen, ecstatic he'd completed the first platform. When I asked him how, do you know what he said to me?"

"What?" Kai asked, eyes wide as he leaned forward eagerly.

"He said he just breathed and felt his way through it."

Kai stood there for a moment, jaw open, his forehead wrinkling.

"That's it? He just breathed and *felt* his way through it?" Kai asked.

"That's it," Karg replied with a grin.

Kai turned and looked back at the course, even more confused. *It can't be THAT simple. But sure, let's give it a go.* Kai walked around to the front of the course again, grabbing the crank and winding up the gear. The course whirred back to full life as he stopped at the front and watched it.

Alright, relax. Focus. Feel my way through the course. You got this, Kai.

Kai's muscles twitched as he prepared to move. With a spring, he was off again. He watched each bar as it came toward him, feeling himself move out of the way as they came one by one, reacting to each in whichever way felt natural. As he moved closer to the end, his thoughts strayed to the last few bars. He prepared himself mentally for the way they came at him last time. He was getting closer—only a few bars away.

One came at him from low right, sweeping in front of his feet. He jumped just in time to avoid tripping over the lower bar, but as he looked up for the next bar, another one up higher came straight in line with his head. Kai brought his hands up to prevent the bar from hitting his face.

A second later, he found himself on the floor again. Karg came over and reached out his hand. Kai glanced up at it for a moment, then pushed himself up and headed back toward the course.

Feel, right. Kai didn't think it was going to work, but he tried again anyways.

He tried three more times, fell three more times, and earned himself at least three more bruises. Each time happened sooner than the last. He was only getting worse. He was also getting angrier.

"You're still trying to remember and outthink it. You need to let go and just feel. It's almost like a dance," the Scalewarden said.

Like a dance. I hate dancing. Karg's words didn't help. In fact, they were agitating him even more. He didn't like having an audience.

Kai stepped up again. The thoughts of feeling were gone from his mind. His eyes burned with a new intensity, but it was not determination. Anger drove him now.

Like all the attempts before, he moved, pushing himself faster, thinking perhaps he could just push through the course and make it out on the other side. And for a few steps, it worked. But then one slammed into his rib, nearly knocking him down. He pushed through it, barely recovering, and kept going.

A few seconds later, he took another hit. And another. Still somehow managing to hold on, and with only two or three bars to go, he leapt with all his might, hoping to reach the next platform before it was too late. That's when one of the bars he'd failed to notice appeared right in front of his face. With his momentum, the only thing he could do was shield his face with his hands to avoid breaking his nose.

There was a flash of light, a surge of heat rushed through his limbs. His vision clouded. Seconds later, he was crashing into the ground, slamming his head against the hard floor. He hit so hard, he felt himself starting to black out. Staring straight up, he saw Karg's face appear above him. The man's words were muffled, the darkness slowly overtaking him. He heard the Scalewarden shout, he felt hands grabbing him. And then, nothing.

As Kai was hauled off, Karg stood in the training arena with Cyrus, who'd come upon hearing the shouting. The two of them moved closer to the course, Karg pointing at the bar that had knocked Kai to the ground.

The bar was charred, its tip still barely glowing, a small trail of smoke swirling above it.

"How?" Cyrus asked.

"I don't know. My first instinct was Fireblood, but they need a source. There are no torches lit nearby. It's like... it came from within him."

Chapter Thirty-Seven

DREAMWALKER

Mara stood on the precipice of a hill overlooking Eastend. Somehow, she could see the town with her own eyes! *I must be dreaming...*

The hour was late, perhaps sometime just after the evening meal. She watched the sliver of the disappearing sun as a gentle breeze brushed her hair out of her face. The world felt alive, and the hopelessness of the prior day began to fade away like the setting of the sun.

She could see the town below was abustle with energy, people moving about their routines in a steady rhythm, the beating heart of the town humming with the sounds of their greetings as they passed each other in the streets. If there was any fear of war looming just beyond the horizon, it was not felt here.

Mara looked behind her up at the snow-covered mountains, the amber glow of the sun's last rays reflecting off their glistening slopes. The last of the leafy trees had shed their skins some time ago, and there were signs of Winter's arrival, imminent with every approaching dawn. But Mara didn't feel cold.

She knew she was dreaming. Everything seemed so peaceful, she didn't care, nor did she want it to end. *If only I could stay here forever.*

Her thoughts turned to Kai. He was probably out right now, worrying about her. She couldn't stay, but perhaps just a bit longer. She'd enjoy the dream while it lasted. She deserved that, at least, didn't she?

Turning, Mara headed down the hillside toward Eastend's west-facing road, one of the main streets leading into the town's center. She smiled at the townspeople as they passed by, but no one seemed to pay her any mind. She didn't think it too strange at first but as she began to see some people she recognized, offering them greetings as they passed by, their blank, unnoticing stares caused her to think again. It was almost as if she were a ghost, drifting about some long-forgotten memory of her past. But this didn't feel like the past; it felt current. It felt... real. But of course, it couldn't be.

Mara continued to wander about the town for some time, the feeling of hopelessness slowly creeping back in. The world was as blind to her as she would be to it when she awoke.

Standing in the very center of town with dozens of townspeople about her, Mara suddenly felt extremely alone. She hopelessly watched people walk by, completely unaware of her presence. Her breathing intensified and the sounds of the busy streets pounded in her ears. It was beginning to overwhelm her, like before. The dream was turning into a nightmare.

"Excuse me, miss... are you alright?" came a voice from behind her. Mara spun in the voice's direction, her heart jumping and her stomach twisting instantly into a knot. Her gaze met with the voice's origin. It was a man, tall and slender, with wavy black hair and deep-blue eyes. He held his hand out toward her, a warm, inviting smile adorning his handsome face. Mara blushed for a moment, but confusion quickly filled her features and she narrowed her eyes.

"You... you can see me?" she asked the stranger.

"Of course, I can see you," he replied with a continued smile. "And I'm so very glad that I can. But tell me, is everything okay? You seem a bit distressed."

"I'm sorry– I just. I thought I was dreaming. I mean, I am dreaming, right? It's just that it seemed like no one else could see me."

"Ah, I understand. This must be your first time then?" the man replied, standing up straight as he looked around at the townspeople passing by.

"First time?"

"Oh, you don't even know then? Very well," he said, pausing as he put his hand up, scratching his chin. "Let me see then. How do I put this? This *is* a dream, sort of. But also, it isn't a dream. I don't suppose you've ever heard of *stellamentia*? Oh, what is the word for it?" The stranger stood there for a minute, rapping his knuckles lightly against his forehead.

"Stella–what?" Mara asked, her face indicating she was becoming more and more confused.

"I'm sorry, I'm used to the old tongue. *Stellamentia*... it is like you're somewhere else, but not in your physical body–in a dreamlike state. Does that make sense?"

"Oh! Do you mean like astral projection?"

"Ah hah! Yes, that's it. So, you've heard of it, then?"

"I read about it once or twice. But you're telling me that I'm actually in a projection right now? How is that possible?"

"How, indeed? I didn't think there were very many left in the world who knew how to perform it. It is complicated magic, not normally something that one could just stumble upon. Forgive me for asking, but who *are* you, exactly?"

"I'm–" Mara paused, suddenly feeling very vulnerable. Who was this strange man, and what exactly *was* happening here? Mara was hesitant, but also intrigued. She decided to give him the first name that came to her mind. "My name is Calista. Did you say... magic?"

"I see, miss Calista. And yes–magic. Tell me, you must have some knowledge of the arcane to have stumbled across such a spell."

"Honestly, I only know a little about what I have read. I certainly do not know any magic. All I know is that I fell asleep and ended up here, in this dream. Or this... projection, rather? This is all so confusing."

"I see. Hmm..." the stranger said, resting his hand against his chin again. He eyed her curiously, bordering on skepticism. Mara felt her face blush as his eyes examined her. After a long, awkward exchange, the stranger relaxed and smiled at her again.

"Well, it seems that you are good-natured and kind at heart. I would love to know more about what brought you here, but perhaps we will save that for another time. I can see this experience is a bit jarring for you. Perhaps I can help?" The man leaned forward again, waving his hand to the left as he cocked his head sideways, indicating he wanted her to walk with him.

Mara hesitated, studying the man, just as he had done to her. He didn't seem dangerous. And if she really was in some kind of astral projection, Mara wanted to know more. She figured there was no harm in at least talking to him and finding out more about what he knew. Slowly, she nodded and started walking forward, smiling back as best she could muster.

"So, Calista, what I know of astral projection, I read from the ancient texts from my home. It is an old magic, one long forgotten to most. And as I said, there are few who know of it, and fewer still who know how to perform it. Which is why I was surprised to find you here. I've been coming almost every day, studying the people, and... pondering a great many things. I prefer to think in the Dream, because it gives me the only real chance to truly be alone. But then tonight, I noticed a girl who wasn't like the others. They can't see or hear us, of course, as you came to realize. But this is actually what is happening in the town of... Eastend, correct?"

"Yes, Eastend," Mara said, nodding as she glanced around at the people passing by.

"I thought so. So, we are actually walking through the streets of Eastend at this very moment, but it is only our astral selves that are here. They cannot see us, and we cannot do anything but observe. Which, I might add, explains the intended usage of astral projection, but also its dangers."

"Dangers?" Mara asked, suddenly a bit concerned.

"Yes, well, as with all magics, there is an inherent danger to it. With astral projection, since we have left our physical bodies behind, they are vulnerable until we return to them. One must take care not to enter the astral plane unless your body is in a safe place. I trust that yours is, Calista?"

"Oh, yes... safe enough," Mara replied, turning to look up the hill in the direction of the keep. The man followed her gaze, giving her a peculiar look.

"Very good. There is another danger you should be aware of, as well. As I said before, there are few in this world who know of or are aware of the astral plane. Only those with a deep understanding of the arcane normally become aware of its presence—and those who traverse it. But if one were to be aware enough of it, they would also very likely become aware of your presence within it. And if that person were to have ill intentions… well, that would not bode well for you. There have been stories of those who've become trapped in the astral plane, held against their will, unable to return to their bodies. And the longer one remains disconnected from their physical body, the more and more susceptible they become to being swept away into the astral void, losing the ability to find their way back out. Which is the third, and probably most important, danger to be aware of. Do you understand?"

"I– I think so. But how does one come and go freely? I ended up here by accident. What if I can't find my way back?"

"That is a great question, Calista. And one that makes me a bit concerned for your safety, at this very moment. Normally, one would study the magic for years before attempting to actually enter the astral plane. You say you have had no such training, and yet here you are. You must have some innate gift that has been latent until recently. But that may not be enough to ensure your safety." The man paused for a long moment. Mara could see the wheels turning behind his mysterious eyes.

"I can teach you, if you'd like?" he said finally.

"I'd like that very much," Mara replied, slightly taken aback at the hastiness of her own reply. But the truth was, she liked it here. If blindness was her new life, perhaps this astral escape could give her some reprieve from it all. And if she was going to do it, she needed to be well-informed.

"Very well. We will meet here again tomorrow night. I trust you can find your way back to the Dream?"

"Yes… at least, I hope so. I don't know exactly how, though."

"Tomorrow, when you're falling asleep, focus intently on where you want to go. Focus on this place. Focus on me, if you like. The stronger your focus, the more likely you are to enter the astral plane here. Do that, and hopefully you will find your way back."

"Okay," Mara acknowledged, doubt in her voice.

"For now, I think it's best if you get back. You don't want to linger too long."

"How *do* I get back?"

"I can help with that. It's one of the things I learned through my studies. I can teach you, but for now, it's best if I just do this." The man held his hand up, palm facing Mara as he closed his eyes. Mara could sense slight vibrations beginning to emanate from his hand. It was faint at first, steadily growing stronger. Her body began to tingle. Then, the man flexed his hand, curling his fingers in before quickly spreading them apart again as his hand flew toward her face. A strong wave of energy washed over her, everything going dark in an instant.

And then, Mara was awake back in her room, feeling her bed beneath her. *Is this real?*

Her body trembled as she ran her fingers over her sheets. They felt real. She reached up to find the wood of her bedposts. They also felt real. She felt confident she was back in her room, but how was the real question.

A hint of sadness filled Mara, as her vision was still gone, but there was a ray of hope in this newfound possibility of sight through her dreams. Even if it wasn't actually astral projection, and it had just been a crazy dream, it was so vivid, she didn't care. A smile edged into her lips—one that had been missing of late. Even though she couldn't see, she now had at least something to look forward to. She had a reason to get out of bed. Mara was determined to find out if it really was real, or not.

Her first stop would be the library. But how? She was still in the infirmary, and the Bloodmender might get worried if she went missing. She wouldn't be gone too long, though. Just enough to talk to the Mindwarden and see what he knew.

Mara eased herself off the bed, letting her bare feet slowly drop onto the floor. She hadn't gotten out of bed much since her blindness had set in, but little by little she was becoming more comfortable with basic movement without the assistance of her eyes. She stood up, her balance momentarily off and she wobbled a bit. But after a few seconds, she stood up straight, gaining control. She remembered vaguely where the door was, so she turned and faced that direction. She took one step forward, then another. Soon, she felt the presence of the door approaching as she grew close to it. She didn't quite know how, but she was starting to be able to feel when objects were around her. It wasn't very precise, but it was noticeable.

Her hands found the door and she ran them along it down to the latch. She found it easily enough, wrapping one hand around the handle as she pressed down on the lever. She heard the sound of the metallic mechanism as it released, pulling the door open and carefully stepping out of its way. She felt a rush of fresh, cooler air brush against her body as the door opened.

She felt for the wall on the left side of the door, guiding herself out into the hallway as she pulled the door shut behind her. It closed with a clank, sending echoes down the hallway in both directions. She could feel the echo bounce back from behind her, the hallway ending a short ways back there, from what she could remember. But in front of her, the way out, she could hear the echo slowly fade down the split hallways far beyond. She heard muffled voices coming from that direction, but they were too far off for her to tell who it was or how far away they were.

Mara reached out and touched the wall across from her room and found the door opposite of her. Holding her hand against the wall, she walked out toward the other hallway. As she came up to the corner, she began to hear the faint sound of footsteps as they drifted down from out toward the central keep. Rounding the corner into the main hallway, they grew louder.

"Oh my, Mara, what are you doing?" Vi called out, her footsteps hastening.

"Oh, hey Vi. You know, just going out for a morning stroll," Mara said, her mouth forming a half smile. "It is morning, right?"

"Yes," Vi said, sounding concerned as she came up beside Mara, grabbing her right hand and wrapping her arm around Mara's. "It is morning. I just checked in with the Bloodmender and he said you were asleep, but clearly that's not the case. Are you supposed to be out of bed?"

"I, uh... well, the Bloodmender didn't exactly say I couldn't, so..." Mara blushed, and she felt Vi giving her a look. "Anyways, what are you up to?"

"Cyrus sent for us early to help with war preparations. The Scalewarden wants everyone to be prepared in case an attack is imminent."

"Ah, they called for you all. I see." Mara frowned. "And Kai?"

"I'm not sure. I haven't seen him since yesterday."

"I'm sure he's off somewhere sulking about not being able to join the fight. Just hopefully he's okay."

"I can look for him later when I'm free. I'll check with Brol and Dax."

"Thanks. I know Cyrus said he'd look after him, so I'm sure he's fine. Anyways, what preparations are they making?"

"They are readying the main forces to march once definitive word comes back from the scouts. They should be back soon, so we're just making sure all of our defenses are in order."

"I see. It's good they're involving you. It's nice to be helpful."

"I'm sorry, Mara. I didn't mean to-"

"It's fine, Vi. You don't have to pretend like I can't help. I mean, I'm blind after all. How am I going to help prepare for battle?"

"Mara, it's not like that..." Vi started, then hesitated.

Mara reached her hands up and placed them on Vi's face. She couldn't see Vi, of course, but she could feel her. She could tell Vi felt unsure of how to relate to what she was going through. She'd heard it in her voice, too.

"Vi, it's okay. I know what I am now. There are things I just won't be able to do anymore. But that doesn't mean I can't do other things. It's just going to take me some time to figure out what that is. And until then, I'm going to need a little extra help. I know you guys are busy, but do you think you can help me out for a few?"

"Of course, Mara. Want to go get some breakfast?"

"No, I'll eat later. Can you help me to the library?"

"The library? Mara-"

Mara giggled, cutting her off. "Well, that's why I need your help. Obviously, I can't read anymore. I want you to read to me-if we find a book on the thing I'm looking for, anyways. We'll ask the Mindwarden first."

"Oh, okay. Sure you don't want to eat first?"

"Food can wait. I have something I really need to know."

Chapter Thirty-Eight

FIREBLOOD

When Kai came to, he was back in his room in the infirmary. Except this time, he awoke to a handful of faces staring at him. Cyrus was there, and next to him at the foot of the bed, stood the Scalewarden. There were also several other of the more senior knights that Kai recognized. Lastly, Baelin was just off to his right. It seemed they'd been mid-conversation about him when he came to.

He felt awful, but not quite as awful as he had the last time he'd passed out. Still, he felt warm, his throat dry again. With everyone staring strangely at him, it was even more awkward.

"How're you feeling, my boy," asked Karg.

"Terrible," Kai said, unsure how else to answer.

"I'm not surprised. You took quite the nasty fall there after... well, after what you did."

"What exactly did I do?" Kai asked, reaching for the back of his head, noticing the bandage wrapped firmly around it.

"What indeed," Karg replied, looking at the others. "We were just discussing it, and we're not quite sure what to make of it. Tell me, Kai, what do you know about Firebloods?"

"Firebloods? I know a little, I guess. Mostly what my sister has mentioned." At that moment, he remembered Mara. "Where is Mara? Is she okay?"

"She seems to be doing just fine. She left the infirmary with her friend, but with all the stress she's been under, we thought it best to not tell her just yet. It's best not to tell anyone yet. We need to figure this situation out, first. So, what has Mara told you about Firebloods?" Karg pressed.

"Dragonbloods who have the ability to control fire. There have only been a few. It's incredibly rare. That's about it, I guess. Do you think that I...?"

"Perhaps, but that's the thing. Everything you said was correct, but you're missing one key element."

"What do you mean?" Kai asked.

"Every Fireblood who's ever existed has been able to manipulate fire. But you? Well, apparently, somehow, you can summon it. *That's* what happened in the arena. You didn't manipulate some fire nearby, you created your own."

Kai's eyes widened as the Scalewarden spoke.

"I... *summoned* fire?" he asked. "How is that possible?"

"That's just the question we were discussing," Karg replied, eyeing the others again. "No other Fireblood, as far as we know, has been able to do that. The Bloodmender has spent some more time trying to make sense of what's going on within your blood. It all lines up with what he discovered earlier. It seems your overheating is a direct effect of this gift. Your heat source is internal, which is why you've passed out twice now. The problem is, if we don't figure out how to control it, this... gift might end up becoming a curse. I don't want to worry you, my boy, but we must tread carefully until we fully understand what is happening."

Kai was spacing out, absorbing the Scalewarden's every word. *Overheating. Internal. Tread carefully. Curse? I wanted more, but not something that might kill me.* Slowly, he looked back up at the faces around him, finally landing on Baelin.

"What do I do?" he asked.

"I'm still working that out," Baelin replied, shooting a quick glance at Karg. "If we can figure out how it works, then theoretically it's like any other... magic, for lack of a better word."

Magic, Kai thought, the very idea of it seeming near incomprehensible.

"If we can pinpoint what reactions your body has to different events, then hopefully we'll find a pattern and be able to perform certain actions to ensure those reactions don't cause any avoidable damage." Baelin paused for a moment. "Sorry, that probably sounds worse than I intended. I'm still trying to work this out in my head. Does that make sense, Kai?"

"None of this makes sense, but I think I understand the gist of what you're saying," Kai replied. He wasn't entirely sure he did, but perhaps Mara would be able to help him process it. She was always good at explaining things.

His mind wandered to the Scalewarden's previous comments and all the stress she's been under dealing with her own blindness. Perhaps now was not the right time. Perhaps he'd spend a little more time trying to figure this out on his own first.

"Alright, so, what next?" Kai asked, looking to both Baelin and Karg for an answer.

"I'll continue to monitor you closely for the time being. Whenever you have something that triggers your body's temperature to rise, we'll document it. It might take some time, but hopefully within a few months, we'll have a better idea what we're dealing with."

"A few months!" Kai exclaimed, raising his voice.

"I'm sorry, Kai," the Scalewarden interjected. "This is uncharted territory. These precautions are for your own safety, and for the safety of those around you.

Hopefully, one day, you will gain mastery over this and prove a valuable asset for the Order. But for now, we need to proceed carefully."

Kai felt his temperature rising as the words left the Scalewarden's mouth. With everyone watching him, he tried to stop it. Struggling, he reached over and grabbed a glass of water, noticing Baelin eyeing him closely.

"Kai, I'd ask that you, and everyone in this room, keep this quiet for now," Karg continued. "We will share this with the rest of the Order when we are ready, but I want everyone focusing on their preparations. And Kai, like I said earlier, we should probably even keep this from Mara."

At the mention of Mara, Kai felt his pulse quicken.

"She's got enough to worry about, and we're still trying to figure out what's going on with her, too. Whatever's happening to you two, it's clear this is no ordinary situation. Baelin," he said, turning to the man. "Please keep an eye on Mara as well and make sure to inform me and Cyrus right away if she shows any similar powers like Kai."

"Of course, Scalewarden," Baelin said with a heavy nod.

"Kai, can I get your acknowledgement on everything we've discussed?" the Scalewarden asked, turning back to him.

Kai was so deep in his own thoughts he failed to hear Karg call out his name. Kai was thinking about Mara and how it was possible his own problems had possibly added to the onset of her condition. She'd always been a worrier, especially about him. But more than that, Kai wondered if she, too, had some gift developing. Perhaps, like his overheating, her blindness was an adverse side effect.

"Kai, did you hear me?" Karg repeated.

"Sorry, what?" Kai replied, trying to bring his attention back into focus.

"Mara. You're not going to tell her just yet, correct?"

"Uh, yes... sir. I don't like it, but I don't want to burden her with my problem. I'll keep it to myself."

"Very well. Baelin, report to me daily on his progress. And Cyrus," he said, finally addressing the man.

"Yes, Scalewarden?" Cyrus asked.

"Please keep an eye on both of them for me, and make sure word of this doesn't get out until we have more to go on. I want our knights focused on their tasks."

"Of course, Scalewarden. I'll do what I can."

"Very good. Thank you all. I'm exhausted and must get some rest. We'll discuss this soon once we know more."

Nods went around the group–everyone except Kai. He'd spaced out again, barely aware of what was going on in the room. He kept thinking about Mara and the possibility she might have her own powers. He kept thinking about how badly he wanted to talk to her about everything. And at the forefront of his thoughts, he kept worrying that he was somehow the source of all of this. It was his decision to drink the blood, even if Yoren had motioned for him to do it. He wanted to blame his uncle, but even if he could, Yoren was gone. The weight of it all bore down on him now.

All he'd wanted was a better life for him and his sister. Now, all he wanted was to wake up from the nightmare it was quickly becoming.

Chapter Thirty-Nine

QUESTIONS

Part 2

Vi led Mara through the doorway to the Mindwarden's office. As usual, the Mindwarden was sitting at his desk, a pile of books and notes scattered in front of him, muttering to himself. Mara had seen him in such a state many times. She could picture it perfectly.

The Mindwarden didn't notice them enter, so Vi cleared her throat.

"Oh, Vi... and Mara? So good to see you. I haven't seen you since–" the Mindwarden paused. "Since before you and Kai returned from the mountains, I suppose. Oh Mara, I am so terribly sorry for your loss."

"It's alright, Mindwarden," Mara replied as Vi escorted her closer to the man's desk. "I'm trying to cope as best I can. Although, it makes me sad I won't be able to read anymore." Mara's smile faded as she uttered the words, choking back tears. *No, you have a task. No time to cry now.*

"Yes, I know it meant a lot to you. I wish I could help..." he said, trailing off. There was the sound of helplessness in his voice–the same tone everyone had been using with her these past few days. She was really starting to dislike it, but she pushed the feeling aside.

"Well, actually, you can help me," she said.

"Oh? And how's that, Mara?"

"I wanted to ask you about astral projection. Is it a skill that's ever been seen within the Order?"

"Astral projection, eh? That's an odd interest. Might I inquire as to why?" Even though Mara couldn't see his face, she knew the inquisitive look he was giving her.

"I've just been having some vivid dreams as of late and I remember reading about it before and was curious. Plus, I need a distraction." Mara could feel her cheeks turning red and she cocked her head to the side, hoping it wasn't too obvious. There was a silence for a few seconds and Mara presumed the Mindwarden was eyeing her closely. She blushed even more.

"I see. Well, you always were the inquisitive one," he said, turning and walking away from them. "Reminds me of myself, long ago. You'd make a fine– ah, sorry."

Mara's blushed cheeks turned redder, this time in sadness. She kept her head turned to the side, away from Vi and the Mindwarden, trying to hide her embarrassment. She felt Vi squeeze her arm a little. Knowing her friend noticed helped, even though she was growing tired of everyone feeling sorry for her. She didn't even know if this was permanent yet, but it seemed everyone else presumed it would be.

"Ah hah, here it is," the Mindwarden exclaimed, snapping Mara out of her conflicting emotions. "Now, let me see. Astral projection. I don't believe I have ever heard of a Dragonblood possessing such a skill, but I will check, just to make sure. My mind isn't what it used to be these days. If you'd asked me a decade or two ago, I'd probably be able to tell you right away. But I am getting old, and my mind has lost some of its edge."

Mara listened to the Mindwarden as he flipped through the pages, mumbling to himself. His words didn't encourage her, but she was hopeful that perhaps there was something he'd overlooked–or forgotten.

"No, not here. Hmm. Not here either. I wonder..." Mara heard him continuing to flip through pages as he muttered to himself.

"Nope, sorry Mara. It doesn't look like anyone in the Order has ever possessed astral projection as a skill. Not that I'm surprised. From what I've read, it is not only an incredibly difficult magic to master, but it is also quite dangerous. It's unlikely there are many, if any, who can wield it safely these days."

Mara's shoulders drooped as she let out a sigh. She was really hoping something could explain and make sense of what had happened last night in her dreams. However, she wasn't quite ready to give up.

"Mindwarden. You seem to be familiar with astral projection, at least, even if it isn't a skill the Dragonbloods possess. Might there be any books in the library that I can at least learn more about it?"

"I do believe it's mentioned in several books here, though we don't have anything on it directly. You certainly are determined, aren't you? Are you sure there aren't any specific reasons for such an interest?"

"I just need something to distract me from everything going on. You understand, I'm sure." Mara tried to think of anything else to dissuade the Mindwarden from questioning her further. "I've read a lot of the books in the library already, but I must have missed the ones that talk about skills outside of the Order–such as astral projection. I'm very curious."

Again, she felt his stare boring into her. She tried her best to keep her expression flat. Finally, she heard him sigh, followed by a chuckle.

"I suppose there's no harm in learning about it. After all, our books don't go into too much detail. You should find it somewhere near the potions and elixirs section. Shall I escort you there?"

"No, I remember where that is. Vi can be my eyes. Thank you, though," Mara replied, giving a nod of thanks in the direction of the Mindwarden's voice.

"Very well. It was nice to see you, Mara. Hope you find what you're looking for."

"Me, too." Mara smiled, then tugged Vi's arm and the two girls walked off toward the main library. Though Vi guided her, she remembered the steps well.

Once inside the main library, Mara was met with the familiar smell of old leather and dusty parchment. She remembered the smell from before, but not quite so vividly as it seemed now. Apparently, her loss of sight was already enhancing some of her other senses. The smell itself brought warm feelings to Mara, which helped put her a little more at ease. A smile found its way to her lips as they passed between some of the tables, Vi guiding her every step of the way.

"Alright, Mara, we're here. Where to?" Vi asked.

"Where are we right now? What sections do you see?"

"Hmm, let's see," Vi replied, letting go of Mara's arm. She crouched down, examining the nearby books. Mara lifted her hands slowly, reaching up until she felt the familiar feeling of worn leather against her fingertips. She ran her hands back and forth, feeling the variation in texture and the variety of lettering etching the spines of the books. The sensations in her fingers brought mixed feelings. On the one hand, the thought of never being able to read any of these books again coaxed more tears to well up, but there was also a warmth to them that gave her hope. There had to be a way for her to still enjoy books. Somehow, she'd figure out a way.

"What kind of books do you see?" Mara asked Vi, trying to divert her attention away from the struggle between opposing emotions.

"So, there's one here on– umm, Suh... nara architecture? I'm probably not saying that right."

"You mean Sah'naran?"

"Yeah, sure... what you said."

"Okay," Mara said with a giggle. "I might know where we are. Any others?"

"Hmm. So, there's another one here called, umm... Sah'naran geography."

"Yep," Mara said, giggling again. "So, this is the Sah'naran section. They made this section because the original architect of the keep here was Sah'naran – Paren Blackhammer. I read a bit about him before."

"Right," Vi replied. "So, where's the section we're looking for?"

"Right, so if we're here, then..." Mara paused, lifting her hands and waving them around a bit, trying to get a grasp of her bearings. "We need to go back," she continued, pointing to the right. "Back and then left. I think it was maybe three or four aisles over. Somewhere toward the end."

"Okay, let's go see." Vi grabbed Mara's outstretched hand and helped her wrap it around her arm again before carefully walking through to the end of the aisle, rounding the corner and turning left. They walked a dozen steps, then slowed and turned left again into another aisle.

"Alright, what do you see here," Mara asked. Vi kept holding her arm this time, grabbing one of the books off a shelf. Mara listened as she turned it over, reading the front.

"This one is 'Accounts of the First War'," Vi said as she read the title.

"Ah, not far enough then. We need to go one more aisle over–I think."

"Okay," Vi replied, sliding the book back in its place before turning to round the aisle and move one more over. "You said at the end?"

"Not quite the end, but close. I think it's right inside the aisle here. Tell me what you see now."

Vi reached up and grabbed another book, flipping it over to read the front cover.

"'A Guide to Dragon's Breath'," Vi read.

"Okay, we're in the right area then. Dragon's Breath is a flower that only grows in the northern volcanic regions of the dragons' homeland. It often signified that Dragonstone was nearby."

Mara could feel the intensity of the stare behind Vi's silence.

"What?" Mara asked.

"Mara, you are something else. How do you remember all this stuff?"

"I don't know," Mara responded with a blush. "I just like to read."

Vi laughed.

"Yes, you sure do, er– did. Sorry."

Mara tried to pretend the comment didn't bother her.

"Sorry, I didn't mean to bring it up. I'm sure this won't be permanent," Vi added.

"I hope so," Mara replied, trying to sound optimistic. "Even if not, I'll figure out how to live with it. But for now, you'll just have to learn to like it a bit better." Mara smiled and wrinkled her nose at Vi.

"Hah! Sure thing, Mara. Just spread the love, okay? I'd like to think I'm better than your brother, but I can only take so much."

"Deal." Mara continued to smile for a second, feeling somewhat comforted in the thought of sharing her love of reading with others. Perhaps that was one way she could live with this–if it *was* permanent, anyways. "Okay, so we're looking for books that talk about magic. The Mindwarden said they'd be around here. See if you can find anything."

Vi nodded, then let go of Mara's arm again as she moved to start examining nearby books. Mara stood there quietly, listening as Vi pulled several books off the shelf in front of them, before moving on to other nearby shelves. This went on for several minutes.

"Okay, so here's one called 'The Uses of Magefire'. Sound right?"

"Yes, that sounds like you're in the right area. Magefire– that's what they used in the assault on Liotha's Fall during the Great War. I still need to finish that one..." Mara felt Vi's stare again. "Not right now, later. Keep looking. I don't know what we're looking for, but just read me some titles and I'll tell you if it sounds like the right book."

"Okay..." Vi began pulling books off the shelf, one by one, reading the titles as she went.

"'The Magical Uses of Precious Stones'" Vi asked, reading one aloud. "Guessing that's not it."

"Nope," Mara replied.

"'A Study of Leylines'?" Vi asked, reading another one aloud.

"Interesting, but no," Mara said hurriedly, knowing what Vi was thinking.

"'Arcane Disturbances and Theories'?"

"Also interesting, but I don't think it would be in there. Would love to read that one though!"

Vi picked up a dozen more books, reading off a variety of potential titles. None of them seemed to be the book they were looking for.

"What about this one? It's called 'Delving into the Obscure'."

"Hmm," Mara said, pondering the title in her head. "Yes, that could be it. He did say astral projection was known by only a few in the world."

"He did?" Vi questioned.

"Yes, he– I mean, the Mindwarden. He said it was... rare, right?" Mara blushed.

"Sort of." There was a hesitation in Vi's voice that told Mara she wasn't entirely convinced. Mara blushed again.

"Anyways, let's open it and see if we can find anything."

"Sure," Vi replied. "Let's see..." Mara listened as Vi flipped through the first few pages, pausing between each to read what was on the page.

"What does it say?" Mara asked eagerly.

"So, it says here that this book was written entirely by some woman named Lyrielle Vesarian. Says she was a professor at Valewind University..." Vi paused and Mara felt her breath on her cheek.

"Lyrielle? Interesting," Mara said. "I've read about her before in another book. She seems to have quite the extensive knowledge of the arcane."

"Okay, right, so, it says here she was head of the Scolastia de Magia–some kind of magical department at the university. She was a scholar of magic, and apparently a friend to some in the Order. Says she had a great deal of knowledge about the arcane, and that the Order had requested she enlighten them on her knowledge of magics that they could potentially come up against in their fight against the dragons. It seems that some of the dragons were just as dangerous with magic as they were with–well, you know. The Order wanted to be prepared for anything."

"This is definitely the right book. Let's go sit down at a table and see if we can find the part on astral projection."

"Hey, I'm all for reading this for you, but can we go eat some breakfast first? I'm starving, and going to need some food to focus."

"Oh, right–breakfast. I almost forgot. Yeah, sure Vi. I guess I am getting a little hungry anyways. Let's go eat, and then we can look through it."

"Awesome, thanks. And yes, afterwards I'll read you that whole book until we find it. I just need some food in my stomach so I can concentrate."

"This isn't the first time I've prioritized knowledge over food," Mara admitted. "Sorry. I can get carried away with this stuff. I'll put the book in my satchel if you want."

"It's okay, Mara. That's what friends are for. And sure, here you go." Vi gently handed Mara the book, which she tucked neatly into her satchel besides the other book that was in there. Surprised, she grabbed the other book and pulled it out, trying to remember what it was.

"Oops!" Mara exclaimed, remembering.

"What is it?" Vi asked.

"You know the other book I mentioned–the one about Lyrielle?"

"Yeah?"

"Well, I kinda borrowed it without permission a while back and just realized I never returned it," Mara said with a sly smile, her face all red again.

"Oh, look at you Mara. You do have a little bad girl in you then, I see," Vi chuckled as she lightly pinched Mara's arm.

"Hey, it was really interesting, and I meant to return it. Please don't tell the Mindwarden."

"Mara, I'm only kidding. It's a book. I'm sure it's fine. I'm doubt anyone's going to miss a book or two."

"Right, of course," Mara said, still feeling a little guilty.

"So, this book. What's so special about it, anyways?"

"Oh, yes. It's very special," Mara said, perking up at the mention of the book. "Here, take a look."

Vi took the book from Mara with her free hand and opened it awkwardly, flipping through it as they left the library.

"Mara, this is just a book of herbs," Vi said, sounding confused.

"Huh?" Mara asked.

"Yeah, it's all just basic information about various herbs, most of which I've never even heard of before."

"Are you sure? I don't remember ever taking any books about herbs. I only just took the one."

"Yeah, I'm sure. Maybe you forgot and actually returned that other one?"

Mara thought for a moment. Her mind was a bit of a mess still from everything that had happened. She thought hard, trying to remember what could have happened to the other book. But try as she might, she only remembered finding it in the herbalism section, and– *Wait, the herbalism section? Coincidence?* She'd read the book many nights in her room. She'd read the entire journal, in fact, and there had been some really interesting information in it. Some things that made her want to know more. *This has to be the book. I never returned it.*

"Ah, I can smell breakfast now. Good. I was hoping we didn't miss it," Vi said, interrupting Mara's train of thought. Mara decided to push the thoughts aside for now, as the smell of the food made her stomach grumble.

"Mmm, yes. It smells delicious."

A minute later, the girls entered the dining hall and found a table close to the entrance. It sounded mostly empty, from what Mara could tell. Because of their delay, Mara assumed most had already eaten. She felt a little bad for delaying Vi so much.

The girls talked as they ate, finishing in short time, Mara finally realizing how hungry she'd been. Once they'd each had several servings and were feeling stuffed, they put their dishes away and left, heading out to find a cozy corner to read the new book.

They spent several hours talking about the book as Vi read section after section. They were both so engrossed in it they lost track of time, going well past lunch. To Mara's disappointment, though there were some exciting entries in the book, it didn't go into too much detail about astral projection. While it was interesting, Mara had only come to it seeking specific answers. By the time they were done, she realized she wouldn't be getting any. At least, probably not from a book. Her mind drifted to the strange man from her dream.

"Well, it's been a long day and I'm getting sleepy," Mara said.

"Going to bed already?" Vi asked. "You don't want to eat dinner with us?"

"No. I'm feeling a bit tired. I've been lying in bed a lot and all the activity from today has got me exhausted. Besides, I'm not sure I'm ready to see everyone yet. But will you at least tell everyone I said 'hi'?"

"Sure thing, Mara. Will do, and I understand. You're dealing with a lot right now."

Mara nodded, trying to keep her mind off it. She hoped her dreams would be a good distraction.

"Thanks, Vi. And thanks for today. I needed to get out of the infirmary for a bit. Thanks for helping me with the book, even if we didn't learn much about astral projection."

"Of course, Mara. I'm here for you."

Mara smiled sleepily in reply as Vi stood up and reached out to take Mara's hand. Mara took it and stood up, placing the book back inside her bag, then hooking her arm into Vi's. Together, they headed out of the cozy nook they'd found and back to the infirmary.

"Alright, Mara. Do you need anything else?" Vi asked once Mara was in bed, her satchel sitting on the nightstand.

"No, I think I'll rest now. Thanks again, Vi."

"Of course. I'll come get you again tomorrow morning for breakfast."

"Sounds good," Mara replied. As the door clicked shut, Mara settled and tried to make herself comfortable. It was a little early, but perhaps the man would be there already.

She focused on Eastend and the town square, just as he'd told her to do. It seemed to take her some time to calm her mind fully, but when she finally dozed off, it seemed she instantly awoke again, opening her eyes to see she was standing in the middle of Eastend, people passing by without so much as a care for her presence. She stood there in awe of it all for a minute, the ability to see again feeling so surreal.

"You're early," came a familiar voice from behind her. Mara turned to face the stranger again. He was smiling the same smile at her as before. "I'm guessing you're eager to begin your lessons, then?"

"Yes, I am," Mara responded without hesitation.

CHAPTER FORTY

BAIT

Sorn trudged slowly toward the portion of the ruins that had been rebuilt and purposed to house his sisters. Even though he was family, due to being male, he'd been ordered to take up residence across the way in his own section nearby. Part of him resented it, but it also allowed him more solitude, so he didn't complain either.

Nalaen had summoned him to her chambers. He assumed she was going to scold him for his absence in their activities. As he came up to the doorway, he nearly bumped into Mykael, who was on his way out in a hurry. Sorn gave him a flat look as Mykael flashed a devilish smile at Sorn before hurrying off toward the portion of the ruins the guards occupied.

"I see I'm not your first visitor today," Sorn mused as he entered the room, seeing his sister across the way brushing her hair. She was wearing a silky nightgown, draped low over her shoulders.

"That is none of your concern," Nalaen retorted as she pulled the nightgown up higher. "So, do you want to tell me what you've been up to?"

"Up to? Whatever do you mean, Sister?"

"You know what I mean," Nalaen said, placing the brush down and turning to face him.

"Just getting some extra rest is all, nothing more," Sorn offered. "Is that a problem?"

"Extra rest? For what? You've been sitting around here being rather useless. How could you possibly need rest?"

"I have been... meditating," Sorn replied as he looked up at Nalaen. He knew she didn't believe him. "Thinking about our plans, how we might avoid needless bloodshed," he added, hoping it might steer the conversation a different way.

"Bloodshed is never needless when it's human blood," came a scoff from a nearby doorway. Talesa entered the room and stopped, eyeing her sister with a smirk before turning her attention to Sorn in distaste. "I killed a handful more of those devils while you hide away and *meditate*. But you always were... softer. I know you don't have the stomach for it."

"For killing innocent humans, you mean?" Sorn jeered. "Don't mistake compassion for weakness. Ravaging the countryside is not what we agreed. I will not partake in these plans."

"You will do as you're told," Nalaen interjected, her tone deadly serious. "You are part of this family. Despite your disinclinations, we have an objective to achieve. You should be soaring the skies beside us, not sitting idly by, taking naps."

"I am sorry that my... inclinations are so different than yours," Sorn sneered as he looked at Nalaen's bed. "But I will not help incite another war."

"So, you would side with them!" Nalaen roared, her eyes flashing a brighter red as she pointed out the door. "Would you prefer for Kyrian to sit on the throne, too?"

"Of course not, Sister," Sorn conceded, realizing he'd pushed her too far. "I simply mean that we came here with a goal. Which, might I add, we already achieved. I can't help but think our goals have stretched too far."

"We already discussed this. His family must pay for his sins, along with any who get in our way."

"Then let us focus on the real threat and be done with it."

"And how exactly do you expect us to do that, Brother? Are we just going to attack the Order head on? Mother underestimated them, I will not. So, we attacked their towers, and maybe burned a few homes along the way. We need to draw them out. And so far, it's working. We've already ambushed their scouting party. It won't be long before they send others, hopefully the twins among them." Nalaen paused, her anger subsiding. "You would know that if you had been present and not sleeping the days away."

"So, what is the plan then?" Sorn questioned, ignoring her snide comment. "If you want me to help fight the *sangures*, then that, I will do."

"Yes, you will. We will move out tomorrow morning to set up an ambush. With Mykael in control of Kyrian's lackeys, we should be able to operate without any resistance. That is, as long as you fall in line."

"I will do my best, Sister." Sorn bowed, a snarky smile the best he could muster. He did not enjoy killing, as his sisters did. But at least if he had to do it, it should be for a reason. And he was less opposed to killing the knights of the Order than farmers.

As Sorn left, Talesa watched him with disgust.

"He will be the downfall of us," she hissed. "We should have left him at home."

"Sorn has no love of violence, but he is not without his uses. I suspect he will prove useful before this is all over. I just need to keep a closer eye on him."

"Let me do it, Sister. I've always wanted to have a reason to slit his throat."

"You will leave him alone," Nalaen ordered. "As much as he is a nuisance, he is still our brother. And as I said, he has a great many talents—ones that you would know nothing about. I will watch him. He's up to something."

"Up to something?" Talesa asked. "Like what?"

"I'm not sure yet, but I might have an idea."

***

It was nearly evening when Sorn lay down to rest. The sun had not quite dipped below the peaks of the mountains to the west, but he had somewhere to be. He was set to leave with Mykael and the others in the morning, so this would be his last chance to meet with her for a few days, at least.

Over the past several days, Sorn had grown quite fond of the girl from the Dream. He still didn't know exactly who she was, but he felt that she was somehow important–important beyond what he understood at the present. He knew she'd been keeping things from him, but he didn't blame her for it. He was a stranger in her dreams. He would not have trusted himself either.

But even though she'd been somewhat secretive, Sorn believed he could trust her. He felt it in his soul. Her identity was quite a dilemma, however. Very few humans could perform magic, and as far as he knew, even the Dragonbloods have never possessed such a gift as Dreamwalking. She obviously didn't have any real training, as she seemed to have stumbled upon the magic by mistake. He believed her, even though it seemed quite unlikely. But that fact made her all the more intriguing.

Over the past few days, he'd gotten to know her a fair bit. Not entirely, but they'd met daily, sometimes more than once. They'd only had an hour or so at first, but it lengthened each visit, the girl showing a remarkable mental resiliency against the effects of being in the dream world. If she was able to stay within the Dream for hours on end after just a few days, there was no telling what she could achieve given months of study. Sorn wanted to know more.

And so, they were set to meet again tonight. Sorn felt like he was building trust with her and was on the verge of a breakthrough. He hoped that perhaps tonight, she would reveal more about who she truly was.

As Sorn drifted off to sleep, Nalaen watched him from the nearby shadows. Though she herself hadn't learned the art of astral projection, she knew vaguely how it worked, as well as the signs of one who was under its effects. Tiredness was one. And for someone who seemed to be getting an excessive amount of sleep as of late, Sorn was abnormally tired.

Though she didn't have enough practice to enter an astral state on her own, she knew there was a chance she could piggyback off Sorn's descent into the dream world. She knew it took some time for one to get into a deep enough sleep state to enter. The trick was to fall asleep at just the right moment, near to him, and in doing so hopefully she would be able to follow him into the Dream. She had to fall asleep quickly if she wanted to catch up with Sorn.

Nalaen lay down on the ground nearby her brother. As she closed her eyes, she focused deeply on him. One thing she could try was to hypnotize herself. It was a trick that she'd seen Velicos perform hundreds of times when she was a little girl struggling to sleep amidst her nightmares. She held her hand up, pressing her two fingers together as she waved them back and forth in front of her. She followed her fingers with her eyes, whispering the words she remembered so clearly.

"En talos verren noxus, en talos verren noxus."

A gentle wave of light appeared at her fingertips, its colors like the departing of the evening sun. Staring at it, she started to feel sleepy, but it didn't work right away. She focused harder, repeating the words.

"En talos verren noxus, en talos verren noxus."

Nalaen's hand dropped to her side as she crashed, a deep wave of weariness washing over her into sleep. She lay there motionless for a minute as sleep overcame her, sinking deeper into her slumber.

Nalaen woke suddenly, sucking a deep breath in. Sitting up, she tried to orient herself. She felt strange. She felt herself, and not herself, at the same time. Looking around, she noticed she was on the outskirts of a town. She peered down at it and smiled an evil smile. *Eastend.*

She'd observed it safely from a distance many times, but this was the closest she'd ever been.

Nalaen stood and walked toward the town. Having only seen it from the mountaintops above, she was eager to peruse the town that sat under the watchful eye of the Order–the town that would burn soon, once the skies were safe from the Order's ballistae. The engines they'd crafted specifically to knock her kind out of the sky were one thing she knew she should fear. It was the same machine that took the great Queenmother Liotha down, all those years ago. It was the reason Nalaen would not attack the keep directly, nor the town that lay within the range of its weaponry. Soon enough, all would burn.

As Nalaen entered the town, she started to see those who called it home. She knew from her studies they would not be able to see her, which was confirmed by their lack of reaction when they walked by. She towered over them, eyes ablaze in their normal red glow, but they couldn't see it. Even though they couldn't see her, she knew her brother would be able to, and she wanted to see what he was up to without him noticing.

She wasn't exactly sure how it worked in the Dream, but it was similar to other magic she'd performed. She walked down a nearby empty alleyway and focused, trying to conjure that same magic to alter her form now. Slowly, she felt herself shrinking, decreasing to the same height as the humans nearby. Once she was satisfied with that, she focused on her hair, intending to change it to black, like her sister's. She could see the strands of red hair resting on her shoulders. She watched as they shifted, waiting until all were completely black. Lastly, she focused on her eyes. She thought about their glow, trying to dim them, unsure if it would work. It was the only thing they couldn't hide in their human form. But perhaps the Dream's rules were different?

Nalaen wasn't sure it worked, but she crept out of the alley, looking around for some way to check. She spotted a nearby pond near the middle of a large, central square. She walked up to it and gazed into the waters. What she saw made her stop and stare. *It actually worked.*

It felt strange, the way she looked. To see her eyes not glowing felt very odd but she ignored the feeling for now, looking up and scanning for any signs of her brother.

The central square of the town was quite busy, humans going about whatever business it was they did. Nalaen wasn't sure what that was exactly, but as she studied them, she felt the distaste of their kind welling up in her throat. Being around them, even in the Dream, made her feel sick.

Finally, she spotted several people who appeared out of place. It was a man and a girl. They didn't quite fit in with the surroundings. The girl, Nalaen didn't recognize, though she couldn't see the girl's face from this angle. But the man, though he looked different, she was certain it was Sorn. She could tell by his mannerisms. Plus, overall, he still looked the same. Just like Nalaen, he'd changed his hair and his height. She needed to get a better angle of their faces, however, to confirm.

He's been meeting with someone? Who could it possibly be?

Nalaen crept closer, trying to remain out of sight. She'd changed her appearance, but just as she saw through Sorn's, she knew if given the chance, he'd likely see through hers, too. Plus, if the girl was gifted enough to be here, she might notice Nalaen, too.

Nalaen turned her attention to the girl who was with Sorn. She could still only see her from behind, but there was something familiar about her. She carried herself in the way of someone who seemed to have low confidence, hinging on his every word. She giggled as Sorn mouthed something. Sorn smiled back at her, sincerity in his eyes.

The girl is coy—or incredibly naïve. Maybe a bit of both. Either way, Sorn would fall sway to a girl like that.

Nalaen continued to watch as they walked down the main street. They stopped momentarily as the girl looked down a side street, then back at Sorn. She nodded to him, pointing in the same direction. They started down the road, walking for a minute until they stopped in front of a large house on the western edge of the city. There were still some other humans around, but it wasn't as busy here as it was in the square. Nalaen slid into the shadows of a nearby alleyway, watching them intently.

They stood outside for some time as the girl pointed at the house and talked. It seemed to have some special meaning to her. Perhaps, it was her home.

She seems to have developed some level of trust in my brother. But I wonder, does she truly know what he is?

Nalaen needed to know who this girl was. To enter the Dream, one had to have some level of skill. After all, it was a skill that not even Nalaen knew how to do on her own. The girl seemed to act naïve and frail, but if she was here, she must have some level of power. This perplexed Nalaen, but it also brought disturbing ideas into her head.

How is someone of this power here in the area? It was unlikely she'd traveled far, though not impossible. If she was someone of great power, she could be a real threat to Nalaen's plans here. But from what she'd heard, all of the other races had all but vanished. Could this girl be some remnant of them in hiding? Nalaen was almost sure the girl wasn't from the Order. She'd studied the powers of the so-called Dragonbloods in her many years. Dreamwalking was not one of them.

Nalaen decided to try to get closer to hear their conversation, and to try to get a peek at the girl's face. She moved silently from shadow to shadow, pausing and waiting to make sure her movements weren't noticed. She was able to get close enough to begin hearing muffled words. She moved through another alley and came up behind them, at last able to distinguish their words.

"So, you've seen now where I grew up," said the girl.

That voice. It sounds familiar, too.

"Will you tell me something more about yourself?" she finished.

"I will, but not right now. We've already been in the Dream long enough, and I am having this strange feeling... almost like an extra weight is wearing on me this time. I cannot explain it, but I feel as though I shouldn't linger much longer."

"I understand. Well, will you walk with me up to the hill, and then we can part ways for the night?"

"Yes, that sounds lovely. A few more minutes shouldn't hurt."

Sorn and the girl began to stroll out of town, headed in an eastern direction. Nalaen continued to follow them from the shadows, careful to keep a good distance. She suspected it was her presence that Sorn felt, and she didn't want to push her luck, but she still needed to catch a glimpse of the girl's face before they left.

Once they were out of town, there were far fewer good options for cover. Nalaen had to move carefully, hiding behind trees and fence lines separating the fields on the outskirts of the town. Eventually, her brother and the girl stopped at the top of a nearby hill, overlooking the fields on the other side. The light of the sun was still bright enough she could see them clearly as she settled in behind a half-stone wall. She wasn't close enough to hear what they were saying, but she could see Sorn's face clearly enough. The girl's face still eluded her.

They talked with each other for another minute or so. Nalaen tried to read Sorn's lips, but she couldn't really tell what he was saying. A few seconds later, he took the girl's hand and kissed it, giving a short bow. Nalaen knew he was about to leave. And when he woke up, he'd bring her with him. She glared, upset that she would likely miss her opportunity to identify the girl.

As Sorn faded out of the Dream, the girl turned and looked back. Nalaen's eyes flashed wide when she realized who it was. Her mind returned to the memory of the day she'd killed her mother's murderer—the day she'd learned of his niece and nephew. She recalled the bloody girl being dragged away by her brother. She'd recognize those faces anywhere.

Nalaen jumped as she awoke, glancing over to see Sorn stirring. She leapt up as quickly and silently as she could, hurrying out of his tent before he spotted her.

As Nalaen entered her quarters, she heard Talesa sharpening her knives on her side of the wall that divided their temporary living space. She came through the doorway, a wicked smile directed toward her sister. Talesa looked up in her direction, noticing it.

"Now that's the smile of my sister I love the most. What have you discovered?"

"As I told you earlier, I knew Sorn would prove useful... even if he has completely stumbled upon this use by accident."

"Oh?" Talesa asked, perking up in her seat.

"Yes. Plans have changed slightly. We will still spring the trap. But now, we have the perfect bait."

CHAPTER FORTY-ONE

TRUST

Jarren paced the halls of Dragonscale Keep, recanting each room he passed by. He'd been studying the full interior of the keep, as she'd instructed. There was still the matter of the secretive Heart, which he'd heard little of. He'd seen the doors, even asked to see inside, but apparently it was a sacred place for the Dragonbloods, and not one outsiders were allowed in.

There was also still the matter of the twins. Mother had reached out to him last night to say the girl was no longer important, and that the boy named Kai, her brother, was the one Jarren needed to get close to. The only question was how.

The boy had been quite elusive. When he asked, all he'd gotten from the other knights was the boy had been in some kind of trouble, possibly with his health. Jarren had no idea what any of it meant, but assumed if that was the case, perhaps he'd catch sight of Kai around the infirmary.

As Jarren cautiously approached the main entrance, it seemed his instincts had served him well. Watching from around the corner, a little way down the hallway, he spotted the boy emerging from the infirmary and heading directly toward Jarren. He ducked back quickly, hoping the boy hadn't spotted him, though it seemed he was lost in thought at the moment and wasn't paying much attention to his surroundings.

Jarren's mind raced, trying to think about what to say. He heard Kai's foot-steps growing louder, knowing the boy would round the corner any moment. He hadn't planned for what to do next, and now he had no idea what to do.

Kai turned the corner, hurrying along as so quick a pace Jarren didn't have time to move out of his way. Jarren tried to get out of the way, but in doing so, he tripped over Kai's foot.

"Oh my, I didn't see you there. Sorry," Kai said, reaching down to grab Jarren's arm and help him up.

Jarren dusted himself off, looking up at the boy and smiling.

"It- it's quite alright," Jarren said. He reached his hand up to his jaw and rubbed where it had smacked into the hard floor.

"You're the messenger, right? From the Lodge?" Kai asked, eyeing him curiously.

Jarren nodded, continuing to smile, ignoring the pain pulsing through his jawline.

"I heard about what happened to the other guy. Aerin, was it? Do you think he really ruined the meat?"

"I– I don't know, for sure, but it s-seemed so."

"Unfortunate, that. He seemed alright, from what I'd heard."

"I guess you just never know," Jarren said, trying to hide his guilt.

"Guess so... well, again, I'm very sorry about tripping you," Kai apologized. "Got a lot on my mind at the moment. But, I should get going." The boy's face was long, and Jarren could tell he seemed burdened by something.

"I'm fine," Jarren said. "I'm n-not doing anything. Just wandering the keep, if you want to t-talk about it."

Jarren watched as Kai seemed to weigh his offer.

"I don't know," Kai replied. "It's a lot, and I don't want to burden anyone with my mess."

"I understand, Kai," Jarren said. "I don't have many f-friends, so I understand what it's like to feel like you can't... can't talk to anyone about your p-problems."

Jarren understood exactly how the boy felt. Without needing any compulsion, he sympathized with Kai, hoping his words might bring the boy some measure of comfort.

Kai's eyes glazed over for a moment, staring blankly at Jarren before he spoke again.

"I... suppose I *could* use someone to talk to, and I don't know that I can talk with anyone else about it right now. Mara always says it's good to talk through my feelings, much as I hate it. But maybe that's exactly what I need right now."

Jarren nodded and smiled even bigger than before. *Well, that worked out.*

The two of them continued down the hallway, and before Jarren realized it, they'd ended up walking in circles around the keep until late into the evening. Kai talked a lot about what had been going on with him–about passing out several times, hitting his head, and worrying about his sister's health. He talked about everything that had led up to this moment in his life, and how, now that it was happening, it was not at all what he'd expected. Jarren got the idea Kai wasn't telling him everything. The boy kept skirting around some topics and specific details, but either way, the boy had somehow bestowed a great deal of trust in him to share what he did. It was exactly what Mother had asked him to do.

Late that evening, Jarren sat patiently in his room, excitedly waiting for her to reach out to him. He couldn't wait to share his success in earning the boy's trust. Mother was going to be so proud, though he did have to wonder what her purpose for the request was. The boy seemed nice, and he was kind to Jarren in a way that few ever were. He hoped her interest in the boy wasn't going to lead to anything bad.

Chapter Forty-Two

FRACTURES

Kai was deep in thought about the conversations he'd just had with the hunter named Jarren. He surprised himself with how much he'd been willing to share with the man who was a complete stranger. Perhaps, there was just so much that had built up that Kai needed to get off his chest. Perhaps, it was just the simple nature of the peculiar man that had put him at ease. Either way, he felt a bit better after having verbalized much of his frustrations. Plus, the man was an outsider, and he didn't seem to fully grasp everything Kai had shared.

Maybe Mara was right. Maybe talking really does help...

He still felt a bit guilty about not going straight to Mara with all of it, but he was worried he'd caused enough harm. He didn't want to burden her with any more of his problems–problems he'd mostly brought on himself. And he'd been told not to tell her, anyways.

Even if he was going to wait a bit longer to tell her what was really going on with him, he still needed to check in on his sister and see how she was doing. She was going through a lot, probably even more than he was. Kai couldn't imagine what it would be like to go blind. He imagined it was far worse than what he was going through, and despite his own issues, he needed to be there for her.

Vi had found him earlier, letting him know Mara seemed to be doing okay, but she was still worried about her. Apparently, they'd gone to the library looking into something called astral projection. It wasn't something Kai knew much about, and Vi hadn't really focused on it. What she did emphasize was Mara seemed overly sleepy and, when she was awake, didn't seem to be prioritizing her well-being over other distractions. Vi worried Mara's condition was weighing on her much more than she let on.

This, Kai understood. As such, Kai was on his way to check in on her. It was early evening, and he hoped to catch her before she went to bed.

Approaching her door, he knocked gently. When no response came, he knocked louder.

"Hello?" he heard faintly through the door.

Opening it, he poked his head inside, spotting Mara lying on her bed.

"It's just me," Kai said, coming all the way in.

"Oh, Kai. I wasn't expecting you. I was just dozing off."

"It's barely past supper," he said. "But I was worried about you, that's all. Does a brother need a reason to check in on his sister?"

"No, of course not," Mara said, sitting up in her bed and turning her head his direction. "But I'm fine, really."

"That's not what Vi says. She's worried about you. We all are."

"Vi said that? Why is she worried?"

"Come on, Mara. You know why," Kai replied, sitting down on the bed next to her. "What you're going through, it's... it can be easy. I thought me being– having my issues was bad enough, but I doubt it compares to going... blind." Kai watched Mara's demeanor shift. He worried about bringing up the topic. "Sorry, I just–" he continued. "I just want to know you're okay."

"I am, Kai. I mean, it is a lot, and it's hard, but I'm working through it. At least my problems aren't trying to kill me–not like yours are. How are *you* doing?"

"I'm..." Kai started, deciding what he wanted to say next. He still really wanted to tell her the truth. "I'm working through my issues as well. Seems like it's getting a little better every day. So hey, maybe this won't be permanent. Maybe you'll get better, too?"

"That's great, Kai. And... I hope so."

Mara's face betrayed her words. Kai's mind raced, wanting desperately to talk about something more optimistic.

"Did you eat dinner, Mara?"

"No."

"Do you want to go get something to eat? I can take you."

"That's okay. I'm not that hungry. Just tired, really."

"I heard you've been sleeping a lot. How are you still so tired? Maybe we should go see Baelin about it. And you really should be eating."

"I'm fine," Mara said, a hint of anger in her voice, catching Kai off guard.

"Okay, sorry. Just don't think it's healthy sleeping this much. Might be a sign of something else going on."

"I just need a lot of rest, that's all. Like you said, I'm going through a lot. It's draining."

"Okay, okay," Kai said, feeling a hint of his own anger rising. "I just wanted to make sure you're okay."

"Well, I'm sick of everyone asking if I'm okay. I'm blind, not helpless. And I think I know when my body needs sleep or food or whatever," Mara said, raising her voice.

"Mara, that's what friends do. That's what *family* does. I'm sorry I care so much about you?"

Kai sat there, staring at Mara in disbelief. He could see she was fighting tears when she turned away from him. He wanted to reach out, to comfort her. He knew she was hurting, but he also felt like it was his fault, and now he was only making it worse. How was he able to talk to a complete stranger so easily, but had no idea the right words to comfort his own sister? Maybe he just wasn't the right person to comfort her right now. Maybe it was better if he gave her some space.

Kai stood and walked toward the door. He stopped short, turning his head to the side.

"I'm sorry, Mara—sorry this happened to you. Sorry for everything that's happened. We both have things to work out. Maybe once I figure out mine, I'll be more suited to help you with yours. Hopefully..."

Kai closed the door behind him, not sure what else to say. He heard Mara's sobs begin as soon as the door clicked shut. He hesitated, even thought about going back in, but he couldn't now. He'd come to help and just made things worse. *I guess they were right. I should just leave Mara alone to grieve right now.*

Kai stormed down the hallway, feeling himself warming up. He only had one thing on his mind now. He had to figure out how to control the fire in his veins, lest it consume him. He just needed to keep trying. He pushed aside the growing fear in the back of his mind, telling him that perhaps it wasn't something that could be controlled.

***

Over the next few days, Kai struggled alone.

He spent his time in continued pursuit of some manner of understanding over his newfound curse. He made more attempts at the Grinder, as it was the first thing to coax the fire from within his veins. And though he felt he'd come close on several occasions, all further attempts ended in disappointment.

He grew flustered and confused. He tried getting angry, and he thought it might have been working, but it wasn't something you could force. Plus, his focus was off, often thinking about Mara and how he'd possibly hurt her even more. At first, he'd been angry about it, telling himself it wasn't his fault, and it might have helped a little, but his anger quickly faded into guilt. He asked Vi to look after Mara, assuming she'd do a much better job than he did. Vi reported to him, telling him she'd been able to get Mara to talk to her on several occasions, but it seemed to be getting harder and harder to get Mara to be honest with her. Kai was growing more and more worried, but he didn't know what to do. Maybe, if he could gain a mastery over his own body, then perhaps somehow, Mara could too. It was a longshot, but it helped Kai stay focused on his task.

And so, Kai trained harder and harder every day. Despite being unable to summon fire again, his body was at least becoming more resilient to the effects of the heat within. He found he could push himself a little longer and a little harder before he started to feel overwhelmed by it. He still had a long way to go, but at least there was some progress.

On the third day since he'd left Mara's room, Kai took a break from his training to watch the procession of knights heading out to battle. The scouts had never returned, and fearing the worst, Karg ordered the main force to march out to hunt down the dragons. A small contingent was left within the walls of the keep to man the ballistae and keep watch over the valley. To no one's surprise, this included his friends, who still had no dragon's blood within their veins.

Part of Kai was glad of it, for he, too, had been ordered to stay back because of his health. But the other part of him wished they would have gone. He was getting tired of dodging questions about what he was up to, and how he was doing. He cared for his friends, but right now, they were distractions. His only comfort in companionship came from the estranged hunter who had taken a liking to him, and who didn't fully understand what was going on with Kai. It was nice to have someone to talk to who neither judged Kai nor offered advice. The man simply listened.

He'd spent more time with Jarren, having talks about the man's past, which was not so unlike Kai and Mara's, though he had no siblings of his own. People generally looked down on Jarren, so Kai took it upon himself to act as the man's friend. It gave Kai comfort that he was at least helpful to someone for the moment.

He still hadn't told Jarren about being a Fireblood. He wanted to, and the man was simple enough he probably wouldn't even really understand, but every time Kai meant to, he just felt something in the back of his mind telling him to hold back.

Kai's attempts to understand his condition continued for a couple more days, becoming more and more discouraged. He'd heard stories of a sand in the desert that, once you fell in, you had little hope of escaping without help. Though he'd never even seen a desert, he presumed how he felt was much like being stuck in that sand, slowly being dragged under with no way out. Kai was losing hope he would ever escape this curse without help of his own. And in his case, help was a luxury he would likely be hard pressed to find.

***

Mara wrestled with how she'd spoken to Kai for days. He had only come to help, and she'd pushed him away. She wanted to seek him out, to tell him she was sorry, to tell him she needed him, but her shame wouldn't let her.

She felt guilty for Kai's own condition, one that had nearly killed him. She worried it was his own need to protect her that might have led to him pushing himself too hard, and she didn't want him to do it again. Mara decided maybe it was better if she just let him process things on his own for a while. Maybe they both just needed a bit more time to come to terms with their own impediments.

Mara was also a bit distraught over missing the man from her dreams. He said he may not be able to visit her for some time, as he had some important things to do. At first, she'd just wondered why, but after nights of not seeing him, her questioning turned to worry. What if something bad had happened to him? What if he'd decided he didn't want to help her anymore? Who else would be able to continue her training? What if she possessed other powers–others that required her to use caution. She still had so much to learn.

The stranger had had a greater influence on her than she thought, and night after night, she wandered into the Dream in hopes he'd be there waiting for her. There was a certain allure about him, this mysterious man who helped her learn how to safely navigate the dream world. Who was he? How did he know so much? He didn't seem to be a threat, and yet, she practically knew nothing about him.

The more Mara found herself spending time in the dream world, the more it caused her to grow weary–a side effect the man had told her would happen. And though he'd warned her to not stay too long, Mara was staying longer and longer. Which meant, during the daytime, she needed to take naps to recover.

Vi had come by on a few occasions, and while Mara had felt the urge to tell Vi what was going on, she feared doing so would only cause more concerns. Mara was tired of everyone worrying about her. She had to assume Vi was telling Kai about their conversations, and Mara didn't want to add any more worry to his load, so she was careful what she said. He wouldn't understand, after all. Entering the Dream seemed safe enough, and she was taking precautions. She could handle it, but Kai would only try to dissuade her if he found out. She grew more resilient by the day. Perhaps, eventually, she would tell him, once she was confident she'd gained a mastery over it. But in order to do that, Mara needed to learn more.

Her forays into the Dream grew lonely. Without the man to keep her company, Mara caught herself staring off into the distance or roaming the city and nearby hills. Often, she would lose track of time. Though it had felt good at first, to see again, she found that the Dream was unpredictable. Nothing was always quite as it should be, mirages and strange shadows moving across the land, and people behaving in ways that sometimes didn't make sense. On occasion, even their faces would look different, almost like they were someone else. It was all Eastend, the city and people she'd grown up with, but at the same time, it wasn't. The man had described it to her briefly in one of their talks, but Mara hadn't really noticed until all this time spent aimlessly wandering and observing for longer periods of time.

The colors weren't quite right, either. They were softer, more muted. And the longer Mara stayed in the Dream, the darker they became. It was beginning to drain her hope that this dream world might somehow be her way to escape from the nightmare of being blind, if it was indeed a permanent condition. And that, too, was a hope quickly fading away.

And so, Mara sank into a deeper despair. She wanted to leave the Dream behind, but she felt this inescapable pull to return over and over. It was a downward spiral, like the stories of boats being swallowed by a raging torrent out in the far reaches of the oceans. It pulled and pulled, and no matter how hard she tried to fight it, it was dragging her down into the deep, dark oblivion of the world beyond her own. If the man didn't return soon, Mara feared she might one day go in and not be able to find her way out.

CHAPTER FORTY-THREE

DECISIONS

J arren searched the halls of Dragonscale Keep, looking for the boy Kai. Mother had given him direct orders to try to persuade Kai to head out to join the fight in the field. Jarren did not know why, but Kai had expressed great distress in being left behind, so it seemed everyone's objectives aligned. Still, he had his suspicions that Mother was up to something and was a bit worried for Kai's safety. He'd grown quite fond of him. Kai had been the first one to really notice, much less speak to Jarren, in some time. Though he was timid, Kai had been kind to him. Not many were kind to him.

He started searching in the training arena, which he knew Kai visited every day. He didn't know exactly what the boy was up to, but the few times he'd caught a glimpse of Kai in action, he'd been impressed. Jarren didn't fully understand why Kai hadn't joined the fight with the others. Based on what Kai had spoken about, it seemed the others looked down on him, too, which had something to do with the way he was feeling. Despite their personalities being quite different, Kai and Jarren shared some things in common. Jarren looked up to Kai, wishing he could be stronger, more determined, just as he was.

Not finding Kai in the training area, he checked the outdoor arena next. Though Kai seemed to prefer training in private, Jarren had seen him outside on occasion. As he stepped out into the light of day, he lifted his arm up to shield his eyes from the bright sun overhead. Once his eyes adjusted, he glanced around the area. There were two knights walking across it together, heading toward him, and one other performing his own training against the left wall, but there was no sign of Kai.

Jarren's eyes scanned the wall above. He noted two knights patrolling either side, but neither of them looked like Kai. He walked out a few steps further, moving out of the way of the knights headed inside, both of whom eyed him with an air of distaste. He took a few more steps out further, turning away, trying to ignore them.

Taking one more glance around the arena and the walls, still not spotting Kai, he turned to head back in. A movement in the shadows below him caught his eye.

Glancing up toward the balcony over the arena, Jarren spotted a shadowy outline against the bright light of the sun. It was Kai. He was standing on the balcony where the Order's leader, Karg, had addressed the knights before riding out for battle.

"Kai," he called out, grabbing the boy's attention from whatever he'd been staring at off in the distance. As Kai looked down at him, he nodded, but his face remained expressionless.

Since Jarren had surveyed most of the keep, he knew how to access the balcony above. There was a set of stairs just back through the gate and down a short hallway. Once inside, he turned to the right and hurried up the steps. After two more doorways, he emerged back out into the sunlight on the balcony. Kai's attention was elsewhere, but he turned his head slightly on Jarren's approach.

"Hey, Jarren," Kai said quietly.

Jarren joined Kai on the railing, reeling back a little at the height of the balcony. It didn't seem as high looking up at it, but it was the first time he'd been out here to its edge. Ignoring the sensation, he turned his attention to Kai.

"What are you doing, Kai?" Jarren asked.

"Just... thinking," Kai said, his words somber, followed by a heavy sigh. He was quiet for a few moments, Jarren trying to decide what to ask next when Kai spoke again. "You said the Lodge told you to stay put after you returned from the mountains, right?"

"Yes, th- that's right," Jarren replied.

"And yet you're here. Why did you leave?"

"Well... I... wanted to help," Jarren lied, hoping Kai wouldn't think anything of his hesitation.

"And how is that going?" Kai asked in return.

"Okay, I'd say. I– I met you, after all, so I'm glad I left. You have been kind to me, Kai. I... appreciate it."

"Hm," Kai said, turning to him, smiling faintly with a nod. "You're welcome, Jarren. I'm glad you left, too. It's been nice to have someone to talk to, to get some things off my chest. I feel like everyone around here just doesn't understand me. Mara always understood, but she's got her own problems now, and I just needed someone else. I'm glad you came along."

Kai looked back toward the horizon for a minute, looking like there was more he wanted to say.

"I think I need to do something. I think I need to do what you did," Kai admitted.

"What I did?" Jarren asked, slightly confused.

"I think I need to leave. I need to go out there and help. I feel like I'm wasting away couped up in here, and I just need to get out and do something. I need to know I can make a difference. I think you, of all people, understand that, don't you?"

Without even realizing, Jarren had come to exactly the position he was supposed to be in. And without needing to follow his compulsions, he again sympathized with the boy. That certainly made his next words easier.

"I do, Kai," he said. "I... know how hard it is to question between what you want to do and what you must do. I find myself in this same position... quite often of late. In such cases, I– I believe you should do what your h–heart tells you to do. It's the only way to be free of that which haunts you."

Jarren felt himself pained by every word he spoke. Part of him wanted so desperately to be free, and he believed his words. He struggled to fight her presence out. He struggled between two sides of his conscious. One side told him to warn Kai, the other side still wanted to please her.

"Thanks, Jarren," Kai said. "I think those were the exact words I needed to hear to make up my mind. I'm going to go get ready right away, and I will probably leave at nightfall. I have much to do to prepare. You are a good friend, and I hope I will see you again upon my return."

Jarren nodded, forcing a smile, hoping his internal struggle for dominance was not apparent in his face. He stayed facing forward as Kai placed his hand on Jarren's shoulder, shook it gently, then walked back toward the balcony's exit.

Jarren continued to try and fight. He wanted nothing more than to turn around, to warn the boy, to tell him to be careful. His willpower felt like it was gaining and losing ground every second.

"Kai," Jarren called out, still facing away.

"Yes, Jarren?" Kai asked, stopping in the doorway to turn back.

"I want you to know..." Jarren started, forcing every word despite the screaming voice in the back of his mind. "...that you are–" Jarren continued, every word causing his head to wrack with pain. "You are in–" He felt himself losing control, her voice pressing deeper into his mind. "...you are invaluable to the Order." Jarren's thoughts calmed. "They are lucky to have you, and soon, I feel, they will all see why."

"Thanks, Jarren. You, too. I'm sure after all this, the Lodge will better understand your worth, as well," Kai said. "I'll see you soon, friend."

Kai nodded one last time and disappeared into the shadows of the keep beyond. Jarren stayed facing forward, a lone tear sliding down his cheek. He let out a deep breath when he was sure Kai was finally gone, sniffing.

Good luck, Kai. May you face your demons better than I.

***

A short while after sunset, Kai crept slowly into Mara's room. She was asleep and he took extra care not to wake her, though part of him wanted to. He'd debated it, but in the end, decided a letter would be best. He couldn't leave without saying something explaining why, but if he woke her, she'd just try to persuade him not to leave. But he had to. It might be the only way to unlock his abilities, and either way, Kai needed to do something.

Carefully, he set the piece of paper on her nightstand. In it, he detailed his decision to head out and try and help in whatever battles remained. He would do his best to help push back the blight of the dragons and repay them for what they'd done to Yoren—for what the dragon princess had done to Mara. He would gain a mastery over his powers, and through it, would prove he was more than everyone had given him credit. And, hopefully, he'd return to Mara and help her figure out her own gifts, whatever they might be.

He apologized for everything that had happened so far, taking the blame for much of it. He apologized for what had happened to her. He apologized for how distant he'd been, ending it all with a promise that he would do better upon his return. Somehow, some way, it would be better. He would be better.

Kai moved to the side of Mara's bed and stared down at her. He tried not to think of the possibility this might be the last time he'd ever see her. *No. I'll be back.* Still, he bent down and kissed her ever so gently on her forehead.

Mara didn't stir. Kai thought it weird, as she'd been somewhat of a light sleeper before. A great many things had changed, it seemed.

I'll see you soon. Sleep well, Sister.

As quietly he'd come, he left the room, closing the door behind him. Kai sighed heavily, apprehension filling his gut. No more questioning himself. He'd made his decision. It was time to walk his own road. Ready or not, it was time to face his destiny.

CHAPTER FORTY-FOUR

ASHES

It had been roughly a week since Aerin had been unfairly expelled from the Order's gates. He'd intended to head back home right away but decided to stay in Eastend for a few nights instead. A few nights turned into a few more. Part of him still hoped there was somehow a chance to go back.

He'd debated going back and trying to talk to Cyrus to see if the man had discovered anything in his favor. But though he tried on several occasions, his guilt kept him from following through. He'd replayed the last time he'd used the storehouse over and over, and the more he did, the more he began to believe that it had been his fault. It didn't make sense, but he didn't think the Order, who willingly protected the lands from the dragons, would wrongfully place blame so frivolously.

No, it had to be true. And even if it wasn't, Aerin's last hope, Cyrus, was seen riding out with a large host of nights just the other morning. If there had been a chance, it was gone now.

Aerin presumed they were riding out to face the dragons head on. They had no time to worry about the woes of a lowly hunter. And so, Aerin decided to stay one last night and finally head home the next morning. Plus, he was nearly out of coin. By his count, he should have enough to stop at Jeb's Post for some supplies before making the final trek home. It was one thing to look forward to, at least.

Late the next morning, Aerin thanked the innkeeper for her hospitality. With a kindly offer of one last meal on the house for both Aerin and Essie, Aerin figured it couldn't hurt to fill their bellies up before heading out. When he finally left, it was a bit later than he'd have liked, but he figured they would still be able to make it to Jeb's by nightfall. With one last look back over his shoulder at the keep on the hill overlooking Eastend, Aerin and Essie were finally on their way back home.

The ride was uneventful. The woods between Eastend and Jeb's were quiet, only a few sparse homes, slowly dwindling the further he got from Eastend, until, after a short while, he and Essie were alone in the woods. The ride would be like this until Jeb's, which was just a small cluster of abodes surrounding the homey post.

Aerin pat Essie as they road along through the forest, whistling to try and cheer himself up. It didn't work, so he decided to just ride along in silence. It had been a few hours ride already, and he was tired, greatly looking forward to stopping for the night to get some rest. His mind was heavy with everything that had happened.

After a few minutes of silence, Aerin realized how incredibly quiet the woods were now. On his ride out, even though this section had been lonely, there had been a chorus of woodland birds to sing to him as they'd passed through. But now, all was strangely silent.

"We should be coming up to Jeb's soon, girl," he said, trying to fill the awkward silence with something. He patted Essie, who seemed to be a bit uneasy herself. "Maybe they'll even have some apples!" At the mention of apples, Essie picked up the pace, though her demeanor stayed the same.

Fortunately, it wasn't long before they came into view of Jeb's Post. Aerin could make out the outlines of buildings through the fading daylight, the distinguishable shape of the post's main building a memorable sight. But something was different this time.

Why are there no lanterns lit? Jeb always has a light in his window.

As they got closer, Aerin could see the outlines of the buildings looked jagged, distorted, and abnormal.

Something is very wrong.

Jarren rode into the middle of Jeb's Post, but instead of finding the inviting inn surrounded by a small row of houses, he saw only ruins. Something had destroyed the entire village.

"What happened here?" he said out loud as Essie shifted nervously underneath him.

His eyes were instantly drawn to small, scattered lights amidst the buildings. After straining his vision, he realized they were embers—hundreds of them, littered about the ruined village. It was then he spotted something else amidst the rubble and dim glow of the smoldering ashes.

Skeletons, at least a dozen.

Some of them still had singed flesh gripping to the bones, others were black and barely distinguishable amongst the rest of the rubble. Aerin jumped off Essie, grabbing his torch as he sprinted toward the main inn. Inside, dust and debris covered everything. A silence hung in the air, as still as the bones of the dead.

Aerin walked into what used to be the main tavern area. Images of drinks and laughter flashed before his eyes, only to be replaced by the horrific scene of melted steel and ash, barely recognizable from when he'd passed through what seemed like just a few days past. For some reason, he saw no skeletons or corpses here. *Where are they? Where's Jeb? Maybe he made it out before...*

Aerin eyes were drawn to an opening near the back corner, behind where the remains of the tavern's bar counter stood blackened and half-crumbled. There sat the door to the cellar, which was almost wholly burnt and barely hanging on its hinges. He walked over to it, peering down into the darkness.

An awful stench reached his nose. He lifted his hand, covering it, a terrible feeling setting in his stomach. He fumbled in his pocket, pulling out a piece of flint. He struck it on a nearby piece of broken metal, the sparks igniting his torch as the area around him began to glow from its light.

Slowly, he moved down the stone steps of the cellar. With each step, the feeling of dread in his belly grew. Several steps from the bottom, he stopped, lifting his torch to get a better view of the dark room. On the edge of the light cast by the torch, in the back of the room, he saw all the inn's residents. They were all dead, their flesh melted and rotting. They hadn't been burned directly like the others above.

They must have hidden down here, trying to escape the fire. But even here in the damp cellar, they could not escape its wrath.

Aerin felt vomit rising in his throat. He turned and ran up the stairs, out into the middle of the street. There was no stopping it. The stench still lingered in his nose, and the terrible sights of the cellar were on the forefront of his thoughts. The vomit made its way up and out, and he heaved it onto the ground next to him. He breathed heavily for several seconds, making sure he wouldn't hurl again. Finally, he wiped his mouth with his sleeve, and looked up at Essie, who was giving him a strange look.

As Aerin looked back, he noticed something behind her, down the road leading to the west, toward the mountains. Burnt trees. He remembered the talk circling throughout the Order before he'd been forced to leave, how the dragons had attacked the towers. He realized what had happened to the town. It should have been obvious.

He glanced down the road that led home, then back at the road heading toward the tower, then toward Essie, his face revealing the turmoil within. He'd been too timid. He'd been too afraid to stand up for what he knew was right. No more. Now, he was angry, and it was time to do something about it. He walked over to Essie and jumped up into the saddle, holding his torch high.

"Sorry, girl, but you're not gonna like what we have to do."

Essie snorted, shifting her feet. Aerin kicked her, and together they rode off down the western road, the light from Aerin's torch fading until it was but one more ember in the growing darkness of nightfall.

Chapter Forty-Five

DREAMCATCHER

"Make sure the others are ready," Nalaen commanded. "We begin preparations at sunset."

Mykael bowed his head to her, turning with a sly grin as he lifted off the ground, his scarred wings propelling him toward the guards' encampment that had been constructed near the mouth of the cave they'd claimed as their temporary outpost against the Dragonbloods. Mykael had healed well enough in the past few days since the fight with Galen, but it was apparent his wounds still ailed him. Nalaen hoped it wouldn't prove a burden.

She returned to her section of their cave where Sorn and Talesa were already waiting for her. She nodded to them both as she entered, coming to stand before them. Sorn was sitting on a large stone, Talesa was standing in the corner, sharpening her claws on the cave wall. As Nalaen approached them, Sorn sat up straight and Talesa retracted her talons.

"The humans are in position, camped in the woods nearby the tower. We launch our ambush at first light. Are you two ready?"

Sorn looked at Talesa, who returned his gaze with a smirk, rolling her eyes at him. Sorn made his own face, then turned and nodded to Nalaen.

"I am ready, Sister," Sorn said with a tilt of his head. Talesa scoffed in the background. Sorn's eyes shifted her direction, but he otherwise ignored it. "What would you have me do?"

"The humans have a sizable force," Nalaen replied as her mouth formed a crooked smile. "It is not to be trifled with. I have word the boy may be there, as well, if he arrives in time. My informant has done well. They'll be expecting a trap and will likely have scouts watching for us. That's where you come in."

Sorn's ears perked up as he raised an eyebrow.

"You are going to take Mykael and all the guards with you and hide at the base of the mountains to the northwest of the tower. Meanwhile, Talesa and I," Nalaen continued as Talesa walked around to stand beside her sister, the light in her eyes flickering brighter as she looked at Sorn, "will spring the trap while they are distracted. Hopefully, they will assume the whole of our forces are waiting in ambush at the tower and not be expecting an attack from behind."

"Interesting plan, Sister," Sorn said as he contemplated her words. "Seems you've learned much. Still, I advise caution. They only had a dozen or two when we fought them in the ruins. This time, they will be fully prepared to face us. The majority of their forces will be a tough fight."

"Just worry about your task, Brother. Talesa and I will tend to ours. I have a plan to guarantee our victory," Nalaen finished.

"Oh? And do you plan to enlighten us on this guarantee?" Sorn asked.

"In due time, but that's enough questions. It's time to rest for the battle ahead."

"Very well," Sorn replied, eyeing his sister through narrowed eyes. "I suppose I am a bit tired."

***

Mara had little hope the man would show tonight, but like every night, she consistently came and sat beside the pool in the middle of town. She was weary, even in her sleep. She wasn't sure how much more of this she could take. She needed to take a break from her dreams.

Perhaps the man had truly abandoned her. Perhaps it was time to return to the real world and try to get her life back in order. She felt guilty for avoiding Kai. She needed to tell him she was sorry. She needed to tell him everything.

Just as Mara was about to stand, she felt a strange sensation against her forehead. It almost felt like a kiss. She reached up and pressed her fingers against it, drawing them back to look. There was nothing there. *Strange.*

"Right where I expected I'd find you," came a familiar voice, startling Mara. Mara spun to see the stranger standing before her with a smirk. "Did you miss me?"

Mara blushed. She wanted to rush up and wrap her arms around him and it made her feel stranger still. She barely knew the man, wasn't even sure who he really was. Her emotions were in such turmoil she couldn't help but think it. She desperately needed to feel seen and heard and understood. He was the first one since everything happened that just saw Mara for who she was as a person, even if he didn't know the full truth.

"Good to see you, too," he said, chuckling. He offered a warm smile as he gestured toward the nearby bench. Mara smiled back and took a seat, trying to contain her excitement.

The man sat down and stared into the water with Mara, sitting in silence for a minute. Mara waited apprehensively, wondering what was going through his mind. He seemed to be staring at his own reflection in the water nearby, as if contemplating something. Mara wondered if perhaps she should start the conversation.

"I–" the man started, just as Mara began.

"How..." Mara trailed off, then laughed, her nose wrinkling. "Sorry, you go."

"No, it's not important. You go."

"Oh, well," Mara said, blushing, "I was just going to ask how your days have been going. I've missed seeing you here."

"Ah, yes. I am sorry for my absence. In truth, it has been a trying few days. My sisters and I are up to some matter of importance, and I'm afraid I have mixed feelings about the whole ordeal."

"I see. Well, do you trust your sisters?"

"Hah," Sorn let out a quick chuckle before his face turned more serious. "That is quite the complicated question, Miss Calista. We are family, yes, but my sisters and I don't exactly see eye to eye. In fact, we rarely see eye to eye on a great many things. You see, my sisters are much more impulsive than I am. In some ways, that serves them well, but in others... well, let's just say it can cause problems," he finished, ending with a crooked smile toward Mara. "But enough about that. Let's talk about you. How have you been?"

"I guess you could say we're somewhat having the same sort of week. My brother and I haven't been exactly getting along. I wanted to tell him about all of this, I just didn't think he'd understand. But he was trying to be helpful and I kind of pushed him away. A lot has happened recently, and he feels responsible for all of it. I can see the change in him, even if..." Mara trailed off, not wanting to finish her sentence. She hadn't yet revealed to the man that she was blind. "He's still my brother, of course, but I see him heading down a dark road, and I don't know how to stop it. I just figured maybe I shouldn't burden him with anything else right now."

"I guess we are more alike than we realize," the man said, smiling again at Mara, though this time his gaze lingered, staring deep into her eyes. "Has anyone ever told you that you have beautiful eyes?"

Mara blushed, averting her gaze at his kind words. It felt odd to her that such a stranger she barely knew could say something so incredibly meaningful at a time when she was feeling the most vulnerable. Mara began to cry softly.

"I'm sorry, did I say something wrong?" he asked.

"No... no," Mara replied as she wiped the tears away. "It's just... so much has happened, and I know that we don't really know each other, but you have no idea how much these conversations have helped me deal with it all. You are a kind man, and I am so glad to have met you."

A broad smile formed on the man's face for a few seconds before it slowly began to fade. Eventually, he let out a long, drawn out sigh.

"Calista, I need to tell you something," he said. One last tear streaked down Mara's cheek, and before she could wipe it away, Sorn reached out and gently lifted it off her face with his finger. "I–"

Before he could speak another word, his appearance altogether changed in an instant. His hair flashed white, he seemed larger, and his eyes turned a brilliant blue, and for a split second, Mara saw the features resembling a dragon's face and teeth. She gasped and withdrew immediately, her eyes filling with fear and confusion.

The man saw her face and reeled, pulling his hand away quickly.

"Is everything alright? I'm sorry, I just wanted to-" he started, clearly confused.

"What just happened?" Mara asked, scooting toward the other end of the bench.

"Whatever do you mean?"

"Your face. It just... changed. Who are you?" Mara asked.

"My face? What?"

Deep, ominous laughter echoed from somewhere within the crowded square. Dread took hold of the man's features as the maniacal cackle pricked the hairs on the back of Mara's neck. The man stood and peered into the crowded square, his eyes seemingly searching for the laughter's source.

"Who is that?" Mara asked, her voice emanating the fear welling up inside her.

The man's eyes stopped searching, his gaze focusing on a woman slowly walking toward them. Her hair was dark, like his own, but there was something about her eyes that caused Mara's heart to race faster. She was the only one in the busy square who was looking at them. She walked slowly their way, an off-putting grin from ear to ear. *Someone he knows?*

"What are you doing here, Sister?" the man demanded, taking a step toward her. "How did you get here?"

"Though I do not know the ways of Dreamwalking, as you apparently you do, you forget I have read many of the same texts as you, dear Brother. I know it when I see it. And as such, I know I can accompany someone with the right timing."

The man's face twisted in contemplation.

"I think I should leave..." Mara quivered, now standing, taking small steps backwards away from the two.

"No," the woman said as she looked straight at Mara. "I believe my brother was just about to tell you who he is—*what* he is. Go on, Sorn. Tell her." She kept walking toward Mara, making Mara feel more and more uncomfortable, but her words struck a chord.

The man, apparently named Sorn, stepped in front of the approaching woman, blocking her path.

"You need to leave, now," Sorn said, his tone infinitely more serious than any he'd used with Mara in their talks. His sister's eyebrow raised and she stopped, looking back and forth between Sorn and Mara.

"Well, you've really grown fond of this human, haven't you. My dear Brother, are you really so naïve?"

"What does she mean, human?" Mara asked from behind him, her eyes wide with the sudden implications of everything. The image she'd seen before flashed before her eyes. *Is he...?*

Sorn sighed heavily, turning around to face Mara, his appearance changing. Her vision. It was true. Mara's face twisted in horror.

"This is what I was going to tell you. I... am a dragon, Calista. I am sorry for the trickery. I didn't want to frighten you."

Mara backed up several more steps, focusing her mind on her bed. The woman's eyes flared to life, her own features transforming to reveal fiery red hair that matched the intensity of her eyes. Just as Mara was about to depart the Dream, the woman snapped her fingers and Mara froze, unable to move.

"Well, it seems that was all for naught, Brother, now wasn't it?" she snickered, coming up closer to him. Sorn spun and faced her, his anger with her fully apparent.

"What did you do to her, Nalaen? Let her go. She's done nothing."

"Nothing?" Nalaen laughed, a deep, throaty laugh. "Oh, dear Brother, you *are* naïve. She told you her name was Calista, did she? And you so trustingly believed her."

Sorn turned and looked at Mara, his brow furling. Her body was frozen by Nalaen's magic, but she could still move her eyes, and she looked back at him, her pupils growing more dilated by the second.

"The snow-covered ruins, the image of claws around a throat," Nalaen started as she began to circle Sorn and Mara. "Uncle comes to the rescue and a young boy drags his bloody sister away, trying to save her from the same fate dear Uncle would soon meet. They disappear into the darkness of the blizzard as he draws his last breaths, painting the snow a deep red."

Nalaen continued walking until she came up behind Mara, grinning at Sorn as she brought her cheek in close. Mara tried to move, to scream, but she was still bound by Nalaen's dark magic. All she could do was listen and observe.

"I knew this day would come. I knew we would find our quarry. I just did not think it would be you who brought them to me. Sorn, I would like to introduce you to Mara Grayscale, niece of the murderer, blood thief, *sangure*." Nalaen spat, looking at Mara as she pulled back her hair.

Mara's eyes darted sideways toward her, then back to Sorn, her eyes begging for Sorn to help her in some way. He looked at her for a moment, his face full of confliction. He averted his eyes after a long stare.

Sorn looked back at Nalaen, his demeanor turning grim.

"I am sorry, Sister, that my eyes were blind to this. I must take more care." Sorn paused, glancing back at Mara briefly. "What do you plan to do with her?"

"Her brother is marching toward our impending battle as we speak. We will still carry out our plans, but with one additional piece on the board now." Nalaen smiled, a diabolical grin directed at Mara. "I told you I had a guarantee. It's her. I will ensure the boy understands that if he wants to see his sister again, he and the other humans will leave, and he will come alone to the ruins. And when he does, the Grayscale line will end."

Sorn's shoulders dropped, his features melancholy. Mara tried to interpret what he might be thinking. *Is he really just going to let this happen?*

"Why so grim, Brother?" his sister asked, seeming to notice. "After all, you are the one who wanted to end this without unnecessary bloodshed. Appropriate that you should be the one to provide the means to make it so, even if it was by dumb luck. So, you see, only they must die. Then, we can return home victorious."

"I thought you wanted to kill them all."

"Yes, well, my pet has told me, thanks to your brother," Nalaen sneered, walking around to look in Mara's eyes, "that the Order is dying. They have no more blood, and many of them are old and grey. Their leader himself has declined of late. They will die off and disappear, back into the dust from which they came, as the dragon empire continues as it always has."

"What will you do with her in the meantime?" Sorn questioned.

Nalaen looked at Mara, then back at Sorn.

"Her tether is strong—much stronger than I expected. I do find it funny that the blind girl is the greater one to fear, even if her brother had managed to master his talent. Nevertheless, you will help me sever that tether and she will remain trapped here forever."

Sorn glanced at Mara, a look of understanding hinted in his eyes. It quickly changed and he looked up and nodded to his sister, walking up to stand in front of Mara, as Nalaen walked around behind her. He raised his hands in the air, matching Nalaen's movements until she was out of Mara's sight. They began to speak words unlike any Mara had ever heard. A terrible fear raged within her, her heart beating at a near painful rate, its thrumming pounding in her ears. She tried to close her eyes, to wake herself up from this nightmare, but there was nothing she could do. She was trapped. More tears ran down her cheeks as she directed her eyes at Sorn, begging for him to somehow stop this.

His face remained expressionless, but he held her gaze firmly. The deep blue intensity of his glowing eyes was the last thing she saw before everything faded to black.

CHAPTER FORTY-SIX

FIRE

The first rays of sunlight brightened the night sky, casting a luminous glow across the snow-capped mountaintops towering above him. Kai had ridden hard all night and was exhausted, but believed he should arrive at the first tower shortly. So far, there'd been no sign of where his fellow Dragonbloods were, but Kai had found their trail easily enough, even under cover of dark. The Order always rode four horses abreast.

As Kai began to climb the slope of the next hill, he felt an odd chill run down the back of his neck. He reached his hand up, looking back the way he'd come. Something felt wrong. Kai sensed something bad had happened, though he had no reason to be worried. So far, everything was going to plan, and as best he knew, no one had seen him leave. He double-checked his side bag, saw the large water pouch he'd filled to the brim before leaving. He grabbed it and took a long drink, just to be sure.

Feeling the sensation fade away, Kai turned his attention back toward the slope before him. Cresting the hill, he came in view of a large, wide-open plain. It swept away and up to the feet of the mountain, disappearing into a thick tree line at its base. And there, just a little further to the right around the foot of the mountain, stood the crumbled remains of the first tower.

As Kai scanned the fields and woods nearby it, he spotted several glowing spots amidst the trees. *Campfires.* He'd found them. *But why have they lit the fires so close to the tower?*

He scanned the skies, looking for any signs of the dragons. Though the light of dawn was just waking, he could see clearly enough, spotting no shadows in the sky. Still, not wanting to ride out into the open, Kai decided it was best to head straight for the tree line closest to him and ride along it to meet his brothers and sisters.

He took one last scan of the woods, seeing if he could see if anyone had already spotted him. Just as he was about to turn his horse, he realized the campfires had grown. *No...*

Kai's eyes widened in sudden realization. The forest was on fire!

He kicked his horse, taking off into a full sprint, just as billows of smoke began to pour out of the woods. He held tight to the reins, focusing his attention on the edge of the forest, his adrenaline kicking in, his heart pounding. He saw figures emerging from the smoke, one by one, waving their arms in front of their faces. Kai rushed onward, hoping to get there in time to help in whatever way he could.

As he raced closer, the smell of smoke filled his nostrils. And he could now hear shouting, more of his comrades pouring out of the woods, forming some semblance of a cohesive group. Some watched the skies, others guided more out past the burning trees.

Several of them spotted Kai as he came up, leaping from his horse. They waved at him, probably glad to see someone approaching, though he could see the disappointment in their eyes as they looked past him, realizing it was only Kai who'd come.

"What happened?" Kai shouted, running up to the back of the group. A knight he recognized, but couldn't place the name, greeted him with a firm shake.

"They came out of nowhere. We were just waking, some were still not up yet. We'd barely started eating when they attacked. They must've already known where we were camped."

Kai eyed the tree line, seeing a few more stragglers emerge. He did a quick mental count of the group before him. Only about sixteen. More had left with the main host.

"The rest?" Kai questioned, growing concerned. He did not see Cyrus or some of the others he would have expected.

"I don't know. It was pure chaos in there. I think some were cut off by the flames," the knight said, shaking his head. "I know some of the more experienced knights were putting up a fight."

Kai scanned the line of faces in front of him. Most of them were younger knights, never having faced an elder dragon. The feral dragons that roamed into the Vale were not much of a threat. But to face real, elder dragons, with cunning and strategy–that was something else entirely. The looks on the faces before Kai showed their uncertainty.

He glanced back toward the woods, peering through the now roaring flames. Something stirred within him. A chance. An opportunity.

"It was Vaelor, right?" Kai asked the man, finally remembering.

"Aye," Vaelor nodded.

"Get these knights to safety, Vaelor. Out of the smoke," Kai said, trying to sound confident. "The dragons have a plan, maybe it was to split us up. Protect each other, watch the skies. Stay together."

"Yes, sir," the knight said. "What about you?"

"I'm going in for the others," Kai said, turning toward the flames.

"It's too hot. You'll never make it through," Vaelor said, his face full of shock.

"I'll be fine," Kai said. To be honest, Kai didn't know if he would, but he had to believe that everything he'd gone through these past few weeks would mean something. Maybe he didn't have a mastery over fire yet, but maybe, just maybe, he had a higher tolerance being near it, at least.

Without hesitation, Kai stepped forward, nodding to the others as he passed. "I'm going in," he called out. "Assist Vaelor. We need to clear an opening in the woods to get everyone out. Use whatever you can, just make an opening."

Kai faced the raging torrent, already feeling its heat licking his face. It was hot, but bearable. Still, he needed to be careful. He doubted he was fireproof, so he looked for whatever openings he could find within the flames.

There were a couple options, none of them great. Kai turned around and walked back a dozen paces, then turned to face one of them. Digging his heel in the ground, he hunched over. It was time to see if all his struggles were for naught.

Kai bolted, sprinting straight toward the gaping mouth of flames. There was no more time to think. He said a quick prayer as he sprinted forward, straight toward the small opening. He closed his eyes and hoped the gods had heard him.

The roar of the flames engulfed him, the heat licking at his exposed skin. The Order's armored helped, but he still felt the hint of pain in his extremities. The heat was more than he'd expected.

Inside, Kai opened his eyes. The world was ablaze all around him. Surrounded on all sides by fire, he imagined this was what being inside an oven felt like. Kai felt his flesh writhing against the heat, and yet, the pain was minimal. He wiped the beading sweat from his brow and peered through the walls of flames, looking for any signs of movement. He saw remnants of the camp nearby, some tins and what looked like a kettle, but there was no sign of any of the others.

He moved forward, spotting more of the camp. Then he saw armor, like his own. Only in this case, the armor's wearer hadn't been so lucky.

He turned away, his stomach lurching slightly as the sight. He spotted several others, all having met the same fate. There were three of them, in total. *The others must have made it away.*

He heard it faintly then, just a whisper compared to the roaring flames. Shouting. Straining his ears, he listened, trying to ascertain where it was coming from. He heard it again, somewhat confident the direction. He took one last glance at his fallen brethren and moved toward it.

Kai reached down and brought a small piece of cloth up, wrapping it around his face. It had been crafted into their armor, a shield to help with breathing through the smoke. It didn't work perfectly, but it was better than nothing. pressed on carefully through the flames, sticking to the patches of dirt as best he could where the flames could not touch him directly. Fortunately, the vegetation was mostly sparse here this close to the mountain, so he followed winding paths between the burning trees, navigating toward the shouting.

After a few more turns, he came into view of several knights kneeling over what looked like a third. Kai ran up to them, one of them spinning at his approach, the tip of his spear held at Kai's throat for a few seconds until recognition filled his features.

"Kai?" the knight questioned, obviously confused. Kai remembered his name was Gelias. He was one of the knights who was often by Caliena's side.

As Gelias pulled his spear back, Kai focused his attention on the knight on the ground. It was Caliena. She had a nasty slash across her cheek, and she was holding rag to her side, stained red with blood.

"What happened?" Kai asked.

"Ambush," she said between gritted teeth. "Bastards caught us off guard. Should have known. The others are further up the hill, still fighting... I hope."

Kai glanced up the hill, unable to see anything through the thick smoke. He covered his mouth, realizing his lungs were now burning from all of it.

"The others were cut off from the group," Kai said, turning back to Caliena. "They're outside the forest. We need to get you out to them."

"I'm fine," Caliena said gruffly. "They need help up the hill. We need to get everyone together."

"I barely made it through," Kai said. "Not sure we can get them up there, but they were trying to clear a way out. Maybe we can get the others to retreat out to them."

"Probably a better idea," Caliena said, gritting her teeth again in pain. "I'd rather not burn to death in here if I can help it."

Kai nodded, looking back up to Gelias.

"Can you get her out of here?" he asked. The knight nodded, looked to the other knight with him, she nodded as well. Kai spent a minute describing the way he'd come in and the approximate direction of the opening he'd come through. When he was confident Gelias understood, he leaned back down to Caliena.

"I'll find Cyrus and the others. Just get out of this damned inferno and prepare everyone for the inevitable fight that will follow us."

Caliena's lips formed a straight line, her mannerism shifting from the usual looks she gave Kai. With a nod, she reached up to take hold of her comrades' outstretched hands.

"Hurry, Kai. Get them out. I'll make sure we're ready when you arrive," Caliena said.

Kai nodded, his own lips drawing a line, and without hesitation, he set on a path up the hill. He glanced back only once to see the two knights helping Caliena around a burning tree and disappearing in the smoke and blaze. *Alright. Let's save the rest.*

As before, Kai wound through burning trees and debris, shielding his face from the smoke as best he could. Fortunately, the further up the hill he got, the fewer the trees and the more spread out they were. After a short while, he began to hear the sounds of fighting. Kai drew his spear. A few seconds later, Kai saw the first signs of battle. A dragon lay on the ground, its maw open wide, its eyes staring blankly his direction. Kai froze for a second, the eyes seeming to be staring right at him. He gripped his spear, leveled it, eyeing the dragon more closely. There was blood pooled around its neck, several puncture wounds along its underbelly. It was dead, but the sight still sent chills through him. This was it. His enemy was close.

He rushed up the hill, past the massive corpse, heading for the sounds. After several dozen strides, he saw them. The rest of his fellow knights. They were huddled around a cluster of trees, several sitting on the ground, looking to be in similar shape to Caliena.

Kai didn't see any dragons, but he heard them. Every few seconds, over the roaring blaze, he heard and felt a strong gust of wind. He could barely see up through the smoke and fiery canopy, but he caught a glimpse of what looked like scales soaring overhead.

One of the knights spotted Kai and waved, bringing his hand up to his mouth, his finger over his lips. As Kai crept closer, more of the knights spotted him. Curious expressions were exchanged, Kai coming up to greet several of them.

"Kai? Where did you come from?" asked Thorlan, stepping out from amidst the group and unwrapping his own face covering. "Are there others with you?" He looked past Kai, down the hill.

"Just me," Kai admitted. "I came to help."

Thorlan's expression shifted from confusion to discontent. He frowned, glancing at several of the others nearby.

"Well, come then, since you're here. Cyrus will want to speak with you," Thorlan said, turning to approach a separate group hunched over several knights lying on the ground.

"Cyrus," Thorlan said, touching his shoulder. "We have a visitor."

"A visitor?" Cyrus said, placing his hands on his knees and standing upright. "How could we– Kai! What are you doing here, my boy? How...?"

"I came to help," Kai said, reiterating his previous statement.

Cyrus's face softened, but his look of confusion stayed.

"You were supposed to stay back to–"

"I'm feeling much better. Besides, I couldn't just keep sitting there waiting. I needed to do something."

Cyrus glanced over at Thorlan, who still wore a frown. Cyrus turned back to Kai.

"It is good to see you, Kai, but I'm afraid we're going to need more help to get out of this mess. As you can see, the situation is... dire." Cyrus turned to show Kai the knights on the ground.

Kai saw three lying there, eyes closed, no signs of breathing.

"We got split up from the rest, and without our full force, I fear the dragons have greater numbers."

"I can help with that," Kai said, turning back to Cyrus. "I made it through. I can guide everyone out. The others should be out there waiting, if the dragons haven't found them already."

"How *did* you make it through?" Cyrus asked.

"Luck?" Kai said, shrugging.

A broad smile formed as Cyrus raised his hand and placed it on Kai's shoulder.

"Good enough for now, I suppose," Cyrus said with a smirk. "Thorlan, get two men each to help the wounded, and two to carry our fallen brothers out. You take the lead with Kai, I'll take up the rear and make sure no one falls behind–and that we're not followed."

Thorlan glanced at Kai, his face twitching slightly before nodding to Cyrus and heading over to start assigning knights their tasks.

"I don't know how you got here, Kai, and when we get back, you'll have to answer to the Scalewarden about disobeying orders, but get us through this damned maze of fire and I'll make sure any punishment takes your bravery here into account."

Kai nodded. He'd expected he would probably get in trouble. Whatever it was, it would be worth it.

"Now, go my boy. Lead Thorlan and the others to safety. I'll be right behind you all."

Kai nodded again, turning to Thorlan, who was now standing by, waiting, the host of knights behind him.

"Follow me," Kai said, turning and heading back down the way he'd come.

It was easy at first, with the trees spread out. But after a short while, it grew more difficult to navigate. By himself, Kai hadn't had much trouble, but with two or three knights side by side, and the gaps between burning trees and shrubs growing narrower, they had to slow their pace.

Kai kept a careful eye on them, all the while trying to remember the path he'd taken. It was difficult to follow at times, and slowly he began to question if they were on the right track.

"Are you sure you know where you're going," Thorlan said from behind him.

Kai's eyes shot sideways, but he kept his head forward.

"This way," he said, still unsure if it was correct.

They navigated back and forth between the trees, the intensity of the heat beginning to weigh on Kai. He glanced backward, seeing most of the others were struggling even more than he was.

"I hope you're right, Kai," Thorlan said, his brow heavy with sweat. "Not sure how much longer we can take this."

"Just a bit further," Kai urged. He had no idea how much further. He was certain they should have made it by now.

Kai focused, scanning every direction. The heat made it difficult to discern where paths were open. His eyes hurt from the smoke. He blinked hard several times, trying to clear his vision.

He stumbled forward, checking several possible directions. They all seemed to end in fiery dead ends. Kai raised his hand for the group to halt and he backtracked the way they'd come, hoping perhaps he'd missed something.

"Well?" Thorlan said, coughing.

Kai ignored him, trying to remember. He walked another dozen steps, noticing a batch of fallen trees. *Those weren't there before...*

"We need to clear these trees," Kai said, turning back to the group. Everyone stared back at him blankly.

"We're lost, Kai," Thorlan said. "We don't have time to break through walls of fire in hopes it's the right path. We should go back."

"No, it's through here. I know it."

"I can't take that risk. I'm ordering everyone back up the hill."

Kai grunted and stepped forward, using his spear to try and chop apart the tree closest to him. It merely sparked but made no sign of breaking. Kai shielded his eyes, tried again. The wood was still solid in the middle.

"What's going on?" asked Cyrus, stepping through the group.

"We're lost," Thorlan replied. "We need to–"

"No, we're not," Kai interjected. "We need to get through these trees. I'm sure of it."

Cyrus looked back and forth between the two of them.

"Are you sure, Kai? We're not going to last much longer in here."

Kai nodded.

"You four, help Kai with the trees," Cyrus ordered, pointing to several knights nearby.

The four stepped forward, spears at the ready. Kai nodded to them, turning back to face the fallen trees. Since the prior idea hadn't worked, he thought perhaps they could push them over, using their spears as leverage.

Kai dug his spear in the ground underneath the lowest tree, propping it up at an angle so he could try to lift it. He turned to the others, giving them a nod indicating he wanted them to do the same.

The four stepped forward, each taking a similar position, all looking to Kai for the go ahead.

"Okay, all together," Kai shouted, everyone pressing their spears forward.

The tree started to shift, steadily moving upward until it came into contact with another tree in the gap. They moved both now, just slightly, but there were several more trees crisscrossed across each other. The weight was too great. They let the trees fall with a grunt.

Kai turned around, looking to Cyrus for help.

"Thorlan, get in there and help," Cyrus barked. "And you two... I'll hold the wounded, you help, too."

Thorlan and the others stepped up, adding their spears to the group. The fire raged all around them, sounds of other trees falling nearby filled the area. The forest was slowly coming down around them.

"Hurry," Kai yelled, pushing with all his might.

The trees lifted again, one by one, until they had three moving upward. They heard the crack of the wood as it started to split, spitting sparks in every direction. Kai glanced toward the sound, saw the trees were lodged in between several still standing.

"Harder," Kai yelled, hoping they could push through it. Another tree fell, this one a bit too close for comfort.

They continued to push, followed by more cracking, but still the trees wouldn't budge.

"Okay," Kai said, catching his breath. "We've got one last shot at this. On three, everyone together with everything you've got left."

Everyone nodded.

"One. Two. Three!"

On three, everyone pushed as hard as they could. Sparks exploded around them with a thunderous crack, one of the trees splintering in a shower of flames.

"We're getting it," Kai yelled.

With a fresh surge of adrenaline, everyone heaved again. More cracking, more sparks, some of them singing Kai's flesh, others landing and burning his facemask. He gritted his teeth and pushed through it.

The wall of trees exploded forward as one of the trees off to the right broke, falling out of the way, everyone trying to stop themselves from falling forward as it did. Kai grabbed a nearby knight who was about to faceplant into the burning pile of wood.

"Thanks," the knight offered once they'd recovered. Suddenly, his eyes shot upward and behind Kai.

Kai spun around to see a falling tree headed straight for the group, Thorlan standing right beneath it, unaware.

Without thinking, Kai jumped in its path, raising his hands up to catch it before it came down on Thorlan. Shouts from some of the others caused Thorlan to turn, just as the tree came within feet of his head. He ducked, Kai coming up next to him. Kai caught it, and with a surge of fresh strength, a strange sensation shooting through him, he pushed it up and tossed it forward, away from the group.

Thorlan looked up at Kai from his crouched position. He stared at the tree, then back up at Kai and slowly stood.

"Thought I was a goner there, Kai. How did you...?"

Kai examined his hands. There should have been burn marks, but aside from being extra hot, there were no visible signs of damage. He turned and looked at the group, everyone staring at him wide-eyed.

"I don't..." Kai started.

"Look!" someone behind him shouted.

Everyone's eyes followed the path past where the burning wall had just been. There, just a short way further, was a large opening in the forest. They'd found it.

More cracking sounds around them, another tree falling just behind the group.

"Right, let's get out of here," Kai said, waving his hand forward. He put his spear away and helped one of the nearby knights who was stumbling a bit, something wrong with his ankle.

They all rushed toward the opening, crashing through the burning debris, out into the light of the day. Everyone gasped for breaths of fresh air.

"Well, well, well," came an ominous voice off to the side. "I'm surprised you made it out of there. And Kai's here, too. How perfect."

Kai lifted his teary eyes, squinting away the damage the smoke had done, and stared as the image of the voice's speaker came into view. Flowing red hair, eyes burning with malicious ecstasy, and a twisted smile across her lips. He was face to face with her again, at last. This time, he wouldn't be running away.

Chapter Forty-Seven

RAGE

Kai glanced around, hearing the sound of wings. The smoke began to swirl violently around them.

Kai stood, along with the others, all of them forming up in a tight line, spears aimed outward. As the smoke cleared, Kai saw they were faced with six of the biggest dragons he'd ever seen, forming a half circle around the princess, who was still in her human form. All of them stared at the group of humans, their fangs dripping, their mouths formed in what looked like smiles. It sent chills down Kai's spine.

His eyes scanned the surrounding area. He saw no sign of Caliena and the others. Had the dragons already killed them?

Kai felt a bump against his shoulder and turned, Cyrus stepping up next to him.

"The Princess Nalaen, I presume?" Cyrus said, standing as tall as he could.

"You presume correct, human," she answered back with a smirk. "You know me, but I haven't had the honors."

"Cyrus Bladesong," he replied coldly. "I am the leader of this group."

"Excellent," she said, smirking again. "Well, Cyrus. I have an offer for you. It seems you and your men have been through quite the ordeal." She peered past Cyrus, examining everyone with her eyes. "Some of them aren't looking so good. And despite our surprise attack, you managed to slay one of mine as well. So, here's my deal."

Her eyes dodged back and forth, landing on the dragon nearest to her momentarily—a darker dragon with green hues, its expression seeming a bit more devious than the others. She turned her eyes back toward Cyrus.

"To avoid any further bloodshed, all I ask is one thing in return."

"And what's that?" Cyrus asked, a hint of suspicion in his tone.

"Kai."

Kai looked at Cyrus, his heart dropping into his stomach. Cyrus placed his hand on Kai's chest, pushing him backward, taking a step out in front of him.

"No," Cyrus said, gripping his spear.

"No?" she replied. "So, you'd rather you all die…"

The darker dragon stepped forward, its claws grinding the dirt beneath it. There was a look of pure rage within its eyes. The princess held up her hand, shooting the dragon a stern look.

"As you can see, we'd happily oblige that request. However, I'd urge you to reconsider. For it is not just the lives of these brave souls on the line. I have someone on the inside, right now, his bow is trained on your Scalewarden, lying blissfully unaware in his chambers."

Nalaen's eyes flashed, a momentary distance behind them, before she came back to focus on Kai.

"And I also have your sister…" she finished with a grin.

Kai stepped up beside Cyrus, gripping his spear tightly.

"What do you mean?" he asked, feeling a surge of anger.

"Don't worry, she is alive… for now. But she is trapped in the Dream world. She will never awake, unless you do as I say."

Kai's eyes softened momentarily as he remembered his sister lying on the bed in her room, deathly still, as if she were no longer living. He remembered the words that Vi had spoken to him, of her concerns for Mara and her strange dreams. And for a moment, his rage subsided as fear took hold.

"So, you understand, then," Nalaen said.

Kai looked back at her, clenching his jaw and raising his spear to point it at her.

"What do you want, dragon?"

"It's quite simple, really," Nalaen replied, beginning to pace back and forth as she looked at all before her. "I want your lives. Much as I'd like to slaughter you all, I'm giving you the chance to be the man you so desperately seek to be, Kai. Give yourself up and none of them," she said, waving her hand in the direction of Kai's comrades, "need to die. Isn't that what you've always wanted? To be a hero?"

The words struck Kai, cutting him to his core. *How does she know?*

"You wouldn't want your uncle's sacrifice to be for naught, now would you?"

Kai's expression shifted again at the mention of his uncle. He wanted to take a step forward; he wanted to end this now, but he forced himself to remain calm. Still, he could feel his body warming up, the rage begging to be unleashed. He wanted to set it free, but needed to be careful.

"Return with your comrades. Mourn your dead. And then, in three days' time, Kai must come alone to the ruins. There, I shall give you the fight you crave. Face me, and me alone. If you win, then I will be dead, and you can force my dear brother to help you bring Mara back from the Dream. If you lose, well… *you* will be dead, and your sister will wander the Dream for eternity. However, I will be satisfied with my revenge and leave the human lands forever. I am soon to be Queen of the dragon realms. If you do this, then I will ensure dragons never set foot here again for as long as I reign—as long as the humans stay on their side of the mountains, of course. Seems like to me, your people win either way."

The realization of her words hit Kai hard. The fury in his soul wanted desperately to fight her, but the thought of defeat–and of Mara left on her own forever–it was a heavy price to pay. His eyes moved to Cyrus, unsure of exactly what to do.

"And what happens if I refuse?" he asked, turning back to her, his eyes narrowing.

"Careful, Kai," Cyrus said, grabbing his shoulder.

Her eyebrow rose again, briefly, before her face grew deathly serious.

"If you do not agree to this, then your dear sister may never awake. And if we somehow don't kill you here and now, I will haunt these lands to the end of my days to find you, killing every last human who gets in my way. A thousand deaths will be on your hands. And dear Mara's mind can only last so long in the Dream. I'm guessing any more than three or four days and she will be lost to you forever."

Kai slowly relaxed his grip. He knew what he had to do. There was no other choice.

"Alright..." he said, looking up at her with a glare, though there was a certain hint of defeat on his breath.

Kai looked away from the princess's grin and back at Cyrus and the other knights. He saw something entirely different there now. For the first time, they looked at him with sympathy. It seemed he was right. They would all see him differently after today.

"Kai," Cyrus said, stepping forward, quiet enough so the princess couldn't hear him. "You don't need to do this. You're one of us. I don't presume to understand all the dangers she spoke of, but the Order will not stand idly by while its own are threatened. If you want to fight now, we will stand by you."

Kai glanced at the others. Some seemed to have heard Cyrus, nodding their agreeance with his statements.

"You brought us through the fire, Kai," Cyrus continued, waving his hand toward the group. "Let us face this next fire together."

More nods moved through the knights, followed by brief words of encouragement. Even Thorlan showed his support with a firm nod.

"I'm still waiting, humans. Give me your final answer, Kai, or face our wrath here and now."

Kai glanced at her, then back at Cyrus.

"Mara..." Kai said. "I can't risk it. I can't risk her."

He turned back to face Nalaen, the brief feeling of pride in what the others had shown him fading quickly back into defeat.

"I will come," he said with a heavy sigh, staring coldly at Nalaen.

"Good choice," she said with a snicker. "Think of all the lives you'll save..." she added, waving down the menacing dragon, which looked ready to pounce at any moment.

The disappointment was clear in the other dragon's features. It was at that moment Kai finally focused on it, realizing who it was.

Just then, the princess let out a terrifying screech. Kai watched her writhe in pain, the light in her eyes flaring to life, her dragon features fluttering before his eyes. She tried to assume her dragon form, tried lifting off the ground, but something was preventing her from doing it. She fell down into the dirt on her hands and knees. Everyone, including the dragons, looked back and forth between each other, clearly confused.

And then Kai saw what the problem was. There was an arrow lodged deeply in her back, near the top of her spine. Kai searched the nearby hills behind her for the arrow's source.

He saw a man step over the crest of the hill behind the dragons, a line of knights appearing beside him. He saw Caliena, still supported by one of her friends, raise her spear and yell. The knights began rushing past her, straight down the hill toward them. Next to Caliena stood a man who wore no armor. It was Aerin, the hunter who'd been cast out.

Some of the dragons turned to face their new adversary, others started rushing forward toward Kai and their group, Talesa leading the latter charge.

Kai braced for impact, the others huddling around him as three of the dragons barreled down on them. Kai saw their throats glowing, knew what that meant. He shot a quick glance to Cyrus, saw he'd seen it as well.

"Ready on my mark," Cyrus yelled. "Fire incoming. Split forces, half right, half left, one with me and Kai in the middle. Thorlan, coordinate the other groups."

"Aye," came a shout from behind Kai.

Everything was happening so fast. He knew his training, but had never performed it in such numbers, and never facing an elder dragon, let alone three. The dragons continued rumbling toward them and would be there in another few seconds.

"Just follow my lead, Kai," Cyrus said, quieter, almost in his ear. Kai barely had time to acknowledge before the dragons were upon them.

Cyrus dove left, Kai followed, feeling one more presence doing the same right next to him. They rolled out of the way of the charging Talesa, streams of fire pouring from her and the others' throats, her claws barely missing. Kai scarcely had time to see if the others were okay before Talesa reared and turned back on them, claws raking, coming straight at his chest.

Kai felt a firm hand pulling him backward, the claws narrowly missing him by inches. As he stumbled back, he saw Cyrus and the other knight leap forward, one on either side of Talesa. Her attention shifting to a more defensive stance, she eyed them warily, waiting for their next move.

Kai glanced to his left, saw a large, lighter colored dragon with blue scales bending over the princess. It scooped her up carefully in its jaws and glanced around, watching the others. It saw Kai, stared intently at him for a moment, an almost sorrowful look in its eyes.

It nodded its head, spread its wings, and lifted off at great speed.

With a sudden rage welling up inside him, Kai bolted after it. He could not let her get away.

Kai heard Cyrus call out behind him, but he ignored it, rushing forward at a blazing speed—running faster than he ever had. If he could just get close enough, he might be able to launch his spear at the dragon before it got away.

Kai leveraged his spear for a throw. It was something he was told never to do. *Lose your weapon, lose your life*, they'd trained him. This was no ordinary fight. He couldn't risk the princess surviving.

Just as Kai was about to throw, there was a terrible screech and he turned, just in time to see Talesa hurtling down to the ground, landing with a crash that sent earth parting below her. He barely dove out of the way, rolling up to face her. She lifted her neck, eyeing Kai, shifting into her human form, her devilish smile even more haunting than normal.

Kai's eyes shot up behind her, seeing the blue dragon growing smaller. There was no chance he could stop him now, but there were other debts to pay. One was standing before him.

"You..." Kai said, glaring as he walked toward her, raising his spear with one arm. "You're the one who killed Uncle, stabbing him in the back like a coward. You'll pay for that."

"Hah!" Talesa laughed, her smile widening even further, resembling her dragon maw. "Is that so?" she jeered. She began to circle Kai. "You're not ready, boy. I'll fight you here, on two legs, with nothing but my daggers."

Kai gripped his spear tightly as he began to run, diving at Talesa who stood unmoving as she smiled at him. Kai pulled his spear back, swinging just as he came within range of her. He barely saw her move as his attack hit only air, the momentum of his run causing him to stumble past her. He felt a tinge of pain in his shoulder as he came to a stop, spinning his spear around toward her. He looked at her smile as she flashed her newly unsheathed daggers at him, then looked at his shoulder. A slight trickle of blood was dripping down the metal covering his arm.

How did she hit me so precisely between the armor?

His mind told him to stop and think, to be cautious, but the rage was still burning hot in his veins, and it clouded his judgement. He ran again, this time keeping his spear forward as he drove it straight toward her. At the last second, Talesa moved out of the spear's path, grabbing it with one arm as she pulled Kai forward, sending him flying through the air before crashing down into the ground. Kai felt another sharp pain, this time in his leg. He rolled over and up onto his feet, spinning to face her again. He glanced down at his leg, seeing another trickle of blood.

Kai's face changed from anger to concern. *She's playing with me. I can't beat her like this.*

"Yes, that's fear you're feeling. I can taste it," Talesa snickered, flicking her tongue out in the air and licking her lips. "Along with your now defiled blood, which I will slowly drain from you until it has been returned to the earth where it belongs."

Kai and Talesa began circling each other, Kai finally understanding his aggressive tactics were not working. He tried to focus his mind–tried to remember all that Cyrus had taught him.

The offense comes through the defense, Kai heard. *Mind your feet, and keep your back foot firmly planted. Don't step too far forward. Patience is key. Let your adversary make the mistake.*

Kai clenched his jaw and planted his feet, squaring off against Talesa. He kept his spear on her as she continued circling him.

"Ah, learning, are we?" Talesa jested. "Good. I didn't want this to be *too* easy."

Kai's anger flared, but he kept his stance, moving his feet carefully to match Talesa's movements. They continued circling each other, eyes focused, muscles tense. Kai watched her movement, trying to decipher what her next move was going to be. At last, he saw her muscles twitch. She was off, dashing toward him at an alarming speed.

Kai tried to keep his spear focused on her, but she was so fast, her movements so erratic, he couldn't keep it on her. He saw her dagger coming straight for his face. He dodged as best he could, but it grazed his cheek, coming within an inch of his eye. He reeled from the nearly deadly assault, trying to keep her in his view as she danced around him, bringing her dagger back in toward his midsection. Kai dropped his spear down and attempted to parry her attack with the handle. It was a successful parry, but his feet got tangled up and he lost his balance. Talesa kept moving, dropping low and under a weak swing by Kai, coming around behind him, her dagger catching the back of his neck.

Kai regained his footing and came around to face her again. He felt the pain on his cheek and neck and reached his free hand up, seeing smeared blood when he brought it back.

Come on, Kai. Focus.

His thoughts were interrupted by her evil laugh. Talesa lifted her knife, licking the blood off it.

"Tastes like vermin," she spat. "After I drain all your blood, perhaps I will find that dear sister of yours. It will be easy to drain her blood as she lies sleeping." Talesa laughed again as she gazed at Kai's cold stare in reply.

Just then, Cyrus and the other knight arrived, joining Kai to face down Talesa once again.

"That was foolish, Kai," Cyrus scolded him. "But I see you remembered some of your lessons. Good. Now, *together.*"

Kai nodded, feeling a hint of embarrassment but quickly pushing past it.

Talesa eyed all three of them, hissing as she paced back and forth.

"Just as well, I suppose. Kai wouldn't have lasted much longer without aid. Guess I'll just have to kill the two of you, first." Upon her last words, Talesa lunged sideways in a blur. She covered the gap between her and the other knight, the man leaping to the side, but not quickly enough. Kai remembered his name was Erlich.

Cyrus dove in, spear trained at her back, but she anticipated it and spun around, getting behind Erlich. He tried to stab her with his spear, but she easily deflected the blow, brushing the weapon aside and coming in close. One of her daggers slashed his wrist and he dropped the spear, her other dagger coming up and straight across his face. In a burst of blood, Erlich reeled backward and toppled to the ground. Kai wasn't sure if he was still alive, but he rushed forward, following Cyrus, who was now only a few feet from Talesa.

Talesa spun to face him, bringing her daggers up to deflect his incoming jab. But it was a fake. Cyrus feigned a jab and leapt over Talesa, spinning in the air as he came down, bringing the head of the spear down on top of her. As Kai sprinted to help, he saw a red line across Talesa's arm.

Cyrus landed between her and Erlich, his face remaining dead serious, his eyes locked onto hers. Talesa licked her wound and laughed.

"Ah, this one has some skill," she goaded.

Seeing his opportunity, Kai pressed faster, hoping he might catch her unaware. Cyrus's eyes met his own, and for a split second, Kai thought it was going to work. Mere feet from his target, he drove his spear forward. He flew through the air at a furious speed, but his spear hit nothing.

Talesa side-stepped at the perfect time, dropping low and bringing one of her daggers around and catching Kai in his leg. He came down on the cut leg, which caused him to stumble and roll forward, landing on his back. He rolled over, saw Erlich lying next to him, his face a bloody mess. There was no question the man was dead.

Hearing a grunt from Cyrus, Kai sat up and leapt to his feet. He winced in pain when he landed, glancing down, seeing another small trickle of blood seeping from his left leg. She landed her dagger between a gap in his armor again. How could she have been so precise when she didn't even see him?

Shrugging it off, Kai ran forward to help Cyrus, who was locked in combat with Talesa. He ignored the pain, focusing on the growing anger building up. He knew he was letting it get the better of him, but right now, he needed it. It was time to let it loose.

Kai came up, just as Cyrus was being driven back. The speed of Talesa's daggers was staggering. A spear was the best weapon against a dragon in its true from, but against daggers, and someone as skilled with them as she was, it could prove challenging if she got in close.

Cyrus was just trying to keep her from getting past his defenses. Despite it, she kept pressing in, trying to find a gap or wait for him to make a mistake. As Kai came up, he tried to get behind her. Cyrus shot a quick glance his way when Kai came into view.

Without hesitation, Talesa burst forward, using one dagger to brush his spear aside while bringing the other in for the kill. Seeing it, Kai charged ahead, only a few feet away, as Talesa drove at Cyrus. He dove backward, the blade narrowly missing his throat, bringing the butt of his spear up and smacking Talesa across the face with it. As she reeled from the blow, she managed to bring her other hand back around, swinging it wildly at Cyrus as he continued to fall backward. The edge of the blade caught his cheek, a spurt of blood flinging into the air.

Talesa kept running to the right, hearing Kai coming in just behind her. She dropped, spun, and came up to face him, changing directions much faster than Kai had expected. The speed at which she recovered threw Kai off, allowing her a momentary chance to come up and get in close before he brought his spear around. With a blur, it was all Kai could do to prevent her from slicing her dagger across his own face. The dagger still made contact, drawing another small gash across Kai's cheek.

Kai brought his spear around finally, swinging it for her head. He missed again.

He continued spinning, trying to plant his feet firmly and keep from falling again. He barely did, running around and coming up beside Cyrus, who was now back on his feet.

"Together," Cyrus yelled and they rushed forward.

Talesa stood confidently before them, daggers held out to the side, a sadistic smile directed their way. She seemed to be barely breaking a sweat.

Kai felt another burst of anger as they rushed toward her. It propelled him faster, inching ahead of Cyrus with every step.

"Kai," Cyrus said. Kai kept running at full speed. The rage was consuming him now. He couldn't stop it.

It was like the fire of the burning forest. Though he knew he should stop, there was no containing it. It was in control of him now. He couldn't stop it. He didn't want to stop it.

With a burst of strength, Kai drove straight at Talesa, anticipating her dodging at any second. He was ready for her to jump right or left out of his path. When she instead jumped into the air, straight up, flipping over his head, he was caught unaware yet again.

Kai ran straight past her, staring up at her smile as she flipped over the top of him, his spear thrusting upward, but too slow and too late.

Kai dug his heels into the ground and came to a stop. Spinning, he turned around just in time to see Talesa drive one of her daggers into Cyrus's leg. He stumbled and fell, toppling over himself.

Kai's muscles twitched as he felt a sudden rush of energy in his bones. The pain of the cuts Talesa had given slowly faded. He reached up and wiped his finger across his cheek where she'd cut him. The gash was gone. He looked back at Talesa with a smile.

Talesa took a step back, a momentary confusion showing at Kai's sudden change before she smiled, assuming a ready stance with her daggers.

At once, both of them exploded forward.

Kai came in low with his spear as he kept it aimed up and toward Talesa's stomach. Talesa kept her stance high, her daggers coming in from two separate angles, aimed down at Kai's head.

As they came together, Kai twisted to the side and jumped, flying to her right as he stabbed upwards. Talesa wasn't expecting him to move as such, and her daggers missed him completely. Then, she saw the tip of his spear coming straight for her chest. She reeled, bending backwards to avoid it. The angle of her movement kept the spear from penetrating her, but it still danced across her chestplate and came up, causing a small prick with its point under her chin.

Kai bounced past Talesa and rolled up onto his feet, greeting her with a smile as he saw the blood drip from her chin. Talesa let out a furious yell, immediately coming for Kai. Kai kept his feet planted, bracing for her attack. As she came in, he shifted backwards slightly, calculating the distance of his strike without moving his foot. Once she was in range, Kai struck hard and fast.

The strike was true, impaling Talesa in her right shoulder. She screeched in pain, dropping her daggers as she grabbed Kai's spear with both hands, tossing him aside as he tried desperately to keep hold of it. Kai scrambled to get back to his feet as he saw her walking toward him. She ripped the spear out of her shoulder and tossed it far off to the side. Her features shifted, her eyes glowing brighter as her claws stretched out and her teeth grew longer in her mouth. Kai tried to roll away from her as she came up, but she still was moving fast, even for someone who'd just been impaled. She grabbed him with her left arm, lifting him up as her grip tightened around his throat. Kai gasped, struggling for air.

Time slowed as Kai felt his life flash before his eyes. He closed his eyelids, feeling the lifeforce leaving him. Her grip was strong; so strong.

Kai.

His eyes flashed open, and he looked around.

Kai!

It was Mara's voice. He didn't know where it was, or how he could hear it, but it was clear as day.

Fight, Kai. I need you.

Kai looked down into Talesa's hateful gaze. The same energy from before welled in his bones. Except this time, it felt like a hundred-fold. Kai grabbed Talesa's arm, her face shifting to a look of confusion as her grip loosened slightly.

Power and energy exuded from Kai as his entire skin became hot to the touch. The veins in his neck bulged with a red heat. The non-metal pieces of his clothing began to smoke. Talesa tried to let go of him, the pain evident in her face. Kai grabbed her arm tighter. She hesitated momentarily, unsure of what to do and Kai slowly came down to the ground, planting his feet firmly. In one last desperate attempt to end the fight, she swiped at him with her left hand, claws aimed straight at his face. Kai reached his other arm up and caught her wrist, holding it firmly in place. A look of disbelief filled her eyes, and for once, a look of fear.

Talesa tried to shift into her dragon form. As her arms began to grow, Kai's eyes flashed, a raging fire engulfing his hands. Talesa's sudden shift in size knocked Kai backwards as he finally let go.

Talesa started to fly but quickly found that she couldn't. Her right wing was scorched and misshapen. She fell to the ground, instantly turning back into a human. Her hand was now gone, a singed stump of burning flesh in its place.

Talesa tried to crawl away as her mouth foamed in agony. She shifted back into her dragon form again, trying desperately to get away from Kai's fury. Kai walked slowly toward her, his fists still on fire, his skin and eyes glowing red. She bolted, trying to get distance from his fury.

Kai took a few more steps, stumbled, feeling his consciousness fading. The fire dissipated, though his skin remained hot. Thirst overtook him and he stumbled himself. He heard shouting around him, saw spears sailing through the air, heard heavy footsteps run past. Talesa roared and took to the sky, barely lifting off, only gaining a little ground before crashing back down again. Spears soared after her, at least one of them hitting their mark. She disappeared from sight beyond the hill as darkness closed in around Kai.

He blinked, trying to remain conscious. Caliena's face appeared above him, shouting for the others to pursue Talesa. Her deep blue eyes were the last thing Kai saw before the world faded to black.

CHAPTER FORTY-EIGHT

SINS

S orn stood over Nalaen as she lay asleep on her bed. He'd gotten her safely back to the ruins, but she'd lost a lot of blood on the way. They were more fragile in their human forms. Still, the hunter had gotten an exceptionally lucky shot, the arrow piercing Nalaen's spine in just the right spot to prevent her transformation to her real form. If she'd been able to do that, the wound would have probably been nothing but a minor inconvenience. But in this case, it caused some decent damage.

She would be fine with some rest, but it would take a bit longer than normal to heal. Once she recovered enough to shift back into her dragon form, she'd heal much faster. Which meant Sorn didn't have long if he was going to help Mara.

Sorn gazed at Nalaen's face for a moment longer. She was his sister after all, and he did love her, but he didn't always agree with the things she did. The girl Mara was a Grayscale, yes, but she should not have to pay for the sins of her uncle. She was a good girl. She was kind and gentle. She did not deserve to be trapped in the Dream forever. If he could save her and help her stop her brother from coming to the ruins, then perhaps there was some way Sorn could convince Nalaen to return home and forget this whole vendetta; perhaps, even convince Mara to try and keep the Order from pursuing them. Maybe there could somehow be peace through all of this. He had no idea if it would work, but he had to try.

A commotion outside Nalaen's quarters brought Sorn's attention to the doorway. He left his sister's side and went to see what it was. Stepping outside, he saw two of the guards landing as they shifted into their human forms, entering their quarters on the other side of the ruins. Sorn ran over to them as he looked in the sky for any signs of the rest.

"What happened? Where are the others? Where's Talesa?" Sorn asked when he reached them.

They looked up at him with blood-crazed eyes, panic and terror behind them. Both just shook their heads.

Sorn's eyes grew wide at the thought his sister might be dead, yet a small part of him also felt a hint of relief.

"How?" he managed to ask, still stunned.

"The boy. He commands fire. He gravely wounded your sister; the others chased her down. Everyone else is dead, including Mykael. It was a blood-bath. We did not sign up for this."

Sorn felt conflicted. He knew his sister, knew what she was capable of. He knew she had attacked as Sorn fled with Nalaen. She probably deserved her fate. But it was Kai who had hurt her, perhaps mortally, and Kai was Mara's brother. Sorn felt pulled in two completely different directions. He remembered the look in the boy's eyes when Nalaen told him what they had done–what Sorn had helped Nalaen do. A flood of guilt washed over him.

This is partially my fault.

Sorn would never forgive Kai for what he had done, but he also under-stood why the boy had done it. And the more important thing now was to prevent another conflict that would see either him or Mara lose another one they loved. No, this had to be stopped, and saving Mara was the only way.

"Are you leaving?" Sorn asked, suddenly realizing the two drakes were packing all their belongings.

"Of course we are. The Princess is on her own. She's not worth protecting anymore–not from that... devil. We will return to *Dor'dragos* and inform Kyrian of what's happened here. Perhaps he will send reinforcements."

Sorn wanted to stop them but he had more pressing matters at hand. With Mara being trapped in the Dream this long, it wasn't going to be an easy feat to free her, much less find her. If he hurried, he could get Mara out *and* get Nalaen back home before things escalated.

Sorn nodded to the two drakes before exiting their part of the ruins and hurrying back to his own quarters. As he entered, he heard his comrades lifting off. He saw them flying away through a crack in the canopy overhead as it waved in the wind. Sorn looked down at his bed.

"Better hurry, then."

***

Mara's state of mind was teetering on the edge of a knife.

As she walked through the once peaceful fields surrounding Eastend, an eerie hue crept slowly across the land. Like a great shadow without a source, this aberration of darkness descended, changing everything it touched. Mara's heart pounded in her chest as she searched for some escape from it. It didn't seem aggressive in nature, but Mara was sure she could feel some sense of intelligence behind its actions.

Mara had no idea how long she'd been trapped in the Dream. Within, there is no concept of time. There is no changing from day to night. There is only the here and the now. And what happened from moment to moment was not so much a fluctuation of time, but of state.

Initially, the Dream had remained much the same. Though there was some strange magic keeping her there, it was not apparent, and it had not altered the world. But the longer Mara stayed, the more things began to noticeably change. The light of the world dimmed, until it eventually became what it was now. The shadow was not cast by any one thing, it just seemed to exist in small pockets, growing and spreading. At first, it was the alleys and side streets. Then, it began to cover parts of the square. And by now, it had surrounded the whole of the countryside. As the light faded, so did the people of Eastend. Mara was sure she still saw their shadows, but it was as if it were only that–soulless husks barely resembling anything human.

Mara still found pockets of light, like rays of sunshine during a heavy storm, but they never remained long and were constantly shifting. She feared soon the light would cease to exist entirely. Mara had spent her time–be it hours or days–chasing these rays of light. She was slowly becoming exhausted by it. Her mind was growing weary.

I've got to get out of here. The echoes of her thoughts boomed in her head, reverberating throughout the world. *I've got to get back to Kai.*

She saw another beam of light over the hill ahead and quickened her pace toward it. Somehow, the light helped keep her mind at ease–kept it from slipping further into madness. But with it becoming so scarce now, she wasn't sure how much longer she could keep at it.

As she crested the hill, she looked down into the valley beyond. The point where the light met the earth was at the bottom of a large basin. Peering through the darkness at it, she saw something she did not expect.

It was a boy.

He sat on the ground, his back turned to her. It looked as if he was playing in the dirt.

Mara began walking toward him but suddenly stopped. Out of the shadows next to the boy came another figure, this one taller and foreboding. As this new figure entered the light, Mara saw it was a woman. She was not a normal woman. She seemed quite tall, even from this distance. She had a pinkish shade of hair and wore a regal crimson gown. She carried herself with the air of royalty.

The woman came up to the boy and knelt down beside him, speaking to him as she investigated what he was doing.

Mara was still a long way off, but she could hear their voices carried on the wind in incomprehensible whispers. She continued to walk slowly toward them, unsure of what exactly was happening. The thought of someone else in this forsaken realm made her continue to step forward, even though a small part of her wanted to turn and run.

Closer now, Mara began to be able to discern words. They didn't sound like words she'd ever heard before.

"*Beinor factium, mai dro,*" the woman spoke, her voice powerful, but calming.

"Hello," Mara called out as she drew closer.

The woman immediately stood up straight but still faced away from Mara.

"Hello?" Mara called out again.

The woman slowly turned toward her. Mara held her breath. Her instincts told her to flee, but she felt like she couldn't move. Her eyes grew wide as she saw the woman's face.

The woman had glowing purple eyes that pierced the darkness, sending a shiver up Mara's spine. She had a look of malice about her, but there was also something else—something deeper, something resembling pain.

She's a dragon.

Suddenly, the image of the boy vanished, and Mara gasped. The woman continued to stare at Mara, her eyes unmoving, her body deathly still. Mara wanted to run, but she felt slow. She wanted to get to the light. She could feel herself slipping further into madness. She wasn't even sure if the woman was real.

The light behind the woman began to wane, flickering, as if it was a torch being blown out by the wind. And then, it was gone. Darkness covered the space all around Mara. All she could see were the dragon's eyes staring up at her.

Panic set in and Mara turned, beginning to crawl slowly back up the hill. When she glanced back, the woman was gone. Mara crawled faster, terror taking hold. She picked up speed, nearing the top of the hill.

As she crested it, she looked back again, fearful of the woman's pursuit. She tripped on something on the ground.

"Ah," Mara cried out in pain as her knees hit the dirt. She rolled over and turned, looking for what had tripped her.

There, on the ground, was a metal helmet, half-buried in the dirt. Mara tilted her head, puzzled.

That wasn't there before...

She turned and saw there were other debris scattered about the ground around her. As she spun, looking back down the hill toward where the town of Eastend had stood just minutes before, she now beheld a giant battlefield littered with corpses.

Mara gasped again, startled by the sudden change of landscape as the echoes of battle rang in her ears. She panicked and looked for their source, but they seemed to come from all around her, out of thin air. There was no sign of movement, no battle. The sounds continued but slowly lessened over time.

Carefully stepping forward into the fields, all around her were the bones of the dead—and not just men; there were also dragons. Their massive ribcages stood several times taller than Mara. She watched her step so as not to trip over the bones and scattered armaments, eyeing all of it as she passed, searching for anything familiar. It all felt foreign, and as far as she could see, there were only miles of the same. There was no Eastend, no sign of anything she knew. Only death.

Another beam of light appeared far off in the distance, somewhere in the middle of the battlefield. Mara picked up her pace as she shuffled toward it, dodging the ghostly remnants of long-lost souls, her thoughts haunted by what she saw.

What battle was this? The Great Wars? Or before that?

Mara pushed past her thoughts and focused her attention on the light. She began to see shadows–formless shapes that twisted and turned–moving throughout the corpses of the dead. She wasn't sure if they were really there, or if it was just her mind continuing to descend deeper into madness. Either way, she didn't want to find out.

As Mara drew closer to the light, she saw a massive mound of dragons' bones up ahead. Once closer, she realized it was the bones of dozens of the creatures, piled one on top of the other, forming something of a wall, blocking her path. She tried walking around it, but the bones continued, as if they were circling the light. Spotting a gap, she squeezed between the ribs of one of the dead beasts. Inside, it was like a thick forest. Glancing up, she could see the massive spines of the beasts, barely able to see the sky with so many of them piled on top of each other.

She continued moving through any gap she could squeeze through. It took her a few minutes to find a way, but at last she spotted the light's glow through the crevices. She found an opening large enough to pass through, emerging in the center where the light rested.

She again saw the dragon from before. Except this time, she was knelt over, and it looked like she was crying. Mara crept slowly around to get a better angle. As she moved, she began to see a body on the ground in front of the dragon. Mara kept moving until she saw that it was the body of a man–no, another dragon, like her, but in his human form as well. It had to be, as it was too large to be a normal man. But he lay still, seemingly dead.

Mara looked up at the woman again. She could see tears streaking her cheeks, and her eyes were closed. Mara took another step, accidentally kicking something metal on the ground. There was an audible *ting* as Mara cringed and held her breath, watching the woman intently.

Slowly, the woman lifted her head and opened her eyes. After a momentary pause, she began to turn her head toward Mara. Their eyes locked again, and Mara felt a cold grasp take hold of her. The woman stood and began to move toward her. Mara wanted to scream, wanted to run, but as before, she felt trapped by some invisible force. It felt much the same as what Nalaen and Sorn had done to her to trap her here.

Step by step, the woman inched closer, all the while keeping her eyes locked on Mara. Her face still carried a look of pain, but there was a greater rage now, and her eyes seemed to glow brighter.

When the woman was almost to Mara, she suddenly stopped and looked up over Mara's head. And then, as before, the light flickered and went out, leaving

Mara in a momentary darkness before she felt a light behind her. Able to move again, she turned around.

Before her stood Dragonscale Keep and a hint of relief touched her. But seconds later the scene changed, flashing before Mara's eyes, causing her to jump. As the new scene set in, she realized the keep was in ruins. She stood on the precipice of the massive main gate, but it had been smashed in, pieces of it littered about the main courtyard. There were more bodies–both men and dragons–scattered around the courtyard and the walls. There were scorch marks everywhere, and much of this part of the keep was crumbling and destroyed.

Mara walked inside, surveying the wreckage. It felt familiar, but also different, despite the fact everything was in ruins. Her only guess was that this was some previous version of the keep from long ago–perhaps around the same time as the battle outside.

Ahead of her she saw a massive hole had been smashed through the wall below the overlook. The castle was pitch-black inside.

The sounds of crumbling rocks echoed out, startling Mara, as more sounds of battle reverberated through the courtyard. Mara eyed the walls, but there was no sign of movement. As the sounds continued, she turned back to the hole in the wall. This time, she saw the shadow of the same dragon woman as she disappeared into the darkness of the keep. She glanced back at Mara before disappearing into the shadows.

Mara waited to see what would happen, but everything fell silent as she stared into the darkness. She inched closer, trying to decide if she should follow.

Mara heard another sound. This sound felt familiar. It was crying, but it wasn't the woman. She'd heard this crying before. She felt compelled to follow.

She slowly stepped into the darkness beyond the gate. As she did, the walls of the keep lit up, illuminating the halls around her. She stood in the center of the keep, staring down the hallway leading to the Heart. Torches lined the walls, and beyond them sat the great metal doors. The inside of the keep was in ruins, and while the main infrastructure remained intact, signs of battle were apparent. There were a few bodies on the floor, but nothing like outside. And here, it was only the corpses of men.

A sound came from down the hallway. Mara snapped out of her thoughts and peered down toward where it had come from. She saw one of the large doors at the end of hallway was now open, and she just barely caught a glimpse of the dragon woman disappearing behind it. Mara hurried to catch up with her. As she hastened down the hallway, she heard the sounds of torches going out behind her. She turned and saw they were disappearing into darkness as she passed. She hurried, moving into a near sprint.

As the light behind her faded, Mara could see a flickering light coming from within the Heart itself. She moved around the giant metal door that hung open and came into the room, immediately noticing the light was coming from a fire near the back. It was where she remembered the statue of Garn Dragonblood ought to be. She looked at the other statues; all of them had blood dripping from their faces. Mara's eyes darted between them. All twelve were the same, save for Garn, who was somehow replaced by fire.

Mara looked down at the table in the center of the room. A skeleton sat in each chair, armor glistening, mouths open as if they were smiling, even in death. In front of each was an ornate silver cup with some kind of dark liquid inside. Mara walked up to the nearest one and bent over to inspect it more closely.

As she leaned in, the image of a dragon's face flashed in the liquid and a cry of pain echoed throughout the room. Mara stumbled backward and fell onto the floor behind her, sitting there stunned for several moments, trying to understand.

The sound of a creaking door came from the other side of the room. Mara leaned to the left, looking underneath the table and between the chairs toward the door in the back of the room.

The door from my dream...

Mara stood up and peered through the short, dark hallway at the back of the room. The fire burning above the entryway made it hard to see, but as she strained her eyes, she saw the door was cracked open. There were tiny specks of white fluttering through it. Mara made her way around the table and approached it slowly, beginning to feel a cold draft coming from within. And then she heard it, just as vividly as she remembered. The slight howl of the wind, and faintly amongst it, a chilling cry.

Mara looked backward as she approached the door, feeling a shiver run down her spine. The room behind her was now pitch black. She pressed onward, moving within feet of the door, stretching out her hand, remembering the pain it had caused her before. Peering around the edge of the door, it was dark, but she could make out steps spiraling downward. The door wasn't wide enough for her to squeeze through, so she put both hands on it and pulled quickly. The door creaked as it slowly opened. It was much heavier than it looked, and the metal felt extremely cold to the touch. Mara reeled from the intense cold, but the gap in the door was now wide enough for her to squeeze through.

Carefully, she side-stepped around it, trying not to touch the cold metal to her skin again. She stood on the top step staring down. The stairway was narrow, with walls close on either side, and they spiraled downward, only letting her see a handful of steps before they disappeared to the left. The cold wind was coming from below; so much so it blew bits of snow up from underneath.

Cautiously, Mara took a step down. And then she was falling.

Everything was dark. There were no steps, no walls, only darkness. Mara screamed as she fell, closing her eyes tightly, sure her life was over. Panic and terror took over her, and her heart felt like it was pounding in her head.

But then, as quickly as it started, everything calmed. Mara opened one eye. She was still in darkness, and still falling, but it felt more like she was floating, as if some invisible force was slowing her descent. She began to hear sounds. They were muffled at first, but as she opened both eyes and listened, they began to come into focus. It was voices.

"Do you ever wonder, Mara, that this is not the way things were supposed to be?" It was Kai's voice. "What if we were supposed to do something else?"

The voice faded and a new one took its place.

"This is an accounting of the study of Queen Liotha and her kin's blood." Mara heard her own voice, reading off the words of the mysterious book she'd uncovered.

"We'd like to ask you and your sister join the party that's going to investigate the missing hunters." Yoren. Just hearing him again brought tears to her eyes.

"What do you think killed it?" she heard Brol ask, remembering the scene clearly in her head.

"I sure as hell know I don't wanna stick around to find out..." came Dax's voice, the familiar twang in his tone.

"Princess Nalaen, Heir to the Dragon Throne." The last voice was deep and sinister. Mara remembered vividly the night in the ruins when they'd first met.

"Where?" the voice roared again. It had been just seconds before Mara's face had been clawed. She reached her hands up, still feeling hints of the scars.

The sounds of battle echoed through the darkness as the night Yoren died ran vividly through Mara's mind. The pain of that day, and the days following, washed over her like a flood. A tear crawled down her face, resting momentarily on her chin as she saw her uncle's face looking up at them as they disappeared into the whirlwind of snow.

The tear dropped, falling down into the abyss below her. For several seconds, there was silence.

She began to hear Kai's voice again, but as she listened to hear what he was saying, something changed slightly around her. There came a roaring sound. It sounded like a raging fire. She heard shouting and more sounds of battle. She did not recognize this memory.

The voice became clearer in her mind.

"You..." she heard Kai say. "You're the one who killed Uncle, stabbing him in the back like a coward. You'll pay for that."

"Hah! Is that so?" This voice sounded familiar. Mara's thoughts returned to the night in the mountains. It was the dragon with the black hair.

Is this real? Is Kai fighting her?

Their voices were replaced by grunts and shouts. Mara heard Kai gasp in pain.

"She's playing with me. I can't beat her like this," she heard Kai say, though its sound echoed more than normal.

Mara's heart began to beat faster as more sounds of fighting ensued. It sounded like Kai was losing. Mara's fear grew. She was trapped in this nightmare and there was nothing she could do to help Kai. He was going to die, and she couldn't save him.

In that moment, Mara felt something stir within her—something she couldn't quite explain. There was a slight change in her body. The darkness didn't feel so dark, and she was almost sure there was a slight glow emanating from her. She closed her eyes and focused on Kai. A vision of him came to her. He was standing in a field, facing the princess's sister. He looked like he was hurting. Suddenly, the scene shifted and he was in her grasp, her claws around his throat.

"Kai!" Mara called out instinctively. There was a dull hum as she felt her body pulse with energy.

Kai struggled to breathe in her grasp.

"Fight, Kai. I need you," Mara said, feeling a ring of energy leave her as the hum intensified, illuminating the darkness all around her. A brilliant flash of light surrounded her, forcing Mara to shield her eyes.

As the light faded, Mara blinked, her eyes taking a moment to adjust. Once in focus, she found herself standing in a dimly lit room, surrounded by stone walls. The walls were the same as before. Mara turned and looked at the room, noticing a spiraling staircase leading upward just behind her.

Back in the keep? What just happened?

Mara took a second to orient herself. Her mind was still spinning with the thoughts of all that had just happened–with the all the memories, with her uncle's voice, and the thoughts of Kai in potential danger. And the light. It had come from her. But how? Despite her confusion, she felt a strange sense of peace that calmed her nerves. She took several deep breaths, trying to focus back on the present.

"Mara," she heard a voice call out. Mara froze. The voice was deep, and it echoed around the room, but there was a hint of familiarity in it, too. "Mara, is that you?"

The voice was coming from up the stairs. Mara turned and backed away, looking for a place to hide. A shadowy figure came into view as it descended the stairs. Mara took another step backward as the figure edged toward the light, the image of their face still obscured in darkness.

"Mara..." the voice said again.

After another couple steps, the stranger came into the light.

"You! What are you doing here?" Mara asked. There was both anger and fear in her voice as she glared at Sorn.

"I came to find you, to help you get out of here."

"I trusted you, and look what happened. Why should I believe you?"

"Mara, I'm sorry. I was foolish. If only I'd known..."

"What? That I'm a Dragonblood? You hid your true nature from me, too."

"Yes. And for that, I am sorry. I guess we both didn't fully trust each other, and for good reason. But Mara, I've come to right that wrong. I came to get you out of here. We must hurry."

"Hurry back to your sister so she can manipulate me to get to Kai?"

"No. My sister is hurt. She's resting, but she won't be resting for long, and if we don't get you out of here before she discovers what I'm up to, you'll lose your chance to stop your brother and end this bloodshed."

"What do you mean *stop* Kai? And why is your sister hurt?" Mara's eyes narrowed as she studied Sorn's face.

Sorn sighed and began pacing around the room. After a minute, he stopped and looked up at her, sighing again.

"We set a trap for your brother and the others near the tower. It was a near flawless plan. I went along with it reluctantly. I shouldn't have, but my sister is... persuasive. I did not agree with her killing innocents, but this was our chance to end the conflict and be done with it."

Mara's eyes grew wider as Sorn continued.

"The trap was sprung, and we had the knights cornered. But they had help. And, something happened, it seems... something my sister did not expect. Your brother. His powers are stronger than we thought. It seems he may have even killed Talesa."

Mara relaxed a bit at the mention of her brother, but powers? What powers?

"They killed most of our kin. My sister, being the clever one that she is, well, she already had a backup plan–you." At the mention of that, Sorn's expression turned to embarrassment. "A plan I helped secure, unknowingly. Again, I am sorry..."

"Kai? Is Kai okay?" Mara asked, suddenly worried again as she processed Sorn's words.

"I don't know–" Sorn started. He saw Mara's expression shift and corrected himself. "I think so. He gravely wounded my sister." As he spoke those words, there was a change in his demeanor, and his anger became apparent.

Mara backed up again, wary of Sorn's change in emotional state.

"I... do not blame him. My sister was a vile creature, and she attacked first. Everything was going to plan until that hunter showed up," Sorn hissed, remembering Aerin. "He shot Nalaen and then everything went to hell. I got my sister out of there, but Talesa and the others– only two survived, and they're gone. Which is why we need to hurry."

"Why?" Mara asked, trying to decipher everything Sorn was telling her.

"Because they're going back to the dragon kingdom to inform the current leader there of all that's happened. I do not know what his reaction will be, but when none of us return with them, things could escalate. They could send a larger force back here. This could incite another war. We must find a way to stop this."

Mara was still processing everything Sorn was saying but was finally beginning to realize the implications his words were suggesting. She didn't like it one bit.

"I still don't trust you, but..." Mara hesitated. "But I understand." Mara let her shoulders drop as she came to the realization she needed his help. "What do you suggest we do?"

"We must stop this fight between my sister and your brother. She gave him three days to come alone to the ruins if he wants to save you. She may be fully recovered by then, but I don't know. She needs to get back into her dragon form to fully heal, which, as of the time I left her, she wasn't able to. The arrow was an incredibly lucky shot."

"Three days? How long has it been?" Mara asked, a bit concerned.

"I don't know. Time runs differently here, and it took me some time to find you. I can feel my mind beginning to grow heavy, so it has been half a day at least, possibly even longer."

"How *did* you find me?" Mara asked, wary again of Sorn's presence.

"Well, I searched the town for some time, checking all the usual places. I felt traces of your essence, but it was sporadic and kept moving. I finally gave up trying to follow it, figuring you'd probably retreat to someplace familiar. The only logical place was the keep. It took me a bit to navigate the halls–there is a strange magic about this place that clouded much of my view. But when I saw the doors leading into the room above, I began to sense your presence much more intensely. And then, I saw a light."

Mara's expression changed as she eyed Sorn closely.

"Did you see the woman, then?" she asked.

"Woman? What woman? There were women in the town, and a few in the keep," Sorn replied, seeming confused.

"What? How? There was a battlefield, and the keep was in ruins. The woman led me here..."

"Mara, what are you talking about? Everything was fine–" Sorn stopped, a look of understanding appearing on his face. "Mara, you've been in here far too long. We need to get you out. Hopefully, the anchor I created is still functional. We must get you there right away."

Mara heard Sorn's words, but they were like a buzzing drone in her ear. Was she really going mad? Had all this been a creation of her spiraling state of mind? It seemed so real. It seemed to have been telling her something. As Sorn's words droned on, unintelligible to her, her mind searched for meaning. She heard something again. Mara stopped and turned, looking at the back of the room where it was darkest.

"Shhh," Mara said, trying to silence Sorn. He stopped and they stood in silence for several seconds.

"Mara, what–" The sound came again.

"Shhh... did you hear that?"

"Hear what?"

"Listen..." Mara said, pointing toward the darkness in the back of the room.

They both listened intently. After a short time, there came the faint sound of crying, just as Mara had heard before.

"Is someone else here?" Sorn asked.

"I don't know, but this is what I was trying to tell you. The woman I saw; she seemed sad, and in pain. I followed her here. And this isn't the first time. I've dreamt of these cries before. I think... I think there's something I need to see here."

"Okay," Sorn replied awkwardly. He moved over and retrieved two torches from the wall, bringing one over to Mara.

Once they both had torches, they began moving toward the back of the room. There were several desks on the way, and bookshelves lined the walls. The place was a bit of a mess, and there was a thick layer of dust covering much of it. As the glow of their lights illuminated the back of the room, they saw there was a narrow corridor leading back further. It would have been barred by an iron gate, except the gate was smashed and lying on the ground. Mara and Sorn exchanged puzzled glances.

Mara stepped ahead into the corridor, minding her footing as she stepped into the cracks of the downed gate. She continued moving forward as Sorn did the same. The corridor ran for a short way before opening into a much larger room, a faint ray of light in the center of it.

As they stepped out into the room, Mara could tell it was quite large as both the outer walls and the ceiling were beyond where the light could reach. As she looked up toward the ceiling, she saw a small, grated hole in the very center, a trickle of moonlight coming through down to the floor below.

Mara and Sorn looked at each other again in confusion, then around the room. Since their lights didn't reach the outer edges of it, they both walked off in different directions to see what mysteries the room held.

As Mara followed the left edge, she saw her side of the room was lined with large metal cages. The cages were about fifteen feet wide, with a door in the middle. As Mara lifted her light and peered inside the closest one, she saw it went back to the wall, maybe twenty-five or thirty feet, possibly more. The cage was empty, as were the ones on either side of it. Mara began walking counterclockwise down the line of cages, one after the other. All of them were empty.

Suddenly, Mara stopped, her heart skipping a beat. There was something inside the next cage. Moving closer, lifting her torch, she realized what it was. Bones. Mara gasped, both horrified and perplexed by what she was seeing.

"What is it, Mara?" Sorn asked as he came over.

"Look," Mara said, pointing.

Sorn's eyes grew wide as he came to realize what he was looking at. His expression shifted to sadness after several moments.

"So, the rumors were true."

"Rumors? What rumors?"

"Back home we have great libraries accounting the conflicts we've had, primarily with—with humans," he stated, glancing sideways at her awkwardly. "There were accounts dating back to the time of Sha'Liotha. I'm assuming you know who that is, given she's on the door out there."

"Yes," Mara replied.

"There are accounts from that time, that some of our kind were taken alive by the Order. That they were kept somewhere secret, and that vile things were done to them. But this is not something we ever confirmed, and most dismissed them as hearsay. We knew our slain brothers and sisters were mutilated and sold for parts, but we couldn't have known why they would have been captured alive. But now I see... it makes so much sense."

There was anger and sadness in Sorn's voice as he spoke. His head dipped low, and he rested his forehead on the cage.

"There are tools and stations on the other side of the arena for harvesting blood. I know Sha'Liotha first attacked the humans. I know she and other queens have brought death and destruction to your people. But this... this isn't right."

"What are you saying, Sorn?" Mara asked. She was trying to understand what he was getting at. She looked back at the bones in the cage, thinking again on his words.

"They kept the dragons here alive to drain their blood," she said, finally understanding. "Sorn, I– I didn't know."

"It seems both our kind have dark secrets," Sorn said. "This is exactly why we must stop this. We have to put an end to the bloodshed."

A cry echoed throughout the room and both spun, looking to the right. It sounded like it was coming from several cages down. They glanced at each other and moved toward it.

After several more cages, they came across a row of smaller ones. Several of them were empty, but others contained smaller bones. Mara choked back a sob as she saw them.

"Even the younglings did not escape this fate," Sorn said, pausing to look at them with glazed eyes.

"But how?" Mara asked. "How did the Order get younglings?"

They felt a shift in the light behind them. Turning, they saw the image of Liotha drift into the light at the center of the room. She stopped just short of it, looking as though she was speaking to someone. From out of the shadows on the other side, a man stepped out. Mara recognized him instantly as Garn Dragonblood.

"Is that... Liotha?" Sorn asked.

"She's the one I've been following. What's that she's holding?"

It was a small, shiny object dangling from a chain. It looked like a vial of sorts, some kind of liquid inside. She stepped forward into the light and handed it to Garn.

There was a large bang and sound of metal grating against stone, the images of Liotha and Garn instantly fading. Mara and Sorn's attention moved to the hallway they'd used to enter the room. Liotha appeared from the hallway, bursting into the room at a full sprint.

She ran over to the cage next to Mara and Sorn where the small child was being held. As Mara and Sorn's stepped aside, they now saw the child lying motionless on the ground. It looked thin and pale. Liotha checked the other cages. The other children appeared worse, possibly even dead.

Liotha tried to force the cage door open, but the metal seemed to weaken her when she touched it. Even being near it seemed to have some adverse effect on her.

She tried to shift into her dragon form, but she struggled. Her appearance twisted and shifted in a chaotic cloud, but she kept returning back to her human form, her breathing heavy, sweat on her forehead. She finally gave up and looked around the room, searching for something. Spotting the extraction tables on the other side, her anger flared. She went over and began smashing them, one by one. She screamed in her rage, her eyes flaring in intensity as her features morphed into a draconic shape.

Once she had wrecked several of them, she paused in exhaustion, breathing heavily. Her eyes moved across the scene, spotting a piece of metal lying amongst the wreckage. Grabbing it, she returned to the cage with the child and started using it to try and pry open the lock. After straining herself to exhaustion again with no luck, she yelled and swung the metal at the cage door, trying anything she could to break it open.

After several more swings, the locking mechanism snapped, and the cage door creaked open. Liotha threw the metal piece aside and entered the cell, scooping up the child in her arms. She held it up to her face, checking for breathing or signs of a beating heart. The child was unresponsive, still limp in her arms. She looked down at it in sadness, the shimmer of a tear reflected in the dim moonlight.

As Mara and Sorn watched intently, they saw Liotha carry the child to the center of the room. She stood in the middle of the moonlight and gazed upward. She looked down at the child again as a tear left her cheek, falling onto the child's face. Finally, the child stirred, ever so slightly, though it never opened its eyes. The sounds of shouting and metal against stone echoed from the hallway. Someone was coming.

Liotha looked up in anger, her features shifting yet again as her eyes began to glow brightly. With a surge of her strength, she shifted into her dragon form and sailed upward, straight for the small grate in the ceiling in an attempt to flee. Mara and Sorn saw cracks form in the ceiling as she smashed into it. They heard the crumbling of stone, but the ceiling didn't give, and Liotha fell down with the child, trying desperately not to drop it as she was forced back into her human form.

More shouts came as the light of torches began to glow down the hallway. Liotha looked down it, then up again. She launched up yet again, trying to break through. Again, Mara and Sorn heard the sounds of cracking stones. Some of the roof began to cave in, but there was still no way out as Liotha fell back down. It was apparent she was in a great deal of pain, and it seemed to be taking every ounce of her will just to go into her dragon form for a few momentary seconds.

Sounds from the hallway grew even louder. Light flooded into the large room as Liotha braced again. Her muscles tensed and her eyes flared. And as before, she flew, crashing into the ceiling with all she had left.

This time, the ceiling gave way and Liotha burst out into the night just as a storm of knights flooded into the room. They looked up and watched as her moonlit shadow faded from view.

And then, the room was dark again, only the light of Mara and Sorn's torches and the small beam of moonlight still remaining, the hole in the roof restored, as it was when they first entered. They turned to each other in shock and disbelief.

"It would seem the great queen came to rescue them," Sorn admitted. "But why? This changes everything." Sorn said, his eyes staring off across the room.

"We can't change the past, Sorn, but we can change the future. We need to share this with everyone. We need to put a stop to this fight once and for all," Mara said, a fresh determination in her voice. "You mentioned a way out?"

"Ah, yes," Sorn replied, snapping out of his trance. "When me and my sister trapped you here," he said, eyeing her again with embarrassment. "I tried to redirect the magic to an anchor point that should allow you to escape. We just have to get to the town. It's there, in the square."

"Okay, but the town was gone for me. I don't know if I can find it."

"I will help you. If you take my hand, I should be able to share some of the toll the Dream has taken on you. Together, we should be able to find it, but we must hurry. Every moment we linger our minds grow weaker."

Sorn stretched his hand out to Mara, bowing toward her, just as he'd done many times before. Mara eyed him, still feeling the effects of his prior betrayal. But what else could she do? If they were going to mend the bond between man and dragon, it would have to start with her and him.

"Very well," Mara said, slowly reaching out her hand. When their fingers touched, his face shifted slightly, as if he could feel the pain of her mind's burden. For Mara, the walls felt a little less dark, and a relief set in that restored some measure of peace. She smiled at him. Sorn replied in kind, but Mara could tell there was a struggle behind it.

"Ready?" Sorn asked.

"Yes," Mara nodded. "Let's go."

Chapter Forty-Nine

DUTY

A horn sounded in the distance, rousing Kai from dreams of fire and rage. He felt warmth against his face, and though his eyes were still closed, he could see the rays of the sun trying to pry them open.

He forced himself to sit up, carefully, slowly opening his eyes. It was bright, late morning or mid-day perhaps, and he was sitting in the back of a wagon as it rolled along at a steady pace.

Kai saw the village of Eastend off to his left. There were a handful of townspeople standing on the northern edge of town watching the procession. He didn't know how much they knew of what was going on but assumed that rumors had surely spread of the attacks by now. If only they truly knew the threat of what Kai and the others had protected them from. If only they knew of the sacrifices that had been made–that were still to be made. Kai remembered the princess's words. He felt his anger growing as he watched them from far off. He'd won, and yet, it still felt like he'd lost.

"Ah, you're awake," came a familiar voice, the sound of horses hooves intensifying behind him.

"Cyrus?" Kai said, trying to turn around. His whole body hurt. He saw Cyrus had a cloth drawn around his head, covering part of his face where he'd been cut by Talesa.

"Aye, I'm here," Cyrus said. "And so are you, it seems. Gave us quite the scare, though. Wasn't sure you were going to recover this time, but seems you've grown more resilient since the last time I found you in bed. You've grown stronger. No less reckless, might I add."

Kai blushed, turning away, his thoughts returning to the fight in the fields. He looked back to Cyrus. "Is she dead?"

"She got away," Cyrus replied. "Barely. You struck quite the blow before passing out. If she lives, she will carry those wounds for the rest of her life."

Kai's eyes moved to his hands, remembering the fire his anger had called forth, the power flowing out of him in those moments. It was dangerous. It was intoxicating.

The sound of heavy hooves drew Kai's attention to the front of the procession. Four riders were approaching quickly, most likely an envoy to escort them in.

Cyrus pulled on his reigns, kicking his horse forward to greet the riders. Kai watched him ride up, speaking with the knights. Turning back, Kai noticed the hunter Aerin was riding a little way behind his cart.

"You," Kai said, pointing at him. "You came back. Why?" Kai remembered Jarren's words. He was conflicted seeing Aerin again, and to make matters worse, Aerin had taken his fight from him when he shot the princess. Possibly even put Mara's own life in jeopardy.

"Call it a hunch," Aerin responded. "I saw their destruction in the woods. I couldn't return home without trying one last time to help."

Noble words. Kai wanted to believe them, but he still hesitated. Making no reply, Kai merely nodded to the man, then turned back forward. He knew what he was going to find when he got back. He knew he needed to get his head straight if he was going to save her. The hunter may have given him an opportunity—if he hurried. The sooner he left, the better chances he had of finding the princess before she had a chance to recover.

***

Kai knelt beside Mara's bed as he stared at her motionless figure lying there, the only indication she was still alive the faint rise and fall of her chest. Memories returned of the last time he'd found her like this. Except this time, there was no waking her; at least, not until Kai confronted the dragon princess and forced her brother to help him save her. Only then would he get his sister back.

He'd heard her voice clearly when he needed it most. He didn't know how, but his sister had somehow helped him. It was his time to help her.

Kai's mind was still ablaze with the fires of revenge, and any tears he might have shed had otherwise been expelled by the intense heat in his veins. And not just figuratively; Kai suddenly realized he felt incredibly thirsty.

"I'm coming for you, Mara. Stay strong," Kai said, leaning in to kiss her forehead.

Kai stood up and headed for the door, taking one last look at his sister's still form before leaving and closing the door behind him. There was no point in waiting, and he did need to speak with the Scalewarden before he left. But first, water.

Kai moved down the hall at a quick pace, leaving the living quarters and making straight for the dining hall. There was a fountain just outside that always had running water—a drinking station for thirsty knights. As Kai rounded the corner and it came into view, he picked up his pace and, ignoring the cups, ducked down and put his mouth below the flow of water.

It felt cool as it rushed down into his belly, instantly satiating the intense heat he felt in the back of his throat. The water splashed everywhere, but he continued to guzzle it at an alarming rate.

"Well, if that ain't a sight for sore eyes…"

Kai paused and looked up, seeing Dax standing in the middle of the hallway, a splitting grin from ear to ear.

"You do know what a cup is, right Kai? Or maybe we should get you a trough. Course, don't think I ever seen a lorix drink as much as you are, and that's sayin' something, 'cause they can *drink*."

Kai finished one last big gulp and stood up, wiping his mouth as he turned to Dax.

"Just thirsty, I guess," Kai said.

"Thirsty? Kai, a horse without water for a whole day in the desert is thirsty. What you just did; that's on a whole 'nother level. When was the last time you had water?"

"I don't know. I passed out, so…" Kai shrugged. "What's a lorix?"

"Ah, shoot. Wait, you don't know what a lorix is?" Dax asked as he started following Kai down the corridor. "Ah, well, I guess you wouldn't know if you've lived here your whole life. They only live on the southeastern plains, past the capital. That's where I'm from. Back there, we had a farm with thousands of 'em. But how to describe a lorix…" Dax paused as the gears in his head spun. "They got some o' them big mountain cats around these parts, right?"

"Yeah, so I've heard," Kai replied.

"Well, if you cross one of them with a goat, I guess that about sums up a lorix. Oh, and they produce the sweetest milk you ever did taste. Mmm, mmm. It tastes like heaven in a bottle. If we ever get to travel that way, you definitely gotta try some."

"Sounds gross." Kai's mind was on other things and he imagined his face reflected it. Besides his sister, he'd heard a rumor that some of the knights had caught Jarren snooping around near the Scalewarden's quarters. Kai hoped it was just a coincidence, but the princess's words about an insider still burned in the back of his mind. *It couldn't be Jarren, could it?*

"Well, everyone I know likes it, but… anyways, enough about that. What's going on with you Kai? You look like someone just killed your dog. Is it Mara? I heard Vi talkin' with Cyrus and it sounded like something was wrong."

"*Everything* is wrong," Kai muttered.

"Everything? What do you mean? What happened out there, Kai? Can I help in any way?"

"No, not really. It's just–" Kai cut short when he saw Dax's empathetic expression. "It's fine, Dax, really. I just have to do something and I have to do it on my own. I appreciate the offer. I do." Kai tried to smile, but he could see Dax wasn't really buying it.

"Well, I sure wish you'd let us help. Whatever it is, I doubt you have to do it on your own."

"Well, I do," Kai responded with a raised voice. "I do," he repeated, softening his tone a bit. "You wouldn't understand, and I don't have time to explain it. I have to go talk to the Scalewarden about Jarren."

"About Jarren? The hunter?" Dax asked.

Kai was already on his way down the hall, nearing the Scalewarden's quarters. As he turned the corner, he saw Dax watching him, a look of hurt about him, which was a rarity for the usually perky boy. Kai's mouth formed a thin line. *Good job, Kai.*

He felt bad for brushing Dax off, but there was too much on his mind and he didn't have time to waste. He hoped his friend would understand.

Inside, Kai made straight for the Scalewarden's door. It was open, so he walked in right away, barely noticing Yuri at his desk outside.

"Ah, excuse me, Master Grayscale," Yuri called out, hopping down from his pedestal. When he came through the doorway after Kai, he saw the Scalewarden was already talking to him. They both looked up at Yuri.

"It's quite alright, Yuri," the Scalewarden said, waving his hand. Yuri left and closed the door behind him with a grunt.

"Cyrus told me what happened," Karg continued. "He and Thorlan just left a few minutes ago. And I heard about Mara. I'm sorry, Kai. I didn't expect things to go this way–none of us did. How could we have foreseen this?"

"It doesn't matter," Kai said. "I will do what I must to save my sister and end this. If the princess is anything like her sister, then I know I can win, especially if she was injured by Aerin's arrow."

"Kai, you don't mean to go through with this, do you? You shouldn't go alone."

"What choice do I have? Either way, even if I lose, then she will leave the Order alone. This is why I must go. You understand, don't you?"

"I... do," Karg said, smiling softly. "I don't like it, but I understand. Do what you must, my boy. Whatever happens, just know the Order will hail you a hero. Before you go, is there anything I can do for you?"

"Yes, actually," Kai replied, a seriousness in his words. "Jarren."

"The hunter?"

"Yes. It seems he's been accused of being a traitor," Kai questioned.

"Yes, that's what they've told me. I was not aware..."

"I've spent some time with the man. He's simple, and a bit odd, but I don't think he's acted maliciously in any way. I hope you'll consider my testimony if it comes to any sort of punishment."

"I will consider it, of course, Kai" Karg said, dipping his head forward. "I understand your concern, and I will weigh the gravity of your words carefully. We will discuss his fate soon."

Kai continued pacing but slowed and nodded to Karg. After gazing at Karg for a moment, words swirling about his head, he decided there was nothing left to say and started for the door.

"You're leaving right away, then?" Karg asked.

"Yes, might was well get this over with," Kai said, turning back to look at Karg. "Thank you for your faith in me, Scalewarden. I hope it was not misplaced."

With one last nod, Kai was gone.

"Godspeed, my boy. Godspeed."

Out in the hall, Kai nearly bumped into Cyrus as he rounded the corner.

"Oh, Kai, sorry," Cyrus apologized.

"It's fine," Kai murmured.

"Just talked to the Scalewarden?" Cyrus questioned, his brow furling.

"Yes."

"I was just coming to talk to him about you. How are you doing?"

"Fine."

"Kai, with everything that's happened–everything that *is* happening, I'm sure you're anything but fine."

"Yeah, well not much to say, really."

"Can we go talk for a minute, Kai?"

"I don't know what there is to talk about. I really should get going." Kai tried to look around Cyrus, fidgeting, not wanting to look the older man in the face.

"Tell you what. Let's just go for a short walk up on the wall. I could use some fresh air, and I'm sure you could too. What do you say?"

"I need to get some rest."

"Just a short walk, I promise. Then you can get ready," Cyrus persisted, offering his usual smile.

"Okay," Kai sighed, realizing Cyrus probably wouldn't give up. "I guess I could use some air for a minute."

"Excellent. There's a staircase just down here."

Cyrus turned and started down the hall, Kai reluctantly following him. Every so often Cyrus turned his head to make sure Kai was still following, but he said nothing more. Once they reached the stairwell, they turned and began ascending it as it spiraled upward, the sounds of their footfalls and heavy breathing echoing through the narrow passage as they climbed.

Up top, they came out onto the wall, taking a minute to catch their breath. Cyrus looked over toward Kai with a raised eyebrow.

"Well, that's one way to get air, isn't it?" he chuckled. Ignoring Kai's unamused expression, he continued. "I'm not quite as young as I used to be, but I'm thankful to see another winter, nonetheless. It sure is beautiful, isn't it?" he said, looking toward the mountains.

"Sure," Kai said as he leaned on a nearby part of the wall. He could feel Cyrus staring at him.

"What do you see?" Cyrus asked, breaking the awkward silence.

"Mountains?" Kai replied, more of a question.

"Aye. And what else?"

"Snow?"

"Aye. Winter is nearly upon us, Kai. Harsh winds blow from the west. It's clear now these winds bring more than just the cold." Cyrus turned to Kai, placing his hand on his shoulder. "The bitter winds of winter should be for those of us who've lived our lives long enough to grow grey. You are still in your spring. You've yet to experience the changing of the seasons, as I have, and all that which comes along with it. The burdens of winter should not be yours to face just yet. Do you understand what I'm saying, Kai?"

"I... think so," Kai said, though he wasn't quite sure he did.

"It would seem this winter has brought with it a terrible storm. And this storm is headed straight for you. I know it may seem like there's no way around it–that you must weather this storm, no matter the cost, but that simply isn't true, Kai. I've seen many winters, and some of them have been terrible. Some of them seemed like they would tear me apart. But in the end, it was through the support of my friends–my brothers and sisters–that I weathered those storms. You don't have to do this alone, Kai. Let us help you."

"But I *do* have to do this alone. You heard her. And you've seen Mara. This won't end until I do what she wants me to do, even if it means my death."

"Aye, and I understand why it must seem this is the only way. But trust me when I say that rarely in life is there one, and only one, choice. There is always another path through the woods. Sometimes it is hidden and obscured, shielded from our view. Sometimes it is a path we must forge ourselves, and we must seek the courage to find it."

"I understand what you're saying, Cyrus, but this is different. I don't see any other choice, and I don't have time to look. This isn't a path through the woods, this is my sister's life we're talking about. I don't have the time to find another way to save her. It's going to take me over half a day's ride to get up there, barring any more slowdowns. I need to do this, and I need to do it *now*."

"I understand, Kai. This is your choice, and ultimately it rests with you. All I'm asking is that you give me until tomorrow morning to come up with an alternative solution. If I don't have any answers by first light, I will concede and let you go. You should probably take the time to prepare, anyways. So, take tonight to gather what you need. The princess will be a formidable warrior, especially if she recovers. Her sister was formidable, but she was also reckless, and she underestimated you. Now that they know what you're capable of, I can only assume she will take the necessary precautions to avoid making the same mistake."

Kai continued to gaze off into the distance for a minute, withholding his response. He felt his jaw clenching, knew Cyrus could probably see it.

"I know this is a heavy burden to bear, Kai. I will not stop you, but just remember, the princess will be prepared, and she may not fight fair. Remember all that you have learned–all that we have taught you. If you come face to face with our enemy, it might just save your life."

Cyrus turned back to face Kai, staring deep into the boy's eyes.

"The greatest strength of a warrior is not knowing how to fight, but when, and why. You know how to fight Kai. I know because I've seen it. You have a fire inside you that cannot be tamed. It will aid you, but take care, lest it consume you. Not every battle need be won in the moment that it is fought. Choose your battles wisely, and more often than not, you will be victorious."

"I've said much already. Whether you take heed or not is up to you, but I'd like to end with one final question. Everything I've said is pointless if you don't understand the reason why you fight. So, Kai Grayscale, what is your reason?"

"To protect the realm from the dragons..." Kai responded quickly.

"Aye, that is a noble cause, yes, but I believe the true answer lies deeper than that. Why do *you* fight, Kai? What passion lies behind the strike of *your* spear?"

Kai thought for a moment, the question seemed simple, yet was proving difficult to answer.

"I fight for my parents, and for Uncle–to avenge their deaths. And for what they did to Mara. I fight to correct those wrongs."

Cyrus nodded his head at Kai's words.

"The road of revenge rarely leads to the destination of our heart's truest desires. That's closer to the answer, perhaps, but think on it some more. Anyways," Cyrus said straightening up and looking toward the door. "I've said enough words for today. Hopefully, they have at least helped a little, no matter what you choose."

"I appreciate it–all of it," Kai finally admitted, trying to relax. "I probably should go prepare. After all, I intend to win this fight."

"That's the spirit, Kai," Cyrus said as he firmly grabbed Kai's shoulder again, giving him a sincere smile. "And I've no doubt you can, but I'm going to try to figure out a way for you to have the best possible chance of stopping her and saving Mara. For now, ready yourself and get some rest. Tomorrow is going to be a long day, and you're going to need your strength. I shall come find you at first light."

Kai nodded, turning to leave.

"Oh, and Kai..."

"Yes?"

"Your uncle–and your parents–would be proud of you. No matter what happens, remember that, alright?"

Kai nodded again. He hesitated, wanting to reply, but after several moments he nodded again and turned to head back down the staircase of the tower. Kai sighed heavily once he was out of Cyrus's sight. He admired the older man, looked up to him, even. His words had struck a chord. However, Kai couldn't afford to wait. By first light, he would be well on his way.

CHAPTER FIFTY

AWAKE

Sorn had told her it may take some time for her body to fully recover before she could wake up. He'd told her there might be some weakness and strange sensations in her body as it revived itself. Everything he'd said had been an understatement, at best.

Mara knew she wasn't sleeping, could feel herself back in her own body, but no matter what she did, it was unresponsive. She felt the weakness and even some aching in her bones. It felt like she'd lain there for days in darkness, waiting for it to come fully back to life. It was reassuring to have escaped from the Dream, but it still felt like the nightmare lingered.

It was subtle at first, moving her fingertips and toes. She felt the familiar sheets of her bed beneath her. As the sensations grew, she found she could move her arms, then her legs. After what seemed like another eternity, she could finally move her entire body, though it was still perhaps hours more before she was finally able to sit up.

She'd tried calling out earlier on, but her voice was faint and hoarse. If Sorn hadn't warned her, Mara would have been in a much worse state of panic than she was right now. It wasn't so much that her body was weak, or that it would barely respond to her, but she had this growing fear something was wrong with Kai. She knew he had fought Nalaen's sister. She knew her sister was fierce. Kai was strong, and a good fighter, but the last time she'd seen him, he hadn't looked so good. Certainly, not up to facing an elder dragon.

As Mara was finally getting herself up, able to swing her legs off the side of the bed, she heard footsteps coming down the hall. A few seconds later, the door swung open.

"Mara? Oh my, Mara, you're awake," Vi said, rushing to her side to help steady her on the bed. "Cyrus, she's awake!"

"Mara, by the gods. What happened to you?" Cyrus said, coming up to her side. She felt him reach for her hand and squeeze it gently.

"I..." Mara started, unsure of exactly where to start. "I don't suppose you would believe me if I told you," she said weakly.

"With everything that's happened, I'd believe anything at the moment. But the princess already told us what happened. Something about the Dream? And being trapped?"

"Astral projection," Vi said, her eyes going blank. "You mean you actually did it?"

"I have been for some time, actually," Mara replied, feeling her cheeks turn red. "But this time... this time was different. I *was* trapped."

"Just like the Princess said..." Cyrus pondered. "I can't believe it was true. But you managed to escape. How?"

"It's a long story," Mara replied. "And I think I'm ready to tell you about it, Cyrus, but first–where's Kai?"

The room grew silent for a moment, Mara's heart beginning to beat faster. "Cyrus?"

"He's gone, Mara," Vi answered. "He left sometime before sunrise. He left... to go save you. Cyrus, you need to leave now. We need to stop him."

Mara's heart pounded in her chest as she waited for Cyrus's reply.

"Right. We were heading out anyways, but this certainly changes things. We will leave right away. Mara, I'd love to hear your story, but I think you understand. When I bring Kai back, and I will, we'll all have a long discussion about everything that's happened."

"Please save him, Cyrus," Mara said. If there was anyone in the whole keep she trusted to do it, it was Cyrus, but she still had this terrible fear that it was not going to be enough. Perhaps, somehow, she could help. Perhaps there was some way she could reach him in time.

It might be possible, but she needed to recover first. She needed to get up and moving, get her body back to normal. She'd been lying in bed for far too long. The Dream had taken its toll. Once she felt like she could get around, she'd reach out to the one ally who, above everyone else, understood exactly what she was going through. The one ally who really could help her stop the bloodshed between man and dragon. The one who could help her save her brother.

Chapter Fifty-One

BETRAYAL

Nalaen sucked in a deep breath and sat up, her head instantly spinning. There was a sharp pain between her shoulders, and her muscles felt stiff. She flexed and tried to stretch, the pain intensifying. As the dizziness in her head slowly faded, her mind floated to the last memory before she'd blacked out.

The battle!

She stood up, taking a few seconds to get her balance, feeling the world start to spin again. She blinked and forced her eyes open, trying to regain composure.

How long was I asleep?

Steadily, she moved toward the door, her legs regaining their strength with each step. By the time she reached the doorway and stepped outside, she felt a bit better. Outside it was quiet, a gentle breeze blowing from the north that brought a slight chill to her bones, but the crisp air felt good in her lungs. Her eyes swept across the ruins. It was sunny and seemed to be around midday. There should have been signs of some activity, but it was far too quiet.

She turned around and walked back inside, checking her sister's side of the living area. It was empty, with no sign of her presence. Most of her things were as she'd left them before the battle. It was as if Talesa had never returned.

Worried, she went back outside and headed straight for Sorn's tent. Inside, she found his place was much emptier than Talesa's. All his prized possessions were missing. Growing more and more concerned, she ran out of his tent and over to where the guards' quarters were. Again, there was no sign of anyone, but the place was a mess, and some of the things seemed to be missing. It looked like someone had left in a hurry.

"Hello?" she called out, waiting in silence for any reply. "Sorn?" she called out again. There was nothing but the whistling of the wind as it carried her voice down the hill. She waited a few more seconds, trying to contemplate what might have happened. It was obvious some had returned, including her brother, but what about the others? What about Talesa?

Nalaen?

Sorn? Where are you? What happened?

I'm... somewhere safe, for now. I had to leave.

Somewhere safe? What do you mean? Why did you have to leave?

Nalaen... I think Talesa might be dead.

Shock overtook Nalaen, a shooting pain in her chest arcing to her injury in her back. She stared at the ground in disbelief. Her sister, dead? How? Slowly, the look of shock faded, and she came back to her senses.

How?

It was the boy, Kai. She attacked after you were injured. I got you out of there, but Talesa tried to kill him. She lost.

"Kai..." she said out loud, a deep malice in her voice. Her eyes closed and a dark expression spread through her features. When she opened them again, they flared brighter as she felt her bones shift beneath her flesh, the inner beast begging to be let loose. *Talesa underestimated him, just as I did. She was foolish. Are you sure she's dead?*

I went looking but found no signs of her presence. I don't know.

What about the others?

Only Drae'lak and Qa'naran returned, and they're the ones who told me about Talesa and the others' fates. They left for home as soon as they came back to the ruins.

So, you were here, then? Why did you leave me alone?

For my own safety.

Your safety? Why- Nalaen stopped as she started to think about what Sorn might be insinuating. *What did you do?*

I've discovered something, Sister—something that changes everything.

What did you do? she repeated.

Everything we've been told, everything we've known... it's all a lie. Sha'Liotha is not who we thought she was. She was a traitor to our kind.

What? What are you talking about, Sorn? What happened?

I saw memories of Liotha. She was here, in the human lands. She was working with them—the original Dragonbloods. She was working with Garn. She gave them... something. I don't know what, but we must find out.

What? How could you possibly see that? How do you know it was her?

In the Dream... I know it was her. I've read the books. I've seen the drawings of her face a thousand times.

What were you doing in the Dream, Brother?

I... Sorn's voice paused. *I was doing what I thought was best—to end the blood-shed, for all our sakes.*

You didn't...

I'm sorry.

You would betray me so readily? I should have known.

I already lost one sister, I cannot lose you, too.

You lost me when you betrayed me.

Sister, please listen to me. Drae'lak and Qa'naran returned home. When they return without you, what will everyone think? They could send our army here.

Let them come.

We do not want another war. And even if they do come, what if Kai kills you?

Do you doubt me so much? You really are soft, just as Talesa said. At least she had a spine. I wish you had died instead of her.

I know you don't mean that.

Oh, but I do. Once the Grayscales are dead, I will hunt you down. You always were smart, Brother. I'll give you that. You were right to not give this news to me face to face.

Nalaen, please! We must end this. What if I come back? You can do with me what you will, just promise me we'll return home and forget about the humans.

So, you're protecting them now, are you? That human girl really got to you. I should have trusted Talesa and never let you come. I have made far too many mistakes already, and it's nearly cost me everything. No, Brother. I will take what is mine. And if I am satisfied, then perhaps I will let you live–as long as I never see your face again.

Nalaen, don't do this. It's not worth it.

I've had enough of your treacherous words, Sorn. Enjoy your banishment. And good luck with your pets. They'll turn on you before long. They'll probably kill you in my stead. How poetic that would be.

Nalaen!

Goodbye, Sorn.

Nalaen focused her thoughts, blocking out Sorn's presence in her mind. She could feel him still trying to reach her for another few minutes, but once the attempts slowed, she began to reign in her focus.

Everyone had abandoned her. She had no more allies. Kyrian would likely be waiting for her return, ready to use all these failures against her. If she was going to return, it wouldn't be empty-handed. No, she was going to return as Queen, bathed in the blood of her enemies, with no alternate heir to the throne, and her traitorous brother banished forever.

The thoughts swirling around in her skull fanned her growing rage. She felt her bones quiver. The dragon within was ready to come out.

She felt an arc of pain as the tightness in her muscles resisted the change. She tried to push past it, but she was still too weak. She needed more rest, but first, she needed to know if Kai was coming. And if he was as powerful as Sorn had said, she'd need a solid plan that worked to her advantage.

She still had one ally left, even if he was unwitting. She might at least have the strength of mind to reach out to him, to get one last update. That is, if the Order hadn't already discovered what he was.

Chapter Fifty-Two

TESTIMONY

"Jarren of the Lodge," Thorlan said. "You have heard the testimonies. The crimes of conspiring against your fellow man by working with the dragons who've invaded our lands. Through this service, you have abetted their cause, bringing about the death of dozens of civilians and eleven knights of the Order, including the death of Yoren Grayscale and the endangerment of his niece and nephew. And this is not counting the potential deaths of more knights as they race to save the boy Kai, whom you befriended under a guise. Additionally, you have endangered the lives of the entire western Vale. For these crimes, you are here today as we decide your fate. As the Scalewarden of the Order of Scales, Karg Wyrmsbane has been bestowed the right to judge this proceeding by Emperor Nerius the First, 13th Ruler of the 16th Age. This is a right that has been continued through his father, and his father before him. As such, his verdict is final. Justice will be served today by his hand. Do you understand all that I have said?"

Jarren looked around the room, his expression sullen, confused about his fate. Turning his attention to Thorlan, he nodded slowly, a quizzical look about him.

So, the boy has left to come here. Good. Jarren's expression shifted slightly when he heard her thoughts enter his head. She'd been quiet for some days—ever since he'd been caught near the Scalewarden's chambers. It had been a nice reprieve to hear her voice less often, but it always came.

"Very well, then let us proceed," Karg spoke, his voice sounding hoarse and weak. "Brother Thorlan, please see to the final witnesses," he finished, nodding to Thorlan. Thorlan returned his nod, stepping forward to address the crowd.

"Brothers and Sisters of the Order," Thorlan started. "As the Scalewarden just said, we are here today to judge this man. We have already heard many testimonies against him. The grievances placed against Jarren are severe, and the consequences demand justice... in whatever form that may come, even death."

At the mention of death, Jarren quivered, realizing the situation may be more serious than he fully understood.

"But to be fair, we must seek several more testimonies. Aerin of the Lodge," he said as his gaze fell on the man. "As a fellow member of the Guild, you have known this man the longest of any in attendance. The Order calls you forth to bear witness against his crimes."

Aerin rose and somberly walked up to where Thorlan stood, glancing over at Jarren as he passed. Jarren returned his gaze with an almost childlike manner, begging for his friend to speak good on his behalf.

"Aerin of the Lodge. You've known this man for many years. You are also the one who initially brought words of the strange events in the mountains. Please, inform the Council of all that you know. What, if anything, could possibly explain this man's behavior, in the off chance that it might sway the Council in favor of a lesser punishment, should that be deserving."

"Thorlan, Council members, Scalewarden," Aerin said, nodding to each as he directed his attention toward them. "It is true, I have known Jarren for some time. We served at the Lodge for many years together. In all that time, I never knew him to bear any ill will toward any of the other members, nor to anyone else... that I am aware of. He is alone in the world. His father died some years ago, and he has served the Lodge faithfully. He has never given me reason to question his integrity, nor his nature. That is, not until some weeks ago."

Eyebrows raised and quiet murmurs went through the presiding council.

"I'm sure you all remember the tale I told when first I came to the Order. It caused quite a stir, and it was the first indication you had that the dragons had returned. But for those who may have forgotten, or missed all the details, I shall recount the basics."

"Jarren was sent out on a mission to try and track down the strange disappearances of the wildlife around Northreach. He left with two others. He returned to us a week later, alone, and he was not the same man who'd left. I cannot explain it, but something happened to him in those mountains. He talked about a woman... a woman with red hair and burning eyes. I believe now that he was referring to the dragon princess—the one I put an arrow in."

So, he was the one. I should pay him a visit before I leave.

Murmurs of approval went around the room at the mention of that fateful moment. Aerin gave a half-smile and nodded in acknowledgment of it but continued.

"Whatever happened in those woods, whatever encounter they had with her, it changed him. I cannot begin to understand it. There is a great deal about the dragons that I do not know, but we do know they have many mysterious powers. Jarren is not a strong-willed man. In fact, it is quite the opposite. But to say that he willingly agreed to serve this princess? I do not know if that is a question I can answer, but I don't think we can rule out the possibility that some kind of compulsory magic may be involved."

Voices raised at the suggestion that Jarren might have been acting out of some level of compulsion. It did not seem this was a favorable opinion. Jarren watched Thorlan, who raised his hands, trying to silence the crowd.

He's a clever one, he is. But will they believe him?

"If Jarren was indeed forced to serve them against his will, then that brings this trial to a critical decision. I have been through a great deal due to his alliance with the dragons, and like everyone else, I, too, have grievances. I saw Jeb's Post burned with my own eyes. I saw the death of friends and the destruction of homes wrought by the dragons. Like you, I want to see justice served for the innocents slain by their hands. But I also do not want to see more innocents killed in the pursuit of this justice." As Aerin finished, his gaze moved to Jarren. Jarren felt pride in that moment, and hope.

Shouts arose from around the room, cries of outrage rose up amongst many in attendance. As Thorlan tried to calm them, Aerin looked deeply into Jarren's eyes. Jarren felt embarrassed. He wanted to leap up and confirm Aerin's words, but her presence still compelled him to silence.

Well, it seems your fate is teetering on the edge of a knife. Don't think this is going to turn out well for you, delisae.

As the words settled in with Jarren, his expression changed again, as if a slightly deeper understanding of what was happening around him had taken hold. He returned Aerin's gaze, an almost pleading look as he studied his face. Aerin seemed to note the change, but after several seconds, he wrested his gaze away, turning to look over the crowd, who were mostly still in an uproar.

Jarren's eyes followed. He noticed a few who were sitting quietly amongst the others. It was the blind girl Mara and her friends. Jarren fixed his gaze on Mara as she sat there, seeming to be listening to everyone. After a few seconds, Mara turned her head toward Jarren, as if she'd felt his gaze directed at her. Feeling uncomfortable, he turned his eyes away and stared back up toward the Scalewarden.

Karg was sitting quietly on his raised seat, staring intensely down at Jarren. When their eyes met, Jarren averted his gaze, casting his eyes at the floor in front of him. It seemed everyone was angry with him. But he hadn't done anything wrong, had he? He'd only done what she'd commanded him to do.

As Jarren stared at the ground, a silence fell over the chamber. He looked up, trying to see why. Karg had finally risen, raising his hands as he waited for the hum of the room to fully subside. When it did, he nodded to Thorlan, who came over and they spoke quietly for a minute. After they finished, Thorlan turned to face Aerin.

"Aerin of the Lodge," Thorlan said. "You came to us some time ago with news of the dragons' arrival. You helped the Order when you did not need to, and we cast you out under unfair judgement. Yet still you returned to aid us again in the hour of utmost need. You have proven your loyalty to the Order, and you have proven a protector of the people. We appreciate your words spoken on behalf of your friend, though they implicate an alternative that is obviously not very popular amongst those in attendance here today. But because of all you have done, we will take your words into consideration. You may be seated."

Jarren watched Aerin return to his seat.

"We would now like to call forth another witness. Mara Grayscale, niece of the Spear, and sister to Kai. We humbly request your testimony, should you be willing."

So, my brother really did rescue her. Traitorous bastard.

Mara stood slowly, turning her head toward where Thorlan's words were coming from. Her face was somber as she slowly nodded. She appeared to be a bit sluggish, too. Thorlan moved toward her to help escort her up. Holding his arm out, she took it and walked with him slowly toward the center of the room. As they walked, she turned her head toward where Jarren sat. There was no malice or ill-will in her features, only sadness. Still, it made Jarren shift in his seat, and he could feel the stares of those sitting around him as it happened. Unlike Aerin, she had more reason to speak against him than the rest.

Once they were in place up front, Thorlan slowly let go as Mara stood on her own. He moved to stand at her side, just a few feet away, waiting on the nod from Karg to begin. It came a few seconds later.

"Mara Grayscale," Thorlan started. "Of all those in the room, you have felt the wounds of the dragons' presence the most. Losing your uncle, the Spear, would have been grievance enough to want to see the execution of the conspirator Jarren. And yet, even now your brother is in danger of the same fate. And your blindness may very well be a direct result of the scars given to you by the princess herself. For these reasons, the Council wishes to hear your thoughts on the matter, which will weigh heavily on the determination of this man's fate."

Mara stood silent for a few moments as she stared blankly toward some point on the ground in front of her. Eventually, she raised her head.

"Scalewarden, Council members, Thorlan... thank you for your kind words, and for considering my humble opinion in this matter. What you said is true. I have a lot that weighs on my heart and my mind. Even now, I fear for Kai's life. I pray that Cyrus and the others will reach him in time to avert any more death, but I am worried that he got too much of a head start. I am worried I will lose my brother, too, before this is all over." There was a deep sadness in her voice. She paused for a moment, trying to collect herself and keep from tearing up. Jarren felt tears coming to his own eyes. Had he really helped send the boy Kai to his death?

"But even though all of that has happened, my eyes have recently been opened. I know that is a strange phrase for a blind girl to say," she added, a flutter of chatter emanating from the room. "But it's true. Because of my blindness, life has changed drastically for me. And though my vision is gone, I have come to see some things more clearly. I am not sure that it is something I can talk about just yet, but I have come to understand things are not always as they seem, and that war brings out the worst in us. It is hatred that has led us here to this moment—a hatred of those who are different. Just because we are different, doesn't mean we need to fight. There is bad, and good, on all sides of the conflict."

A renewed turmoil began to move through the room as whispers of protest were exchanged. Mara quieted, and even from his seat, Jarren could see her blushing. He felt bad for the girl, felt sorry for any pain he'd caused her and the others.

"That's enough," Thorlan shouted, trying to calm the room yet again. "Let the girl speak. Mara, we appreciate your sentiment, but we are here to decide Jarren's fate. I'm sure there is a point you are getting to that relates to that?"

"Yes, there is," Mara said with a sigh. "My point is that the bloodshed needs to end. Killing this man will not end this fight, and it will not save us from whatever is to come, nor will it bring back that which we have lost. If there is a way to end this war, it is not this. I hurt for what has happened, but I do not want his blood on my hands. The only justice I want to see is peace. All I want is for the hatred to end."

All eyes turned to Karg as he sat on his chair, eyeing Mara closely with a discerning look. After several long moments of silence, he shifted, sitting upright, preparing to speak.

"So, you do not want to see the traitor condemned, then?" he asked.

"No, I do not," Mara replied, blushing again.

"And what of these suggestions that Aerin put forth? Do you think the man has been under the sway of the princess's magic?"

"I..." Mara started. "I cannot say for sure, but I– I know the dragons have powerful magic. Even now, I can sense a cloud of confusion over his head. Call it blind intuition, I guess, but it seems like it is possible she has some hold on him, but I do not know enough about such things to say for sure."

Hah, blind intuition. The girl is stronger than she thinks. How unfortunate that she escaped. We will have to be more clever to capture her a second time.

Everyone in the room began whispering to each other, waiting to see what Karg would say. Meanwhile, Jarren's face contorted as Nalaen's words pierced his mind. Though his thoughts were not wholly his, he felt conflicted between what Mara had said and what the shadows in his mind were telling him. As if sensing this turmoil, Mara turned and gazed his direction. Though she could not meet his gaze with her eyes, he felt a strange sense of her presence about him. It was calming, but not enough to rid him of his captor's thoughts.

"Very well, Mara. Your words are noted. We thank you for your participation in this endeavor. You may return to your seat," Karg said, nodding to Thorlan to help her again.

Thorlan took Mara's arm as before and helped her back to her seat. Jarren watched with a smile, happy that Mara had taken a stance in his favor, but still worried it wasn't enough. Thorlan returned to his position up front and nodded to the Scalewarden.

"The Council has heard the testimonies of those we had intended to hear. We all know the crimes this man is being charged with, and did not intend to call on any others. However, if there is anyone here today who can provide anything additional that the Council does *not* already know, speak now." Thorlan scanned the crowd for any who would wish to speak. It seemed everyone was eager to get to a verdict, most of whom likely saw things differently than Aerin and Mara did. As such, after a few more moments of silence, he carried on.

"Very well. The Council will adjourn to discuss this issue in private, and to decide Jarren's fate. We will ring the call bell when it is time to reconvene. Thanks to all who bore witness today, and for those who've already voiced their opinions on the matter elsewhere. You are dismissed."

Jarren buried his head in shame as everyone stood, chatting amongst themselves, some of them still casting dirty looks his way. Everything they had said, it was all because of him. So many deaths, so much pain. He hadn't wanted any of it. He'd only ever done what she made him do. He had no way of knowing it would lead to all of this.

All Jarren had ever wanted in his life was to be helpful. But this, the sudden realization of what his help had wrought, it was almost too much to bear.

CHAPTER FIFTY-THREE

SEVERANCE

Aerin skipped lunch, insisting on staying with his friend during the hours after the trial. He didn't know how long until the final verdict would be called, but Aerin knew he needed to be there for Jarren as long as he could.

The knights guarding Jarren's temporary holding cell in the guest quarters didn't allow him to stay with Jarren for very long, but fortunately Cyrus, at Aerin's request, had given him permission to get the man some food and water and make sure he was comfortable.

"Are you hungry, Jarren?" Aerin asked as the man sat quietly in the far corner of his bed, his head against the wall.

Jarren had so far refused to look at Aerin, much less respond. He'd just sat there, facing away, gently banging his forehead on the wall, whispering to himself. It was mostly incoherent mumbling, Aerin only making out fragmented words, though it didn't make much sense to him.

"Mother left... hear the others now... I didn't know..."

"I'm going to get you some food, Jarren. Is there anything in particular you'd like?"

Jarren stopped rocking momentarily, seemingly the first time he'd acknowledged Aerin's presence since they'd returned to his room. He turned his head sideways, Aerin seeing his eyes turn his way. He seemed for a moment as if he was about to speak but gently shook his head and returned to his rocking.

Aerin frowned, but stood, deciding he'd get Jarren some food anyways. As Aerin reached the doorway, he heard a faint voice speaking his name. He turned and saw Jarren's head tilted to the side again. Aerin came back closer so he could hear what his friend was saying.

"Some potatoes, please?" Jarren said weakly.

Upon hearing the words, Aerin smiled warmly.

"Of course, Jarren. I'll fetch them right away."

Jarren nodded and turned back to the corner, resting his head on his knees.

Aerin smiled again and turned to leave, nodding to the guards outside to close the door.

"I'll be right back with some food and water for him."

One of them nodded to Aerin, his expression cold and flat. Aerin frowned again when he turned around and headed for the dining hall. He understood why the Dragonbloods were upset with the man, but didn't understand why many of them cast judgement so quickly. Jarren had yet to be proven guilty, and even if he was, there was a very good chance it wasn't even his fault.

Aerin's thoughts continued as he made his way to the dining area. When he arrived, the hall was still bustling with the sounds of dinner and talking. He glanced around the room, noting how everyone seemed to be going about their day and chatting with each other as if nothing bad had happened. Nearly everyone in the keep had been at the trial, had seen and heard all that had been said.

Ignoring a few stray looks, Aerin headed to one of the nearby tables and grabbed a plate, piling on some potatoes, plus a few pieces of meat, just in case Jarren decided he wanted to eat more. Some of the knights nearby watched him load up the plate to take with him.

He turned to leave, ignoring their whispers behind his back. He could feel himself getting more and more upset. They didn't know Jarren like he did. How could they sympathize with his plight? But then, Aerin expected more from the knights who willingly protected the land from the dragons at their own peril. Perhaps years of fighting had hardened their hearts, especially when there was a human who might have possibly betrayed their life's work, even helped kill some of their own.

Aerin tried not to think about it on his way back to Jarren's holding room. He tried to ignore the distasteful looks from the guards outside the room as he approached with the plate. He tried not to get agitated when they insisted he only leave Jarren a spoon to eat his food. He tried to put on a smile as he came in, Jarren still facing the corner, and placed the food on the bed, only for Jarren to nod quietly but otherwise ignore it. He tried to remain hopeful that his actions had mattered, that Jarren would enjoy his food after Aerin left and that his words earlier had had an actual impact on the outcome of the council's decision. But try as he might, once he finally left and rounded the corner, out of view of the guards, Aerin slammed his fist against the wall in a fit of anger.

He was sick of people judging, not just Jarren, but also himself. They'd cast him aside so quickly before, and then they embraced him as a hero, only to be shunned again for testifying in Jarren's favor. He was tired of the people living safely behind the Wall, people like Lord Valeheart and his pompous steward, living without fear of dragons and enjoying the fruits of all the Vale had to offer, without a care or second thought for the people beyond the Wall's border. The world was unkind, and unfair, and now that Aerin had journeyed out into it, he was finally beginning to understand just how cruel and unfair a place it could truly be.

And yet, despite it all, there was one shining beacon of hope. Mara.

After everything she'd been through, after losing her uncle and her sight, and the current threat of losing her brother, she still saw the world for what it should be. She, who had every reason to judge Jarren the harshest, instead vied for peace and an end to the needless violence.

There was something special about her, and whatever it was, Aerin wanted to be a part of it. Perhaps now, in his darkest hour, she could be the light he needed to continue seeing the good in the world. Her and others, like Cyrus or Captain Garlan. Despite how dark the world could be, there were still bastions of hope keeping the light alive.

Aerin began wandering the hallways, looking for Mara. He didn't know where he'd find her, but it shouldn't be too hard. The girl was blind, so she likely wouldn't wander far from the usual places.

Aerin worked his way back to the dining hall, double checking to make sure Mara or any of her friends hadn't come in or been there before and he just hadn't noticed. As he scanned the room, several knights emerged, one of them tossing a cooked potato into the air while joking with the other knight he was with.

Aerin watched it float through the air, thoughts of Jarren coming flooding back to him. He had specifically asked for potatoes. *Mother left... hear the others... I didn't know...*

As the knights passed by, both of their brow's raised in a questioning manner toward Aerin as the sudden realization of everything washed over Aerin like a tidal wave. *He's back!*

He turned and bolted down the hallway, heading straight toward Jarren's room. He flew around the corner, coming into view of the two guards. They were sitting on chairs in front of the door, laughing together, eating some food that someone must have brought for them. They glanced up when they heard Aerin approaching, his breathing heavy.

"Open... the door," Aerin huffed between breaths.

"You already brought him food," one of the knights said in a gruff tone.

"Please..." Aerin added.

"We're eating. He probably is, too. Just come back in a bit, if you must," said the other knight before taking a large bite of his meat.

"No... I need to check on him. I need to see him now," Aerin said, finally starting to catch his breath.

Both knights rolled their eyes, the one who was chewing his big bite of meat looking at the other as if he were wagering with him as to who would acquiesce Aerin's request. Finally, the first knight grunted and stood, grabbing the ring of keys from his belt and heading toward the door.

Aerin waited, trying to be patient, watching him take his time. As the knight fumbled with the keys, searching for the correct one, Aerin felt a growing apprehension building. Jarren was in a pretty bad state when he'd left, and if he was back to his old self, there's no telling what he might be doing with his misery.

The man finally got the right key, sliding it into place and twisting, the locking mechanism clicking a few times before the man pressed the lever and the door began to swing open. Aerin watched the man as his gaze turned inward, his eyes moving upward and opening wide in a look of astonishment.

Aerin pushed his way past the knight, who was standing transfixed in the open doorway. As he pushed through, his eyes came to behold the same thing that had grabbed the man's attention.

Jarren was hanging about a foot off the ground, one of his bedsheets wrapped tightly around his neck, looped around the wooden beam running along the ceiling. He was still twitching, ever so slightly.

Jarren's eyes blinked, then locked on to Aerin's. The world stood still, and for a few seconds, Aerin was stunned, held in Jarren's gaze like a moth drawn to a flame. His mind drew blank, his legs and arms limp.

Aerin blinked and came to, rushing forward to grab Jarren's legs, hoisting him up to try to allow his friend to breathe. He struggled, looked toward the open doorway, both knights now staring blankly at him.

"Don't just stand there," he yelled, still struggling.

They came in, both of them helping lift Jarren up while Aerin hopped up on the bed and reached over, trying to untie the bedsheet. It took him a minute, but he finally got it untied and they all brought Jarren down, resting him on the bed.

Aerin inspected his friend, but Jarren was cold and stiff, no longer twitching, his eyes staring blankly at the ceiling.

"Jarren" Aerin said, grabbing him by the shoulders.

No response.

"Jarren," he pleaded again, shaking.

"I think he's gone, lad," said one of the knights, placing his hand on Aerin's shoulder.

Aerin shrugged the man's hand off, leaning in closer to check Jarren's mouth and watch his chest, hoping with every fading second he'd see or hear signs of breathing. When, after what felt like several minutes, he got no such signs, Aerin laid his chest on Jarren's and began to sob, hugging the poor man.

Through blurry vision, he saw the spoon he'd brought lying on the nearby dresser, bent and misshapen, scuffed along the handle. His eyes moved up to the wall next to Jarren's bed, noticing something had been scratched there. In crude lettering, he read Jarren's final words.

Mother left us. I can hear the others I hurt. I didn't know what she was making me do. Tell everyone I'm sorry. Tell Kai I'm sorry.

Aerin's tears flowed as he read the words. He was traumatized by what had just happened, but there was also anger boiling within his soul. He was angry with the Order for being so blind. He was angry with the dragon princess for using his friend as a tool. He was angry that he had not done more to stop all of this atrocity–that he had been too hesitant, not bold enough. He began to understand why Mara had said what she had said in the trial. Only the blind girl had truly seen.

This war needed to end. And in the pursuit of its end, Aerin would always remember the unnecessary sacrifice of the quirky and curious man, his fellow hunter and, in some ways, his friend, Jarren.

CHAPTER FIFTY-FOUR

PRESAGE

"Sorn, are you there?" Mara called out. As Mara looked around the city square, everything was back to the way it was before she'd been trapped in the Dream. It was weird to think how lingering so long could change so much. Mara never wanted to relive those experiences, but it had been for a purpose. For without those dark visions, Mara would not have learned the truth—at least, part of the truth. There was more to unravel in this mystery, but first things first, she needed to stop the fighting and save her brother.

"I'm here, Mara," replied Sorn. Mara turned and saw him approaching from one of the side streets.

"There you are. I was worried you'd left or... or something bad happened with your sister."

"Mara, I'm not leaving. I plan to see this through. Besides, it seems I must stay either way, as my sister made her intentions on never seeing me again quite clear."

"That bad, huh? But you're here, so I guess it could've gone worse."

"I told her from a safe place using *tele'soné*. I don't really know how to translate that into human, exactly, but basically, it's how we dragons can communicate using only our minds. I knew she wouldn't be pleased. My sister can be... arduous, but I don't really have to tell *you* that. Anyway, we need to figure out how we're going to stop her—and your brother. I can deal with the family drama later."

"I understand. My brother can be difficult, too. And that's why I'm here. I don't know if the knights are going to catch up to Kai in time to stop him before he reaches your sister. And even if they do, we still need to stop them from trying to kill her. We need some other alternative. Any ideas?"

"Yes, actually, but it's a long shot," Sorn said, sitting down on the bench by the pond.

"Let's hear it," Mara said, sitting next to him.

"Seeing your mental resolve while trapped in the Dream for so long gave me the idea," he said, staring into the quiet waters. "I'm not sure I could have lasted staying as long as you did. Taking on even half the burden of the weight you bore when we got you out of there was enough to put me on the edge. I think you have a real gift, Mara. I don't know how, but your strength is truly impressive. But all that aside, it's still just raw power, and you've yet to learn how to fully bend it to your will. The mind can be a powerful thing, but it is also incredibly fragile. If we push you too far, it could cause irreparable damage... or worse. It makes me struggle to even mention this path."

"Sorn, I understand what you are saying, but if we have a way to save our families and put a stop to this war, then I'm willing to do what it takes. Please, tell me."

Mara rested her hand on Sorn's shoulder, looking at him with a determined smile. At the touch, Sorn jerked slightly. Mara could tell he still felt bad about everything. But as her hand rested there, he gradually relaxed, looked at her hand, then into her eyes, smiling in return.

"Alright," he said with a sigh. "So, during my studies growing up I spent a lot of time reading about the ancient magics. Most of the magically gifted dragons that I know of are aware and practice many of these magics, but there are a few that are considered... forbidden, and for good reason. I know of these magics because my sister was infatuated with them. I don't know how much she knows, but I saw some of the books she took from the off-limits sections of the archives. While hiding, trying to decide what we could do to stop my sister, one of these books came to mind. It was titled '*Nefa'tili Venatus*'. There was a spell in that book called *dicerevis*, which essentially translates to mind-control in your tongue. My sister knows this magic. In fact, she–"

"Jarren?" Mara exclaimed as the thought hit her.

"Yes. So, you know?"

"He was just put on trial. I thought I felt something, but I didn't know what it was exactly. I tried to warn them that might be the case, but now it's too late. He killed himself because of the weight of all he'd done, all he'd helped your sister do. I can't believe it... Aerin *was* right." Mara's demeanor grew grim, the full realization setting in. "I should have tried harder to understand what I felt. I should have–"

"Mara, it's not your fault. It's my sister's. She must have let him go. It pains me to hear how things ended for him, but you can't blame yourself. You haven't been trained. You couldn't have known. Either way, this is all the more reason to put a stop to her. No one else needs to get hurt–if we can pull this off."

Mara looked back up at Sorn, sadness still in her eyes, but she knew he was right. The best way to honor Jarren's sacrifice was to stop it from happening to anyone else.

"Right, okay. So, what's the plan exactly?"

"We're going to do it to my sister," Sorn said, his expression grim.

"Do what? You mean...?"

"Yes. We're going to mind-control her."

"What? How? Won't that be–"

"Incredibly difficult? Yes. Yes, it will be. But like I said, you are strong–stronger than you know. I think together we could pull it off. My sister knows the magic, yes, but she is only able to use it on weak-willed individuals. There were three hunters in the woods that night. Only Jarren was weak enough to come under her sway. That being said, it still won't be easy. I essentially know how to do the magic, but I've never actually done it. And of course, you know nothing. But if you can figure out how to channel your strength through me, then I may be able to perform it long enough to gain control of her mind and stop her before she kills your brother. Once she's under my control–if we even get that far, then we'll have to figure out somewhere to keep her where she won't be able to hurt anyone until we figure out what to do next. And that's if I can actually keep her under control long enough."

"What about the cages in the Order basement?" Mara asked. "Not to hurt her, just to keep her safe until we figure out what to do."

"Hmm," Sorn thought. "That could work, assuming the cages are still there *and* functional. And assuming the Order promises to let her live. I trust you, Mara, but everyone else, not so much. They were ready to condemn Jarren, and that was just for helping us, even unwillingly. What do you think they would do to *her*?"

"Yes, you're probably right. With what I just saw, I don't think there would be any sympathy for your sister." Mara paused as a thought came to her. "Unless..."

"Yes?" Sorn asked, his eyebrow raised.

"Cyrus. I could convince him."

"Who is Cyrus?"

"He's one of the few at the Order who has enough compassion and reasoning to understand what we're trying to do. If I could just talk to him, I'm sure he could help. But he's on his way out now to try and stop Kai. I don't know how we're going to reach him."

"I see," Sorn acknowledged. "But you're sure he would be sympathetic to our plan?"

"Yes, I believe so. He's a good man, Sorn. Like..." Mara paused, her mood turning sad again. "Like Uncle."

"I am so sorry, Mara," Sorn apologized. He seemed as if he wanted to put his arm around her, to console her, but she could tell there was still a lot of hesitation from him.

"It's okay. I miss him, every day, but we're doing this in his memory. Him, and Jarren, and everyone else who's died in this war. That is why we must succeed."

Sorn's face softened and he smiled at her.

"Right, okay. So, we just have to get out there before they kill each other, subdue my sister, transport her to the Order's cells, and convince your friend to keep everyone from killing her long enough to figure this whole thing out. Easy."

"Well, when you put it like that," Mara said with a smirk.

"We can do it. Like you said, we must. But there is one more matter we need to consider..."

"What?" Mara asked.

"Your brother. I'm not going to allow him to kill my sister. We have to figure out some way to stop *him*, too. From what I heard, he's powerful enough in his own right, though it sounds like he barely knows how to control it, like you. But if he were to unleash it, he might even have a chance against my sister in a fair fight."

"Yes, and he's not exactly thinking straight right now. But if I'm there, I think I can convince him to stop. Like every other part of this plan, it won't be easy, but we must succeed."

Sorn sighed, a deep, heavy sigh. Mara looked at him in complete understanding. They had a loose plan, but it was going to take nothing short of a miracle to see it through.

"Wait," Mara added with an increased confusion. "All of this hinges on us getting out there before Kai does. He's got more than half a day's ride ahead of us. How are we going to beat him?"

Sorn smiled and Mara's face twisted into a confused smile.

"What?" she asked.

"Mara, I'm a dragon. We're going to fly."

Mara's face turned pale and Sorn laughed.

***

Kai pulled on the reins of his horse, coming to a stop. He'd ridden along the mountains on nearly the same route he had taken to the tower, continuing past that toward the north-central tower. It was the safest way to get to the ruins of Liotha's Fall, stopping just before the second tower to veer northeast, giving him a straight shot to his target. When he'd ridden past the site of the battle from just over a day ago, he'd spent a moment looking for any signs of Talesa. He hoped they had missed her body by some chance, but it seemed she truly had gotten away. This brought him little satisfaction, given the circumstances, but he hoped she at least felt some of the same pain he did. Perhaps she had died from her wounds, just somewhere else. Even if she didn't, she'd think twice before facing him again. And if it ever came to that, hopefully, the next time, Kai would have a better grasp on his abilities.

From where he had stopped, he could see the north-central tower was in the same state as its southern twin–broken and burned. It wasn't smoking anymore, but even from where Kai sat, he could see the scorch marks and black soot covering the top half of it.

Their destruction knows no end. It's time to put a stop to this...

Kai pulled his reins to the side, pointing his horse toward the mountains. He knew the path to take because it was the same one they'd used to flee the mountains on the night his uncle had been slain. Staring at it now, memories of that night came flooding back to him; the agony of losing his uncle, the pain of feeling it was all his fault, and his sister's bloody tears as he held her closely all the way back to the keep. He felt his temperature rise the longer he thought about it. *No, save it, Kai. You'll need it to fight her.*

He kicked the sides of his horse, sending her into a gallop, heading straight for the snow-covered path that wound between the frost-ridden trees under the shadows of the looming mountains.

***

Far away, atop one of the highest peaks along the Spine, Nalaen perched watching down below. She'd finally been able to assume her true form, and it was fortunate timing. From where she lay hidden, she could see both towers. And with her exceptional vision, she'd been watching Kai the entire time. He was a small speck to her, but she knew it was him. He'd come exactly along the route she'd predicted.

Of course, she'd known he was on his way, along with a group of knights at his heels. The final use of her delisae had proven fruitful. She had yet to spot the knights, but she'd been formulating a plan to get Kai alone, to keep them from interfering. She turned her eyes northeast, spotting dark grey clouds rolling in.

Perfect. Nalaen smiled, the droplets of her saliva dripping from her fangs and freezing as they hit the ground. Up this high, she needed to be in her dragon form just to withstand the cold. But that was not the only reason to assume her true nature. She wouldn't make the same mistakes as her sister. Today, *she* was going to end the Grayscale line. And she would do so with a swift snap of her jaws.

A glint of light caught her eye to the southwest. Peering at it, she saw it was the knights, who were just now passing the south-central tower and heading up the road toward Kai. They weren't far behind. *Time to move.*

She needed to draw Kai away from the ruins and toward the approaching storm. She needed to draw him into her trap. Thanks to the storm, hopefully, the others wouldn't be able to follow.

Nalaen flexed her wings, stretching them out and lifting off the ground as the strong winds instantly propelled her forward. She dove along the cliffside and down to the trees below, hovering just above them, making her way toward her prey.

***

"So, what are we doing out here exactly?" Vi asked as she walked down the main road leading from Dragonscale Keep to Eastend, Mara holding her arm.

"I need you to take me to meet someone," Mara answered.

"Meet someone? Who are we meeting?"

"I'll tell you when we're closer. I promise, this is important. Just take me to the woods on the other side of Eastend. We'll meet him there."

"Him? So, you're meeting strange men now, Mara? Didn't think you were that kind of girl..."

"Vi, please. It's not like that. Besides, he's a friend. I– I'll explain once we get there."

"Okay, fine. Keep your secrets."

"It'll be fine, trust me. Also, thanks for getting rid of Aerin for me, and for sweet-talking that guard to let us out. You have a way with people, Vi."

"Hah," Vi chuckled. "Yes, well when you come from one of the Families in the capital, you learn how to deal with people. Call it a gift, I guess."

"Well, it's useful. I like Aerin, but he's been following me around everywhere and I just don't think he'll understand at the moment. He's too fragile with... well, with you know what."

"Yes, well you can mostly thank Brol and Dax for that. They had the idea of asking him to teach them how to shoot. And honestly, they even seemed pretty excited about it, especially Dax."

"Yeah, that's perfect. From what I hear, Aerin is amazing with a bow. But anyway, thanks for that. And also, I thought for sure the guard wasn't going to let us out. Whatever you did worked there, too."

"Yes, well one thing I learned growing up is that being a woman has its advantages, especially against men who don't get out much." Vi chuckled again, squeezing Mara's hand.

"What *did* you do, Vi?" Mara turned her head toward Vi with an inquisitive look.

"Oh, nothing like that. I just talked him up a bunch and pretended to flirt. It didn't take much, really. He's just a bit lonely."

"Okay..." Mara said in a sly manner, scrunching her nose.

Within a short time, the girls entered the outskirts of the town. They continued through, making their way into the central square. Mara could feel the stares of the townspeople as they passed by. It was vastly different from in the Dream, when none of them could see her. She didn't know how she felt about it. Perhaps, it was just more hints at the gifts she'd come to understand better once all this was over.

Past the busy part of town, it didn't take them long to reach the other side of Eastend. Beyond the border, Mara remembered, there were some fields and then the edge of the forest just a little past that. Vi cleared her throat as the sounds of the town faded behind them.

"Alright, we're almost there. So, now are you going to tell me what's going on?"

Mara started squeezing Vi's hand tighter, a bit of sweat forming on her forehead.

"Okay, yes..." Mara paused, her eyes darting around uncontrollably. "So, you need to promise me you won't freak out."

"Freak out? Mara, you look like you're terrified. What's going on?"

"Oh, you noticed?"

"Of course, I noticed. You're squeezing my hand pretty hard, and you're sweating. Should I be worried?"

"Oh, sorry," Mara smirked, relaxing her hand. "No, it's not like that. I'm just a little nervous about meeting him, and for what we're about to do."

"Meeting him? I thought you said he was a friend. Mara... what aren't you telling me?"

Mara could smell the scent of pine as they started passing trees on the way into the woods. It was pleasant, reminding her of simpler days. She was still formulating the words stuck in her throat when she sensed Sorn's familiar presence.

"Vi..." Mara replied, "I'd like you to meet Sorn."

Vi instantly squeezed Mara's hand.

"Mara, that's– He's a–"

"A dragon? Yes."

Mara felt Vi swallow hard.

"Is he bowing?" Mara asked. Vi said nothing, but fidgeted slightly, perhaps in a nod. Mara giggled.

"Are you ready to fly, Mara?" Sorn asked.

"Fly?" Vi said, turning to her. "Did he just say, fly?"

Mara swallowed hard this time. In truth, she wasn't ready, but they had no other choice.

"Yes. It's the only way to reach my brother in time," she replied. Turning toward Sorn, she said, "Ready as I'll ever be, I suppose. How will this work, exactly?"

"Well, I forgot to bring my saddle, if that's what you mean?" Sorn said with a snicker.

"Oh, I didn't–"

"I know. I'm kidding. This is a first for me, too. I guess just hop on and we'll figure it out together."

Mara's face portrayed her lack of confidence in his reply.

"Don't worry, Mara. I've got you. You'll just have to trust me." Sorn paused. She heard him move a little closer to her. "Do you trust me, Mara?"

Mara hesitated for a second, but after a moment, slowly nodded.

"Yes, I trust you. Let's get this over with. I'm worried we've already wasted too much time."

"Hold on," said Vi. "Can I get an explanation here? For starters, how are you friends with a dragon, Mara?"

"It's... a long story," Mara said. "But basically, he's the one I've been meeting in the Dream. I will be safe with Sorn, I promise."

"Okay..." Vi said. "I don't like this, but if it's to save Kai, then I guess I'll just have to be okay with it."

"Thanks, Vi," Mara replied, trying to reassure her friend. "I promise, once this is all over, there will be plenty of time for explaining everything."

"Yes, indeed," Sorn said, butting in. "But right now, we must hurry. I'm ready when you are, Mara. Just give me a moment to transform," he said, moving away from them.

Mara listened as Sorn shifted into a dragon before them, a truly strange image propelling into her mind. She wished she could see it herself. Vi tugged on Mara's arm, pulling them a few steps backwards as Sorn grew in size, assuming his full stature. Though she couldn't see it, she felt his presence growing larger, as if the magic surrounding him grew in size with it.

"I'm not sure if this is the most terrifying or the coolest thing I've ever seen," Vi said, her tone more serious than joking. Mara chuckled again.

"I wish I could see it," Mara sighed.

"Alright, I'm ready," Sorn said, now in a deep, guttural tone.

"Thanks for your help, Vi," Mara said, turning to her friend with a smile. "Just remember to keep this quiet. Hopefully, we'll be back before anyone starts asking too many questions."

"Of course, Mara," Vi replied, squeezing Mara's hand. "Now, go save that reckless brother of yours. And be careful," she said.

"I will," replied Mara.

"I was talking to *him*, but yes—you too."

"Oh, right. Well, we will both be careful. Can you help me up on Sorn's back?"

"Sure."

Vi walked Mara forward as she lifted her arm, her hand outstretched. Mara felt a tingling sensation in it for a few seconds before finally feeling his scales against her fingertips. She paused there for a moment, feeling their connection strengthen. It was odd to be finally meeting him in person, and in his true form, yet Mara felt a peace come over her. Even though she was terrified at what was about to happen, it felt right.

"You good?" Vi asked, pulling Mara from her thoughts.

"Em, yes... sorry," Mara replied awkwardly. She felt Sorn's conflicted thoughts as well.

Mara reached out her hands, trying to find something to grab hold of. She found the ridges along his spine and pulled herself up, Vi using her hands to give her something to push her foot off of. It took a minute for her to nestle into a spot along his back, fidgeting until she felt as secure as she was going to be.

"You ready up there?" Sorn asked.

"I'm terrified, but yes, I think I'm comfortable."

"Well, don't get too comfortable. I don't expect this to be a regular occurrence."

"I hope not," she replied, smiling weakly.

"Just keep low and hold on tight. I will keep you steady up there as best I can," Sorn reassured her.

"Okay..." Mara still felt uneasy.

"Thanks, Vi," Mara said, turning where she thought her friend was standing. "We'll see you soon."

"You better," Vi said, taking steps backwards.

Sorn crouched his hind legs, and Mara felt his body moving, widening, a slight wind pushing her hair to the side. Feeling her panic increasing, she sensed Sorn's reassurance in her mind. She felt her nervousness lessen, though she still gripped his spines firmly.

Quickly, Sorn moved, picking up speed, the gentle wind from before now swirling about Mara rigorously. She felt her heart sink into her stomach, felt the ground lifting away from her, heard the sound of the trees struggling against the beating of his wings. It was chaos all around her, like being caught in the middle of a storm, and then, calm. The cool wind brushed against her face, and the world fell quiet. It was thrilling, and terrifying, at the same time. Perhaps not being able to see it herself was a unfortunate stroke of luck.

Mara could never have imagined how drastically different her life would be from the hopes and dreams she'd had as a child. Yet, despite nothing seeming to have gone as planned, it somehow felt right. There was still much fear in her chest at what was yet to come, but her thoughts drifted to the conversations she'd had with Kai just a short while ago. Perhaps, this was the purpose her and her brother had been searching for. However, there was still much to do. She needed to save Kai and end this war. And that, she thought, would probably be even harder than flying blind on the back of an elder dragon.

CHAPTER FIFTY-FIVE

CLOUDS

Kai gazed up at the sky between the thickening tree cover. The sun was moving further west, and by now, fewer and fewer of its rays penetrating the thickening greenery above. As he moved deeper into the mountains, the trees had grown thicker and larger. The snow was also deeper–much deeper than the last time he'd been here, his horse slowing a little because of it. The sky was mostly clear at present, but the clouds of winter had obviously been busy.

Apart from the sounds of his horse's breathing and the metallic chinking of his gear as he rode, the woods were deathly quiet. The thick snow made even the horse's footfalls barely audible. Kai tried to focus his own breathing, thinking on the task ahead. He hadn't really devised any sort of a plan other than to ride out and face her, hoping his powers would serve him again when needed. But he still didn't even know how to control them, let alone summon them. And then there was the matter of him potentially passing out again. Now that his goal was much closer, he realized he needed to have some sort of backup plan should things go wrong.

He turned and glanced at his spear, which was fastened to a holder on the saddle. The Order had them custom made, just for the knights. As he looked at the spear, he heard the words of Cyrus in his head.

The spear is a Dragonblood's greatest weapon...

He'd gotten quite good with it over the years, but would it be enough to face an elder dragon alone?

A sound, like a heavy gust of wind, drew Kai's attention, the trees ahead of him shuddering momentarily as it twisted their limbs, sending snow floating to the forest floor. It seemed to have come from above, but as he looked toward the sky, he saw nothing.

A stray gust of wind?

He rode along for another minute before the sound came again, off to his right. Kai thought he caught a hint of movement in the sky up above it, but the gaps in the trees were so small he wasn't even sure if he had seen anything. His horse snorted and shifted underneath him, slowing its pace.

"Easy, girl," he said, patting her neck as he pulled her to a stop. He looked around the woods again, both at the ground floor and the treetops. But still, he saw nothing.

He wanted to believe it was just stray winds in the mountains, but he knew better. His horse snorted again, acting a bit jittery. Kai patted her some more, turning his head around to look behind them.

As his eyes scanned westward, he saw it. It was a slight hint of movement on the forest floor, and it was moving fast, the billowing of trees and flurrying of snow following it. It was erratic, and hard to pin down as it circled directly behind Kai. There was no questioning what it was now.

The beast was moving in the sky, casting shadows in the small traces of sunlight on ground. It was moving directly toward him—and fast.

Kai kicked his horse, the action causing her to jump before starting at a full run. He glanced up just in time to see the form of a dragon soar directly above them, heading in a northerly direction.

The dragon craned its neck down and to the side as it flew over, locking its gaze with his own as it passed over a larger opening above. Its fierce red eyes emanated malice, and he was certain he saw it grin, as if she were mocking him. Even in a different form, Kai knew those eyes well. He returned her gaze momentarily with a distasteful expression until she sped up and soared out of his view.

Kai kicked his horse to speed up, though he could feel her resistance now that she knew of the dragon's presence. Kai continued to look up as he raced through the woods, catching glimpses of the princess Nalaen, dodging and weaving overhead, their gaze meeting several more times.

She's luring me out into the open. She can't land with the thick tree cover.

Kai thought he knew what she was playing at and decided to stay where the trees were thickest. He continued to pursue her but remained cautious. He did not want to be caught off guard by whatever strategy she was trying to employ. He would stick to the trees until he knew more.

This game of hide and seek continued for some time before Kai realized they'd strayed far from the path that wound to the old ruins. From underneath the trees, he couldn't tell where they were exactly, but it felt like they'd gone a bit more north than he would have expected, which put them further east of the ruins.

Where is she taking me?

Kai tried to remember the maps of the region. He remembered vaguely where the ruins were, but north of the ruins there wasn't much of anything except mountains and forest for miles, so he had no frame of reference to navigate with. He slowed his horse to a trot, trying to listen for the sounds of Nalaen's flight. He hadn't seen her in at least a few minutes and was worried he'd lost her.

It was hard to hear over his horse's heavy breathing, but the woods were silent again. Giving his horse a brief rest, they continued at a steady pace, Kai's eyes constantly scanning the skies.

"Sorry girl, I know you're tired. Catch your breath. You're doing great."

Now that he had a minute to slow down and pay more attention to his surroundings, Kai noticed the wind had picked up a bit. The sky was still mostly clear, but he noted some thicker cloud cover through the trees that hadn't been there earlier. He knew storms could come out of nowhere in the mountains and was worried they were about to be caught in one, but he still couldn't see much from the ground floor. However, there was a mountain to his right, and he figured maybe now was a good time to try and get some elevation and see what he could observe.

Just as he was about to pull on the reigns and veer right, he heard another gush of wind, Nalaen flying overhead again. He waited, trying to decide if he should alter his course and get a better view, or if he should continue to pursue her. His thoughts were mixed, but the frustration building inside him caused him to kick his horse, continuing the chase.

He rode on again, as before, for some time, all the while catching glimpses of scales and wings overhead. It seemed as though Nalaen was not aware of his exact location. The trees were still thick, and their gaze didn't meet anymore. Kai figured she had to know he was down there. Either way, he tried to keep whatever advantage he could, even if it was small.

At last, Kai saw the trees thinning, and what looked like a clearing up ahead. He slowed his mount and approached cautiously, not wanting to lose the tree cover. Needing to get a better view of the clearing without exposing himself, he decided to dismount and approach on foot. He tied his horse to a nearby tree, some thirty feet back from the edge of the clearing, and pulled his spear from its holder, placing it at his back. Once secure, he crept slowly forward, using the trees as cover.

At the edge of the tree line, Kai peered out into the open field before him. It was a large area, a hundred or more feet from one side to the other. To Kai's right, he saw the slope of a mountain starting upward. He could see part of the cliff facing him, littered with large boulders, their outlines only broken by sparse trees and shrubs. To the left, down where the field ended, sat more forest. All in all, it was the perfect place for Nalaen's ambush. Kai's eyes moved to the sky, looking for any signs of her, but she was nowhere to be seen.

Definitely an ambush.

He scanned again and thought about what to do, now realizing the sky was almost completely covered in clouds. The wind blew colder now, too. A storm was surely approaching, and from the looks of it, wasn't far off. He knew going out in the open was a bad idea, so he decided to skirt the edge of the clearing and head toward the hills to the right. If she was in hiding, that was most assuredly where she'd be. Perhaps he could get around her and take her by surprise.

Kai looked back at his horse, who was standing nervously, watching Kai in return. He needed to be quiet, so he left her there and moved forward on foot. It took him a few minutes to get to where the incline of the mountain's slope started, and once he did, he stopped there for a short time to take note of every possible route he could take.

The land split here. To his left, the slope of the mountain rose steeply, lined with large boulders and plenty of places to hide–both for Kai, and for Nalaen. But to the right, the land descended downward below a sheer cliff that reached up high to the mountain above. If the threat of imminent danger wasn't so great, Kai would have considered this a beautiful place to rest for some time. But there was no time for rest; Kai needed to decide which course to take.

He eyed the path to the right, his eyes following the cliffside up to its top. He wondered if it would be possible to scale it. The thought of creeping around large boulders, just waiting to get ambushed, was not exactly appealing, but the cliff looked like it would be difficult to scale, especially with his gear and the approaching storm. He looked back and forth between the two routes, trying to make up his mind. Finally, with a look of indecision, he decided to head right, getting a closer look at the cliff before making the call.

He moved quietly, watching the top of the cliff high above for any signs of movement. The path wound downward toward the base of the rocks, Kai moving from tree to tree at a steady pace until he came within a couple dozen feet of the cliff's base. Peering out from behind the tree in front of him, he saw a small opening at the very base of the rock wall. It looked like a cave, but from this angle, he couldn't quite tell. Taking one more gaze upward for any signs of his foe, he stood and carefully approached the opening.

Kai quietly pulled the spear from his back, skirting to the right to get a better view of the opening, keeping his spear pointed toward it. It was dark inside the hole but appeared to go into the mountain beyond the few feet he could see inside. Kai stopped, looking up at the cliffside above him. It was a straight ascent up. He looked back at the cave, the wheels in his head turning as he started to devise a new plan.

It could work. If I can take away her advantage, then I can win this. If it's safe, maybe I can lead her inside, set up my own ambush.

It seemed like the best option, but he needed to check out the cave further to see if his plan would actually work. Apprehensive, and keeping his spear raised, he stepped into the darkness of the narrow passageway.

High above, waiting patiently atop the cliff's edge, Nalaen hid, watching Kai enter the cave below. When he disappeared into its shadows, she grinned.

***

"How are you doing up there?" Sorn asked, turning his head to the side to get a quick peek at Mara. She looked pale, as if she was going to pass out at any moment.

"I'm... fine," she replied, a quiver in her voice. Sorn laughed.

"Mara, you look anything but fine. You almost look worse than when you were trapped in the Dream."

"Right, well, I guess mild dementia and dark delusions aren't nearly as bad as flying blind."

"That bad, huh?"

Mara simply nodded.

"Well, good news is I can see the ruins now, so we're not far off. I can have your feet back on the ground momentarily. We'll need to be ready, though."

"I'll do my best. Might take me a second to compose myself."

"Fair enough," Sorn replied, straining his eyes, scanning for any signs of his sister. They were still a way off, but if she was flying around, he'd be able to see her. So far, there was no sign of her. He did notice the dark clouds brewing beyond the ruins, however.

They continued for another couple minutes, Sorn swooping down low to just above the treetops to try and gain the element of surprise. His sister would not be happy to see him, especially considering the passenger he was carrying.

Much closer now, Sorn surveyed the area around the ruins. It didn't look like there was anything going on. That was either a good sign, or a very bad one.

"We're coming in for a landing," Sorn noted for Mara. "Hold on tight."

"Do you see them?"

"I do not."

Sorn felt Mara's grip loosen slightly when the words left his maw, but as he spread his wings, slowing their descent, he felt her squeeze again. He tried to land as softly as he could, touching his hind feet down first, easing onto the front, keeping his back as straight as possible. It was a feat more awkward than he'd anticipated, but he managed well enough.

Relaxing his feet in the fresh snow, he turned around to check on Mara.

"How are you–"

Mara slid off his back, smacking the ground with a light thud. The snow softened her fall, but it still looked a bit painful. Sorn cringed, watching her roll up on her hands and knees. He watched in dismay as Mara turned the snow in front of her a brownish-green color.

"Sorry..." Sorn offered once she appeared to be finished. "Did I come in too fast?"

"No..." Mara replied, taking a deep breath before wiping her face with her sleeve. "No, it's fine. I just don't think I'm cut out for flying." She took another minute, trying to collect herself as Sorn scooted away from the stink that was now hitting his nose.

He focused back on the ruins, spotting no signs that his sister or Kai had been there. Sorn grew puzzled, wondering what could have happened. They should have been here. It's where his sister told Kai to come.

Sorn's attention was drawn to the northeast, noticing again the heavy clouds rolling their way. He took one last look around the ruins before turning back to Mara.

"There's a storm coming," he said to her.

"They're not here, are they?" Mara asked, ignoring his previous comment, standing up and turning her head his direction.

"They are not. And it doesn't look like they've been here, either. Do you know what route your brother would have taken to get here?"

"Southeast, most likely, from the road between the towers."

"I know the road. I remember seeing it. Perhaps my sister intercepted him somewhere along that route?"

"We better check, and fast. I'm getting a sinking feeling in my stomach that something is very wrong."

"You mean besides the pile of your last meal in the snow there?"

Mara frowned, turning her head his direction.

"Sorry, sorry. I shouldn't joke. Well then, do you think you can manage more flying?"

"I'll have to. No other choice, really," Mara said, starting to take a step toward him.

"You might want to step to the right a bit further," Sorn interjected.

"Right... thanks," Mara said, scooting carefully to the right, holding her hands up to find his side. She found it and felt her way over to his midsection, surprisingly finding the spot on her own where she'd climbed up previously. As her hands skimmed his scales, the strange sensation teemed through Sorn again. He could feel the power emanating through her fingertips. While they searched, perhaps they could work on his plan.

"Are you ready?" he asked once she had found her previous sitting spot and settled in.

"Yes, let's go."

"No more hurling now."

"Don't worry, I think I'm good. I feel much better."

"That's good," Sorn replied with a slight chuckle. Mara replied with her own uncomfortable laugh.

Sorn spread his wings and flapped them gently, leaping with all four of his legs, sending them effortlessly into the air. It was only his second liftoff with a passenger, but he felt like it was already an improvement over the first.

"Mara," Sorn said once they were back in the air, and once he felt Mara's nerves calm again.

"Yes?" she asked.

"I had a thought about how you can channel your power through me."

"Oh?"

"I don't mean this in a weird way, but when you touch me, I can feel it flowing into me ever so slightly. I think, if you focus, you can create a channel of energy that I can tap into. Without any sort of training, this might be the only way."

"Okay. So, just focus and channel my power into you with my hands. That's it?"

"Theoretically, but of course there's more to it than that. We can give it a try now if you want."

"Sure. So, create a channel..." Mara said out loud, more to herself than to Sorn.

Sorn could feel her hands holding him firmly as she concentrated, though that wasn't much different than before. He thought he felt a few short pulses of energy as she continued to try. He reached out in response, hoping to tap into it, but the pulses came and went too quickly, and he wasn't able to establish a connection with it.

"I can feel small pulses of energy, but I don't think you're focused enough," Sorn advised.

"I'm trying to focus, but I don't really know what to focus on."

Sorn thought for a moment. In truth, he didn't really know either.

"Just try to focus on me; the feel of my scales, the wind as it whips around our bodies, the sound of my voice. Try to focus on my thoughts and see if you can reach out to them."

"Okay..." Mara said, doubt in her voice.

Sorn felt more short pulses, none of which he could tap into. There was one longer one, and his window was better, but he still couldn't seem to connect with her. Finally, Mara grunted in exasperation.

"I don't know what I'm doing wrong. I just don't know how to do this. It's no use."

Sorn could hear the defeat in Mara's tone. He wanted to reassure her, tell her to try again, but wasn't sure what to say. He turned his attention to the landscape in front of them, searching for any signs of movement.

"Any sign of them?" Mara asked quietly after a little while had passed.

"No, nothing yet."

"Where are you, Kai?" Sorn heard Mara speak quietly. "I wish I could feel your presence."

Mara's words struck Sorn in a peculiar way, giving him an idea.

"Mara, let's try one more time." He heard her sigh in response. "I have an idea. Pretend I'm Kai."

"What?"

"You obviously have a strong connection with your brother. Maybe if you pretend that I'm him, you can focus on me and generate a stronger connection."

"Umm, okay..." Mara said. "Not sure that's going to be easy, but I guess I can try."

Sorn felt Mara attempting again. The pulses resumed, as they had before, flashing erratically, with several longer pulses. But as before, it still wasn't enough.

"I can't," she said, sounding as though she was about to start crying.

"It's not your fault. I know I'm not even close to your brother, so how about this. Don't pretend I'm your brother. Just think about him. Think about how much you want to find him. Think about the last time you were with him and were happy. Try to conjure those same feelings."

"Fine, I can try that," Mara said somberly, though there was a hint of hope in her voice.

Sorn waited as she focused. Slowly, he felt the pulses start. Again, they came sporadically, but as the seconds went by, they seemed to grow slower and steadier, pulsing longer and longer, a little bit at a time. Sorn decided to wait this time, not trying to tap into them right away, but instead just letting Mara continue to focus her energy.

Over the next minute, the pulses of energy got longer and closer together. It still wasn't a steady stream, but it was a promising improvement. Sorn eventually began to feel a tingling sensation. It started in his back where Mara had her hands, and it slowly began to spread outward to his extremities. He wanted to speak up, to tell her she was doing great, but he also didn't want to interrupt what they had going on. So, he continued to fly in silence, waiting for the right moment.

And then the moment hit.

It was like a jolt of lighting in Sorn's body, a wave of energy rushing through him that sent him hurtling through the sky at an increased speed. He felt Mara flinch as they took off, and the bond wavered, but didn't break. Sorn tried to get this new energy under control, but it was so intense he felt himself struggling to steady it.

Suddenly, there was a stark sensation, like a tingling sense of danger coming from their left. Both Sorn and Mara sensed that the other had felt the same thing. The stream of energy between them flickered, then died out. After another few seconds, Mara seemed to snap out of whatever trance she'd fallen into.

"Did you feel that?" she asked, sounding a bit confused.

"I did. What was that?"

"I think it was Kai."

Sorn turned his neck, looking at Mara, then in the direction the sensation had come from. He nodded, tilting his left wing downward as the other rose, sending them twisting in a sharp turn and headed in a northeasterly direction.

"Hurry, Sorn," Mara said, gripping him tightly. "My brother's in trouble."

Sorn raised his wings, pushing them downward with a strong force, the remnants of Mara's energy still flowing through them. He felt Mara's strong grip as they sped up. But now, it wasn't fear so much as it was renewed determination and concern.

Sorn, having also felt it, knew they needed to hurry.

***

Cyrus dropped off his horse and inspected the impacts in the snow, trying to discern what had happened. They'd been following Kai's tracks for a little while now, and they had been steadily following the path that he'd expected Kai to take. But looking at the scene before him, he was trying to understand what had happened.

"What do you make of it, Caliena?" he asked as she came up beside him on foot.

"I'm not sure, sir. There doesn't seem to be any signs of a struggle, but something definitely caused him to stop here. And whatever it was, probably made his horse nervous."

"The tracks lead north, but the princess told him to meet her at the ruins."

"Aye, she did. I don't know why he'd head north. Maybe he wanted to come at the ruins from a different direction?"

"Yes, that's possible, and a good idea. She'd probably expect him to come this way, but we're still a good hour or more ride. Seems like this is a bit too early to head north."

"Can't be too cautious, especially with dragons."

Cyrus nodded his head at Caliena's remark, but he had his doubts. He studied the tracks in the snow for another minute in silence as she ventured a little further up the path in the direction of the ruins, all the while his eyes scanning the skies.

After a few minutes, Cyrus turned back and glanced around at the rest of the knights, most of whom were scouring the woods nearby for any other signs of what might have happened. As he watched them for any indication that they'd found something, he saw Caliena returning, a look of concern about her.

"What is it?" he asked as she approached.

"Storm's comin', and it looks like a big one. I imagine there will be a fresh coating of snow here within the hour. If we don't hurry and catch up to Kai, we will likely lose his tracks."

"Where's it coming from?" Cyrus asked, growing concerned himself.

Caliena frowned, then turned and pointed. It was exactly the way Kai's tracks led. A very real fear gripped Cyrus.

"Mount up!" he yelled. "Storm's coming, and we're running out of time. We need to move now."

Everyone climbed back on their horses and started after Cyrus as he raced off, following Kai's tracks into the woods. Wherever Kai had gone, very soon, they'd have no way of finding him. They were running out of time.

Chapter Fifty-Six

DARKNESS

Kai trekked through the darkness of the cave for some time, wondering how deep it went into the mountain. Fortunately, thanks to Cyrus's behest, Kai had prepared before he'd left, which meant he had a torch with him. Kai smiled momentarily as he looked at it, thankful for Cyrus's friendship, even though he felt a hint of embarrassment at not waiting. His smile faded quickly, thinking about how disappointed Cyrus must have been that he had left before he could offer any sort of plan. He wondered what Cyrus was doing at this very moment, wondering if perhaps they had followed him to try and help. Perhaps even now they were on his trail, trying to catch up to him. Kai stopped and hesitated, looking back the way he'd come.

No, I can't go back. This is my fight. I need to be the one to end this. No one else needs to get hurt.

He continued for another few minutes before he felt the narrow cave start to open wider into what seemed to be a much larger cavern. He couldn't see beyond the ring of light cast by his torch, but he could tell it was much bigger because the sounds of his movements were echoing, where before they'd been quite muffled.

Kai explored this new cavern, trying to understand just how large it was. As he moved about, he was surprised by its size, not having expected to find anything this extensive based on the first part of the cave. Again, a part of him wanted to go back. A part of him wanted to leave this place, feeling he might have made the wrong decision to come inside.

"This is much bigger than I expected," he said aloud, voicing his inner thoughts, continuing through the large, open space. "I don't know if this will work, and I don't want to get lost." His voice echoed, the reverberations of it a haunting sound that sent chills down the back of his neck. He turned back toward the way he'd come, looking for the hole that would lead him out. But when he went to where he thought it had been, he only found a solid wall.

"That's funny. I thought it was right here." Kai walked a dozen paces to the left but found no exit. He walked back even further to the right. Still, there was no way out.

"I didn't walk that far, did I?" He paused, thinking. *Did I?* He continued to walk around the edge of the room, dodging boulders and pillars of stone that seemed to fill the huge cavern.

Finally, after another minute of searching, he heard the slight sound of wind up ahead. As he drew closer, he saw the hole in the wall that led out of the cavern. He let out a sigh of relief, moving to step into it.

"So sure that's the way out, are we?"

Kai's heart skipped a beat, freezing in fear for a brief moment. Regaining himself, he spun, drawing his spear, peering into the darkness for the source of the deep voice. He held the flame higher, trying to cast the light as far as possible.

"Who's there?" he asked, mustering up the courage.

"Come now, you're smarter than that, Kai. Surely you must know." Her voice was much deeper, but it still carried the same undertones he'd heard before.

"I know it's you," Kai replied, admitting what he already knew to be true. He glanced around, trying to locate her position, but all he could see was darkness. With the echoes, it was hard to pinpoint exactly which direction her voice was coming from.

"Very good. Now that we have cleared that up, let's have a little chat, shall we?"

"Why? We both know why you're here. Let's get this over with."

"So hasty to die, are you? But what about dear Mara? Don't you want to know how to find her?"

"You already told me," Kai said, sounding irritated as he continued to move about the cavern looking for her.

"Yes, well, things have changed. But you're here, so I'm guessing you don't know. How unfortunate. I suppose I'll enlighten you. Oh, and you can stop looking for me. You won't find me like that."

"We'll see."

"You won't get to your sister without finding my brother. She's with him."

"Right, like I said, you already told me. Find your brother, force him to release her from this... dreamworld."

"Oh, but he already has."

"What?" Kai stopped looking momentarily, confused by this new revelation.

"Yes. It seems my dear, traitorous brother has decided he quite likes your sister. So much so that he would betray me, setting her free from my trap. Right now, they are probably together doing who knows what, apathetic about what befalls us."

"No, you're lying. She wouldn't."

"Why would I lie? I have nothing to hide from you... not anymore, at least. Only one of us is leaving this cave alive. In the off chance it's you, better you know the truth. That's all I want."

"The truth, really? You just want to turn me against my sister. Maybe your brother did betray you, but I saw my sister asleep when I left. She wouldn't wake. No, she would never betray me."

There was a deep sigh from the darkness as Kai continued to search the chasm for any sign of Nalaen.

"Don't believe me? Fine, I'll show you..."

A dim light flickered up ahead of Kai. He froze, eyeing it warily, his spear trained on it. It was like a swirling mist of light, slowly morphing into a picture before him. At first, it was incoherent waves of color, but gradually the picture became clear. It was an image of his sister riding on a dragon's back. The dragon was blue in color, and Kai's mind went back to the fight near the tower. He had been there; he was the one who flew the princess away as her sister attacked. It was her brother, and he saw Mara smiling at him.

"No..." Kai said.

"I told you."

"No, this can't be real."

"Oh, it's real. I'll admit, even I didn't know what we'd see. But like I thought, they are together. Seems they've bonded rather quickly. Makes me sick that he let her ride him, like he's some kind of... animal."

Mara, why? Kai's thoughts were clouded. He struggled to believe what Nalaen had said–what she'd shown him. But it felt real, and for some reason Kai believed the dragon was telling the truth.

"Yes. It hurts, doesn't it–the betrayal of your own flesh and blood. They've been meeting for some time, too. I'm guessing she never told you."

Was that what she was dealing with before? Why didn't she tell me?

"Of course, why would she? You were busy trying to figure out your own powers. She needed you, and you left her alone. Hence why she sought refuge in my brother's arms."

No... Mara, I'm so sorry.

"I knew my brother was weak. I didn't expect him to betray me so boldly, but I can't say I was all that surprised, either. But your sister... well, do you know the only reason I had her trapped in the first place was because of my brother?"

"What do you mean?" Kai asked, hints of despair creeping into his voice.

"She was meeting him in the Dream. They spent some time together there before I discovered what he was up to. And once I invaded the Dream with them, it was he who helped me trap her there. Of course, he saved her in the end, but it's a wonder she survived that long at all. Many would have gone mad staying in the Dream for days. Your sister is strong–much stronger than I expected. Perhaps, even stronger than you..."

Kai's spear arm dropped, his body's tension beginning to melt away, the weight of Nalaen's words piercing him like a dagger. He knew the danger he was in, but what did it matter if his sister wasn't even in danger–if she didn't even care? Everything he'd been thinking, everything he'd been holding inside, it had all led to this moment. Everything he'd blamed himself for was true. Even the princess, who knew nothing of his past, could see it so clearly.

Kai shook his head, trying to keep the intrusive thoughts out. *She wouldn't...*

"Sorry to be the one to break it to you."

"Don't pretend like you care about me," Kai said, suddenly more aware of her presence again. There was a hint of anger in his tone now, like the voice of one who felt betrayed.

"I... understand you, Kai. You and I are more alike than you realize."

"We are nothing alike."

"Oh, but we are. Our parents are dead, our loved ones have betrayed us. Both of us have been told lies our entire lives."

"Lies? What lies?" Kai asked.

"I just found out that my kind and yours, your Order, we used to work together. We were allies, even, though I can scarcely believe it myself."

"There's no way that's true," Kai said in disbelief. "I've had enough of your lies. Come out and face me."

"Oh, believe me, I wish it wasn't true. My brother was the one who told me, and I didn't believe him either. I was furious, even, but after I calmed myself, it hit me. I've been searching for truth for many years, and I've known the history of the world is not always what has been written. What Sorn and your sister found, they saw it firsthand in the Dream. I won't explain it to you, but I believe it now, though there still remains many more lies to uncover. If only you hadn't pushed your sister away, like I did with Sorn, then perhaps she would have trusted you and told you herself. And yet, he still told me in the end."

"Enough!" Kai shouted, dropping to his knees, the tip of his spear hitting the stone floor as he fell, his torch also coming to rest on the ground. His eyes flashed ever so slightly when he shouted, fading quickly as he slumped to the floor.

Kai felt defeated. He wanted to be angry, but everything he had heard weighed on his thoughts. He expected the princess would lie to him, but what if she wasn't? What if all of it *was* true? There were bits and pieces of it that made sense. Mara had been acting strange, and Kai knew she'd been withholding something from him. And if the princess wasn't lying about those things, then it made sense that all of it might be true. And if it was, then what was the point? He was still the same failure despite all that had changed.

As Kai sat there on his knees, drowning in his conflicted thoughts, he failed to notice the pair of glowing red eyes that were watching him intently from high above in the cavern. Nalaen had remained concealed up above on a ledge, careful not to let her eyes show as he'd searched for her.

Slowly and quietly, Nalaen spread her wings and descended to a ledge much closer to Kai. There was a small gust of air as she did so, but it was mostly muffled by the sounds of wind already echoing through the cavern. She paused, crouching, waiting to see if Kai noticed.

She placed her claws down the side of the rocks and leaned forward, accidentally knocking loose some small stones, creating a noise in stark contrast to the dull howl of the winds in the tunnels. She stopped as Kai stirred, holding his torch up a bit higher, looking around for a moment.

"So, where does that leave us then?" he asked. His voice was soft, his tone callous. "If what you say is true, then what's the point of all of this? What's the point of even fighting?"

"That is a fair question, human. You want to know the point? It's simple, really." Nalaen continued to inch over the side of the ledge. "I am soon to be queen of all the dragon realms—a position I will assume only because my mother is no longer here to sit the throne. Your uncle and the others in your so-called Order stole her from me. But that is not why I want you all dead. I know that when I sit on that throne, I will not become all the queens who've sat on it before me. My actions will not be determined by the past. Whether we worked together ages ago or not, I will make my own decisions. I will rule as I see fit. But in order to ascend to that which is mine, I must prove to the world I am not bound by the same failures as all the queens before me. They were weak... even my mother. So, you must see."

Nalaen descended the ledge as she spoke, creeping ever closer to Kai. Her jaws were mere feet away from him now, his back still turned away from her as he sat and listened. If only he'd turned around, he would have seen the light of the fire reflected on her face. The malice in her eyes glowed hot as she emerged from the darkness behind him, so close to her victory.

"Even if I wanted to spare you, I can't."

Nalaen spread her jaws, turning her head to the side, ready to bite Kai in half within seconds.

"Fine. Just get it over with, then..." Kai said, closing his eyes, dropping both his torch and the spear on the ground. "Take your vengeance and leave my people alone, as you promised."

Nalaen paused for a moment, a bit surprised by his utter defeat. It seemed her plan had worked even better than she'd thought. Her jaws moved past Kai's head, ready to bite. But when she went to close them around him, something stopped her.

It was as if an invisible force was holding her jaws open. Her mind raced with thoughts, trying to understand what was happening. And then she felt it—the tiny prick of energy in the back of her skull. She focused on it, following the trace of its pull to wherever it was coming from. An image of Sorn flashed in her mind's eye, and on his back sat Mara. They were flying over the mountains, looking down on the one where deep below, in the darkness of the cave, Nalaen was inches away from her victory. Somehow, they'd found her. Somehow, Sorn was keeping her from ending Kai's life.

Using my own magic against me, Brother? You have grown bold, she called out to him.

Nalaen, you need to stop this. This isn't right. This isn't going to bring Mother back.

You still think this is about Mother? And I thought you were the smart one. What else could this possibly be about?

This is about showing the world that I am fit to wear the crown–that I am fit to rule the dragon kingdoms, and maybe even more. Mother was weak, just like her mother, and all the Mothers before, all the way back to Liotha herself. If what you said before was true, then she was the weakest of us all. I will not make the same mistakes. I will not be weak.

Nalaen... Sorn's hold on her weakened, just momentarily, her jaws inching closer to Kai. She felt a surge of power and her jaws stopped again.

You can't fight me forever, Brother, she said, using all her might to fight him. *I will have blood.*

"Mara, you must hurry," Sorn said, straining under the connection he was maintaining with his sister. "I don't know what's wrong with Kai, but he's just sitting there. Can't you reach him?"

"I'm trying," Mara exclaimed, her voice wrought with desperation. "Kai! Kai, please hear me. I'm here, Kai. Get up!"

Mara couldn't see Kai with her mind, but she could feel his presence under the mountain below them. She could feel the aura of despair that surrounded him. It was like he'd given up. She tried desperately to use her mind to reach him–to punch through the barrier of hopelessness surrounding him.

"Mara, you need to hurry. I can't–" Sorn pleaded, straining himself further. "I can't hold her much longer like this. They're too deep underground."

Nalaen's jaws began to quiver, continuing to resist her brother's attempt to stop her. Within moments, she would be free.

"Kai!" Mara called out again, understanding the urgency.

"You can do it, Mara," Sorn said. "You are strong enough. Focus your mind solely on him. I'll hold my sister, but you have to reach him now!"

Kai... Mara's words drifted through time and space, pouring every ounce of herself into this last attempt.

Mara? Clear as day, Mara heard her name.

Yes, Kai. I'm here. You're in danger. You need to get out of there, now.

Mara, why would you betray me? You chose him over me?

What are you talking about, Kai? I didn't betray you. We don't have time for this. You need to get out of there!

The dragon... you're with him. Why didn't you tell me?

Kai, I would have, I promise. But everything has been so complicated, and I didn't even know what Sorn was at first. I didn't understand what was happening until you were gone. Kai, please... get up!

It doesn't matter. I understand now. I've failed you. I've failed everyone. Just let me have this one last chance at doing something right... Kai's words hit Mara hard. It broke her heart to hear the despair in his voice. Why had he lost all hope? She scrambled, knowing any second his life could be over, trying to think of what to say to snap him out of it.

"Mara, hurry..." she heard Sorn grunt. He was about to lose his hold on Nalaen.

Kai, do you remember when I was thirteen and you fought those boys off who were making fun of me? Kai didn't reply, but she could feel that he was listening. *You took a serious beating for me that day. I know you've always been protective of me, and I always told you I didn't need protecting. But that was never true. I wanted to be strong when Mom and Dad died, but I just... wasn't. I barely held it together every single day. That is, until the day you fought those boys. That was the day I finally believed I could live without Mom and Dad... because I had you. And the real reason that I wanted to be strong was so that I could protect you, too. I know you never showed it like I did. I know you held it in, but inside, you felt the same. You felt like it was somehow your fault. And if I could be there for you like you were for me, and we could both believe it wasn't either of our fault, then, together we'd somehow survive this. So, you see, I need you, Kai, just like you need me. If there's any piece of my brother left in there, then I need you to grab hold of that, get up, and get back to me. I'm holding out my hand, Kai. I just need you to take it. I need you to let me save you this time.*

There was silence for several seconds, though it felt like an eternity to Mara.

Deep in the dark of the cave, Kai still knelt passively, listening to Mara's words. As the last of them hit him, something stirred within. Kai had been on the brink of a deep darkness, far beyond the darkness of the cave around him. Mara's words pulled him back.

Kai's eyes flashed open, glowing a bright orange, just as Sorn's grasp on Nalaen slipped away. Sensing her presence finally, and faster than he thought was even possible, Kai bent forward and rolled away, reaching out with his hand to the dying flame of his torch still lying on the ground. Pulling it up and growing it in intensity, he flung the fire directly into Nalaen's open jaws as she lunged for him.

Nalaen reared her head backward. She scanned the now dark room, looking for any sign of Kai. It seemed the fire had blinded her temporarily, so she couldn't spot him.

Mere feet to her left, Kai crouched behind a large stone pillar. For some reason, he could see a bit better in the dark now. He spotted his spear on the ground where he'd left it, directly under Nalaen's chest. There was no way he was going to get it. He tried to think quickly of what to do. He had no weapon and needed to get out of the caves.

"That was a lucky break, now wasn't it?" Nalaen said. "Too bad... but you should know," she paused, turning her head toward where he was hiding. "I can see your eyes now!" she bellowed, lunging straight for him, slamming into the pillar, the brief sound of stone cracking before it gave way and crumbled onto the cavern floor around him.

Kai barely had time to dive out of the way. He got up and scrambled toward the closest wall. He didn't even realize his eyes were glowing. No wonder he could see better. He quickly scanned the edges of the cavern, looking for a way out, even as Nalaen was recovering.

There, he thought, spotting the exit. But then other gaps in the cavern walls drew his eyes to two other potential exits. *Which one was it?*

Nalaen, seeming to now be fully recovered, spun around searching for him. She spotted him and leapt, trying to catch him in her jaws as he took off across the cavern. He was moving quickly now, his resolve renewed.

Kai could hear Nalaen behind, clawing her way after him, bouncing into pillars and scattering rocks as she rushed in. He didn't want to fight her down here in the dark, and he had no weapon now. He needed to get up to the surface–back to Mara. But with the princess on his heels, he had to make hasty decisions.

He chose the closest opening, diving into it, hearing Nalaen's jaws snapping right behind him. He rolled as he landed, coming back onto his feet and spinning around to see her trying to reach into the smaller opening. Unable to get through, she locked eyes with Kai for a second. Kai smirked, but saw her grin as she backed up a few feet. Her body began to shrink, morphing into her human form. Kai had almost forgotten, and his eyes grew wide. He turned and began to sprint down the narrow passageway.

I sure hope this leads out, he thought.

Kai ran as fast as he could manage in the dim light of the tunnel. It was a grace his eyes were at least working in his favor at the moment. If they weren't, it would have been nearly impossible to navigate the twisting tunnels in a hasty manner, which by now he realized was probably not the same one he'd used to come in. He shot quick glances backwards, but so far, he hadn't seen Nalaen in pursuit. He thought he heard sounds of movement behind him, but the way the tunnels altered sounds, it was impossible to tell while he was still moving, and he didn't want to slow down to verify.

Up ahead, Kai spotted a divergence in the tunnels, splitting into two paths.

I don't remember that coming down. Definitely a different path. Kai cursed to himself.

He paused only for a second before darting down the right path, no idea if it would lead him to safety. He continued to run, hoping that maybe the split paths would throw Nalaen off his trail.

He continued down the new corridor for a minute before it began to open up, leading into a much wider area. This area, like the cavern where Nalaen had been, was large and riddled with columns of stone, some of which looked to extend from ceiling to floor. Fortunately, there was a small shaft leading upward, letting a bit of light into the room. Though it wasn't much, he could see a bit better. Kai looked around at what he could see, trying to spot a path forward.

This place is a maze.

"I can smell you, Kai. I can hear your breathing. You can't outrun me." Nalaen's voice echoed down the passageway behind him, and he half expected to see her emerging at each word.

Kai began to run again, sprinting down the middle of the cavern, glancing right and left for any signs of where to go next. He was so busy looking for a way out that he almost didn't notice the chasm he was running straight toward.

Kai skidded to a halt, his heart racing as he slid up to the chasm's edge, leaning backward to avoid falling in. Steadying himself, he peered down, but it descended far beyond what his eyes could see.

What is this place? Kai questioned, backing away from the ledge.

He turned his attention up and across the chasm. There was a ledge on the other side, and what looked like a way out, but the gap across was at least twenty feet, probably more. Kai debated attempting it, but quickly decided he didn't want to try. It was too far.

"Where are you?" Nalaen called out.

Kai ducked behind a nearby pillar, peering out to see where she was. He saw her walking out into the cavern, scanning for him.

"You should have gone left. There's no way out of this cavern, except down. Unless, of course, you think you can jump across . But I'm not sure even your kind can make that leap."

Kai eyed it again, judging the gap across the chasm. Was she lying? It was far, and Kai wasn't sure he could do it, even if he believed he could. If he failed, that would be the end of it. Either way, he only had two options–back the way he came or face her. Which was worse? He knew what he'd normally do.

Kai...

It was Mara's voice again. He heard it in his head, but also felt like it was coming from behind him–from the chasm.

Mara?

I'm here, Kai. We're going to get you out of here. But you're going to have to trust me.

Okay. What do you want me to do?

Jump...

Mara, it's too far. I can't jump across that.

Not across. Down.

What? Mara, you can't be serious...

Kai. I know what I'm asking, but you have to trust me. We'll catch you.

Kai looked back at the chasm, swallowing hard, the thought of descending down into its depths twisting a knot in his stomach. He wanted to trust Mara, but the thought terrified him.

Kai, please. You're running out of time.

Kai glanced around the pillar again. Nalaen was getting closer. It was now or never. Kai stood and moved out of hiding, staring Nalaen down as her gaze met his.

"Ah, there you are. Made up your mind then?"

"Yes," Kai replied, glaring at her, his fists clenched.

"Finally found your fight then?"

"Finally making the choice I should have all along," Kai said, slowly stepping backward toward the ledge.

Nalaen frowned, seeming to not understand what he meant. She took several steps toward him, eyeing him warily as he got closer to the chasm. She looked at it, then back at him, her face showing her suspicion.

Kai shuffled as the back of his foot found the ledge. He turned and looked down, swallowing again.

"That's not going to work out well for you," Nalaen offered, still a bit confused.

"We'll see," Kai responded, giving her one last glare. "You may have lost all faith in your family, but I won't give up on mine. I won't give up on Mara. So long, Princess..."

Kai gently let himself fall backward into the void, his heart pounding as he twisted to look downward into the endless dark below. He closed his eyes and felt the wind as it swallowed him whole.

I'm coming, Mara.

I've got you...

Nalaen walked slowly up to the edge, just in time to see Kai disappear into the deep, dark below, beyond what her vision could see. She knew these caves, knew where they led. There was a massive cavern below—one that scaled anything beyond comparison to where she stood now. There was no way he'd—

Then it hit her, what he'd said before. She reached out and felt Sorn's presence somewhere down there in the dark.

Screaming in rage, Nalaen instantly turned back into a dragon, the cracking of bones and stretching of muscles echoing through the darkness, the sound of her wings spreading and beating against the stale cavern air, diving down the abyss's throat in pursuit of Kai. Her eyes flared with a renewed rage, and she pushed herself faster to catch up to him.

Deep below, Mara and Sorn flew through the massive underground cavern. Though Mara couldn't see it, she could feel the enormity of it. Sorn had said these were caves used by the dragons eons ago, and they spanned miles of underground areas below the Thousand Peaks, stretching nearly to the edges of the dragon kingdom itself. Apparently, this cavern was one of the largest. Mara was glad Sorn was so well versed enough to navigate them.

Mara felt the whirl of Kai's emotions as he leapt. She knew he was falling up ahead of them somewhere, and she could feel his presence drawing closer.

"He's coming. Do you see the gap?"

Sorn looked up, scanning the ceiling. There were a dozen gaps, his eyes dodging between them.

"There are multiple. I'll need you to try to guide me."

"I will," Mara replied, focusing as she'd done before, power emanating through her fingertips and into Sorn's body. She still didn't fully understand how she was doing it, but so far, it was working.

After a few seconds, Mara felt Sorn speed up and alter his course. It seemed like it had worked. He had sensed Kai through their connection.

"Got it," he said, reassuring her. "I can feel him now."

Mara sighed, tightening her grip on his spine. Her heart was racing, but she tried to stay focused.

"There he is. Hold tight," Sorn bellowed.

"I'm trusting you, Sorn. Catch my brother!"

Mara felt Sorn tapping into her energy again, speeding up even more. It felt strange but exhilarating at the same time. Either way, right now it served a critical purpose.

Suddenly, Sorn's aura pulsed, and Mara felt a brief moment of fear rush through him.

"What's wrong?" Mara asked.

"Hold on" Sorn bellowed again, tapping into more of Mara's energy. Mara's heartbeat intensified, her thoughts syncing with Sorn's. She instantly understood what was happening.

The race was on—brother against sister. Nalaen had the downward advantage, but Mara's energy was strong. Still, it was going to be close.

Sorn and Nalaen eyed each other as they drew closer. Sorn saw the hate in his sister's eyes—hate for him and the humans alike. It made him sad to see her so, but this was no time to fret over it. She'd made her choice, and he'd made his. All he could do now was see it through.

Time slowed as the two of them came within a wingtip's difference of each other and Kai. Sorn could hear his sister seething, pushing herself to get to Kai first. Sorn aimed just below Kai, trying to get under him so Mara could grab hold of him. He didn't have time to see if she was ready, but he still felt her thoughts in sync with his.

He glanced up at Nalaen as he flew under Kai, her claws outstretched, ready to draw blood from whomever was in reach first. He felt Kai ease gently onto his back as Mara embraced him, a sense of relief as she did. Nalaen's jaws were just feet behind. Sorn didn't think he could avoid her attack. The only thing he could do was swerve at the last second, flinging his tail upward at her.

His tail smashed into her face as he felt her claws latch onto him. He gritted his teeth in pain, spinning, using her downward momentum against her to fling her off and toward the ground. It worked, but she didn't let go of him without tearing off some of his flesh. He cried out as she did, the pain of it more than anything he'd felt in a very long time.

He could feel Mara and Kai shifting on his back while he swirled in the air. He tried to push past the pain, steadying himself, but it was almost too much to bear. He turned, seeing the stone pillar just before they crashed into it, Mara and Kai thrown from his back.

When the black cloud faded from his mind, Sorn lifted his head, looking around at the scene before him. Both Mara and Kai lay unconscious nearby.

At least, he hoped they were only unconscious. He couldn't feel Mara's energy anymore.

He tried to stand, the pain shooting up his back leg, causing him to stumble. He stopped, looking around for his sister. She was on the cavern floor below them, a thirty-foot drop below the rise Sorn had fallen on. She lay still for the moment. Despite what had just happened, he felt fear that she might be dead, too.

Moments later, there was a slight movement in her body, and Sorn sighed, but a new fear quickly took hold. Slowly, she rolled over and back onto her feet, lifting her head to look for them. She spotted him, the same rage still in her eyes, though he could tell she was in pain too. He glanced back at Kai and Mara, who so far hadn't moved. He crawled toward Mara, who was closest to him.

When he was close enough, he nudged her with his snout. She was still warm, and he could feel the energy through her skin. But it was faint now. She was alive, at least.

Kai started to stir, groaning in pain as he forced himself up. He rolled over and looked at Sorn next to his sister, noting her appearance. His expression shifted and he crawled over to her.

"Mara? Mara, are you okay?" he asked. He looked up at Sorn in desperation. His face looked much like Nalaen's, but there was something else there, too. It was as if he wanted to be angry with Sorn, but his sister's life was more important.

"She's alive," Sorn reassured him. "I can feel her energy, though it's faint. We need to get her out of here."

Kai looked down at Mara, grabbing her head and cradling it in his hands.

"Can you get us out of here?" he asked.

"I think so. I'm badly hurt, but I think I can–"

"You're not going anywhere…" Nalaen said, clawing her way on top of the short cliff. Sorn and Kai both turned, watching her as she scaled the edge and stared them down, only a short way away. She stood awkwardly, breathing heavily and carrying herself as if her wounds ailed her greatly.

"Sister, please stop this madness," Sorn pleaded, trying to stand as best he could. His leg throbbed, sending shooting pains up his spine.

"Madness? Oh Sorn, the only madness here is you siding with them. Nevertheless, I'm glad you're here. Saved me the trouble of hunting you down. How fitting that you die at their side."

"I'm not taking sides. I don't want to fight you. I want peace."

"Peace?" Nalaen let out what sounded like a laugh, spitting out some blood. "Peace is an illusion. Peace is a tool the strong use to control the weak. No one really wants peace; they want power. The power to change the world is governed by those strong enough to wield it. Peace only serves passivity. You've read the histories, Sorn. They are written by the powerful. We have a chance to alter the very course of the world–to change history itself. I thought you, most of all, would appreciate that, at least. I guess I was wrong."

Nalaen was pacing along the cliff's edge as she spoke. Sorn watched her, eyeing it as he stayed between her and the twins.

"You're wrong, Sister. Power is only the tool of the oppressor. It corrupts the mind, giving a false sense of control. You can't rule through control no more than you can control the tides. In the end, it wash over you. Abandon this path of vengeance before it leads to your destruction."

Nalaen stared at him, hatred burning in her belly. It seemed as if his words might have changed her attitude momentarily, but suddenly her demeanor shifted and she lifted her head.

"No..." she said. A light grew in her belly, rising to her throat. She turned toward the twins and opened her mouth, sparks spewing forth, a sign of imminent purgatory.

Sorn started to move forward to block her path, but when she went to unleash it, she couldn't. Confused, Sorn looked around. Kai was standing next to him, his hand raised, his eyes bright with their own fire. He realized what the boy was doing. Without hesitation, Sorn dove straight toward his sister, crashing into her, launching both of them over the cliff's edge to the floor below.

The fall wasn't that far, but with all the injuries he'd sustained already, pain spiked through Sorn's body. They rolled when they hit the ground, tumbling over each other until they came to a halt, Nalaen on top. She grabbed him with her claws, pinning him to the ground as he tried to throw her off. He fought back as much as he could, but with his hind leg badly injured, and her digging her rear claws into it, the pain pulsating through his veins caused his muscles to seize up.

"It's time to die, Brother," she said, lifting her head, her jaws open and aimed for his throat.

Sorn closed his eyes, waiting for death to take him, but no bite came.

He opened his eyes, gazing up at her. She was just sitting there, staring at him, her mind seemingly elsewhere. Confused, Sorn moved his head to the side to look past her. There, up on the side of the cliff, was Mara. She was standing at its edge, Kai holding her one arm in his as she stretched out her other toward Sorn. Her face was contorted in concentration.

Sorn looked back at his sister. There was a distant look in her eyes as she struggled against Mara's assault. Sorn couldn't believe it. Somehow, Mara had done it. Somehow, she'd been able to pierce Nalaen's mind on her own.

Nalaen tried to fight it, but she'd left an opening in her defenses. Plus, her body was weak. The stupid girl had awoken and figured out how to use her own magic against her. And try as she might, Nalaen couldn't shake it. How many times had she underestimated that damned girl? Both of them.

It was all Nalaen could do to fight the assault off as the darkness slowly enveloped her, sending her into a deep, nightmarish state of subconsciousness.

So, this is what it feels like.

CHAPTER FIFTY-SEVEN

TEMPEST

"Mara, you should give me control," Sorn said, noting Mara's visible struggle as she focused on maintaining her hold over Nalaen.

"Yes, I think that's a good idea," Mara replied, her voice indicative of her distraught. "Not sure how long I can keep this up. It's a miracle I'm even holding her at all. I can feel her... trying to fight me," she finished, grunting.

"Yeah, we need to do this right away. Give me your hands."

"Okay." Mara reached her hands out, waiting for Sorn to take them.

Sorn took hold of Mara's hands and closed his eyes. He reached out, touching Mara's energy and followed it. It was a twisting mass of tangled threads, but all of them led to the same place. Deep down within her consciousness, Sorn saw the convergence of all Mara's power. It looked like it was throbbing, growing and shrinking as it flickered. Sorn could tell it was all Mara could do to keep the tide of his sister's power at bay. If Nalaen hadn't been injured and weaker than she normally was, she would have likely already broken free.

Sorn gently nudged his own strands of power in place of hers, gradually severing her connection to Nalaen and taking the burden upon himself.

Hearing Mara's voice, Sorn was pulled back to reality.

"What are you doing?" Mara asked, her sigh of relief quickly turning to concern.

Sorn turned, noting Kai was standing feet away from his sister, eyeing her suspiciously.

"Why are we keeping her alive?" Kai asked, eyeing Sorn out of the corner of his eye.

"We don't need to kill her," Mara replied.

"Mara, she killed Uncle, or did you already forget?"

"Of course I didn't forget..." she replied, clearly hurt. "And I don't know if I will ever forgive her for that, but this is much bigger than my feelings, or yours. If she's killed, we could incite a war with the entire dragon nation. And that is something none of us want. Can you agree on that at least?"

"I suppose, but she's still dangerous. How are we planning to keep her from killing anyone else? It's clear we're barely containing her right now, though I won't even begin to try and understand how. But what happens if you can't control her?" Kai looked back at Sorn as he finished speaking, watching the visible strain on his face.

"I can hold her," Sorn said through clenched teeth.

"So you say..." Kai chided. "But for how long?"

"Your brother does have a point, Mara. I can hold her, but not forever. We need to get going. Can you explain this further on the way?"

"Yes, of course. We should get going," Mara acknowledged.

"How is this going to work exactly?" Kai asked, doubt written all over his face. "Can you even fly?"

"Yes, I think so. I'm already starting to heal, though it is slower now with my energy focused on her. Luckily, she didn't damage my wings. It's probably going to hurt, but with Mara's power added to mine, that will help."

"And how does *that* work exactly?" Kai asked.

"You ask a lot of questions, you know that?" Sorn retorted, growing more and more annoyed. He saw Kai give him a discontented look.

"Well, forgive me if I'm not exactly ecstatic to climb on the back of a dragon who just recently found his conscious and who's not only injured but also focused on mind-controlling his sister while we fly miles over mountains and razor-sharp rocks."

"Kai..." Mara said, moving toward him. She was holding out her hand.

Kai relaxed, reaching for it. When she took hold, she pulled him off to the side and spoke softly. Even though they tried to be quiet, Sorn could still hear them.

"It's okay, Kai. I know you don't know Sorn—not like I do, but I'm telling you that you can trust him."

"Mara, weeks ago, he was our enemy. His sister killed Uncle, and he helped! You can't expect me to just... *trust* him after that. Granted, he saved my life back there. But for what? I don't know how someone has a change of heart just like that. I'm still not sure I understand what's happened between you two."

"I know, it's a lot to explain. Much has happened. I didn't trust him either... for a time. But we've seen things. It's too much to explain right now, but I can try on the way back. And if you can't trust him, then just trust me. Can you do that at least?"

Kai rolled his eyes, then looked at Sorn. Sorn glanced away, pretending he wasn't listening.

"Fine," Kai said. "I'll trust *you*."

Mara smiled at Kai, then tugged on his arm, pulling him back toward Sorn. As they approached, Sorn shifted his attention to the two of them with a questioning expression.

"Come to an agreement then?" Sorn asked, a hint of sarcasm in his voice.

"As close as we'll get," Mara replied. "Do you think you two can get along for the ride home?"

"Of course, Mara," Sorn answered, bowing.

"And Kai?" she asked.

"Yes... I suppose," he answered begrudgingly, rolling his eyes again.

"He's rolling his eyes, isn't he?" Mara directed at Sorn.

"Yes. He is," Sorn replied with a smirk in Kai's direction.

Mara let go of Kai's hand and elbowed him in the rib.

"Hey!" Kai exclaimed, glaring at Sorn. Sorn offered a smug smile in return.

"Alright, I'm going to transform. Might want to stand back a bit."

Kai grabbed Mara's hand and pulled her backward a handful of steps. He watched Sorn's body contort, then grow. Sorn tried not to show his pain as he shifted, but it was clear by the boy's face that it wasn't working. His injuries still affected him greatly. After a dozen seconds, Sorn managed to settle back into his dragon body.

"Alright," Sorn said, his voice deeper now. "I'm... ready."

"Are you sure?" asked Mara. "Are you sure you can make it?"

"With your help, yes. With your power flowing through me, that should help in the healing process, too."

"I hope so. Alright, Kai, are *you* ready?" Mara asked.

Sorn noticed Kai had wandered off somewhere behind him. Turning, he saw Kai approaching an oddly straight object protruding from the ground near the cliff's edge.

"Kai?" Mara repeated.

"Is that–?" Sorn started, noting the object looked oddly familiar.

"I think it's a spear," Kai replied.

"A spear?" asked Mara.

"Yes," replied Kai, grabbing hold of it and pulling. It seemed to be lodged quite firmly in the ground. Sorn watched as he grunted, pulling on it with both hands. He shifted his weight, his muscles straining. After a few seconds, Sorn felt a small pulse of energy from the boy, and the spear finally came free.

"What's a spear doing here in the middle of these caves?" Mara asked.

"What indeed," Kai said, trying to wipe what looked like centuries of dust and rust off the weapon. "This thing looks ancient. I lost mine up there when..." he said, looking at Nalaen. "Anyways, it seems we aren't the first Dragonbloods to be down here."

"Another mystery," Mara said, her face contorting in confusion. "We'll add that to the list of things to figure out once we get out of this mess, but for now, I think we should focus on that bit first."

"Agreed," Sorn chimed in, though he eyed the spear, not fond of the idea of Kai having it while climbing on his back. Still, it was a peculiar thing to find way down here, and he had to wonder.

Kai strapped the spear to his back and helped Mara up to Sorn's side where she quickly found her way up. Kai watched her, his face indicative of his inner turmoil. Before climbing up himself, he shot Sorn a sideways glance.

"Coming?" Mara said, drawing his attention.

"Yep," Kai answered and climbed up. It wasn't as graceful as Mara had done, partially because he wasn't familiar, but Sorn figured it was also just awkward for the boy. It was awkward for *him*, too.

Once Kai was seated behind Mara, he looked around confused.

"So, where do we hold on, exactly?" he asked.

"I'll hold on up here, you can hold onto me," she replied. "But really, other than the takeoff and landing, it's pretty smooth."

"If you say so…" Kai's expression did not portray much confidence. "What about her?" Kai asked, gazing toward Nalaen, who was still sitting off to the side, minding little of what was going on before her.

"I'll carry her," Sorn replied. "Unless you'd prefer she sat behind you?"

"Yeah, no thanks."

Sorn let out deep chuckle.

"Alright, time to fly. Hold on." Sorn spread out his wings, stretching them one at a time, prepping himself for liftoff. "Okay, Mara. You know what to do," he added, once he was satisfied with everything.

The takeoff wasn't exactly smooth, but Sorn managed despite the pain it caused him. Once he was a few feet in the air, he turned and reached down for his sister with his good leg, carefully grabbing her. Once he had her securely, he pressed his wings harder, taking them away from the cavern floor.

It took them a few minutes to get going at a steady pace, Sorn taking it easy with the multiple tasks he was juggling. After a few minutes, he began to pick up the pace as they moved through the large caverns. Hopefully, everything would go better from here on out.

Mara focused on transferring her power to Sorn as they lifted off, but she already felt a bit weak, plus she was getting distracted by Kai, who kept altering from gripping her tightly to not enough, then tightly again. She presumed he was nervous but also felt awkward at the whole ordeal. She wasn't surprised. Kai was strong, and brave, but he also liked to be in charge, and whenever he wasn't it made him uncomfortable. Mara didn't want to make it worse, so she kept her thoughts to herself. He'd get used to it, the same as she had.

"Storming something fierce outside," Sorn said, drawing Mara's attention. "I was afraid of this. Going to fly up and see if I can get above the clouds. Hopefully, the storm is relatively low."

"Okay," Mara called out. She couldn't see how bad, but she heard the wind howling viciously as they approached the exit of the caverns.

Mara felt the cold before it began blasting her from all sides. She felt Sorn pull up, moving them into a climb to gain altitude, the wind turning even more fierce. Sorn made a sound like a cough, slowing his descent. A few seconds later, he coughed again, this time causing them to dip swiftly.

"Are you okay?" Mara asked, speaking for both her and Kai.

"I'm fine, just… struggling a bit, is all," Sorn offered in reply. Several moments later, he coughed yet again. They were sounding worse.

"Yeah, I'm gonna go with he's not fine," Kai said.

Sorn turned his head and glared at Kai, but quickly altered his gaze and let out what sounded like a sigh.

"Sorry, Mara, I–" Sorn winced, dipping again and reversing his ascent. Mara tightened her grip on him and Kai held tighter onto her.

"We need to land, now," Mara said. Sorn nodded, moving faster toward the ground.

They dove faster than Mara would have preferred. She could feel the ground getting closer, and, a few seconds later, she heard the distinct sound of pine trees whipping in the wind. Sorn fumbled the landing, crashing into the ground. Fortunately, the fresh snow softened the blow.

Kai hopped off immediately, helping Mara down after a moment. Once she was off, Mara made straight for Sorn's side.

"Are you okay?" she asked.

"I think we've already answered that question, Mara," he said. "I'll be okay, but I can't fly and keep control of my sister. Apparently, my injuries are worse than I thought."

"Great, okay. So, now what?" Kai asked. Mara gave him a judging look.

"He's hurt, Kai. But... I don't know. Sorn, can I help you heal with my powers?"

"It should help, yes, but it's going to be slow with using all mine to contain my sister. I don't know if it will be fast enough to get us going again. I can already feel her gaining ground on me."

"My horse!" Kai exclaimed. "I almost forgot. She's out here, somewhere. Maybe I can find her and get help?"

"Of course," Mara said, her eyes growing wide. "Cyrus might be close by, actually. He came out looking for you."

"Wait? Cyrus is out here?" Kai said.

"I don't know. He left the same day you left. They were coming to try and catch up to you. Obviously, they didn't make it, but they might still be out here."

"You said we're going to need him, anyway, right?"

"You're right..." Mara said, just now remembering how essential Cyrus was to their plans. "Sorry. I forgot with all that happened. We *do* need Cyrus. Perhaps if you can find him, he can help us get back."

"Alright. I'll try to find Cyrus. You do what you have to do to keep the princess subdued, and... help him."

Mara made a stern expression but nodded.

"Don't worry. We'll take care of that. Just hurry, Kai. We need to find Cyrus quickly. I don't know how long we can contain her."

"I'll find him. Be careful."

"I will," she said, letting go of his hand.

"Alright, let's see if we can get you feeling better, Sorn," Mara said, turning away from Kai and going to Sorn's side. She felt Kai's presence slowly fading away, hoping the storm wouldn't make his task impossible.

***

"There's no sign of his tracks, Spear," Caliena stated, coming up to stand beside Cyrus.

Cyrus sighed, looking up into the sky, large flakes resting briefly on his cheeks before melting as he squinted away at others.

"We've got to keep looking. He's out here somewhere," he said, avoiding eye contact.

"Brother Cyrus... I know that finding Kai is important. I don't want to give up on him either, but the men are freezing, and if we don't find shelter soon, we're going to have a rough night. We won't do Kai any good if we freeze to death."

Cyrus paused, considering her words, staring at the dejected faces of his comrades. He knew Caliena was right, but the idea of giving up on Kai didn't sit well with him, either. Finally, he looked her in the eye and nodded.

"Take the men and head east. You should be able to find the ruins. That's probably our best bet for shelter. Plus, maybe you'll get lucky and Kai will be there."

"What about you?" Caliena asked, looking concerned.

"I'm going to look a little longer." Cyrus glanced back at her, noticing her expression. "Don't worry, I'll be fine. I'm just not willing to give up on Kai quite yet."

"Brother, I didn't mean–"

"It's okay, Caliena. You're looking out for the others. Take them and go find shelter. I'll be along in a bit."

"Understood. Be careful, Brother," she bade, offering him the standard salute of the Order.

"Thank you, Caliena. You, too, Sister."

Caliena bowed, retreating to join the others. Cyrus could hear her explaining the plan to them as he set off on the way Kai's trail had been headed before they'd lost it in the snow.

***

Mara sat as still as she could, trying to focus her thoughts on Sorn while resting her hands on his side. There wasn't much she could do to help him other than lend her strength, which was something she was starting to get better at. However, she was still having trouble focusing. Her thoughts kept drifting to Kai, and the storm was chilling her to the bone. Luckily, being close to Sorn helped shelter her from the weather to some degree.

She took a second to reach out with her energy, checking on Nalaen, who sat quietly nearby. She could sense the struggle and the internal push and pull of the connection between Nalaen and Sorn. It was a fight, for sure, but it seemed Sorn was maintaining his hold at least.

"Is it working?" Mara asked, turning her attention back to Sorn.

"Yes. It's slow, but it's progress. I already feel a little better."

"How does it work, exactly?"

"You mean the healing?"

Mara nodded.

"Not really sure how to explain it. I don't actually *do* anything. We just heal faster as dragons. Our bodies are innately more magical in this form, which is a large part of it. Given the power that flows through you now, it's possible you might experience the same thing, to some degree."

That thought gave Mara pause for a moment, instantly thinking about her eyes. But it had been weeks already with no sign of change. Perhaps some things just couldn't be healed.

"How come you heal faster as a dragon?" she asked, pushing her thoughts aside.

"That's a good question. I suppose that we're more relaxed in our true forms. Some have hypothesized that when we're smaller, our capacity for magic decreases. I don't think that's ever been proven, but it's possible, I suppose. Others just believe that we are stronger when we are our true selves. Back home, there are even many who avoid human form until it's absolutely necessary, considering it a sign of weakness."

"And what do you think? Why do you take human form at all?"

"It's a necessity," Sorn replied. "We cannot stay in our dragon form forever or risk expending all our energy. If we do, there's a chance we might not come back. Some say it's a curse the gods placed on us so we would never grow too powerful. Others believe it is merely the balance of the world, two halves of the whole, so to speak. I understand both sides of the argument. As with all things, I believe it's not quite so simple, though I suspect the second way of thinking is much closer to the truth. Things are very rarely black and white in our world, if you know what I mean."

"Yes, I think I do," Mara replied, drifting off, her thoughts wandering.

Mara yawned, suddenly realizing she was becoming quite tired. Apparently, the lengthy transfusion of power was beginning to wear on her. Her arms felt weak, and she was still cold, so she scooted in and rested her body against Sorn's warmth.

The rhythmic rise and fall of Sorn's belly made her even more sleepy. His breath seemed to slow along with hers as she steadily drifted off into a deep sleep.

Mara woke sometime later, sitting up, an odd sensation in the back of her head. She felt Sorn, who hadn't budged. His breathing was slow and steady. He was still asleep.

Mara realized she was covered in a layer of snow, her skin damp. Sorn's warmth had kept her from getting too cold, but the snow was still coming down steadily.

Feeling that same strange feeling again, she reached out with her mind, searching for Nalaen. There was nothing. Confusion set in, but Mara was still sleepy. She sat up straighter, trying to force herself more awake. She still felt a bit weak, too, but she scanned the area again, stretching her senses further out. Still, there was no sign of Nalaen's presence.

Mara's confusion turned into fear.

"Sorn. Sorn, wake up!"

Sorn roused, shaking his head lazily.

"Sorn!" Mara shouted.

"Huh, what is it, Mara? Is something wr–"

"Your sister is gone!"

Mara felt Sorn fidgeting, probably looking for any signs of his sister. His heart began to beat faster, Mara sensing the fear welling within him. And then there was a brief moment, a shift in his demeanor, and Mara felt something far worse was happening.

"Sorn?" Mara cried out, trying to understand the change. "Sorn, what's wrong?"

"I'm sorry, Mara," Sorn replied, his voice sounding strained. "I can't... resist."

Every fiber of Mara's being twitched as a jolt of energy pulsed through her. She understood now what was happening. Sorn, in his weakened state, had succumbed to his sister's will. Mara suddenly felt extremely vulnerable. She could feel Sorn's internal struggle–a battle he was losing quickly.

"Mara, run!" Sorn warned her. They were the last words he could get out, the tide of his sister's magic about to overtake him any second.

Mara stood up and began to run, stumbling several times, tripping over herself. She didn't know where she was, didn't know where she was going. All she knew was that she had to get away.

She had to get to Kai. She reached out for him, but there was no sign of his presence. He was probably too far away, which meant she needed to keep moving. Every step was moving closer to her brother and further from Sorn. At least, she hoped.

Mara kept moving, holding her hands up to check for objects. She was getting better at spatial awareness, but this was an entirely different scenario. This wasn't back home in the safety of the keep with its familiar halls. This was out in the real world, with a real threat at her heels.

She managed to do okay, only running into the occasional tree branch, but she felt like she was going too slow. She tried to listen for any signs of Sorn's pursuit, but the sound of the wind as it whipped snow against her drowned out almost everything else. The one thing she could do though was attempt to search for him with her mind.

She could feel his presence behind her still. So far, it had remained steady, with no indication he was coming. It was reassuring, but the fact she could still feel him also made her nervous. And there was still no sign of Kai's presence.

She trudged on for another minute before she felt a strong pulse of energy from behind. *Sorn's coming!*

Mara quickened her pace, a renewed panic setting in. She could sense him drawing closer. She could sense the anger driving his thoughts.

The trees were getting thicker. She could tell because she was bumping into them much more frequently, sometimes several at a time. It forced her to slow down, but it also meant she probably had more cover from Sorn, which gave her a small measure of comfort.

She heard and felt a stronger gust of wind, sensing Sorn very close, somewhere up above her. She stopped, pulling herself close to a nearby tree. She stood there for a moment, catching her breath as she waited and listened. Sorn's presence faded for a few seconds, then spiked again, accompanied by another gust of wind. She thought she even heard him snarl.

"I know you're near, little bird," Sorn bellowed. His voice sounded different, deeper and more sinister.

Mara gasped, the notion hitting her that if she could feel his presence, then he could most certainly feel hers, too. He must have known she was close. Her thoughts raced, trying to decide what to do. If he knew where she was, then hiding wouldn't be safe. No, her best bet was to find Kai, hopefully before Nalaen found him—if she hadn't already. That thought alone got her feet moving again.

She moved from tree to tree, stopping every few to listen for Sorn. She could hear him flying overhead, a continuous pattern of zigzagging. Mara just hoped the tree cover would stay thick enough to prevent him from landing. She hoped she wouldn't stumble into a clearing.

Mara felt a stronger wave of malice emanate from somewhere overhead. A few seconds later, she heard the roar of flames. Her heart skipped a beat, realizing what was happening. Sorn was razing the forest. Her heart began to pound even harder in her chest.

Mara ran like she'd never run before.

She heard the sounds of more flames as Sorn scorched the forest around her. Even with the storm raging, and the bitter cold of it still biting at her skin, she felt the heat as trees started to burn. She navigated away from it as best she could, but it was seemingly everywhere. She started choking on the smoke, too, doing her best to keep low.

Sorn, please! Stop this, Mara called out, trying to reach him with her mind. She didn't know what else to do. She waited, sensing a slight hesitation in his thoughts, but it only lasted a few seconds before another wave of fire lit up the forest nearby. This one was close enough that Mara instantly felt the heat, causing her to reel away in the opposite direction.

Mara curled up in the snow and began to cry as more flames engulfed the area around her, blocking her in.

"Where are you, Kai? I need you," she sobbed, trying not to cough amidst the encroaching smoke.

***

Kai felt an urgent sense of danger. He pulled on the reigns of his horse, bringing her to a stop, looking back up the hill he'd just descended. Something was wrong.

Mara?

He eyed their tracks through the torrent of snow. They were being covered nearly as quickly as he made them. He turned and faced forward, back toward the way he'd been headed. He was torn between finding help and this new fear that his sister might be in trouble.

Kai set his jaw, furrowing his brow in a determined expression. No matter how much they needed Cyrus, his sister was more important. He pulled on the reigns, turning around and heading back up the hill, following his fading tracks until he reached the top, noting they were quickly fading in the fresh fallen snow.

"Damn," Kai cursed under his breath.

He grunted and kicked his horse to keep moving, trying to remember the way he'd come. He traveled in the correct direction for some time, noticing a few familiarities, but after a while, he wasn't sure if it was right or not.

Kai stopped again, shivering from the cold, searching in all directions. He had no idea which way to go now. Everything looked the same in the snow, and he could only see so far anyway.

"Damn this blizzard," he yelled out loud. He thought for a moment, remembering how Mara had somehow reached out to him before with her mind. "Mara, can you hear me?" he called out, having no idea how it worked. When no response came, he tried again, this time in his head. *Mara?*

Still, there was no response. Kai cursed under his breath again.

"Maybe I need to calm down and focus," he said, letting out a deep breath and closing his eyes. He tried to focus his thoughts on Mara. He tried to sense which way to go to get back to her.

After a long, quiet pause, he opened his eyes, facing a specific direction in front of him. He couldn't say for sure if it had really worked or not, but for some reason, it felt like the right way to go.

He rode on for some time before he began to feel the same sense of danger again. Only this time, it felt different. It wasn't coming from in front of him, and it didn't feel like Mara. He stopped his mount and scanned what he could see, holding his hand up to keep the snow from hitting his eyes. There was nothing but a swirling vortex of white all around him, only contrasted by the stark grey of the tree trunks in his direct vicinity.

Kai continued moving, albeit a bit slower as he continued to scan the forest around him, still feeling the same strange feeling. He rode on for another minute, spotting nothing unusual, but just as he was about to stop looking, assuming the feeling was just a remnant of what he'd felt before, his eye caught a flash of color off to his right. He took a double take, but whatever he had seen was no longer there. *Strange.*

He blinked, shutting his eyes forcefully and reopening them to look again. Perhaps the cold was just getting to him. He frowned, picking up his pace as he continued moving, his fear for Mara growing.

Soon, the sensation of nearby danger spike again. Kai tried to push it aside; tried to tell himself it was probably nothing, but he couldn't shake it. He thought he heard a sound behind him and spun around to look, staring into the blizzard.

As he turned back forward, a blur of red came from his left. Kai saw it just in time to hold up his hands as it got hold of him, ripping him off his mount and sending him crashing into the ground.

Kai rolled, trying to shake off his attacker as his horse took off at a full gallop. He looked down his body into Nalaen's rage-filled eyes. He kicked her in the chest, her clawed fingertips scraping against his armor, narrowly missing their target as she was pushed away. She was in her human form, but her hands resembled her dragon claws. Kai scrambled, trying to get up and away from her, even as Nalaen reeled from his kick and came back in to attack.

Kai felt her grab his leg and turned, seeing her raised arm coming in for another swipe. He twisted around in the snow and brought his other foot straight into her face. Nalaen let out a cursed howl, sounding more like a dragon than a human.

Kai rolled over again and forced himself up on all fours, moving as quickly as he could onto his legs. He scanned the woods for his horse, but she was nowhere to be seen. He'd holstered the new spear to his saddle holder, so he had no weapon. Kai shot a glance backward as he took off in the direction he'd last seen his horse headed, hoping he could catch up to her. He saw Nalaen getting up behind him, a half-cocked smile on her face as she spat blood, beginning her chase.

Kai ran as fast as he could, dodging trees and trying to avoid the mounds of snow the heavy winds had scattered about the forest. He glanced behind him again, Nalaen still in pursuit, seemingly gaining on him.

"What's the matter, boy? Was it really so easy to eradicate the fight inside you?" Nalaen bellowed through the woods. "The great Kai Grayscale, Fireblood, running for his life. Peh! You don't deserve such a gift. You're nothing but a scared youngling with power he's barely able to wield."

Kai gritted his teeth at her words. He wanted to stop; he wanted to turn and face her, but she was partially right—he hadn't mastered his powers. Even if he had, Mara was still in danger and needed his help. Though, if the princess was here, then what possible danger could it be? Either way, debate wasn't a luxury Kai could afford right now. He continued, trying to ignore Nalaen's taunts as best he could.

"A chase it is, then!" she called out. "You know you can't outrun me, even if you do find your mount." Nalaen laughed as she continued to gain ground on him. She was fast, even in her human form, and she was catching up.

At this point, Kai's lungs were on fire, and his legs were getting tired. Running full speed through the deep snow in armor, breathing in blistering cold air as small shards of ice pelted your face would do that. Kai's resolve was strong–it had to be, but he still had his limits and wasn't sure how much longer he could maintain his lead on her. The storm was still in full swing, but seemed like he could see a bit further up ahead now at least. And fortunately, because of it, he spotted his horse. She looked like she was boxed into a corner, large boulders blocking the path she'd been set on. Kai altered his course and made straight for her, angling himself so he could jump up on the saddle. From there, he had a narrow escape path off to the left, with Nalaen closing in behind him.

Kai heard another scream from behind. She must have noticed where he was headed. Kai didn't have time to look back. His horse heard Nalaen's scream and started panicking, looking for a path of escape. Just as Kai closed the gap and leapt for her saddle, she bolted in the only real direction there was to go. Kai didn't land on top, but he did get a hold on the saddle, trying to pull himself up.

His legs were weak, but in one quick surge of strength, he pushed off the ground and launched himself up onto the saddle, settling into place, kicking her and pulling on the reigns. He heard another scream from behind and ducked just in time to see Nalaen launch over the top of him, narrowly missing him with a swipe of her claws. She slammed into one of the rocks, letting out a grunt, followed by another scream.

Kai grabbed his spear and pulled it out of its holder. He didn't want to make the mistake of not having it again. He cocked his head backward, spotting Nalaen getting up and shifting, growing to her full size, he eyes burning with a renewed fury. He kicked his horse, hurrying her as fast as she could go.

The woods were still dense but began to open up. Kai was worried that would give Nalaen the opportunity to easily spot him.

He emerged from the forest into a large open area. His stomach turned as he pulled on the reigns, swinging his horse back to the left toward the tree line. Headed in the new direction, he glanced back up their path. He heard her screech overhead before he saw her, glancing up just in time to see her barreling down toward him. He flicked the reigns sideways, sending them through a narrow gap between several trees. The trees behind him let out a loud crack upon her impact, splinters erupting all around.

Nalaen screeched again, roaring as she prepared to let out a fury of flames aimed directly at Kai. Sensing it, he jerked the reigns again, quickly altering their course. Flames erupted behind him, narrowly missing Kai, but his horse squealed, her stride stuttering. Kai stole a quick look backwards, seeing some scorch marks on her hind leg. It didn't look too bad, but it didn't look good, either.

"Almost got you there, boy!" he heard her roar above the wind and crackling forest. He knew she was somewhere overhead. He could hear the sound of her wings beating the cold air, even above the howling tempest winds.

Kai continued to stick to where the woods were thickest. At the very least, it would buy him some time. He still needed to find Mara and had absolutely no idea where he was now.

"You're not getting away from me this time. You got lucky before. Your sister won't be able to save you."

Kai suddenly realized the gravity of her words. What if something had already happened to Mara? What if he was too late? If Nalaen had escaped their grasp, then that could only mean...

"I made sure they would not interfere. It seems my traitor of a brother still has his uses, even if they are not of his own volition."

What was she getting at? What had she done?

"Of course, I wanted to do it myself–kill your sister, that is. She's been a thorn in my side, but I figured it would be much more ironic if my brother was the one to do it. He opened himself up to me. It was only a matter of time before I figured out how to reverse the connection. And now, he's my puppet. It's much more useful to have one of my own on a string than that weak human Jarren. Even now, he's burnt down half the forest at my command. It's only a matter of time before your sister is dead–if she's not already."

Kai heard what sounded like a laugh overhead as she swooped low, seeing her scanning the forest for him. *Did she say Jarren? He was–?* Kai shook his head, focusing on what mattered most.

I felt Mara not that long ago. It can't be... Kai's heart sank, his thoughts turning grim, his hope fading.

No, he thought. She already discouraged him once. He wouldn't give up on his sister–not again. He would keep looking for her as long as he drew breath. He slapped the reigns, pushing his horse even more than she was already going. Kai began to feel his body temperature rising. He was tiring of this chase, and of her constant gloating. His jaw set and his expression turned to anger as they raced onward.

In his growing rage, Kai almost didn't hear the voice in his head. It was faint, and his blood was beginning to boil with his own hatred as thoughts swirled. It was like a whisper at first, but slowly, it grew louder until finally he heard it.

Kai.

It was Mara. When he finally noticed it, Kai's anger subsided, and he strained to hear her.

Kai, are you there?

I'm here, Mara, Kai thought, hoping she could hear him. He waited several seconds, calling out her name again in his head when he heard nothing. *Mara.*

Kai. Is that you? Please... hurry!

I'm coming, Mara. Where are you?

I don't know. I'm hiding. There's smoke and fire everywhere. He's looking for me. I sense him very close. You need to hurry. His mind is not his own.

Kai clenched his teeth and tried to sense where she was, like he'd done before. He felt a tug in a specific direction and turned, steering his horse that way. Up ahead he saw that it was directly through another clearing of trees. He'd have to cross out in the open to get to Mara.

I'm coming, Mara. Hold on!

Ignoring his own safety, Kai burst from the trees and headed straight for where he'd felt Mara's call come from.

"There you are," Kai heard Nalaen roar. She was coming.

He saw her as she swooped around, altering her course in his direction. The storm had cleared a bit more, and he could see a bit further. There was another tree line up ahead, but he wasn't sure if he was going to make it. He pushed his horse, ignoring her wheezing and the slight limp in her right leg where she'd been burned. If they didn't make the trees, it likely wouldn't even matter.

It was a race. Kai could see Nalaen in his peripheral, barreling down toward him from the left. He saw the raging malice in her eyes as she lifted her claws, stretching them forward, ready to rip Kai to shreds. The trees were growing closer. Kai began to notice a faint smell of smoke. He was going in the right direction. Mara was close.

But the trees were still too far away. He wasn't going to make it before Nalaen was upon him. He saw her grin, probably coming to the same conclusion. Kai lifted his spear, pointing it directly at her, twisting his body to face her. It was the only option he had left. Perhaps he could score a lucky blow. But with the speed at which she was diving, even if he managed to land a strike, the impact of her force alone could crush him.

They were now seconds away from impact. Kai braced himself, letting out a deep breath. This was it. This was his final moment.

Just as Kai went to release his spear, Nalaen winced, turning her head to the side in a look of pain. Her course altered slightly to the right, just barely enough so that she whizzed past Kai, only a few feet behind him before crashing into the ground.

Kai spun in the saddle to look at her, trying to understand what miracle had just saved his life. He noticed a familiar handle sticking out of her side. It was an Order spear. He pulled on the reigns, bringing his horse around, scanning for where it had come from.

There, along the tree line, stood Cyrus. His expression was stern, but he also looked incredibly relieved. Kai kicked his horse, moving in the man's direction as Cyrus began to sprint toward him.

"Cyrus!" Kai hailed, waving on approach. "By the gods, your timing couldn't have been any better. I thought for sure I was done for. How did you find me?"

"Good to see you too, Kai," Cyrus said, smiling. "I smelled the smoke and followed it. I was just headed north when I heard the screams. That's when I saw her coming in for the attack. And just in the nick of time, I see."

"Indeed, but Mara's still in trouble. I have to get to her."

"Mara's out here? How? I left her at the–"

Nalaen began to stir, and both Cyrus and Kai heard her moving. They looked at each other, then back to her.

"No time. Go, Kai. Help your sister. I'll deal with this one."

"Cyrus, are you–"

"Yes!" Cyrus yelled, slapping Kai's horse. "Go. I'll catch up."

Kai didn't wait for Cyrus to tell him again; he was off. Mara was close now, he could feel it. He looked backward one last time, seeing Nalaen standing, reaching around with her jaws to rip the spear from her flesh before she bent it slightly and tossed it aside, Cyrus slowly walking toward her.

Kai said a short prayer for Cyrus before disappearing beyond the trees.

It didn't take long before the thick smell of burning pine filled the entirety of the air. He slowed his horse and leapt off, trying to get below the cloud of smoke. Kai crept forward a few feet before he heard his horse collapse on the ground behind him. He looked at her, her eyes rolling backwards into her head, her chest falls frantic and pained. He'd run her too hard. There was nothing he could do to help her now, so he crept onward in his search for Mara.

Mara? Are you here?

He didn't get a response. Was he too late? He stopped and focused again, trying to feel for her presence. He wasn't sure, but his thoughts carried him forward.

He could hear the trees burning up ahead. He thought he also heard irregular gusts of wind above. *Sorn?* He stayed low and quiet.

After a little bit further, he heard a soft noise. It sounded like coughing. He quickened his pace, heading toward it.

He peered through the smoke, approaching the source of the coughing. Slowly, the smoke cleared, and he spotted an odd shape up ahead, half-buried in the snow. After a few more feet, he saw the distinctive face of his sister.

Mara coughed, opening her eyes halfway, as if she somehow knew he was there. She smiled faintly, then closed her eyes again.

"Kai?" she said weakly.

"Are you okay?" Kai whispered, rushing up to her, hearing another gust of wind overhead.

Mara coughed but didn't respond. Kai reached out and grabbed her hand. Her skin was frozen to the touch and pale, with blotches of reddish purple. Kai leaned down and put his hands underneath her, carefully picking her up and holding her close. He was warm and hoped some of that warmth would transfer to her.

He heard another gust overhead, followed by what sounded like a large thud somewhere nearby in the smoke. Kai couldn't see anything, but assumed he knew what it was. He held Mara tightly as he crept back the way he'd come, hoping to get her away from danger.

Mara coughed again and Kai froze.

"I hear you, little bird. Where are you hiding?" Sorn's voice.

Kai stood and ran, holding his breath as long as he could to avoid breathing in the smoke and coughing. He didn't manage to make it far before he had to breathe, trying to duck down again for cleaner air. He took in a big gulp of smoke, trying to hold in an impending cough. He pressed his face into Mara's stomach, suppressing his cough as best he could and kept moving.

Soon they made it out of the worst of the smoke and Kai found his horse. She was still alive, but her breathing had slowed considerably. Fortunately, her body was still warm. Kai nestled Mara up against the horse's belly, hoping it would be enough while he tried to figure out a plan.

He stood and walked a few feet away, looking up the hill. His thoughts instantly drifted to Cyrus, but a sound behind him drew his attention. He turned, seeing a massive blue dragon emerging from the smoke.

"So, my sister didn't manage to kill you yet. At least you two are reunited again. I'm sorry, Kai, but I have no choice," Sorn said. His face appeared to reflect whatever struggle was happening in his mind. His pupils dilated unnaturally, the light in them flickering several times, before finally glowing stronger. Kai watched his neck crane, his vision focusing on Mara. Kai knew what was about to happen.

He stepped directly into the path of Sorn's attack, raising his hands and closing his eyes. He had no idea what he was doing, but had to believe he could do it again. A thundering torrent of flames spewed forth, enveloping Kai. The flames continued for a handful of seconds before gradually depleting. As the fire died, Sorn surveyed the damage.

Kai stood, eyes closed, not a burn mark on him. The snow all around him was melted, singed all the way down to the dirt. Sorn's face contorted and confusion took hold.

Kai put his hands down and stood up straight, opening his eyes. Holding his hands up in astonishment, he saw a bright orangish glow, seemingly emanating from his eyes. Sorn saw it too and took a step back. Kai's eyes had glowed red when he'd fought in the battle at the tower–when he'd fought Talesa. But now, they were brighter. But why?

As Kai locked his gaze with Sorn's, something shifted slightly in the dragon's demeanor.

"Kai, I am sorry. It's my sister. I can't... resist her," Sorn said, taking several more steps backward. "I feel her hold slipping, but I..." Sorn grunted, closing his eyes, wrestling with the thoughts in his head. "I'm trying, but–"

There was another loud thud behind Kai and he whirled, seeing Nalaen drop the limp form of Cyrus on the ground. There were several fresh wounds in her hide, but Cyrus looked much worse. Kai quickly glanced over Cyrus's body, noticing a great deal of blood. Was it his, or Nalaen's?

"Stop resisting me, Brother," she said, shifting back into her human form, sneering at Sorn. She bent over and grabbed Cyrus by his armor, lifting him up in front of her to face Kai. "And as for you... your friend fought bravely, Kai. But in the end, he was weak, just like the rest of your kind."

Kai stared at Cyrus, seeing the man's bloody, swollen face. Cyrus could only open one eye, and he gazed back at Kai, trying to force a smile. A drop of blood squeaked through his lips, dripping down onto his chin.

"I see you've found some of your powers. Good job, Brother," she said, scolding Sorn with her eyes. Sorn bowed his head in shame. "But will it be enough?" she continued, eyeing Mara unconscious on the ground. "Looks like it's just you and us now."

"And what about you? Any last words?" Nalaen said, placing her head down besides Cyrus's face as she looked at the man.

Cyrus tried to speak. More blood splattered out of his mouth, followed by a slight gurgling sound.

"What's that? Speak up now." Nalaen's lips curled in delighted contempt.

"Why..." Cyrus muttered.

"Why what?" Nalaen laughed.

"Why, Kai? Why do you fight?"

Nalaen looked at Kai, her face still adorned with a malicious smile. She raised her eyebrow, prompting Kai for the answer.

Kai stood there silently, contemplating Cyrus's question. He remembered the conversation they'd had, which now seemed forever ago. He looked down at Mara for a moment, his thoughts swirling. Kai raised his head and looked back at Cyrus. Kai smiled and nodded at the man, who returned the gesture with a pained nod. Kai's gaze moved upward, locking eyes with Nalaen.

The orange glow in Kai's eyes slowly grew brighter until they were a light yellow. Nalaen's devious smile turned to confusion for a few seconds.

"Kill him, Brother!" Nalaen commanded, tightening her grip on Cyrus.

Kai felt the heat growing behind him, but he stood resolutely, staring Nalaen down. He felt the pulse of heat when it left Sorn's mouth, but still he remained. At the last second, Kai lifted his hands and pulled on the flames, whipping them around as he spun. He wanted to direct the flames at Nalaen, but she was still shielding herself with Cyrus. So instead, he kept spinning, slamming the attack back into the side of Sorn's head. The force was so strong, it nearly knocked Sorn off his feet. Sorn reeled, taking several steps away from Kai.

"Don't stop you idiot!" Nalaen shouted. Sorn hesitated only a second before preparing for a second attack. The fire rose in his throat and Kai raised his hand.

Just as Sorn was about to unleash the flames, Kai clenched his fist and slammed it downward toward the ground. In concert with the movement, Sorn's head followed, slamming into the dirt, his eyes rolling into the back of his head. Several seconds later, he blacked out entirely.

Nalaen grunted behind Kai, tossing Cyrus aside, sending him tumbling on the ground.

"I have to do everything myself!" she screeched again, morphing back into a dragon. She lifted as she did, instantly diving at Kai.

The intense fury of her attack would have caught anyone else by surprise, but with this new power coursing through his veins, Kai was moving faster than he'd ever moved before. He rolled to the side, bringing his spear up and whipping it around, ready for her next attack.

It came in just as fast, but Kai was ready. She swiped with her claws, hitting nothing but air. Kai was already out of the way, diving under her arms and sliding past her belly. As he did, he stuck out his spear. It scraped against her scales with a clinking sound but otherwise did no apparent damage.

Still, Kai was moving, wasting no time as Nalaen dove back in again, claws raking. He moved away from Mara and the horse, wanting to draw her attacks as far away as possible.

She kept coming, diving in and out, each time pressing him back. Kai used his spear to deflect her blows, trying to comprehend what she was doing. Her strength was incredible, but Kai somehow managed to keep his grip on the spear, though he had no opening for a counterattack.

The offence comes through the defense. Kai heard the words of Cyrus in his head. And so, he planted his feet firmly, waiting for his opening.

It came moments later.

Nalaen seemed to be getting frustrated that Kai was somehow holding his defense, and dove in again, this time even faster. As she did, Kai ducked under her attack and came around on her right, jabbing his spear into her side. The tip of his spear found a gap in her scales and sank into flesh, drawing a gush of blood as Kai yanked it out, continuing to move forward and out of the reach of her tail as she swung it toward him.

Nalaen reeled, looking at her side before turning and hissing at Kai. Kai smiled, gripping his spear firmly as he waited for her next move. She looked to the sky, deciding on a new strategy. Lifting her wings, Nalaen rocketed upwards, into the billows of smoke overhead.

Kai watched, following her until she disappeared into the thick smoke. He kept his spear trained upward, watching for her return. He caught glimpses of her shadow as it raced through the clouds, trying to keep track of where she was.

Finally, it grew quiet. Kai waited, knowing her attack was coming any second.

He heard the slight whisper of wind behind him, spinning to see her barreling down. He barely had time to dive out of the way before she rose back up and disappeared again.

Kai waited, expecting her to attack from behind again. But this time she dove in from his side. As before, he dove out of the way, trying to bring his spear back up for a hit, but she was moving too quickly.

Nalaen tried several more times, her jaws coming within inches of Kai on the last attempt. He was trying to get a hit on her, which he almost did, too.

Kai decided to try something different.

Kai stood and didn't move, hoping she would come from behind him again. His eyes moved sideways when he heard the slight shift in the wind behind him. She'd taken the bait. Instead of diving to the side, Kai bent his knees, jumping with all his strength. As he did, he spun in the air. He saw Nalaen's back as she swept underneath him. Kai stuck his spear out, driving it straight down as hard and true as he could. He watched it drive through her wing, the audible sound of flesh ripping as it tore all the way through.

Nalaen hissed in pain and tried to rise again, but the attack had done too much damage. She fumbled briefly before crashing down into the ground, a tangled mass of scales and blood that slowly morphed back into her human form. She was getting weaker. She lay there for a moment, holding up her slashed arm, grunting in pain and anger. She looked at Kai, the anger slowly turning into something resembling fear.

Kai walked slowly toward her. Nalaen's gaze turned to the side. She looked back at Kai with a smile before jumping up and sprinting toward where Mara lay.

Kai, seeing what she was doing, sprinted, but Nalaen was much closer, and she soon had Mara's limp body in her grasp, just as she'd done with Cyrus. Kai slowed, keeping his spear aimed at her.

Nalaen raised an eyebrow, looking at his spear and sneering. Kai stopped, holding it up a few seconds longer before dropping it and glaring at her.

"Good boy," Nalaen smiled. "Now, stay. Come any closer and I rip her to pieces."

Kai held his hands up, looking around for any way out of this predicament. His gaze scanned the area, searching for Cyrus. His body was gone. Kai's brow scrunched, but he quickly saw Nalaen studying him and focused back on her.

"What do you want?" Kai asked, trying to get her talking.

"Hah!" Nalaen laughed. "This again? I thought you would have figured that out by now."

"I already bested you, so now you resort to cowardly tactics. You aren't strong. You don't deserve to be queen of anything."

"Quiet, fool! You do not know strength. You stumbled upon a stolen power you know nothing about. Everything I have, everything I am, I've earned. The blood in my veins is pure, unlike you creatures. You are an abomination—an abomination I shall rid the world of. I don't expect your feeble human mind to understand it."

Mara coughed and started to rouse. She slowly opened her eyes, a look of terror in them. It was just like before. Kai tried to reach out with his mind. *It'll be okay, Mara.*

"We know more than you think," he said, focusing on Nalaen. "Maybe not me, but my sister understands the world better than you ever will. She understands that compassion and mercy are not weakness. You say you want to prove to the world you are strong, but you have everything backward. You want to know why I beat you? When I fought your sister, I was angry. That anger gave me power. It was enough to defeat her, but today, I found something stronger. It was the love I have for my sister that made me strong. It was the desire to protect those I care about that gave me a strength even greater than my rage. And it was with that strength that I bested even you, Princess. So, leave my sister out of this and come face me. Your anger against my peace. At least if I die, I will know it was protecting my family. You only want to use yours to further your thirst for power."

Nalaen glared at Kai, her hatred seething with every word he spoke. Her grip tightened around Mara's neck, causing her to begin to choke.

"Are you going to face me or not, coward," Kai said in a desperate attempt to get her to stop.

"Fine," Nalaen said, smiling again. "But as you said, I will use all my resources." Her eyes looked up and behind Kai.

Kai turned, seeing Sorn diving straight toward him through the clouds above. Without hesitation, and faster than Kai thought possible, he rolled forward, grabbing his spear and coming up with it. He pulled his arm back and let it loose with all his might. It was aimed straight for Nalaen's face. He only had one shot to make it count.

The spear flew as Sorn dove. There was no fire coming this time. Sorn was meant to crush Kai. Nalaen's eyes grew wide as she watched the spear sailing straight toward her. It was so fast, she didn't have time to react.

Suddenly, a bright pulse of blue light erupted, exploding in a brilliance that blinded everyone for a few seconds. The spear flying at Nalaen was diverted from its course, deflecting off harmlessly in the distance. Nalaen staggered and fell.

Kai glanced up at the last second, his vision returning, seeing Sorn divert his course just slightly before crashing into the ground, mere feet away from Kai.

As the cloud of snow settled, Kai trying to understand what had just happened, his eyes landed on Mara. She was standing, her hand raised. Her eyes were filled with a gentle blue light. They flickered for a few seconds, then slowly faded. The ground around her was bare, the snowing having been scattered in every direction in a large circle.

Nalaen tried to stand, shaking her head. When she realized what happened, she screamed, lunging toward Mara, her hand raised and formed in a claw. Out of nowhere, Cyrus tackled her, jumping on her back and forcing her to the ground, quickly clamping something around her neck. He fastened it with a click and a dull hum filled the air around her. Nalaen tried to shrug Cyrus off but couldn't. She struggled under his grasp, but he continued to hold her firmly.

"What have you done?" she screamed, grasping at the object around her neck.

She raged, still trying to resist Cyrus, who continued to hold her. She managed to roll over, finally, just in time to see his fist come barreling down into her face, instantly knocking her unconscious.

"Well, I wasn't wholly sure that would actually work!" Cyrus exclaimed as he stood, looking at both Kai and Mara, his face still bloody and swollen. "But I have to admit, it felt damn good."

Chapter Fifty-Eight

RESPITE

Mara held Kai's arm, shivering. She was still a bit cold, but it was more her nerves that just wouldn't relax. It was hard to believe the nightmare was finally over. Her lungs still hurt, too, but at least her coughing seemed to have subsided.

"What is that?" Kai asked, bending over to investigate the item around Nalaen's neck, who was still lying unconscious in the snow.

"It's what the craftsmen from the capital call a 'dampener'. They made them specifically to subdue magical beings—namely, dragons, of course. Most of ours were lost during the war, but the Order still has a couple. When I was thinking of a way to help you, I almost forgot we had them. I figured it might prove useful, though you left before I could tell you." Cyrus finished, giving Kai a stern look as he raised an eyebrow.

"Yeah, about that..." Kai muttered.

"What does it look like?" Mara interjected, reaching her hand out toward it. She could feel a slight vibration in the air coming from it.

"You've seen the metal before," Sorn chimed in. "In the Dream."

Cyrus eyed Sorn up and down, his one good eye squinting. Mara could sense the tension in the air, even though she'd told him Sorn could be trusted.

"What does he mean, Mara?" Kai asked, diverting his attention from the entrancing metal. "How have you *seen* it?"

"When I'm in the Dream world, I can see. I don't know how, but it's like... a miracle. And I saw it under the keep. There were cages. We saw—" Mara paused, turning toward Cyrus. "We saw a vision of the past there. Dragon children were kept in cages under the keep, harvested for their blood."

"What!?" Kai exclaimed, standing up. "So, that's what she told me about..." he added, glancing toward Nalaen. "Cyrus, is this true?"

Cyrus's eyes glazed over a moment as he stared at Mara.

"It is true the cages were meant to hold dragons, but never children. Mara, you saw this in this dream world? I think it's time we finally had that talk we were discussing."

"It's a long story," Mara said. "Perhaps I can try to explain more on the way home?"

"Yes, that could do. We should get going, anyway. Caliena will be worried."

"The others are out here?" Mara asked, perking up.

"Yes. I sent them to the ruins to seek shelter. I imagine they'll be out looking for me now, since I didn't return."

Cyrus turned, focusing his attention on Sorn.

"I presume you'll take care of her," he asked, tilting his head toward Nalaen.

"Yes. I can carry her. I'll follow your lead."

"Very well, then. Are you two ready to head out?" Cyrus asked, directed at Kai and Mara.

"Yes," Kai and Mara answered at the same time. They turned toward each other and sighed with a smile.

"Mara, you can ride with me," Cyrus said. "I left my horse tied up in the forest. Hopefully, she's still there. And I'm sure you two are fine walking... or, flying, I presume?"

"Uh, walking is just fine for me, thank you," Kai answered hastily, followed immediately by a stifled chuckle from Sorn.

"I'll walk too, actually," Sorn said as he recovered. "My leg's feeling a bit better now, but I still need some rest. Plus, we don't want to startle your friends. I've had enough fighting for one day."

"Let's hope it's much longer than that, but yes, probably for the best," Cyrus said with a smile. "Well, off we go then. So, Mara, tell me about this dream world..."

***

Caliena paced the ruins, waiting for the others to return.

Once the storm had subsided, she'd taken the liberty of grouping the knights in pairs to scout. They were ordered to walk five-hundred paces, covering a specific section of the woods in the direction they'd left Cyrus behind. So far, there'd been no sign of him, and the last patrol covering the final section was slated to return any moment.

She continued pacing, keeping a watchful eye for their return. When she finally saw them, she headed their way, hoping to catch a glimpse of Cyrus among them. She quickly realized they had no such luck. When they spotted her, they both shook their heads.

Caliena's spirits faded. She knew Cyrus was one of their best. He was probably fine, but she worried, nonetheless. He was getting on in years, and the storm had been brutal.

"Sorry, Sister," one of the scouts spoke as they approached. "We searched as best we could but found no signs of him. As the others reported, the snow covered everything. We didn't–"

"Look!" shouted one of the nearby knights, pointing. Everyone's eyes veered north, grabbing their spears and heading to the edge of the ruins.

Beyond the hill there was a slight hint of movement. Everyone put their hands over their eyes, shielding them from the sun as it reflected off the freshly fallen snow. Slowly, the forms came into view, cresting a hill a short way off.

"It's Cyrus. And it looks like he found Kai. And... is that, Mara?" shouted another knight.

"Who's that with them? Is he carrying someone?" questioned another.

Caliena walked briskly toward Cyrus and the approaching group. As they drew closer, she moved to his horse's side and extended her arm. Cyrus grabbed her forearm as she grabbed his, giving each other a firm shake.

"I was worried about you," she said, smiling at her elder.

"Aww, you shouldn't have," he replied with a large grin and a wink with his good eye.

"Seems it was founded. You look dreadful."

"Is it that bad?" Cyrus asked, reaching up to poke at his puffy eye. He smirked, cocking his head to the side with a slight shrug.

"I see you found Kai. And apparently Mara was out here, too? I sense there's quite a story behind all of this. And who do we have here?" she questioned, eyeing Sorn, whose cloak was covering the top half of his face. Caliena's eyes landed on Nalaen next. "Is that?"

"The dragon princess? Sure is," Cyrus replied. "And this is Sorn–her brother." Sorn lifted his head at the mention of his name, revealing his glowing blue eyes, an apprehensive smirk on his face.

Several of the knights gasped. All of them gripped their spears tightly, raising them toward Sorn. Cyrus put his hands up and slowly lowered them, gesturing for them to stand down.

"It's alright. He's here to help."

"Help?" Caliena questioned, her face twisted in confusion.

"Yes," Cyrus chuckled. "I know. I was a bit surprised myself, but Mara has informed me of a great deal. He was instrumental in helping her earlier, and he saved Kai's life. He is no threat to us."

Sorn made a slight bow toward Caliena and the others, though she could see the hint of shame in his features as her eyes met his. For good reason, as most of the knights with her didn't seem too convinced by Cyrus's words.

"Well, that is not something I ever expected to hear, but you are all here and alive, so I won't press the matter any further. I guess this means it's time to return to the keep? Kai can ride with one of us, but I'm not so sure about them..." she noted, flicking her head as her eyes moved back to Sorn and Nalaen.

"No need. I'll be flying," Sorn chimed in. Everyone held firmly to their spears, still feeling a bit unsettled by his presence.

"Very well," Caliena acknowledged, less affected, but she imagined her face still revealed mixed feelings. "That settles it, then. Is there anything you all need before we head back?"

"No. I think we can get going," Cyrus offered. "Everyone is tired and eager to get home. Although, I will take some healing salve if you have any. My face is hurting something fierce."

Caliena nodded with a smile, then turned and signaled for the others to prepare to mount up. She dug in the sack on her saddle, locating a small glass vial filled with a semi-clear, greenish liquid. She handed it to Cyrus, who took a few dabs and rubbed it on the outside of his swollen eye before handing the vial back to her.

Everyone packed hastily and was prepared to go within a short while. Kai saddled up with one of the knights and nodded to Cyrus and Caliena that he was ready.

Cyrus clicked his tongue and kicked his horse gently, sending them off at a trot in a easterly direction. Caliena followed suit, and everyone else fell in line behind her.

She glanced back, hearing Sorn as he transformed and took to the sky, the princess held tightly in one of his claws. The horses whinnied all along the line, echoing their own discomfort as Sorn's shadow covered the snow around them. It was the first time any of them had the shadow of their enemy cross their path without instant fear taking hold, even though it was apparent that its effect was still unnerving to more than a few. Even Caliena felt an odd chill run down her spine at the sight of it.

***

The ride back home was mostly uneventful, other than Sorn being spotted by a traveling merchant caravan, who had recently left Eastend and were headed for Valehold. Cyrus had to talk them down, trying his best to explain why a dragon was under the protection of the Order. Needless to say, Sorn was more worried about the rumors that would undoubtedly spread.

There was also the point at which Nalaen woke up. She started raging something fierce, so Sorn, feeling much stronger now, used his powers to control her again. With her own powers subdued by the dampener, it was quite easy. He didn't like doing it, but it was for the best.

As they came into view of Eastend, Cyrus called down Sorn and suggested it would be for the best if he walked from there. While Cyrus and the present group understood his presence, the rest of the world might not. At least, not yet. Cyrus had already voiced these concerns to Sorn in private, worried the other knights with them might be problematic enough. Sorn waited patiently off to the side while Cyrus had a stern talk with them, ordering vows of silence by all until he could figure things out, at which time he, or the Scalewarden, would make an announcement.

Finally back on their way, the procession still attracted onlookers from the town, but Sorn kept his head low and his eyes hidden. It felt strange to be so close to so many humans. He walked amongst them freely in the Dream, but this was entirely different. He wasn't sure if he should feel happy or ashamed. Their fear of his kind, was, after all, founded in an unfortunate truth. He tried to force his thoughts aside, focusing on the fact that he was trying to make things right, and this was the first step of many along that path. And it would probably be many more labored steps before the world saw the error of their ways–if such a thing was even possible.

Mara seemed to have sensed the conflict of emotions in Sorn's head and turned, looking his direction. Sorn noticed and smiled. At least he didn't have to do it alone. If there was anyone who could help them see, it was the blind girl. She was special. Just when Sorn thought he'd come to understand the world better, here she came, graceful and full of mercy. He did not deserve her companionship, much less her forgiveness. Nonetheless, it had been given. With every waking hour, he wouldn't stop trying to earn it.

Drawing near the outskirts of Eastend, Sorn was given some chains and a rope to tie around Nalaen's wrists, just to make her capture more convincing. Her presence there alive would be reason enough to raise concerns with the others. Her image as a prisoner needed to be abundantly clear. Again, Sorn didn't like it, but he trusted Cyrus in his promise she'd be well taken care of once they had her safely inside the keep. For a human, he seemed trustworthy. Like Mara, he seemed to have a good heart.

The guards on the wall sounded the horns at the party's approach, signaling for the gates to raise. Vi was standing on the wall herself, waiting for Mara's return. When she heard the horns, she came straight away to the gate, along with Brol and Dax and all the others. In fact, the entire keep had been on edge, apprehensively waiting to see what had happened to their comrades. As such, there was a large gathering in the courtyard when they arrived, Mara and Kai's friends front and center. Aerin was there, too.

The crowd split, making a path down the middle as the column rode through. Most eyes landed on Sorn, whose head was still bowed, and to the prisoner he was toting in front of him. Murmurs spread, most undoubtedly recognizing Nalaen for who she was.

In her present state, Nalaen seemed to care little, though Sorn could sense the shred of contempt lurking behind her thoughts.

When they came to a stop, Kai hopped off the back of the horse and came over, helping Mara do the same. Together, they embraced their friends and exchanged greetings.

Thorlan pushed his way through the crowd, which had pressed back in toward the new arrivals. When Cyrus saw him, he offered his hand in greeting.

"Hail, Brother Thorlan. I return with good tidings," he said, looking over his shoulder at Kai and Mara.

"I see. That is comforting, Brother Cyrus. Unfortunately, I do not bear the same. The Scalewarden is very ill."

Cyrus frowned, noting the seriousness in Thorlan's tone.

"Understood. I'll come see him right away, but first we need to secure our prisoner."

Thorlan peered around Cyrus, noting Sorn and Nalaen. His brow furled, his eyes studying Sorn.

"Prisoner? And who's this?"

"Yes. We need to take her to the undercroft. And this... is a friend. He helped us subdue the princess."

"The undercroft. So, we mean to–?"

"Yes. We'll discuss her fate later... in private."

Thorlan eyed the crowd, then nodded.

"Very well, then. Shall we?" he said, spinning and heading toward the inner gates.

Cyrus looked back and nodded to Caliena, who returned the gesture and whispered to several of the nearby knights. They dismounted and started clearing the path through the crowd so Sorn could walk through. Everyone eyed him, and Cyrus began to hear their whispers amongst each other.

"Alright, that'll be enough," Cyrus called out. "Back to your duties. Kai, Mara, with us."

Kai and Mara both turned away from their friends, Kai holding out his arm for Mara as they made to follow the others into the keep.

It didn't take them long to reach the Heart with the keep mostly clear. Once there, Cyrus dismissed the rest of the knights, other than Caliena, leading them to the back doorway and down the stairs. It was strange for Mara to be there. Though she couldn't see it, it all felt familiar. It was surreal for her to realize that her time in the Dream had actually been real, which further confirmed the truth of her other discoveries. She had so many questions, but those answers would have to wait. She worried the Order still wasn't ready to hear what she had learned. Fortunately, Cyrus was a good man, and she was glad to have him on their side. She hadn't told him everything yet. But hopefully soon, she would.

Mara smelled the dust and distinct scent of rusting metal as they entered the lower room. She remembered the general shape of it, heading to the back and into the narrow corridor. As they passed through, Mara reached out her hand and ran her fingertips along the wall. The events from her time there in the Dream came flooding back to her.

She felt the space grow and the walls spread out, assuming they'd entered the holding chamber. The smells there were different. There was no rust smell, like before. It was still a bit musty, but there were other strange scents she couldn't place.

But more so than the scents, she could feel the hum of the cages. Sorn said it was the same metal that was around Nalaen's neck. Now that she was near it in the real world, she could feel it. It was like a dull vibration that emanated from all around her. It wasn't strong, but it did make her feel slightly uneasy. She imagined those children—or, younglings, as the dragons called them—imagined what their terror might have been like, being trapped in this dark place with that constant humming, waiting for the knights to come take vials of their blood.

Mara's legs began to quiver, a feeling of weakness overtaking her. Kai caught her and held her upright.

"Are you okay?" he asked.

"Yes, I'm fine. It's just... I think I just need a rest. And I don't like this place. Can you feel that?"

"Yes. It makes me feel strange. Is it...?"

"The cages, yes," Mara replied.

Mara felt Sorn's presence as he came up beside her. She knew he felt it, too.

"We'll be done here soon, Mara," Cyrus said, noting her actions. "Sorn, if you will." Cyrus pointed to the cage that Caliena had just propped open.

Sorn turned his attention toward it and slowly walked forward, entering the cage and placing his sister down on the hard floor. He could feel the power being sapped from him, making his knees quiver slightly. It was a feeling quite unlike anything he'd ever felt in his entire life. He didn't envy his sister for what she was about to endure, but he knew it was necessary. He just hoped she would somehow come to reason so he could take her back home eventually. That was asking a lot of his sister, but somehow, he hoped it was achievable.

Nalaen began to stir, Sorn's lack of powers severing his hold over her. Getting her full consciousness back, she gazed around in confusion. Sorn stood and rushed out, Cyrus closing the door quickly before Nalaen realized where she was and what was happening.

As she came to fully realize what was happening, she immediately spun around, her eyes quickly landing on her brother. She came over to the edge of the cage, gripping the bars and pressing her face through one of the sections, glaring at him. Her eyes were still glowing, but much more faintly now, as if the power was being drained from them, too.

"A traitor to the end, I see," she spoke, her voice much calmer than Sorn would have expected. "In the end, you'll get what you deserve."

"I'm sorry, Sister, this—"

"Do not call me that. Family wouldn't do this to each other."

"It's the only way to ensure you don't hurt anyone else," Sorn sighed. He didn't think his words would matter, but felt he needed to say them anyway. "I wish there was another way, but I've been given their word that no harm will come to you while I'm gone."

"Gone?" she asked, eyeing the humans warily.

"I must return home to tell them of all that has happened–to tell them that their future Queen will return, in time... *if* she comes to find a better version of herself, that is."

A sinister smile formed on Nalaen's face. Her eyes scanned everyone again, finally landing on Mara.

"You really did a number on him, didn't you? My congratulations. It seems you've won... for now."

Mara tilted her head to the side, understanding that Nalaen's words were meant for her.

"It was never about winning, Princess," Mara said, her voice a little shaky. "It's about finding a better way to live in coexistence with each other. There is no reason to fight."

"There is always a reason to fight. This conflict extends far beyond your and my lifetimes. I do not think our ancestors would agree with your sentiment. I doubt those persecuted and enslaved by the humans would agree, either."

"I cannot speak on that, but whatever wrongs have been done, we will seek to right. And perhaps, if our ancestors knew the truth, then many more of our kin wouldn't have needed to die. There is more to our story–dragons and humans. I suspect there are wrongs on both sides, but I– *we*," Mara corrected, turning her head in Sorn's direction, "are going to find out the truth. Maybe we will even find a commonality amongst us that could lead us into a new era of peace."

"Peh!" Nalaen spat, cringing. "You're naïve, girl... you and my– and Sorn. The only commonality we have is the stolen blood flowing in your veins. Once you take that away, we are nothing alike."

"You're wrong, Sister," Sorn interjected. "Mara is much more than she seems. She has extraordinary gifts, yes, and I suspect they stem from more than just our kin's blood in her veins. But even if you take all that away, and even without her sight, she sees more of the world as it could be than all the rest of us. And I know there are others," he added, eyeing Cyrus, "who will come to share her sentiment. If I have chosen a side, then it is the side of compassion and understanding. You are free to choose your own path. I only hope you come to abandon this path of misery before it costs you everything."

"This doesn't look like free to me," Nalaen retorted, eyeing the metal cage around her.

"Yes, well, actions have consequences, and all freedom comes at a price. You'll have to earn yours, now. Goodbye, Nalaen."

Sorn bowed, then turned on his heel and started walking away, the others following him. He looked back one last time before exiting into the hallway, seeing his sister watching him behind her cold, unchanged eyes, the last of their light flickering one last time before fading entirely into the darkness of the room that would serve as her prison for the foreseeable future.

As Sorn turned away, a single tear crawled down his cheek. He wiped it away before anyone noticed. Now was not the time to be weak. He had a tough road ahead, and he had no time to shed tears for his wayward sister.

The group stopped once they again reached the Heart, Cyrus gathering them together before they joined the rest of the keep.

"I need to go see the Scalewarden. I'm told his health is not well. Sorn... thank you for your words. Though it is still an odd thing—to have a dragon walking these halls without fear of its fire—I, for one, am glad you are on our side. I knew that Kai and Mara were destined for great things the moment they walked through our gates. It seems so long ago, now, but really it was only yesterday. However, none of us could have foreseen events of this magnitude. I scarcely believe it myself. I don't mean to ramble, but what I mean to say is... thank you," Cyrus said, bowing to Sorn. Sorn returned the gesture.

"I know you have work to do. There is much that we must attend to as well, and I suspect Kai and Mara's story is merely just beginning. But is there anything you need before I leave you?"

"No... sir," Sorn answered with a bow.

"It's Cyrus, please."

"No, Cyrus. I will be leaving right away. I fear it's already been too long. I must return to ensure there are no repercussions for all that has happened. I don't know how things will play out, but I will do my best. I only ask that you uphold your promises and see that my sister is protected and taken care of until I return."

"You have my word, Sorn. No harm will come to her while I yet draw breath."

"My thanks. I will be off then. Mara... would you escort me out of the keep? I should very much like to say goodbye before I'm off."

"You're leaving so soon?" Mara asked, looking as though she was choking back tears.

"Yes. I wish I could stay, but I must go. Besides, it's probably better if I'm not around while Cyrus and the others work things out here."

"Aye," Cyrus said. "For the best. Just, uh... don't turn into you know what until you're out of view of the keep, eh?" Cyrus added, winking with his good eye.

"Naturally," Sorn replied. "I understand the effect my presence can have. I'll make sure I'm in a secluded area. Shall we, Mara?" Sorn said, offering his arm as he shot Kai a quick glance.

Kai glared at him, keeping his grip on his sister, but after a few moments, he rolled his eyes and let go, helping Mara find Sorn's arm.

"Are you coming, Kai?" Mara asked, tilting her head backward as they made for the exit.

"Sure," Kai sighed. "Someone's gotta help you get back."

Mara smiled, turning forward to start chatting with Sorn. Cyrus smiled at Kai, placing his hand on the boy's shoulder as they left the room behind Sorn and Mara, parting ways once they hit the main hallway.

Kai followed behind his sister, eyeing Sorn the entire time, but giving them the space to talk. He didn't like how close Mara and Sorn seemed to be but knew that there wasn't much he could do to change it. Sorn was going to be a part of their future, whether Kai liked it or not. Although, having a dragon on your side wasn't the worst ally one could have. He just hoped the creature would not get *too* close to his sister.

Kai saw his friends on the way out. He tried to talk them out of following, but they were adamant about tagging along. Besides, Vi had already told them all about Sorn, so there wasn't really any harm in it. Aerin was there, too. His attitude seemed more skeptical of being in the presence of a dragon than the others, but he still wanted to tag along.

"He's really a dragon?" Dax asked as they left the keep. "I mean, he's tall 'n all, but doesn't seem very dragony otherwise."

Sorn turned, noting the boy's words, lifting his hood slightly to reveal his glowing blue eyes. Dax's own eyes grew wide, his mouth dropping in stunned silence for a moment.

"Alright, fair enough. That proves it," Dax said after another moment. Everyone laughed. Even Sorn chuckled.

"So, what do we do from here?" asked Brol.

"Well, Mara's found some things out about our past," Kai said. "Seems like there's a lot that we don't know. It's complicated, and I don't even understand half of it, but we believe there are answers. It's just going to take some time to figure everything out. Sorn's going back to the dragon kingdom to try and explain everything to them. Mara and I were talking, and we think we might need to do the same thing. An alliance with the dragons won't come easily. The Order *might* be made to understand, but the rest of the Vale? That's an entirely different matter. We'll have to talk to Cyrus and the Scalewarden about it. No idea how this is going to work, but we've got to figure out something."

"Dragons and humans living in peace? Now, wouldn't that be something," Dax noted, his eyes revealing the contemplation behind his words. "Hey, Mara," he hollered, his attitude changing in an instant.

"Yes?" Mara said.

"I heard you got to ride on his back. What was that like?"

Mara's face turned red, followed by Sorn's awkward expression.

"Um, well, I'd rather not talk about that," Mara replied, her face turning redder.

"Alright, fair enough," Dax chuckled. "I've ridden plenty of beasts back home, including the lorix," Dax continued, elbowing Kai. "But never anything like a dragon before. Er... no offense, Mr... uh, Sorn, sir."

A slight chuckle went through the group.

"None taken," Sorn bowed, trying to hide his discomfort but failing miserably.

Dax began running up the hill, holding his arms out as if they were wings, hooting and hollering as if he was flying himself. Everyone laughed harder this time, especially Kai. It felt good to smile and laugh again. It felt good to feel like his old self again, even if he—and his sister—would never be quite the same again.

But in truth, it excited him. He didn't know what the future held for them, but he knew it was something far beyond anything he could have imagined.

Kai sighed. It was a good sigh this time. He let it out, joining Brol up ahead to watch Dax's ridiculous antics as their temporary celebration continued, everyone's spirits exceptionally high.

As Kai and the boys moved ahead, Vi came up beside Mara and nudged her gently.

"Hey, Mara. You don't think you'd go to the capital, do you?" Vi asked.

"I don't know, Vi. Maybe. Why?"

"Oh, just curious."

"Aren't you from there?" Riesara asked excitedly. "Could you show us around if we go?"

"*If* we go, I suppose."

"Oh, Vi, wouldn't you like to go see your family? I'd love to meet them," Mara exclaimed, getting excited herself.

"Yeah, sure," Vi commented.

Mara caught the hesitation in her friend's voice but decided not to dwell on it. She turned her attention back to Sorn as Riesara began peppering Vi with questions about the capital.

"Do you have a plan?" Mara asked Sorn.

"Not really. I'll have to go see the Council first thing. And deal with Kyrian."

"Who's Kyrian?"

"He's head of the High Council, and the interim ruler of the dragon kingdoms. He's not a friend, and he will do everything he can to twist this to his advantage. The good news is, he's not a warmonger. He's more the stab you in the back kind. So, at least I should be able to keep this from escalating to war. If anything, he'll be pleased with my sister's continued absence, though he'll undoubtedly deny it. But it's what he'll do in that absence that worries me. He already has considerable sway over the kingdom. I fear that will only grow now."

"I see..." Mara said, feeling worried for Sorn's safety.

"Don't worry, Mara. There is hope. We have friends there, even on the Council. It's going to take some time, but I believe we can enact change. My biggest fear is that my sister will never change her own ways. And if she doesn't return, with no other female heir, they'll have to choose a new Queen from amongst the Scions. If that happens, it could cause even greater divides than there already are."

"How long will they wait to decide?"

"I don't know. We'll just have to see how things go and do our best to convince them that things can change for the better. It won't be easy, but together, we can do it."

Mara's expression turned to sadness. Sorn must have noticed because he reached down, gently touching her chin.

"What is it, Mara?" he asked.

"You said together, but... we won't be together. When will I see you again, Sorn?"

"Mara. We always have the Dream. We'll just have to figure out a way to find each other there. It might be harder over the longer distance, but your power has grown considerably. I'm sure we'll find a way to keep in touch."

Mara perked up at the mention of that possibility. She'd almost forgotten about the Dream and how it could aid her in the future.

"Can it work that far?" she asked.

"It can. It will take more effort, but it's possible. You will have to practice, continuing to hone your mind. Just remember what I told you. Be careful how much time you spend in there. You were lucky last time that I came to help. If you get lost like that again, I may not know how to find you."

"I understand. I will be careful."

By now, the group had moved out of view of both the keep and Eastend, traveling along the hills as they ascended into the first of the mountains. The smaller mountain sloped down into a valley before the next mountain rose back up even higher. It was the perfect place for Sorn to take off.

"Well, this looks like as good a place as any," Sorn said, gazing up at the mountains.

"I guess this is goodbye then," Mara said sorrowfully.

"For now..." Sorn corrected. "We both have much work to do. I trust the next time we see each other, we will have much to discuss. I look forward to that day."

"Me too," Mara said, a gentle smile forming. "Be careful, Sorn."

"You too," Sorn said, taking Mara's hand. "I am so very glad to have met you, Mara Grayscale. Until we meet again..." he finished, bowing and placing a gentle kiss on the top of her hand. Mara blushed as he let go.

Mara listened as Sorn walked out ahead of the group, preparing to make his transformation. She heard gasps as he shifted in front of them, assuming his true form in a swirl of magical energy, Mara sensing it even as the others watched in amazement. Mara still wished she could see it—what he truly looked like as a dragon. Maybe one day, she would.

"Okay, now I definitely ain't got no doubts about him being a dragon..." Dax exclaimed, his eyes looking like they were about to fall out of their sockets. The others nodded, jaws wide and mesmerized by Sorn's change. Kai and Mara laughed at their friends.

Sorn turned his head back toward them, winking at Dax. He nodded to Kai and Mara before lifting off into the air with his powerful wings. Kai came up to stand beside Mara, taking hold of her hand.

They stood there for a minute, everyone watching the shape of Sorn slowly grow smaller, Mara quietly imagining it as she felt his presence fade away. Their friends came up beside Mara and Kai, forming a line on either side, silently watching together. When Sorn finally disappeared beyond the distant mountaintops, Kai squeezed Mara's hand again, letting her know it was time to go.

"Quite the day, wasn't it?" Mara asked.

"Quite the past few weeks, I'd say," Kai replied.

"You can say that again," added Brol.

"So, what now?" asked Dax.

"Well, I for one would love a nice, long hot bath. And then I'm going to eat a whole loaf of cinnamon bread. What about you, Mara?" Kai asked.

"A hot bath does sound nice. I think my toes are still frozen from the mountains. And I'm a little hungry, but I want to hit up the library."

Kai tilted his head and smiled inquisitively, eyeing Mara with a raised brow.

"Library? But you–"

"Yes. I'm going to need someone with working eyes. Care to join me? We've got some answers to start looking for."

"I can come with you, Mara," Vi chimed in.

"It's alright, Vi. I'll take my sister," Kai said. "But thanks for the offer," he added, smiling at her. Mara felt Kai's hand warm up a little. He cleared his throat after a few seconds.

"Well, shall we?" he asked, clearing his throat again.

"Yes, let's," Mara replied, smiling, a warmth filling her heart. Despite everything that had gone wrong, they'd made it through, together. She still worried about the future but felt confident now that she had her brother back at her side, and her friends, both old and new, around her. Even Aerin, who had so far remained quiet, seemed to have some part to play in whatever was coming. And for that, Mara was beyond grateful.

Kai held Mara's hand tightly as they walked back to the keep. The group walked and talked together all the way back, discussing everything that had happened, as well as the possibilities of what their future might hold. It was going to be hard, and it was going to take work. Mara and Kai still had so much yet to discover–about the world, about themselves, and there were so many other uncertainties. But one thing Kai knew for sure was that whatever they had to face in the coming days, he would no longer try to face it alone. He'd learned that lesson the hard way.

Cyrus had been right. He didn't have to do this alone. At last, he finally understood why.

CHAPTER FIFTY-NINE

AWAKENING

"Viscont, Rikkan is here to see you. He arrived from the site just moments ago, and I told him you would want to see him right away. Is now a good time?"

"Yes. Send him in," replied the shadowy figure sitting on the dais above.

The attendant disappeared through the doorway, returning a minute later, Rikkan at his heels. The attendant bowed, motioning with his hand for Rikkan to enter and approach the raised platform where the Viscont was sitting. As soon as Rikkan passed, the attendant left, promptly closing the door behind him. Rikkan flinched at the sound of it, swallowing as he turned to face his superior.

Rikkan had been in this exact position a handful of times before, but it never got any easier. A visit to the Viscont was an unnerving experience. At least *this* time he had good news.

Rikkan offered the customary bow as he approached the raised dais where the older man sat. Though the dais was already high, the massive marble chair the man sat on was even more impressive, twice the height of Rikkan standing fully upright. It was a marvel how the Viscont even got into it. Perhaps, he never left.

The Viscont's face was mostly obscured by his hood, shadows cast by the dim light of the room further hiding all but his mouth and nose. Rikkan assumed the lack of lighting was meant to further enhance the discomfort of all visitors. Even if that wasn't the case, it was the effect.

Looking now at the Viscont's shadowy features, he could barely make out the man's eyes, a hint of the malice burning beneath the hood. They seemed to stare into one's soul, as if they stole the very essence of life from anyone who held their gaze for too long.

Rikkan shivered, taking a moment to compose himself, attempting to formulate the words he was about to say. He did not want to stumble over them and make himself any more of a fool than he already felt.

"Speak, Rikkan. Or have you forgotten?" the old man uttered, his voice seeming to spur Rikkan's muscles into a twitch.

"Apologies, Viscont," he offered, bowing again. He felt uncomfortable as he met the man's gaze, immediately casting his eyes downward. "I have good news. We've uncovered another text, and the translators are making good progress of their own. I have scribes working day and night to generate copies to be sent over for you. They should arrive within the week."

"Which text have you found?"

"We believe we've found number six. That makes five now–almost half of the presumed twelve. Decent progress, I'd–"

"No. That is not good enough. We need to find the rest, now. Double the excavations. I want every man and woman working all hours of the day."

"But Viscont, that's–"

"You will do as I say. Or should I find another to lead the recovery efforts?"

"No, no Viscont. I will do it. Forgive my lack of faith."

"And I want those translations by sundown in two days' time."

Rikkan's mouth opened, wanting to object, but he knew it was folly.

"Yes, Viscont. It will be done." It was going to be near impossible to achieve a timeline like that, but Rikkan couldn't afford to disappoint the man again. "Is there anything else, Viscont?"

"I will not tolerate failure, Rikkan. Do not disappoint me. Find the rest of the tomes. We're running out of time."

"Is there news, my lord?"

"Yes, from the East. The dragons have returned–the Princess, along with her brother and sister and a small contingent of escorts. I believe she is the third queen the tomes speak of. If that is true, then we may already be out of time. We must find him before it is too late."

"I understand, Viscont. I will... *encourage* the workers to move faster."

"Yes, see that you do. Now, go."

Rikkan bowed one last time, every muscle in his body ready to get him out of the vile man's presence. He wanted nothing more than to return to the excavations and get as far away from this place as possible. At least there, it was they who feared him.

As Rikkan left, closing the door behind him, the Viscont watched in silent appraisal.

"What do you think?" the Viscont asked out loud.

A shadowy figure emerged from the darkness, coming up to stand beside him on the platform. The figure was also cloaked, standing nearly as tall as the Viscont on his raised seat. This put him considerably taller than most men.

"I think he is weak," the man spoke, his voice deep and guttural. "I could see his knees shaking from the back of the room."

"Yes, most of them are, but they serve their purpose. His fear will ensure results. And if he doesn't deliver, I will find another."

"You should let me go and ensure they stay on schedule."

"No," the Viscont hissed, turning toward the man. "I have another purpose for you."

"How can I serve, my Lord?" the figure offered, turning to look him in the eyes.

"The scouts sent word of two young knights within the Order. Twins, who they say seem to possess exceptional gifts, even for... Dragonbloods. But so far, I have heard only rumors. I need to know more about their origins. I need the truth."

As the Viscont spoke, the shadowy figure's eyes darted back and forth, his mind racing with understanding.

"What would you have me do?"

"Go and find these twins. The news surrounding them is most interesting. If the rumors are true, we would very much like to meet them here. Their appearance now, at this juncture, may be more than mere coincidence. And if so, we must keep a close eye on their activities in the days to come."

"Very well. I will see it done."

"Report to me as soon as you know anything. It's necessary that I be kept abreast of *every* detail."

The man bowed, fading back into the shadows.

Once the Viscont could no longer sense his presence, he reached inside his robes and retrieved a small, metallic object hanging from his neck. Holding it up in front of his face, he examined it, as he'd done a thousand times before. It was a medallion, and on it's face was a symbol—an eye, wreathed in flame, and what looked like a drop of blood at it's center. He eyed the medallion, the faint light in his eyes growing slightly stronger. He had yet to fully understand the symbol's significance, but he sensed he was close to more answers. And somehow, it seemed these mysterious twins were a part of it. But who they were, and what part they would play, remained to be seen.

He sat back in his chair, his cold eyes flicking back and forth as the shadows seemed to darken around him.

"It would seem the Awakening has already begun."

THANKS

...AND WHAT'S NEXT!

First, I'd like to take a quick second to offer one final "thank you" to any readers who've made it all the way through this book. You are amazing, and it means a lot to have you here with me. This is just the beginning, and we have one heck of a wild ride coming up ahead. I hope you're ready!

Speaking of, where *should* you head next? So glad you asked...

If you haven't read it yet, Dawn of the Queen is a prequel novella set some time before the events of When Blood Burns. If you have read it, just skip down past the links to the "Future Books" section.

While it is from a much earlier time, Dawn of the Queen's relevance to current events can't be overstated. You heard about Liotha in this book. Now, go see for yourself who she was and what events unfolded that led to her involvement, not just with the first Dragonbloods, but with events that will have repercussions throughout the entire series to come. It just might answer a few questions you have in the back of your mind, too!

You can get Dawn of the Queen either directly from me (preferred), or from Amazon, and even a few other popular retailers. It's totally up to you where you get it. I will appreciate the support no matter what.

Here's where to find them:
Direct – https://payhip.com/AwakeningBooks
Amazon – https://www.amazon.com/dp/B0FG8J1VMX
Other – They are also sometimes available with other retailers, like B&N, Kobo, and more. Check out links at the bottom of the direct shop.

Future Books:
If you've already read Dawn of the Queen, then your next stop will be A Flame to Guide Them, another novella set even further back in Velasia's history. This novella will focus on an entirely different backstory, detailing what life was like for humans before they settled in the Vale. It's an interesting story giving us another

piece of the puzzle to Velasia's troubled history, leading us just a little bit closer to the real truth lurking in the shadows of the past.

You can get writing progress updates via the newsletter, or directly from the "Books" page on my website. This novella, as well as all future books, will all be detailed there.

Thanks so much for your support!

CONNECTION

If this book is your first venture into the Awakening, I'd like to extend you a quick invitation to make a deeper connection with me and my world. As an indie author, I want to make sure I'm as accessible to my readers as I can possibly be. Besides just telling great stories, I want to build a shared world we can all thrive in, and I can't do that without you. So, if you'd like to join us in this endeavor, the website should be your first stop. It will have all the information you need to become a true Seeker and member of this community. Keep an eye out for a pop-up for the newsletter, but you you can also click the link at the top to open it directly. The newsletter is your way to keep up to date on everything Awakening, and my way to give back to you in whatever way I can, be that sneak peeks of what I'm working on, early announcements, promotions, and anything else I feel is to your benefit. It will also get you a copy of a short prequel story featuring one of When Blood Burns prominent characters and their viewpoint of twins Kai and Mara as they prepare to join the Order and become Dragonbloods!

Website: https://astevenswrites.com

You can expect one regular monthly update via the newsletter, and then occasional announcements like cover reveals and launch dates as necessary.

If you're familiar with Discord and want to join us there, that's another great option for getting connected! We already have a small community started, and it's slowly growing. Details are on the website, but if you want to dive right in, here's the link to join. This will be where the majority of our community is built, but there may be other options in the future, like Patreon.

Discord: https://discord.gg/DRu2vZnBsz

Whatever you choose, I sincerely hope you'll join us in one form or another. I look forward to meeting all of you who do!

REVIEWS

How YOU can help!

Now, on to the most practical way for YOU to help me continue telling great stories. If you enjoyed the book in any way, it's one small thing you can do to help me out in a BIG way!

Reviews are the lifeblood of books. And as an indie author, it's one of the best ways for word of mouth to spread about what I'm creating here. Because, at the end of the day, word of mouth is the main way new readers find my books. And when they do, they need to know what to expect. That's why your <u>completely honest</u> review will go a long way in helping me build this passion into a lifelong career.

In order to make reviews as seamless as I can for you, I've created a special page on my website. It contains both a "thank you" video from me and some details about reviews, with links to both Amazon and Goodreads pages so you can get straight to it. Also, if you're not exactly sure what to write in your review, there are a few questions that might help guide you in the right direction.

Just scan the QR code below, or click directly on the link to check it out!

https://www.astevenswrites.com/thank-you-reviews

Thanks so much for taking the time to leave an honest review!

AUTHOR
WHO I AM AND WHY I WROTE THIS BOOK

My name is Andrew Stevens, and I am many things. Husband, father, son, gamer, author, veteran. There is a lot more to me than just that, but those are the presiding words to describe what I am. But who I am, well, that's an entirely different question. I'm not sure I can answer it fully, but here's a brief attempt.

I am a creative, a dreamer. I am a wordsmith. I am a lover of stories, writing my own and even the occasional poetry. I am a searcher, always questioning the nature of my reality, always looking up to the stars, ever wondering what vast secrets lie beyond that which my eyes can see. I am a believer in a God who I will never claim to fully understand, yet trust to have my best interests in mind. I believe my gifts come from somewhere, and if not him, then where? I am an errant hopeful, always seeking the good in the world, though I still get discouraged when it seems hard to find.

I am all these and more. I am also a man who believes I can make the world a better place through stories. And that brings us to why I wrote this book.

I wrote this book because it is something I must do. Writing and creating is a part of me that I didn't realize to its fullest for many years. Once I found the means and the will to see it through, the result is the blood, sweat, and tears you have just read. It's not perfect, but like my soul, it is deeply intertwined with who I am. It is a mirror—a brief glimpse into the reflection of my deepest self.

Whether the words resonate with you or not, I appreciate you taking a chance. I appreciate your willingness to invest some of life's most precious resource into me and the past few years of my life. At the end of the day, no matter how you feel about it, know I am eternally grateful.

Again, thank you for your time, and if you've made it this far, you given me much more than I deserve. Hopefully, the pages have at least reinvested some of that gift back to you. From the bottom of my heart, I sincerely hope so.

Cheers,
Andrew Stevens

Shadows stir, the world trembles.

Steel yourselves, Seekers.

The Awakening has begun...

https://astevenswrites.com